THE FOUR SUNRISES

Book One of the Endellian Saga

JC MAYNARD

ISBN-13 — 979-8-7927-0070-3 Paperback Edition
ISBN-13 — 979-8-7947-8709-2 Hardcover Edition

Story, Text, Maps, and Design by JC Maynard
Editing by David S Taylor
Cover Artwork by Creed Bauman
and a special thanks to DL Orton

Independently Published 2022

~For my first readers, who have stuck with me
through countless story iterations,
and for my characters,
who have gotten me through my darkest days~

MAPS

*Not all geographic features shown, including unmarked rivers, forests, and settlements
WESTERN ENDELLIA
N
W
E
S
DARUSEMARE
The Meande
The North Sea
(The Northlands)
Landevore
Lac Lariet
The White Rivers
Seawatch
Dothram
Lake of Duloret
Dawne
Saerasong
Lac Lucera
The Taurbeit-Krons
Longbrush
Duloret Post
Monta Licelle
FERRAMOOR
WESTERN ENDLEBARR
Farwater
Oakfoot
Hills of Duloret
Bellerush
The Spring Rivers
Camp Stoneheart
Ifle-Laarm
Willowwood
Camp Auness
Wallingford
The Inlet
Aunestauna
Nottenberry
The Auness Sea
Greenwash
The Green Rivers
Abendale
Southern Pass
Diphabee
Sundale
Highhill
River of the South San
The Burning Hills
The Taurbeit-Krons
Pyrot
THE SOUTHLANDS

*Not all geographic features shown, including unmarked rivers, forests, and settlements
EASTERN ENDELLIA
N
W
E
S
THE NORTHLANDS
The Wildrush
Northpost
Chendoff Lake
The North Sea
The Iced Bank
The Northlakes
Lowtown Nocht
Vashner
The Winter Woods
The Snowbite
Fkishk
Patczeckiv
ELISHKA
Fordcross
The Erricurr
Whitetree
The Seirns
Seirnkov
Blackpine
Bordertown
Teirvar
EASTERN ENDLEBARR
CEREBRIA
Tallwood Watch
Fellsink
Shadowfork
Weirkoff Nocht
The Valley Rivers
Woodshore
Ontraug
The Shirr
The Sister Cities
Lake Kiettosh
Gienn
Roshk
Endgroth
Tangle Took
Port Dellock
Lakeholt
The Fjordlands
The Kettlerush
Fennenbogg
Terraneirishwine
THE CRANDLES
Findinholm
Shweedlund
Bellmostva
Dindibore
Brasmiccin
Kettlehoggen
Catteboga
The Taurbeir-Krons
The Southern Sea

TABLE OF CONTENTS

PART ONE

PART TWO

PART ONE

The Strangest Memories

PROLOGUE

~Night, October 4th
Aunestauna, Capital of the Endellian Empire

Prince Tronum gazed down at the moonlit city of Aunestauna sleeping below him. As his eyes wandered the streets, he tried to gather a sense of fortitude in his heart. He needed to be strong, he told himself. Strong like the huge stone column he leaned against — like his father.

A chill sighed through the palace breezeway where he stood, his stern gaze examining the capital below. His father's funeral would be tomorrow morning, his coronation the following hour. Tronum — the Heir to the Throne, the Heir to the Empire. Tomorrow, he would take command over the entire continent of Endellia.

Tronum stole one last cold breath from the night before turning and crossing the polished marble of the open-air corridor, his path illuminated dimly by torches. A frigid breeze blew out the fires, and the hallway went dark, lit only by the moon. Another chilling gust of air blew behind him, followed by the searing pain of slicing flesh. Burning like red hot coals, a knife punched out through his abdomen. Tronum coughed blood and fell forward onto the marble floor.

A strong arm flipped Tronum onto his back, revealing the cloaked figure above him. The dark shadow raised its bloody dagger into the air for a final strike when a ferocious roar ripped through the hallway; a storm of white wings collided with the silhouette. Another roar shook the stone corridor and Tronum glimpsed the massive, winged lion chasing after the fleeing assassin.

Tronum convulsed in pain, his blood pooling around him, his heartbeat pounding in his head, and his consciousness slipping away. The roars of his winged lion echoed as it chased the attacker until all was silent but the sharp coughs sending waves of pain through his chest. Tronum's vision began to dim. Struggling to stay conscious, he heard faint footsteps rushing toward him from the other end of the corridor.

To his right, a young woman sprinted down the dark hallway. "Your Majesty!" She knelt by his side, searching for the wound. She looked around the scene, almost checking to make sure no one else was there — distant voices were approaching, running toward the commotion she had heard; but she still had time. She tore apart his tunic and placed her palm on his mutilated stomach. A stream of pure white light poured out of her hand, swirled above Tronum's skin, and seeped into his body. The bleeding stopped, and large scars appeared in place of his gashes.

His eyes flickered open and slowly focused. They stared at the woman from a ghostly pale face. "Who are you?"

"Forget I was ever here," she whispered, "Your Majesty."

Down the hall, a group of palacemen rushed toward the Heir to the Throne in a panic.

The woman quickly moved away from Tronum and turned to one of the men, who looked horrified at the sight of all the blood. "Janus, take him to the infirmary."

"Yes, right away," the man replied as he slung Tronum's arm over his shoulder.

The woman stepped farther away. "The assassin's dagger went deep. He's lucky that Fernox flew in to save him." She turned her gaze to the massive lion perched in the far window, glistening white in the starlight. The beast raised its head, a slight breeze whispering through its mane; rippling muscles across its back caught the starlight and threw it against the walls of the corridor. With a guttural rumble and a thrust of its mighty wings, the lion leaped out into the night.

The echoes of anxious words filled the stone corridor as servants surrounded their soon-to-be-king, gently helping him rise. Tronum's breath shuddered, and a name fell from his lips. He repeated it, spitting it into the blood at his feet. "Xandria."

Janus seemed to hesitate. ". . . I believe so."

"Where is she?"

"Your Majesty, I—"

"Where is my sister?!"

Janus paused again, trying to decide what to say. "Xandria hasn't been seen tonight, Your Majesty . . . she might be in the city, but we'll send out the Guard to find her." Suspicion gathered in Janus' eyes. "Do you think—"

Tronum nodded grimly. "Xandria tried to kill me and take the throne."

"If she's responsible for this and finds out you're alive, she will probably flee to the Cerebrian territories. When we realized her men were gone, we came looking for you."

Tronum grimaced in pain. "Summon the Council." He looked out through the columns of the corridor, out to the glistening lights of the capitol below. Turning back to the palace, Tronum searched for the woman who had healed him, but she was long gone. His fingers traced the newly formed scar on his stomach, and his heart hardened. "She'll be preparing for war . . . we must do the same."

THE FIRST FOUR SUNRISES

Chapter One

~Twenty-Two Years Later, Morning, August 22nd
Southeastern Endlebarr

The forest fog swirled and ebbed, whispering quietly between the trees. A squirrel hopped along a fallen trunk covered in moss, sniffing the air. Raising its nose, its hair stood up, and it darted beneath a rotten log. Galloping hooves crashed through the underbrush and bounded over the earth. Three horses with riders, clad in the scarlet armor of Ferramoor, tore through the forest. Moments later, three more horses trampled through, carrying soldiers adorned in the dark green of Cerebria.

Tayben Shae adjusted the grip on his spear, tracking the Ferramish soldiers through the fog ahead – stragglers fleeing the battle. He and his horse bounded between fallen logs and moss-covered boulders, guided by the dim light filtering through the dense canopy above. Blood from his shoulder dripped down his spear arm.

"Tayben!" shouted Gallien, the soldier riding behind him. "Take the ridge and cut them off before the river while Birg and I trail them!"

"I'm on it!" Tayben called back as Gallien and his white stallion split off to the right with the third Cerebrian.

Tayben spurred his mount forward and galloped around another ancient tree. A crack sounded beneath him, and his horse collapsed, sending Tayben hurling through the air. He hammered hard into the ground below, hitting his head on a rock. Everything went black.

Tayben moaned, his head felt like it had been split in two. He tried to rise, but gentle hands grabbed onto his shoulders.

"Easy, Tayben, you took quite a knock." Gallien settled him gently back down. "He's up, Birg."

Hunching over beneath the canvas roof of their soldiers' tent, Birg walked over to Tayben with a bowl of broth. "'Ere ya go, Tayben," he said, handing it to him along with a wooden spoon.

Tayben inclined his head to drink the steaming broth.

Gallien chuckled. "A year fighting alongside you and you still can't ride a damned horse."

Tayben's head pounded with every pulse of blood rushing through it. "I don't know what happened."

"Oh he's jus' givin you grief," said Birg. "Your horse fell through a rotten log and jacked up its leg."

Tayben sighed. His eye focused a bit more and he saw blood spattered on the tent canvas. Gallien's face bore cuts from the skirmish, and Birg's eye was blackened, but Tayben saw them mostly in silhouette due to the fading light of day. Gallien had dirty blonde hair, long enough to move around in the wind as he ran, but short enough to see his eyebrows. His face was narrow and strong, and his deep blue eyes mirrored a cool winter sky. At twenty-one years old, Gallien was just two years older than Tayben, but had joined the army at the same time.

The tent was cold and dark, hidden beneath the impermeable canopy. Slowly sitting up, Tayben took the bowl of lukewarm broth. "How long have I been out?" he asked.

"It's still the 22nd," said Birg. "You've only been out for 'bout half a day."

"Those Ferrs cut you up?" said Tayben, noting a few of Birg's gashes.

"Oh, Gallien and me had a little trouble takin' them on our own while you was lyin' on yer arse, but it wasn't anythin' we couldn't 'andle." Birg laughed. "At least we can stay on our horses long enough to put up a fight!"

Tayben rolled his eyes and tried to sit up a bit more.

Gallien put his hand on Tayben's shoulder and spoke softly. "You sure you're alright, Tayben? That was a nasty spill you took there."

Tayben nodded. "Yeah, thanks, I'm fine – head just aches quite a bit."

Gallien shook his head as Birg left the tent. "You weren't the only one who took a hit."

"The other platoons?" Tayben asked while sipping the disgusting concoction of native roots and hardened jerky.

"I'd say about forty men are gone with at least that many also wounded," replied Gallien. "It wasn't our most successful attack, but it sufficed. Word has it that our battalion will be moved north to meet with the main front. Fenlell has told us that come late autumn, the Ferrs will no longer be able to travel across the Southern Pass."

Tayben thought for a moment, but his head still throbbed. "I hope someone has a grand plan in this whole thing. I have no idea what we're doing here picking off these small Ferramish battalions." Tayben shook his head. "I don't know, Gallien. I think Queen Xandria might be casting her eye on securing the mountains."

"Maybe," Gallien sighed. "We force Ferramoor back, and then they force *us* back. And then again, back and forth." Gallien paused and looked Tayben in the eyes. He seemed to be digesting the words, and they seemed painful, almost disgusting to say. "I've gotten used to the sight of blood, Tayben."

Disturbing memories flashed through Tayben's mind, but he had learned to push the images out quickly.

Gallien shook his head and took the empty bowl from Tayben. "You still look pretty dazed, catch some sleep while you can. The captain won't want to see you stumbling around like a drunk."

Tayben laughed and shook his head. "Through six different partnership transfers, Gallien – a whole year – we've stuck together; and yet, you've still managed to never be a klutz like me and get yourself concussed."

"Just rest up," said Gallien.

Tayben closed his eyes and drifted off after a short while, dreaming of a small, silver ornament and a beautiful castle; but the dream began to blur into an image of fire.

~Morning, August 23rd

Tayben awoke just before the sun rose. Only a dim light reached the forest floor and passed through the fabric of his shared tent. With his head no longer throbbing, he stepped up and gazed out of the tent flap. Very few soldiers out of the hundreds had risen yet. He took in a deep breath of the cold, wet air. Water droplets from the fog coated the hair on his arms and covered his body in a refreshing morning chill. Tayben donned his green uniform, strapped on his shoes, and headed for the trunk of a tree the width of a small house. Wanting to actually see the sun once today, he began his ascent up the trunk.

Guided by small wooden planks and holds that had been nailed into the tree, he pulled himself up step by step. The notches in the tree were crafted by the Cerebrian army to provide a path up to the sentry posts – wooden platforms around fifty to a hundred feet up in the tree. Sentries stood guard here watching the surrounding forest, but Tayben knew this platform was vacant for the hour.

Once Tayben reached the platform, there was nothing but true climbing left – branch after branch, notch after notch. An enveloping darkness hung over the Great Forest of Endlebarr. Fog caressed the trunks of the giant trees that stood hundreds of feet tall, blocking the sun from reaching the lush vegetation below. The cool, humid air of the forest felt alive, winding its way between every fern and moss-covered log, climbing up to the bridgelike branches. Hundreds of feet of leaves blocked most sunlight from ever meeting a man's eye. The eternal twilight, the ever-present mist, in time drove even the strongest minded men mad. More orange light filled Tayben's eyes as he rose above the leaves, and the lurking fog of the forest soon dissipated.

As he reached the top, he scanned the horizon; a flat line of dark green stretched for miles in all directions, save for the white peaks of the Taurbeir-Krons in the West – a north-south mountain range that bisected Endlebarr into two halves. Clouds of fog jumped up above the trees and then dipped back into the depths of vegetation. The golden sun peaked above the earth and Tayben felt a dizzying throb in his head.

§

~Morning, August 22nd
Royal Palace, Aunestauna, Ferramoor

Prince Eston stood on his bedroom balcony as the rising sun cast a golden glow on the vast city below him. Aunestauna, the bustling capital of Ferramoor, lay between emerald hills and an inlet of the ocean. The streets of the capital were a criss-crossing jumble creating triangular buildings that looked familiar even though Eston had never ventured into the city. Snaking its way through the center of the city was the Spring River that emptied into the inlet. Beyond the cluttered mess of streets rose countless groves of oak and cottonwood trees, and far away to the south drifted rolling dunes of desert sand – or so the prince had heard. Though Eston had just risen, it felt like days passed from his bed to the balcony. Eston's butler entered his room with a knock and greeted the prince on the balcony.

"Good morning, Errus," Eston replied without turning.

"Good morning, My Liege. Have a nice rest?"

Eston hesitated. "It was . . . rest."

"Let me know if I can do anything to help you."

Errus began to exit when Eston turned to him. "Oh, what is today?"

"Why, Your Majesty, it's your mother and father's anniversary, August 22nd."

"Thank you, sir." Eston breathed in the saltwater air blowing in from the west, thinking about the oddly vivid dream he had during the night – a foggy forest, the smell of blood, clashing swords, a sharp pain in his head.

Errus raised an eyebrow. "Are you alright, My Liege?"

Eston rubbed his eyes. "Yes, just . . . a strange dream I guess."

"Strange dreams are never good for the mind . . . it's best not to think about them."

Eston shook his head. "I'm not sure . . ."

"Well, your mother and father are expecting you at their celebration."

The prince thought for a moment. "I thought that wasn't until the afternoon."

"The winds predict a day of light showers, My Liege; so the King and Queen moved the celebration to breakfast. They seek your presence soon."

"I'll be there shortly," said Eston.

"Is there anything you need of me?"

Eston shook his head and Errus exited through a great wooden door, followed minutes later by the prince.

The hallways of the Royal Palace arched far above even Eston's tall figure, each decorative pillar of stone reaching seventy feet in the air. Countless open windows – each twenty to thirty feet tall – lined every hallway, letting in the summer ocean breeze. As the saltwater air drifted into the palace, it rustled the towering white and scarlet curtains. A dozen giant courtyards and gardens filled the castle, providing natural light to its hundreds of rooms and halls. Paintings of the Ferramish countryside, famous historical figures, and royal ancestors hung in alcoves along the walkways. The places Eston was told about but never shown were illustrated all around him.

Every corner Eston turned brought greetings from passersby. From the servants and younger courtiers came a "My Liege" or "Your Majesty" accompanied by a quick bow which he met with a nod. Older senators and important members of the government nodded as he passed by with a "Good morning, Prince Eston." Eston knew most of the wanderers of the halls by position if not by name. He grew up surrounded by these diplomats, artists, and important citizens, all of whom filled the palace with an imperialistic air.

An energetic eighteen-year-old ran up from behind him and punched him in the shoulder. "Hey, Eston, did you get that florist we wanted for their anniversary?"

"Yes, Fillian, mother will be happy; and are you capable of looking respectable for one second?" Eston grinned at his younger brother's messy brown hair, similar to his own. Fillian was barely a year younger than Eston and equally as tall. Together, the princes walked to a western courtyard that overlooked the inlet to meet with their parents.

The palace sat atop a cliff face, a few hundred feet above the vast Auness Sea, which narrowed its way through the Hills of Duloret and expanded into the valley of Aunestauna. Scenting the seaside air with salt, the inlet hosted a large port that connected the city with the rest of the world. Far to the southeast, dunegrass and windbreaks lined the seashore that stopped most of the southern sandstorms from reaching Aunestauna.

Walking into the courtyard for the celebration, the princes hardly drew much attention. Queen Eradine, however, noticed them and approached in a thin silver crown and long flowing dress. "Boys," she said, extending her hand, "come and join us." Queen Eradine smiled and guided them over to the table with a breakfast feast at which the king sat proudly. King Tronum shared a jest with advisors and senators also sitting at the table. The king sported a full head of white hair, a silver beard and bright blue eyes, adorned with scarlet robes and a silver crown. The table stood in soft grass looking over the ocean, and its attendees rattled off political opinions.

Noting Eston's arrival, Senator Nollard, a handsome young man with olive skin declared confidently, "—and twenty-one years of marriage later, the Wenderdehl family has still never disappointed . . . Of course, we'll see if that statement is true once your son here sits on his father's throne."

Eston laughed. "Hopefully you'll have a head of gray hair before you see *me* on the throne." Eston would be the third Wenderdehl to rule, succeeding his father, King Tronum, and grandfather, King Gallegore the Great.

A tall man with dark hair and a narrow face sitting beside King Tronum gave a slight cunning smile. His name was Sir Janus Whittingale, and for nearly as long as Eston could remember, he had served as his personal mentor and teacher, showing him the arts of everything from swordplay and battle strategy to mathematics and history. Eston had always been intimidated by Whittingale's intellect and often coldhearted demeanor, but it was from him that Eston learned everything he knew.

Whittingale spoke to the table, slightly quieter than the rest. "Well, if history may serve as any indication," he said, "I believe the blood running through this young man's veins is the very thing the world will need when the time comes." He gestured to Eston, glancing at him in the eyes. "Your father and his father have guided this world from decay into life. Over fifty years have passed since King Gallegore rose from nothing and united a continent torn apart by the rise of dark magic." He spoke to the whole table. "When all seemed lost, he led the Great War to vanquish the evils of sorcery forever from this continent and unite us into one Endellian Empire. Since Gallegore's death, King Tronum has ruled with might and power, keeping the peace and securing our futures. And, though those are large footsteps to fill," he turned to Eston, "my days teaching this one have given me confidence that he will leave even larger steps."

The table was silent; Eston was surprised by the rare compliment from his mentor. Senator Nollard broke the silence and stood. "Well then, to the royal family and their happy anniversary!"

Eston politely retreated as the circle of diplomats celebrated, and Prince Fillian directed palace servants bringing bouquets of flowers out of the castle and into the courtyard. He stopped by the rail overlooking the steep precipice that plunged into the ocean below as Fillian approached.

"Are you going to ask him about the Council meetings again, Eston?"

"No," said Eston, looking over at his father. "He doesn't trust us yet and he's not going to increase our power in the Council. Plus, I have to go get my books for my lesson with Whittingale today, just like every other day."

"Whatever you say," said Fillian.

After greeting a few more guests, Eston left the party and jogged across the palace to the library to gather his books for his lesson with Sir Janus Whittingale. Just as the clock struck eight in the morning on a clocktower in the city, he stopped as he saw a great plume of smoke rise far off in the distance – in the Third District.

§

~Morning, August 22nd
Aunestauna, Ferramoor

Kyan awoke facing a ceiling that seemed ready to crumble on top of his scraggy body. He looked around the cluttered, stuffy attic in the Third District of Aunestauna. Just for a moment, the cozy habitat of stolen goods that Kyan had created seemed claustrophobic, a feeling that he rarely got. Having long black hair and sour breath, Kyan's appearance matched the ramshackle state of his little home. The early morning sun streaming through the rotting wood panels of the attic bounced off little floating dust particles. Kyan pried open two boards with his skinny but toned arms to look at the clocktower across the square.

Seven o'clock, the 22nd . . . Strange, I thought yesterday was the 22nd.

Kyan shook his head and crawled out of the attic door onto the roof of the theater. Taking out a few boards and building it up, he had extended the attic of the theater up into a small, jagged shack that sat half above and half below the roof.

In the open morning air, up above the streets, he looked at the palace shining above the city with scarlet banners streaming in the wind. Up on their hill, the repulsive pricks laughed and drank without a care in the world. He spit toward the palace and began walking from roof to roof.

Kyan wore cut-up pants and a shirt that was too small. Around his tanned neck hung a very small makeshift necklace, bearing a small Olindeux, a silver-colored metal piece. Although it was summer, he also wore a jacket to conceal his identity. But for a homeless street dweller, Kyan carried himself surprisingly upright. Long boards of wood stretched from roof to roof, making traveling through the city quite easy. Nimble and agile, Kyan never fell to the streets below while journeying up there. His whole life had unfolded in and over these streets. The day was hot, and over the salty ocean breeze, he whiffed the golden prize

– bread, the warm scent wafting upwards over the angular houses of the Third District.

Kyan jumped down to a balcony in an alley, dropped to the street, and then turned the corner onto the avenue. The scent he was following came from a bakery that he had stolen from before. Approaching the stand, he pulled up his hood and tried to remain inconspicuous. Kyan stood beside the stand, waiting for the plump baker – Mr. Ruben Tumno – to turn his back. Kyan reached out and grabbed a small loaf. Placing it beneath his shirt, he casually walked around another street corner and tore into the warm bread, ripping off lumps and gorging it down as he walked through the city.

Though not as ramshackle as the Fourth District, houses of the slums still leaned in toward each other, casting deep shadows even at midday. Shingles regularly tumbled off of rooftops; bricks from the tight cobblestone streets were often missing; and doors hung crooked on their hinges. Most citizens carried a knife at their waist. On this side of the city, teeth were yellowed, and steps were limped.

In the distance, Kyan could hear a cacophony of squealing southern instruments, rattling jewelry, and shouting. The alley opened up into a large city square in which a throng of Gypsies waved their hands and scarves as they danced. A group of similar-looking foreigners – the Zjaari – cursed at the Gypsies as they moved in their elaborate gowns of beads, gems, and colors. The Gypsies and Zjaari were all immigrants from the deserts of the Southlands, but the two groups hated each other viciously. The Gypsies were a nomadic people of the deserts and plains, while the Zjaari were the coastal city-dwellers who ruled the Southlands.

Amidst the yelling, a Zjaari man took hold of Gypsy girl's black and red head scarf, ripped it off as she screamed, and threw it over a torch he held in his bracelet-covered hand. Four Gypsy girls grabbed the man and kicked out his knees. Pinning his arms behind his back, they dug their long nails into his neck gashing it open so that blood stained the cobblestone street. As he collapsed, his torch rolled behind him into a tailor shop; the curtains caught fire. The dancing morphed into a brawl as every man and woman started cursing and fighting each other. Kyan watched as men poured oil in the other shops and lit them on fire.

A group of Gyspy women took hold of one of the younger men and threw him in the flames. Screaming, thrashing, and burning, the man barely fought his way out, rolling around on the ground to try and extinguish his flaming clothes.

Instruments rang their tune throughout the square, the tempo quickening with every crash and yell. A bare-chested, tattooed man sat right beside fires and blew into a curved shaft that emitted an eerie harmonic tune of the desert. An old woman adorned with beads and carved tokens screamed out in chant as she was kicked on the ground; and others drunkenly laughed and danced to the strange music of disarray.

Kyan observed the chaos closely, smiling at the beauty of dysfunction. A column of black smoke began to stretch for the sky, filling the air with a haze that blocked out the hot sun. The Third District clocktower struck eight, ringing out in loud bashes of bells that clashed with the crackling fire and the clatter of the Scarlet Guard's horses.

Gleaming gold bracelets fell off of a man while he was brawling with another. Kyan quickly swooped down and grabbed them before walking away from the incoming Scarlet Guard. Looking back at the pillar of darkness reaching for the sun, another flash of déjà vu overtook him, and he almost thought he had seen that same cloud of smoke before.

The slums had given him nothing but poverty, hunger, and disdain for humanity. There was nothing redeeming about anyone – it was only live or die. Turning back, the dark-haired thief trudged against the flow of yellow teeth and drunken eyes that hoped to catch a glimpse of the fire and chaos.

§

~Morning, August 22nd
Seirnkov, Cerebria

Calleneck Bernoil awoke after hearing his name being hollered, followed by a "Come downstairs now!" It was the irritated but protective voice of Aunika, his older sister. Calleneck stumbled out of bed and folded up the sheet, looking outside at the clouded morning sky of Seirnkov. Even in summer, the days in Cerebria's capital never grew hot, just warm. He opened his window to the noise of jabbering city-goers. Narrow streets carved through a maze of ivy-covered wood houses. All the streets eventually reached the center of the city – Queen Xandria's black fortress.

Dalah, his sweet younger sister, opened the door. "Some new view out your window, Cal?" She gave a friendly chuckle. Her freckled cheeks were still rosy in the summer, and her light and wavy brown hair flowed gently over her delicate figure.

"Just taking in some fresh air, Dalah." Calleneck sighed with a hint of sadness.

Dalah walked up to him and hugged him from behind as he looked out into the city. He smiled at her and she let go, jumping onto his bed and staring up to the ceiling. "Aunika wants you downstairs."

Calleneck rolled his eyes. "Tell her I'll be down in two minutes." Calleneck laughed. "Also, our mother gets to tell us what to do, not our sister."

Dalah sat up on the bed. "It's fine, Cal. Just get changed and come down when you're ready. She wants us to leave early today."

"I know," he said as Dalah left the room for him to change.

Calleneck pulled off his tunic, revealing a large white scar on his chest — severely burned and wounded. Going back to the place that gave him the mark always felt a little unsettling, but he knew he had no choice. He carefully dressed in day clothes and grabbed his bag. He unzipped it carefully to make sure all of the new maps he had made of the underground tunnels were still there . . . they were. He closed up the bag and quickly walked down the narrow staircase to the kitchen where his mother and two sisters were talking. Dalah was born three years after Calleneck, while Aunika was three years his senior. Isolation from the family had been Aunika's preferred mode of handling tough situations until she had recently returned. Mrs. Bernoil's face had recently started to show wrinkles, and her hair was far along its path to gray.

"Morning mum," Calleneck greeted as he readjusted the strap around his shoulder. "Is father home?"

"He's on the other side of town selling his new sets of shoes today," his mother informed him. "Woke up at dawn this morning to get a head start." Her face often rested in a stubborn gaze, but however cold she looked on the outside, she always had loving intentions.

"That's alright," said Calleneck, "we'll see him in three days when we're back."

"Cal, grab some eggs before we leave," said his younger sister. "I cut up some green onions into them for you."

Calleneck smiled and kissed her on the head, "Thanks, Freckles." It was a name Calleneck had given Dalah many years back. He reached for the small plate of eggs by the fire.

"Eat them quickly," said Aunika. "We need to get going. *Uncle Gregt and Aunt Shelln are waiting for us.*" That, of course, wasn't true, but Calleneck quickly finished the food and said his goodbyes to his mother.

The three siblings headed out the door and onto the wet cobblestone streets. A misty rain drizzled down from the gray skies — the usual weather. The siblings turned a street corner and walked down a puddle-covered avenue with overhanging buildings on either side. As they crossed an intersection, a horse drawn wagon and its driver came barreling down the street. Calleneck grabbed Dalah's arm and pulled her out of the path of the cart as it whizzed by.

"Watch it!" he yelled at the driver, but the cart was already halfway down the next street. Calleneck shook his head. "Great Mother . . ."

The siblings continued walking forward into an alleyway shortcut, but Dalah stopped before entering.

Calleneck looked back. "Dalah, you alright? That cart driver was probably just drunk."

"Yes, I'm fine," she said, "it's just . . ."

Aunika stopped too. "What's wrong?"

Dalah avoided eye contact and looked down the street, folding her arms. "I . . . I don't know, I guess I just miss being with Mum and Dad more."

Calleneck walked back to Dalah and leaned against the wooden wall of the alleyway. "We got to see them the last few days . . . You've been fine with it before."

Dalah rocked back and forth in her boots and looked down. "I just can't keep lying to them. How long are we going to say we're going to Uncle Gregt and Aunt Shelln's place when we're not?"

Aunika put her hand on Dalah's shoulder. "Mum and Dad can't know about this; it would put them in danger. You know we don't have a choice."

"*You* had a choice," said Dalah, looking her in the eye.

Aunika turned to Calleneck and sighed, looking to him for advice. "I don't know, Dalah . . . if you really feel like you can't do it this week, I might be able to talk to the Council of Mages and excuse your absence, but—"

"No," said Calleneck, looking at Aunika. "We stick together. Remember? We're not splitting up again . . . not like last time."

Dalah's face turned pale, and she fidgeted with her hair. "It scares me going down there. Have you forgotten what they've done? Your scars, Cal, they're—"

Calleneck stepped forward and hugged Dalah. "You'll be okay."

Tears streamed down Dalah's cheek. "They hurt you . . ."

Calleneck pulled her close. "It doesn't hurt anymore." He pulled back and smiled. "It'll be okay . . . let's keep walking."

Dalah took a deep breath and nodded, and the three siblings trudged through the misty rain to their destination.

When the siblings reached the *Ivy Serpent,* a low-class inn, they entered in two-minute intervals to avoid drawing suspicion. Calleneck entered first.

The *Ivy Serpent* reeked of musty air and smoke. The first-floor lobby harbored men smoking pipes and playing cards. From under her black cloak, a woman with long, silvery-blonde hair and a piercing gaze watched Calleneck pass. A heavy man with one eye glared at him through a mirror on the wall and grunted while he flipped a knife in his deformed hand. Locating the short innkeeper, Calleneck stated the code, "Excuse me, sir, would you happen to know if there's any place I can find a spotted horse to take to Ontraug?"

The hunched-over innkeeper smiled and guided him down a back staircase to a room with three locks on the door. The man's wrinkled hands shook as he handled the rusty keychain. Looking over his shoulder down the hallway to be sure no one was there; the innkeeper opened the door and Calleneck slid inside the room. He heard the locks shut and the man limp away on the wooden floor. The room was covered in mirrors and the only light was a small crimson flame that Calleneck formed in his hand. The flame was certainly real, but its magic prevented it from burning Calleneck's hand. Calleneck extended his hand upward and placed the flame in the air. Hovering in place above him, it flickered back and forth, gently emitting light.

Taking his bag off his shoulder, he changed into long black robes. Calleneck took his crimson flame from the air back into his hand and pressed it against the correct mirror. Quietly, it began to hum with vibration, and its edges turned a pale green. The glass moved around like liquid silver suspended in the air. Calleneck glanced at the locked door, knowing that Dalah would soon follow, and stepped through the mirror.

Two guards in long black cloaks and hoods stood in front of him and bowed. "Greetings, Mr. Bernoil," they said.

Calleneck bowed back, and the tall sentries allowed him to pass, permitting him into the miles of subterranean tunnels and cities in which the Evertauri and their sorcerers dwelled.

THE CEREBRIAN GIRL
Chapter Two

~Afternoon, August 23rd
Royal Palace, Aunestana, Ferramoor

Angry voices echoed in the senate chamber as Eston watched in silence. Biweekly senate meetings held by King Tronum brought matters of concern to the attention of the government. His Majesty, along with Queen Eradine, their eight senators, and various officials – generals, scholars, and ambassadors – sat in a large round chamber. From the height of the palace hill, Eston turned and looked through the countless windows and gazed out upon the wealthiest parts of the city – the First and Second Districts – and then to the poorest slums – the Fourth. Far in the distance were forests of willows and fields of berries. The Council decided the fate of Ferramoor here, beneath a towering domed roof with a giant stained-glass skylight.

"That's exactly what Xandria expects us to do!" Senator Qarra An'Drui shouted from her seat in the chamber. Her dark skin made her fierce eyes pop as they hit the sunlight. "I agree with the queen. The best action to counter these attacks is to ensure the security of the inlet. We must continue our efforts to build Fort Duloret."

Prophet Ombern laughed. "You believe Xandria is foolish enough to attack the capital? She will bleed our forces in Endlebarr and push through central Ferramoor so she can hit the major centers of our power from the east. What we need now is to be bold, bold like in the days of Gallegore. We have the numbers; it's time to come out from behind our walls and take the initiative. Xandria will only win if we allow her to choose the field of battle, allow her to keep us forever on the defensive. We need a threatening assault on the Great Cerebrian Gate. That wall is keeping us from driving east, and if we take it, we would have the numbers to overwhelm her."

"We would lose all of our men trying an operation like that!" said Senator An'Drui.

"We must take risks!" affirmed Prophet Ombern.

"Please, Prophet," said Tronum, "I know Xandria's ways well. It is in our best interest to never assume what course she will take. If we do not approach these matters with clear minds, she will destroy Ferramoor. Our generals have advised us to continue the advance of our northern campaign in Endlebarr, but Xandria is reorganizing her battalions to counter. She knows that we will not be able to press forward fast enough to support all of our troops in the southeast quarter of the forest. Once winter hits, the Southern Pass will be impassable and our forces in Eastern Endlebarr will be cut off from us. We need to withdraw them soon and wait out the winter. Caution will not lose us this war, Prophet, but risking all on a single throw of the dice just might."

All the while, Eston could not help thinking about a swirling crimson light – crimson fire. He shook his head and turned his attention to the discussion. He thought hard about ways to help. *I could bring up the peace treaty with the nation of Parusemare and ask to extend it to a military alliance in exchange for tariff-free trade with Ferramoor.*

"Father," he said, "if I may–" The instantly raised hand of Tronum ended his attempt to offer input. Eston sat in silence for the remainder of the meeting, embarrassed by his inability to address the members of the government.

Eston approached his father after the senate meeting. "Father, I–"

"Eston, the reason I allow you to attend the senate meetings is strictly for you to observe and gain experience, not to govern."

"Of course, father," said Eston. He shrunk down in the presence of his father, who nodded and walked off. Eston closed his eyes and clenched his jaw. *I need a walk,* he thought.

Eston strolled through the courtyards and breezeways to the eastern wing, where massive gates blocked the upper tiers of the palace. Ascending a narrow stone staircase, he passed a sentry who gave a nod and "Your Majesty." Eston felt his hand along the white stone wall of the palace grounds, lost in thought. He knew the war was important, and Ferramoor must stand for reuniting all the nations of Endellia once again in a continental Empire, but what was being done to help the people? *We send sons and husbands off to war, and if they're lucky enough to make it out, they return to a home worse off than the one they left.* Eston rubbed his temple and stepped up onto the wall.

The prince sat on the arch overlooking the lower levels of the royal hill with his arms crossed. I'm next in line to the throne of this kingdom and I have done nothing to help it. Eston hadn't left the palace in years because of his studies with Whittingale and his father's perpetual disapproval of Eston's desire to do real work. It had never seemed much of a restriction given the immense size of the castle and the abundant resources that poured through its gates every day. A great sadness rushed over Eston as he looked back at his home, and out toward his kingdom. *If, one day, this will be mine, I must be a part of it.* But from somewhere in his memory, he felt that he already knew the city, from the mansions to the slums. *How could I?* he asked himself. *I have seen it all before, but not as myself . . . it's like I've been through the city and ran over its roofs in a dream. Still, I must see it.*

Using a messenger, Eston summoned his friend and the palace overseer — Lord Benja Tiggins. Not a half hour later, Eston met him on the archway above the gate to the palace. Atop the palace wall, the whole city glistened below them, bustling like a hive of bees.

Benja Tiggins had thick black hair that, if not brushed aside, would hang below his nose. He was not too much older than the prince — in his early twenties — and the two were close. Benja had ascended quickly in government due to his late father's position as general and his mother's famous engineering works in the palace. Many called the position he held the "Scarlet Lord," as he also served as commander of the Scarlet Guard. One might say that he had more control over certain things in the palace than King Tronum himself; Benja Tiggins had keys to all the vaults and authority over all the servants and guards. Yet, with all his power, Benja's pale face stared somberly out into the city as if something very deep within his heart troubled him.

Eston informed his friend that he wanted to travel beyond the gates of the palace, telling him how much he hated the mundane routine of sleeping, eating, studying, and sword fighting, how embarrassed he was by his inability to affect policy or communicate with upper members of the government. "I just want to actually make a difference for once. I'm supposed to represent my people, but I don't even know them."

Benja Tiggins replied quietly and winked, "Your father would be quite happy with you missing." Eston chuckled but thought twice about Benja's words; they contained a drop of truth. Benja continued, "But it would be very difficult to exit this palace without anyone noticing you."

"That's exactly why I would need your help. You're the Scarlet Lord — I'm confident that you're able to make arrangements to cover my absence."

Benja put his hands in his pockets. "But Eston . . . that would be misusing my powers."

"It would just be this one time," said Eston.

Benja shook his head. "You know that's not true."

"Benja, I'm not going to destroy Ferramoor by going into the city. I just want to . . . I want to know what it's like. It wouldn't be dangerous. Most commoners don't know what I look like . . . please?"

"I really don't think that you should," he said, noting Eston's longing gaze toward the city. Benja sighed and turned toward the prince. "Alright, this one time . . . but only if you take a guard with you."

Eston shook his head. "I go alone. I don't want to see my people behind the sword of another . . . I want to see them as they are."

Benja sighed. "Just know that it's me who gets in trouble if you decide to act stupid down there and get yourself caught or hurt."

"Thank you."

In the Second District of Aunestauna, Eston glided along with the crowds of thousands of people, moving like ants on a forest floor. The streets here were filled with countless colors and sounds. People of every color scurried along, talking in warm, rhythmic dialects; the women's gowns of scarlet, turquoise, and gold waved as they walked. The city lived and breathed. Deep, hearty laughter sounded from within every tavern, bank, and shop. Merchants on each side of the street shouted prices and offers at him as he passed. "Half off on any nails and knives today! Only fifteen argentums for a winter coat!" Eston kept walking, headed to the place he wanted to see most – the light and life of Aunestauna, the Great Ferramish Bazaar.

In the middle of the Second District lay the grand marketplace that stretched over dozens of blocks. Barrels of maize, zucchini, and potatoes lined the walkways. The soft smell of bread meandered underneath the canopies of red and yellow. Even berries and melons from beyond the southern edges of the kingdom reached the markets of the capital. Cooks sizzled seasoned meat over fires for the wealthy to purchase. Children ran around, knocking over the occasional bucket or basket, causing both laughter and shouting from the swarm of people entering and exiting the markets. Rows of beads and jewels hung from the edges of the tents, ready to be sold to the hundreds of city-goers. Eston felt an urge to snatch one, but he backed away, not knowing what possessed him to even think it . . . he had never stolen.

A young, handsome man eyed him and approached him quickly, causing Eston to turn away in case he had been recognized. The man grabbed Eston's shoulder and turned him around. "Buy some flowers, sir!" the man practically yelled above the noise of the square. "Only a quarter argentum for 'em." Relieved, Eston laughed and purchased a large dahlia with the coins he brought in his pocket, surprised at how little it cost.

The prince left the Bazaar and walked through many more avenues which were shaded by flamboyant awnings before ducking into *The Little Raven*, a street-level tavern with a welcoming atmosphere. Deciding to take the risk of revealing his identity, he ordered a small glass of wine. Because of the prince's limited experience with common folk, his interaction with the bartender was too awkward to be comfortable for Eston, though she didn't seem to care. As he waited for his drink, he couldn't help but hope that whatever plan Lord Benja Tiggins had dreamed up was a sufficient distraction for his disappearance. Eston considered the possibility that Benja had Guards following him to make sure nothing happened. He looked around the tavern, but nothing seemed suspicious, and no one seemed to know his identity.

Luckily enough, the only papers posted on these walls and in the avenues were issues from the Scarlet Guard. No average citizen had ever seen the prince. The only royal figures that could be seen in paintings were King Tronum and Queen Eradine. Even those, however, were inaccurate depictions of his family. In the paintings, his parents looked close to gods, with smooth skin and bright eyes, healthy hair and soft gazes. His father seemed everything but that.

Although it was just late afternoon, reddish light flooded in the square windows because of the scarlet banners that often stretched between the roofs of the First and Second District. The color was not only used for city and kingdom pride, but also for unity under his father's throne.

Eston compared the calm atmosphere in *The Little Raven* to the bustle of the Bazaar. Both men and women sat in chairs over tables either sitting in solitude or quietly discussing small matters. A young woman — just around Eston's age — sat intently reading a roll of parchment at a table in the corner. The first thing Eston noticed was her hair — a brilliant blonde. The pale color was particularly unusual in Ferramoor. The light from behind her made it glow pure and soft, so bright that it could've been the snowcapped mountains of the far north — but no, it was warm like the white sands of the Southlands. But the hair was tattered and had remnants of dust and dirt — like she was trying to hide the brilliance of its color. The foreign hair fell in front of her face in a way that made Eston want to lift her chin to see who she was. But amidst the light, he sensed there was something dark and unnerving hidden deep in her pale blue eyes. He turned away to avoid being thought rude.

Just as the bartender returned with a glass of white wine for the prince, the girl rolled up her parchment, placed it in a small handbag and approached the counter, sitting two stools away from Eston. He looked down at his glass and couldn't help but eavesdrop on her conversation. The bartender asked if she could help her.

"Yes, I'll have another glass please." There was something a bit strange about the way she spoke. It was as if she was trying to subtly make her voice sound warm, like most of the speech in Ferramoor; yet, there was a hint of a colder dialect with which she was more comfortable. This tone was barely noticeable, but it was there.

He angled his wine glass in such a way that he could catch another glimpse of the girl's face through the reflection. This time, he felt like he knew her face. He immediately turned the glass back.

The bartender came back with her drink.

"Thank you, ma'am," said the girl.

As the girl was brought her glass, he glanced sideways again. *Where have I seen her before?* . . . After a minute or two of internal debate, Eston plucked up the courage to say something.

"Excuse me," he said, turning to her a few stools over.

The girl's eyes settled on him, and Eston could tell from her unchanged expression that she did not recognize him.

He tapped the counter. "I'm sorry, have I seen you before?"

The girl shook her head. "'Don't think so."

"Oh, sorry, I— you must look like someone I know."

The girl shrugged and took out a piece of paper from her bag to read. The writing was small and sideways, allowing Eston to only read the title, "Servant Registry for 784 AHL." 784 AHL was Eston's birth year. He couldn't shake the feeling that he had seen this girl before. *Why is she looking at a palace registry?*

"I'm sorry," he said, "have you been around the First District?"

The girl turned her paper over. ". . . I've been around the city a lot, First District a couple of times."

"What's your name?" asked Eston.

She paused for an unnerving silence before deciding to ask for his name. "Endra," she said. "Yours?"

He replied with the first name that came to him. "Umm . . . Gallien." Eston took a sip of his drink. "You seem to have an accent," he said.

The girl hesitated. "Well I guess . . . my father grew up in Cerebria and moved to Nottenberry before the split of the Empire. I got a bit of his speech wrapped up in my own." The door chimed as another customer entered *The Little Raven.*

"What made you come to Aunestauna?" said Eston.

The girl nervously chuckled. "You ask many questions, Gallien. I'm here for some business for a collection of farms in Nottenberry."

Eston took a sip of wine. *Why would farms want to know about the palace servant registry?* "What do your farms grow?" he asked.

"Look," said the girl, "I don't want any trouble, I have to go." She lifted her bag and set an argentum on the table to pay for her drink. As she packed up, she took a letter from her coat pocket and stuffed it in her handbag. Eston couldn't help but glimpse parts of the addressed front.

To- Seirnkov, Cerebria, . . .

From . . . R.N.

R.N.? He thought. She said her name was Endra . . . and why is she sending mail to Cerebria during wartime? The girl pushed in her stool and exited the tavern door, sounding a chime. Eston couldn't shake the strange feeling he got from her. *Her accent . . . she's a Cerebrian.*

IN THE UNDERBRUSH
Chapter Three

~Morning, August 23rd
Southeastern Endlebarr

Tayben stood on a large branch of a tree overlooking the Great Forest of Endlebarr. Full of morning energy, the sun had just come over the horizon. The only sounds above the canopy were the slight breeze that rustled the leaves of the giant trees and the occasional bird that darted up above the forest. He felt as though days had passed since he climbed up here, but he shook his head remembering the skirmish the day prior and falling off his horse. *Probably just because of the concussion.* He looked out into the painted sky, glistening with oranges and yellows, lighting the vast expanse of forest with a warm glow.

A morning fog rose up from the forest and partially obscured the sun, seeming to lift him into the sky itself. All around him, the trees rustled and the forest wakened. He imagined it was almost like standing over a vast city, vibrant with people and winding streets. The fog glowed yellow and orange around him and reminded him of the fire from his father's blacksmith's shop. He breathed deeply, taking in the sunlight and the air, and turned back down.

He began his descent to the forest floor by grabbing the moss-covered branches of the three-hundred-foot tree. Toned from army training, his arms and back lowered him through the canopy with ease. As he descended, the sounds of vibrant songbirds, countless buzzing insects, and the bubbling creek that ran through the camp wound their way through underbrush.

About halfway down the towering tree, Tayben stopped and stood on a bridge-sized branch to look around at the canopy surrounding him; the light had already dimmed and the air had become cool and wet. Thick willow-like leaves filtered out the steamy air of summer and the frigid winter air, remaining cool year-round. Tayben liked the freshness of the air, it reminded him of home by the woods and the lake. Though the winter brought freezing temperatures, some force kept every plant full of yellow leaves that would turn green come spring. A year in the forest had deprived him of sunlight; his skin was pale, and his pupils could never fully adjust whenever he climbed to the sky.

As he lowered himself through the under canopy, Tayben tensed as he felt a cold draft of air slowly settle around him; the muted colors in the wood around him seemed to get darker and the sounds of birds and insects became distorted. He had a very strange feeling that he was not the only person in the tree.

With heightened awareness and apprehension, he put his hand on his sword and turned around, thinking he saw a shadow shoot past, only to see a black squirrel that was watching him from a branch up.

Relieved, the soldier ambled toward it on the branches that grew as wide as Tayben was tall; he never needed to worry much about falling off them. The squirrel scurried away, and Tayben continued descending back down to the sentry platform. From his vantage point, he could see that many people had awakened to begin their day during the time that Tayben had been gone. Usually, the camp would come to life before the sun was up, but the summer brought days so long and mornings so early that even the toughest troops would wake after sunrise.

He looked around at the wooden platform on which he stood. The sentries had the luckiest job in the army, he thought, getting to spend all day high above the world in the magnificent trees. He would have given anything to spend his time up there, away from the death and battle. But of course, he could never bring himself to leave his companionship, especially Gallien — his one consistent friend in the last year on the front lines.

Tayben finished his descent down to the forest floor and walked back to his tent, which was nestled between two of the massive eight-foot-tall roots. Like the banyan trees of the southern jungles, this giant was one of many whose roots formed cages and webs before entering the ground. Flowered bushes and thick grass decorated the underbrush with green. Yet, where Tayben and his battalion camped in the south of Eastern Endlebarr, the dense underbrush didn't come close to the thickness and near impenetrability of the deepest parts of the forest

Just as Tayben unbuttoned the door flap, Birg burst out of the tent.

"Oh, there you are, Tayben! I was beginin' to wonder if you and Gallien had ran off without me."

"I went out alone. Is Gallien not here?"

"No, he left without folding his blanket, didn't do nothin'. Left his shoes by the door as well. Thought it was a bit strange for a neat freak like him to be off like that without tidyin' up. Didn't go with you? That's strange."

Tayben raised an eyebrow and looked around to the other tents nearby. "He must have gone somewhere else in camp, I'm sure he's nearby."

The soldiers retrieved their portions of stiff and dry breakfast for the morning and warmed a pot of water over a fire with their troop, which consisted of nearly a dozen partnerships. Tayben and Birg had not yet seen Gallien at breakfast, meaning their partnership of three soldiers was incomplete. The troop commander, Captain Fenlell of Endgroth, assessed the condition of the forty-some-odd young men. Fenlell himself was not much older than twenty five, but he swaggered around like he was king. An experienced fighter, he loved yet hated his troop and had a habit of referring to the boys as bastards. The platoon supervisors never fell in love with "his style of bloodying up the bunch" mostly because he rarely listened to them, but they let him command the troop nonetheless. When he came around to Tayben and Birg he counted, "One, two, and *not* three. Gallien Aris is not with you. Care to . . . *elaborate?*" The last word bounced off of his tongue in a harsh Cerebrian accent.

Tayben saluted, "Sir, we woke up and he was not in our tent. He left his shoes in the grass outside of the tent and his things were not packed. We have not seen him this morning."

"The leader of your partnership gone missing . . . Well even the good ones get driven mad in this forest. We'll find a replacement soon enough." Fenlell walked to the next group. Tayben and Birg looked at each other with worried expressions, fearful of what might happen to their friend.

Fenlell finished his last check, grabbed a very young soldier's rock-of-a-hardtack biscuit and a pot, strutted over to the center of the troop and banged them together repeatedly, summoning the attention of the group with a ring and clang. Walking around and hitting the pot, he yelled above the noise, "All right bastards! Shut your traps!" The talking ceased and he tossed the pot down on a rock – making it ring loudly again – and chucked the biscuit at the young soldier's head. "The *honorable* supervisors have asked us to meet at the barracks over the ridge for drills and training in half an hour! Please act like you know how *not* to die in battle."

The armory was one of the few permanent structures in the surrounding forest, and one of only a few dozen of the kind in the eastern forest of Endlebarr. Boasting training grounds and a small mess hall, the bold wooden structure still sat like an ant beneath the towering trees, whose canopies reached such great size that they completely arched over the wide field which fit hundreds of troops. Fire lamps hung around its edges to provide light in the dim underbrush; alone, the little light that found its way through the trees did not fulfill the needs of a battle training ground. Soldiers had to cut down and burn plants daily to keep the forest floor from growing back. Tayben's troop lined up with the ten others in his platoon, forming a line of soldiers clad in dark green. Officers ran the platoon through drills and formations, preparing them for battles to come.

Archers shot volleys of arrows over the backs of swordsmen, who each crawled on the ground to various locations. For hours on end the drills continued, with few breaks for rest and water. But after the forest darkened even deeper with the fading light of day, the troops were dismissed for the day.

Tayben and Birg headed off along the lightly beaten pathways back toward their troop campsite for dinner. The trails in the forest never stayed for too long; after being flattened by soldiers and horses, the grass, moss, and undergrowth would spring back almost overnight.

Tayben stopped by the small brook that wrapped around the tents and eating area to clean off the dried dirt from his face and hair. Not ten yards away, his troop's soldiers were starting the dinner fire and adding timber to build it up a bit. Birg knelt down with him too, but both were awfully silent. They were both thinking about the same thing – Gallien was still nowhere to be found.

Tayben dipped his head in the water again, feeling the cold, wet stream clean off his sweat and muck. When he lifted his head out of the water, he overheard Captain Fenlell in the distance informing the circle of gathered officers of Gallien's disappearance. "Yes, sir; Gallien Aris. My best guess is that the *aristocratic* wimp realized he isn't fit for battle. Probably fled camp in the middle of the night to go back to his mansion." Tayben spit out the cold water on the grass. *Gallien wasn't a Crat . . . was he?*

Birg approached him and sat down; he was slightly older and taller than Tayben with chocolate skin – rare for a Cerebrian. They discussed the day and the new formations, and also the absence of Gallien. Tayben thought back to Fenlell's statement.

"Say," said Tayben with a concerned gaze, "is Gallien a Crat?"

"That I couldn't tell you for sure," said Birg. "But it's not the first time someone's asked me – 'think it's the way he carries himself. He's smart, but not full of himself like the Crats."

"Well even when I would tell Gallien about my childhood in Woodshore, he never did explain much about himself, other than the fact that he lived in Gienn and his father was an inventor . . . Maybe he could be. But Fenlell over there is telling the supervisors that he fled out of cowardice. I just can't see that . . . even if he was a Crat."

"Oh to hell with 'em Shae. My guess is as good as yours as to what happened to him. And I know it'd be a sour thing if he was one of them, but it doesn't matter who he is as much as what he' done."

Tayben nodded. "He's done a lot." Tayben played back memories. "A few months before you joined the army," he told Birg, "there was a day we ran out of flint to make a fire for our meals." Tayben chuckled. "So he walked around the entire camp collecting reflective things like the backs of shields and he made them into this giant curved thing that reflected the sunlight from a break in the canopy onto the firewood and then *phoof* . . . it ignited and we got our meal."

Birg smiled at the story. "Gallien taught me how to read."

Tayben looked up with surprise.

"I mean I knew a li'l . . ." said Birg, "But yeah . . . My family said I 'ad to work for 'em first and then I could go to school."

Tayben nodded. "Then you joined the army."

The two of them sat there next to the babbling stream and listened to the quiet, haunting sounds of the forest.

"Well, I'm starving,'" said Birg. "Let's get some food in our stomachs to take our minds off everything, aye?"

Tayben sighed. "Yeah."

The two stepped over the stream and sat down around the fire with their troop. They were all removing their armor and boots to relax and turn in for the night. A pot sat cooking over the fire as the last few soldiers funneled into the group, except for Gallien.

One of the older soldiers went ahead and began serving portions of dinner out, since Fenlell was still talking with other captains across the stream.

"Thanks," said Tayben as the soldier to his right passed him a bowl of broth and chopped potatoes.

Birg, to his left, began shoveling down what little portion of food he had. Within thirty seconds, he had downed the dinner. Looking over to Tayben, his eyebrows furrowed. "You've gotta eat somethin'."

Tayben shook his head. "He's out there, Birg. He's probably alone and . . ."

The other soldiers around them spoke in low voices to each other, but Birg focused on him. "I know . . . but I'm not sure what we can do. Just try to get your mind off it for now."

Tayben ate a few mouthfuls of his meal, but Birg wasn't satisfied with his efforts. Birg slowly began tapping his foot and muttering.

"What?" said Tayben as Birg began to sing.

"Well I know a man across the wild, foul as any seen!" he sang with a big smile on his face.

Tayben rolled his eyes and smiled.

"With a heart as cold and bone as frail as a Goblin, yes indeed!"

Tayben chuckled as the other troops around the fire, recognizing the tune, joined in jubilantly. After just another line, they were clapping their hands on their thighs and thundering out the lyrics to lift their spirits.

A greedy lad, he killed his dad,
To steal the kingdom throne!
The thief, the cheat, who hates our queen,
The evil man named Tronum!

Tayben laughed and joined in for the chorus.

We'll sack his city and take what's ours,
As long as we'll be free!
The untrue king will want no more,
As he flees from Ferramoor!

Suddenly, screaming broke out in a pavilion across the stream. The soldiers jumped to their feet.

"Another one's gone mad!" Birg yelled. He and Tayben stood up as people rushed toward the commotion; the officers across the stream behind him didn't seem to notice the rampage occurring.

"It's coming!" screamed the man running through the camp. "For all of us!" He fought off several people and tried to escape. The man flailed and cried and punched and kicked, shouting gibberish about blood and omens. More and more soldiers ran to contain the chaos; he attempted to grab someone's sword. Just as the soldier regained possession, the fear-crazed man wrenched free of the men trying to wrestle him down and snatched a spear, hurling it right in the direction of Birg. Instinctively, Tayben tackled Birg and ducked under the spear just in time for it to pass over their heads.

Suddenly, a cold shiver ran down his spine and the air around him seemed hazy. The fire not too far away blew out in a wisp of smoke. He remembered the tree in the morning and had the same unnerving impression that he was being watched. A very strange force drew him toward an opening in a bush. Right as he thought he saw a black shadow and a pair of silver eyes, Birg grabbed his face and asked him if he was alright.

"Yes, I—"

"Thank you, Tayben," said Birg.

Soldiers finally tackled the deranged man to the ground and a captain approached them.

"You alright, soldier?" said a general named Korkov, speaking to Tayben.

"Yes, sir."

"Contain him!" he shouted to the soldiers. He turned back to Tayben. "That was quick thinking, soldier. Your name?"

"Tayben Shae, sir."

"Glad you're alright," stated General Korkov.

The deranged man across the brook growled and yelled nonsense as soldiers gagged him, and the general headed back to his headquarters.

Once Korkov was gone, Captain Fenlell turned to address the crowd. "See that, boys? That is the lovely sound of madness! We are not welcome in this forest. Endlebarr is a nasty bitch. She watches you from every corner; she takes weak men at her leisure and drives them loopy; she doesn't care if you live or die. But of course none of you brave bastards would *ever* succumb to the strangeness of the underbrush." He raised his sword parallel to the ground. "A sword is a quick death, but that's not what's happening here. So wake up and smell the mist! It's hiding what'll kill you." He pointed over to the thrashing soldier. "If one of you bastards finds yourself lured by disturbing visions, do me a favor and slit your own neck . . . There are strange things here boys. Don't let the fog cloud your mind."

As they walked back to their tent, Birg put his hand on Tayben's shoulder. "I can't thank you enough, Tayben. You saved my life. That was quite somethin' back there."

"It's hardly close to other things we've faced . . . I'm still worried about Gallien."

"Well, there isn't nothin' we can do about that."

Tayben shook his head. "Look, you don't understand. Gallien has been by my side ever since I joined the army. He's saved my life more times than I can count, and he's the smartest person I've met. I just don't think he'd ever run off like that."

Birg put his hand on Tayben's shoulder. "You heard Fenlell . . . this forest makes people do crazy stuff. People aren't in their right minds here."

Tayben looked out into the foggy forest and shook his head. "Not Gallien." Tayben sighed and opened the tent flap.

"I think you're overthinkin' this business. You look dreadful and you just need rest." Birg entered the tent and Tayben stood outside, holding the flap open.

"It's not just Gallien . . . Birg, did you feel something when that man was going insane?"

"Well I felt a bit creeped out if that's whatcha mean."

"No, I mean, like a cold and unnerving draft."

"I'm not sure. It was probably just a breeze that blew out the fire, Tayben."

Tayben shut the flap of the tent, tired of Birg misunderstanding him. *I'm not going crazy!* he thought. The night was far fallen, with only faint, filtered moonlight and distant torches lighting the underbrush. The scene of the soldier driven mad replayed in his mind as he stood outside the tent for a while. Fenlell's warning echoed in his head and he heard Birg turning over in his sleep. He looked down and saw Gallien's shoes next to his feet. *Could he have been driven mad? Wandering in the forest with no shoes . . .* He looked into the forest and whispered, "Where are you?"

While looking out into the underbrush, his body suddenly turned cold and the dark fog around him seemed to swirl. He stepped forward from his tent and the tree roots to try and see better. The chirps of insects faded to silence; he could hear Birg's breathing in the tent. He could barely see anything in the twilight—just faint silhouettes of the tree trunks. Just as Tayben was about to go back to his tent, he stopped dead in his tracks. A man adorned in a black cloak stood in the mist not ten yards off, staring straight at him. The mist swirled in the slight breeze and enveloped the shadow-like figure. When it settled, the cloaked figure had vanished.

AN EVERTAURI
Chapter Four

~Sometime, August 23rd
The Network, Seirnkov, Cerebria

Far beneath the city of Seirnkov lay a network of subterranean tunnels and vast caverns. The air stood still there, and drips of water echoed off the dark stone passages. Stuffed with stalactites and bioluminescent cave insects, the tunnels twisted through the gray rock beneath Cerebria. But in the darkness, these chilling tunnels occasionally lit up with blinding flashes of light produced by the sorcerers of the Evertauri.

A jet of crimson embers burst out of Calleneck's hand and hit a stalactite on the roof of the cavern.

"No. Again," commanded his older sister from behind him.

"Aunika, I can't—"

"Again . . . Focus."

The cavern was pitch black, and the cold rock surrounding them echoed their voices. Calleneck closed his eyes from within the hooded black cloak that he wore. Summoning the magic in his flesh, crimson sparks slowly emerged out of his palm, swirling together to form flakes of light. They spiraled and flew chaotically in all directions in a burst of energy before fading away.

"Calleneck! What did I tell you?"

"I know! I just need practice."

"But we don't have time for this. You've been in the Evertauri for what, two years now, and yet you can't control your—"

"Emotions, yes I know! Aunika, we've been at this for an hour."

"Oh, I'm sorry," she said, "is there something more pressing that you have to do? Sometimes I think you forget we are fighting a war; even Dalah understands that. Queen Xandria's only disadvantage is our existence; we all have to be ready to do anything we can to overthrow her."

"I know," said Calleneck.

"Then show me you care. You're gifted compared to others your age. I'm just trying to help you; I can't see you dead in battle . . . Focus. Focus on the energy. Focus on your mind."

Crimson embers erupted from his hand, lighting the cavern. He channeled the column of light into the rock wall in front of him, causing it to glow red. He pushed harder, forcing the energy through the stagnant air. A deep rumbling could be heard over Calleneck's heavy breathing. A fracture appeared in the wall, and soon hundreds of pounds of rock instantly shattered, falling to the cavern floor ahead of him. He stopped the flow of energy and caught his breath.

Aunika looked satisfied. "I'll be back." She left through the entryway of the cave, and Calleneck sat on the cold stone floor next to a stalagmite to rest.

The caves were unfinished sections of the abandoned underground city created by the once powerful Goblins of Cerebria. They had toiled over hundreds of years building the massive subterranean Network, but a few years before Calleneck was born, their race had been hunted to extinction by Queen Xandria. Inhabiting the Goblins' home without their consent made Calleneck feel unwelcome, but it was the only place where the Evertauri could operate in secrecy.

Hot and covered in sweat, he took off his cloak. The skin on his chest was severely burned and contorted from his branding. The Evertauri did not tolerate mistakes.

He thought back to the day he was marked. It was after Aunika – unbeknownst to Calleneck – joined the Evertauri that he discovered his gift, or rather, curse, of sorcery; but the way in which he learned was not a pleasant memory. He remembered the explosion from his chest that threw him to his knees, crushing him into the wet cobblestone. He remembered the columns of crimson flames violently circling his crouched figure at great speeds and the glass shattering from street windows cutting through the air. He thought of the air drumming in his ears like thunder, the crimson embers erupting from his chest and reentering through his back, screams slicing through the cloud of smoke that stretched to the sky.

As soon as the incident occurred, the Evertauri came to the scene and rushed him into the tunnels beneath Seirnkov to hide him. Unwilling to show mercy, President Madrick Nebelle, the leader of the Evertauri, branded him to show that he was now a part of them, that others could never know of their existence.

Snapping back to reality, he covered himself as Aunika returned through the entryway with two cloaked sorceresses and a skinny, ugly pig on a rope. Calleneck stood up and bowed to the guests as Aunika guided the pig to a stalagmite and tied him to it.

"All right, Calleneck, obviously you can't practice on a human, but this is close. Kill it quickly."

Calleneck looked at the pile of broken rock ahead of him and took a deep breath in. Crimson sparks sprung from his hand. He channeled them into a column of energy and forced them into the pig. The pig squealed in pain and writhed on the floor. He hated the sound. He hated the screaming and the pain and he almost forced himself to stop the stream of embers. He knew what the burning felt like.

"Don't torture it," Aunika said, "just kill it."

Calleneck drilled the sparks into the bones of the pig and shattered them, sending fragments of bone slicing through its organs. It flopped on the stone, lifeless.

"An efficient way to kill a man," said a woman watching. "Once mastered, it will take only seconds to take down a dozen enemies. You are exceeding expectations. I think we are done here. Thank you, Ms. Bernoil, for aiding your brother in his training."

"Of course," Aunika replied as she exited the cave. Drained from the exertion of the magic, Calleneck followed her out, passing by tunnels and rooms, each glowing with various colors. Violet flashes, golden waves of light, and green flames dotted the corridors.

Calleneck halted when a wave of liquid-like yellow light beat in pulses along every corridor. *Summonings of the whole Evertauri by President Nebelle are usually silver,* he thought, *but this is yellow . . .* Something was off. He changed direction and headed toward the Nexus.

The Nexus towered fifteen stories high, yet still remained far under the surface of Seirnkov. It was the central underground city square, the heart of the Network to which all tunnels led. Open like a giant foyer or courtyard, it was lined with balconies, halls, libraries, and dorms on each floor of the central square.

It was a truly enormous cavern, an engineering marvel, hundreds of feet beneath Seirnkov. Light from thousands of torches burning in all colors filled the giant underground city square where hundreds of cloaked figures began to gather. On a balcony above the central square stood Sir Borius Shipton, whose body emitted waves of yellow light with each of his heart beats. Sir Borius, second in command to President Madrick Nebelle, had ebony skin, a stern face, and a strong regard for justice. The crowd of sorcerers stood in complete silence as the last of the Evertauri funneled in. Calleneck squeezed next to fellow cloaked rebels to listen. The beating yellow light stopped, and Sir Borius Shipton stepped forward.

"I have come to address you on behalf of our leader, President Nebelle." The stone of the Nexus amplified his voice. "The reason for his absence today

– the Council of Mages has received word from our spies that his son, Shonnar Nebelle, has been murdered."

Gasps and muttering filled the Nexus.

Sir Borius continued, "President Nebelle has asked me to take command for the next week to allow him to clear his mind."

A yelling voice echoed from a side hallway; many of the Evertauri looked over to see the source. A man, being dragged by guards, emerged from the tunnel with green ropes of energy binding his feet and hands. His face bled and he let out cries of anguish, screaming for help. "Please, I beg you! It wasn't me!"

Sir Borius scanned the crowd gathered in the Nexus. "The Council of Mages also would like to remind you that any disloyalty or breach of the law is punishable by death."

The man was then tied to a stone column underneath Sir Borius's balcony.

"One of our Evertauri, Mr. Klytus Kraine, accompanied Shonnar Nebelle on a routine mission through the Network tunnels. And once they were far enough away, Kraine stabbed Shonnar and left him to die alone in the dark."

Calleneck shook his head. *Why would anyone do that? And to the President's son?* He looked over and saw his sister, Dalah, covering her mouth with her hand.

Sir Borius continued. "This murderer will now suffer his victim's fate."

"Wait! Please!" shouted Kraine, tied by ropes of light. "I didn't kill him!"

"You were found running through the tunnels away from his body with his blood on your hands," said Sir Borius.

"For the Great Mother's sake, listen to me!" said Kraine.

The rest of the Evertauri stood still, and Borius nodded. "Speak."

Kraine looked to the Evertauri. "This was not a routine mission we were on. Shonnar Nebelle, who has been like a son to me, he – he asked me to follow him deep into the Network. 'Said he had found something – traces of – of dark magic . . . glowing flowers growing out of nothing but cold, dark stone. I was the first person he found, and he told me I needed to see, to report back to the Council of Mages with him . . . he was saying that we were almost there when we were attacked."

"By whom?" said Borius.

Kraine shook his head. "I don't know, they wore masks – horrifying masks and blood-red cloaks. They wielded powerful magic, they overwhelmed us. They took my knife and stabbed Shonnar. They left after they had killed him, didn't see me as a threat. I tried to stop the bleeding with my hands, but when I couldn't, I ran for help."

"You ran away from the Nexus, the opposite direction," said Borius, "farther into the tunnels – you were trying to escape when a supply train caught you."

"I was disoriented," Kraine pleaded, "the fight made me lose sense of direction."

"How many attackers were there?"

"I don't know."

"You have no estimate?"

Kraine muttered and looked at the ground. ". . . Maybe seven or eight."

"But you conveniently saw no faces."

"They wore masks, I— I couldn't see."

"Did you fight back?"

Kraine shook his head. "It all happened so fast . . ."

Sir Borius shook his head. "So you claim that the president's son asked you, and only you, to go with him because he saw signs of *dark magic* deep in the Network. And then you were ambushed by masked sorcerers who took *your* knife and stabbed him, and then left *you* unscathed. They disappeared and you ran for help in the *opposite* direction of the Nexus."

Kraine fell silent.

Borius Shipton spoke to the rest of the Evertauri. "Does anyone find any truth to his story?"

The hundreds of Evertauri stood still.

Sir Borius nodded. "Then I sentence you to die, on the charges of murdering the president's son, Shonnar Nebelle, and committing high treason."

As screams of protest erupted from Kraine, Borius Shipton raised both of his hands and emitted streams of yellow light that spiraled down into Kraine's body.

"Please! I swear to you!" he begged.

Because it was everyone's duty to stand for justice, the crowd of cloaked figures raised their hands. A collage of colors soared from their hands and into the body of the traitor.

Calleneck watched as his own crimson beam pounded into Kraine, who screamed in pain. He glanced over at Dalah; she held a stream of shimmering gold in the air and reluctantly sent it gently into the air with everyone else. The energy inside of the murderer grew until it was too much to bear, and he fell limp on the stone column.

Calleneck stood stunned. The sight of death sickened him, and he had contributed to it. His stomach lurched, but he shook the feelings away.

Borius Shipton looked out into the sea of black cloaks. "Dismissed."

Calleneck and his closest friend in the Evertauri, Tallius Tooble, waited in line for a dinner portion. The cold eating hall hung high, and many torches and candles illuminated its stone walls flickering in blue, violet, and green. Little Dalah sat quietly on a cart of food, handing out rations — one of her duties in the Evertauri. She looked upset but put on a brave face like she usually did. Tallius stood a full hand taller than Calleneck with dusty blonde hair. Just a year older than Calleneck, Tallius had long, strong legs, and his eyes shone blue.

"What coward would kill President Nebelle's son?" said Tallius. "What has to be going through your head to commit treason like that?"

Calleneck took a step forward in line. "You forget that this whole operation is treason itself."

"You know what I mean, Cal . . . and he was spitting nonsense about dark magic and masked sorcerers. He must have been driven mad."

"I think they could have looked into his story more at least before so quickly deciding to kill him," said Calleneck.

"The Council of Mages isn't exactly forgiving; you know that well. I mean for Great Mother's sake they *branded* you."

"Tallius—" Calleneck looked sideways at his best friend.

"Sorry," said Tallius, forgetting that Calleneck surely didn't want others around him knowing.

When he stepped in front of the cart with Tallius, Dalah reached down to get a plate of large carrots, noxlimes, and bread for each of them. Calleneck looked back at Tallius. "Anyway, do you know who will replace Shonnar?"

"No clue, my guess is that—"

Dalah turned around. "Aunika will."

Calleneck took his food from her and raised an eyebrow.

"I was surprised too," said Dalah, "but she told me herself about twenty minutes ago."

"Are you sure she wasn't just pulling your leg?" asked Tallius with a smile.

Dalah handed him his food. "Why would she do that?"

"Well . . . she's your sister," he replied.

"Even so," said Calleneck, "Aunika wouldn't kid. Dalah, did she tell you anything more?"

"Yes," she peered over at the other sorcerers who were standing within earshot, "I'll tell you later."

The boys found a table by a glassless window that looked into the Nexus. A blonde woman sat behind them, and three burly men in front of them. Two horses pulled a cart of food through the street; they were some of the very few horses the Evertauri owned. Few horses tolerated an absence of sun, but the ones who did were used to ship supplies in and out of the Network.

Tallius and Calleneck discussed the day and their assignments. Tallius chomped down on his bitter carrot and then held it up to examine it. "You know, Cal, I thought after two years of this that I would get used to the food." Calleneck laughed, but soon stopped; for some reason that he couldn't place a finger on, his mind kept flashing with images of a dark forest with massive trees.

The images were dreamlike, almost like memories. "Cal?" said Tallius. "You're daydreaming again."

Dalah approached the table and smiled. "He tends to do that."

"Sorry, just thinking," muttered Calleneck. "So, tell us what else Aunika told you."

Dalah began her meal at the table. "I didn't get to talk to her much, but she just told me that Borius Shipton had approached her and asked her to fill Shonnar's spot. I mean, she's qualified, she's one of the best sorceresses her age, and better than many who are older."

"What will she do?" Tallius asked Dalah.

"Probably the same as Shonnar did . . . spying on distinguished Crats, relaying information back to the Council of Mages, stuff like that . . . it's truly horrible, what happened to him. I wonder when Raelynn will find out – losing her brother like that has to be awful. They were the closest siblings I've ever seen, especially since President Nebelle spent all his time with Selenora instead of Shonnar and Raelynn. I just can't imagine getting that news."

"I mean, she's undercover in Ferramoor," said Tallius, "so it could be some time until word gets to her. Her father would have to be the one to tell her since only he knows why she left, and it's classified. What's strange to me is that he didn't seem pleased that she left. Maybe it's not a mission."

Calleneck felt like he had spoken with Raelynn recently, even though she had left for Ferramoor weeks ago. The daughter of President Nebelle, Raelynn would surely be devastated to learn of her brother's death. "Yeah, maybe it's not. Is President Nebelle okay with the slot being filled this soon? I mean it's his son that he's replacing."

"Well, I think he has to be," said Tallius.

A short man with a lazy eye and a girl with rosy cheeks approached the table. Sir Kishk Kaubovfier, the overseer and trainer of newcomers into the organization, addressed the three of them as the girl stood beside him. "If I may have a minute of your time Calleneck and Aunika, oh and Tallius too." The three nodded.

Calleneck often found it hard to focus when Sir Kishk talked to him. He felt bad, but he didn't ever know which eye to look into, as one was always staring in another direction. It didn't help that the eyes were lopsided and different sizes as well. The girl beside Kishk, however, was quite pleasant to look at, and he could tell that Tallius thought quite the same. She looked about the same age as the two of them with silky chocolate hair and rich blue eyes.

Sir Kishk went on in a high voice still laden with a heavy Cerebrian accent, "I am late for a meeting with the Council of Mages – details about Shonnar's death and things of the sort – so I don't have enough time to show this young lady around – she's quite friendly you know. I need you three to sit with her and help her adjust – it's a cruel place down here – oh, don't tell anyone I said that – so just show her around. All right?"

"Of course," said Dalah. Kishk the Trainer left the dining hall and the girl sat down next to Tallius and across from Dalah, who introduced the three of them.

"I'm Lillia Hane," said the girl. She looked just older than Calleneck – most likely twenty or twenty-one.

"How did you join?" Dalah leaned forward and put an elbow on the table.

"Well, my family – they live about halfway between here and Ontraug in Fellsink – they needed me to go find work to help support them, so I came to Seirnkov looking for a job. I was recruited by a woman named Selenora Everrose; she told me they would send money to my family from a fake apprenticeship."

"Wait, you were recruited by *the* Selenora Everrose?" Calleneck interjected. He smiled at the others and returned to Lillia. "You must be promising, Selenora is the best sorceress in the Evertauri. I'd even say she's more talented than Borius Shipton; he's second in command here."

Tallius nodded. "Selenora is an extremely powerful sorceress. President Madrick Nebelle trained her himself. I've only heard stories of the things she can do – topple buildings, disintegrate ships, some say she can even manipulate time."

Calleneck rolled his eyes. "That's a myth, Tallius." He looked back at Lillia Hane. "Anyway, how much do you know about us?" he asked. "The Evertauri."

"A decent amount, I guess. They interrogated me for hours and told me what I would be assigned to do. Both the Council of Mages and the guards are intimidating. And that– that execution of that man just made me sick to my stomach; this whole place scares me. But times are getting tough and the war is spreading resources thin. This is the only way that I've found to take care of my family, so I'm willing to do it."

"It scares you because we're serious about what we do," said Calleneck. "It's treason to be part of this; but we use our sorcery only for the benefit of Cerebria and to ensure its safety against Xandria."

"How can you pull off this huge movement directly underneath Xandria's capital and get away with it?"

"Secrecy and skill," said Tallius. "President Madrick Nebelle is the leader of the Evertauri and he founded it some twenty years back, after the split of the Empire. He thought that sorcerers and spies living in the capital of Cerebria would be the only way to take down Xandria."

Lillia shook her head. "But if you dethrone Xandria, won't Ferramoor just take over the government and make us a part of their old Empire?"

Tallius nodded. "We think that if we successfully take down Xandria, Tronum will be satisfied with the defeat of his sister and not risk another war. Ferramoor has already lost so many men, and if Tronum can have an amicable relationship with Cerebria, he'd be daft not to take it."

"Plus," said Calleneck, "if he discovers that sorcerers took Xandria down, he'd be leery of our power and back off."

"It sure caught me off guard," replied Lillia. "But that's another thing, the *sorcery.* I always thought it was a myth and then I was taken and told I was a sorceress. How did they know when I didn't? And how is this even possible? I've never done anything like magic, I—"

Tallius jumped in. "What do you know about the Great War?"

Lillia paused, unsure if she was answering his question correctly. "I know that around a hundred years ago, sorcerers started appearing all across Endellia. People say they came here somehow from the Lostlands, the old forgotten continents of ancient history plagued by war and magic and monsters. They terrorized cities and tried to gain territory, gathering armies." She stopped again to look at the others, then continued talking. "And after fifty years of that, they were close to ruling the continent. I know there were lots of warring kingdoms and chaos, but out of it rose Gallegore Wenderdehl, and he led the people to victory to eradicate the sorcerers and rid the world of the evils of magic."

"Atop his giant winged lion with a flaming sword," laughed Tallius.

"I'm just saying what I've heard," said Lillia, "and those stories don't seem too unreal now that I've met you all and seen this— *this place.* But I don't understand, what does the Great War have to do with it?"

Calleneck smiled. "Because Gallegore *didn't* kill all the sorcerers. When the battles were nearly over, thousands of sorcerers gave up the fight and chose to hide their powers – hide in plain sight. They lived normal lives and had families and bred with the people of Endellia."

"Most settling in the Cerebrian territories," added Tallius.

Calleneck nodded in agreement. "So their magic blood, their powers, it was all passed down through generations, and we," motioning a finger around the table and then the Nexus beyond, "we are their descendents. Oftentimes it will skip family, one sister or son may have the gift when another brother or daughter doesn't. But somewhere in your bloodline, in mine, there was a sorcerer living in hiding who passed along their powers to us."

"And magic users have kept living in hiding," Tallius cut in. "Since the Great War, anyone who has discovered their own magic has concealed it for fear of being found and killed."

"Until," said Calleneck, "Madrick Nebelle began finding them – outcasts. He gathered sorcerers for the first time since the old days to use magic for something good – the Evertauri. Powerful Evertauri can sense magic in others when they may not sense it in themselves. Selenora Everrose must've sensed your magic, investigated whether you'd be likely to join our cause, and then recruited you."

It was obviously a lot for Lillia to take in all at once. "How am I supposed to use it? Magic?"

"We're still learning ourselves," said Dalah. "Kishk the Trainer will teach you the basics soon, and then you will receive training from various other people. They'll teach you how to use it carefully and know your limits – if you cast a spell too powerful for you to control, you can lose your magic completely."

Calleneck leaned back in his chair. "But basically, every human has a sort of . . . 'energy' flowing in them, though few can harness it and use it. Now, I don't know how the recruiters know, but they can tell who can use that power and who cannot. Selenora recruited you, so you're obviously capable of it. Every sorcerer or sorceress has a Taurimous." He looked at Dalah for help. "How should I put this?"

"It's kind of like your soul." Dalah put her hand out; a shimmering golden flame danced around her finger tips. "See, this flame? It isn't matter, and it's not really energy; we just call it that. It's part of your Taurimous, a manifestation of your soul that some of us can control." Dalah continued. "Every person's Taurimous portrays itself in a different color. As you can see, my color is gold; Tallius's is sapphire and Cal's is crimson and so on."

"And what determines that?" Lillia asked.

Tallius put down his bread. "Nobody really knows. I suppose President Nebelle may have an idea."

"But you *can* produce energy that isn't your Taurimous' hue," said little Dalah as she wrinkled her forehead and changed the little flame in her hand to deep purple. "It doesn't carry nearly as much energy and power though, and it takes a lot more strength, focus, and skill to control. It's quite difficult, so most of the Evertauri just stick with the natural color of their Taurimous." Her flame turned back to gold. "You'll find yours soon I bet."

Lillia Hane put a finger on her temple. "How does the Evertauri supply itself? It doesn't seem to have very many people."

"We have about a thousand members I think," said Calleneck. "Most of them are here in the Nexus or above ground on missions in Seirnkov. The rest are stationed throughout the Network."

"We're shipped supplies through secret donors and supporters," said Tallius. "Some people who aren't sorcerers grow us food and get us horses. But you're right, the number of actual sorcerers is several hundred."

"That's another thing," said Lillia. "The 'Network.' What is this place?"

Dalah extinguished her flame. "I'm sure you've heard about what Xandria did to the Goblins about twenty years ago – The Day of the Underground Fire, the complete extinction of an entire race."

Lillia nodded. "Of course. It's one of the reasons she has no right being our queen. Some people say it was necessary but I just . . . Wait, *are these the Goblins' tunnels?*"

"Well, President Nebelle needed a place where the Evertauri would never be found," said Tallius. "After all the Goblins were killed, this network of underground tunnels and cities went dark. President Nebelle and a friend of his named Mordvitch Aufenschiess found hidden entrances in Seirnkov, and he brought his followers down here to live. But to this day, we're still figuring out how the Network was used. One of Cal's jobs is to help map the tunnels. It's so complicated that we still have trouble navigating it twenty years later."

"He's right," said Calleneck. "The Goblins were extremely skilled architects. These tunnels span across all of Cerebria and even into the Crandles and Endlebarr. The routes and distances sometimes seem to defy all logic; it's a maze of impossible passages."

Dalah jumped in. "Cal helped discover an entrance to the surface in Gienn just four months ago."

"Anyway," Calleneck continued, "we use it to avoid being seen, and to move around Cerebria quickly."

"Why wouldn't Xandria have taken control over it after she exterminated the Goblins? If it's truly so expansive and fast to use, why didn't her army occupy it and use it to travel around the country?"

Calleneck nodded. "What we think – or rather the theory that we've been told, is that the Goblins must have made a last ditch effort to either survive or preserve their history by sealing the entrances with magic. They were not as gifted as we are in the art of sorcery, but they used some mixture of magic and science to seal them so that only sorcerers could get through – and that's how President Nebelle made it in. We don't think Xandria has any way of getting back down here, but of course you saw the guards as you entered. We're cautious, but we're safe here for now."

Tallius finished his bread. "You know, it's marvelous – given how quickly supplies get around in these tunnels – that the food can still taste this bad."

Lillia laughed. "At least the noxlimes are fine."

"Well we eat those with every meal since we can grow them here in the dark," said Tallius. "Of course these two don't have to deal with all of this every day." He pointed at the Bernoils.

"You have a life on the surface?" asked Lillia.

Dalah nodded. "Cal, Aunika, and I live up in Seirnkov with our parents. We generally stay there for three or four days and then come down here for another three or four days. It's rare for the Evertauri to be that lenient for us, but Aunika convinced the Council of Mages before Cal and I joined that it would work."

"It was a condition for our loyalty," said Calleneck. "We didn't want to be cut off from our parents."

"Most Evertauri who live on the surface run businesses that directly aid the Evertauri," said Dalah. "But some like us live there because of family; we live with our mum and father. We have had some quarrels with them in the past, so they think that half the time we are staying with our Aunt Shelln and Uncle Gregt just to get some space. Our uncle was never very close to our father and didn't ever tell him that he and his wife and our cousin moved away – out East near Bordertown and the Erricurr. They worked as doctors and charged next to nothing because they wanted the poor to have access to medicine; but that eventually forced them to move out of the city three years ago."

"Your parents never found out they don't live in Seirnkov anymore?" asked Lillia.

"No," said Calleneck, "our parents aren't in touch with our aunt and uncle due to the falling out; and the few letters they send to each other go straight to the Evertauri's mail and are delivered to us. We forge letters back to them. Our aunt and uncle and cousin now think that our parents know they moved, and our parents are convinced that we are staying with them half the time."

"Lillia, do you have a room to stay in yet?" asked little Dalah, changing the subject.

"Sir Kishk was supposed to assign me one, but he didn't have time."

"You can room with Aunika and me tonight. We should be able to find out more about what she'll be up to . . . or maybe not, since high-level operations are usually classified."

Lillia agreed and the girls left the eating hall, followed shortly by Calleneck and Tallius.

Tallius looked up at a high balcony on which Dalah Bernoil and Lillia Hane walked and brushed his hand through his hair. "Say Cal, what's the likelihood her cheeks flushed red when she glanced at me?"

Cal punched him in the side and shook his head. "The last thing you want is a relationship in the Evertauri."

Tallius smiled like he was the cleverest man alive. *"No one would have to know."*

"What makes you think she'd be into you?"

"What makes you think she wouldn't?"

"Do you have a spare hour?" Calleneck laughed.

As they walked, both tried not to look at the bloody corpse of the murderer that still lay on the cold stone floor of the Nexus.

NIGHTSNAKES
Chapter Five

~Evening, August 23rd
Aunestauna, Ferramoor

Kyan's feet dangled off of the theater rooftop. A simple chain with a small silver ornament hung around his neck in the shape of a diamond, like all Olindeux were. He had seen others on some of the Gypsies in the city, but all of them had different carved lines embedded in the token. It was the only thing his parents had given him before the orphanage took him in, though he had been too young to remember them. He had heard the Gypsies in the streets saying the Olindeux had the power to hold families together. *Ironic,* thought Kyan, who had been alone his whole life. But something inside compelled him to keep it, maybe out of a vain hope that it could bring his family back.

The sun was starting to set over the palace hill, where the white and scarlet palace sat high above the city overlooking the entire valley and the sea beyond. The sun lit its many banners that waved in the breeze, and even beyond that, the waves of the sea rolled in and out. He imagined the senators and aristocrats peacefully watching the city in their long, flowing gowns, and he thought of that wretched royal family on their thrones. Standing, he picked up a rock from the roof, and hurled it toward the palace.

Kyan's long dark hair hung wild and unkempt; his dirty and blood-stained tunic covered his thin frame. Looking in his pocket, he pulled out the golden bracelets he had stolen from the brawling Southlandi the day before and smiled. The clocktower chimed seven and he walked across a wooden board to an adjacent rooftop. He looked south and headed toward a gloomy region of buildings that rose crammed and crooked.

The Fourth District was the only place where he could trade his loot without being caught by the Scarlet Guard, the men in armor and red capes who policed the streets of Aunestauna and kept a lookout for suspicious behavior. The Scarlet Guard rarely ventured into the Fourth District, as they thought it was too dangerous and a lost cause. Kyan chose to live in the Third District because of the higher concentration of jewelry and goods; one couldn't steal anything in the Fourth District worth more than five or six argentums, the cost of a wool blanket. The slums housed the poorest people trying to get by — those plagued by gangs.

Kyan hopped down off a roof and splashed into a puddle. A scrawny rat shot out from a hole in a building's foundation and scurried over the broken stones and murky mud of the dark street. People with somber faces and missing teeth passed by him, sometimes bumping into him. Everyone dressed in dark colors, causing them to blend in with the dark, gnarled wood of the ramshackle houses. The sky was beginning to turn dark blue, and a single star appeared overhead.

He turned into a shop with a shattered window and a leaning doorway. A small chime rang as he walked in, and a man who must have been seven feet tall opened the back door and entered the room. Little ornaments sat on shelves in the shop, and the man towered over it all. His ink black beard hung below his belly, and his eyebrows sat like bushes jutting out on his forehead. His name was Zogo Blackblood, but something told Kyan that no one had ever gotten the chance to draw blood from him to check its hue. Just recovering from a coughing fit, the man greeted Kyan in a deep, raspy voice.

"You're back. What've you got for me?"

Kyan reached into his pocket and threw down six gold Gypsy bracelets on a table. "Picked these up yesterday."

Zogo smiled and sat down at the table; he couldn't fit his knees underneath. "These look like a Gypsy's." He looked at Kyan, who stood a foot and a half shorter than him, and chuckled. "Got a bit of blood on your tunic." He eyed the gold closely. "This all?"

Kyan reached in his pocket and pulled out a pile of watch parts, an intricate wooden talisman, three iron rings, and a jewel-lined pocket mirror and threw them on the table. Zogo inspected the objects. And looked up at Kyan under his comically bushy eyebrows. "It's worth eight argentums, but I'll give you ten because I'm generous."

Kyan clenched his fists — the loot was worth at least fifteen; ten argentums would only buy food for a week. He took a step forward and the giant stood up from his chair, immediately dwarfing Kyan.

Zogo drew a knife. "Or I can keep everything and force you out with no payment."

Kyan hesitated, then took ten argentums from Zogo Blackblood, put them in his pocket, and walked out the door and down the dark and dreary boulevard. Old men hunched in corners of the street whispered to each other about death and plague coming as Kyan walked by. He heard a woman scream in the distance as he turned into an alley between two tall, abandoned buildings. May as well take a look around while I'm here. He looked behind him before opening a door into one of the buildings.

He could barely see inside of it; it appeared that he was in a kitchen of some sort. He opened cabinets and looked through the shelves, all of which had nothing in them. The usually creaky stairs made no sound underneath Kyan's light feet. On the second floor, Kyan slipped into a large room lined with shelves and decorated with a few sitting chairs. On the shelves sat just three old books so faded that the spines could not be read. Cobwebs hung across the ceiling beams and the furniture; there was nothing to be stolen.

Kyan decided to take one last look in the attic, where he found a spyglass that he shoved in his coat pocket. Opening a window, he effortlessly jumped onto the shingled roof of the adjacent house, opened a window below him and swung himself in. Same result – nothing worth stealing except a quill and ink and a rusty compass. He jumped from the window to a pole on the opposite wall, from the pole to another window, and onto the street. Bending down to tie his shoe, he noticed someone standing right behind him.

He spun around and was instantly shoved into a wall; a hand and rag covered his mouth. He tried to punch his attacker, but hit after hit could not bring him down. Some strange odor in the rag made the world tilt sideways. Kyan's mind went fuzzy, then blank.

He woke up in the middle of what seemed to be a vacant room in a manor – his body and limbs were tied to a chair. A curtain hung over a window to his right so he could not orient himself but for a strip of moonlight that shone on the dusty wooden floor. He looked around the unlit room and quickly gathered that he was alone. Blood still stained his tunic. He could tell that the coins in his pockets were gone, along with his knife. He unsuccessfully tried twisting his arms out of the rope, and kicked and turned in his chair, but it was nailed into the floorboards. He looked around the room again, able to pick out tables, mirrors, and paintings as his eyes adjusted to the dark.

Waiting in silence, he jerked his head when a door behind him creaked open; multiple sets of footsteps clicked on the floor. A dark-haired man just a bit older than Kyan – mid twenties – grabbed a chair and sat directly in front of him. The man was tall and slender with a scar on his angular face. Although he was much bigger than Kyan, his steps barely made a sound. The other figures, who illuminated the room with candles, stood off to the side. The young man in front of him wore a very long, black cloak with the collar turned up around his neck; on his feet were extravagant leather boots; on his wrists were countless bracelets. Black gloves concealed his hands and his bright blue eyes pierced straight through Kyan. He scooted his chair so that their knees touched.

The man took in a breath that sounded like a strained hiss. "We've been looking for you."

Kyan glanced at the older boy's pocket where the knife rested. Kyan scoffed and shook his head, smirking. "What do you want? Trying to intimidate me isn't going to work." But Kyan's heart rate steadily increased; his bluffing wasn't working.

"Is that so?" said the young man sarcastically. "Just a minute ago, you were trying so violently to get out of your bonds. And you were searching so frantically for your knife."

Kyan furrowed his eyebrows – he wasn't there a minute ago. He walked through the door just now.

"And yet, when I pretended to have only now entered the room, your demeanor changed . . ." The man in his dark black outfit let his words hang in the air like a cloud of ice waiting to seep into Kyan's body. "It's . . . only natural to be afraid."

Kyan remained silent in his chair, but his fists started to clench and sweat.

The man smiled. "Each one of us has been here since you awoke . . . Yes, yes . . . Quite unfortunate, really, that we had to put you under; we feared that you would not listen had we not tied you up . . . You just didn't notice us slipping in and out of the room . . . Oh, you think I'm bluffing?" The young man looked to the side; Kyan's eyes followed. Everyone who was previously there was gone, and the candles sat on the tables.

Kyan stared at the man. "What are you playing at?"

"Just chipping away at your sense of superiority . . . you're not the only one who's good at stealing." The man pulled back his sleeve to reveal even more jewelry; he pulled off six gold Gypsy bracelets and played with them in his gloved hands.

Kyan's eyes widened.

"Don't worry, I didn't jeopardize your relationship with Mr. Zogo Blackblood, I just thought they were . . . pretty. That old giant won't realize they're gone. They aren't his to own if he can't keep them safe." The man paused and smiled a smile that made Kyan's insides turn. "You're full of hate, Kyan . . . You're obsessed. But with what? That's the question . . ."

"Who the hell are you?" Kyan leaned away from him and realized that the others were once again standing right next to him, but he couldn't remember them entering.

The man ignored him and went on, still smiling and peering into his soul. "You're talented, and young too. I've been watching you for a couple months now. You're rarely detected; although there was that one little slip with the old hatter two weeks ago. Nimble; you've never fallen off of a roof and you got down from that old building tonight very nicely. You just lack a certain . . ." he smiled again, ". . . charm."

"I don't play well with others," said Kyan.

The young man laughed. “And you think I do?” He pulled off one of his gloves; the hand only three long-fingers and a thumb – what remained of the index finger was nothing but a vein-covered, yellow stub. The man took a sharp breath in and grabbed Kyan’s chin, pushing the deformed stub onto his lips.

Kyan tried to turn his head away, but the menacing man laughed and tightened his grip. Pressure built inside his mouth and jaw as the man squeezed; he felt trapped, unable to turn his head.

The other man smiled, stretching the distasteful scar across his face. “You’d be surprised how many people I’ve maimed or killed with these four fingers. This one here was cut off by my mother . . .”

Kyan grunted as he tried to pull away from his hand. He managed to slowly slip his left hand out of its binds but did not want to use it yet.

The sinister man breathed in sharply through his nose, like a hiss. “Where is your mother?” He peered at Kyan from within his collared cloak and moved his face inches from his, with a hand still grabbing Kyan’s face and his other, gloved hand stroking his ruffled black hair. “I like your work, your style . . . You’re smarter than you think you are. I can tell that you have figured out who we are . . .”

Kyan glanced sideways – the others had vanished once again without any visible trace or sound.

“Look at me!” He continued to stroke Kyan’s hair. “Yes, I see your free hand. Yet, you have not tried to hurt me . . . you've figured us out, but you need confirmation, don’t you? . . . Go ahead. Do it . . .”

Kyan thrust his hand toward the man’s neck and pulled down the collar of his cloak, revealing a large, red snakebite.

He grinned with a scarred face. “Very good . . . very good.” He released his hold on Kyan’s face, leaving white finger marks on his skin.

“You’re the Nightsnakes,” said Kyan.

“Indeed . . . my name is Riccolo . . . the Lord of Thieves.”

Kyan shook his head. “Thousands of reported robberies, hundreds of murders, an unknown number of thieves, no confirmed sightings, no names, but thousands of argentums worth of loot; I’ve seen the Scarlet Guard’s notices. You’re wanted all over Aunestauna, but I’m sure you know that.”

"I love it," said Riccolo, closing his eyes like he was dreaming, "the panic it causes, the fear we inspire . . . It's a beautiful thing really."

"You're mad," whispered Kyan.

Riccolo opened his eyes. "Not any more than everyone else."

Kyan sat silently.

“And really," Riccolo hissed, "the Aunestaunans do not give us enough credit – it should be twelve thousand robberies and four hundred kills. The Scarlet

Guard won't catch us. Especially when we erase their records of us in the palace."

"And what makes you so confident that you'll never be caught?"

"If you were me, you would be confident," said Riccolo. "Nobody realizes, but we control this city. People ask us to do dirty things, Kyan. We've never gotten caught."

"Why steal when you have so much?" Kyan asked.

"Why do you steal?"

"To get by."

Riccolo shook his head. "And it has nothing to do with trying to take back the warm and safe life that the city stole from you? Nothing to do with trying to plunge the world into the darkness in which you so often find yourself? Nothing to do with hurting the city that rejected you? Nothing to do . . . *with anger?"*

Kyan sat still.

Riccolo put his black glove back on. "The Nightsnakes want you. You can do so much more here than as a street rat."

"And you're not a street rat?"

"I'm a rich street rat — a King of Vermin perhaps."

"And what if I say no?"

"We can persuade you . . ."

Kyan shook his head. "How do you do it? Steal thousands of argentums worth undetected like magic."

"Is it magic, Kyan, that you can run from rooftop to rooftop without ever slipping? Or is it skill? We have pulled off thousands of crimes because we are the best, Kyan. You have not noticed us watching you because we are the best."

"You want me to get the snakebite."

"We believe you would be valuable."

Kyan looked at the knife in Riccolo's lap. "I work alone."

Riccolo reached out and caressed his hair.

Kyan tried to grab his arm but found that his hand had somehow been retied to the chair.

Riccolo whispered, "Now, there, I'm a bit disappointed in you." He sat up, put on the Gypsy bracelets, grabbed Kyan's knife and placed it on the ropes in his lap. "Release him."

Two Nightsnakes came and untied him while Riccolo reached in his pocket and handed him the ten argentums Zogo Blackblood paid him. "I'll have Bay guide you out then. I'm afraid we'll have to blindfold you until we get you further away from our . . . sanctuary."

Kyan raised an eyebrow — it should not have been this easy to say no to the Nightsnakes. He agreed to be blindfolded.

As he was turned toward the exit to the abandoned pub, Riccolo grabbed him and whispered in his ear, "You have pretty hair." Riccolo took out a knife and cut off a strand. "For me."

Kyan shivered, and the nightsnake Bay guided him to an alley far away and removed the blindfold. When he turned around to see Bay's face, he was gone. He turned the corner, orienting himself, and began walking by moonlight back to the Third District.

Riccolo's words rang in his ear, *"You'd be surprised how many people I have maimed or killed with these four fingers. This one was cut off by my mother . . . Where is your mother?"*

Kyan turned perpendicular to the Third District and trudged down a dark street until he got to a faded wooden sign that read, *Pebblebum Orphanage*. He looked into a side window at a sleeping boy with curly hair and stood there for a minute. In the corner of the old window was a scratch mark – a backwards 'K' read normally from the inside. He carefully pulled out the necklace strung around his neck to see the Olinduex. The point of the diamond-shaped silver token had been sharp enough to scratch that 'K' in the glass all those years ago. He looked at the Olindeux in his hands, just larger than a coin with three curved engraved lines running down from the tip. His blood turned icy cold and he turned his back to the building, walking by moonlight back to the Third District.

After depositing his coins in a jar, he sat in his attic staring up at the stars through the gaps in the rafters. Soft orchestral music played in the theater below him, but it did not help to lull him to sleep. He knew one thing at that moment – Riccolo would not have let him leave that easily without a reason, and that meant that Kyan needed to be cautious. *Extremely cautious.*

WINTERDOVE LANE
Chapter Six

~Evening, August 28th
Seirnkov, Cerebria

Seirnkov housed hundreds of thousands of Cerebrians. Unlike Aunestauna, with jagged, unorganized streets, Seirnkov's infrastructure was built like a spider web, with some streets moving outward from the middle and others stringing them together; its heart was Xandria's fortress. The whole city rose higher toward the center, and bordering it towered a ring of white mountains, The Seirns. Even in the summer, the snowy peaks remained white and completely enclosed the city, save for a southwestern valley that led out to the vast evergreen forests of Cerebria.

Around Xandria's giant fortress rose stone mansions with great redwood doors – the homes of the aristocrats, or 'Crats' as the commoners would say. They paraded around their gardens and courtyards filled with flowers, statues, and fountains, talking to government officials, trying to change the laws according to their will. Controlling the rule of law and taxes of Cerebria only made them more powerful.

Twenty blocks down from these white mansions stood a house on the corner of a little square – 138 Winterdove Lane. Tall, narrow houses joined together with no space to travel between them lined the lane. Each household had potted flowers in window boxes that hung over the stone street. Men and women greeted each other from windows while they pounded dust out of floor mats or hung clothes to dry. In the house on the corner, Mrs. Sheilla Bernoil sat knitting by the kitchen window, catching the last of the day's light as the sky took on its full sunset red tint.

Having to exit the Evertauri's underground Network a different way than they entered, the Bernoil children emerged above ground through a fake tree behind a set of houses in a nearby neighborhood – one of Seirnkov's entrances to the Network. Similar to the mirrors which they had used to enter the Network, Calleneck had held his Taurimous flame to the trunk, and the bark revealed itself to be an illusion of matter – a floating image – which they could then step through. To ensure security, guards awaited at the bottom of the ladder inside the hollow tree trunk.

The three never tired of feeling the golden light of the sunset on their faces after they exited from the dark and cold underground. It made them feel like they were children again; but the strictness and darkness of the Evertauri had stolen their innocence. They were rebels, traitors, and liars; and as much as they loved their parents, they were sworn to secrecy. *We are coming back from our aunt and uncle's,* they all thought to themselves as they walked home.

Mrs. Bernoil smiled and stood when she saw the children walking up the sunlit lane. Aunika opened the door and they walked into 138; Mrs. Bernoil crossed the room and placed two pots into the fireplace to cook. "I was beginning to think you weren't coming back today."

"Sorry, we always try to be here on time," said Aunika.

For some reason, Calleneck felt as if he had been gone from home for much longer than just a few days, but he couldn't figure out why. "Where's father?" he asked.

Mrs. Bernoil brushed dust off of a counter. She had salt and pepper hair, and her daily stern face lightened up periodically while talking to people and knitting. "He stopped by a customer on the way home from the market, but he should be back before dark. Put your bags upstairs and then help prepare supper. Oh, Calleneck, get two buckets of water from the well, will you?"

Calleneck grabbed two buckets off the wall, and headed out the door into the square. He stopped for a royal carriage and its horses, carrying an aristocrat up into the heights of the city. Their hooves clip-clopped along the street as many others passed by, returning to their homes for the evening. In the middle of the small square next to their house stood a well from which the surrounding residents drew their water. In the summer, the water supply was abundant, but it was often either dry or frozen in the winter. Calleneck hooked a bucket onto the rope, and lowered it down. A girl came from behind and walked around him; she set down a bucket and leaned on the well. "Nice to see you back, Cal," she said.

"Oh, hello Gilsha, how are you?"

"I'm well. And you?" she asked.

Calleneck shrugged. "I'm alright. Just figuring life out I guess."

She smiled at him with remarkably white teeth for a commoner. Her hair loosely curled in waves; it was a golden mixture of blonde and light brown hair. Just a winter younger than Calleneck, Gilsha had been his friend as long as he could remember and had gone to the same school until they graduated at the age of sixteen. Gilsha pushed a strand of hair from her face. "I'm assuming you were at your aunt and uncle's again."

Calleneck lifted the bucket out of the water. "They're doing well too." He unhooked the bucket and put the second on the well at the same time Gilsha lifted hers onto the well.

Gilsha pulled her bucket off. "Oh, sorry, you go . . ."

"No by all means . . ." Calleneck chuckled, and she smiled back. She tilted her head to the side – a habit of hers – and lowered her bucket in the well. He looked at her as she looked down into the well; her face glowed in the light of the setting sun, and a white blouse that hung on her shoulders moved slightly with the breeze, as did her hair. She looked up at Calleneck, and he looked away and watched another wagon and its horses roll by. When she finished, he drew his last bucket of water and asked how her family was doing.

"Oh, just the same. Mum and I are handfulled with the little ones like always."

"Has Gline still not learned to tie his shoes?"

Gilsha laughed. "No, not yet. But his brothers are picking on him for it, so he keeps trying."

"And your father?"

Her smile faded a bit but her blue eyes quickly lit up again. "Well, he's the same too I guess."

They heard Mrs. Bernoil say from inside the house, "Where is that boy?" She stepped outside and called out. "Calleneck, how long does it take to fetch me water?"

He chuckled and started walking back to the house with Gilsha.

"You two are just *chattering* away while the supper burns. Oh, Gilsha, I did accidentally make extra and would appreciate your company."

Carrying a bucket of water, Gilsha looked at Calleneck and then to Mrs. Bernoil. "Maybe, but I'd have to take this back and ask mum."

Mrs. Bernoil crossed her arms and smiled at her. "You wouldn't turn down *my* stew, now would you?"

Gilsha laughed. "I guess I just have to join then don't I?" She turned to Calleneck. "See you soon then."

Mrs. Bernoil called after Gilsha. "Hurry, dear, don't be long now!"

Calleneck carried the buckets inside and poured them into a large tin tub in the corner. Aunika walked down the stairs. "Calleneck, help me with father's things."

"What?" Calleneck was looking out the corner window, lost in thought watching the horses pulling wagons trot along the cobblestone street.

"He just walked in with supplies for his shoes."

"Sorry . . . just–"

"Thinking, yes."

Otto Bernoil walked into the room. He stood tall and had white hair. His gaze looked solemn, and the brightness had left his eyes from years of constant work as a cobbler. Removing a gray flat cap from his head and placing it on a wall hook, he asked them to move some boxes into his workshop in the backroom. Mr. Bernoil's voice was calm but commanding, and when he was angry, he whispered rather than yelled. The children respected him, for he always knew what to say, and when to say it.

Dalah and Mrs. Bernoil pulled out the pots of stew just as Gilsha knocked on the door. Mr. Bernoil opened it and stepped aside. "Well if it isn't the famous Gilsha Gold."

"Nice to see you, Mr. Bernoil."

Dalah and Aunika greeted her as they sat down at the table; the Golds had been friends with the Bernoils for quite some time, and Dalah often helped Gilsha and her mother with the three younger boys.

"Gilsha darling," said Mrs. Bernoil, "we haven't had your company in a while!"

Mr. Bernoil scooted his chair in. "But I'm sure your father is busy."

Gilsha glanced up at Mr. Bernoil. "Yes . . . And your work, sir?"

"Oh, quite fine. Same as ten years ago, and twenty, and thirty. Everybody needs a pair of shoes. If he's any smarter than a horse, a cobbler can't lose business . . ."

After dinner was cleaned and Gilsha left, Calleneck went to get more water from the well with Aunika. It was dark enough to see a few stars, and the auroras from the north cast a green glow over the city. Aunika hooked a bucket onto the rope and began to lower it.

"Have you thought about what you're getting Dalah for her birthday?" asked Calleneck.

Aunika shook her head. "I hadn't thought of it."

"I saw a scarf over on Pinewood Street. It's red; I'd think she'd like it. Could you lend me two argentums to help pay for it? I'll cover the rest so you don't have to."

"Why?" asked Aunika.

". . . well, it's not like you've been here every year to give her something. I'm used to paying."

"Calleneck–"

"Would two argentums hurt you?"

"Calleneck," she sighed. "Two argentums is fine, but you're starting a conversation I would really prefer not to have right now; we've had a nice evening and a nice dinner, and I want to get some good sleep for once."

"Well, when is the right time to talk about it?" Calleneck placed his bucket on the edge of the well. "I don't *need* two argentums, but I think it would be fair if you showed a little care."

Aunika dropped the rope and her bucket splashed into the well. She rubbed her forehead. "I told you I'm sorry. But I think it's unfair of you to say that I don't care, alright? I left for a couple years, yes—"

"Just because you were fighting every day with mum and dad didn't give you an excuse to leave!" Calleneck's face flushed red.

"Don't shout at me. I saw that my relationship with mum and dad was hurting you and Dalah, so I left; and in some ways, I think that was the more caring thing to do." Aunika pulled the bucket of water from the well. "But now that we gave ourselves space, it's much better. When was the last time you heard me argue with them? Not for months. And you have issues with them too; that's why they let you stay with 'our Aunt and Uncle.' After that it was simple to say that Dalah needed to come with us to be with her big brother and sister."

"But ever since we've been in the Ever—" Calleneck watched some people passing by them, "you know what I'm talking about."

"That wasn't my fault that you had to join. Just because I left didn't give you an excuse to lose control of your emotions and destroy a street corner!"

Calleneck stepped close to her and whispered. "I didn't know that I could wield sorcery; how could I? Nobody does unless another sorcerer senses it, or if they let their emotions boil like I did. I was angry that you left, and I let my emotions get the better of me, like most brothers would."

"You blew up half a building, Calleneck!"

"And you dragged me underground when I was unconscious, and they branded me!" he whispered. He unbuttoned his tunic and tore it open, revealing the crimson scar on his chest. "They had no right—"

"They had every right."

"Says who? Who gives them authority, Aunika? No one; it's a rebellion! There's nothing to keep them in check. We keep hearing how terrible Xandria and this war is, but did you forget they executed someone just days ago? We all helped too."

"Because he murdered Shonnar Nebelle."

"There wasn't a trial, Aunika!" he whispered. "What kind of justice is that? Is that the kind of world you want to live in? Is that the world we're helping create? For all you know, they could have executed me just as easily as they branded me. That's a scar I'll live with forever; and it's a hell of a lot less painful than the scars you *can't* see."

Aunika whispered through gritted teeth "They made sure that an outburst like that wouldn't ever happen again. When you have the ability to cause that much harm, you have a moral obligation to control yourself."

"You think that *you* controlled yourself? Controlling yourself doesn't look like running away from your problems. And now you want to act like the hero and be there for Dalah. You're forgetting that you took away her childhood."

A man in the distance hammered a nail into his house as Aunika spoke. "*She* followed *us*; it wasn't my fault."

"She could've had somewhat of a normal life if you hadn't left mum and dad for a band of failed rebels. You shouldn't have picked revolution over family, Aunika. No matter what, you never give up on family!"

The two turned when they heard Dalah's voice, "Just stop it, you two!" They were too angry to have noticed their younger sister approaching them. Her freckled cheeks were twitching, trying to hold back tears, and she walked away.

Aunika turned to Calleneck and shoved two argentums into his hand. "I never gave up."

Aunika ran after Dalah, and Calleneck sat down next to the well. He folded his arms on his knees and put down his head. *Control . . . breathing . . . quiet.* An image of crimson flames and sparks circling his body and shattering windows. *Calm . . . quiet . . . breathe.* He heard the screams from that street corner in his mind and pushed them out.

Mr. Bernoil was sitting in the kitchen reading a book when Calleneck walked in. His father set it down and rubbed his chin stubble, and he could see that his eyes were red. After pouring the buckets of water into the tin tub, Calleneck sat down across from his father and ran his fingers through his light brown hair. "Are you alright, father?" The girls were outside talking, and a small burning log crackled in the fireplace.

"Cal," said Mr. Bernoil in a calm, soothing voice. "Have I ever told you that my mother was an artist?"

"No, sir."

His father flipped through his book and pulled out a folded piece of parchment. "Your grandmother drew this over forty-five years ago." He slid it across the table.

Calleneck unfolded the wrinkled parchment carefully; on it was a charcoal drawing of two little boys in wool hats sitting on a porch playing some game with a wooden cube.

Mr. Bernoil sighed. "You probably don't know who this is . . . he was a very close friend of mine named Rushki. I found out today that he was killed by the Jade Guard." He sniffed. "Seems like he got tangled up with some bad Crats."

The Jade Guard was the Queen's top regiment of soldiers, a counterstatement to Ferramoor's *Scarlet Guard.* The Jade Guard had a habit of raiding homes, stores, barns, and shipyards in search of traitors of the crown or evidence of disloyal countrymen. "What happened?" Calleneck asked.

"Well the government doesn't like news like this getting around, but word around town says that he outed some Crats for taking citizens' taxes for themselves. He published the paperwork and everything . . . he tried to stay anonymous, but nothing gets past the government. He was just always trying to make the world a happier place." He smiled and looked down again at the hand drawn picture for some time. "'Day after this was drawn, I broke an old widow's kitchen window when we were throwing rocks around. When I ran away to avoid being caught, he knocked on the woman's door. He was a good man . . . and to be killed for getting on the Crats' bad side." He stared out the window. "Overall, yes, the queen has done good for the country, but sometimes I worry about the cost."

Calleneck shuffled his feet. "Well, I think there are people who'll try to make it right. I'm sorry about your friend." Calleneck was reminded that the Evertauri was not just trying to take down Xandria, but every scheming Crat and corrupt government official that backed her. "Father, what was the Empire like?"

Mr. Bernoil sat up in his chair. "Gallegore's Empire?" Calleneck nodded. "Why do you ask?"

"Just wondering."

Mr. Bernoil sighed and searched back into his memory. "It was peaceful, I remember – every nation on the Endellian continent united. I was about your age; I remember when Xandria was appointed by her father to govern the Cerebrian Territories of the Empire. Everyone was happy to see a smart, daring young woman take control. That was around thirty years ago. The Cerebrian Territories prospered under her rule, the schooling here was the best, our technological innovations were the best, our pride as a people was the best; and it was thanks to her. People oftentimes felt more of a connection and loyalty to Xandria than her father."

"What about Tronum?" asked Calleneck.

"What about him?"

"Well why did Gallegore choose Tronum as heir to his Empire rather than Xandria?"

Mr. Bernoil crossed his arms. "That, I couldn't tell you. Tronum might have had the birthright if he really was the eldest twin, but most people doubt he actually was. I don't know if it was a good choice, or a bad choice. At the same time Xandria governed the Cerebrian Territories, Tronum governed the northern Parusean and Ferramish territories from Aunestauna to the Parusean Channel; if Gallegore had chosen Xandria, who's to say that Tronum wouldn't have seceded with *his* land. That's the danger of twins in a royal family, there could've been war either way . . . I do think Xandria was the eldest – at least that's what she claims, but there's no way to know for sure. It was just a dangerous situation." Mr. Bernoil's voice trailed off and he stared blankly at the table.

"Father, are you alright?"

"Yes, I'm fine," he said, snapping out of his trance. "Anyway, twenty-two years ago in late 781, the announcement was made that we were our own country. They paraded down the streets, hoisting up banners and blaring horns. The following years were . . . quiet."

"Quiet?" said Calleneck.

"It was like the silence in the air before a storm. The peace on our continent rested on the tip of a blade. For years, everything went on as normal . . .

"Then what?" asked Calleneck.

"Then the storm hit," said Mr. Bernoil. "The first crack of thunder – they called it the Day of the Underground Fire; Queen Xandria had been silently gathering her forces, and in one day, the entire race of Goblins that lived underneath us was slaughtered."

"Why?"

Mr. Bernoil scratched his chin. "I suppose they threatened her dominance. Xandria couldn't exert her full power over Cerebria until those who lived underneath its surface were exterminated. At the time, there were lots of writings and stories of the awful things Goblins did to Cerebrian citizens. But I don't know how much of that was true and how much was propaganda to spread fear of the Goblins. After all, if you've never met a certain race or species before, your image of them can be easily molded by words and lies from someone you do know."

"Did *you* ever see one?" asked Calleneck. "A Goblin?"

"I may have when I was little, but I don't remember it clearly. But after that day, our army started to build camps in Endlebarr. A month later, we were at war . . . It's been long and bloody, Calleneck; I wish you grew up in a more peaceful time."

Calleneck looked at his hands. "So do I." He sat for a while thinking about the war when a thought crossed his mind. "Father, we were never taught in school why Tronum only declared war on Cerebria and not any of the other new nations in Endellia that seceded from the Empire."

Mr. Bernoil nodded. "I think the reason King Tronum only chose to fight Cerebria was partially because Queen Xandria was the start of it all – he thought she was the most to blame because her territories seceded first. The vast majority of the Imperial Navy came from Cerebria because of our tall pine forests that provide the lumber for great masts and ships. We clung on to all of those warships and vessels when we seceded. Tronum did try to send naval forces into the Crandles and Southern Elishka to maintain power in the East before they broke off too, but the Cerebrian fleet blockaded them and turned them back.

His fleet tried to resupply on the Island of Guavaan, but they gave no aid. The few ships that sailed back to Aunestauna were raided by Crestellian Pirates – Tronum lost control of the seas."

Calleneck connected the dots. "So, without a large naval force and an inability to create one, Tronum had no way of attacking the Island of Guavaan when it seceded soon after, and it would have been impractical to take on Elishka or the Northlands without ships – he would have to go through Endlebarr and Cerebria first to get to either of them."

Mr. Bernoil nodded. "Exactly. He also didn't attack Parusemare because Queen Eradine, his wife, grew up Parusean, the daughter of the Governess Anette Lameira. Their marriage went a long way in securing peace in the west, though Tronum couldn't avoid the split between Ferramoor and Parusemare. And down south of Cerebria, the Crandles posed no threat to him and were peaceful and isolated. As for the desert Southlands, their military and population exceeded Ferramoor's when they declared independence – Tronum had no chance of winning against them until he had secured the East."

"Why did the other nations besides Cerebria break away?" Calleneck asked. "I know Xandria wanted to secede because of her claim to the throne, but what about the others?"

"Well," began Mr. Bernoil, "There have always been fairly distinct differences between them – different cultures and languages and races. People don't like people that don't look or speak like them. So, in truth, it seems fairly logical that the others broke off from the Empire. Tronum's claim to the throne was weak at best, and they figured that while he was preoccupied with his sister, they could take their chance to develop their own freedom. They knew Ferramoor couldn't fight all of them, so they stepped back and let the siblings war over the right to rule."

Calleneck leaned back in his chair. "So then is Xandria just fighting for Cerebrian independence and freedom, or is she trying to take over Ferramoor and the rest of the kingdoms?"

Mr. Bernoil smiled. "Now that is the question, isn't it? Many will tell you that it is the first, that all she wants is peace from her brother and a land of her own – a land for our people." He shook his head. "But I think her ambitions hold much more than that. Content with one nation? Not her . . . not Xandria."

"Do *you* think she's dangerous then?" asked Calleneck.

Mr. Bernoil's smile had disappeared. His gaze was back on the drawing of his old friend, Rushki. "If she is, we're living in the right country."

Calleneck paused for a moment, then went on asking his father about times before Calleneck was born – even so far back as the Great War, when Gallegore triumphed over warring nations to defeat the sorcerers of the Lostlands and the corrupted kings to unite Endellia into an Empire. They talked for a long while, until they reached a lull in the conversation. Calleneck looked across the table at a letter from one of Mr. Bernoil's customers. It seemed as if in a strange memory, he saw a letter addressed to Seirnkov. Suddenly, a sense of curiosity overtook him. *I feel like I forgot to get a letter from the mailtower. But what letter? When did I see it?* Calleneck shook his head and then asked his father, "May I go on a walk?"

"Don't be out past ten," said Mr. Bernoil.

Calleneck nodded and headed out of the house and up the street.

The mailtowers were some of the tallest buildings in the regular parts of the city. *The Orchid Mailtower* was the nearest to Winterdove Lane and also the one which the Evertauri used. Some voice inside of him was guiding him toward it. *Why the Evertauri mailbox?* he thought.

Once at the circular tower, he walked up its central spiral staircase. *Floor fourteen.* He opened the door and stood outside on an open balcony lined with a stone railing and large columns that supported the next floor. Mailboxes covered the inner wall as it wrapped around the staircase. Looking out across the balcony, he could see much of the city and the white Seirns glistening in the moonlight. Messenger birds occasionally flew into the balcony area and dropped a letter in a mailbox slot. These birds were the safest and most efficient way to send information. They flew hundreds of miles in days, and if the message couldn't get to where it was supposed to, the birds shredded it in their talons.

Because the Evertauri primarily used the Network to transport information, their mailbox was not often used or checked. He knew the location of the mailbox because once Kishk the Trainer had assigned him to pick up a letter from a sorcerer in Elishka. *Number 1431bn.* President Madrick Nebelle had placed a security measure on the mailbox, similar to the entrances of the Goblin Network. Like all the other compartments, the mailbox had a slot wide enough for letters to pass through, but small enough to prevent anyone from getting inside it. However, the Evertauri mailbox's keyhole was fake, and therefore, could only be opened with a Taurimous – the flame-like energy of a sorcerer. Calleneck scanned the floor to make sure he was alone. Like with the mirror and the tree, he formed a crimson flame in his hand and placed it on the mailbox, which, in turn, hummed and shimmered. He reached his hand out and it seemed to disappear into the metal. Once one's Taurimous was placed on these 'objects,' their solid appearance vanished, and one could pass through it like a ghost. He felt around the cold metal and placed his fingers on a single letter. He pulled it out and the metal shimmered back into its solid form.

To- Seirnkov, Cerebria, Orchid Mailtower, Box 1431bn, Madrick
From — Aunestauna, Ferramoor, R.N.

R. N. he thought. *Raelynn Nebelle.* Calleneck furrowed his eyebrows, unable to remember why he thought to look for the letter in the first place, or if he even did. He seemed to recall talking with her in a tavern, but he couldn't think of where or when. *Something weird is going on in my head.* Calleneck tried in vain to think of why or how we could have spoken to Raelynn recently. *That's impossible though . . . she's been in Ferramoor for over a month. But I definitely saw her . . . I know I did.*

He shook his head again, wondering if he was going mad. *Put it back,* he told himself. As he extended his hand toward the insert slit in the mailbox, a messenger bird screeched and dove for the letter, grabbing it in its talons. Calleneck ripped it back and shooed the bird, but the envelope was torn open, and the letter inside had fallen out.

Calleneck looked around. *No, no I- can't read it.* But as he picked it up, he couldn't help but scan the first lines.

Dear Father,

I have searched through the palace archives to see if what you said about Mother is true. I think I'm on to something, and I may be close to finding the file that explains where she went. I don't know when I will come back to Seirnkov and the Evertauri, but I think my time is better spent finding Mother. I wrote another letter to Shonnar that explains what I've found so far. I haven't received a response from him yet, but I hope both of you are doing well . . .

Calleneck's subconscious interrupted and halted his reading; he needed to stop. He stuffed the note back into the envelope and sealed its rips and tears with his Taurimous, then slipped it back in the box, ashamed. But on the way home, he couldn't stop the thoughts circling in his head. *She's searching for her mother? And she still doesn't know her brother is dead. She's in Ferramoor, but I could have sworn I spoke to her recently.*

Calleneck continued to walk down the moonlit cobblestone streets of Seirnkov, back to his house on Winterdove Lane.

THE HOLLOW
Chapter Seven

~Afternoon, September 2nd
Southeastern Endlebarr

Down beneath the canopy of the Endlebarr, Tayben and his battalion began their relocation to the northern front. When they packed up camp, Birg and Tayben left Gallien behind, along with any chance of him returning. They donated his things to soldiers in need. The last days of summer were fading on the continent of Endellia, and autumn would soon set in, but the enchanted leaves of Endlebarr remained green until winter, where they would fade into reds and oranges, before turning green again for spring.

Tayben was told by his commanding officers that because snow would soon start to fall in the forest mountains, the Taurbeir-Krons, the Southern Pass would soon be impassable, thereby hindering Ferramish advances through the southeast quadrant of Endlebarr. While Xandria began to move battalions on the southern front north to counter Ferramish attacks, the Ferrs traded offense for defense and began to move their ranks back to the Southern Pass. Tayben's battalion marched north to take post at the Great Gate of Cerebria. At the fall of the Endellian Empire and the secession of Cerebria, Xandria's forces constructed a massive wall between two mountains in the Taurbeir-Krons. It was the only accessible pass by winter, and therefore, the only pass needing large scale defense.

Tayben trudged forward through the forest with his battalion with half closed eyes. When he lay his head down to rest on the forest floor, he could not forget the disturbing image of several nights prior. A dark mist, a man clad in black, a gust of wind, and it was gone. Again, Tayben heard Fenlell's words in his mind. *Should I succumb to the visions the forest has been giving me? Is it my duty to end my life before I go mad? No, no, I'm not going mad.*

The forest's dark magic and cunning had gotten to Gallien, gotten him lost or killed. Surely by now he was dead. Both Tayben and Birg had accepted the fact that their friend would not return; whatever led him to leave camp must have been compelling. The battalion officers filed his disappearance as desertion. Even if he fled, the journey to civilization would take weeks on foot, and no one could survive that time alone in Endlebarr. Strange beasts or other mysterious, dark things would take him quickly. Gallien was gone.

Tayben decided that the man he thought he saw in the mist was a hallucination, or at most, an animal that he mistook for a man. *But that cold draft I felt three times that day – in the tree, after I dodged the spear, and outside the tent . . . No, it's just the forest . . .*

Horses with dark green blankets over their backs carried the soldiers' armor, food, and essentials. Both animal and man trod through lush vegetation; on either side of them rose trees hundreds of feet tall. They were journeying into a deeper, darker part of the forest. Far fewer birds chirped here, and a heavy air seemed to compress the lungs of the soldiers; it was not a place for the claustrophobic.

As Tayben stepped over damp soil and moss, he put his free hand on his horse's soft neck. Lost in thought, his mind wandered to images of fire and screaming. An awful feeling filled his gut, the feeling that he was doing something wrong, that something was a danger to him and the Cerebrian army. Images, like memories or a dream kept coursing through his head. Crimson fire and sparks filled his vision as the feeling in his stomach grew worse. Inside his head, something screamed, *They're trying to overthrow us from the inside!*

Tayben froze, unaware of how that thought had entered his head. *What the hell was that?* he thought. *What am I thinking?* More fire filled his mind. *Why can't I get these memories out of my head?!* Tayben's body turned cold. *Memories? I– I feel like these are memories. He felt like vomiting. What the hell is going on?*

"Birg," he said, "can you take my horse's reins for a second?"

Birg nodded. "You don't look so good."

Tayben tried to breathe. "I– I just got a really bad feeling that–" Tayben stopped as images of faces flashed through mind that he swore he knew. He felt claustrophobic, like he was in a cold, dark tunnel buried deep underground.

A worried look crossed Birg's face. "That what?"

Tayben tried to force the images out of his head. "That the queen – Cerebria – is in danger . . ." Tayben's breathing quickened. "I need to talk to the captains." Up ahead, the officers rode on white stallions near the front of the brigade. Walking through the soldiers and cavalry, Tayben approached Fenlell and requested a discussion with him at the next stop.

"What's the trouble, soldier?" Captain Fenlell stood in front of him.

"Thank you for your time, sir." Tayben saluted him.

"Get on with it, Shae." Fenlell flipped his hair back and folded his arms.

Tayben hesitated as the images of dark tunnels and fire swirled in his mind. "Are you aware of any rebel groups in Cerebria?"

Fenlell furrowed his eyebrows. "Should I be?"

Tayben thought quickly. "Umm, no sir. I— I was just thinking that we should be watching out for those, you know. Just something I was thinking about."

Fenlell shook his head. "No need to worry, Shae, our army has everything contained."

"I just think we should be vigilant about—"

Fenlell raised his hand. "Shae, there is nothing out there."

Tayben nodded. "Of course. Thank you for your time, sir." Tayben slowly walked back to Birg, composing himself. *Everything will be fine . . . it's just the forest putting these memories . . . no, images in my mind.*

He returned and sat down next to Birg.

"Aye, what was that all 'bout, Tayben?"

"Oh, it's— it's nothing," said Tayben, lost in thought. "Sorry if I've been keeping you up at night lately. I just have a lot going through my head right now."

"It's no trouble."

A blonde boy, probably not older than sixteen, walked up to them. "Are you Birg and Tayben?"

"Yes, can we help you?"

The boy shuffled his feet. "My name is Hasht, I'm in with the new group of soldiers; there was overflow so the officers told me to join your companionship, seeing as you are short a man."

Tayben tried to smile to show welcome, but he didn't like the idea of replacing Gallien. "Sure thing, sit down with us."

"I'm from Whitetree," said Hasht, "just a long day's ride from the capital. What about you two?"

"I grew up in a little town called Woodshore," Tayben explained, "it's on the north end of Lake Kiettosh, near Endgroth. It's small . . . everyone knows everyone there."

"What does your family do?" the boy asked.

"My father is a blacksmith; my mother helps out, but I have no siblings. So, when recruiters came to our village asking for volunteers, I was the only person in my family who could fight."

"Tayben's the best spearman around," said Birg.

The boy nodded. "What about you?"

"My father's running one of them docks in The Iced Bank, tradin' with—" His speech was cut off when a cold draft of air circled around the group. The fog that surrounded them began to swirl and ebb.

Tayben stood up and grabbed his spear from his horse. "Birg, are you seeing this too?"

The boy grabbed a knife. "What's going on? It's just a breeze." Other soldiers seemed not to notice much, but a few horses started shuffling their back hooves.

"It's not just a breeze." Tayben looked out into the forest. "Stay with our horses," he said to the boy. "Birg, let's check it out."

Hasht grabbed the horses' reins. "What are you two doing? If you step away from the battalion, you'll never find your way back in this forest. It'll eat you alive."

Birg grabbed a longbow. "Don't think we're goin' far."

The two walked away from the stopped brigade and made their way through the dew-covered shrubs and leaves. Mossy vines hung between the massive trees, whose canopies blocked almost all sunlight, hundreds of feet above them. Daytime did not look much different than night; the green of the forest appeared grayer in the twilight. As they walked farther off the game trail the army was following, the fog settled, and their bodies began to warm. They stopped under a tree with cage-like roots that grew above the ground.

Birg looked around. "Tayben, I really don't think anyone is here. We need to go back."

Tayben jammed his spear into the ground. "I just have a feeling that we aren't alone. Don't you feel strange?"

"Yes, but it's the forest. Remember what Fenlell said? The forest is trying to drive us mad. Endlebarr's full of strange things that we don' know what they are. If we get lost, the battalion won' wait for us. Once someone loses the troop, they don' never come back; look what 'appened to Gallien."

The insects stopped buzzing, and the air grew cold. Both soldiers grabbed their weapons; Birg strung his bow. Tayben strained his eyes and couldn't see anything through the fog.

"Tayben! In the tree!" yelled Birg.

Tayben looked up and saw a black figure dart like an arrow into the canopy.

"To hell with this Tayben, we have to go back! This is freakin' me out and we'll get lost if they leave."

"No," whispered Tayben "someone is still here, I can feel it."

"Tayben–"

"Shhh!" Tayben stepped forward through ferns and wildflowers, his boots sank with each step over moss and black, wet soil; Birg stayed at the tree.

"Tha's it, Tayben, I'm goin' back with or without you!"

"I'll follow you in a minute." Tayben readjusted his grip on his spear. He knelt behind a mossy rock and looked into the dark forest. He heard Birg start to walk back to the brigade, which was no longer in earshot. He jumped when an owl screeched from a vine hundreds of feet above him. When he looked back down, a dark shadow darted from behind a tree then out of sight with incredible speed. *What the hell was that?* Tayben picked up his spear and sprinted into the forest, where the shadow had gone.

Watery leaves and bendy branches slapped his face as he looked back, running clear underneath the twenty-foot arch of a gigantic tree root, the foot of which was surrounded by more plants and mist. He danced between boulders and dodged through cages of tree roots, and looking to the side he saw a dark shadow disappear far up a gigantic tree. He stopped at a fallen tree trunk that was four times his height in width; it angled up and leaned on the tree where the figure had been, shooting up into the canopy.

Tayben took hold of the damp, rotting bark and pulled himself onto the trunk which cracked and peeled as he ran up the side of the fallen tree, ninety feet in the air. From this vantage point, he could see that the colossal branches weaved and wound like a system of streets and bridges in the canopy of the forest. Mist swirled ahead of him, and the air was cold. Almost. He ran forward on six-foot wide branches. He saw the dark shadow in the tree next to him, but when he scanned his surroundings, there was no way for him to get to the tree . . . *unless I jump.* Tayben lay on the branch and looked over the edge, nearly a hundred feet down to the forest floor. *I must be going mad.*

Tayben latched onto a thick vine that hung on an upper branch halfway between the trees — the gap he would have to swing across was nearly twenty yards. He saw another shadow dart around in the tree. *Just don't look down.* Tayben spotted a branch slightly below his height where he would land; he sent his spear straight into the branch. After a few steps back, he ran forward and leaped off the tree.

His stomach plummeted as he shot through the air and his calloused hands held the vine so tightly his knuckles turned white. The vine suddenly jerked to the side. Tayben looked up — the vine caught on a branch. He began spiraling around the tree, getting closer and closer until his body smacked into the side of the trunk like a bird hitting a window. With over sixty feet still below him, Tayben lost his grip and began sliding down the vine. His hands burned as slivers jammed into his palm and fingers. Tayben cursed as the vine ended and his body slammed into a branch below and bounced off. The world spun around him as he searched for something he could catch. He spotted a small branch as he fell and caught it; the momentum of his body tore at his shoulders. After just a few seconds, the branch snapped, and he plunged toward the forest floor. He hit the lowest trees, the branches cutting his body and spinning him like a ragdoll. With another smack against the trees, his mind went blank.

Tayben tried opening his eyes — one eyelid was sliced, and the blood obscured his vision. He lay on the forest floor on top of several ferns. No air was filling his lungs; he felt as if he was suffocating. One of his ribs was broken, and convulsions sent sharp pains through his chest. As soon as he lifted his head, he turned to the side and vomited. Blood pooled on the ground; he saw that his uniform was shredded to pieces and his body was scraped and cut everywhere. A gruesome gash ran from his shoulder to his thigh, his right forearm was bent and bleeding – broken. He groaned and tried to stand up, but immediately lost his balance and fell.

Panic spread through his mind – he couldn't remember from which direction he had come; it all looked the same. Moreover, he couldn't walk. *I've lost the troop.* He screamed for Birg for minutes but heard no reply. Clutching the branches of a bush for support, he successfully stood onto his feet and began stumbling forward, leaving a trail of blood behind him. His only weapon hung stuck in the tree branch a hundred feet above him.

He wandered for several hours, clutching his chest and trying to walk upright. His body told him to rest, but he had to find the battalion. Each step was a hill, each slope a mountain. He limped for what seemed like miles in what he thought was the direction of the troop. After coming to a patch of table-sized red mushrooms that he had already passed, he finally sat down and leaned against a tree root. *I'm going in circles!*

Tayben hit the ground in anger and tears began to well up in his eyes. Before he knew it, he was sobbing. *I'm sorry, Birg . . . I should have listened and stayed with the platoon.* Fenlell's warning filled his head as his erratic breathing worsened. *"We men are not welcome in this forest . . . She watches you from every corner . . . she doesn't care if you live or die."*

He looked down at his shredded body and screamed out into the dark forest, "I'm sorry!" He breathed in sharply as tears streamed down his face. Screaming out in frustration, he punched the black wet soil again. Again. Again. Again, until his knuckles pained him too much. Letting out one last pitiful cry into the endless forest, he collapsed onto the wet ground, resting his face on the mud. A feeling of utter hopelessness filled his broken and bloody body as he slowly whispered once more, "I'm so sorry." He closed his eyes and tears dripped down his bloody face into the cold mud. Memories of his hometown filled his head. He tried not to think of his parents. *What will they do once they hear that I–* He couldn't finish the thought, but he slowly let the words sink into his broken body. *I'm going to die here.*

After a while, he opened his eyes and looked into the distance – nothing was there but forest and settled fog, save for a very faint white light that he had not noticed before. After a couple minutes, Tayben realized that this was not a hallucination. The white light was shining on the ferns around it. He hobbled toward it and peeled back the giant leaves revealing a glowing white flower. A strange light emanated from its petals, flowing down through its stem and into the soil below. Sparks of light traveled beneath the dirt and vanished into the surrounding plants. Curious, Tayben touched it with his bloody finger. A searing pain shocked him, and he pulled back. When he looked at the tip of his finger, he saw that the blood had vanished, and the cut was gone. *What in the world?* He touched his palm to it and an even larger shock of pain rippled through his body, causing him to yell. But, when he turned his hand face up, it looked as if he had never fallen out of the tree.

In the corner of his eye, another white light was glowing. He picked himself up and staggered toward it, collapsing right in front of another glowing flower. Because a rib was broken, each breath sent waves of agony through his body. He leaned forward and was about to touch it when he saw a bed of glowing flowers far in the distance. *They heal . . . I could lie in the flowerbed . . .* He used his unbroken arm to get back up. Lightheadedness had begun to affect his ability to walk in a straight line – he had lost too much blood from the fall. As he looked around, he could see more and more of these flowers lighting the mist. Just a few steps before he reached the bright light of the flowerbed, someone grabbed him from behind and slipped a dagger in front of his neck.

Tayben froze; he was defenseless. He could not see whoever was holding him except for a hand in a purple robe. A woman's voice whispered harshly behind his neck. "Don't move! Who are you? . . . Answer, now!"

Tayben coughed. "I am a soldier for the Cerebrian Army."

The woman pressed the blade to his neck. "Why are you here?!"

"I veered away from our brigade and I'm lost."

The woman pressed the dagger to Tayben's skin, drawing a thin line of blood. "Why is the army in this region of the forest?"

"We're on orders from the Queen. The army is just passing through to get from one location to the next." Tayben winced with pain. "But I'm hurt; those flowers–"

"Those won't heal you permanently," said the woman.

Tayben could tell that the woman was looking around. "Who are you?

She ignored him. "I can make most of the pain and the bleeding subside," she said. A little burst of light in the back of his head lit the forest for a brief moment like a lightning flash, and most of the pain he felt was immediately lifted. Blood stopped running down his body. "Come with me now," she ordered.

Intimidated by whatever she had just done to ease the pain, Tayben did not question her. She pushed him through the forest with a dagger hovering close to his neck. He walked like a drunk man for a half hour as he clutched his broken arm. The farther into the forest she led him, the more plentiful the glowing white flowers became; soon, they lit up the underbrush with the power of a thousand blazing torches. The woman pushed him past a barrier of light and into a field of these glowing flowers which stung at his feet. Tayben had to squint his eyes, as he was not used to this kind of light in the dark forest.

Adjusting to the brightness, Tayben's eyes widened when he saw an immense tree on an island in a small, glowing lake ahead of him. What amazed him was not the sheer size of the tree — which was well over forty feet wide and hundreds of feet tall — but that there was a door in the bottom, and open windows in the trunk glowing with firelight — a house inside a tree.

Tayben gazed into the lake of iridescent light that surrounded the central tree; in it swam glowing minnows of all colors. A shimmering rainbow of light danced underneath the surface of the water; it seemed like the water was sprinkled with starlight. On the forest floor, not just the white flowers glowed; but white, orange, and red toadstools, patches of moss, and ferns all emanated light. Somewhere in his delirious state, Tayben found himself being surprised that the hollow's light had not permeated the surrounding fog. In the glade, the grass grew perfectly green, like an aristocratic lawn. He felt a strange desire to jump into the pond and swim with the luminous creatures. A violet butterfly glowing with light gently fluttered down and briefly landed on Tayben's hand before softly taking flight again. For a moment, Tayben's mind was so enchanted by his surroundings that the lingering ache in his body failed to intrude his thoughts.

A deer pranced on the other side of the glade, and three rabbits ate grass beside Tayben's feet. Whenever he stepped, the grass beneath his feet would light up in a blue-white glow, leaving footprints of light on the forest floor. The woman — of whom he had not seen more than an arm — pushed him forward to the edge of the pool of enchanting water, facing the tree with the house built inside. He looked down into the water casting ripples of light on his bloody face — the pool seemed to be bottomless. From one of his unhealed cuts, a drop of blood fell into the water, but there was no splash or sound. The blood simply vanished as soon as it hit the surface. A turtle-like creature swam up to the shoreline and floated in front of them. It was black — the size of five or six shields with a shell that had thick, low-lying spines, and its head looked like a horned lizard.

"Step on," said the woman behind Tayben.

"I'm sorry?" Tayben tried to look back, but she turned his head and forced him onto the floating creature. Once they were both on its back, it turned and began swimming toward the island. The hollow sang with the calls of birds and hummed the buzz of pollinating bees. His attention was drawn to the water below. All sorts of glowing creatures, which Tayben never imagined could exist, swam in its depths. Another purple butterfly briefly touched down on the black turtle and then flew off, with little flakes of light shedding off its wings with every flutter. On the opposite side of the lake, Tayben could have sworn he glimpsed a white, winged lion.

As they approached the shoreline, Tayben noticed that the rooms within the giant tree rose four or five stories high. There was no glass in the windows which were curved and irregular like the grain of the tree bark. In fact, the door and everything about the house seemed to flow with the growth of the tree.

The spiny creature stopped at the island to let the woman and Tayben off before dipping below the surface. She pulled the dagger away from Tayben's neck and allowed him to turn around. She looked strangely old and young at the same time – almost like she should have been in her forties but hadn't aged since her twenties. She was Tayben's height and wore a purple cloak. Her dark, curly hair flowed over her shoulders and contrasted her pale, angular face.

The woman looked intently at him with wondrous green eyes. "You're wounded. I'll take care of that. I apologize for the dagger; it was to ensure you wouldn't run away. If you try to swim across the lake, the water will kill you and my Krackleback will only take you back across the water if I tell him to. Sit down and stop wasting your energy."

He sat on the grass and clutched his side.

"You won't live unless I heal your wounds . . . this may give you a scare, but don't run away. Take off your tunic."

He did as he was told but flinched when the tunic tugged on his broken arm.

"How did you get hurt this badly?"

"I fell from the canopy."

She placed her hands over his bloody chest. A white light flowed from her hand and onto his skin. Tayben flinched out of surprise when the blood on his chest disappeared. His flesh began to grow and stitch itself back together; the scratches and cuts all vanished. "This will hurt a bit," she said before the white light snapped his rib back together under his skin. Tayben yelled in pain through gritted teeth. She repeated the same procedure with his broken forearm and cleared up the rest of his body from cuts and bruises. The only thing that scarred was a gash that ran from his shoulder across his chest.

"Who are you?" he asked.

"It doesn't matter, you won't remember any of this anyway."

Tayben raised an eyebrow. "I'm sorry what did you say?"

"No one would live here without a reason. I want to help you, but no one can know about me. I'll alter your memory so that you think you never injured yourself in the forest and never saw this place."

"That's impossible—"

"So was healing your wounds."

"Are you a sorceress?"

". . . If that's what you'd like to call it," she said.

Tempted to ask her why he was seeing memories of sorcery and fire, he resisted, instead asking. "Why did you do this for me?"

"You were going to die if I hadn't done anything."

Tayben stood up with ease. "I don't know how to thank you . . . This all seems so strange . . . so dreamlike . . ."

"The life force of the world flows freely in this glade," she said. "That energy blossoms here because of what I have given it, hence all the glowing. I grew this tree in the shape that I wanted, with hollow chambers inside to make my house. This is my home, where I can live in solitude from the rest of the world. That's also why I will have to search your memory to make sure you aren't lying about who you say you are and where your people are going."

"I swear I'm—"

"I don't care," she said.

Minutes later, Tayben lay on the ground with white ribbons of light shooting through his head. She was prying into his mind for glimpses of information. Flashes from his childhood passed by, and suddenly, he saw memories of what felt like other childhoods . . . two sisters – one older and one younger, a brother and a palace, an orphanage. The memories became so vivid he could almost swear they were his own . . . but they couldn't be. The prying stopped.

The woman shook her head. "How does it work?" she wondered aloud.

"I'm sorry?" Tayben had no answer and wasn't even sure he understood the question.

"Your mind, your Taurimous, it inhabits four different bodies simultaneously. I've never seen anything like it. How do you control four bodies at the same time?"

"I– I don't think I do . . . it's almost like I see different memories or dreams from . . ." A wave of questions arose. "What's happening to me?"

"You think what you've been seeing are dreams? That's all real. Your consciousness must jump back and forth between your bodies . . . Your perception of time isn't linear; it must be like you're living each day four times . . . When does the clock reset?"

"I– I think," Tayben's head spun, trying to say anything, "it seems like sunrise when the memories shift, and it always seems like days have passed – but I can't be sure."

"It would be like you're traveling back in time a day, but all the events would still appear to an outsider to occur at the same time. Can you change the past once you've lived it?"

Tayben looked at his hands, "I– I don't know . . . how– how is that possible?"

"It shouldn't be possible . . ." The woman paused for a moment, thinking hard, then looked at Tayben in fear. She muttered something under her breath that Tayben could barely hear. "Wait, I saw a memory of Seirnkov and the palace of Aunestauna. No . . . can it be?" She put a hand to his face. "You're a Cerebrian . . . is your name Calleneck or Tayben?"

"What? What are you talking about?"

"Which one are you?!" she demanded.

"Tayben," he said. ". . . How do you know my name?"

She shook her head and whispered. "Names . . . Eston, Kyan, Calleneck, Tayben. I see you tell the truth, although you did not tell me the whole truth about why you ran away from your brigade. Don't follow things in the forest, Tayben. It will only bring you harm . . . I see conflict in your head. Figure out what you believe, or you will find yourself on opposite sides of the same war."

"How do you know me?"

The woman stood up and stepped away. "No more questions; you must leave this place now."

"But I barely—"

The woman raised her hand. "Do not speak." She escorted him across the lake again, with a dagger to his neck; then she walked him far into the forest, where no glowing flowers could be seen. She asked him to lie down so he would not hurt himself when he lost consciousness; he obeyed out of fear of what she might do to him. "I'm sorry, but I must wipe your memory of this encounter."

Tayben apprehensively pushed away, but a force stopped him and held him down. "Wait! Please!" he said. "If you're going to change my memories, just please keep what I know now about my mind, the connection . . . my other three bodies . . . please . . ."

The woman paused. ". . . some, not everything. You'll have to figure out the rest on your own." She stepped forward. White ribbons of light shot from her hand into Tayben's head. His eyes closed.

When he awoke, he scanned his misty surroundings. *I shouldn't have taken a nap. I need to keep searching for the battalion . . . Where is my spear?* He stood up and walked through the forest in the direction he thought he came from frantically trying to find his spear, and after five or ten minutes of looking, he still had no luck. But he couldn't help but feel like something was missing, like he had forgotten something. *It's the forest again. Don't panic, you'll find your way back.* It was hard convincing himself that he would be the only one out of two thousand missing soldiers to return to the battalion after being lost in Endlebarr.

Tayben had not been walking long when he ran across what seemed to be a trail of two sets of footprints walking in the direction he had just come from, dotted with drops of blood on the ground. Tayben looked back, trying to remember if he had seen anyone in the forest. *That's so strange, I would've seen someone if they were here.*

He moved along, interpreting the scene as another way the forest was trying to trick him. Then a shiver ran down his spine. The air seemed to sit completely still, and a bird stopped singing. In the mist, twenty yards ahead of him, a black figure stood like a statue. He grabbed a stick on the ground and walked toward it. An unknown voice in his head said, *Don't follow things in the forest, Tayben. It will only bring you harm.* He ignored it and kept walking toward the figure. As he got closer, he saw another black figure standing beside the first. With every step, more and more figures appeared out of nowhere; he looked back and found himself surrounded by over a dozen cloaked people. They began slowly walking toward him, closing the gaps in the circle.

Tayben called out, "Who are you? Stop right there!" The figures did not stop; they made no sound as they stepped through the lush vegetation. They were like ghosts the way they moved. Tayben's heart raced, and his lungs convulsed rapidly. His bones turned ice cold and he tried to yell but couldn't. The figures were now each twenty feet away from him, but he could not see their faces underneath their cloaks.

The figures stopped, and one stepped forward and removed his hood. "Tayben, lower your guard; we are not here to hurt you." Tayben fell to his knees, for before him, cloaked like the others, stood Gallien Aris.

"Gallien — where have you been? What's going on? Who are these people?"

"Your questions will be answered soon."

Tayben looked around the circle at the cloaked figures who had not made any sounds. They were the shadows he had been chasing . . .

Gallien opened his arms and smiled big. "We are the Phantoms of Cerebria."

THE SCARLET PALACE
Chapter Eight

~Afternoon, September 2nd
Royal Palace, Aunestauna, Ferramoor

Lightning flashed outside the palace window, briefly illuminating the Great Library, which was otherwise lit by candles. Rain pounded on the glass and thunder shook the stone walls that arched into a towering, vaulted ceiling over two hundred feet tall. Lined with decorative mahogany and elaborate murals of the Ferramish countryside, the Great Library of Aunestauna hosted millions of scrolls, letters, and handwritten books. Taking up nearly the entire North Wing of the Royal Palace, the library hosted scholars, senators, and wealthy citizens alike. At a small reading table, Eston sat across from Sir Janus Whittingale.

Whittingale looked young for his fifties, with a narrow chin and slick hair so dark brown it was nearly black. His eyebrows were perpetually furrowed, causing his forehead to wrinkle. Eston had noticed from a young age that the man never flinched or jumped, like an immovable gargoyle meant to ward off bad spirits. As Tronum's First Advisor, Whittingale had been Eston's mentor from the time he was ten years old. Whittingale had taught him in the arts, language, science, politics, history, and physical skills; but most importantly, he was preparing Eston to become King of Ferramoor. One day his father would die or voluntarily pass off the crown to his eldest son. Either way, Eston could not escape the immense responsibility that awaited him.

It always seemed unreal to the prince that one day he would rule over a kingdom of which he had seen so little. He never liked thinking about how Fillian would not have a chance of taking the throne even though Fillian was only a year younger. Unlike when Gallegore withheld information regarding who was the eldest twin and chose Tronum to rule over Xandria, Tronum had no choice but to hand the throne to his clearly eldest child. The king had appointed trusted mentors for Fillian and Eston, for he could not teach his children day to day.

Whittingale turned over a scroll on the table. "Name the two ways to delay a senate order for a general's resignation."

Eston leaned back in his chair to think.

"Back straight, Eston."

"Yes, sorry sir. The order can be delayed if the general doesn't have an immediate successor — preventing a security issue — but the senators have a right to appoint that position. I forget the second."

Whittingale shook his head. "The second is if the general's home district senator is not in favor of their resignation — then the decision goes to the King. You have to know this, Eston. Read through this scroll again tonight and make sure the information is solid in your head."

"Yes, sir," said Eston.

"You've read up on your lineage? Last session was an embarrassment."

"Yes, sir," Eston repeated.

"Who was Kliera Dellasoff?" asked Whittingale.

"Kliera Dellasoff was from an aristocratic Cerebrian family in Ontraug. She was the only wife to King Gallegore, making her my patriarchal grandmother. The match was likely made to help Gallegore keep hold of the eastern nations — marrying a Cerebrian was a sure way to do that. Shortly after they were married at the end of the Great War, she died giving birth to my father and then Xandria."

"In which order?"

"That order," stated Eston.

Whittingale gave a slight smile that made Eston shift in his seat. "Anette Lameira?"

"My matriarchal grandmother. She was Parusean like my mother and served as Governess of the Parusean territories during the peace of the Endellian Empire."

"And what was her territory?" asked Whittingale.

"The western coast, the port cities," Eston said confidently, "Illora, Port Impere, Cota Lume, Luquette, and the others."

"And who were your grandfather Gallegore's parents? Where did he grow up?"

Eston paused. "No one knows."

Whittingale let another small smile appear. "Interesting, isn't it? . . ." He let the question hang in the air like a feather fluttering to the ground. But as soon as the silence peaked, he shattered it. "Let's see if you know your Northlands tundra clans . . ." Whittingale continued testing Eston on everything from other languages, to war history, to medicines and sums, to subjects he knew Eston had not yet studied. Once Whittingale finished, he stood and pushed in his chair. "Meet me in the Maple Courtyard in fifteen minutes. Get changed and ready to duel."

"Another in the pouring rain?"

"You won't always get to choose when you fight," said Whittingale as he left.

Eston took the scroll and glanced over at the other reading tables in his section of the library. Out of the corner of his eye he saw a girl with silvery blonde hair leaning over scrolls. *That's her! The one from the Little Raven, the one I've been looking for. Her name . . . it's- Ra- Raelia-, no, Raelynn, Raelynn! That's it! . . . How do I know that's it?*

Vibrant colors of light coiled through his memory. *She's a sorceress . . . She's here to find her mother . . . I read her letter to her father . . . Those dreams about sorcery, they can't be real. Sorcerers were killed off by my grandfather. It wasn't real. But then how could I have read her letter?* Eston thought hard. *I could've dreamed that I read it. But I have memories of seeing her in Cerebria even though I've never been there. I could ask her again why she's here; if she says she's trying to find her mother, then that means those visions actually could be memories. That means that there is a rebel group within Cerebria . . . the Evertauri.*

As soon as Whittingale exited the library, the prince stood up and walked over to Raelynn. "Excuse me?"

Her eyes widened when she saw him. "Hello." She looked around apprehensively.

Eston grinned. "You were in the tavern on Monarch Street, *The Little Raven*, were you not?"

"I was," she responded. "Why are you here?" she asked, brushing aside a strand of her blonde hair.

Eston paused. The scholars behind him seemed occupied enough not to notice their conversation. He pulled back a chair and sat down across from her. "My name is Eston Wenderdehl."

Raelynn tried to shuffle to her feet. "Your Majesty, forgive me, I didn't know."

"You don't need to stand, miss. I was just wondering what you were studying over here."

She hesitated. "I . . . I'm looking into some of the history of King – um, your grandfather – just for my studies." Before Raelynn pulled her papers into her lap, Eston was able to read the title of a scroll that read, *Government Positions under King Gallegore the Great.*

"Pardon my bluntness," said the prince, "but I suspect there's more to who you are and where you're from. Nevertheless, I promise I won't get you in trouble."

"Like I said, I'm from—"

"Nottenberry. I don't think that's true. You're here looking for something and based on the manner of your dress and hint of accent, I think you're from far away." Eston leaned in and whispered. "Trust me, I have no interest in getting you in trouble. In fact, you could get me in trouble with the Scarlet Guard and the government if they knew I was sneaking out into the city. Just . . . tell me the truth."

Raelynn flinched as a thundercrack shook the library windows. "I'm from Cerebria," she whispered.

Eston's stomach turned cold. She was from his enemy nation, but why would she disclose that if she truly was his enemy? "I don't think it's wise for you to be here. More than a few people here would want to see you dead if they found out."

"And you're not one of them?"

"Well, do you work for Xandria?" said Eston.

"No."

"You're a commoner?"

"Yes," said Raelynn.

Eston looked at her intensely. ". . . Bloody strange commoner."

Raelynn sat in silence.

"Why are you here?" Eston continued.

Raelynn scanned the surrounding tables and whispered. "My mother used to work here; she vanished shortly after I was born."

It's true . . . Thoughts that he felt had to be memories of underground tunnels, the letter, colored flames, two girls who felt like family – one older, one younger – circled through his head. *The Evertauri is real?* Eston felt dizzy.

"Where are you staying here in Aunestauna?" he asked.

Raelynn paused. ". . . *The Westflower Inn.*"

He paused for a moment. "I need to leave, and you should stay away from the Royal Palace." Eston walked away, through the stacks of books and scrolls and past the windows that pattered from rain. *Would it be possible to have another body that I live in?* He tried to shake the thoughts from his head. *I'm going mad.*

"You're late," Whittingale called out. Rain still poured into the courtyard. He handed Eston a wooden longsword and shield like his own that he held in his hand. Water flattened their hair and poured off their lips as they took stances opposite each other. Eston struck forward, and Whittingale dodged the sword, slashing at Eston, who met the sword with his shield. "Eston, I feel that your mind is not clear."

"Yes, sorry sir," said Eston, as he thought about the tunnels. He also couldn't shake the images of Endlebarr from his head, nor the images of the slums of Aunestauna and a small shack.

Eston forced his mind back to his training. "Can I practice with my sword? How can it ever be a Queenslayer if I never use it?"

Whittingale shook his head. "You need to practice with this one . . . and who calls your sword Queenslayer?"

Eston shrunk. "Fillian."

Whittingale sighed. "Then show me you're capable of brandishing a simple one like this."

Eston lunged at Whittingale, who swept the blow aside. The two dueled for nearly an hour in the courtyard, alternating between Ferramish and Cerebrian styles of fighting. Ferramish hit hard with their swings, with wide arcs, while Cerebrians kept their swords close to their torso. Whittingale had been training Eston in combat since he was ten and wanted him to be fluent in all types of swordplay so that he could "slay any enemy, no matter the attacker."

Eston slipped on a puddle and quickly attempted to recover. Before Whittingale could land another blow, Fillian ran into the courtyard and called out for Eston. "Hey, Eston!"

Eston looked at Fillian, distracted, as Whittingale clipped his elbow. "Ouch!"

Whittingale shook his head and put down the sword.

Fillian laughed. "Good day, Sir Janus." He had probably just finished his own lessons with his mentor – Sir Endwin Bardow, brother of Senator Erdwey Bardow. "Eston," said Fillian, "Father would like to talk to you. He says thank you to Whittingale, but the lesson is done for the day. He's in his study."

"What does he want me for?" Eston put down his sword and Fillian stepped into an alcove to avoid the rain.

"He didn't tell me."

Eston groaned inwardly. *What is it this time?*

A guard opened a giant walnut door, and Eston entered the King's Study nudged between the North and West Wings of the palace. The room was tall and cylindrical, with shelves of maps, gadgets, and ornaments. A chandelier hung in the center. King Tronum stood on a balcony above the large, cushioned chairs, looking at a chart. His white beard hung only an inch down from his slightly wrinkled skin. A scarlet robe brushed on the floor behind him. He noticed the prince enter and glanced up, removing a monocle from his eye – a fine accessory only for the wealthiest. "Ah, Eston. You were out in the rain I see – your curls are flattened. How was your lesson today?"

"Oh, it was fine, normal."

"Good." Tronum placed the scroll on a desk and stepped on a sliding ladder.

"Father you can just take the stairs—"

"I'm fine, Eston." The king's hands shook slightly as he stepped down the ladder, which rattled against the floor. He reached the bottom and sat in a large, pillowed chair, and requested Eston sit across from him. With slightly twitching fingers, he sipped a mug of coffee, a rare delicacy, shipped all the way from Guavaan. Tronum sighed. "Eston, look at me . . . I'm getting old . . ." He held out his hand which twitched every few seconds. "I know you've been wanting to move up in the chain of command and take matters into your own hands."

Eston leaned forward, trying to look calm, but his insides were turning with not only excitement for more responsibility, but also sadness for his father's condition. *It's time for me to ask.* "I want to lead a regiment on the frontlines. If I have good war experience, the kingdom will be in safe hands when I'm king."

Tronum continued, "I'm not comfortable with you going out on the front with our soldiers, but you can participate more in the Council. You need more experience here, more instruction with Whittingale." Eston's heart sank and the slight smile turned into a disguised frown. "Being King is the hardest responsibility a man can bear, and his advisors share that hardship. I want you on my Council, Eston, but you still have much to learn . . . I just want what's best for you; you know that."

"Yes, of course." *He wouldn't have changed his mind from a few months ago.*

"I won't be able to do this forever, Eston. My youth is gone, and I'm fading out like an old scroll. You will take my throne one day. I can't give it to Fillian. My point is, you'll share that throne with someone. Marriage is not as far away as you think."

"Father, we've talked about—"

"We have not discussed specifics. Listen, as a diplomat, you have to think strategically about your marriage. You're nearly twenty, Eston; you should be married by twenty-two at the latest. Look, I'm not going to force you to marry anyone, we aren't old traditionalists from the west. However, I will require you to open your mind to possibilities. It must be done with care."

Eston shook his head. "You married mother just because she was born in Parusemare? So you could maintain a good alliance with the Paruseans during their secession from the Endellian Empire?"

"*And* because I loved her, Eston . . . all I'm saying is that you need to start thinking about it."

Eston looked up at the chandelier and outside at the stormy afternoon sky. "I assume you have someone in mind then."

"Qerru-Mai An'Drui," said Tronum. "She's the Council Scrivener and she's got a good head on her shoulders. Her late father, Lord Jarro An'Drui, was one of my closest friends. He was governor of southern Ferramoor during my father's reign, and my top general before he was killed in the Battle of the Burning Hills. Her mother is a Senator and has been one of my closest Council members from the time I took the throne. Senator An'Drui values the right things and cares deeply for the nation. She has taught her daughter to follow in her footsteps as you are following in mine. I had a brief conversation with Senator An'Drui and she approved of you spending time with Qerru-Mai."

"Qerru-Mai?" Eston leaned back and sighed, relieved it was a girl he was already familiar with. "She's wonderful don't get me wrong, and so incredibly smart, it's almost scary . . ."

"She would make a good queen, Eston. Even if she's not the future queen I have no doubt she'll be your First Advisor when you take the throne. Sometimes I think she could challenge even Whittingale's intellect, and she's less than half his age."

"I guess I can consider it; but right now, if you want me to focus on my studies then I'll mainly focus on that . . . If that's what will allow me to rise up in your chain of command."

"It's not about your studies, Eston . . ." Tronum sat up and walked to the window. "This is about more than you; it's about the millions you will affect who need someone strong . . . Give it a try with Qerru-Mai."

"Yes, father."

Lightning lit up the cloudy sky outside the rain-pelted window. Tronum put a shaky hand on the glass. "Your Aunt Xandria will stop at nothing to see us fall. It will soon be up to you to defend Ferramoor. We must succeed, Eston. We must."

Eston paused for a while, thinking deeper until he almost forgot where he was.

"What is it, Eston?" His father gave off an obvious air of impatience.

"I– I don't understand your war." He didn't know where the words came from, but they couldn't be unsaid.

King Tronum's face grew red with anger. "*My* war?"

"The war, the war between Ferramoor and Cerebria. What is the goal? What does the bloodshed accomplish?" Eston could tell he had already gone too far, but something kept him going. "In the beginning, when your sister declared independence with Cerebria, trying to preserve the Empire and take it back made sense; but it's since split into eight different kingdoms and we're no closer to uniting them back together than we were a decade ago. What does fighting Cerebria do for us? What would you have me do as king once the war is won? Stop there, or keep trying to conquer all of Endellia?"

Tronum's clenched hand was shaking, but Eston could not tell how much was from anger and how much was from the king's disease. "Xandria—" Tronum breathed in deeply, trying to suppress his rage. "Xandria did not just declare independence, she killed my father Gallegore and she tried to kill me. She tried to take the throne, Eston, the throne that is mine and will be yours. She will not hesitate to try and kill me again and this time she has you and Fillian to get to before her claim is legitimate. She won't stop until you and I and the Ferramoor we know do not exist."

The rain pattered on the windows and the air felt colder. Eston breathed slowly and purposefully, not knowing what to say.

"This is about protecting our right," said Tronum, "our bloodline."

"A bloodline how long?" said Eston. "The great families ruling the other kingdoms go back hundreds of years . . . where did our right come from? Where did Gallegore come from? . . . He didn't ever tell you, did he?"

Tronum looked down at his desk. "My father rose from— He was more powerful than you can understand. He united a broken world. He defeated the sorcerers and the false kings, and he brought peace to the world with strength and—"

"—and a flaming sword?" said Eston. "A winged lion?"

Tronum looked up at his son with disdain and spoke in slow, short words. "You don't know what you mock . . . Your behavior is inexcusable. Childish! If you even think about acting this way at the ambassadors' dinner tonight, I swear—" He shook his head. "I've had enough of this. Out!"

Eston left without question and shut the door behind him. As he walked away, past the Scarlet Guards outside the study, he replayed the conversation in his mind. *This war won't end until Xandria dies . . . or until we die.*

A roaring fire filled the Great Hall with a warm yellow light, by which the Wenderdehls and high officials gathered for dinner. On most occasions, the seats were occupied by some permutation of senators, generals, the Scarlet Lord, the First advisor, or the Prophet; but tonight featured as guests the Ferramish Ambassador to Parusemare – Thomet Changereau – and the Parusean Ambassador to Ferramoor – Cheveir Fontigne.

Eston heard Whittingale's voice in his head, telling him to recite the names of all eight nations' ambassadors to each of the other nations. With vacancies, that number neared fifty diplomats charged with the politics between the squabbling kingdoms of Endellia.

The guests surrounded the table, King Tronum and Queen Eradine at the head. The ambassadors shook each others' hands across the table and then turned to the royal couple. Ambassador Fontigne gave a deep bow to the queen and kissed her hand. "Ah, ze beautiful Eradine Lameira, how ve miss your presence in ze great Kingdom of Parusemare." His hair was dark like most Paruseans, but it had begun to turn gray in scattered places.

Queen Eradine nodded in return. "Your words are kind, Ambassador," she said, with a greater hint of her own accent emerging in the presence of another Parusean.

"Oha, please, call me Cheveir . . . ve are family after all, no?"

Eradine smiled as she sat, prompting the whole table to take their seats. "Indeed." They were, of course, family – Eradine's elder brother, Philar Lameira, sat on the throne of Parusemare with his wife Charletta Fontigne, Cheveir's elder sister.

Eston unfolded his mess cloth into his lap as Fontigne continued, "King Philar sends his best to you and hopes to maintain Endellia's strongest alliance."

King Tronum scoffed. "A strong alliance, he says." Servants entered the room with dishes of roasted ham and baked vegetables.

"Your Majesty," said Ambassador Changereau, "We have made a great deal of diplomatic progress today, and we are eager to share that with you."

"Is Parusemare prepared to lend us troops to fight Cerebria?" asked Tronum, carving out a slice of ham and placing it on his plate.

Ambassador Fontigne took a sip of wine. "It regrets me to say zat ve cannot officially support you in your war against your sister. However, ve are happy to donate our excess wheat to your granaries free of charge. And of course, if zis bread happens to feed your soldiers in Endlebarr, ah, vell ze Parusean government vould have no vay of knowing." Fontigne smiled and winked.

"And what is this in exchange for?" asked Tronum.

"Rights to fishing on the entirety of the Lake of Duloret," said Thomet Changereau. "Lac Lucera has a much larger fishing need than Duloret Post. Feeding both of our kingdoms better only makes sense. Your Majesty, this is a wonderful deal for us that we desperately need. Our granaries are not prepared for the winter and we're trying to feed mothers at home and fathers at war."

King Tronum nodded. "What else have we got?"

As the ambassadors continued their discussion, Fillian whispered to his brother beside him. "What did Father want earlier?"

Eston cut open a squash. He knew Fillian wouldn't leave satisfied without some answer. "He wants me to spend more time with Qerru-Mai."

"Senator An'Drui's daughter?" Fillian chuckled. "Sorry, brother, but she is way out of your league."

Eston looked sideways at his brother. "Fillian . . . I'm a prince."

"Sure, and you have the muscles of a twelve-year-old girl."

"Oh, hush . . . She's the Council Scrivener and father sees her as a potential First Advisor to the King. Father wants me to have a capable wife."

Fillian placed a fork on his empty plate and stood; beneath his messy brown hair, he glanced at his father at the far end of the comically long table, lost in conversation with Queen Eradine and the ambassadors. "Or maybe father trusts Qerru-Mai to make decisions for you."

As they walked out of the hall after dinner and rounded a corner, Eston grabbed Fillian's shoulder and turned him around. "Father keeps hinting to me he doesn't think he has much time, yet he's refusing to give me any responsibility. Doesn't that make no sense? It's because I know he doesn't trust me, and I know he doesn't want me to take his place."

Fillian shoved Eston off. "The question isn't whether he wants to give you the throne. It's a question of whether you want it."

"Of course I want it. It's my responsibility and I plan to do my part in protecting Ferramoor. But he would rather you have it."

"You *want* to become king?" asked Fillian. "You *want* power? Do you not see father? Every day he grows weaker and weaker from his illness, and he demands more and more power. That's what got us into this bloody war in the first place; a war against our aunt, Eston! But now he realizes who he has become. We're on the brink of collapse. The reason he isn't giving you power is because *you are asking for it,* and he thinks that's dangerous."

Eston pointed to the city. "You and I aren't changing anything. We aren't making a difference in the world. People are dying to defend our lands and take back what's ours, and we just ate a feast. You don't realize what—"

"I hate it just as much as you do, Eston."

"Am I supposed to just sit idly by then?"

"Yes," was Fillian's simple answer.

Eston turned away and walked across the night courtyard through the downpour. Benja Tiggins ran up and met him in the middle of the courtyard.

"Good evening, Benja."

"Evening . . . Eston, you look upset." They crossed into the palace and walked through its halls.

"I will be taking another absence from the palace tonight, Benja." Eston wanted to go to the *Westflower Inn* to find Raelynn to help confirm if the visions he was having were real. "Can you see to it that I go unnoticed?"

"You said it was only that one time."

"I know I did . . ."

"Promise me you are thinking through your decisions, Eston."

". . . I promise."

"Okay . . . I'll give you *maybe* two hours, but that's all I can guarantee." They walked to the main entrance to the palace which was lined with hundred-foot marble columns. The prince put on a brown cloak and messed up his hair. Benja looked around to make sure nobody was watching. "Eston, I couldn't help but overhear you and your brother."

Eston stepped forward into the pouring rain. "I know . . . Fillian is just apathetic. He just doesn't understand what the real world is like."

"And you do?" Benja's pale face stared out into the dark city below. "I wouldn't be so quick to dismiss what he says. A great king is a great listener . . . Fillian is doing a great deal of listening. I would advise you to do the same . . ."

Eston looked back, his cloak now soaked. He descended the palace steps, through the giant gate and into Aunestauna, headed toward the *Westflower Inn*, hoping to find Raelynn.

People ran from building to building in the dark, trying to avoid the downpour; puddles of water reflected flickers from candles inside houses. Eston looked up into the sky; rain fell on his face and ran down his embroidered tunic. Faint voices slipped through the rain pelting on the wooden buildings. He trudged through the soaking city, down alleyways and through narrow streets headed toward the inn. Lightning flashed through the sky, illuminating the cobblestone streets. After asking for directions, he crossed a bridge over the Spring River and into another part of the city.

The rain continued to fall hard, and the gutters poured out into the streets. After a crash of thunder faded, he heard a group of men on a covered tavern porch up ahead laughing and singing a bawdy sea chantey. As he approached, one of them pointed at him. "Whatcha doin' in the storm?"

Another man slammed his wine down on the table. "By golly! It's a Crat! What's 'e doin' here?"

Eston's stomach lurched as he realized that under his coat, his expensive clothes showed, along with his golden watch - an extraordinarily expensive invention from the engineers of Elishka. *Oh no, please don't make a scene. I need to get out of here right now.* He tried to hide the watch, but the man spoke again to him directly. "*Mr. Rich Boy*, you looking for trouble?" He stood up and stepped into the street in front of him.

In less than a minute, a swarm of a dozen people gathered around him. A big loud "Hey you!" rang out from the crowd. A giant man stepped out from the crowd with a raging face, ready to attack. He jumped on Eston, grabbed him and shoved the crowd aside. The man pulled him aside into an alleyway. A smaller man tried to pull the attacker off Eston, but he knocked him out with a side hook.

He slammed the prince into a wall and grabbed his neck. Eston tried to tear the man's wrists off him. The frightening face looked straight in Eston's eyes. "You bastard palace Crats! My two sons died fighting in your army! You shut my business down and sent my wife to a whorehouse! You took everything!" Eston felt the veins bulging in his neck and his face turning blue. He could barely hear the screams from the crowd. "And I swear to the Great Mother I'll slit your high and mighty throat good an' proper, you son of a bitch!"

The man drew a knife and pulled his arm back, ready to strike. A blur of scarlet passed in front of Eston and the grasp around his neck released. His vision closed, and when blood returned to his head, he saw the attacker dead on the ground and four soldiers of The Scarlet Guard standing next to him;

adorned on their shoulders were scarlet capes and, on their heads, tall, feathered helmets. One of them grabbed Eston. "Your Majesty, are you alright?"

Eston nodded, seeing his attacker's corpse soaking in the rain.

The Scarlet Guard sheathed his sword. "We've been on your tail since you left the palace."

"On whose orders?" said Eston. He realized Benja had probably had the Scarlet Guard trailing him. He recognized the man in front of him as Liann Carebelle II, son of the Ferramish general with the same name.

"Lord Benja Tiggins'," said Liann. "He wanted to let you roam but needed to protect your safety. But it's clearly dangerous for you here, and we must escort you back to the Royal Palace. I'm sorry My Liege, but this is our duty. It's not safe. You almost got killed." Liann pushed Eston away from the crowd and wound through the streets until they climbed up the steps of the palace and stood at the front gate in the rainstorm. A messenger was sent to retrieve Tronum and Eradine.

Tronum stood straight in front of him. Silent. He was rarely silent. The king raised a slender, shaking hand, and slapped Eston hard across the face; it stung more in his heart than on his face.

Eston's mother thanked the Scarlet Guards, and the three walked back inside the palace. Eston's head hung low, and Tronum refused to say a word. As he passed a giant marble column, He looked back to see his brother watching him. Behind the next column stood Benja Tiggins who mouthed to Eston, *"I'm sorry."*

A PHANTOM
Chapter Nine

~Before Sunrise, September 3rd
Southeastern Endlebarr

Gallien stood before Tayben in the thick fog; a group of fourteen other cloaked Phantoms encircled them. Dark and hooded, the shadow figures blocked every avenue of escape. Gallien raised his hands toward Tayben. "There's no need to worry," he said, "I too was both afraid and curious when I began to see the shadows."

"What happened to you?" whispered Tayben.

"Like you," said Gallien, "I stepped out of my tent one night to go look for the shadows. But before I did, they found me, and I was seized and knocked out to avoid creating a ruckus in the camp. I awoke to a scenario just like this; where General Lekshane," Gallien motioned to a figure on his right, "informed me that I had been recruited as a Phantom."

"But I don't understand. Who are the Phantoms?" Tayben leaned forward, his eyes glazed in enchanted curiosity.

A forty-something man to Gallien's right, General Lekshane, stepped forward and pulled back his hood to reveal a face that drew Tayben's attention. His chin, which was covered in a short but thick reddish-brown beard, was slightly raised. "The Phantoms are Cerebria's most elite soldiers, for reasons you will soon find out. Our operation is under the direction of Xandria herself, and our existence remains a secret to the world . . . even to the army and its highest commanding officers. We recently lost two of our soldiers in battle. For purposes of maintaining a consistent structure of sixteen members, one slot has been filled by Mr. Aris here, and one will now be filled by you. As I understand you are friends with Mr. Aris, we wanted you to first speak with him to make the transition from soldier to superhuman seem more . . . natural."

Tayben looked around at the fifteen cloaked figures around him and still felt chilled inside. "Sir, I'm – why do you want me?"

The general smiled slightly. "That, you must discover for yourself, Mr. Shae."

Tayben looked back at Gallien. "Are you the shadow figure I've been seeing?"

"We all are, Tayben," said the general. "Our mission is to accomplish what no others can, to ensure the safety of Cerebria and our families. You want to do what you can to protect Woodshore, do you not?"

Tayben stumbled. "Of course I do . . . but what is it you want me to do?"

General Lekshane spoke. "You will see soon enough. And Tayben . . . this may be difficult at first to hear, but all Phantoms have been reported as dead by the army . . . that will now include you."

"I'm sorry?"

"Your parents will receive a letter soon, stating that you have lost your life. We don't leave you much choice, I know. But if you truly want what's best for this country and for your family, you will become a Phantom soldier. Look around at your new brothers; we have all paid this price."

Tayben sat in silence. *This can't be real.* "Surely you're joking . . . my parents have to know I'm alive."

The group did not respond, giving him a clear answer. He wasn't *going* to have a choice in this matter.

General Lekshane extended his hand. "Walk with us. We haven't much time. I'll hand you off to your company leader, Thephern Luck."

A cloaked figure stepped forward from behind Tayben. Two long, slightly curved swords hung from his belt beneath his cloak. He was taller than the general, and his thick hair was wavy on top of his head. "Greetings soldier," he welcomed. "Thephern Luck. I can answer your questions as we walk."

The fifteen Phantoms began walking behind General Lekshane. They moved like ghosts, eerily seeming to glide over the vegetation. The black parade of silent soldiers followed the general up a half-fallen tree trunk like the one Tayben had used to enter the canopy. Vines, mushrooms, and moss covered the trunk, which was wider than several door frames, rising so high that the forest floor was no longer visible through the fog. "Sir . . . Thephern, was it?"

"Yes, Thephern Luck of Shadowfork."

"General Lekshane said that you were my company leader."

Thephern stepped over a gigantic knot in the tree. "There are sixteen Phantom soldiers – General Lekshane and three companies or platoons of five. I am one of the three company leaders. Alongside you in our company is Gallien Aris of Gienn, whom you already know, Chent Vantte of Tangle Took, and Ferron Grenzo of Vashner."

Tayben raised a hand to greet the soldier named Chent, who carried a bow. His face was flatter than most and his eyes were narrow. *He must be descended from the Guavaanese people of the south,* thought Tayben. Chent gave a slight nod and nothing more.

"Yeah," said Thephern. "Chent doesn't talk very often."

Tayben turned around and met the eyes of a very dark-skinned, toned man around twenty-three. He introduced himself as Ferron Grenzo and patted Tayben on the back, much friendlier than the others in the company. The people of his dark complexion, Tayben noted, did not seem to have one nation of origin such as the olive-skinned Gypsies of the Southlands – rather, they seemed to be mixed among all the Endellian nations, immigrating there from islands in the Shallow Green Sea. Ferron smiled with wide eyes. "You're in for a journey my friend. I saw you dodge that spear the other day, sorry for spying. I can't imagine how good you'll be once we get you to the Nymphs."

"The what?"

"Oh, you'll see," Ferron said.

"So am I not returning to my battalion?"

"We told you, Tayben. In a day or two they will file you as dead. You *are* dead to the rest of the world. You are a ghost . . . a phantom . . . well not yet."

"Why are we traveling up into the canopy?" Tayben's foot slipped on a wet patch of moss, but he caught himself.

Thephern glanced up at the leaves above the Phantoms. "The canopy's the fastest way to travel when you're like us."

"Like you?"

Thephern stopped and chuckled. He looked out into the fog and jumped off of the tree into the air, plunging into the mist below.

"Thephern!" Tayben yelled as Thephern's body fell and disappeared. He heard laughter behind him and saw Ferron shaking his head and smiling.

"He's just showing off," said Ferron, "don't worry."

"What do you mean, don't worry?" said Tayben.

"Tayben, remember when you tried chasing us through this forest? We probably seemed to disappear and shoot around from tree to tree. You weren't hallucinating." Ferron laughed and then sighed. "You have no idea what's possible . . . but soon you'll know."

"What do you mean?"

"It's hard to explain," said Thephern.

Tayben flinched when he realized Thephern Luck was standing right where he had jumped off.

Thephern answered Tayben's unspoken question of – *How?* "I spotted a vine, jumped, swung around the tree on it, jumped onto a branch, and climbed back up."

He thought Thephern was joking at first, but soon realized he wasn't.

"We are Phantoms because, well . . . we can control what you would call 'magic' inside of our bodies – an enhancement of normal capabilities." His voice was warm but sounded dangerous. "Our eyes penetrate both fog and the night. Our legs allow us to jump twenty feet in the air and run twice as fast as a horse. Our arms can outmaneuver any swordfighter we come across."

"You are telling me you're superhuman?" Tayben raised an eyebrow.

"I'm telling you we are Xandria's best soldiers, exceeding the natural physical capabilities of any other. We are, in a sense, superhuman," said Thephern. They stepped from one giant tree branch to another, hundreds of feet above the forest floor. "General Lekshane takes his orders from her. She formed us to help set things straight, defend the forest, and fight to create her Empire. The only original Phantom here is Lekshane, the rest have been killed off in battle or fallen out of favor with the Queen's vision."

"Where are we going?"

Thephern sighed. "Who do you think rules this forest?"

". . . Mankind?"

Thephern laughed in response at the apparently preposterous idea.

"No one then?"

Thephern followed the Phantoms in front of him and stepped over a branch, followed by Tayben and Ferron. Ferron chuckled. "I take it you don't believe in fairytales."

Tayben shook his head.

"Do you believe in Nymphs?"

"Don't tell me that you get your 'magic' from fairies."

Thephern spun around and slapped him across the face, causing Tayben to stumble back in shock. "Mr. Shae . . . I think you forget that I am your company leader. You will not be so arrogant in a few hours. The Nymphs you hear in stories are nothing like these."

"You're telling me they're real? You've seen a Nymph?"

"Yes. But these . . . these are beings of perfection. They rule over this forest, but you do not see them. The Nymphs of Endlebarr are the most powerful beings in the world, Mr. Shae, and they could kill all sixteen of us in a blink; we could do nothing to stop them. However, their being and their energy is pure, and under no circumstances will they inflict harm upon any living thing. But King Tronum's tyranny threatens the safety of Endlebarr; the Nymphs needed something or someone to protect the forest – their home, their sanctuary. In exchange for the protection we can provide them and their forest, the Nymphs gave each of us just a fragment of their power, which allows us to control what we see as magic, inside of our bodies. The Phantoms are the protectors of peace."

"Why did that arrangement take place?" asked Tayben. "How did they agree to it?"

Thephern looked around almost as if he wasn't supposed to say anything. "It's something I don't think anyone but Lekshane knows. Xandria has some history with them; she's been in this forest before, and the Nymphs came to her . . . It's a story long forgotten."

Tayben decided it was best to drop the conversation, especially if even Thephern didn't know the answer. He continued to walk alongside them under the dark cover of the endless forest.

The Phantoms stopped after a couple hours of winding through the night canopy. "Here we are," said General Lekshane. Tayben looked around at the forest, which looked exactly like the forest had for the past several hours. Maybe the trees had gotten wider, and the fog may have thickened; but the consuming dark of the forest still lingered. The general walked over to Tayben on the giant branch. "This is where you become one of us. I assume Thephern explained it to you. The Nymphs will come. Do not speak to them, for they cannot speak. Do not run away from them. Simply relax your mind."

"But sir—"

"No time," said General Lekshane. "The Nymphs will transfer a piece of their power into your body. Do not panic once this happens; it may take you a while to adjust."

"I'm sorry, I just don't understand—"

"These creatures are infinitely more powerful than you. Respect them. We will leave you here for the time being. Don't move until the Nymphs arrive. You could say that this is your initiation; you are now under Thephern's command who, in turn, is under mine." The bearded general then stepped around Tayben, followed by every other Phantom. Gallien patted Tayben's shoulder as he passed. The black-cloaked soldiers descended two hundred feet down and disappeared into the fog below, while Tayben stood silently on a mossy branch. His body warmed to normal temperature as the Phantoms left. His stomach grumbled, and he could not figure out what time it was. *I left the battalion in mid afternoon, I probably wandered in the forest for six or seven hours. Then I tried to kill a deer and fell asleep . . . though I feel like I'm forgetting something.*

A light appeared far away – a dim, white light in the foggy forest. To his right, another light appeared; to his left, another. The glowing lights slowly moved toward him. He obeyed his orders not to move or speak. As the lights approached, Tayben discerned figures in the fog – not separate from the lights; the lights made the figures, and the figures made the light. Slowly, the three Nymphs became more defined, with an energy that flowed over their bodies in an ever-changing manner. The Nymphs walked on branches that converged where Tayben stood, but their feet never touched the ground and seemed to walk on an invisible barrier. He looked down and saw dozens of lights approaching from in the fog. When the lights were close enough, he could see the glowing Nymphs walking on air, like they were climbing an invisible staircase.

The forest was silent . . . completely and utterly still, save for Tayben's rising and falling chest. Lights began to descend from above him – more Nymphs emerging from the leaves above him. They filled the forest like stars, and the reflection from Tayben's eyes glistened in the otherwise darkened canopy.

As the brightness in the mist increased, Tayben began to hear an enchanting shimmering sound, like thousands of tiny wind chimes. The sound filled the roots of the trees and its branches and seeped into Tayben's body. A feeling overwhelmed all of his senses. It was sweet, like the pastries in the old bakery just two doors down from his father's blacksmith shop. It was vibrant, like the colors of a Woodshore sunset. It was immense, like the roots of the massive tree he stood in. It was powerful, like the fire in which he used to thrust metal ready to be hammered and shaped into a sword. It caused him to turn and look into the eyes of the Nymph standing before him; deep, endless eyes in which his mind lost its way and found it again a thousand times over. The shimmering sounded like millions of stars pulsing in and out of existence all around him. They radiated pure ribbons of light that circled around Tayben. His heart began to pound. In his mind, the forest was singing, and it sang to his heart louder than the roar of a thundercrack.

Dozens of Nymphs now circled him, some standing on air just an inch above the branches, and some hovering in the mist beyond the tree. Around the Nymphs fluttered glowing butterflies. Tayben fell to his knees before the strange creatures. The Nymph reached out a hand and slowly placed it under Tayben's chin. When it made contact with his flesh, he took a sharp breath in, but then immediately relaxed. The hand felt warm against him; an energy flowed through it. The song winding silently through the forest told him to rise; he did so, standing before the Nymph, which was only slightly taller than he. The forest around him was filled with a light that moved around him in streams like waterfalls without gravity. He looked once more into the Nymph's eyes – bottomless, shimmering pools of power and purity. Lost in awe, his mind went blank, and the song took control of his body. The Nymph turned Tayben's head toward the empty fog and let its hand fall to its side. The song swirled inside Tayben's brain and urged him to step forward, off the tree branch. He closed his eyes and stepped into the air.

His foot felt like it touched on a soft, mossy hillside. He took another step, and another, his feet climbing up through the air, as if on an invisible staircase. He opened his eyes and saw mist below his feet, and nothing else. His body slowly turned on its back, suspended hundreds of feet above the forest floor by millions of beads of light coming from the bodies of the Nymphs, who gathered in a sphere around him. A wind rustled around his body and cloak. Droplets of light swirled around his head before entering his chest. An energy began to grow inside of him. All he could hear was the shimmering, all he could see was light, and all he could feel was an unfathomable energy blossoming throughout his being. He could see himself in his entirety — his arrogance, his love, his hatred. The song and light and energy flowed through his body like a flood. Tears began streaming out of Tayben's glistening eyes; they dripped down his face and fell into nothingness. The beads of light formed a shell around his figure and drew closer and closer to his body until he could no longer see his own nose, only light. He could feel a new power in his bones, his ears, his legs, his arms, his eyes, his mind. He sobbed with an overwhelming joy as the cocoon of light around his body exploded and sprinkled the canopy with a galaxy of shimmering specks. His floating body descended back down to the tree branch.

As he lay still on the branch, staring straight up at the leaves above him, the Nymphs still circled him and cast a blinding light throughout the forest. A Nymph bent over Tayben's body and laid its lips of light on his forehead. The song flowed from Tayben, back into the Nymph. And just as they came, the figures of light walked out into the air and vanished.

Tayben's body lay there on the mossy branch in the darkness, tears still streaming down his face. After several minutes, he stood up and noticed a newfound strength in his muscles. He felt as if he could lift a house, and sprint faster than a hawk flies; he no longer hungered and no longer sought rest. He gazed out into the fog . . . which wasn't there. . . no, it was still there; Tayben's eyes just penetrated the dense mist like it was a clear, sunny day. The sky far above him spread a deep golden light over the world. He peered into the forest and located a leaf one hundred yards away, on which he could count the individual droplets of dew. He listened. He listened closely. What used to be a silent forest now rang like trumpets in his ears — the scratching of animals hundreds of feet below, the drip of water off of ferns, the faint chirps of birds a mile away in the dark forest.

He heard a voice behind him. "Are you feeling alright, Tayben?" said Gallien.

Tayben turned back at Gallien's grinning face. He didn't know what to say, but he found himself standing up and embracing Gallien, smiling, laughing, and crying all at the same time. "Did this happen to you?"

Gallien laughed with him and pulled back, looking at Tayben with teary eyes. "Yes." He nodded with a smile. "Yes, it did."

Tayben examined his hands and arms as Thephern Luck approached them on the branch. "I feel limitless."

"You should," said Thephern.

"What do you mean?"

"Your powers help you only to the extent that the Nymphs want. If you stop believing in your cause, their magic in you will fade."

"How do you know?"

"I've seen it happen," said Thephern. He put a hand on Tayben's shoulder. "Go on . . . see what you can do."

Tayben looked at his body. Eyeing a branch to his left, Tayben carefully pushed off with his legs, but the amount of power in them sent him flying ten feet beyond it. As just a blur of black in the air, he quickly grabbed onto a branch above him and swung up. Tayben sprinted on the branch and rocketed off, catching a vine. He climbed it as fast as he could normally run. He felt alive.

Behind him, he could hear Gallien following him, laughing and cheering. Tayben raced up to the top of the tree, darting up between branches effortlessly. He broke through the canopy like surfacing above water and gazed out into the orange sunrise sky, where the wind blew through his hair and over his smiling face. Closing his eyes, he took a deep breath in, allowing the cool open air to fill his lungs. The world was turning into day and the forest bustled with sound and movement. He could almost feel the plants growing around him, stretching into the fresh air and the light.

Gallien emerged from the tree and pulled himself up onto a branch next to Tayben. He watched as Tayben's smile slowly faded. "Tayben?"

Tayben turned toward Gallien, sensing that he knew what he was thinking about.

"Tayben, I—" Gallien tried to smile. "I know how hard it's going to be. Letting go of family and . . . everything. Hell, the only family I had left was you. So I'm glad you're back."

Tayben nodded. "I should have known you wouldn't abandon me after a year of fighting together . . . Everything is going to change."

Gallien smiled and looked out into the eastern sky. "It already has."

After a minute or two, the golden sun peeked over the horizon, and Tayben's mind was transported in a flash of light.

OLINDEUX
Chapter Ten

~Morning, September 6th
Aunestauna, Ferramoor

A mound of coins sat on the shelf next to Kyan's pile of blankets that made up his bed. Beams of light shone through holes in his attic, reflecting off stolen jewelry and argentums. He had woken up, but stayed beneath the thin layer of cloth, lost in thought. It finally began making sense to him after days of piecing together memories. Although he tried to find every other possible explanation, only one remained, one that made him think he was going insane – that his mind inhabited four bodies. Each day at sunrise, his consciousness traveled into another body. At the next sunrise, he would travel back in time to the day before to live as another one of these four persons.

Today was the 6th of September, and he had already lived it once as Calleneck. The sun had risen today – the morning of the 6th, and he awoke staring at the ceiling of the shack. Once the sun rose on the 7th, he would essentially jump back to the sunrise of the 6th and live the day again as either Tayben or Eston; but there was no way to know which. *But that means that right now, I know what will happen later tonight to my body as Calleneck – I'll eat baked bread and potato stew for dinner with the family; and right now, as I lie here, I'm doing things as Eston and Tayben, I just don't know what I'm doing . . . what would happen if I saw myself? I could either see my past or my future, depending on if I have already lived the day.*

As Eston and Calleneck and Tayben, he would despise his thief life. In his other bodies, he knew stealing was immoral; but as soon as he awoke in the body of Kyan, his mind changed. *I have a right to do this. I take from the world what it has taken from me.* The coins on the shelf had mostly remained untouched for months, for Kyan had no need to spend them when he could steal his meals and clothes. But yesterday, without thinking about what he was doing, he had bought a loaf of bread.

Kyan's eyes were closed, and his hair was ruffled more than usual. Although he learned to sleep through the racket of the night by tuning out the world and listening to his breath, he had gotten little sleep the past two weeks. Just as the

Phantoms spied on Tayben before recruiting him, Kyan felt as if Riccolo and his Nightsnakes were right outside his makeshift door. He felt the need to watch the blanket doorway as it swept aside in the wind to see if someone was stalking behind it.

Understandably, no one had ever seen his shack before – roof running was quite an uncommon practice among the citizens of Aunestauna. Only twice before had Kyan seen thieves running atop the city, and that was at night. Sheets of metal ran over the largest holes to protect his shelter from common summer rains; but now, the first cool breezes of autumn had begun to sweep through the valley. On the clearest of days, Kyan would wake to a salty waft of air coming from the large inlet of the Auness Sea, which connected the capital to the rest of the world by sea trade.

A leaf on an oak tree under the clocktower yellowed, and most children would now start schooling again. All children in the First and Second District attended a primary school from the ages of seven to fourteen. Most children had some sort of schooling in the Third District, but many of them were orphans, and even more were homeless in the Fourth District, where few parents elected to keep their kids past the age of ten. Whenever the winter months rolled over, he liked to watch the school children who threw snowballs at one another in the square below his ramshackle home. There would be familiar faces from time to time, and Kyan sometimes felt as if he knew them and their personalities, even if they had no idea he was there.

A month prior, Kyan could not read or write better than he could as an eight-year-old at *Pebbleburn Orphanage*, but memories and knowledge from his other lives kept flooding into his mind every day. In a matter of two weeks, he absorbed over a decade's worth of knowledge. He knew the intricacies of the Ferramish government and what it felt like to be prince; he knew what it felt like now, to be a Phantom soldier and jump twenty feet in the air and sprint through the forest fast enough to dry sweaty hair; and although, as Kyan, he could not visibly control his Taurimous, he knew what it was like to be a sorcerer. Even though he thought of many explanations, he decided the only one that made sense was that somehow, the reason he lived four lives was because he shared the same Taurimous between his selves – one mind in four bodies, or four people with shared memories.

As Kyan, he hated living parallel lives; as Tayben, he hated Calleneck; as Calleneck, he hated Tayben; as Eston, he tried to make sense of it all. It felt as if several doors had been opened in his mind, revealing a whole new world of information . . . new rooms in an endless castle. Kyan felt as if he had found a way to unlock his mind and access what was truly there – three other lives, with things and places and relationships as real as any that he had now. But trying to wrap his head around it only brought up more questions. He let himself drift back to sleep, dreaming about falling through the misty forest, feeling droplets of water on his skin before snatching a vine and swinging from it.

The air was slowly warming after the cool night, and Kyan slept shirtless on a pile of blankets. The silver Olinduex rose and fell on his bare chest, strapped around his neck by a thin chain. He never took off the small metallic token, even to sleep. The clocktower across the adjacent square struck eight in the morning and a rat scurried away from the blanket-covered doorway which blew open. A set of footsteps clicked on the wood outside the attic and an eye peered through a hole in the beams. A delicate hand drew open the makeshift door and a girl silently stepped inside the cramped rooftop shack; Kyan remained asleep.

Her skin glowed dark olive, and her soft, almond-shaped eyes bore resemblance to the people of the Southlands, the people of the desert. Long, thick hair hung over her slender shoulders. She wore a Gypsy-like headscarf, which she slipped off to reveal a large, red snakebite on her neck.

The girl, trying not to startle him, whispered, "Kyan . . . Kyan, wake up."

Kyan's eyes shot open as he jolted back, instinctively grabbing his knife. "What the hell are you doing? Who are you?!" The girl held her hands up as Kyan stood and pointed his knife, his head nearly touching the ceiling. "I said who are—" Before he could finish his words, the light bounced off a bite mark on her neck. Kyan whispered, "Nightsnake . . ."

The girl looked at Kyan's knife. "Please, lower your knife. I'm here alone and I am not trying to hurt you. If I was, I wouldn't have awakened you . . . Please."

Kyan hesitated, then slowly lowered his knife, and blood returned to his knuckles. Her skin color and accent hinted to Kyan that she was from the Southlands – like the Gypsy and Zjaari immigrants that lived in Aunestauna. Her words were hot like the burning sands, ebbing and flowing like the dunes. Kyan surmised that this was her second language. Kyan's mind rattled back to the snakebite on her neck. "I told your gang that I work alone. Riccolo won't—"

"I know," the girl said, "I know. If any other Nightsnake sees you or talks to you, you must swear not to mention that I was here, or that I talked to you." Her expression was serious, but sincere.

"Why should I?" he asked.

She ignored him and glanced at the pile of coins behind him. "My name is Vree Shaarine. I work for Riccolo; and when I signed up, I had no idea what I was getting myself into. Once you get bitten, you stay stuck in Riccolo's grasp for life. If you join, you live in your own hell. Riccolo uses me as . . ." she paused. "I've killed too many people for him."

"So why did you join?"

"I needed good work," said Vree.

"I wouldn't call thieving for someone else good work."

"I didn't know I would be stealing . . . And now I have no choice. I fought back once and almost escaped from him. He no longer trusts me much; but he trusts me enough to think that I'm scouting out places to hit. I know you won't give in to Riccolo, but he's dangerously persistent, and he will kill to get what he wants." Vree paused and felt her long black hair with two fingers.

Kyan chuckled and shook his head. "Then what the hell are you suggesting I do?"

"Leave the city," Vree said quickly. "That's your option. Leave the city within the week. Otherwise, I'm afraid that he will come after you."

Kyan put a jacket over his bare chest. "Why are you telling me this?"

Vree folded her arms and looked sideways. "Because I know what it's like to have to serve him, to be unable to escape. I want to help you before it's too late."

"Why me?"

"Why not?" Her eyes darted sideways at the door when she thought she heard something. "I want to save someone from my same fate, no matter who."

"Why don't you leave if you hate him so much?" asked Kyan.

She gave him a sour stare. "I can't . . . it's complicated."

"Oh, I see," mocked Kyan. "Maybe you're scared of him, but I'm not."

"And you're a fool because of it," snapped Vree. "You would not sleep easily if you knew what he does to people who cross him . . . You don't know him."

"I'm not leaving Aunestauna," said Kyan. "I can deal with Riccolo."

"No you can't," she said in her exotic accent. "I know how good you are and that's exactly why he wants you. You've memorized half of the city – the streets, the turns, the roofs, the alleys. You're smart, but you should have the humility to accept that against Riccolo, you don't stand a chance. Not only is he the best thief in the world, but he has almost forty others just like him. You won't see him coming. The only reason he didn't kill you when you turned down his offer is because he knows that you won't tell anyone. The only people you've talked to in the past month are me, Riccolo, and your dealer. He still thinks he can win you over. He also tells me that somehow, he's erasing all the records the palace and the Scarlet Guard have of our existence. He's not worried about exposure."

"If he doesn't see me as a threat, why should I worry that he's gonna kill me?"

Vree's face went cold, and she stared right into Kyan's eyes. "Because death is too quick a punishment to him. He makes a game out of torture; it amuses him. No matter how you try to outsmart him, he'll always be two steps ahead of you. If he sees you, he'll act charming and friendly and say he means you no harm, but he will always have a nasty plan in store for any disobedience . . . Please, just leave. What would you really be leaving behind?" Vree followed

Kyan's eyes, which glazed toward his small, diamond-shaped ornament with three curved grooves running through it, connecting at the tip. "Kyan?"

He looked back up at her. "I wouldn't be leaving anything . . . Just get out, okay?"

Vree spun around and swept aside the entryway. Once outside, she turned back and pulled out a necklace from beneath her tunic, "You know, you think that no one understands you," she held up a small silver Olindeux that caught the sunlight, "but I do." The entrance shut, and her leather boots tapped across the theater roof and out of earshot.

Kyan thought for a moment about Vree's Olindeux, but moved on from the image. *If I save up enough money, I could leave Aunestauna and move away . . . I could go far away, maybe to the Crandles or even Guavaan. Maybe I could leave . . .* But he knew deep inside that this dream of his was unachievable. How could he ever bring himself to leave? What in this whole world could compel him to abandon his only chance of ever finding them? He knew he would stay in Aunestauna until he had some answer to why he was left so alone.

Kyan traced his fingers along the silver ornament strung around his neck. About the length of his thumb, it felt cool and metallic in his hand. The three curved grooves beginning at the top point and swinging down let a crack of light through the back if angled correctly. He grabbed a shirt and tied it up over the necklace, hiding it from himself.

A shoulder jostled him aside in the crowd of street goers. Kyan weaved his way through the Third District in hopes of finding dinner. A merchant in a shop called to him; a priest walked by chanting; and Gypsies danced in a kaleidoscope of swirling fabric. He approached the four dancing women with their pierced stomachs and olive-honey skin. Little ruby and emerald gems dotted their skin in a line from the tip of their nose to their hairline. They twirled and swirled and hypnotized people watching. A woman put an argentum in a pan full of coins; another man put two argentums. One passerby after another, the pan filled with money, and his eye fell upon it.

Shimmering gold and silver coins. Not when everyone is watching. *No, I can't do it . . . Yes, I can. I'm good enough for the Nightsnakes to want me.* Like a machine, he took a step forward. Another. Another. He smiled at the Gypsies like a possessed man. He took a silver argentum out of his pocket, knelt down, and set it in the pile so the Gypsies could see; and with a quick movement of his hand, as he stood up, he drew a handful of argentums out of the pile. He smiled at them and turned around, putting his money-filled hand in his coat pocket. He was in a dreamlike state, his mind not controlling the movements of his body.

As Kyan walked away, a little boy holding his mother's extended hand above him stared at his pocket and then at his face. Kyan stopped in his tracks; the boy said nothing, but slowly stepped behind his mother's legs. A jewel-covered hand grabbed his shoulder and spun him around.

A furious Gypsy's face stared at him. "You thief!" she shouted. "You street rat!" She clawed his face with razor-sharp fingernails and rings. He immediately felt his skin tear and blood rush down his cheek, forcing his mind back to reality. "You filthy scum!" she screamed. Panic flushed throughout his body; he threw the coins out of his pocket and bolted away from her and into the crowd, where he ducked and dodged to get away. The Gypsies screamed and told people to catch him, but he slipped through the hundreds of people like a fish through a stream. He removed his jacket and ruffled his hair as he ran, so he could look slightly different than before. Catching a glimpse of an alley, he ducked into it.

From within the shaded back street, Kyan stared out into the lit avenue where big crowds moved back and forth; he lost the Gypsies, and he could no longer hear their shouts. But he also lost his coins. His right cheek streamed with scarlet blood. Wanting to keep a look out from the protection of the alley, he leaned against the brick wall, scanning the crowd.

"Hello . . ."

Kyan shot around when he heard someone speak out. A tall figure stepped forward. He wore a long, black cloak with a scarf to conceal his neck. "Remember me?" said Riccolo.

Kyan stood still as Vree's words echoed in his head. *He's mad; and he's intelligent. That makes him dangerous.*

The Lord of Thieves stepped forward and pulled out a cloth, wrapped around a knife. "Oh Kyan," he clicked his tongue, "you disappoint me . . ." He raised the knife and cloth level with Kyan's neck, causing him to step back.

His heart was beating faster and faster.

"If only you had listened to me . . ." Riccolo inched forward and drew the cloth off his knife with gloved hands.

Kyan took a sharp breath in as the hand thrust forward holding the cloth. Riccolo gently touched it to his bloody face to soak up the blood as he put his knife back in his coat pocket. ". . . I told you that you were the best of the best. You almost had the Gypsies' money." The Lord of Thieves' blue eyes stared down on his cut face. "Why did you stop when that little boy looked at you? You could've easily done it. What a shame . . ."

"Get off of me." Kyan grabbed Riccolo's arm and shoved it away.

The cloth in Riccolo's hand now had splotches of the scarlet Ferramoor red similar to banners that hung in the streets. "Now, now . . . I don't want violence to befall us. I want to help you." Riccolo dropped the cloth on the ground and the horrible scar on his face spread with his psychotic smile.

"Like hell you want to help me." Kyan put his hand in his pocket and touched his knife with a finger.

"Oh, I really do. I see your ramshackle attic and I want to provide a home for you. You see, in the Fourth District – well of course you've been to it – my Nightsnakes have a nice place. It even has a courtyard. There, everyone always has food to eat. I'm really very proud. And I would like you to reconsider joining our team."

Kyan stepped back to the brick wall. "I work alone."

Riccolo inched forward. "I think we got off on the wrong note. I was aggressive back at my manor and I apologize." He raised his palms. "No weapons, no need for violence. Just a friend to a friend."

Kyan clenched his fist.

"Fine; a thief to a thief."

"You expect me to believe you?" Kyan put another finger on his knife.

"I want to help you. I understand you. I was just like you. Trust me." Riccolo removed a black glove from his deformed, four-fingered hand, which he stuck out and ran through Kyan's long, black hair. "Did I ever tell you that you have pretty hair?"

Now, he thought, pulling his knife from his pocket and thrust it forward. Riccolo grasped his arm right before the knife reached him. He punched forward with his other arm and hit Riccolo square in the nose; but, while it bled, he did not move an inch.

As Kyan punched Riccolo again, Riccolo's grasp on his other arm tightened like a clamp, turning his hand purple. The pressure was so great that Kyan yelled and dropped his knife on the stone alley floor.

The Lord of Thieves smiled and slammed Kyan's head into the brick wall, causing him to fall limp. "Now, there, I think you are missing a great business opportunity. We'd work well together." He drew his knife from his coat.

Kyan tried to lift himself up but failed.

"You are a fantastic thief, and I would hate to see your life go to waste . . . What do you say?"

Kyan struggled repeatedly to stand up, falling several times onto the wet cobblestone.

The Lord of Thieves stood in his black cloak like a hungry bat. "What do you say?"

Kyan grabbed the frame to a doorway next to him and pulled himself up. "Go to hell." He kicked his knife up at Riccolo, who dodged the flying blade.

A crash rang out from the avenue next to them and people in the crowd screamed. A window shattered and a group of Southern Gypsies sprinted away from the glass, followed by Guards' whistles that cut through the evening air. A stampede of people ran into the alley to escape the commotion, knocking Kyan and Riccolo against opposite walls. More and more people ran through the alley as more Guards came to tame the Gypsy fight on the street. Through the flash of passing faces, he saw Riccolo on the opposite side of the alley, staring at him with a glare of pure hatred. Kyan glanced to his side as the stampede rolled through; when he looked back, the scarred, menacing face of Riccolo was gone.

The sun cast its orange light over Aunestauna as it set over the sea. Kyan sat in the wooden pews of a grand cathedral in the Second District, close to the rich palace neighborhoods. Needing a quiet place to think, he journeyed there after being attacked by Riccolo. The arches of the nave stretched hundreds of feet above him, decorated with paintings and stonework. Because the cathedral was closed off until the last week of each month, he sat in the pews alone. A bird high up in the cathedral fluttered its wings as Kyan's sniffle echoed through the nave. An enormous stained-glass window depicting the Great Mother sat behind the pulpit of the cathedral, through which orange beams of sunset light streamed, illuminating the entire hall. A reflection hovered on the vaulted ceiling, cast by a small silver token in Kyan's hands.

He traced the diamond shaped metal piece with his fingers and ran them down it's grooves. A tear fell on the ornament, which he wiped off. He closed his eyes, and his mind went swirling back in his memories—

"He's a strange little boy; doesn't talk to anyone," said the orphanage matron, who stood in a doorway talking to a bald man. She went on. "I know, I know, he's in a tough spot and all. I never even met the mother who left him here. At least some of the children here remember their parents, but he was here when he was a baby. I've never heard the boy speak. We know he's not mute, he talks to himself sometimes. Guess he's traumatized by something he doesn't realize is traumatizing him. Kyan? . . . Kyan, will you speak to us? Please talk to us. We can't help you if you don't talk to us."

Kyan remained silent and the man put his beige flat cap on. "I'm sorry, ma'am, but he's a lost cause. Not even the loneliest orphans isolate themselves to this extent. He's really never said a word to you?"

She shook her head. "Not one."

"Ma'am, if he hasn't spoken in the seven or eight years he's been here, I just can't take him. If he hasn't run away from this place yet, he will soon. I'm surprised he's held on for this long here . . . It's all the same. Have a good day ma'am . . . You too, little man."

Another tear dripped down from Kyan's eye onto his hand. He looked up at the hundred-foot stained-glass window and the beautiful depiction of the Great Mother in a long white dress. Her calm eyes projected gentleness and power across the pews and across the city. Kyan looked up through watery, reflective eyes. *Great Mother,* he thought, *given the circumstances I doubt you're really there . . . or listening to me for that matter. Why would you do this to me? Why did you have to rob me of a happy life? You don't care . . . Is it funny to see all this happen? Wasn't it just hilarious when I could see my rib cage in the winter? What about when that drunk—*

Kyan shook his head. "I'm talking to a damn window."

A door creaked open in the back of the nave. Kyan knew he wasn't supposed to be in the cathedral and slid underneath a pew. A single pair of steps echoed toward him until he could see a pair of leather boots. He heard a girl's voice laugh. "I'm not the priest . . . you don't have to hide."

Kyan slowly slid back out from under the pew. His eyes widened when he saw the smiling face of Raelynn Nebelle.

"What?" she asked, noticing his expression.

"Oh, nothing . . . What are you doing here?"

She sat down in a pew. "Probably the same as you, looking for answers. What's your name?"

He swallowed and replied. "Kyan. Yours?"

"My name is Endra. It's nice to meet you, Kyan." Her fake Ferramish accent was better than the last time he saw her . . . except, he had never seen her before – at least not in this body, but as Calleneck and Eston. He noticed again that she had tried to stain her shimmering blonde-white hair with dirt and mud to go unnoticed, but the discoloring had not lasted long. She smiled. "So you also snuck under the 'no entry' sign?"

Kyan let out a quick chuckle. ". . . I tend to do things like that."

"Well, that makes you more adventurous, doesn't it?" Raelynn signaled for him to sit down next to her.

"Why are you here?" he asked. The orange glow of the sunset filtered through the dust in the air and landed on Raelynn's pensive face.

"Well, personally, I'm not religious. But I think this is a nice place to think. Let's just say I've come a long way to answer some questions of mine."

Kyan saw this as an opportunity to find out more about why she was not in Seirnkov with the Evertauri, seeing as she didn't know he was both Eston and Calleneck. He was still shocked by the fact that out of the whole city, he had randomly come across her twice. "And what is it you want to find answers to?"

She stared up at the vaulted ceiling. "I live with my father and my brother," she looked up at the stained-glass Great Mother, welcoming her into her arms, "but when I was very young, my mother vanished, and I was hoping to find clues here as to why."

Kyan's heart sank; both because that was the same reason he was there, and because she still did not know that her brother was dead. President Nebelle did say that his wife had gone missing back after the fall of the Empire. "And have you gotten any clues?"

She squinted her eyes. "A few, but it's all blurred and difficult to connect. Why are you here?"

"I just like the quiet." Kyan looked over at her.

"What's that in your hand?"

Kyan looked down and realized he was still holding the small silver medallion, its weight and shape etched perfectly into his mind like the carvings on its surface. He paused for a moment, feeling the delicate token's edges.

"May I see it?" she asked with an innocent curiosity.

He handed it over to her and she traced the three curved grooves with her fingers as Kyan did. Kyan swallowed, trying not to appear conspicuous, or infinitely worse – look sentimental. "It's an Olindeux."

"I'm sorry?" she said.

"An Olindeux . . . It's sort of like a family crest, but it's a symbol of love . . . Some Gypsy parents give them to their kids . . . they're all unique. People say they have the power to bring you back to family . . . But it's silly, I–"

"No, it's beautiful . . ." There was a sadness in her voice, and the more she spoke, the more her fake Ferramish accent faded into her true tone. "Your mother and father must love you."

"I don't think so." The smile disappeared from his face.

"And why is that?" Raelynn turned toward him, a stranger.

"Because I've never seen them . . . I ran away from the orphanage when I was eight. I've lived in the city all my life."

"You've stayed in Aunestauna waiting for them, haven't you? Don't you think the reason you were given up could be that they died?"

Kyan sat silently.

Raelynn seemed to be thinking about something quite over Kyan's head. "I think . . ." She paused, gathering her thoughts more. "I think if people don't feel love, they start to prioritize the wrong things . . . mainly power, I think. It can be political power or physical riches or just the pleasure of oppression or hurting other people." She looked at her lap. "I don't know if any of that makes sense."

Kyan felt a deep sadness, or maybe even guilt. "I think so . . ." He didn't want to admit it, but something told him inside that he was someone like that. His only companion was the loot he had gathered over the years. And for what purpose? Because he had no other choice? Or was it anger, revenge? He chose to stop thinking about it.

Raelynn placed the Olindeux back in his hand and closed it. "Kyan, was it? Well, I hope you find what you are looking for. You know, sometimes it's the loneliest people who can offer the most love . . . I should be going soon." Her fake Ferramish accent returned. "I need to go check the mailtower. I haven't gotten anything while I've been here, but it's worth a try. I'll be leaving Aunestauna soon anyway . . . I hope we meet again someday." She stood up and walked down the aisle, her footsteps echoing off the cathedral walls like the ticking of a clock.

MORDVITCH
Chapter Eleven

~Afternoon, September 16th
Seirnkov, Cerebria

As usual, the sky above Seirnkov was cloudy and dull. Four Evertauri disguised in civilian clothing stood at a guarded gate to a mansion in the center of the city, near Xandria's fortress. The four Evertauri – Calleneck, Aunika, and another man and woman – removed their hoods and two Jade Guards stepped forward to meet them.

"What is your business here?" they asked.

"We have a meeting scheduled with Sir Mordvitch." The tall Evertauri girl in her mid twenties held up a letter of invitation.

The guards looked at each other. "I'm afraid we can't let you four in without a formal request from the master himself."

A butler walked out of the doors of the mansion and down the cobblestone driveway, which was lined with perfectly cut grass. "Guards, please grant them entry. I was just speaking to the master."

The guards bowed and opened the gate.

"Guests," said the butler, "please follow me inside. My name is Kosov, and I serve the man you seek."

Led by Kosov, the Evertauri made their way through the ornate halls of the pristine mansion. Countless rooms and passages wound through the house's interior. The mansion boasted three separate wings, a library, an observatory, multiple studies, and a large fountain. Their walk ended in the back of the mansion and out the doors into a massive garden, which overlooked the entire south side of Seirnkov. Rows of countless flowers lined the garden as well as marble statues and smaller fountains. The mansion and its hedges surrounded it, as well as the ivy-covered stone balcony overlooking the city.

"The master will see you soon. Please wait here." Kosov began to walk away from them when he stopped. "And, well it's not really in my place to address you but . . . thank you . . . for doing what the rest of us can't . . . the Master will see you soon."

The four Evertauri looked at each other as he returned to the house. Aunika spoke under her breath. "So, this is where all the country's money goes."

A large, muscular Evertauri with dreadlocks and dark skin who looked to be in his early thirties accompanied them. He turned to them and pointed toward the mansion. "Except this is the one 'Crat' who isn't corrupt. Most of our sorcerers think he is third in command in the Evertauri, but nothing is official. He was the first man who joined President Nebelle. He's the best spy in the world, and quite an interesting man at that. He's leaked more secrets out of Xandria's government than all our other intelligence combined. He's also our only spy that we've gotten passed Xandria. You could say he's our poison dart."

"Is he really more powerful than even Borius?" asked Calleneck.

The fourth member of the party, a woman, was tall and slender, with dark brown eyes that stared at you as intensely as a bird of prey. Her name was Selenora Everrose – famous in the Evertauri for being taught by Madrick Nebelle himself, almost as a second daughter, and for being one of the most skilled in their organization, rivaling even the President. She nodded. "I've seen his Taurimous. Few people wield his hue naturally; it's a dark violet or iris. Of course, it's not as uncommon as ours, Mr. Bernoil."

Calleneck's stomach whirled a bit; she was the only other Evertauri with a crimson Taurimous. He felt unworthy of being near her, like her magic was something he shouldn't become involved with. His blood turned cold at the stories he had heard of her skills, and he nervously watched as Selenora knelt and caressed a carnation. A little crimson ribbon of light exited her fingertips and made the flower glow like hot metal in a foundry. Within a few seconds, the flower grew to the size of a dinner plate; its leaves thickened, and its petals shined, almost glowing with a soft red light.

Aunika's eyes opened wide with the unspoken question of '*how?*'

Selenora traced her fingers along the giant petals in a trance-like state, eyes glazed over, searching back through her twisted memories.

Abruptly, the door of the mansion opened and Selenora stood back up with the three others. A man in his forties with tightly curled black hair walked out wearing an expensive coat with long violet sleeves. He stood straight and proper and took his time strolling over to the four like a true aristocrat. When he got close to the group, he took a hand out of a pocket and motioned toward his mansion and smiled. "I'll tell you, no Jade Guards in this part of Seirnkov have let in a bunch of 'commoners' like you in quite some time. Well that is, of course, untrue; you aren't exactly commoners . . . What smells delightful at dawn and putrid at dusk?"

The man with dreadlocks answered the code. "Bread from Roshk."

He smiled and gave a slight bow. "My fellow Evertauri, welcome to my humble abode. For formality's sake, my name is Sir Mordvitch Aufenschiess;

you may address me as such. I am the queen's leading scientist, part of her head political Council, and currently, I am committing high treason by speaking to you . . ." The man's attention was caught by something behind them. "That carnation behind you has grown quite a bit, wouldn't you say?" The four glanced back at the flower. "If it isn't the famous *Selenora Everrose.*" He smiled and stepped closer to them, almost whispering. "*I remember you.* Always something new and . . . imaginative." He nodded at her. "Scholars like me enjoy those types of people. It's a pleasure to meet you again."

Selenora bowed with a "Sir."

Speaking in a heavy Cerebrian accent, the man with dreadlocks and an underbite introduced himself as Sir Grennkovff Kai'Le'a, followed by 'Mr. Bernoil and Ms. Bernoil, brother and sister.' Grennkovff raised an eyebrow. "Excuse me, sir, but your butler . . . is he an Evertauri? He knows who we are."

Mordvitch smiled. "Yes. Though Kosov is no sorcerer, I would trust him with my life . . . Walk with me."

Calleneck and the others did as they were asked, though he felt uneasy in the presence of Mordvitch. He knew he could trust him – after all, he helped Madrick Nebelle create the Evertauri – but nothing erased his obvious status as a Crat. Calleneck could not help but notice the way Mordvitch walked. His hands clasped in front of him, obscured by long, drooping sleeves of violet silk. Each step he took was slow and exact, as if he consciously reminded himself that he owned every blade of grass on which he stepped. His life seemed defined by luxury, but Calleneck knew that it was only a masquerade to hide his work for the Evertauri.

Mordvitch gestured toward the rows of flowers, revealing a large silver watch – a product from the scientists of Elishka. "Please excuse my inability to discuss matters in the Nexus, but the queen is working tirelessly to step up Cerebria's technological advantage against Ferramoor, which means that I have to stay within a half mile of her fortress."

"Sir Mordvitch," said Aunika, taking her gaze off the white mountains and back to him, "if I may ask, what advantage are you giving the Evertauri by furthering the capabilities of our opposing forces?"

"Because," shrugged Mordvitch, "there must be *something* of Cerebria once the Evertauri dispose of Xandria, which is no light task to ensure. Cerebria must be able to function with a new government. We still want it to have a strong army and make sure its citizens are well off. We don't want the Northlands or Elishka invading us after we take down Xandria." He stopped and examined an ivy plant which was growing up the side of his sumptuous manor.

"The queen began the war because she was too prideful to rule over just Cerebria, and she wanted what Gallegore never gave her – an Empire," said Mordvitch. "She is convinced that she would have held the Empire together after her father's death, that its fracturing was Tronum's fault; and I agree with her. Because she and Tronum are twins and their mother Kliera Dellasoff died in childbirth, Gallegore never revealed which was the eldest so that he could have a choice of giving the crown to his son or his daughter. Some even say that Xandria *was* the firstborn, and Gallegore denied her the throne. But had he chosen Xandria to rule the Empire, it would not have split. She's smarter and more capable than Tronum, and Tronum knows that."

Calleneck had never considered it, but maybe it was true.

Mordvitch went on. "*But*, because he did not grant her the throne, former Governess Xandria took her territories and created a seceded nation of Cerebria; the other territories then followed the queen's path." Mordvitch continued winding the group through a maze of statues and hedges. "Many Evertauri and other rebel groups think she only started the war to get revenge on Tronum and her dead father and will stop once she conquers Ferramoor. But she will not stop there. After gathering the Ferramish military arsenal under her green banners, the Queen will invade the Northlands and the Crandles."

Calleneck ran a hand through his hair. "Wouldn't the Northernfolk put up quite a fight?" he asked. "I know the Crans are pacifists, but they and the Northernfolk were originally the ones who controlled the Central East three hundred years ago, and they were driven out when the Cerebrians conquered. While the pacifists were granted the Crandles, the Northernfolk were banished to the tundra because they resisted the invasion. I would hardly believe they'd be taken over again with ease."

"The Seven Clans of the North don't have an organized army or a strict chain of command," said Selenora. "They would fall apart if invaded. But Xandria isn't trying to wipe them out, she's trying to unite the East."

"Exactly," said Mordvitch, leading them to a stone balcony overlooking the city. "We think that she wants to let the Northernfolk back into Cerebria, to heal the wound of the Cerebrian Invasion – giving them back fertile land to develop. With the warriors from the Northlands and the abundant food and manufacturing of the Crandles, Xandria will moved her gaze east to Elishka. It would be a tougher fight, but she could conquer it given a year or two. With the combined military force of Cerebria, Ferramoor, Elishka, and the Northlands, and with the supplies of the Crandles, the vast Ferramish agriculture industry, Elishk wealth and technological innovation, and the new naval force between all five former countries, the queen will sail to the Southlands.

"Their Sultan, Abdu Faazernan, will counter the Cerebrian Empire with a massive army and defend the Zjaari Gulf. But rumors are spreading that Faazernan is violating the Abolition Pact with Guavaan by enslaving Gypsies. If Sijong Yoto of Guavaan doesn't come to Faazernan's aid, the Southlands too will fall. With that quantity of power and resources, it would be too late for the remaining two nations to form a formidable alliance and drive her back. She will proceed to destroy the Kingdom of Parusemare and the island nation of Guavaan. All eight nations would be hers — our whole continent of Endellia."

The four guests stood silently, overlooking Seirnkov on the balcony. Mordvitch's tight curls moved back and forth in the wind. "It's far worse than many realize," he said. A dark purple flame danced around his fingertips as he spoke. "We will thwart as many of her plots we can without causing suspicion, but if we don't dethrone the queen soon, the years that follow will flow with blood, and the continent will be hers. We all want our own Cerebria, independent from the rest of the nations, but we have to stop Xandria.

"The goal for the Evertauri is to take down Xandria and this government, even to help the Ferrs do it, but once it is done, assert our power over Cerebria and order a reform of our kingdom. Even if Tronum survives his sickness and remains on the throne, he would know not to cross us once we're at full strength; he's had experience with sorcerers before . . . But if Xandria wins the war and starts conquering and growing in power, our chance of overthrowing her and creating a new Cerebria will be gone. So, in short, the work I do for the queen will help protect the citizens of Cerebria from foreign powers if the Evertauri succeeds. If we do not, my work will help lay waste to hundreds of cities. It's a bet that I am taking.

"You are wondering why I asked you here today." Mordvitch continued. He looked up at the central hill of Seirnkov and Xandria's looming fortress. It was taller and more daunting than the palace in Aunestauna, but both were situated on steep hills. "The queen has an underground wing in her fortress dedicated to technological developments — primarily for war. Other than the Innovation Square in Gienn, it is the most highly guarded and most important series of vaults in Cerebria. Although I am on the queen's board, I had to do some investigation to uncover her latest project — not including her flying machine prototypes in Gienn, which the famed Aris family is funding."

Calleneck's stomach lurched at the sound of Gallien's last name.

"I believe" said Mordvitch, "that the queen has found something of the Goblins'. You see, her incentive for murdering the entire Goblin race just after the formation of Cerebria, twenty years ago, was not because they posed a threat to Cerebrian security; Goblins did not burn villages and kill children like she says they did. No, instead, she killed them because they were smart."

Calleneck leaned in, intrigued.

"They were *unfathomably* smarter than most humans," Mordvitch continued, "which threatened the queen's dominance over the region. She killed the only beings who could challenge her intellect. The only reason she won was because the Goblins were so few in number compared to her freshly trained army.

"President Nebelle's Network guards have reported disturbances in the Goblin libraries underneath Roshk. Evertauri guards noticed that the entrances to the Network, which were sealed off after the genocide, are now put back together differently. The Goblins were alchemists and they experimented not only with chemistry but with a little sorcery as well. My investigation leads me to think that the queen has found it in her interest to borrow information from her stolen Goblin archives. To little avail, she's been trying to replicate many of the Goblins' wondrous machines and strange devices, hoping to use them in war.

"But recently, the queen's top scientists and scholars stole information from the Goblin libraries on how to use a mixture of chemicals that explode. She is trying to figure out how she can use these explosives to create an even deadlier weapon. I saw a paper pass over my desk for authorization of parts to what was titled 'The Gelltzkreik Device.' After taking a glance at it, I believe scientists are finding a way to launch heavy projectiles through the air without a trebuchet — powerful enough to break down a wall and easily take a person's head off. These weapons could be loaded onto naval ships in droves and give Cerebria a major advantage against Ferramish troops who only have swords and bows."

Aunika nodded. "And what is it you would have us do?"

Mordvitch put his hands in his trench coat pockets and leaned against the stone railing. "There is a woman in the queen's fortress who manages the incoming and outgoing supplies for the science wing — the Technological Advancement Vice-Supervisor, directly under me. We would want to know what she knows, but unfortunately, she is extremely loyal to the queen and is keeping secrets from me. So, we're going to have to take her place in the chain of command. Ms. Everrose and Sir Grennkovff, this is where you two will come in. As some of our most gifted operatives, your assignment is to assassinate this woman." He reached into his coat pocket, pulled out an envelope, and handed it to Selenora. "Her information is in here as well as how we want the assassination to be carried out in order to not cause suspicion. We want to wait at least eight weeks until this is done.

"However, her spot will need to be filled." Mordvitch turned toward Aunika. "This job was originally going to be assigned to Shonnar Nebelle; but I see that after his unfortunate death, you have taken up his duties. A few months after the assassination, you will enter the fortress acting as an official from the Gienn Innovation Square. You will meet with the Science Council in an interview for the job a week after that. Obviously, you will pretend you don't know me once we begin working together." He handed her an envelope.

"In here is all the information you will need. We will have Evertauri with you to ensure your success, but you will be our primary infiltrator. Multiple Evertauri will be sent to Gienn in the next few months to arrange everything for the lie to be believable. Remember, the queen is cunning, so this must be perfectly executed. Over the next week, you will also need to brush up on a great deal more science than you learned in your schooling. Providing the Science Council grants you the position, you will oversee the vaults and report everything back to the Evertauri. This would be a full-time job, except for certain additional missions we will inform you of later."

Calleneck frowned. She would no longer be able to stay with her parents in a few months – the second time she would abandon family for the Evertauri.

Aunika tucked the envelope into her coat. "As you wish, Sir."

Mordvitch turned to Calleneck. "And, Mr. Bernoil, you will now be working with our supply and mission report strategist team. Your credentials show that you are the Evertauri's leading cartographer."

"Well," replied Calleneck, "in my two years I have helped map out much of the Goblin's Network, allowing for smoother missions and an advantage when it comes to transportation of information and supplies."

"Excellent. You will receive Aunika's reports, as well as others', concerning the shipment of weapons and scientific information. You will discuss this with the strategy team and then inform the Council of Mages on the best course of action – specifically if we need to intercept information or destroy supplies. You will also be in charge of navigation for new investigative teams in this operation who will be gathering Goblin information on these weapons, the explosive devices. We expect that a large shipment of the queen's weapons will be sent to the front lines after final testing. If this shipment occurs, we expect the Ferramish front to collapse. We hope that, as the queen starts to push back Ferramish troops, the shipment will travel through the Great Cerebrian Gate in the Taurbeir-Krons." Mordvitch turned toward all four of the guests. "If we can get our hands on the weapons as they travel through, we can use them to destroy the gate – Cerebria's main defense against Ferramoor. Of course, the numbers are not yet sure; I have many more calculations to do."

Mordvitch looked at his luxurious watch, its delicate and precise little gears ticking, moving silver hands around its face. "I must go now." He handed Calleneck an envelope. "My information and estimates for you to give to President Nebelle. This also contains your mission report. And make sure that he reads the report on unusual activity in Port Dellock . . . Let me escort you all back."

He walked the four through the mansion and left them at the front doors. They were halfway down the steps when Mordvitch called out, "And Ms. Everrose. Be careful when you're growing your flowers." She gave a nod, and she, Gremkovff, and the Bernoils made their way to the *Ivy Serpent*, where they each took turns disappearing through an illusion of Taurimous which looked like a mirror of molten silver and reentered the Network.

Back in the Nexus, Calleneck entered Madrick Nebelle's study. Sitting squarely behind a large desk with dozens of little drawers was the President of the Evertauri himself. Madrick was tall even in a chair, with heavy eyes and slightly wrinkled hands. A thin stubble beard of salt and pepper hair ran across his angular chin and matching silver hair adorned his head. But most noticeable of all was the constant scowl he wore. Calleneck had never seen the President smile, and after some time of knowing him, he knew that he never would. Why would he? He had lost his wife, his son, and any ease of life since starting the revolution. Once a man is hardened by grief, the muscles stiffen, and the scowl stays put — day after day, the same lifeless expression devoid of any warmth.

Calleneck still felt uneasy around the President, the man who caused him so much pain for a mistake Calleneck couldn't control — the man who branded him. Calleneck handed Madrick the envelope, the white scar on his chest hidden beneath his cloak. "From Sir Mordvitch."

"Thank you, Mr. Bernoil," said Madrick in a voice as rough as the short hairs on his neck, "this is valuable information. Mordvitch has risked a great deal to get this to us. Some Evertauri don't realize why he does what he does, why he helps Xandria; and they hate him for it . . . Many don't comprehend any sacrifice that is not their own. But because of him, we have a chance. He's gained Xandria's trust over the years."

The Goblin study, which he had turned into his office, was filled with silver ornaments. Some of them perpetually moved in patterns and some were shimmering, ever changing illusions of matter; everything was silver, the color of President Nebelle's Taurimous. Madrick Nebelle was not only the leader of the Evertauri, but also the most gifted sorcerer by far, knowing secrets about sorcery and the Taurimous that no one else knew. With wrinkles in his hands, one would expect little from him, but the stories of what he could do were terrifying.

President Nebelle noticed that a desk drawer was open and shut it. "We step closer and closer every day; every day the sword gets closer to Xandria's throat. Her world will be covered in crimson blood . . . Crimson . . . That's a color of power, Mr. Bernoil." Calleneck swallowed. *How does Madrick know my Taurimous?* The man kept pacing around his office and staring at the silver ornaments. "Crimson . . . reddish hues . . . blood-stained battlefields . . . the rising and setting sun . . . a burning fire forging red metal into weapons . . . those colors are colors of *power*. Why do you think the Ferrs chose scarlet as their national color? . . . It inspires fear. A crimson Taurimous is one not to take lightly . . ." He turned and stared Calleneck in the eye. "Make what you ought to make out of what you have. To do otherwise will destroy you." Madrick formed a shimmering orb of silver flames that danced around his fingers. "*Be careful playing with fire, Mr. Bernoil.*"

"Yes sir," replied Calleneck, wondering whether President Nebelle could have guessed what was going on inside his head . . . the memories, the other lives.

"Is there anything else you wish to report, now that you have a new position?"

Calleneck's mind flashed and remembered sprinting and swinging through the forest with the Phantoms. He knew all of it; he was inside the Cerebrian army, and he knew what they were capable of. He had fought with them – helped them kill. He thought of the awesome power which flowed through Tayben's veins . . . *the Phantoms . . . Xandria's Phantoms . . . the Evertauri doesn't know. The Phantoms could destroy the Evertauri and we wouldn't know how to stop them.*

"Yes, sir, actually there is something important that you should know." *Tell him about the Phantoms.* But then Calleneck thought of the Nymphs and their pure light, like endlessly luminous starlight. They were pure, and they trusted the Phantoms. This was Tayben's secret, not his. Did he have any right to expose him? And if he did, would he expose the Evertauri as Tayben? He liked to think that he wouldn't – he would never reveal the Evertauri. But, then again, did he really have control over what he did as Tayben? He was on opposite sides of the same war. As Calleneck, he wanted to stop Tayben from killing and stop fighting for Cerebria, but he knew that in the body of Tayben he would think the opposite. How could he? How could he be so lost and confused and savage in Tayben's mind? That wasn't his mind, that wasn't Calleneck, it couldn't be, it couldn't. "Um– I will soon start working on mapping the southern Goblin tunnel system which will allow twice as much access to our entrances in The Crandles."

"Good work, Mr. Bernoil. Dismissed."

§

After Calleneck had left his office, President Nebelle leaned back in his chair, thinking back years ago to when he and Sir Mordvitch invited Borius Shipton into that very office. President Nebelle and Mordvitch had successfully started the Evertauri, and it was time for Mordvitch to work for Xandria as an Evertauri spy, and time for Sir Borius to take his place as second in command. Borius was Madrick's most trusted advisor other than Mordvitch, and a powerful sorcerer to fill the role of number two to him.

Thinking back on more memories of those years ago, he extended his hand, producing a little silver flame. He twirled it between his fingers and then shaped it into the form of a little rose petal in his hand. A shiver ran down his spine as his mind flashed back to a memory from over a decade prior – a memory that had haunted him ever since.

A little Raelynn, not more than seven years old ran up to him in an underground cavern.

Madrick's eyes looked scornfully on his daughter. "What are you doing here, Raelynn? I told you not to follow us!"

"Daddy, daddy! Can I practice with you and Selenora this time?"

Madrick looked to his other side at a young Selenora Everrose, just a few years older than Raelynn. Madrick turned back to the little hopeful Raelynn, whose blue eyes beamed in the dark tunnel.

He shook his head. "Not this time."

She furrowed her eyebrows at Selenora and then looked back up at her father. "It's not fair that you teach her everything and not me. And look, I'm getting so much better at magic!" The little Raelynn made a little puff of black fire and smoke from her hand.

Madrick snapped forward and grabbed her hands, looking her in the eye. "Don't do that, Raelynn. I've told you not to practice magic on your own. You could accidentally create a spell too powerful and lose your magic."

She looked on the verge of tears.

Madrick picked up his voice. "Go, now! Go back to the Nexus!" Raelynn cried as she ran away.

Madrick turned to Selenora. "Let's keep going." Selenora nodded her head. Madrick scratched his chin. "Here's something to try. I haven't taught you yet how to mold your Taurimous into objects, have I?"

She shook her head. "I don't think so."

Madrick formed a little silver flame in his hand. "We can use our Taurimous to create objects that we can control." The silver flame formed into a small key. "See?"

The young Selenora stared in awe. "Is it real?"

He shook his head. "It's only a replica; as soon as I want it to disappear, it can." The key in his hand vanished in a wisp of smoke. He looked at the young Selenora. "Why don't you give it a try?"

"What should I make?" she asked.

He thought for a moment. "Well, Ms. 'Everrose,' why don't you make a rose? It'd be fitting."

She thought for a minute and then formed a little crimson flame in her hand. Blood-red fire floated around her hand and danced beautifully between her fingertips. Concentrating hard, she began to form the fire into a rose.

Madrick laughed. "That's very good, Selenora!" But very quickly, his laughter vanished. Behind Selenora on the floor of the cavern, glowing roses — dozens of real flowers — were springing up and growing from nothing.

Madrick's heart raced, and his blood froze with fear. "Stop!" he yelled.

Selenora jumped, making the flower in her hand disappear. "What did I do wrong?" She looked at him with apprehension.

Madrick frantically thought of what to say. A Taurimous creating inanimate objects was common practice, but creating life? No, it couldn't be real. She was so young. Madrick pretended to be playful, trying not to look at the flowers behind her. "Oh nothing, you were wonderful, it's just time to go back now." Grabbing her hand, he pulled her out of the cavern. But just before they rounded the corner, she glanced back and saw the patch of glowing roses growing right where she stood.

In his office, Madrick shivered, remembering the long-gone event like it was yesterday. He shook his head as thoughts raced through his mind. *Manipulating life with a Taurimous . . .* he thought *. . . Selenora is up to something . . . I can feel it.*

WAR COUNCIL AND WINE
Chapter Twelve

~Midday, September 18th
Royal Palace, Ferramoor, Aunestauna

Eston sat at an ornate oak desk below a bedroom window looking out upon the wooded hills of Ferramoor, where the yellowing trees battled against the green. His fingers traced a small black rock he held in his hand; its shape was perfectly circular and thin, ideal for skipping across water.

His mind flashed back to when he picked it up off the sandy shore just five miles south of Aunestauna. His little six-year-old hands dug into the wet sand and held the stone for his father to see. But a large wave hit the little prince and swept him into the water. An arm reached around him and pulled him back to shore. Tronum's more youthful face filled with relief when his son started coughing on the sand, the skipping stone still clutched in his hand.

A knock echoed on his large bedroom doors. Eston quickly opened his top left desk drawer and placed the skipping stone inside of it on a velvet cloth. "Enter," he called.

Queen Eradine stepped inside the doors wearing a long blue gown. She walked over to him and put her hand on his shoulder. "You can come out more, you know." Eradine pulled over a chair and sat next to him. Hints of her childhood accent from Parusemare dotted her speech. She sighed. "It's alright, it's been three weeks."

To avoid the conversation, Eston picked up a scroll on his desk and pretended to read it. "Father doesn't want me around him. He sees me as a disgrace for wandering off into the Second District and getting–"

"Your father was mad, yes, and I was too. Was it a foolish thing to do? Of course. But do we forgive you? Of course."

Eston flipped over his scroll. "If he forgives me, then why isn't he here himself? Mother, you and I both know that Father doesn't want me to inherit his kingdom; he would rather have Fillian sit on the throne. Why else does he refuse to give me any responsibility, or even experience? King Gallegore was giving both Father and Xandria command of whole territories by my age, but Father won't even allow me to speak in the Council."

Eradine looked down with sadness in her eyes. "Eston, I love you with all my heart; you and Fillian equally . . . Your father refuses to see the fine prince that you have become; you're still his little boy. He doesn't feel right giving you a kingdom stuck in war with your aunt . . ." She glanced at Eston's scroll. "I think you should have a speaking seat in the senate meeting today."

He looked up. "You think that after all the shame I got from Father and how it traveled around the palace—"

"I don't care, Eston. I don't care how your father feels; you are a prince, and you are more informed than some of the senators present in the Council."

"And yet I am not allowed to speak!" shouted Eston. He knew he shouldn't have yelled at his mother and promptly looked away while his mother held her gaze. "I'm sorry; that was unlike me."

"You want to help your people, and that's the most important part of being a leader. I don't know where this new-found sense of adventure is coming from, but it's valuable and I don't want you to lose it. You made a mistake; now it's time to show everyone that you're better than that."

He stood up. "The Council decides on matters without taking my advice into consideration."

"Well, soon they will have to consider your thoughts," said Eradine. "You see the way your father moves; it's mechanical and shaky. I have to put on his crown for him . . . He's sick, Eston."

"I know."

The queen walked to the window. "Show your father. He doesn't ignore Whittingale's positive reports of you; he wants to leave the kingdom in good hands. Once your father goes, I too lose the majority of my power and give it to whomever you choose to marry." Eston remained silent. Eradine adjusted the sleeve of her long blue dress. "And concerning your brother . . . he looks up to you. In fact, he convinced me not to demote Benja Tiggins for arranging your absence, even though Whittingale recommended it." She walked to the doors and pushed them open and was stopped by Eston thanking her, to which she replied with a simple smile. "And Eston," she added, "Qerru-Mai will be at the Council." Her blue dress trailed her as she left his oversized bedroom.

A throng of faces reflected in the thousands of crystals in chandeliers that hung around the rim of the senate chamber. Tronum and Eradine sat together on the highest terrace of seats; below them sat Eston. To his right, a very old man, Prophet Ombern of the Church of the Great Mother, stroked his long white beard. On his other side, Qerru-Mai quickly flourished a quill across parchment, taking notes of the proceedings of the meeting. As the Council Scrivener, she kept the records from all the debates, discussions, and decisions occuring in the chamber. She had skin like creamy chocolate and attentive eyes that swept the room, analyzing every second, seemingly unaware of the prince's presence next to her. Sharing her dark skin and curled hair, her mother, Senator Qarra An'Drui stood to address the Council.

"If I may," said the senator. "The Council has seemingly dismissed the fact that our intelligence still does not know how Xandria retrieved this information. The expansion of Camp Stoneheart will be a primary defense in preventing the advance of Cerebrian forces through Endlebarr, and now Xandria knows its location. Do we have any idea who told her? Was it Cerebrian spies?"

"I propose," said Senator Bardow across the hall, "that we mandate our generals their interrogate high ranking officers to find the culprit who betrayed us."

Janus Whittingale stood by a window. "You seem to forget, Senator, that Xandria wants us to lose trust in our leadership. She is not preoccupied with Camp Stoneheart; it provides a fraction of the defense for us than the protection the Great Gate provides for Cerebria. The last battalion in southeast Endlebarr was sent back to be stationed at the Southern Pass on the tenth. For the next four to five months, there will be little to no conflict in southern Endlebarr." Whittingale put his hands in the pockets of his long black coat. "Now that winter has fallen in the Taurbeir-Krons, she knows where our forces are concentrated, and we know where hers are. Now because her forces have been occupied defending southeastern Endlebarr, we have seen little of what advantage the gate will give her. We cannot allow this Council to be distracted with issues that tear apart our command; rather, we should focus on how we can attack Xandria while defending our side of Endlebarr."

Prophet Ombern remained seated, but his voice boomed. "Perhaps we infiltrate her system. I'm sure there is some way to get a spy in her castle and send us messenger birds."

Eston almost laughed but caught himself. *This is my time.* He stood up and placed his hands on the table in front of him. "That is much easier said than done. Out of seven spy missions, one resulted in captivity and no information, and six resulted in the spies' deaths, again with no information. Xandria's system is impenetrable."

"And you have a solution?" asked Prophet Ombern.

"Xandria's military prioritizes weapons and machines over sheer numbers of men, which is our advantage. The next leading producer in the scientific industry is Elishka."

"You propose we miraculously get the Elishk to fight our war?" laughed Ombern, throwing his hands up.

"No," said the prince. He hesitated and his heart beat rapidly. "I propose that we eliminate all tariffs on their products." Murmurs echoed throughout the chamber. "The Elishk will be more incentivized to sell to us, rather than to

Cerebria. By making Xandria pay more for weaponry, we could destabilize her primary advantage. We may lose money, but we may also win the war."

Qerru-Mai raised her head and looked at Eston with wide eyes.

Her mother smiled and gestured toward the prince. "Impressive idea, Your Majesty. I believe the Council should consider this option. Senator Nollard, you are Ferramoor's head of trade; what do you say?"

"I don't like the prospect," said the younger man with olive skin and long black hair, "but it could potentially work. Although we would risk exposure, if we rerouted our military supply chain to run through Nottenberry to our camps at Wallingford and Abendale, we might save enough time and money to partly compensate for the loss of the profits from tariffs."

While Nollard spoke, Eston noticed that a small wave rippled through a curtain on the other side of the room behind Senator Duboiret's chair booth. The man had hung his coat on the back of his seat. Silently, a hand slipped out of the curtain and removed a piece of paper from the man's coat; the hand vanished behind the curtain. Nobody had seemed to notice but the prince.

Above Eston, the queen thanked Senator Nollard and decided to further the research in his department on the issue. "And thank you Prince Eston for proposing the idea, you may be seated." Eston sat but kept his eyes focused on the Duboiret's chair. About a minute later, the hand returned and placed the piece of paper back in the same coat pocket.

Prophet Ombern rubbed his forehead. "Elishk manufacturing and weaponry will only help our army if we get past that damned Gate. Does nobody see?"

Eston remembered what Mordvitch had told Calleneck. "We should expect that a massive shipment of the queen's weapons will be sent to the front lines after final testing . . . If the queen puts the full effort of the science wing into developing these explosives, the government will be shipping enough through the gate, that if we intercept it, we may not only be able to destroy the weapons but use them to destroy the wall." He remained silent.

Senator Elim, and older woman with gray hair to her waist furrowed her eyebrows, causing her to look quite dangerous. "And I'm sure in all your wisdom you know how we could possibly do that?" Her voice grew cold. "She has an entire legion on that gate. It's hundreds of feet tall – solid stone from the Taurbeir-Krons. We have to hold off until next summer when the Southern Pass opens again."

"We don't have time. Xandria's forces grow more powerful by the second," said Whittingale, perpetually standing like a statue. "We have to find a way, Senator Elim."

"There isn't a way."

Prophet Ombern stroked his short gray beard. "Perhaps . . . yes . . . perhaps there is a way." The room fell silent like it was muffled in snow. "There was a time some twenty years ago, Ferramoor created—"

"Ombern!" King Tronum rocketed up from his seat and bellowed. "Absolutely not! Without exception!"

Prophet Ombern shook his head. "It's been so long, Your Majesty . . . *You know* of what I speak."

The king's eyes widened, and his face grew purple. "Silence yourself, Prophet!"

Ombern clenched his jaw and almost hissed through it. "Your Majesty, they are growing restless! I plead that we use what we already—"

Tronum slammed a shaking fist on the table in front of him. "Leave this chamber at once, Prophet! If you refuse, I will have the Scarlet Guard remove you."

The Prophet's face grew dark. "You wouldn't dare."

Tronum didn't blink. "Guards!" Soldiers adorned with scarlet and gold armor entered through the large oak doors of the chamber.

In a hushed voice, Prophet Ombern snarled at King Tronum, "You're afraid . . . your father would've done it . . . *I expected more from a Wenderdehl.*" Ombern stormed out of the chamber, refusing to let the guards touch him.

Once the meeting was adjourned, Eston turned to Qerru-Mai, whom he had known for quite some time. "That was intense . . ."

"Quite. There is obviously something that your father has not told many people; I don't believe my mother understood either. I would be careful." The warm light from the city below the palace caused her warm brown skin to glow.

". . . Yes." Eston remembered the hand from the curtain taking a slip of paper out of Duboiret's pocket and returning it a minute later. "Qerru-Mai, did you notice anything strange behind Senator Duboiret during the meeting?"

"I'm afraid not. Is there something in particular you are referring to?"

"It's nothing, I might have imagined it." The two exited the chamber and turned down a window-lined hall, where the midday sun streamed in.

With messy hair, Fillian ran around the corner. "Hey, Eston!" he panted. "You have to tell me what happened in th- . . . Oh, *hello* Ms. An'Drui."

The senator's daughter nodded, and Eston shook his head at Fillian, "I'll tell you later. Tell Benja that I think there is someone in the palace that shouldn't be here. I saw something strange in the Council." To Eston's side, a girl in a black cloak turned a corner; she stopped in her tracks and a streak of blonde hair fell out of her hood. *Raelynn Nebelle.* She spun around and casually walked back down the hall she came from. Eston turned to Fillian and Qerru-Mai. "I'm sorry, I have to go right now, I just remembered I have to do something."

"It's fine," she said, "I'm just on my way to berate Senator Resbee in his office."

"Yes— have fun— pleasure seeing you, Qerru-Mai. Oh— and don't tell Benja just yet."

She looked slightly confused as Eston bolted away from them.

He rounded the corner and saw Raelynn sneak into a side hallway; he ran after her. But he stopped when he saw the dead end of the isolated hallway; Raelynn was not there. The only sounds came from chirping birds outside of the windows. Cautiously, he walked forward. A large marble statue of the Great Mother stood at the end of the hallway, somewhere he liked to explore as a youngster. Alcoves with statues lined one side of the hallway and windows lined the other. *How did she get away?* He left the hall, abandoning his chase. He failed to notice that where there was once a beautiful centaur statue was now bare stone.

The wall shimmered like liquid, and slowly, it evaporated into mist. Raelynn looked down the hall, relieved that her illusion worked. She quickly made her way through the East Wing hallways, passing a room with the senator's daughter and a man arguing, then out into Aunestauna.

§

Qerru-Mai shook a roll of parchment in her hand as her chocolate eyes pierced into Senator Resbee – an older gentleman with a double chin and a ring of white hair around his balding head. "You, sir," she said, "look me in the eye and tell me that it has nothing to do with Benja."

Senator Resbee leaned back in his office chair. "Ms. An'Drui, I really don't think it does; just because—"

"I can't believe this!" Qerru-Mai threw her hands up.

"I have much more important things to worry about—"

"No, you of all people. Why aren't you on my side about this?"

Senator Resbee put his face in his hands. "Because there aren't any sides, Ms. An'Drui. You're the only person in this whole palace that's concerned about it. What does it matter to you? You're just our scrivener."

"Sixteen missing classified files from the Great Library in a month, Senator, sixteen. Benja is pretty much the only one with access to them. That doesn't worry you in the slightest?"

Senator Resbee shook his head. "It's trivial, it really is. Just as you said, sixteen scrolls among thousands. Who is even keeping track of all of them? I think the reason you're the only one who cares is because you're the only one that's read every bit of parchment in the library."

Qerru-Mai rolled her eyes. "I haven't read every— it doesn't matter how few, it matters that we may have sensitive information being stolen by people infiltrating the palace!"

"For the love of the Great Mother, just ask Benja."

"Why would I ask Benja if he's the one I suspect?"

"Then ask Whittingale," said Senator Resbee. "He's been trailing Benja. He's also concerned about your mother and Ombern, 'thinks they're after something'."

Qerru-Mai threw up her hands. "And for some reason you haven't thought to tell me?"

"Didn't have time," said Senator Resbee.

"You spent an hour yesterday meeting with Lord Shellingdrane about how much of his land out east should be used to grow corn!"

"Ms. An'Drui—"

"Corn is what worries you and not stolen classified information?! You know what, I *will* talk to Whittingale." Qerru-Mai stormed out of the room.

Senator Resbee called out from his office with an annoyed voice, "It's trivial, Ms. An'Drui!"

"Fillian!" Qerru-Mai ran across the golden treed courtyard to the prince. "Are you busy?" she asked.

Fillian shook his head. "Not at the moment."

"I was wondering if you knew anything about those files that are missing from the library?"

"No, why?"

She threw her hands up. "Apparently nobody does. Sixteen files are gone. Something's off, and I think Benja is up to something. Do you know where Whittingale is?" she asked.

Fillian shook his head. "No, but the last time I saw him, he wanted you to start working on a case way out in Abendale."

"In Abendale?"

"For Abendale. Apparently, there were some soldiers of ours who broke into a cellar of wine the night before they were scheduled to be moved to the front lines in Endlebarr."

"And how is this my concern at all?" she asked.

"They're our troops."

"And I'm supposed to do something about this?"

"Exactly," he said.

"What on earth does he want me to do?" she asked.

"Probably write strongly worded letters to the soldiers."

"Thanks, that's a real help."

"No problem." Fillian smiled.

"I'm not giving up on this document issue without a fight, you know," she said as she turned away.

"Wait," said Fillian looking around with as suspicious eye. "I haven't been on the lookout for Whittingale, but I have for Prophet Ombern and –"

Qerru-Mai leaned in. "And who?"

Fillian frowned. "And your mother . . . they're up to something. I've seen them sneaking around in the corridors beneath the Royal Palace. Do you know something I don't?"

Qerru-Mai shook her head. "No . . ." She didn't like the feeling of an additional mystery. People were acting strange around the palace, and she couldn't piece together the secrets. Something was going on but getting to the bottom of it was like trying to catch a shadow. "Well, I'd better be on my way."

As she left, Fillian shouted after her, "You're too stressed, Ms. An'Drui! Go shoot some arrow targets or ride your horse to take your mind off it."

Qerru-Mai sighed and rounded the corner in search of anyone with answers. Fillian had only left her with more questions than she started off with.

§

~Evening

In the Great Hall, a fireplace and the fading light of the sunset illuminated the ornate pillars and ceiling. At the long wooden dinner table, the royal family and a few other important figures stood behind their chairs. As King Tronum took his seat at the head of the table, the others followed.

King Tronum smiled and raised his hand as servers brought over steaming food to the table. "I'd like to thank everyone for their patience today with our rather—" he laughed, "rather unusual Council meeting today."

Fillian, sitting beside Eston, raised an eyebrow. "You never told me what happened."

Queen Eradine shook her head. "It's nothing to be concerned about . . . your father and Prophet Ombern just had a disagreement."

Fillian stared longingly at a sizzling, roasted turkey sitting on a platter in front of Sir Janus Whittingale and King Tronum. "Well, now I'm sad I missed the excitement."

Whittingale, who sat between Tronum and an empty seat, carved off a leg of the turkey and handed it to the king. "Your Majesty," he said. "Now, Eston, your comment today during the war Council meeting concerning Elishka was quite insightful. How would you suggest shipping their supplies to our troops? Would we pay to use their ships or—"

Whittingale stopped when Benja Tiggins rushed into the Great Hall. Walking up to the table, he bowed to King Tronum and Queen Eradine. "I hope you accept my apology for my lateness," he said, obviously shaken up by something. "I believe I mixed up my schedule and I was preoccupied with something that—"

King Tronum raised a hand and smiled. "We understand, Lord Tiggins. Take a seat."

Benja sat in the open chair beside Whittingale. "We've just received reports of a Cerebrian in the Royal Palace, but I can't pin them down."

Eston's stomach turned – he knew exactly who was in the palace – and Raelynn was up to something today. *I told Qerru-Mai not to tell Benja yet.*

Queen Eradine picked off a branch of grapes and placed them on her plate. "If you've notified your Scarlet Guards, they'll be on the lookout."

Eston shook his head. "It's probably nothing."

Benja placed a slice of crispy bread on his plate. "Well, you can never be too careful."

The Royal family, Benja, Whittngale, and other officials discussed the war effort and relations with the Southlands and the Northlands. As the turkey and hams were finished, a series of palace servants brought out wine glasses, setting them around the table to each of them, including Eston and Fillian.

After they left, King Tronum raised a wine glass, prompting the others to do the same. Tronum smiled and looked around the table. "To progress, and our best efforts in sealing our victory."

The others joined their glasses together, and Tronum raised the glass to his lips.

Suddenly, Whittingale's eyes shot open. "Everyone stop!" He had his wine glass an inch from his own mouth.

The room froze and Whittingale sniffed his wine. He turned to King Tronum. "May I see yours?"

King Tronum slowly handed his wine glass to Whittingale.

Whittingale took a whiff of the red wine and nodded. "It's poisoned."

Queen Eradine gasped, and Fillian practically threw down his glass on the table.

King Tronum stood up from his seat. "Nobody move." The king held his glass up to the firelight. Faintly swirling in the red liquid were a few drops of a darker, golden-brown liquid. Tronum breathed out slowly and shook his head. "BlackHolly."

"What?" said Fillian.

Tronum set the glass back down on the table and picked up Eradine's and Whittingale's to see the dark drops of liquid swirling inside. "Poison," he said.

"*My sister* used to be especially keen on using it." He looked over to Whittingale. "Thank you Janus, your nose remains much better than mine."

Eston's mind immediately shot to Raelynn. *Would she . . . no, why would she try to kill us?*

"Are all of them poisoned?" asked Eradine, as Tronum walked around, examining them.

Tronum picked up Benja's, sniffed it, and held it to the firelight. "Not this one . . ." The king spun around and grabbed Benja by the collar, nearly lifting him out of his chair. Tronum looked him straight in the eye and his voice boomed. "Did you have something to do with this?!"

Benja frantically shook his head. "No, Your Majesty. I swear to you!"

Whittingale stood. "Your Majesty, Benja would never hurt you! We'll figure this out, just— just calm down."

"You don't tell me to calm down Janus," shouted Tronum, "not when my wife and sons were almost killed!" Tronum's face was flushed red with anger. "If he didn't, then who did?!"

"Well didn't Benja say that there was a Cerebrian in the palace?" said Whittingale. "This needs to be investigated more before we make these assumptions, Your Majesty."

Eston nodded. "He's right. I think there's something larger at play."

Queen Eradine walked over to Tronum and placed a hand on his shoulder. "It's okay, darling . . . we're all safe. Let him go."

The king grunted and shoved Benja back, shattering Benja's glass of wine on the floor. He looked around the room with a raging face. "I WANT TO KNOW WHO DID THIS!" he boomed, slamming his fist on the table, sending a rattling of silverware and plates echoing through the Great Hall. "This was my sister's doing!" He began to mutter, "Damn her! It's BlackHolly . . . that's hers!" Tronum looked around at everyone's frightened faces. "Someone has infiltrated this palace and I want them hanged!"

Eston's stomach turned. *I need to find Raelynn.*

It was under the cover of night that Eston — dressed fully in commoners clothing — had gotten out of the palace and into the city to find Raelynn. More than a few Scarlet Guards owed him favors, allowing him to discreetly leave the palace hill without involving Benja. *The Westflower Inn is where she told me she'd be staying.* He had wound his way through the midnight streets of the city until arriving at the inn.

Walking into the dark parlor lobby lit by only a few candles, he walked up to an oddly short man at a desk. Eston spoke quietly. "I'd like to know the room number of someone who goes by the name Endra . . . she's probably the only blonde you've got staying here."

The short man shook his head. "I'm sorry, but I can't give that information to you, sir—"

Eston held out a handful of twenty argentums and set them on the desk.

The man stumbled over his words. "The— yes— yes, umm . . . let me look . . . that'll be room twenty-four, second floor."

Eston nodded and thanked him, walking up a staircase to room twenty-four. Standing outside the door, he knocked. After a few seconds, he could hear footsteps. The door cracked open, and Raelynn peeked her head out. Her eyes shot open when she recognized Eston.

The prince pressed a finger to his lips, silencing her. He placed his hand on the door and stepped inside where he saw on her small bed an opened case of clothes.

He shut the door and looked Raelynn straight in the eye. "Did you do it?"

"Do what?" Raelynn stepped back in apprehension.

Eston pointed at her. "You know damn well what I'm talking about!"

"I swear, I don't."

"Did you try to poison my family?"

Raelynn stepped back in shock. "Of course not! What happened?"

"There was an assassination attempt tonight – on all of us. The wine had drops of BlackHolly and— Well then what were you doing in the palace today? You stole something while the Council was in session."

"I think you're mistaken—"

"I saw you take a paper from Senator Duboiret's çoat. Why?"

Raelynn fell silent.

"Why?" pressed Eston.

"Senator Duboiret keeps the password to the lower sections of the library on a piece of parchment. He's quite a forgetful one." She tried to joke to cover her nervousness.

"Why did you want to access the lower library?"

"As soon as I got the password, I went and told the library guards and they let me in for a half hour. I was looking for a document of employment about the time when the Endellian Empire split. My father and my brother have no idea what happened to my mother except that she worked in the Royal Palace."

Eston's heart sank. *No letters from Seirnkov; she is still unaware that her brother has been dead for weeks. I need to tell her. But how could I? I'm not supposed to know. Should I write to her as Calleneck? No, no, it isn't my place.*

Raelynn brushed a strand of blonde hair out of her face. "My father fled with us to Cerebria after she vanished, but he wants to forget about her; he's almost sure she's dead. I caught a ship to Findinholm from Port Dellock and from Findinholm to here. I've been searching in the library for any clues, and the ones I find are vague and hard to piece together. My last hope was a document in the lower, classified sections of the library. When I looked, the document was already gone."

Eston looked over to the bed where she was packing clothes. "You're leaving?"

"At sunrise tomorrow, I'll catch a ship to Catteboga in the Crandles and make my way back to Cerebria."

Eston shook his head. "Nothing makes any sense right now." He looked at Raelynn again. "Are you sure you don't know anything? You're the only Cerebrian who's been in the palace in years at least as far as I know."

Raelynn shook her head. "Your Majesty . . ." She started folding more of her clothes. "I wish I could help. But I wasn't here for political games . . . I was here to try and find my mother."

Eston took a deep breath and paused for a while, before turning toward the door. "I wish you safe travels then."

Raelynn gave a small bow. "Thank you."

Eston turned for the door. "And by the way . . . I know your name is Raelynn."

She stood in shock. "How?"

Eston shrugged. "I have my ways. Get a good night's sleep before your day tomorrow."

"But—" Raelynn stuttered, not understanding. "Yes, Your Majesty . . . I will."

With more questions than he arrived with, Eston turned the door handle and began his journey back up to the Royal Palace, returning safely and secretly. He thought to Raelynn. I'll see you soon.

The sun had been set for hours when Eston reached Fillian's bedroom door. *I have to tell him everything,* Eston thought. *I have to tell him about Raelynn, how I know her, how I know all of these things. Raelynn might be the one responsible for what happened. I have to tell him what I've been seeing . . . these . . . other lives.*

Eston knocked on the door and a few seconds later, it opened.

Fillian stood there with disheveled hair as always. "Evening, Eston. What are you doing?"

Eston stepped into the doorway. "I was wondering if we could go on a quick walk. It won't take long — only to the courtyard."

"Why?" Fillian asked.

"Just come along, would you?" said Eston.

Eston had a hard time trying to broach a subject even he didn't fully understand. By the time they arrived at the courtyard, he had stalled all he could by making small-talk, when he finally asked, "Do you—" Eston stopped. *What was I thinking, I can't say this! I'm a prince. I can't sound like I'm going mad!* Suddenly he switched topics to another minor thing that had been on his mind. "Do you think I should be with Qerru-Mai?"

Fillian gave him a strange look.

Eston stumbled. "I— I mean, have you ever felt, you know, *like that,* toward someone."

Fillian raised his eyebrow. "I don't know why you're asking *me* for advice."

"I just thought you'd have another perspective, that's all." Eston lied. "I just don't know if I'm feeling those things because mum and dad want me to or if . . ." Eston's mind trailed off.

Fillian shook his head. "Don't worry about it. Wait until the war is over, when we have time to dwell on love and all that," he joked. Fillian stopped. "Are you alright, Eston? You're acting a bit strange."

Eston shook his head and sighed. "Just lack of sleep, that's all."

Fillian shrugged, and the brothers spent the rest of the evening engaged in long-deserved casual conversation, something that gave Eston a much-needed break from the heavier things weighing on his mind. He finally remembered how nice it was to forget about things for a while.

MOUNTAIN, RIVER, CANOPY

Chapter Thirteen

~Morning, September 22nd
Eastern Endlebarr

"Tayben, wake up," said Gallien.

Tayben opened his eyes and stared up at the dark leaves of Endlebarr. The Phantoms slept high in the canopy of the trees on massive branches the width of a bridge. Some branches were wide enough to collect dirt, springing forth ferns and shrubs on top of them. "What is it, Gallien?"

Gallien put his hand on Tayben's shoulder. "I found something strange. I want you to come and see." Gallien turned around and jumped off the branch onto another one thirty feet below. His blonde hair flipped back and forth as his superhuman-like body nimbly scrambled and jumped down the tree. Confused, Tayben lifted himself up; the other cloaked Phantoms around him were still sleeping. Still nervous about trusting his new abilities, he reluctantly decided to follow Gallien and jump off the branch. As he descended through the fog onto the next branch, the wind brushed his face like a wave of mountain water, and he could feel his body accelerating the farther he dropped. His heart raced, but his legs were strong as steel and stopped his fall on a branch forty feet below.

When the two reached the forest floor, which was covered in endless groves of ferns and more normal sized trees, Gallien took off running. "Wait up!" Tayben followed after him. His legs were quick as a horse's and rocketed him through the underbrush like a speeding arrow, but his steps were so carefully placed and so light that no tracks could be seen. "Gallien!" he called out. "Where are we going?"

He chased after Gallien, jumping over a river and running through a fallen tree whose inside had decomposed. "Wait up, I'm not as fast as you—"

Gallien had stopped in a small glade. Tayben halted from his lightning-like sprint and had no need to catch his breath; the Nymphs' magic within him provided all the energy and necessary functions of the body for him. He had no need to eat, and little need to sleep other than the occasional naps Lekshane allowed them to take.

Gallien knelt down and lifted the branches of a fern. "Come and see," he said. Tayben knelt next to him and saw a white light emanating from under the fern, the source of which was a small glowing flower. "Give me your knife," ordered Gallien.

"Why?"

"Just hand it here." Gallien took the knife, pressed it against his hand, and slit it open.

"What are you doing?" Tayben recoiled. The wound would heal within the hour because of the Nymphs' powers residing in Gallien, but Tayben still worried as he watched the blood drip from Gallien's hand.

"Just watch." Gallien reached forward and touched the flower; his hand jolted back as if he was shocked. But when Tayben looked at his hand, the blood was gone, and the cut was sealed. A flash appeared in Tayben's mind of a glowing white flower. Gallien asked him what was the matter.

Tayben stared at the white flower. "I just . . . I feel like I've seen this before . . . It's like something I saw in a dream . . . I just remember a glowing flower and then something else . . ."

Gallien's body started to shimmer like rippling water and morph into Thephern. "Wake up, Shae!"

"What?"

"Wake up!" Tayben felt a light slap across his face and his eyes shot open from the dream. "Wake up, it's time to go," said Thephern, who knelt next to him on a tree branch high in the forest canopy. "Come on, Shae, everyone else is awake, we're about ready to be on our way." Tayben glanced around and saw Gallien and Ferron talking on the large branch next to him as Chent adjusted the string on his bow.

Tayben stood up. "Yes, my apologies, sir."

Thephern ignored Tayben's words. "Even though you don't need as much sleep now, that hour there will help with traveling today." The two of them jumped over a two-hundred-foot drop to their troop on the adjacent branch.

Ferron Grenzo, one of only two dark-skinned Phantoms, held a short, heavy sword. Picked for his skills in tracking, his attention to detail had increased exponentially as a Phantom.

Chent Vantte carried a bow. With rippling shoulders to pull the string, which required ten times the weight of a normal bow, he could hit a diving sparrow through dense fog and trees two hundred feet away. He hid his thoughts behind his flat face and slanted eyes, remaining quiet for most of the time — the Phantoms always respected his preference for isolation.

"Alright boys," said Thephern as he looked at Tayben and the three others, "let's join up with General Lekshane and the two other platoons."

"We're traveling over the entire Taurbeir-Krons today?" asked Tayben while the group ran through the building-like trees.

"We have to wait for Vaya Irroy," said Thephern, "she's giving us information on our mission."

Tayben hurdled over a perpendicular branch. "Vaya Irroy?"

"Irroy is one of the few people who know of our existence," explained Thephern Luck. "She is Xandria's top courier. She delivers information to and from General Lekshane and Xandria. Because we are constantly on the move, Xandria must know where we are to send us orders. We consult with Ms. Irroy on our course of action for the next month. Because everyone who knew us believes we are all dead, she's our only link to Cerebrian society."

Ferron smiled. "And our rare link to the fairer sex."

Gallien and Tayben smiled and shook their heads as they traversed through the forest. The platoon came to a tree which sat on an island in the middle of a parting brook. On a branch ahead of them stood the two other platoons of five phantoms each, along with General Lekshane. Tayben had finally learned every Phantom's name, but only knew his own platoon well – Thephern, Ferron, Chent, and of course, Gallien.

"About time, boys!" said General Lekshane. A single stream of early morning light pierced through the fog and bounced off his reddish, brown beard. Of course, the fog no longer impaired Tayben's vision, only his enemies'; he could now see farther through fog than he could before even on a clear day. Tayben and Gallien had not yet battled alongside the Phantoms, but Tayben foresaw a change coming soon. *If I can run faster than any other,* he thought, *jump across any tree, and rarely run out of breath, how will the Ferramish troops stand a chance?*

General Lekshane and the rest of the Phantoms sat down on the tree branch and closed their eyes; meditating until they heard a galloping horse half a mile off. When the hooves stopped underneath them, the Phantoms stepped off the branch and fell toward the forest floor. Now that Tayben's senses were heightened beyond comprehension, he examined the world around him as he fell. A bird fluttering above him, a squirrel scuttering in the distance, and below him – a girl with shimmering auburn hair, not five years older than Tayben. She stood next to a sleek black horse with bulging legs and removed a letter from a bag. He landed softly on the black soil below. When she looked back at the forest, a circle of sixteen black Phantoms stood around her. General Lekshane stepped forward and shook her hand. "Always a pleasure, Ms. Irroy."

"And the same goes to you, General," she replied. The black-maned beast beside her shook its head. "Once you cross the Taurbeir-Krons, it will be harder to access you, so here is your list of coordinates and dates when we will send you messenger birds. And just so we don't forget again," she handed Lekshane a document, "do not send us a letter back with the bird. If it arrives back in Seirnkov, we will know our message has been delivered. This will be Xandria's only way to keep you informed of our latest intelligence. The information on your mission is in this document. A group of Ferramish war spies have gathered intelligence on our army's exact locations and are gathering at these coordinates to trade information. They are heavily protected – most likely around three hundred soldiers, and we need everyone there neutralized." General Lekshane thanked Vaya, and she mounted her horse. "I see you have two new members. Mr. Aris, Mr. Shae, the queen sends her thanks to you for defending our fair nation. The best of luck to you all." Vaya kicked her horse, which bolted away through the underbrush faster than any horse Tayben had seen before.

"Soldiers," said Lekshane when she was out of earshot, "we move westward. The Taurbeir-Krons are not for the lighthearted. No men but Northernfolk can traverse them; but we are not average men. We will run straight over the Taurbeir-Krons, seventy miles in twelve hours over hundred-foot snow drifts and through hurricane winds. Try to regulate the energy inside you to stay warm, it shouldn't be a problem. And watch the cliffs. Despite how far we can free fall without consequence, these mountains are tall enough to kill you. Platoons, stay behind your leaders. Leaders, keep up the pace; it's going to be a long day."

The peaks of the Taurbeir-Krons stood jagged, icy, and foreboding all around them. Even in mid afternoon, the cold pierced through the Phantoms' cloaks, forcing them to focus on regulating the energy inside them to keep their internal temperature normal. Within a period of thirty minutes, the company had seen both beautiful cold blue skies, and a fearsome blizzard that hurled stinging pelts of ice at their face. Tayben had not felt the need to rest or slow down in weeks; but the steep slopes of the snowy mountains caused his heart to quicken. Outside of the forest, he felt like the Nymphs' power weakened. The Phantoms were still stronger than any man, but nevertheless strained.

Although he had been training relentlessly with the Phantoms, the snow weighed heavy on his mind. In the eastern foothills of the mountains, Tayben had trained in the canopy to fully embrace the Nymphs' energy in his body. Being able to dart through the canopy gave him an unmatchable advantage in battle. Carrying just a spear, his mind frequently flashed back to his home in Woodshore, the smell of the fire in the smithy.

The home he loved so much seemed so very far away now. But he would protect it. He would do anything to save it from destruction by the Ferramish. The land Xandria had claimed for the Cerebrian people was the perfect place to call home. Whenever towns would struggle, the capital would help by sending in extra grain and meat. People looked out for each other in Cerebria, in Woodshore. He knew that one day he'd make it home, even if the Phantoms wouldn't allow it. *I'll go back,* he thought. *I'll come home and see my family. I'll take my canoe out one more time on the lake to watch the sunset . . . watch the sky turn from pink to twilight. I'll take walks on the shore again or through the forest groves up the hill.* He chuckled to himself. *Or maybe I'll stay away from the forests for a while . . .*

But troubling thoughts also flashed in his mind — blazes of crimson flames and a grand palace. Kyan was his only self who was smart enough to dislike the Ferramish government. The Evertauri, the Council . . . whenever he would think of his disloyal lives, he would run faster over the snow. Yet, with all the knowledge of threats facing Cerebria, he could not bring himself to discuss it with General Lekshane, Thephern Luck, or even Gallien. *No one would believe me,* he thought.

He looked around at the people with whom he would likely die. Thephern, the strict but strong leader. Ferron, the jester in rough times whose voice was sweeter than the birds. Chent, the reserved, unmatched bowman. Albeire Harkil of Tallwood Watch, the First Platoon leader, who seemed to feel a deep connection with the forest. And of course, Gallien, the true friend and the one constant since Tayben had left his little home in Woodshore to join the frontlines.

Tayben fell sick to his stomach thinking about his other lives — the fact that day to day he was betraying these brothers of battle. The soldier knew that in four hours, his other body would sit in a senate chamber hundreds of miles away, listening to the plans to counter his army. *How could I fight against Cerebria? How could I support the Ferramish army? My* "father," *the king, seeks to lay waste to everything I love. And how can I live beneath Seirnkov alongside the Evertauri, plotting to overthrow Queen Xandria and tear this nation down? It seems like it's me against everyone else — myself.* One final thought rang in his ear like trumpets, *I have to fight.*

The Phantoms' black cloaks whitened in the howling snow, and not until far after nightfall did they reach the dense forest of Western Endlebarr.

Although the late summer night hung cool in Western Endlebarr, the forest seemed warm compared to the otherworldly blizzards of the Taurbeir-Krons. The Phantoms had found their coordinates and stood by the bank of a small forest river until they heard footsteps a half-mile away. They could not tell that the Ferrs were there by the actual thump of their boots, but by their effects in the forest around them like an irregular chirp of a songbird. The Phantoms could see their enemy through the mist minutes before the Ferramish would be able to see them. *It feels strange to be the shadow I saw as a normal soldier.*

How strange it will be to look from the eyes of a Phantom onto the frightened eyes of a Ferr, who in turn will see nothing but a blur of shadow before death takes him.

General Lekshane lowered his head and whispered to the battalion. "Leave no man alive, Tronum cannot know how these spies and their battalion died. However, *do not* kill the spies' messenger, nor his bird, until I say so. Third Platoon – Gerreck – lead your troops up into the canopy and form a wide perimeter around this riverbank; signal Second Platoon with numbers of men and horses. Second Platoon – Luck – station yourselves in this tree; wait for the spies to gather here. First Platoon – Harkil – encircle this riverbend, hide in the brush. As soon as the spies begin their meeting, First and Second Platoon, take out their watchmen." A crack of a branch sounded out not a thousand feet away. "We improvise from there. Remember, we have fear on our side. To us, they're normal soldiers; to them we're nothing but shadow."

Tayben's Second Platoon did as they were told and scrambled like black squirrels up the tree. Waiting on its enormous branches, Tayben, Gallien, Ferron, Chent, and Thephern watched eight scouts converge below them, six male and two female, and one teenage boy holding papers, a quill, and a birdcage. Five Phantoms far in the distant canopy signaled them as to how many surrounding troops they counted – three hundred strong.

A spy with pale, scarred skin spoke out fifty feet below them. "Well, I'm happy that all of us found our way here through this bloody forest. Thank the Great Mother for compasses." He continued to address the others concerning the operation as Thephern nodded at Chent Vantte, who drew an arrow, and let it fly through the skull of a guard below. Below him, Chent's brother Si-Chen from the First Platoon bolted silently across the brush and caught the dead soldier before he hit the ground. Tayben's heart began to beat faster.

Chent drew his bow again and a soft whiz rang through the dark and stopped when it sank into another sentry. A blur of black ran over and gently placed the sentry on the ground. Neither the spies, nor the other hundreds of troops in the distance noticed. Another arrow. Another. Gallien reminded Chent not to kill the teenage messenger. Dozens of watchmen rested silently on the ground, and the Third Platoon signaled Thephern that everything had gone to plan. From the tree, Tayben could barely see a group of cavalry in the distance; their commanders wore scarlet red sashes over their torsos. Once Chent's quiver ran out of arrows, his brother yanked them out of the bodies and silently threw them fifty feet back up to him.

Tayben tuned into the conversation below. "–and that shipment is currently traveling on the Kettlerush."

"And how were the Cerebrians managing that in this bloody forest?" asked another.

"One moment." The man turned around. "Captain, are we still on schedule?"

Tayben's stomach plummeted, and the platoon glanced at one another; the forest stood deathly still. "Captain?" called out the man. "Is everything alright here?" No response. He stood up and began walking away from the group and around a tree to locate a watchman.

Chent frantically looked at Thephern Luck, who nodded in response. Chent quickly loosed an arrow and hit the spy in the neck.

From an adjacent tree, General Lekshane whistled; the signal. A large man from the group could barely ask what the source of the sound was before Chent picked him off, and the First Platoon of Phantoms silently shot out of the underbrush and ran swords through the spies' hearts. Tayben's platoon raced to the ground, but before Gallien could muffle the teenage messenger boy holding the birdcage, the boy screamed, "Assassins!"

The Phantoms heard the gallop of horses and the sound of unsheathing swords heading their way as Ferron gagged the boy and tied him to a tree. In a flash of darkness, the Phantoms bolted toward the trees and the enemy. As Tayben ran with his platoon, General Lekshane gestured across the diagonal of his chest, imitating a scarlet sash, indicating the necessity of killing the commanders first.

Gallien sped ahead of Tayben, grabbed a vine in a fraction of a second, and swung himself up to the first layer of colossal branches. He then dove down and drove daggers into the chests of first one and then a second commander on horseback. Streaks of black were the only indication that death was coming. It was not a fight; it was a slaughter. The soldiers all lay dead on their speeding horses with holes in their backs or arrows in their necks. Tayben ran alongside the horses and drove his spear into man after man. They seemed to move in slow motion, their futile attempts to flee or fight back almost laughable.

A horn sounded in the distance, and the Phantoms split into pairs to take the second group of oncoming soldiers. Beads of sweat that formed on Tayben's forehead flew off as he drove his nimble feet through the underbrush.

Intercepting the oncoming troops, the Phantoms ran like water through the battalion of scarlet. Each Ferr barely had time to turn his gaze and meet the shadow which drove a spear into his body. In the corner of his eye, Tayben spotted a scarlet sash on the shoulder of a commander and flew through the air, meeting his sword with a spear blow. The commander was the only person who stopped Tayben's spear from its path. He swung a longsword in an attempt to split Tayben's spear but failed when Tayben rotated his weapon. Twisting the spear, he hurled it into the wrist of the commander, driving between his bones, and causing him to drop his sword. In a flash, Tayben swung his spear around and leaned back, ready to strike; but because his agile body and mind moved so quickly, it was barely noticeable when Tayben paused after recognizing the face of the commander as one he had been acquainted with in the palace as Eston. Tayben pushed the traitorous thought out of his mind and plunged forward.

Ferron swept past Tayben, signaling there were still more retreating battalions; no one could escape alive. He followed Ferron at the speed of a diving hawk; over logs and streams and under giant arching tree roots. Chent and Gallien joined them, followed by Thephern, and the five black blurs raced forward until they came upon a battalion of sixty men. Before attacking, the five perched themselves nearly invisibly on a tree which overhung a large waterfall and a lush ravine. Although it was night, the water sent small glints of moonlight up through the canopy. As Thephern signaled to the four, a soldier from below called out. "They're in the trees!"

Soldiers panicking, the battalion of Ferrs launched fifty spears and arrows with little aim. In a second, the five Phantoms ducked behind the giant branches of the tree, standing up when the arrows had whizzed by their ears like bees. But a lone spear flew up into the canopy a second behind the others, headed straight for Gallien, who was looking at Thephern. Tayben's stomach dropped, and without thinking, his legs sprung him forward and he knocked the spear aside. Landing on a thin branch that snapped, he fell forty feet into the waterfall below.

Icy water soaked into his cloak and slowed his movements. The current of water pushed him repeatedly toward the underwater boulders, spinning him in a vortex at the base of the waterfall. Tayben attempted to fight the current and breathe on the surface but was lucky when he failed – the Ferramish troops had seen him fall and gathered at the base of the waterfall, ready to shoot him if he surfaced. As tiny bubbles shot all around him, the Nymphs' energy inside Tayben tried to compensate for the frigid black water surrounding him. He kicked his legs and tried to reach the surface, but even the strength of a Phantom could not overcome the tons of cascading river. He closed his eyes and went limp, holding his breath and conserving energy until the current could sweep him along the river.

The troops were waiting for a black shadow to emerge from the river, aware that they could not accurately fire arrows at the base of the waterfall. As Tayben's body finally flowed out of the vortex, he took off his cloak, and let it rise to the surface of the river.

Tayben opened his eyes and saw a hand reach in the water and grab his black cloak. Drifting along with the current, he swam down to stay submerged long enough for the Ferrs to think he was gone. After a minute, Tayben grabbed a branch on the riverbank and pulled his head out of the water. The Ferrs had bought his bluff.

Silently, he emerged from the river and removed his boots to prevent the sound of his sloshing feet from echoing through the forest. As he stood up on the grassy forest floor, he caught a sword that his platoon tossed down to him. Three shadows plunged out of the trees, circling the troops. In an instant, Chent's arrows rained down from the canopy and Tayben's platoon slaughtered the remaining soldiers in a blur of darkness.

The bodies lay dead below them as they rendezvoused back to the riverbend where General Lekshane first ordered them to separate. Gallien put a hand on Tayben's shoulder. "Thank you. I owe you my life. But damn it, Tayben, you're just plain dumb sometimes."

Tayben smiled in response.

They came to the riverbend and heard squirming coming from behind a large bush. General Lekshane pulled it aside to reveal the messenger boy whom Ferron had tied up. General Lekshane pulled out a knife and held it to the boy's throat. Trying to hold back tears, the boy pushed his head into the tree trunk behind him. General Lekshane pointed at the birdcage. "You are a Ferramish messenger?"

The boy didn't move but breathed rapidly.

"I would like you to write a letter to your generals stating that your navigators were wrong, and they led you to a far more dangerous part of the forest where your soldiers went mad and fought amongst themselves. You will tell them that you are fleeing before the madmen catch you."

The boy narrowed his eyebrows in hatred, prompting General Lekshane to take his knife and run it slowly across the boy's shoulder, drawing blood. The boy breathed in sharply through his gagged mouth. "Now let me make this clear, boy. We can make this very difficult . . . *very difficult.*" General Lekshane took his knife and tore the boy's ear in half, causing the boy to scream, muffled in his gag cloth. Tayben flinched, feeling as if it was wrong. A flash appeared in his mind of little Ferramish schoolchildren in Aunestauna who looked so similar to this boy in front of him. General Lekshane frowned. "You think I enjoy causing pain, do you?" Tears streamed from the boy's eyes. "You think I like hurting you? I don't, so write the message." After a long silence, the boy eyed his birdcage and agreed to write the letter.

After it was finished, General Lekshane and the Phantoms examined the style, formatting, and codes of the classified Ferramish military letter so that they could forge them in the future, sending false reports to the Ferramish generals – misguiding their troops into traps. General Lekshane grabbed the boy by the hair. "Thank you, young man. You've done the world a great service." He swiftly sliced through the boy's neck like a butcher.He grabbed the birdcage, petted the messenger bird, and placed the letter in its talons. And as the bird fluttered up through the canopy, Tayben's ears could hear the whispering of the enchanted air hanging over a bloodstained forest floor.

TO ONTRAUG AND BACK
Chapter Fourteen

~Morning, September 19th
Seirnkov, Cerebria

Calleneck flinched when he heard a scream echo across Winterdove Lane; Aunika and Mrs. Bernoil stopped their dusting in the kitchen. Giving them a worried glance, Calleneck set down his book on the Bernoil's kitchen table and rushed out the door, followed by Aunika and their mother.

The cobblestone street was wet, and a thick morning fog hung over Seirnkov. Another shout rang out, and the three could tell whose scream it was. *Gilsha,* thought Calleneck. The three ran across the street and down another and saw Gilsha Gold running after a wagon cart pulled by horses. She screamed "No, please! They're my brothers!" On the cart, three little boys reached out with their hands and called after Gilsha. "Don't take them!" she screamed. "You can't! Father stop!" A man whipped the horses to quicken. "Father, stop! You can't leave! I raised them!" Gilsha slipped on the wet cobblestones and fell onto the ground, scraping her arms and knees. Calleneck and Aunika ran up to her as the horses pulled the cart around the corner, disappearing into the bustling capital.

Gilsha knelt on the cold ground crying and the Bernoils stopped above her. Aunika put a hand on her arm and tried to get her to look up. Finally she did, revealing her disheveled face and swollen red eyes. "He took them," she said hopelessly. Her dirty-blonde hair hung over her face and mud from the street stained her white blouse. "My father took them. My baby brothers; he took them."

Calleneck knelt down. "Why?"

She started crying again. "He has been looking for an excuse to take Garner, Gimb, and Gline from me and mum; he wants to take them out of school and give them to the army to train in exchange for money; and now mum is very sick, she's bedridden." She wiped her tears. "He said he doesn't want my brothers to get sick too."

Mrs. Bernoil had just caught up to them and knelt down. "Oh dear." She took Gilsha's arm, which was bleeding from her fall. "Here," she said, "let's get you inside . . . Aunika, check on Mrs. Gold and give her anything she needs; I'm sure she too will be distraught that her sons are gone." Turning to Gilsha she comforted her. "Calleneck and I will take you back to our house, Gilsha. I'll make some soup. Come, we want to help."

Aunika went inside the Gold's house and Calleneck and Mrs. Bernoil took Gilsha to 138 Winterdove Lane, where Gilsha wrapped her arms around Calleneck and cried.

Mr. Otto Bernoil picked two potatoes off a market stand and handed them to Calleneck, who collected the produce in a basket. The price of food had increased since summer to pay for the war. A potato that cost a one eighth argentum now cost a half argentum; most meats could now only be afforded by the wealthy. The markets in Seirnkov felt bleak and gray compared to the vibrant, bustling Ferramish Bazaar; instead, they were littered with weary men and women. Winter would arrive in a few months, and the poorer folk in the capital valley began to worry that they would not make it through.

Shopping at the market with Mr. Bernoil often prompted memories of his life as Kyan, who, day by day had become less inclined to steal. The savings he had acquired from his deals with Zogo Blackblood had accumulated over the years, and Kyan was able to pay for almost everything he needed. Vree Shaarine had warned him once again to leave the capital, for Riccolo had become increasingly angered by Kyan's lack of compliance. But something tore at him, causing him to stay in his rooftop shack in Aunestauna. And at sunset, Kyan began to tolerate the view of the palace to the west on its steep hill overlooking the ocean. Although he didn't admit it to himself, his view of the government was slowly changing, and he had become used to the idea that once every four times he lived the same day, he wore expensive robes beneath those ornate palace ceilings as the prince of Ferramoor.

Meanwhile, Eston had not been able to find out why Prophet Ombern had made such a scene at the Council meeting, and he had felt a strange absence since Raelynn Nebelle had left for Cerebria. Painful thoughts crashed down on Calleneck – day after day, as Tayben, he trained to take down the Ferrs, infiltrate their system, and disrupt communication throughout the Ferramish army.

"Calleneck," called out Mr. Bernoil, stopping his train of thought, "Come here. You see this price? That's three damned argentums for a loaf of bread; three. We may as well try mining in the Seirns for our money, and if we strike gold, we might just be able to feed ourselves."

Calleneck laughed; his father's heavy Cerebrian accent made him sound more like a grandfather than a father.

"Speaking of gold," said Mr. Bernoil as he begrudgingly bought the loaf for three argentums, "your friend Gilsha Gold, is she alright?"

Calleneck shook his head.

"Mr. Gold was a crooked little man, every deal I made with him, he tried to cheat me. I can't decide whether it's better or worse that he abandoned Gilsha and her mother."

"Mrs. Gold hasn't got long, Father."

"I know; which is why your mother would like to take Gilsha in after Mrs. Gold is gone – until she finds work or a husband somewhere . . ."

Calleneck remained silent as they walked through the afternoon market.

"You need to find a job soon too, as well as a wife. Your aunt and uncle and I can't support you forever. At least Aunika now tells me she's studying medicine. But you're nineteen. It would do you good to find a partner in the next few years . . ." Mr. Bernoil hesitated. "I think Gilsha is a good girl."

"She's a good friend, yes," said Calleneck. Mr. Bernoil turned a corner and he followed.

"I may not be young, but I see how she looks at you . . . I would approve. Of course, that also depends on what you think of her." He hadn't gotten the hint.

Calleneck stopped – he hadn't thought much of marriage since the mental barrier to his other bodies vanished. Would only one of his selves ever find a wife? Could he bring himself to raise multiple families? Could he even raise a family if the Evertauri dethroned Xandria? He knew that Eston had an obligation as a prince to marry; as his minds became more and more alike over time, would three of his bodies live alone? But now that he thought about it, Gilsha did make him happy, and he'd liked her from time to time growing up in Seirnkov together. "I guess I hadn't thought of it. But I do enjoy her company . . . quite a bit."

Mr. Bernoil picked up a rose from a basket and examined its petals. "It's simple to grow something once there's a seed; try it and see. It's as simple as giving her a rose." Mr. Bernoil handed the flower to Calleneck. When he touched it, a petal fell off and landed in a cobblestone puddle.

~September 22nd
The Network, Cerebria

Calleneck looked down at one of his many maps and traced his finger along the underground Network path, reading it by the sapphire light of Tallius's Taurimous hanging overhead in the dark tunnel. "It's to the left," he said, and the two turned at a fork in the stalactite-filled tunnel from Seirnkov to Ontraug. President Nebelle had notified Calleneck and Tallius that an innkeeper in

Ontraug had discovered an Evertauri staying at the inn, and he sent them to either sort out a deal of loyalty with him if he was trustworthy, or kill him.

As they walked, Tallius tried to keep up with Calleneck's fast legs. "Why didn't President Nebelle just ask us to take the regular path?"

Calleneck took another sharp turn, causing Tallius to slip and nearly fall on the damp slope. "He wants me to confirm this other way in case there is a cave in." Calleneck ducked under a stalactite, "We need—"

"—a backup plan, I know," said Tallius, his dusty blonde hair brushing up against the same rock as he tried to duck under it too. "I just think it should be right around here." Tallius looked up at the glowing cave bugs on the top of the tunnel. "These weird glowing bugs on the ceiling creep me out." He swirled his Taurimous up at a group of bioluminescent bugs and burned them; the ceiling went dark.

Calleneck looked back. "What did they ever do to you?"

Tallius laughed and shook his head.

Calleneck grinned. "Some traumatizing event in your childhood concerning cave bugs?"

Tallius's shoulder shoved Calleneck into the cave wall, rolling his eyes. "Oh yes." He deepened his voice like an old man's. "When I was but a wee lad exploring in a dark and *very scary* tunnel, a swarm of cave bugs surrounded me, and slowly, started crawling up my skin—"

Calleneck stopped. "Tallius, cut it out."

"—and they began to gnaw at my flesh . . ."

Calleneck put a hand over Tallius's mouth, "Shut up, we're here." Calleneck pressed a hand covered in crimson flame against a rock wall and disappeared through it with Tallius. On the other side, a spiral staircase wound up several stories until stopping at a door.

Tallius frowned. "After you." Tallius followed Calleneck closely. "Hey, so what do you think of me and Lillia?"

Calleneck shushed him. "Do you hear that?"

Tallius put his head against the door. "Yeah . . . sounds like music. Should we go through?"

Calleneck nodded. The two silently turned the doorknob and stepped out onto what seemed to be a dusty wood floor. All around them were ropes and levers, and the room was relatively dark, save for a little light coming from a crack in a curtain; and the music was much louder now. "I thought this came out in the forest *outside* Ontraug."

"That's the usual one, I've never been this way."

Tallius nodded and peeked through the curtain. "Shit." He stumbled back, grabbing onto Calleneck.

"What are you do—"

Tallius pressed a hand over Calleneck's mouth and whispered, "We're backstage in a theater! An orchestra's playing. Get— go— get out." They climbed through a window and out into an alleyway of Ontraug.

The city was as large as Seirnkov and sat at the confluence of the Valley Rivers. Filled with huge clocktowers and riverdocks, the city sat under a thick cloud of fog that night.

Calleneck and Tallius walked through the foggy night along a lamplit riverside street. The heavy mist obscured the far bank of the river and muffled the sound of creaking boats on their docks. Calleneck pointed ahead at a small riverside inn. "There it is," he said to Tallius.

The inn stood above the water on large stilts and connected to two docks, where dozens of boats were tied up for the night. Named *The Misty Wharf Inn,* it served as a resting stop for people traveling on the Valley Rivers throughout central Cerebria.

Calleneck explained the plan to Tallius. "We'll rent a room first and then try to find the innkeeper."

Tallius and Calleneck walked into the inn just as rain began to sprinkle on the cobblestone street. A small fire crackled in the wooden lobby, and around it sat a few travelers on worn couches. Calleneck and Tallius took off their hoods and looked around the inn, seeing a staircase leading up to bedrooms. Before a minute had passed, a short woman approached them. "A room for you, dears? How many days will you be staying?"

Tallius spoke politely. "One night will do."

The hostess nodded. "And do you have a boat with you?"

Calleneck shook his head.

"Well that'll be ten argentums then for a two-bed room," said the woman.

Calleneck counted out ten argentums provided by the Evertauri and handed them to her.

She smiled and pointed up the stairs, "You'll be just up there, second room on the left."

"Thank you," said Tallius. "But before we retire for the night, we were wondering if we could speak to the innkeeper."

The hostess pointed to a door on the other side of the room. "He should be in there."

They thanked the woman and went and knocked on the door. Shuffling and giggling ensued inside as a man's voice said, "Who is it?"

Tallius looked at Calleneck for help. Calleneck spoke up, "Customers. Just a few quick questions."

Whispering and jostling inside followed and then the door opened. A stout woman with heavy makeup and a nearly-exposed bosom exited the room and said, "Go on in."

Calleneck and Tallius entered the room to find a long-haired man buttoning his wine-stained, yellowed tunic. The man looked to be around forty with shoulder-length blonde hair and a thin beard. He chuckled and stumbled into his desk chair, obviously drunk. "Fine ladies of the night we've got here, aye?"

Tallius and Calleneck sat down in chairs in front of the desk and ignored the innkeeper's comment. A gust of cool night air along with a few drops of rain blew through the open window, joined by the sound of creaking boats. Unsure of how to start the conversation, Calleneck skipped introductions and moved straight to the point. "My colleague and I understand that something strange happened a few days ago here."

The man raised his eyebrow. "What are – who are ya two?"

Calleneck spoke again. "What happened?"

The man shook his head and took a swig of wine from a glass on his desk. "You talkin' 'bout that crazy witch girl? I, uh– 'acciden'ally' stumbled in 'er room one night . . . thought me needin' to get to know our lady guests better if you boys follow, eh?" The man laughed out, his stench filling the air with a disgusting odor.

"What did you see?" asked Tallius impatiently.

"Well, she was makin' fire in her hands."

Tallius nodded to Calleneck. *This is him.* "Yes," said Tallius. "Do you remember anything she said?"

"Somethin' 'bout an Eventari." The man began to laugh so hard he nearly fell off his chair. "Sorcerers! Who'da thought? Apparently ole King Gallegore didn't kill them *all* off, now did he? Ch'ya know, I think you're tryin'a take Xandria down if I 'ad to guess."

Tallius leaned forward. "Have you told anyone about this?"

The innkeeper laughed. "No, 'cause I figured I'd make some pretty good money if *you* paid me to keep yourselves—" he whispered "secret."

"We don't trust you to keep it secret," said Calleneck. He looked at Tallius and nodded. He turned back to the innkeeper. "We're sorry about this," he said. In a fraction of a second, Calleneck and Tallius sent crimson and sapphire flames into his abdomen. The innkeeper fell off his chair and onto the ground.

Tallius walked over, felt his pulse, and nodded. "Dead."

The two of them quickly picked up the innkeeper and slid him out the open window into the cold river below. Climbing out the window, they headed back toward the underground entrance through the rainy night.

As they trudged back through the puddles, Tallius stopped Calleneck in a city square, with tall shops on all sides. "Look at that over there," said Tallius, pointing to a wall beside them where a large poster hung.

All able-bodied men ages sixteen to thirty,
report to town hall for inspection and draft processing.
~From fjords to mountaintops,
the land of Cerebria reigns strong, just, and wise~

Tallius put his hand on the wet poster. "We need to take this back to Seirnkov for President Nebelle to see."

Calleneck looked around the square. It was too late in the night for anybody to be out and about, and the misty rain covered them. He nodded. "Do it quickly."

Tallius tore the poster down and stuffed it in his coat. The two silently made their way through the rainy, dark city and back into the underground Network.

~Late Night, September 24th

On their way back through the deep tunnels of the Network, they rounded a stalagmite-covered corner and jumped back, surprised to see another figure up ahead. As they lit up the tunnel with sapphire and crimson light, the narrow face of Selenora Everrose appeared.

"Oh hello Ms. Everrose," said Tallius, "you scared us quite a bit." Tallius dimmed his sapphire flame.

Selenora nodded. "My apologies."

Calleneck raised an eyebrow. "What are you doing this deep in the Network? We're over an hour away from the Nexus."

"Oh," said Selenora, looking around them at the stalactites, "Just doing some exploring . . . President Nebelle had me look at some of these tunnels in case he wanted to use them for food transportation."

Calleneck nodded, but inside he felt something strange. That would have been his job. *There's something she's hiding.*

Tallius sensed it too, but smiled. "Well, I guess we'll see you around."

Selenora smiled. ". . . Of course."

After she had left, Tallius turned to Calleneck. "She gives me the creeps sometimes, ya know that?"

"Like the cavebugs?" said Calleneck with a smirk.

Tallius shook his head and sighed.

With that strange encounter, Calleneck and Tallius continued through the cold and dark tunnels toward the Nexus.

"You know Tallius, I think you could argue the cavebugs are like a starry sky. A bit . . . *romantic* if you think about it. Maybe you could show Lillia . . ."

Tallius smiled, thinking of his blue-eyed, brown-haired hair.

§

~Later that Night

In the Nexus, Lillia Hane's eyes shot open when she heard a knock on her dormitory door. The room was pitch black and cold. Another quiet knock sounded. She looked over at Dalah Bernoil who lay fast asleep. The knock sounded again, and her heart began to race. She stepped onto the cold floor and cautiously moved toward the door with a small white flame in her hand. She crept past Dalah and slowly opened the door to the main tunnels. Tallius Tooble stood before her sporting a big smile and gave her a hug with arms wrapped completely around her.

Lillia shut the door and whispered to Tallius in the candle lit hallway, "You're back! Great Mother, you scared me. How was it?"

Tallius brushed a strand of hair out of her face. "It went fine, I'm just glad to be back." Tallius looked around. "Will Dalah notice if I take you on a little walk?"

Lillia looked back at her door and then back to Tallius. "Not at all."

Tallius smiled and took her hand, leading her down a series of increasingly crooked tunnels. Tallius held a little blue flame out in front of them, and Lillia a white one to help guide the way.

"Where are we going?" Lillia whispered.

"You'll see in a bit," said Tallius. "Cal and I found it on our way back from Ontraug."

After fifteen or so minutes of walking, Tallius stopped and put an arm around Lillia. He extinguished the little blue flame, plunging them into pitch black darkness.

Lillia could tell they were in some sort of cavern, and she pressed herself close to Tallius. "Where are we? What are you—"

"Shhh," hushed Tallius. "Just let your eyes adjust."

Slowly, a thousand little lights began to appear in strings hanging from the ceiling. Lillia gasped as she began to see it. The faint light of uncountable bioluminescent cave bugs dotted the cavern like the spectacular night sky. Lillia smiled and hugged Tallius close for a while, admiring the galaxy of life, twinkling in millions of little blue and white lights.

She turned to Tallius and looked him deep in his eyes. He met her gaze and slowly kissed her, again and again, his heart beginning to race. Her skin was soft like velvet, and his hand traced along her cheek and down to her shoulder beneath her night clothes. She kissed him back, her breaths growing faster and deeper. Another kiss, and the next, and the next.

After some time, out of fear of falling asleep on the cave floor or being caught, they quietly headed back to the Nexus, guided by their own little blue and white flames.

THE GHOST OF A GYPSY
Chapter Fifteen

~Night, September 26th
Aunestauna, Ferramoor

Kyan paced in the dirty Fourth District outside the pawn shop of his dealer – Zogo Blackblood. Afraid to enter, Kyan stalled by kicking a hardened pebble of mud around. He had bought all his food recently, rather than eating stolen bread. Finally, he got enough courage to walk up to the door and open it. There at the back of the shop was Zogo with his ink black beard. The giant stepped forward and Kyan thought the floor was going to fall through with how heavy the man seemed to be. Zogo Blackblood grumbled deep, "You're here early this week. What do you have for me?"

Kyan bit his lip and remained close to the door. "I don't have anything."

Zogo folded his arms. "What do you mean?"

Kyan swallowed and looked at the wall. "I won't be doing business with you anymore."

Zogo stood and Kyan's body tensed, ready to bound out of the door if necessary. Horrifyingly quiet, the man said slowly, "Excuse me?" Zogo took a step toward Kyan. "You agreed to steal for me for two more years after I saved you from getting caught by the Scarlet Guard," he said as he inched closer. "You wouldn't dare short me on our deal."

Kyan stood his ground and looked the man in the eye. "I am."

"What did you just say?!" Zogo bellowed, who looked at Kyan with wide eyes. When the man stood up, Kyan lunged for the door and bounded out, diving into the alleyways of the Fourth District. With adrenaline pumping, he couldn't help but slip a little smile – the weight felt lifted off his shoulders. In the distance, he could hear Zogo Blackblood cursing out the doorway. "There's a reason your whore mother left you for dead on the streets! You're nothing but a bloody rat! A vermin fucker! You– You–"

Zogo's voice faded away, for good, Kyan thought. He made his way home quickly after that, ignoring the strange mutterings or screams of madmen as he passed by them in the night. Before he knew it, he was back in his rooftop shack.

As he settled down to bed, he held his Olindeux and gazed through a small crack in the wooden planks out at the starry night sky. A soft breeze sang him close to sleep when he heard a footstep outside. He slowly sat up and tried to look out at the rooftop when he saw a figure quickly run off the roof. But he knew the face. *Vree?*

Needing to investigate, Kyan silently put on a coat and exited his shack. Spotting Vree's moonlit silhouette in the distance, he quickly followed to see what she was up to.

Eventually she entered a house in the Second District. Kyan dared not follow her in, so he waited on an outcropping of the rooftop. Within a minute, another figure appeared on the rooftop, seeming to have been following Vree as well. It was a girl dressed in black. *Is she with Vree?* Kyan thought as he crouched behind a chimney so as not to be seen. Thirty seconds later, Kyan saw Vree climbing out of a window near the girl and onto the moonlit roof. She pulled a bag off her shoulder with something large and shiny inside.

Kyan's stomach turned cold as the second girl pounced on Vree, punching her in the temple. In a series of hits and kicks, the attacker grabbed the bag and tried to run, but the jump to the next building was too far. Vree lay badly hurt, and the girl drew a knife. Kyan stood up from his hiding place and sprinted at the girl as she cocked back her arm. Running across the tiled roof, he collided with the girl in one hard hit, knocking them both over the edge.

Instinctively, Kyan reached out and grabbed a windowsill a story down, knocking hard against the wall of the building. Hearing the sickening smack of the girl below him, he knew she was gone. Slowly, he worked his way to the ground and grabbed the bag to look inside, where he found a shattered porcelain decoration of some kind. From the dim moonlight, he could pick out a few letters of the name "Gallegore." *Vree can't steal this, she shouldn't.* He looked at the front door of the house, wishing to return it, but he knew she would be punished if she didn't come back to Riccolo with it. Reluctantly, he tossed up the bag to the roof and quickly left the scene before the Scarlet Guard came.

§

~Earlier that Night

Earlier that night, Vree opened an eye and reached under her pillow, taking out a small playing card. The moon shone through a window above her and onto the card. Written on it in scratchy handwriting was a location and instructions—

2309 Laythelt Lane, Second Floor
Decorative Porcelain Shield with Engraving
Back by 3AM

Vree sighed and lifted a leg out of bed. For the past year, she had been nocturnal, waking when the sun set and going to bed when it got light. She set her feet on the cold wood floor and stretched her arms out, ready to start the new night. It was an easy job. Leave, steal, return with loot. Every night a new target. Tonight, leave, steal a porcelain shield, return by three in the morning. Food was largely up to the individual to find. And, as always, if they found any playing cards, they were ordered to steal them as well — Riccolo loved to gamble, but most of all, to swindle. He often made decisions by drawing cards and letting fate decide.

Vree pulled on a shirt, pants, and a leather jacket, stringing a bag around her shoulders. Fixing her hair in her bedroom mirror, she clasped a necklace behind her red, snake-bitten neck; hanging on it was a small silver ornament — an Olindeux from her twin sister, Venessta. Inscribed in the diamond-shaped metal piece were two V's overlapping each other, one upside down. Vree's memory jumped back two years to the desert.

~Two Years Prior

"Vriisha," said Venessta, calling Vree by her Gypsy name in a warm and heavy Southlandi accent. She held the same silver ornament, "this is an Olindeux; lose it not ever. It contain power to guide back to family. We must stick together when we go to Aunestauna; we must find way to get by. But anything is better than here . . . ay, do you listen to me?"

Vree nodded and looked out her tent at rolling dunes of white sand lit by the midnight moon. Her fingers traced the canvas flap of their meager shelter. "Shkro u baan eht aabu shol."

Venessta put her hand on Vree's arm. "You have to practice speaking the Common Tongue; they all speak it in Ferramoor. We go to Aunestauna soon, and when we arrive, we leave our past behind. You will be Vree Shaarine, and we will never have been Gypsies. Otherwise, we won't ever be truly safe from those who rule. Da'an khora, Vriisha . . . practice."

Vree sighed as she looked out at the desert night. "I said — You not need to tell me this all."

"So you promise you keep this?"

Vree looked back at her sister and gently took the Olindeux in her hand. "Eht paraani . . . I promise."

On top of Riccolo's manor, Vree took out the playing card again, visualizing where she needed to go. Bounding across planks over the occasional torchlit street, Vree wound her way into the Third District where she stopped on the top of a theater. A little shack built up from an attic leaned quietly in the night. *Kyan.* Trying to hear if he was there, she stepped closer to it. He stirred inside, and she left the rooftop.

Reaching a large stone house in the First District, she slipped in through an open window. A little girl lay asleep in a bed beside the window, and Vree stopped. Her mind jumped back again. What are you doing, Vriisha?

~One Year Prior

"What are you doing, Vriisha?" said Venessta as Vree pulled her through the vibrant and bustling streets of Aunestauna.

"I've found us a better job!" Vree exclaimed, "five hundred argentums a month, each! Five hundred!"

"You can't just go around chasing everything. I doubt it's safe."

"Trust me," Vree said, "I know what I'm doing," she pulled her twin past a horse and wagon. "We aren't making enough now, especially since the price of our room at the inn went up."

"What's the job?" Venessta barely dodged a crate being pulled by an ox.

"We would be working for a shipping company that sells textiles to Parusemare."

"Who offered you the job?"

"His name is Riccolo, he definitely knows what he's doing."

Vree brushed her hair out of her olive skin face and briefly picked up a doll at the end of the girl's bed. She walked out of the girl's bedroom and into a hallway from which she could see firelight and the shadow of a man reading on a chair. She peered over the edge of the railing at what she assumed to be the girl's grandfather, an old man with a ring of white hair; the man only had one leg. Silently, she opened the doors of various rooms looking for a porcelain shield. *What's the point of a shield if it's made of porcelain? It can't be solid porcelain . . . can it?*

Vree opened the door to another room, which was bare, except for the prize strung onto the far wall. She closed the door behind her and traced a finger along the pure porcelain's smooth edge until her almond eyes settled on an engraving at the top.

Presented to Sir Laythelt by
His Highest Emperor and King Gallegore Wenderdehl
For Bravery and Courage during The Battle of the Endless Night

Vree whispered to herself, "This is from *the* King Gallegore." *I can't steal this . . .* Her reflected face stared back at her in the porcelain, almost like an image of her twin.

~Eleven Months Prior

They were standing in a dark room in Riccolo's manor, surrounded by Nightsnakes.

"Vriisha, don't do it," whispered Venessta. "It's not worth it. We can run away."

Riccolo smiled with a snake in his hand. "You can never run from me. No matter what, I'll find you." Riccolo carried the snake to Vree. "It will only hurt for a few weeks . . . after that, the venom subsides."

Vree snapped out of her reflective state and gently pulled the shield of porcelain off the wall. It was thin but heavy. The sheer amount of money this was worth could support her for years to come. I could take it for myself . . .

~Ten Months Prior

"Come on!" Vree yelled back at her sister. She jumped onto the back of a horse with a bag of Riccolo's treasure strung around her back. The Aunestaunean street was crowded as usual, and Venessta ran through it and jumped onto the horse, carrying a similar bag.

Together, they rode through a maze of streets and out into the countryside, carried nearly thirty miles by their horse. When they stopped for the night to make camp near Willowwood, the twins fell asleep with a feeling of safety – a comfort they had not enjoyed for some time. Vree drifted seamlessly to sleep, ready for a new life in Oakfoot; but her eyes shot open when a hand with a rag closed over her nose and mouth.

She awoke many hours later back in Riccolo's Manor. Her sister was tied in a chair next to her and Riccolo sat in a dark corner sharpening a knife.

Vree took the shield and shoved it into her bag. *I can never escape,* she thought, *I have to do this . . . I have to get her back.* She exited the room, taking one last look at the veteran below who had helped unite the continent of

Endellia under King Gallegore. She continued on silently down the hall, into the little girl's room, and out the window. Once on the roof, she pulled the bag with the shield off her shoulders, wanting to see it again in the moonlight.

A fist from behind rammed into her temple and knocked her down. The girl who punched her swooped in to steal the shield. She too wore a leather jacket but was masked, as many thieves in the city were. Vree grabbed the girl's ankle, who tried to dive away from her with the porcelain shield. The masked thief kicked her nose and ran away across the roof but stopped on the edge when she realized the next building was too far away to jump. Vree stood up, dizzy and prepared to fight for the porcelain, but her body went cold when the masked girl cocked her arm back with a knife in her hand. Just as she began to throw it toward Vree, a dark figure rammed into the masked girl, knocking both the knife and her off the house to the stone street below.

Vree ran forward on the roof and leaned over the edge. The girl lay sprawled on the street below with blood gathering around her head. The person who had come to Vree's aid had clung onto a windowsill to stop his fall. The figure hopped to another windowsill, then jumped down to the street below, grabbing the bag with the shield. To her surprise, the figure threw the bag up to her on the roof. Vree's heart sank when she caught it and heard dozens of shattered pieces of porcelain clatter in the bag. The figure below looked familiar . . . *Kyan*? Just as quickly as he came, he vanished behind a building. A steady stream of blood from her nose dripped on the bag as she held the shattered shield on the roof.

When she returned to the manor, Riccolo was waiting for her in the moonlit foyer. His glare turned sour when he heard the jingling of porcelain fragments in a bag. With blood from her nose dripping down her whole front, Vree dropped the bag of porcelain on the floor.

"Care to . . . explain, Ms. Shaarine?" Riccolo's stared at her like a snake waiting to bite.

"There was another thief," said Vree with her head down.

"I assume that's why you're bleeding."

Vree nodded.

"Well I'm going to make you bleed a lot more than that." Riccolo paced around her like a hawk ready to dive and snatch its prey. "One small item . . . and you couldn't bring it back in one piece."

"It's still worth hundreds if not thousands of argentums," said Vree.

"Well it's worth a hell of a lot less now that you've shattered it!" he screamed. "Oh, but I'm sure that this other thief was quite tough to handle."

"She was waiting for me on the roof."

"She?" he laughed.

"She threw a knife at me!"

Riccolo stopped circling her. "This thief had a bad aim, did she?"

". . . Someone else stopped her and pushed her off the house."

Riccolo kicked the bag of porcelain. "Oh, Great Mother, please tell me it wasn't Kyan who swooped in to save the day." Riccolo smiled in Vree's silence. "It was, wasn't it? He went with you to steal it because, on the way there, you went to his shack to fuck him! Didn't you, you little slut!" He grabbed Vree and threw her to the floor.

Tears welled up in her soft, brown eyes as she tried to get back up. "I didn't do anything, I swear."

"You lying bitch!" Riccolo drove his foot into her already bleeding face. "Whores like you are all the same; doesn't matter who he is, as long as he's sleeping with you!"

Vree drove her nails into Riccolo's arm, drawing blood. "You monster!" Blood streamed down her face and onto the floor. "You sick creature!"

"Oh, Vree, now my feelings are hurt."

Vree kicked the bag of porcelain away from him. "Go to hell."

He held her and whispered in her ear. "You know what happens when you fight me . . . How will I ever be able to trust you?"

~Ten Months Prior

"How will I ever be able to trust you?" said Riccolo as he paced between the Shaarine twins who were each tied to their own chair facing the other. Another Nightsnake, Bay, stood watching. Riccolo traced a finger along his discolored facial scar. "I gave you a home, and food, and a life free from your wretched past, and what do you do? You try to escape . . . Why girls, that hurts my feelings."

"You're a snake!" yelled Venessta.

"Fitting, isn't it?" laughed Riccolo.

"One day someone will drive a knife through your heart," said Vree.

Riccolo smiled. "Is that so?" He pulled out a deck of cards from his cloak and shuffled them as he paced. "I don't accept disloyalty. You two need to be punished . . . but how will I ensure that this won't happen again? Now, seeing you two are compelled to rebel together, the best option would be to eliminate one of you from the picture."

Vree stared at the playing cards in Riccolo's four-fingered hand.

Riccolo chuckled to himself. "I've learned recently that there is a highly profitable business emerging in the southern slave trade – back where you two are from in the Southlands . . . They're taking Gypsies like you for a nice price." Riccolo stood over Venessta. "I think it's unfair for anyone but you two to decide your fate." He fanned out the cards. "Whoever draws the lower number I sell to the Zjaari slave traders . . . Choose."

Venessta shook her head with tears running down her cheek.

"Fine," said Riccolo, "I'll draw for you." His fingers grazed over the cards and snatched one. Riccolo smiled and showed them, laughing, "Seven . . . right in the middle." He turned toward Vree. "This makes things interesting."

Tears streamed down the sisters' faces and when Riccolo offered the fanned-out cards to Vree, she shook her head.

"You two are just no fun, are you?" Riccolo whipped out a card and smiled. "Ten."

"No! I'll do anything for you," Vree pleaded. "I'll do anything. Just don't take her away."

Riccolo signaled to his henchman. "Gag this one, she talks too much." The Nightsnake quickly tightened a rag around her mouth.

Venessta struggled in her bonds. "You can't do this. We're sisters." Tears streamed down her face. "We'll obey you and we won't try to escape. I promise."

Riccolo shook his head. "Your promises mean shit to me. I'm sick of your lying." A slight smile overtook his face as an idea dawned on him. "In fact, I think the slave traders would be quite appreciative of me if I cut out your tongue before you get the chance to lie to them."

Venessta's eyes opened wide with horror. "No! Please!"

"Bay, grab her jaw and hold her mouth open." ordered Riccolo. The henchman walked over and wrestled Venessta's face as she tried to get away and wrenched her jaw wide.

Vree cried out, gagged. It wasn't real, it couldn't be. She sobbed and looked away as her sister screamed. She heard Riccolo's knife slice through flesh and Venessta's scream pounded on her ear. The sound slowly filled with bubbling from the blood pouring out of her mouth. The Nightsnake held Venessta still as she cried out in pain, and Riccolo stepped toward Vree. Vree refused to look up at him, sobbing. Riccolo tossed a lump of bloody flesh on Vree's lap, making her cry even more. He picked up her chin as Venessta continued to scream.

"You want your sister back?" he said to Vree. "You make double the money for me that I get from selling her, you can take half and buy her back . . ." he sniggered to himself, "if you can find her." Riccolo turned and looked back at Venessta's bloody face. ". . . What a shame it had to all happen like this . . . if you had only listened . . ."

§

~Before Dawn

Riccolo closed the door to Vree's bedroom. It was four in the morning – almost time to go eat dinner and sleep, but he still had his second meeting with *the client.* Riccolo left the manor and walked to the designated abandoned house a few blocks away in the Fourth District.

When he arrived, the client was already there. Sitting at a table beneath a boarded window, the man was tall with a stern face. "Hello, sir."

Riccolo nodded back at the man and sat at the table.

The man spoke in a hushed voice. "All the information you need is in this letter here." The man handed Riccolo a piece of parchment. As Riccolo read it, the man added, "If you have one of your thieves steal it, you must not tell them the reason for my request. Create a lie for why I need to steal it. Say I want it to impress a woman or something of the sort. And keep in mind what will happen if you break a deal with me . . . I can bring down all of this with a simple word."

Riccolo set the parchment down, which had the man's signature on it. There was nothing unusual in the man's desire for discretion, in fact he was surprised he even felt the need to mention it. "When do you need it done?"

"The robbery must be within the month, but you must notify me of the night you plan to do it. If you are successful in the robbery, I will inform you the night for the assasinations. Do you agree to the request and your compensation?"

Riccolo signed the contract – not Riccolo, but *Kyan.* He smiled and shook the man's hand. "I don't normally take chances, *but this deal, I cannot refuse."*

Back at his manor, Riccolo's sighed as he walked over to his bedroom window where his breath was visible in the cold morning air. "Who to send, who to send?" he whispered to himself.

He took off a glove and examined his yellowed, cut-off finger. "Kyan . . . I want him . . . but how to make him comply?" He tapped on the glass. "There's something different about him . . . something bizarre."

EVERROSE
Chapter Sixteen

~Noon, October 1st
The Network, Seirnkov, Cerebria

Alone in his study, Madrick unlocked a drawer from his desk. Inside it, a small white flower glowed. Madrick found a needle on his desk and pricked his finger, drawing blood. He reached forward and touched the flower; instantly, the blood disappeared as an electric shock ran through him. *If you're still with us, where are you?* he thought to himself. A tear formed in his eye, and he quickly wiped it away.

President Nebelle flinched as a knock sounded on his door. "Yes?"

"Our noon meeting Madrick?" called the voice of Sir Mordvitch Aufenschiess from behind the door.

Madrick placed the flower back into the desk. "Yes, come in."

First into the room came Mordvitch, followed by Selenora Everrose and Grennkovff Kai'Le'a, whose foreign surname came from his Shallow Green Islander lineage – as did many with ebony skin. The silver fire candles flickering in Madrick's office began glowing deep violet, crimson, and green, shifting between colors as each of the three powerful sorcerers entered.

"Selenora, Grennkovff." Madrick nodded to them as they took seats in old stone chairs. Selenora's long dark hair streamed over her soft white skin, starkly contrasted by Grennkovff's dark stature. Mordvitch shut the door behind them and then placed a set of papers on Madrick's desk.

"Mordvitch," said President Nebelle, "good to see you after these last few weeks." He looked down at the papers. "But these reports I've been receiving from you don't look good, do they?"

"I am aware, sir," said Mordvitch. "I suspect the queen has been recruiting more and more from the Sister Cities, not much from Gienn yet, but heavily from Ontraug and Roshk. My guess is that she will soon start diverting supplies to Port Dellock."

"She already has," said Grennkovff. The candles sent out little flashes of dark green light. "I just returned from the fjords; supply operations are in full effect in Port Dellock. The Cerebrian army is backing off in Endlebarr, and there have been more recruitments to their navy."

"How do we know?" asked Mordvitch.

"Bernoil and Tooble went to Ontraug; they brought back this poster that hung in a square." Madrick pulled a flyer out from a cabinet that read –

All able-bodied men ages sixteen to thirty,
report to town hall for inspection and draft processing.
~From fjords to mountaintops,
the land of Cerebria reigns strong, just, and wise~

Mordvitch pointed to the bottom corner of the paper, "*Sila Morya,* the seal of the navy . . . I fear they're loading those Gelltzkreik Devices onto their ships. They could rip apart Aunestauna with cannonfire with little to no warning."

"The Ferrs don't stand a chance against Xandria." said Selenora. "Their cause is hopeless. I don't see how Tronum comes out on top."

Madrick scratched his beard and sighed. "Which is why we need to help."

Mordvitch pointed to the paper beneath the one Madrick held. "There's more. I wrote that copy of the September file given to me by the queen. It confirms that the highest members of the Jade Guard have been sent to Roshk."

"For the weapons," said Grennkovff, "the explosives you want us to destroy when they're shipped through the Great Gate."

"Not exactly. However, we now know the date when we can attack at the Great Gate."

"And are we notifying the Ferramish government?" asked Grennkovff as he adjusted his seat, making the whole thing creak.

"We can't," said President Nebelle.

"Why?"

"Because I don't trust Tronum." Madrick leaned back and traced his fingers on the wooden edge of his desk. "It's better that he remains ignorant for now. He'll claim his forces took out the gate if we destroy it, which will help keep us undercover."

"I see," Grennkovff replied. He turned to Mordvitch. "But concerning Roshk, you said I was not fully correct?"

"Indeed. I believe the queen is after something different." Mordvitch paced slowly. "There was a confirmed break into the Network by the Jade Guard in the Goblin capital. They raided the library there. It was actually the week you were gone in the fjords. Take a look at the summary."

Selenora leaned in slowly. "What is she after?"

The candles in the room again began flickering between all four colors. Mordvitch turned to her. "I don't know, but I think *he* does." He was pointing at President Nebelle.

Madrick paused for a long moment, and all the candles in the room glowed silver. "I have my suspicions, yes."

Mordvitch waited for him to continue but was answered by silence. He looked at the small spinning silver instruments on the bookshelves of the study. "You know, Madrick, you didn't used to keep secrets from me." Madrick seemed struck by the boldness of his friend's words. "You've changed . . ."

Before Madrick could respond, another knock sounded on the old Goblin door. Mordvitch, breaking eye contact with Madrick, walked over to the peephole in the door. "It's your daughter," he said to President Nebelle.

Madrick's gaze turned sour, but it was obvious he tried to hide it. "She's back a day early . . . let her in."

Mordvitch opened the door and Raelynn walked in, her white-blonde hair catching every hue of the dancing candles. "Hello, Sir Mordvitch." She turned to see the others and greeted them as well. ". . . I didn't mean to intrude on a meeting." Her voice was cold and natural now that she was back in Cerebria and no longer pretending to be someone she wasn't.

"It's no trouble," said Mordvitch, "We were already finished talking . . . I trust your travels were safe."

Raelynn nodded. "The winds from Aunestauna to Catteboga were strong; made up a day's time. I just dropped my bag off at my dormitory and headed over here."

"Well, it's good to have you back." Mordvitch half-smiled, and there was obvious stress in his eyes.

Raelynn looked to her father who had hardly moved in his chair. "Thanks for the warm welcome."

Madrick set down his papers and looked up at Raelynn. "We are months away from our initial assaults on Xandria, and you leave. You leave *to Ferramoor*! As my daughter, you have an obligation to help lead this cause."

"I was trying to find anything I could about mother," said Raelynn. "Just because you've given up trying to find her doesn't mean I have to . . . You obviously have more important things on your mind."

"You can't understand what family means," said Madrick.

Raelynn folded her arms. "And *you* do? Shonnar took care of me as a child while you were running the Evertauri and— and spending all your time mentoring—" Raelynn had almost forgotten Selenora was in the room. Madrick stared at her without expression. Expecting a retort, Raelynn waited . . . but there was no response. "Father, is Shonnar out today? I haven't seen him."

The silver flames of the candles in the room dimmed. "I didn't write to you because I didn't think you'd come back . . . I thought it was best you didn't know."

Mordvitch raised his eyebrows in shock. *"You didn't tell her, Madrick?!"*

Raelynn stepped back. "Tell me what?" She looked around the group. "What do you all know that I don't?"

There was a long pause. "Your brother is dead," said Mordvitch.

"What?" Raelynn stuttered and crossed her arms. The candle flames turned to black smoke. "W— what are you talking about?"

Madrick looked down at his hands. "He was murdered by Klytus Kraine, who was executed shortly after his death." The candles flickered back.

Raelynn's heart pounded and a frog formed in her throat; her eyes glazed over with a film of tears. She could tell everyone in the room was serious. But she couldn't— it couldn't have happened. "How long ago?" she said, barely speaking and trying to keep her composure.

"Almost a month."

Tears started to drip down Raelynn's red cheeks. "And you didn't tell me?"

The room stood in silence as Raelynn grappled with the reality of Shonnar's death. She had just seen him before she left. He had hugged her goodbye. He had told her to come back safely to him . . . He couldn't be gone. "How— how did—" Her mind was turning over itself and she could barely think. "How could he have been killed he— he was strong, and he shouldn't have been alone." Raelynn was stuck between reality and disbelief, where a floodgate of tears was being held back. "How could you have let him get killed?"

Madrick looked up at her with narrowed eyebrows. "I've been grieving more than you can imagine . . . You think I could have prevented this?"

Raelynn's face turned red. "If you had cared about us! You would've been there, you would've been more watchful, you could've helped."

"I raised you two!" yelled Madrick.

"You raised HER!" Raelynn's finger pointed directly at Selenora. *"She* was all you ever cared about!"

"Raelynn—" She was out the door before he could respond. The room was silent.

Mordvitch turned to Selenora and Grennkovff with pursed lips that held back the full onslaught of angry words he wanted to share. "Leave us, I'm going to talk to the President *alone."*

Selenora and Grennkovff obeyed without a word, leaving the study and shutting the door behind them. The distant sound of crying and running footsteps faded away as Raelynn vanished out of sight.

§

Raelynn wiped the tears from her eyes as she ran down the hallway. The yellow, ever-burning torches of the Goblin tunnels flickered out for a moment as she passed. Although it was always night below Seirnkov, the corridors of the Nexus were cold and quiet. She spun around when someone whispered her name. Looking back, the corridor was empty. She continued to walk forward. A whisper like a long hiss slipped over the stone, "Raelynn!" She stopped again. Nobody in sight.

She turned a few more corners and down three flights of stairs to her dormitory floor. Walking past a group of Evertauri talking in the corridor, she opened up her room and slammed the door behind her. She felt so weak, so defeated. She collapsed onto the small bed in the corner of the room and cried into her hands. He couldn't be gone. Shonnor wouldn't have left her alone in this world. He had to be out there somewhere.

Raelynn's vain attempts to rewrite the truth only made the reality so much worse to let in. But it kept on coming, seeping into her like cold winter air that she couldn't hide from. The one person who had been by her side . . . he was really, truly gone.

She wept for some time before a gentle hand knocked on her door.

"Raelynn?"

She knew the voice, and it was about the last person she wanted to see.

"Raelynn," said Selenora from outside, "I just want to talk." Raelynn didn't respond, but Selenora quietly entered the room and sat down beside Raelynn on her bedside. "I'm so sorry you had to hear that today."

Raelynn could tell she was looking at her.

"I know you've never liked me. Your father gives me attention I've known he doesn't give you. He's treated me how he should've treated you, and treated you how he should've treated me . . . You were right when you said he should've been closer to Shonnar. Maybe if he were . . ." Selenora stopped.

Raelynn's crying had slowed down, and she pulled her face up from her hands to look at Selenora. "Have you lost family? Do you know what it feels like?"

Selenora thought for a moment. "My father and older brothers were killed by the Ferrs in the war. But I was orphaned here in Seirnkov not long after; then your father took me in. So, it's not as fresh."

Raelynn sniffed. "My father was supposed to keep him safe . . ."

Selenora looked at the ground. "Your father has changed." Selenora gazed back up at Raelynn and stood. "Take a walk with me . . . I want to show you something."

Raelynn wiped her eyes with the sleeves of her cloak, and nodded, following her out the door. Selenora led her down a few Goblin hallways of intricate stone, leading further away from the Nexus and into the Network. After a few minutes, they were passing beneath stalactites and walking through bioluminescent caverns. Here, the tunnels moved with the terrain of the underground; they winded and plunged and rose, taking them through caverns and across subterranean streams.

They had been walking for long enough that Raelynn wondered if Selenora was lost. "Where are you taking me?" she asked.

"To my garden," Selenora replied. Raelynn looked visibly confused. The tears had dried on her cheeks and her hair was slightly disheveled. Selenora continued to walk. "Your father took me there when I was little to train. I don't remember it well . . . and there's a reason for that."

Raelynn followed her around a bend in the tunnel. "What do you mean?"

"Your father isn't what you think he is . . . I had begun to figure out ways to use magic that he didn't completely understand. The first time I remember, it happened here." Selenora had stopped in the middle of the pathway in between two stalagmites. She placed her hand on the wall and spread bright crimson flames over it. The wall of rock began to shimmer. "Everything will make sense on the other side." Selenora stepped through the stone like it was mist, and Raelynn followed.

They had entered a cavern that went on endlessly, seeming to have no height or walls. The only light came from a faint red glow in the distance which illuminated the stone in front of them.

"What is this place?" whispered Raelynn.

"It's where I've let my magic run freely. That day when I was young, when I was with your father, I created roses from my Taurimous."

Raelynn turned to Selenora. "Why would that matter? We can create any objects we want with our Taurimous if we focus enough, they're just fake."

Selenora nodded and pointed out into the darkness. ". . . and *these were real.*"

As Raelynn's eyes adjusted, she saw that up ahead, illuminated by the soft crimson light, small bushes appeared in the dark, and farther on, trees grew. From the smallest riverside sapling to towering pines. Selenora began to walk deeper into the cavern, and Raelynn followed. She recoiled, however, at the touch of grass on her feet. She hadn't remembered taking her shoes off. A strange force filled the air and coursed through their feet whenever they stepped. The two walked on the blanket of grass and through the subterranean forest, always toward the crimson light.

"You created all of this?" asked Raelynn.

Selenora nodded and continued to speak. "Your father grew scared of what I could do, so he began to erase and play with my memories. He tried so hard to keep me down and suppress my strength once he realized the gift I possessed."

"Why would he erase your memories?" asked Raelynn. "Is that something someone can even do?"

"Once again, your father is not all you think he is. He's scared of magic, what it can do. He doesn't understand the true power of it, all the good we could do." The leaves and needles on the trees seemed to move toward Selenora as she walked, reaching out to their creator. "If we just had the opportunity to show the world what we can truly become, we could bring peace — *true* peace. Your father just doesn't have the strength to do what's needed."

The light became brighter up ahead, and then they were there; beneath the canopy of trees, a bed of roses lay before them glowing bright crimson, at the center of which sat a swirling pool of light. Selenora produced a crimson flash of light and cut her finger. Slowly, she reached down with her bleeding wound and touched the roses. The blood and cut vanished.

Raelynn gazed in shock. "What did you just do?"

Selenora smiled. "It's the power of healing. The power of life— creating life. Look around you. This is what magic can do; this is what your father is scared to use. You and I are the two people that know your father the best. We can make the change that he can't make. Imagine what we could do together, unlocking the secrets of the magic that flows through us. I've learned to do wonders, things your father could only dream of . . . I could bring your brother back . . ."

Raelynn's stomach dropped. She couldn't find the words. Was she serious? How could that be possible?

Selenora gazed into the pool of light. "We could fix what had to be done and do that for everyone whose mind we need to change."

Raelynn stepped back. "What are you talking about?"

"With our powers, we can set aside everyone who would get in the way of the bright new world we could create— your father, the Council of Mages. While the kingdoms war and stretch themselves thin, we could grow stronger. We could establish the Age of Sorcerers and bring our friends back once we've accomplished it."

Raelynn felt her blood turn cold, and she took another step back. She began piecing it all together, and slowly, she became terrified of the monster standing before her. "Shonnar knew this, didn't he? Shonnor knew this and tried to stop you . . ." Raelynn looked at Selenora's face glowing in the crimson light from below. ". . . you killed my brother . . ." Raelynn's face drained of color.

Selenora sighed. "Raelynn . . . you fail to see the bigger picture. This is all for the best." Selenora peered into Raelynn's eyes with a hypnotizing stare. "I have half the Evertauri on my side already. They're ready at a moment's notice. The revolution is coming, and *you* are the missing piece."

Raelynn tried to turn away but felt her body fight against itself and stay put. Selenora's voice almost seemed to be inside her head instead of coming from the figure before her.

"Join me and we can save this world and bring back our loved ones from the dead. We can do the work they're not willing to do. They will be reborn into a grateful world where sorcerers have taken their place as rulers and keepers of the peace."

Raelynn struggled, trying to produce her Taurimous and get away; but she couldn't. *What is this?* Raelynn looked back at Selenora. *You can hear my thoughts.*

Selenora's face grew fearful.

Raelynn shook her head, realizing it all. *I'm not actually here; this isn't real.* Raelynn fought against the spell on her. "Get out of my head."

"You're not going to win this Raelynn. Join me and we can finish this together."

Raelynn screamed. "GET OUT OF MY HEAD!" With a final push, she willed her way out of Selenora's spell and back into her own mind and vanished from the cavern.

§

Selenora opened her eyes, looking at the stone room around her. Beside her, Grennkovff stood up. "What's wrong? What happened?"

Selenora's face was filled with fear. "I— I didn't think she'd be able to push me out of her head . . . no one's ever done that."

"What do you mean? What is she doing? Where is she?"

Selenora tried to catch her breath. "She's going to warn them! We need to start the attack now!" Selenora touched her black cloak and it slowly turned to crimson, as did Grennkovff's. A horrifying mask of Taurimous also appeared over his face. "Our Evertauri have the signal. Get to the Nexus before Raelynn does! I'll try to hold her off. Gather our followers and kill everyone you can."

Grennkovff nodded and rushed out the door, while Selenora closed her eyes, trying to wind her way back into Raelynn's head.

§

Raelynn opened her eyes and looked around her dormitory room — she hadn't left. Her heart was beating out of her chest, and her body felt chilled to the bone. Trying to remember everything that had happened, she bolted to her feet. *I need to warn them!* Raelynn opened her door and headed for— for— what would be closest? *The Nexus.*

Raelynn turned and sprinted down the hallway, fingertips ready to launch a spell at any moment. Raelynn turned a corner and — no, the other way — where was she? What was the extent of her plan? *Get out of my head!* yelled Raelynn at Selenora, feeling her jabbing into her mind.

Stop this Raelynn, join me and—

Raelynn pushed her out of her head with every bit of magic she could conjure. She bounded down a staircase and into another hallway.

You could have your brother back.

YOU KILLED HIM! Raelynn's legs gave out under her as Selenora toyed with her mind. Raelynn tried to get up, but it felt like gravity was pulling her in all different ways. She tried to hold onto the wall, but she couldn't stand. *GET OUT OF MY HEAD!* Raelynn's vision was swirling, and she felt the world tipping around her in her head. She couldn't run forward. The Nexus was so close. She needed to tell them, but she couldn't open her mouth to scream. She felt helpless, like a puppet on Selenora's strings. But Raelynn fought back harder, pushing the spell back. Raelynn needed to get into Selenora's head. It was like keeping back a flood, but she pushed back until the connection snapped and she was in Selenora's head. Raelynn severed the connection and opened her eyes.

Jumping to her feet, she sprinted toward the Nexus. It was right there. She pounded her feet against the stone floor as she rushed forward into the subterranean atrium. Bounding through an entrance to the floor of the Nexus, she skidded to a halt as a masked sorcerer in a crimson cloak marched into the Nexus with green sparks shooting from his feet with every step. Dozens of Evertauri stood doing their daily business as Grennkovff rushed to the center of them. Raelynn only had time to shout, "Everybody down!"

A massive flash of green light roared through the Nexus. A disk of Taurimous split through the air in all directions as Raelynn ducked underneath it. Screams filled the air as bodies were sliced through and blasted apart. The explosion threw Raelynn's body back into a wall. Her vision collapsed for a moment, then returned. She couldn't breathe, but she stood up to see the carnage before her. In the center of it all stood Grennkovff Kai'Le'a in a crimson cloak with green fire circling his hands. And out from the tunnels, marching into the Nexus with sparks flying from their footsteps, came hundreds of masked sorcerers.

THE BATTLE FOR THE NEXUS

Chapter Seventeen

~Noon, October 1st
The Network, Seirnkov, Cerebria

"Alright," said Sir Kishk Kaubovfier, the short Evertauri trainer with the lazy eye. "It's noon, so let's get started. Calleneck and Tallius have done this exercise before, but the rest of you are new to it."

Calleneck, Tallius, Lillia, and Dalah, along with two other Evertauri stood in a semicircle around Kishk. Filling the dark cavern in which they stood was a massive Goblin building from years ago. It had most likely served as a school or collection of living quarters when inhabited years ago. Half in ruins, the marvelously crafted building stood four stories tall and connected with many other tunnels to the Nexus. Sir Kishk had asked Calleneck and Tallius to join them in a game of "Find and Stun" to demonstrate for the newcomers to the Evertauri.

"The rules are as follows," said Sir Kishk, who stood only a little over five feet tall. "You will enter the building one by one and hide until I send out the signal, then you will try and find your team and disable the other. I said *disable,* not hurt – I'm looking at *you two,*" he said to Calleneck and Tallius.

Kishk paced in a circle. "Use non-burning flames and sparks to fight each other. If you hit your opponent with your Taurimous and they can't fight back, you win, and the loser exits the building and comes back down here. Last one standing wins for their team. It's combat skill practice."

Sir Kishk looked to Calleneck and Tallius. "Since you two are veterans of this 'game,' I want you to be on separate teams – you're captains." Calleneck and Tallius smirked at each other.

Calleneck noticed him eyeing Lillia and before he opened his mouth, Calleneck blurted out, "I call her."

Tallius glared at him and Calleneck grinned. Tallius chuckled and mouthed, *"Watch your back."*

Calleneck laughed and Lillia shook her head with a grin. Lillia had since been appointed to a position overseeing supply shipments. Her training in sorcery from Kishk had gone well, and she had advanced far more quickly than most did.

"Fine," said Tallius, "*I choose Dalah.*"

Dalah furrowed her eyebrows and smiled. "Oh, don't make that seem like I'm a burden."

Tallius laughed. "Of course not, we're gonna run circles around those two."

They selected the remaining two; Calleneck's team member – Eddri – a blonde boy who currently had the hiccups, and Tallius's – Vorrov – a man with a scar running from his eye to his chin. Kishk nodded. "Alright, let's have the ladies enter first, and then you boys can figure it out."

Calleneck was the last to enter the Goblin ruins. Walking up a staircase in near pitch-black darkness to not give away his location, he stepped over the rubble from fallen pillars and walls. He turned into a side hallway and then into a small alcove between two pillars. Thirty seconds later, a bright purple light filled the entire cavern, the signal from Kishk to begin.

Calleneck closed his eyes and strained his ears to try and hear for anything. Tempted to move, he decided to wait until – there it was, a hiccup in the distance. Calleneck chuckled and rolled his eyes – Eddri was close. Slowly, he crept out into the hallway and followed the faint noise of hiccups. After a few turns he settled on the room where Eddri was. He stepped in and the boy gasped.

"Hey, it's me," Calleneck reassured him.

Eddri sighed. "Do you know where anyone is yet?"

"No, you're the first." Calleneck dropped to the floor when he saw a stream of gold light blast through the room.

Turning around, Calleneck saw Dalah launch a golden fireball at him. Not having time to put up a shield, he rolled over and dodged it as Eddri panicked and tried to run past Dalah, who tripped him with a golden stream of Taurimous. Calleneck stood up just as Dalah sent another stream of light to tie up his hands.

Calleneck laughed. "You sneaky little—"

Dalah smiled with her freckled face and shot a stream of sparks at Calleneck, who created a shield of crimson light and pushed her over, tackling her.

Dalah too put her shield up and laughed from beneath Calleneck. "No fair, you weigh like a thousand pounds!"

Calleneck grunted and forced his shield around hers, bending hers and shattering it. Before she could retaliate, he used Dalah's same trick and tied a stream of light around her torso, pinning down her arms. Calleneck stood up and smiled. "Hah. Now both of you get out of here, you lost."

"Ugh," Dalah grunted, following Eddri out of the building.

Calleneck quickly left the scene and headed up another staircase to try and see if he could find any flashes of light. He stuck his head out of a half-crumbled stone turret window. Looking around the ruins, it was mostly dark. Then a flash of white light. *Lillia is still in!* Calleneck traced a quick line in his mind through the ruins and then set out toward it.

Running over a little bridge and through several corridors, he rounded a corner and emerged in a stairwell, where Lillia Hane stood above him battling the man with the scar. "Lillia!" he shouted and began running up the stairs. But just when he was about to reach her side, a giant wave of sapphire blue light threw him into the next room.

With a bruised shoulder, Calleneck stood up just in time to block another one of Tallius's blows.

"Gotcha!" The two of them stood in a large rotunda with a domed roof and stone columns encircling them.

"You'd like to think that." Calleneck smiled back at Tallius, grimacing as he shot a cloud of embers at him like a thousand red fireflies.

Tallius pushed them aside with a tall and bright waterfall of light flowing upwards and charged at Calleneck with a spinning disc of Taurimous. Calleneck quickly dove down behind one of the large columns. As the disc of Taurimous hit the column, it severed a crack halfway through the stone.

Calleneck stood up with wide eyes. "That could've killed me."

Tallius grinned. "But it didn't."

Calleneck swirled fire around his fist and shook his head chuckling, "You son of a–"

"Wait! Ceasefire!" said Tallius.

Lillia entered the room with her hands up. "I lost to Vorrov. Sorry, just passing through."

Tallius pointed at her. "You better not be lying and trying to sneak up on me."

Lillia's mouth dropped.

Calleneck smiled at Tallius. "Looks like someone's in trouble now." He turned back to Lillia, wondering why she was still there. "Great Mother, Lillia, *we're* still in the game."

Lillia giggled. "Oh yes, sorry," and left.

Almost immediately, Calleneck and Tallius launched equally, definitely unsafe, fireballs at each other. In total disregard of the rules, both launched another round of Taurimous embers at each other, resulting in burns on each of their arms. In an attempt to find backup, Tallius spun away from Calleneck and ran down a side hallway to try and find Vorrov – his teammate with the scar.

Calleneck raced after Tallius with a crimson flame lighting the way. Following his sapphire blue glow through the building, Calleneck was nearly out of breath when he heard his scream.

Calleneck sprinted forward after he heard it and came to a dead halt behind him in a corridor. In front of Tallius on the ground, lay Vorrov in a pool of blood. His chest cavity was open, and blood was spurting out.

Calleneck's blood felt chilled. "What the hell did you do?"

Tallius shook his head in shock. "I didn't do anything! He was just lying here like this when I found him—"

"Watch out!" yelled Calleneck as a wave of orange sparks soared right between them. Calleneck looked down the corridor and saw a figure in a crimson red cloak with a horrifying black mask hiding its face. The masked attacker lifted its hands and orange embers slid along every wall toward them like a swarm of fire ants. The sparks filled the hallway with a burning heat as they approached from ahead and behind. Calleneck and Tallius stood their ground and produced massive waves of energy that burst all the embers.

The masked sorcerer sent another fireball toward them, which they blocked with shields of light. Tallius sent a disc of glowing Taurimous toward the crimson-cloaked man which bounced off the wall and sliced open his chest.

They ran over to the man and grabbed him by the collar, ripping off his mask. As the sorcerer coughed up blood, Tallius pounded him into the ground. "Are there more of you?!" he shouted.

The sorcerer coughed up more blood.

Tallius yelled again and smashed the crimson-cloaked sorcerer's head into the ground. "Tell us, dammit! Who are you following?! Is this Xandria's work?"

The man smiled. "Even if you kill us, we'll live forever . . . we'll come back." The man coughed up another spurt of blood and then fell silent, eyes glazed over.

The blood drained from Calleneck's face. "We need to find the others."

The two boys ran away from their attacker whose orange embers beside him fizzled out and died, leaving a corpse behind. Faster than Calleneck thought he could run, he and Tallius sprinted out of the building to find Lillia and Kishk fighting off a group of rebels with crimson cloaks and masks.

As they ran toward them, the boys sent two powerful shockwaves of Taurimous light that rippled through the ground like lightning and sent the group of attackers flying. As soon as they hit the ground on their back, Sir Kishk finished them off with an enormous burst of lilac light.

Tallius hugged Lillia and Calleneck ran up to Sir Kishk. "Where is Dalah?!" Calleneck said breathlessly.

"I never saw her come back," said Sir Kishk. "She might have run off."

"Who are they?" said Calleneck, heart pounding.

Kishk looked at the three of them. "I don't know, but be cautious; they could be anywhere. You three get to the Nexus, I need to find Madrick and Modrvitch."

Tallius, Lillia, and Calleneck all looked at each other in fear.

"Go!" yelled Kishk.

The three of them took off through the tunnels toward the sounds of explosions. The Goblin halls rang with thundercracks of Taurimous hitting Taurimous. Shouts and flashes of colored light shot out from every tunnel. Calleneck's heart began to pound even more. He began to run. "Shit . . . shit, there are more! We're being attacked from the inside!"

Lillia ran after him, followed by Tallius. They turned a corner and in front of them were two Evertauri, one in black, and one in a crimson cloak and a haunting mask – *Crimson cloaks? Could they be connected to Selenora?* The man sent a stream of orange flames into a younger man, throwing him against a wall. When the younger one tried to defend himself against his attacker, the crimson-cloaked rebel launched a ball of yellow embers into the chest of the young man, bursting his ribcage open.

At the same moment, Calleneck and Tallius put their hands on the ground and sent crimson and sapphire bolts of Taurimous shattering through the rock until meeting the traitor, where the floor of the tunnel drove spikes of rock into his feet, lodging him in place. From behind them, Lillia sent a coiling stream of pure white light toward the attacker, who, stuck in place, deflected the stream, exploding a glass window.

As the glass rocketed from the window, Tallius produced a sapphire field of his Taurimous, which deflected the shards from hitting them. Tallius sent a huge blue fireball toward the masked Evertauri and he fell dead on impact. Not knowing why everything was happening, they pushed onward through the tunnels toward the Nexus.

They ducked as a sheet of aquamarine light shot over their heads from an adjacent tunnel. The light rebounded off a glowing shield of golden Taurimous, knocking out the masked attacker. The golden shield dissipated, revealing Dalah. Calleneck wrapped his arms around her in a tight hug. "Are you okay, Freckles?" he said with his face stuffed in her wavy hair.

"I'm okay," she said back weakly, obviously shaken. Calleneck gave her a quick squeeze and then ran over to the unconscious crimson-cloaked Evertauri, whose aquamarine flames still writhed around him. Calleneck knelt, ripped off the traitor's mask, and sent a flash of light into his head. Once the attacker was dead, the four of them ran until they heard voices in another side hallway. They stopped at the corner and listened.

"I killed the guards at that entrance," said a girl in a hushed voice underneath a mask. "We just need to find Borius, Mordvitch, and Madrick; Selenora will be able to kill them."

The four looked at each other with wide eyes. *Selenora Everrose is the one behind all of this.*

"Be careful," said another voice, "we're outnumbered, and we have to hold the Nexus." The two traitors began to run toward the intersection of tunnels, and when they came close, the four ran into the intersection and launched a great glowing ball of crimson, sapphire, white, and gold toward the two Evertauri. Having no time to stop it, the liquid-looking ball hit them and exploded on impact, leaving a charred pile of black on the ground.

"Calleneck, Dalah!" Aunika's voice shouted from behind them.

"Aunika!" yelled out little Dalah.

Calleneck turned to see his sister running toward them with two other Evertauri at her side – a tall blonde boy named Garner and a Guavaanese girl they called Siti. Aunika's lime green Taurimous lit up the corridor with dancing light as she rushed up to them and quickly embraced Dalah. Before Calleneck could speak, Aunika addressed Lillia. "Take Dalah back to your dormitory. Seal yourselves inside with your Taurimous. Don't come out until I come to get you."

Lillia nodded. "I'll keep her safe."

"Aunika, I don't want to leave you!" said Dalah.

"It's not safe . . . Go!"

Lillia lit a white flame in her hand and rushed Dalah to a nearby staircase up and out of sight.

Tallius looked around at the others. "We need to get to the Nexus now."

"It's that way," pointed Siti.

Calleneck, Aunika, Tallius, and the two other Evertauri sprinted toward the convergence of the tunnels, where they could hear explosions shattering through the air like thundercracks.

§

~Minutes Earlier

Raelynn's blood turned cold as the army of crimson-cloaked sorcerers rushed into the Nexus. In a matter of seconds, she analyzed the scene around her. Up in the dozens of stories of balconies encircling the Nexus, flashes of colored light began to light up the air as Selenora's followers commenced their attack on the rest of the Evertauri. Around her, bloody corpses of Evertauri lay sprawled on the stone floor as green flames from Grennkovff's explosion devoured their bodies. A few sorcerers nearby had ducked in time, and pushed themselves off the ground, ready to fight. The enemy was clear – masked and in crimson cloaks.

Raelynn oriented herself and located Grennkovff as spells and fireballs began to fly through the air from the hands of the rebels. A few Evertauri beside Raelynn conjured shields of magenta and golden light to block the bombardment of blasts from the enemy. But there were too many of them; Raelynn had to provide them with some cover to buy them any time she could. Summoning the power of her Taurimous, she produced a ball of energy in her hand in the hue only she had ever wielded – obsidian black.

The ball of swirling black Taurimous grew like a plume of smoke, and she expanded it in seconds to fill the Nexus in a pitch-black haze. Raelynn's spell plunged the sorcerers into darkness as explosions continued to bang and whizzed through the air like arrows, striking into Evertauri and Selenora's followers alike. Flashes of violet and sapphire light lit up the swirling cloud of darkness. Raelynn ducked as a fireball soared over her head. She could tell a few reinforcements had arrived, but she kept holding the spell in hopes that rebels were firing at each other in the dark. But as quickly as she conjured it, a wave of green sparks filled the Nexus and contracted the cloud of darkness. Grennkovff blasted the energy back at Raelynn, who was able to divert the blast just enough for it to smash behind her, exploding into a stone column.

From high above, a girl screamed as she was blasted off a balcony. Her body hurdled toward the earth and before Raelynn could conjure a spell, her body smacked against the stone floor beside her with a sickening sound. Horrified at the sight, Raelynn looked back at Grennkovff, who launched a volley of dark green fireballs at her. She quickly met them with shields and shattered them in mid air as they came speeding toward her. As sparks and flashes of orange and ruby light soared through the air, Raelynn charged back at Grennkovff with a column of swirling black energy that came crashing down on him.

Grennkovff yelled as the spell collided with his hands swirling with fire and he smashed the shockwave into the ground, sending her tumbling backward through the air. Raelynn was sure her body would break on impact, but a shield of yellow light surrounded her and slowed the fall. She quickly stood to see Borius Shipton with yellow fire running into the fray to fight Grennkovff.

A sorcerer in a crimson cloak cut down an Evertauri beside her and raised his hands coiling in bright blue swarming energy. A blue torrent of fire roared toward her from, and she quickly sliced the spell in two as the energy grazed past her on either side. Another Evertauri with a long white beard came to her aid and sent a shockwave of energy into the enemy that looked like lightning. The whole Nexus lit up in flashes of violet, orange, sapphire, and green as black-robed Evertauri slammed against the rebel group of masked sorcerers, and the sounds of screams and shattering stone were deafening.

A ripple through the ground sent Raelynn to her feet as Borius and Grennkovff collided with their spells. A huge wave of yellow light crashed into green sparks as Borius tried to push him back. Raelynn ducked under an arrow of violet light as she ran toward Grennkovff, hurdling over corpses of Evertauri and masked rebels. Grennkovff's storm of green light began to shatter Borius's shield like fractals of glass cracking, and soon, the whole force field gave way, and he was pummeled backward by the impact. Grennkovff conjured a swirling stream of green fire and held his hands up, ready to bring down a final blow.

Just as his hands went down, Raelynn jumped in with her black Taurimous and held off the tremendous wave of energy. The torrent of fire slammed her into the floor as her shield of swirling black smoke absorbed the flames. Her knee crushed down on the stone beneath the weight of the spell as she held it off. A flash of yellow light from behind her screamed over her head like an avalanche as Borius knocked over Grennkovff.

Borius ran up and lifted Raelynn to her feet as Grennkovff stood back up. Raelynn and Borius had separated him from the rest of his masked sorcerers. Behind them, the bearded Evertauri protected them from the onslaught of spells cast by the rest of the rebels.

"Now!" yelled Borius.

Raelynn and Borius charged forward, casting enormous spells of obsidian black smoke and glowing yellow fire that coiled around each other before slamming into Grennkovff's green force field. They continued to fire spells and jinxes at him, tearing his crimson cloak to shreds and ripping off his mask. Grennkovff stumbled back as he tried to fend off the bombardment of spells.

But suddenly, Raelynn's vision went blurry as the world seemed to tumble sideways. Selenora's eerie voice spoke inside her head. *Stop this Raelynn. Join me and we will fix this world together.* Raelynn tried to push her out and conjure spells but could tell that Grennkovff was fighting back now as Borius tried to protect them both. *You and I together can take on your father and rule after Xandria is gone.* Raelynn yelled as she tried to get Selenora out of her mind, but she couldn't do it. The sounds around her all seemed muffled as the explosions went off. Borius yelled as his spell failed and Grennkovff's jinxes surrounded him and slashed at his body. He writhed on the ground in pain as green daggers of light stabbed into him. *Join me,* continued Selenora's voice as Grennkovff turned toward Raelynn and sent a bombardment of green fire.

Just before it hit, Raelynn reached for Selenora through her mind and grabbed a hold of her. Something switched, and out from Raelynn's hands roared a wave of crimson light that crashed against Grennkovff's spell with such intensity it shook the walls of the Nexus. Selenora's Taurimous soared out of Raelynn's hands and surrounded Grennkovff in a storm of red fire that crushed in on him until an explosion of light reduced him to nothing but a pile of glowing green sparks on the floor of the Nexus.

Raelynn's full senses returned and ringing in her ear took over. She looked around at the scene of devastation around her as more Evertauri and masked rebels collided. Beside her, Borius lay coughing up blood. She rushed to his side to see that his left eye had been gouged out by a jinx, and blood pooled around him from stabs.

"Raelynn!" shouted a voice from behind her. She looked up to see Aunika, Calleneck, Tallius, and two other Evertauri rushing out of a tunnel and into the Nexus. The five quickly made their way to Raelynn, blocking spells as they weaved through the fighting.

Calleneck arrived first, seeing Borius's bloody eye socket and stained cloak. He turned to the others that arrived, pointing to the girl and the boy. "Garner, take Sir Borius away from the Nexus! Get him help!"

"Aye!" said Garner, who lifted up Borius with the help of the girl and dragged him away from battle.

Aunika and Tallius made it to Calleneck and Raelynn. The four of them quickly scanned the scene and saw that the Evertauri around them had pushed back the rebels against one side of the Nexus, and more Evertauri in the tunnels behind them prevented their escape. Without a word, they each sprinted forward to the front lines where black cloaks met crimson cloaks.

Calleneck and Tallius rained down fire on masked rebels together with crimson and sapphire plumes of energy. Aunika sent her lime green Taurimous coursing between the legs of rebels, wrapping around their ankles knocking them over as Raelynn pounced on them with black daggers of obsidian smoke. The Evertauri coming down to aid from the balconies on the other side were pushing the rebels into a tighter circle in the center of the Nexus.

Just when the spells began to cease and it seemed as if they would surrender, a shockwave of crimson light rippled through the ground from the center of the Nexus where the stone floor rose into the air engulfed in a blaze of crimson fire. When the flash of light subsided, Selenora stood tall on a mound of rubble with fire circling her fingertips.

Calleneck's blood turned cold as Selenora stood there in a crimson cloak overlooking the scene of devastation. Around him, Evertauri launched spell after spell at her. As each jinx approached her, she effortlessly sent it hurdling back into the crowd of Evertauri. Calleneck and Tallius sent fireballs of red and blue toward her and her followers, but they vanished with little wisps of smoke. Selenora sent another wave of light rippling through the ground, tearing up pieces of stone and stabbing spikes of rock up into Evertauri, impaling them through their chests like stakes. Tallius screamed out next to Calleneck as a stalagmite stabbed through his foot between the bones. Selenora sent waves of spells after spells until no one was attacking her. Aunika held up a shield of lime green light that swirled like water, but a fireball blew her backwards into Calleneck, knocking them both over.

When they stood, they saw that the remaining Evertauri were pulling themselves off the floor, coughing up blood and shaking. The spells had stopped, and Selenora stood at the center. Her followers formed a ring around the base of her pyramid of rock. Dust swirled in the air as Evertauri tried to pick themselves up. A lone Evertauri tried to attack Selenora, but he was quickly sliced open by a flick of her hand.

Selenora raised her hands and spoke. "My fellow Evertauri, a new day has come!" Her voice echoed through the cavern and down into the tunnels of the Network.

Beside Calleneck, Raelynn pushed herself off the ground as blood gushed from gashes on her shoulder. Patches of her white-blonde hair were stained dark red from blood. Tallius breathed heavily and grimaced from the pain of the stone stabbing through his foot as he tried to pull it out.

"You have been fighting for a corrupt idea," said Selenora, "for corrupt leaders. Madrick Nebelle, Borius Shipton, Mordvitch Aufenschiess and all the others — they wish to diminish your power, your strength. They fear what you can do. They don't teach the magic that could truly change the world." Selenora stepped over the pile of rubble, pacing around it. "Once you are taught the true ways of sorcery, the Evertauri could be so much more, so much stronger." Selenora looked Raelynn in the eye, then back to the others. "Madrick Nebelle has told you that the way to bring peace to this world is to take down Xandria and leave Cerebria ripe for the taking . . . He is a fool."

A few more Evertauri had gotten to their feet but saw no chance in trying to take down Selenora alone.

"But there is another way," said Selenora. "If we were to join Xandria and help her win the war, we could proceed to take over all of Endellia. After the work is done, we can take out the Queen and take control of our new Evertaurian Empire. We would be the keepers of peace, ending war, disease, and hunger. We could bring back the dead — all who opposed us will rise again in a changed world — a free world." A small crimson flame danced violently around Selenora's fingertips. It looked barely restrained, like a lion waiting to pounce and kill its prey. "Join me," she continued. "Join me and realize your full power. We are all the descendents of the sorcerers who sacrificed their lives to try and build a better world. We have power running through our veins we haven't even imagined. Join me and create a new world — the Age of Sorcerers."

Selenora stopped when a wave of silver light slipped over the walls of the Nexus, shimmering with sound like thousands of bells and then vanishing in a sigh of whispers. Three hooded figures entered the Nexus on a balcony above and descended through the air on a wave of silver light, landing on the blood covered stone. The two on the side lifted their hoods and ignited purple flames in their hands – Sir Mordvitch and Sir Kishk. In the center, staring directly at Selenora, the girl he raised as his own, was Madrick Nebelle.

"Selenora!" he boomed. "Stop this madness!" His voice filled the air with strength and might. "You have slaughtered hundreds; but it's me you want!"

"The resistance against us won't stop with you," said Selenora. "All those who join me will be heros in the eyes of history, and you and your followers will be nothing but an insignificant whisper from the days of darkness."

Madrick stepped toward her and the circle of her followers. "Look what you've become. I took you in and raised you, Selenora. I raised you as my own daughter!"

"We could rule over everyone!"

"You don't understand!" screamed Madrick with a tear in his eye. "You don't understand that it's not about claiming the throne for ourselves!"

"That is the only way we can have peace!"

"You are lost! Your quest for power has corrupted you. That's why I did the things I did, that's why I held you back! I saw what you could become, and I failed to stop you." He looked around at the carnage on the floor of the Nexus—corpses impaled on spikes of stone, bodies limp and pale, covered in drying blood. Madrick's face was red with anger, veins pulsing on his forehead and neck. "This is my fault for not stopping you before it was too late . . . what happened to the girl I knew so long ago?"

Selenora let a tear drip down her face. "She woke up." And with those words, she hurled countless balls of crimson fire at Madrick. He sent silver ribbons of light bouncing through the air, meeting every ball of fire Selenora produced. Still, the swarm of energy was unlike anything Madrick had ever encountered.

Within a second the Evertauri still standing began to fight back against Selenora's followers. Sir Kishk and Sir Mordvitch launched waves of violet and lilac light into the circle of rebels, punching a pathway through them to Selenora.

Calleneck, Aunika, and Tallius shot jinxes at the masked sorcerers, taking out a few of them while Raelynn battled her way into the center of them to get to Selenora.

Madrick sent bolts of silver light coiling around the perimeter of the Nexus until meeting Selenora's crimson shield of Taurimous. He advanced forward but was stopped by a wave of crimson that shot through the cavern, shattering balconies and columns all around. An endless storm of silver and crimson embers danced around each other as Madrick pushed his way to the center. The storm of light swirled faster and grew in size as the Evertauri around him battled with the rebels.

Madrick's fingers trembled and his teeth clenched as he focused his silver energy on Selenora, who fought back harder than she thought possible. He followed Selenora's eyes — Raelynn had fought her way through to her.

Selenora looked at her. "Raelynn! Help me!" Selenora grimaced as she pushed back Madrick's storm of silver embers. "Raelynn!" She looked at Raelynn's bloodied face. "I know where your mother is! I could lead you back to her!"

"She's lying!" yelled Madrick as he pushed harder. The battle raged on around them as the Evertauri clashed with the rebels. "Don't listen to her!"

Raelynn stood still, heart pounding out of her chest. "You killed him . . ."

Selenora's eyes widened with fear as black fire roared from Raelynn's hands, joining Madrick's silver storm, crushing down on Selenora. The combined force shook the walls of the Network, sending rumbling thunder through the air as blasts of light shot out from Selenora's vortex of crimson fire. With a scream, her defenses collapsed and the fire overtook her, shattering her Taurimous with an explosion that lit up the Nexus in blinding white light.

Raelynn opened her eyes and pushed herself off the ground. The echo of the blast still rattled through the tunnels and a high-pitched ringing filled her ears. She looked around at the Evertauri standing — they were looking in horror at something. She whipped her head around to look at Selenora's corpse, which was slowly turning into glowing crimson rose petals that drifted away over the stone rubble. Raelynn stood up and watched as all the bodies of fallen crimson-cloaked rebels began to do the same. Their burned and torn cloaks caved in as their bodies vanished into clouds of fluttering rose petals, leaving behind nothing but pools of blood on the cold stone floor of the Nexus.

THE PALE GLOW OF STARLIGHT

Chapter Eighteen

~Afternoon, October 8th
Aunestauna, Ferramoor

Kyan's hair blew across his face in the strong afternoon wind. A few brown leaves skipped around his boots as he walked through the Third District. In a square, a group of Ferrs had gathered; men in the middle were handing out fliers and shouting, "More volunteers for the war! More volunteers! Defend your kingdom and fight the Cerebrians! Take back our land! Pay is 270 argentums monthly plus food and clothing! Calling ages 17 to 35!" A man stepped out in front of Kyan and asked him to join.

"No thank you, sir." He was already more involved in the war than he wanted to be, fighting for both sides. Many men he used to see regularly around his part of the city had gone off to Endlebarr. Not only was Kyan still cynical toward Ferramish authorities, but he was a Ferramish authority in another body, a prince; he knew the inner workings of the war. Cerebrian forces pushed back Ferramoor day after day, and Ferramish intelligence's secret missions were failing time and time again. An unknown force was sabotaging every effort to advance their campaign. Of course, Kyan knew the source of the failure – the Phantoms of Cerebria could not be countered if no one knew about them. *And I sure as hell am not telling the Generals as Eston; they'd think I'm mad.* They were truly ghosts, haunting the Ferramish troops, luring them into ravines and killing them off. Of course, the Ferramish government had to publicly attribute these losses to the strange dark forest of Endlebarr; but fear of this unknown force flooded the palace halls.

Lost in thought, Kyan walked away from the square. He had begun the habit of taking walks around Aunestauna. However, these walks had changed from his normal outings to steal to simply . . . walks. Using the money that he had saved up from Zogo Blackblood, Kyan had eaten three meals a day for multiple weeks – an irregular practice for a street rat. And as opposed to avoiding conversation with others at all costs like normal, he only felt . . . well, *mild discomfort* when speaking to fellow Ferrs.

Kyan had gained a bit of much needed weight, making his ribs disappear and unknowingly, his usual dark glare had vanished. The days began to blend together, and oftentimes, he would forget who he was. Thoughts entered and exited his mind from his other bodies, causing him to question everything he thought about the war, the world, his families, and himself.

Kyan turned into an alley next to the theater and climbed up the walls onto the top. He meandered over to his little shack, which looked dreadful in the dim gray light of the seaside city. The wind knocked the door back and forth and the coats and blankets nailed to the inside fluttered around. Kneeling down, he entered his little home. It had a door on the floor leading to the theater attic below, which he sometimes slept in when winter came and brought freezing temperatures to the city. On his shelf sat the little silver ornament he had shown Raelynn when she did not know who he was.

Kyan picked up his Olindeux and ran his fingers over it. He assumed that the three curved lines represented his father, his mother, and himself. Although he had never met his father and mother, for some reason, he could never put the Olindeux away. The chain that strung it to Kyan seemed like more than links of metal; it felt as if it was keeping him in place, forcing him to stay in Aunestauna. Although Vree Shaarine had demanded he leave the city due to the danger of Riccolo and his Nightsnakes, something had kept Kyan there, and the Olindeux served as a reminder of what it was. Kyan dismissed the fact, but deep within him, he longed for an answer to what had happened nearly twenty years ago.

Deciding the silver ornament was clouding his mind, he quickly slipped through the floor door into the attic of the theater, where he could just make out the sound of a choir. Walking through the maze of rafters and beams, Kyan sat down by an opening which looked down into the large theater hall below. A choir sang on the stage in a haunting tune which filled the hall with a ring of minor key. Kyan sat there and listened, trying to rid his mind of thoughts about the war or Raelynn or the Phantoms or the strange behavior of King Tronum and Prophet Ombern. Kyan heard a creak behind him and looked back to see no one. Turning back to the choir, his lined up with Riccolo's. He smashed Kyan's head against the attic rafters, knocking him unconscious.

Freezing cold water rushed over Kyan's face and a hand grabbed his hair and pulled his head out of a water-filled bucket. Kyan coughed as he opened his eyes and examined his surroundings. He was in a moonlit courtyard in the middle of a ramshackle building in the Fourth District. *The Nightsnakes' Manor.* A group of figures surrounded him. Kyan's hands and legs were tied around a post and the night air was cold against his skin.

Riccolo walked forward. "Thank you for waking him, that'll be all." The Nightsnake walked back into the circle, taking the bucket of cold water. Riccolo knelt next to Kyan and put a hand on his dripping face. Tisking his tongue and shaking his head, he talked in a near whisper. "I was upset that we did not finish our last conversation."

Kyan stared into his haunting blue eyes. "Talk to me without tying my hands." Kyan spit in his face and received a hard slap in return. It drew blood from the jewels on Riccolo's hand. "You think I'll listen to you?" said Kyan. "Follow you?"

Riccolo's giant facial scar stretched as he smiled. "I have my ways." He slipped a knife out of his pocket. "Have you ever wondered what it feels like to have four fingers?" Riccolo moved closer and whispered. "I can make this *very* painful, Kyan. And unless you do what I say, I will torture, starve, and kill you right in this courtyard. If you do what I say, I will spare your life, leave you alone, *and* give you something I know you want *so dearly*."

Kyan stayed silent as Riccolo opened his coat and pulled out a piece of parchment in an envelope.

Riccolo continued. "I was walking past *Pebblebum Orphanage* the other day and saw you there. When you left, I entered and inquired about you . . . You've looked for your orphan files, haven't you? It turns out they like to hide them in case the Scarlet Guard comes to shut them down. But they always give you what you want if you pay them enough. They gave me something very interesting, dated back seventeen years ago." He read from the envelope. "Orphan File of Kyan Alda." Riccolo turned it around to show Kyan the writing on the front. He pulled out the parchment from the envelope. "I read your story, Kyan. I know why your parents left you. It's right here and it's yours if you do what I say."

Kyan clenched his fists. *Riccolo bought the file from the orphanage? I've been looking for it when I could have paid them . . . but maybe I never had enough for them.* Kyan stood still and looked over at Vree Shaarine who stood in the group of Nightsnakes. Her eyes were wide, and she gently shook her head. He read off her lips, "*Don't listen to him.*" She turned to Riccolo. "Would you allow me a minute to talk with Kyan? I may be able to persuade him."

Riccolo hesitated, but then backed away to let her speak with him. Vree came up to Kyan and whispered almost inaudibly, "Do not agree to help him. You have to escape."

"What does he want me to do?"

"I don't know, Riccolo hasn't even told me. But he wants you to steal something . . . something very hard to steal. He wants you to do it because if

Riccolo gets caught, it's all over for him, but he doesn't care if you get killed. *Run away.*"

Kyan's heart began to pound. "Is the file real?"

Vree spoke in her desert accent. "It doesn't matter, Riccolo will kill you."

Kyan tried to move his hands out of his ties. "Vree, is the file real?"

She looked down. "I was with him when he took it from the orphanage . . . but it doesn't matter, Kyan. It's not worth your life. Say you'll take the deal and then escape. You have to get out of the city."

"I can steal anything, I'm not afraid. I'm getting that file . . . Call Riccolo back."

"You're not listening–"

"Call him back, Vree."

Vree stood still, looking Kyan in the eyes. After a pause, she pulled out her Olindeux necklace. The token had four lines carved into it forming interlocking 'V' shapes, one upside down. It glistened in the starlight, and Kyan felt the urge to lean back from her and hide his own Olindeux.

"My sister has the other," she said in the quietest whisper Kyan had heard. "After we realized who Riccolo was, we tried to escape. He found us, cut out her tongue in front of me, and sold her to the Zjaari slave trade. I'm working for Riccolo to buy her back."

Kyan didn't know what to say and looked away from her eyes.

She tucked the Olindeux back beneath her tunic. "So if you don't think I know what it's like to want your family back . . ." She stopped, looked at Kyan's necklace, and then to his eyes. "Get out while you still have the chance." With that, she turned away and nodded for Riccolo to come back.

Riccolo smiled as he approached, his gold and silver bracelets jingling over his cut up arms. "What do you say? Do you want answers?"

Kyan hesitated, thinking about what Vree had said. He didn't want her to be right, he needed the answers. He looked down at his Olindeux, then back up. "What do you want me to do?"

The Lord of Thieves laughed. "I'm glad you're smart. I have people that will pay a whole lot of money for what we steal. I have one client in particular that would like something very impressive to woo a woman he desires. He wants something that money can't buy, and I have an idea of what to steal." He fiddled with the deck of cards he always carried. "You see, our government likes to keep Ferramoor's finest jewels and precious artifacts to itself. They store everything in a vault in the Royal Palace. You're the best thief around besides us, and if you get us rich, you'll get your life back, privacy, and answers to your questions. I will not lay a finger on you unless you try to bring us down. No matter what you may think of me, I do not break my promises. Now do you have an idea of how to get to the palace's vault?"

Kyan hesitated. In another body, he was the prince of Ferramoor, of course he knew how to get to the vault. The only problem was that Benja Tiggins was the only person with the key to the vault; but he knew where to go. However, there would be countless Scarlet Guards – the mission would be unlike anything he had stolen before. And he hadn't stolen anything in weeks and didn't have a desire to do it; but then he thought of the file that Riccolo held. "I can figure it out," said Kyan.

Riccolo smiled. "Bay, untie our guest. Everyone, we will accompany Kyan until we near the palace to make sure he doesn't run off. We leave in a half hour."

The crooked roofs of Aunestauna cast an eerie glow in the moonlight, and twenty or so shadows bolted across them. The Nightsnakes ran across beams and jumped off chimneys, quickly making their way toward the sea, and toward the coastal hill atop which stood the Royal Palace. Beads of sweat dripped down Kyan's forehead, for running in this body was much harder than running in the body of a Phantom.

They stopped on the roof of a mansion near the edge of the palace walls. Riccolo turned to Kyan. "Stay in the vault for as little time as possible. Steal only what we've asked so as to make an escape easier. You meet us here immediately following your departure from the castle. Do not tarry. The Scarlet Guards cover the gates and the wall, but the wall has far fewer men." He handed Kyan a light gray cloak.

"What is this for?" asked Kyan

"To get in," said Riccolo, "you need to climb the palace wall, the grooves of the stone blocks are big enough to wedge a finger in. The gray cloak will help you blend in with the wall. It's night so it'll be hard for the Scarlet Guard to see you. Once you're over the wall, use the cloak as a carrier. Unless you know a better way."

Kyan nodded.

"If you fail," said Riccolo, "They'll hang you before I can torture you. Now go."

Kyan was halfway up the wall when he looked down – fifty feet of drop to the city below. The clouds moved quickly overhead, and the city was quiet. His fingers burned from holding onto the gaps in the stone blocks and his boots barely clung to the small cracks. A strong gust of wind blew his gray cloak and swung his body which he pressed firmly into the wall so as to not be blown off. Raising his foot onto another crack a fragment of stone broke off, causing his foot to slip out from under him. His stomach dropped as he regained footing. If he fell, he could die. Another stone block. Another. After several minutes, he managed to put his hand over the top of the wall; but he quickly put his fingers back on the last gaps between stones when he heard voices approaching from over the wall.

Two Scarlet Guards walked toward Kyan, their armor clanking lightly as they walked. Kyan let out a soft sigh of relief as they passed him without noticing his presence. When they had walked out of earshot, he pulled himself over the ledge, briefly gazing down at the hundred-foot wall and the Nightsnakes surrounding the palace at two block increments.

Kyan took off his gray cloak and ran across the pathway on top of the wall. He dug through his memories as Eston and tried to visualize where the arches and walkways would take him. He ran across a stone bridge. *After this, two lefts, down the staircase, another left.* As he approached the main keep of the palace, a moving torchlight appeared in the hall ahead. Kyan ducked behind a stone block on the edge of the bridge, holding its side so as not to fall a hundred feet down. A caravan of finely dressed men walked onto the bridge twenty feet from Kyan, led by Senator Mar.

There was no way to hide. The men drew nearer, and they were sure to see him hiding behind the stone block. Kyan frantically looked around and located an outcropping windowsill ten feet down from the bridge on a large turret of the East Wing. Ten feet away; the men walked toward him. Kyan breathed in and jumped.

His mind went blank as he fell through the air; like a Cerebrian Phantom, he grabbed onto the windowsill, his legs swinging and hitting the wall. The men went on and crossed the bridge. Kyan lifted himself onto the windowpane and pressed lightly on the window; it was unlocked. He swung himself inside the palace and into a bedroom where he saw an old woman sleeping. He silently crept across the room and out the door into a dimly lit corridor. *I need the key to the vault. I need to find Benja.* Taking a moment to visualize where he was in relation to Benja's study, which sat near a central courtyard, he sprung forward into the dark hallways of the Royal Palace.

He bolted around the corner in a hallway lit only by moonlight; Benja's door lay just ahead. But Kyan ducked into an alcove when he saw Senator An'Drui turn into the hallway far in the distance. Gliding in her fine purple dress, the senator approached the door and knocked, prompting Benja to emerge. "You wanted to see me, Senator?" asked Benja as he shut the door.

"Yes. Now walk with me," she said. Kyan eyed the keys hanging on Benja's belt; *he would never leave the keys alone in his room . . . I'm going to have to steal them off of him.* Kyan followed them silently from alcove to alcove, using the shadows cast by the nearly full moon as coverage. He listened in. ". . . The King will not let Prophet Ombern authorize it and we must follow his orders.

Ombern fails to recognize the danger of using those weapons if they were to fall into Xandria's control; but we *do* need to use them. Tronum is afraid, and I've been here long enough to know he will not concede. We are being pushed back toward our borders, and they grow restless. We have to give them to the army and make it look as though Prophet Ombern did it. This is all for the greater good."

Benja stopped. "The greater good can be interpreted in many ways, Senator, ways which demand much more control on *my* end as Scarlet Lord. Unleashing these things will ruin us. We don't know how to control them."

"We are losing, Mr. Tiggins!" she whispered. "And unless we act, Aunestauna will burn. Fight for it in the Council and you will have the power to commence the plan."

"This is a war of attrition, and we would contribute to the death toll! My responsibilities and capabilities are designed to keep Ferramoor safe, not to gamble."

Desiring to listen more, Kyan had to shake his head to remind himself that the longer he waited, the more likely it was that he would be caught. He had picked pockets before and removing the keys from Benja's belt was no different. But Benja had been his friend since he was just a toddler of a prince. Then he thought of the files Riccolo held. So, standing in an alcove, Kyan reached out and snatched the keys as Benja passed, putting a finger between each one to prevent them from clattering. Benja and the senator walked on, and Kyan ran silently across the floor.

Down the stairs, a right, a left, a back passage to circumvent a populated area of the palace, more stairs, a left, second corridor, around that bend, down more stairs, through another passageway far beneath the palace; the vault. Marked by a large wooden door most likely two feet thick and twenty feet tall, Kyan had only seen it twice before as the prince. It sat in a large, plain arch. Kyan lifted the ring of keys; time was running out; soon Benja would return to his room and realize the keys were missing.

Frantically, he put a key in the large golden lock on the door. He tried to turn it without success. Another key, no success. *Please open.* Another key. *Turn, damn it! Open! Open!* He froze; he could hear yelling far up the staircase leading to the rest of the Royal Palace, and it grew louder quickly. *Shit!* He thrust the next key into the door and turned it hard. *No! Come on! Open!* Three more keys. No success, and the yelling came closer. One key remained. He jammed it into the lock and turned it, but it did not budge. *No! Damn it! Open!* He took the key out and turned it over, jammed it in, and turned it. The lock spun around, and the door creaked open. Kyan closed and locked the heavy wooden door behind him, causing a thundering echo.

From the length it took the echo to return, Kyan guessed that the room was as large as a cathedral nave. It took his eyes a moment to adjust to the darkness, for the only light in the room was a small candle, almost burned out. *Still a few inches left on the candle . . . someone must have been here within the past few hours.* The darkness slowly faded into firelight, and after a few seconds, he began to make out a massive wall of gold ornaments and jewelry underneath an arched ceiling.

Hundreds of shelves, each fifty feet tall, held countless necklaces and goblets of bronze and silver. Illuminated by the single candle, the shelves reflected so much light that he could easily walk through the chamber. The room was a great chamber of treasure and riches, seemingly as ancient as the earth itself. Eight hundred years of history lay dormant in this chamber — relics from every age of man.

Kyan bent down next to a stack of dozens of crowns and picked one up, blowing the dust off. If he took it for himself, he wouldn't have to steal anything for a decade. The door of the vault shook, and yelling echoed outside of the giant room. He opened his gray cloak and placed the priceless crown inside, but he stopped when he saw a great longsword encased in a glass box. Gingerly, he opened the lid and reached inside, touching a finger to the rusted, dusty steel. As Kyan moved closer, the blade shone different colors, as if it had been scorched by hot fires even after its forging. Engravings of vines and leaves ran up the fuller, and the wide hilt boasted a head of a lion on its pommel and wings for the guard. Then he noticed the writing etched in gold on the outside of the case — " *Vaeleron, Sword of King Gallegore the Great.*"

So it's true, he thought, *the stories of Gallegore are true — the flaming sword, the winged lion. He held this as he united Endellia . . .* He reached forward to touch the blade again but stopped when he saw a pale glow out of the corner of his eye. Closing the glass case, he slowly rounded the corner of an aisle, blowing out the candle. Far in the blackened distance emanated a soft glow of white tinted blue. It looked as if all the stars in the night sky had settled into one spot and their light shone like a barely noticeable beam.

He dropped the candle on the ground and didn't flinch when it clattered, nor did he pay heed to the ceaseless pounding and yelling at the vault's door. The light seemed to move slowly toward him . . . no, he moved toward the light. His eyes glazed over as he stepped forward. He began to make out a wooden chest on a stand with a blue-white light streaming out from it. Another step closer, and he thought he could hear a voice speaking to him. His head felt light as if he were dreaming. Another step and he could see the lock on the box. More pounding on the door — Kyan did not quicken his pace. He reached forward and placed his hand on the splintered oak box, cool to the touch and seemingly vibrating with a current of energy. Looking at his key ring, he picked a strange, twisted key and slowly put it in the lock. Twist. The lock clicked and Kyan drew open the lid only to be momentarily blinded by the light that came out.

After a few seconds, not only did his eyes adjust to the light, but the actual intensity of the light weakened. He sat on his knees and looked into the box, where, sitting in a blanket of velvet, lay a large glowing stone. It looked as if it had no edge and its interior was swirling ribbons of white smoke; it shimmered like water, yet it resembled a glass orb. Starlight danced around inside of it and seemingly melted into Kyan, who reached down and picked it up. A strange sensation passed through his arm and the stone felt cold to the touch. Kyan shook his head out of the trance when a gigantic boom rang out and the door to the vault burst open followed by shouts of the Scarlet Guard.

Kyan's stomach dropped as he put the stone in the gray cloak and shut the box; he looked up at the shelves reaching to the ceiling and only one thought entered his mind – *Hide.*

Twenty or so Scarlet Guards walked through the archway into the vault carrying torches. They scanned each aisle without success. Above their heads knelt Kyan on one of the stone arches that spanned the width of the room. No Guard had yet thought to look up, and if they did, they would barely be able to see his thin figure above the beam. *There are too many of them to go unseen,* thought Kyan as he watched around twenty torches wind through the alleys of gold. Kyan silently slid himself along the beam until it curved enough downward for him to reach a bronze goblet embedded with rubies. He cocked his arm back and hurled the goblet as far into the room as he could; it sailed above the alleys of treasure and landed with an enormous clatter in the back of the hall, knocking down stacks of glass.

A guard signaled to some of the others. "You men go over there; we'll block the doorway." A majority of the soldiers slipped to the back of the room and dispersed throughout the isles.

Kyan jumped from arch to arch, silently landing on the stone beams above the soldiers, until he reached the arch above the doorway, where five Scarlet Guards stood, looking around in the darkness. Quickly, Kyan thought up a way out.

Slipping the key to the vault out of his pocket, he pulled up his hood so they would have no chance of seeing his face. He grabbed the ledge with two hands and swung himself down, hanging just a few feet above the soldiers' heads. Holding his breath, he lurched his body and landed softly behind them. One heard him land and turned quickly. The others spun around and lunged forward to catch him. But before they could grasp him, Kyan leaped back and heaved the door shut behind him, slipping in the key to lock it just before the soldiers pounded against the door.

Kyan stood still for a moment as the door held shut, locked from the outside as the soldiers tried to wrench it open. He spun around and bolted up the stairs and into a hallway, carrying in his pockets a whole assortment of treasures and jewels – as well as the faintly glowing stone. Clamoring broke out behind him as another group of Scarlet Guards saw him streak by.

Kyan raced into a marble hallway and slid across the floor. Around the corner came twenty more soldiers running after him. Kyan sprang up and flew through the hallways of the palace toward a large balcony, which overlooked the main bridge. The cloak in his arms holding the stone softly glowed.

The Scarlet Guards tailed him a hundred yards back. Kyan rounded a corner and before he could react, his body slammed into another person wearing a similar black cloak, causing them both to fall over. He looked at the man he had just ran into – *Benja.*

Benja looked at Kyan without knowing he stared at Eston in another body; and then he looked at the glowing bundle he held and then at the gold necklaces that had scattered all over the floor. "Thief!" he yelled and pounced on Kyan, who quickly twisted over, ripping Benja off his body. Kyan kicked Benja into the wall and ran toward the balcony. Knowing there was a balcony below it, he grabbed the cloak, jumped off and held onto the edge to swing himself below. Just as he landed, he heard the Scarlet Guard round the corner on the floor above him, but they stopped and there was much yelling and cursing. *They lost me,* he thought as he hastily made his way to the gate.

Hiding behind a cart near the front gate, Kyan had waited for ten minutes for anything to pass by, for the sky was just beginning to lighten and the activity on the palace grounds was low. Finally, a horse driver and carriage rode by headed for the gate, and seeing it as his only way out, Kyan ducked down low and ran behind it, grabbing onto the back and swinging himself under the carriage, hooking his feet onto a crossbeam of wood, the ground less than a foot beneath him. He managed to hold onto the stone under one arm and hold himself up with another, but it tested his strength.

The carriage stopped. Kyan could hear footsteps approaching and the clanking of armor. "Good evening, boys," he could hear the driver say.

"We'd like to inspect your carriage before you exit the palace sir," said the watchman. "It's just before sunrise and we've just had a robbery from the palace vault."

"Oh, why of course. Go about your checkin' then," said the driver, followed by a mumble of "–damn government."

The Scarlet Guards circled the carriage and opened multiple compartments; Kyan held his breath and tucked himself higher under the cart. A guard stopped right next to Kyan, his shin almost touching Kyan's hand. Kyan held his breath and the Scarlet Guard stepped back. "All right then sir, you're free to leave." Kyan slowly let out his air in a sigh of relief, and once the carriage was out of the palace gates, Kyan rolled onto the street, taking the bundle with him – he was safe; though he'd had too many close calls for comfort. *It's a miracle I made it out,* he thought. His luck had been unmistakable, almost as if the Scarlet Guard had let him rob them. But one thing he knew – his luck was up.

It was only a few minutes from the palace by rooftop, and when he arrived, the Nightsnakes were waiting for him. They stood in a semicircle, cloaked, and impatient. Riccolo stepped forward. "Congratulations Kyan. I had my doubts, but you made it out alive. Now do you have the Stone in that bundle?"

"Set down the file first," said Kyan.

Riccolo hesitated, his stare unnerving. But he smiled and gestured with his hand, "As you wish," setting the file down on the roof. Standing beside Riccolo, Vree refused to make eye contact with Kyan.

Kyan stepped forward and opened the bundle to show Riccolo, revealing the glowing stone, which seemed to absorb and amplify the starlight that surrounded them on the rooftop.

Riccolo stood still with wide eyes. He took the stone into his hands. "It's–" he gaped but did not have the words to describe it. "The deal is almost complete," he said. He shoved the file toward Kyan with his foot. "Your reward, Kyan. I keep my promises. But do not test me . . . *Do not test me.*"

Kyan looked at the file – the answers. Without a word, he put it under his coat and ran off the roof, his nimble feet carrying him over the crooked rooftops of Aunestauna.

A BLACK MORNING
Chapter Nineteen

~Dusk, October 8th
Royal Palace, Aunestuna, Ferramoor

Eston couldn't help but think about the events that would unfold that night. He would, as Kyan, break into the palace vault on Riccolo's orders. He didn't know if he should try to stop it, or even if he could. If he remembered it happening tonight, could he even change it – change the future?

Throughout the day, Eston's apprehensive attitude drew the attention of Sir Janus Whittingale. "Is something worrying you?" he said as they walked across a bridge – the same bridge from which Kyan, later that night, would jump off to a window below and into the palace. The sun had just begun to disappear over the ocean, and the sky blazed crimson.

"Not particularly," said Eston. He didn't want to think about his mission to steal from the vault that night, but seeing as Whittingale looked concerned, he thought back to a question that *had* bothered him. "Actually, sir, I was wondering if you knew anything about why Prophet Ombern was removed from the last Council meeting."

Whittingale stopped and leaned on the wall of the archway, looking out on the inlet. "Ombern is a mysterious man and has been here since before your father; he served as an advisor for your grandfather. There are many things he knows that I do not. Nevertheless, I have speculated that your father did something that he regrets, and somehow Ombern wants to use it to Ferramoor's advantage in the war. But beyond that, my knowledge fades along with the many lost documents from the time of the split of the Endellian Empire."

"I'm sorry, lost documents?"

Whittingale closed his eyes as if searching deep inside his memories. "At the time of your grandfather's death, there were many strange things happening in the Royal Palace, many whispers of darkness threatening the Empire. It was the night you were born, about three years after Cerebria seceded from the Empire. I saw your father standing in a chamber deep within the castle in front of a raging fire of burning paper. The smoke hung heavy and dark in the halls of the palace the next day. Of all the details from that night, your father's face remains the clearest in my memory. It looked as if he had lost something, but his gaze was also filled with anger. Those were very strange times indeed . . . To this day, no one knows what happened there. But for your own good, I would urge you not to ask your father."

"Why would he be so secretive?"

Whittingale looked him in the eye. "Is secrecy an uncommon trait for a Wenderdehl?"

Eston lowered his head.

"There are things in the world that may be best not to seek after, whether it be answers to certain questions that may just hurt you, or material things, or even power. You leave a large footstep, Eston, and not just because you're tall like me." He looked out into the harbor at a ship leaving on its voyage, skimming softly over the waves with a scarlet banner waving above. "You may not be able to control what your father has done, but you must control yourself, and soon you'll not have my help."

"Why?" said Eston.

"You're nineteen. I've taught you nearly everything your father has asked of me."

"Except how to be him."

Whittingale smiled, a rare occurrence. "Don't be like your father. He used to be just like you . . . Gallegore didn't want Tronum to ruin his perfect Empire, but Tronum was ambitious and wanted power. So when Gallegore died and gave Tronum the Empire instead of Xandria, his pride got in his way; he wouldn't stand to let Xandria and Cerebria peacefully secede. And now we no longer have an Empire. Without the right leadership, *all* of Endellia could fall into disarray, chaos."

"I guess I don't have as much to ruin," said Eston, dispirited.

"If you think that, Eston, you fail to appreciate the greatness of this land. Ferramoor may struggle at times, but it is prosperous. I would hate to see it in flames." His voice got low. "Don't be your father, Eston . . . you have the power to unite and not divide." With that, Whittingale turned and left the bridge, and Eston was left questioning what he meant.

The dinner was late that night and more guests than normal were invited by Queen Eradine to the Great Hall in the West Wing. A musician played in the corner while the royal family and others ate at a large table. Qerru-Mai sat next to Eston. Always slightly intimidated by her but wanting to become more acquainted with her as his parents had requested, Eston had enjoyed a rather lengthy conversation with her, ranging from her interests in politics to her travels with her mother to Highill and Pyrot.

"Your mother," said Eston, "is she not here tonight?"

"No," said Qerru-Mai, "she mentioned that she had business to attend to. She's not been around much lately with everything going on in Cerebria and Endlebarr."

Eston thought back nervously to stealing Benja's keys as he and Qerru-Mai's mother were arguing. "Lord Tiggins is also not present here, I've noticed."

"It's been odd," said Qerru-Mai, "I mentioned Benja the other day, and my mother's gaze went sour. I think they may have some major disagreements, but over what, I don't know . . . Changing the subject, I heard the king is planning on making a trip to Willowwood and Ifle-Laarm next month, and there is to be a ball to celebrate it. I've never had a dance partner and I was—"

Each talking over each other, they danced around the question. "Yes, I was wondering if you'd—"

"—maybe we could go—"

"—want to go together."

Qerru-Mai laughed. "Yes, that's what I was thinking."

"I'd love to," said Eston.

On the other side of the table, Fillian rolled his eyes. "Yeah," said Fillian, "and while you two are waltzing, I'll be content to be anywhere else. Although I may intercept the wine cart as it leaves the Grand Ballroom. Why not make studying history in the library a bit more entertaining, aye?"

Eston twiddled his fork between his fingers. "Oh sure, and after one sip you'll be stumbling off the north balconies."

"Who is it, brother, that fell flat on his face in the courtyard the other night? I know it's quite hard to walk on grass."

Qerru-Mai chuckled as the brothers went back and forth, and it was a while until Eston and the royal family had retired to bed. He almost fell asleep without thinking of who was climbing up the palace wall that moment, who would soon become the first thief to ever enter the palace vault.

Eston's eyes popped open, and he threw himself out of bed when he heard a commotion outside his door. He quickly put on clothes, sheathed a sword on his belt, and burst out the door. A swarm of chattering people moved eastward through the hall. "Thief!" they yelled as people in nightgowns pushed by, trying to figure out if they were in danger. *Kyan is in this castle right now, or leaving it —probably at the front entrance . . . What have I done?* The image of the strange glowing stone filled his mind, and so did the fear of the Scarlet Guard pursuing him. Through the commotion, he heard a voice call out for him. Fillian burst forward through the throng and ran across the floor to Eston. "Eston!" he said breathlessly and grabbed Eston's shoulder. "It's— it's Benja, Eston . . . They've got Benja. There's been a robbery in the vault, they think he's involved."

Eston stopped. "They think Benja was the thief?"

Fillian took another quick breath and swallowed. "Or an accomplice. Father ordered the Scarlet Guard to get the gallows in the amphitheater on the East Wing." Eston's mouth hung open for a moment before he took off, his boots pounding against the marble floor below. "Wait, Eston!" yelled Fillian as he ran after him.

While the crowd moved up the stairs to organize themselves on the top of the amphitheater to see the ordeal, the two princes flew down a flight of stairs and into the hallway in which the entrance to the amphitheater was located. Scarlet Guards stood at the large doors which led to the floor of the theater and raised their weapons when the princes ran to them. "Open the door!" yelled Fillian with a hand on the hilt of his sword.

The guards hesitated, but cautiously opened the door.

A noose hung in the center of the arena, casting no shadow, for the sun had still not appeared over the horizon, but the clouds above had turned orange. Benja stood in the front of the theater with his hands bound and two armed guards on his side. His face was blank and bloodstained, his mouth was gagged, and his eyes did not widen when the princes burst through the door with guards running after them. "Stop!" yelled Eston. "Stop! He didn't do it."

The judge – Judge Ratticrad – stood up from his seat in the amphitheater. "What in the name of the Great Mother is going on?" he said.

Eston ran to him. "It wasn't Benja, we're sure of it."

"Eston!" boomed a voice. Tronum stood up. "You stop this instant. This is out of your hands, boy."

Eston threw his sword to the ground. "But Father, you must know that Benja would never do this. What purpose would he have? What evidence is there against him?"

Judge Ratticrad, a small, crotchety man who boasted a large wig and a peculiarly high voice read off a paper. "Lord Tiggins has much evidence against him, Your Majesty. Firstly, he was not at the royal banquet last night like he stated he would be. Additionally, on his drawing board in his study were maps of the tunnels beneath the castle, including the vault from which an invaluable item was stolen – one that could put us in more danger from Queen Xandria if put in the wrong hands. The Scarlet Guard also recovered Benja's keys to the vault on the floor, and only *he* had possession of those. Moreover, Your Majesty, Benja was found next to a balcony, claiming he 'saw the thief' and 'had him in his hands, but the thief got away and vanished over the balcony.' Now tell me, Prince Eston, how could a thief vanish into thin air by escaping off a fifty-foot balcony?"

The crowd watching the scene from above began to whisper and mutter, while Eston stood silent.

The little judge continued. "It does look— well it looks rather *convenient* that, as Scarlet Lord, Benja Tiggins commands the Scarlet Guard and they so happened to be in just the wrong places last night to catch him — the thief. Also, Your Majesty, why was there also a trail of gold and gems behind Benja, and why was there gold in his pockets?"

Eston remembered using the gold coins to distract the guards, and he remembered them falling out of his coat as he ran. When he collided into Benja, the gold spilled everywhere, including into Benja's pockets. "I— I don't know he could have been gathering gold to bring it back to the vault, but— but what about the item you say he stole. You couldn't find where it went, could you?"

"He could easily have had an accomplice aid him in whisking it away before our Scarlet Guards caught him. But you're also missing another important event," said Judge Ratticrad. "There is strong evidence that at a dinner feast less than a month ago, the failed assasination attempt of your parents — the King and Queen — as well as Whittingale and multiple senators, was the scheming of none other than Lord Benja Tiggins himself. He reportedly showed up late and distraught to the dinner, and when poison was discovered in many of the wine glasses, his remained untouched. Tell me now, Prince Eston, why you think we shouldn't have this man hung for attempted murder of our King *and* the stealing of sacred items from our palace vault."

Eston shook his head. "We don't know that it was him. There could be another thief out there or someone working for Xandria."

"He is guilty, My Liege," said the petulant judge. "You must still explain why there were no guards stationed at the vault. As the Scarlet Lord, Benja is the only one who could have authorized them to leave the vault . . . *unguarded*." Eston thought of the walk that Benja and Senator An'Drui took. "Tell me then, if Benja Tiggins was not the thief . . . who was?"

The whole amphitheater stood still; the only sound was of the scarlet banners flapping in the cool predawn air. Eston couldn't move or think clearly.

"Well, who is it?" yelled Judge Ratticrad.

A tear slid down Eston's face as he muttered, "*I don't know.*"

"What was that, My Liege?" mocked the judge.

"I said I don't know!" screamed Eston.

His voice echoed off the walls. "Then we will proceed with our vote." Eston's heart raced as he looked at Benja, who had his eyes closed. Judge Ratticrad spoke back to the jury. "All with the vote that he is innocent, please indicate!" The jury behind him including the Council and important figures stood still. Slowly, Senator An'Drui raised her hand, which shook in the air. "One," said the judge. "All in favor that he is guilty of robbery, attempted murder of the

King, and treason, and shall be sentenced to death, please indicate." The entire jury slowly raised their hands, including King Tronum, but Queen Eradine stood still. The judge slammed the gavel on his podium. "Guilty. Guards, please escort Lord Benja Tiggins to the gallows."

The crowd above them broke into chaos, and Eston looked up at Tronum. "Father! Stop this, you can't allow it! This is a farse of a trial! You decided he's guilty before it even began! This is Benja – our friend! Send him to a cell for now, anything else! This is madness—"

Tronum raised his hand and silenced the prince.

Fillian stood in disbelief, and Eston rushed forward to Benja. The Scarlet Guards surrounding Benja pushed Eston away as he tried to get through.

"Benja!" he yelled. "Benja!" Eston fought his way into the swarm of guards and grabbed Benja, who looked at him with wide eyes. "Benja, I'm sorry. I'm sorry."

The guards pushed Benja forward toward the gallows in the center of the circle. "I know it wasn't you!"

Benja tried to say something under his gag, so Eston ripped it off, causing a guard to yell at him. The Scarlet Guard forced Benja onto the first stair up to where the noose hung, and Benja fought and turned around to speak to the prince. "Eston!" he said. He writhed in the hands of the guards and Eston tried to fight his way onto the staircase to hear him. With the crowd in commotion, Benja managed to turn around toward him. "Eston, listen! There is a scrap of paper beneath my mattress; read it and then burn it! Things in this palace are not as they seem. Trust no one, Eston. Trust no one!"

A huge Guard put an arm around Eston and pulled him off the stairs. The guards hung the noose around Benja's neck as the judge crashed his gavel into the podium to order silence; a hush overtook the crowd. The sky was lit brightly in orange, and the sun was close to rising. "Lord Benja Tiggins will now have a final word!" ordered Judge Ratticrad.

Everyone stood silent and a crow screeched high up in the palace. Benja stood still on the trap door with the rope around his neck. He raised his head, closing his eyes, allowing all of his worries to drain out of his body. And in a loud voice, he shouted "Long live Ferramoor!" Benja lowered his gaze to Eston on the ground and looked him in the eye. "Long live the King." The trap door opened and Benja's body jerked for a minute and then hung still. The sun peeked over the horizon, and Eston opened his eyes to see himself standing as Kyan next to his shack in ragged street rat clothes holding an orphan file.

§

Kyan knelt, watching the sun rise over the city. For a reason he did not want to admit, he had not yet opened the file from the orphanage. He sat in silence, unable to comprehend what he had done. He looked at the file again, for which he had stolen the stone from the vault, resulting in his friend's execution. A tear slid down his face as he whispered out loud, "I killed him."

He looked at the file and clenched his fists, for he hated himself with all the might he could muster. He hated himself for stealing, he hated himself for hating everything else in the world, he hated what he did. He felt the Olindeux that hung from a chain on his neck and traced his fingers over it. The silver medallion had kept him in Aunestauna, and until now, he did not know why, or maybe he could just not admit it. The false hope that he would find his family bound him to the streets, and it weighed on him now like a mountain.

All the answers lay in the file in front of him, but he didn't open it. Without reading a word off it, he grabbed the file, the answers, and ripped it in half. He ripped it again, and again, tearing it to shreds, and threw it into a gust of wind. He watched, breathless, as the cloud of white parchment fluttered above the roofs of the city.

Wiping the tears from his eyes, he began to run across the roofs. In his mind, he saw Benja staring at him as the trap door in the gallows opened beneath him. Kyan ran faster, harder in the direction of the rising sun, over a plank and across a street. *I'm more than a street rat,* he thought as he began to climb up the side of the clocktower. And with regret in his heart but feeling free for the first time in his life, he stood on the top of the chiming clocktower with his hand around the spire, and with the other hand, he took off the chain that held the small silver Olindeux. Kyan looked into the rising sun, closed his eyes, and threw the necklace with all his might into the city below.

THE THUNDER OF ENDLEBARR

Chapter Twenty

~Evening, October 18th
Western Endlebarr

Throughout the days, Tayben grew ever more frustrated with his other selves, who had all fallen in some way or another into supporting Ferramoor. He couldn't see why they were so insistent on ripping away the independence and freedom Cerebria gained. Xandria had helped them all escape from a corrupt empire and prosper. His little hometown of Woodshore was never left to suffer – the government always came in to help. Xandria sent food into town when the winters got rough and helped her people. He couldn't stop his mind from rattling around. *Why can't they let Cerebria be free?*

The anxious fire that burned in him somehow failed to capture the attention of his fellow Phantoms. Tayben's thoughts had been distracted by fleeting images of home, which now seemed farther away with each passing day. When he dreamed, the image of a glowing flower always appeared.

Endlebarr had turned cold, but as always, the lush undergrowth crowded the forest floor, and the plants fought each other for the chance to catch a ray of light in the twilight beneath the canopy. But there was something else in the air, and the Phantoms could feel it. The fog that twisted and contorted the minds of ordinary soldiers tickled the Phantom's skins like it hadn't before, and a dark, looming presence seemed to be slowly filling the forest.

Reports that the Ferrs had stopped the Cerebrian advance into Western Endlebarr had been sent in the past week; yet Xandria had not sent a sizable number of reinforcements to help the exhausted Cerebrians, who had come within thirty miles of placing their boots in the less dense forest and rolling hills of Ferramoor. Concerned, Lekshane planned to take matters into his own hands. Because of their scarce success in the last weeks, Lekshane led the Phantoms north to strike a deeper wound into the enemy – an assault on Camp Stoneheart, which housed seven thousand Ferramish troops.

The Second Platoon sat in a cage of roots that was likely large enough to fit a whole other tree inside. Having been granted no time to relax for a whole month, the Phantoms were allowed to rest by Lekshane who demonstrated a burst of confidence on the eve of the attack. Tayben sat across from Chent, who, more withdrawn from the circle, carved a beautiful wooden figure of a merperson out of an oak branch. Ferron, Gallien, and Thephern sat around a tiny fire that provided little warmth. Ferron, the entertainer of the group, enjoyed sparking up conversation with the others, usually concerning his need for women in his life – a specific Vashner girl to be exact.

"Three years in this forest has burned you out this much, aye?" said Gallien.

"You'll know the feeling, Aris. Once you've had it with fighting wars in this canopy, leaping between branches like a– like a damn treefrog, nothin' in the world will be better than the idea of goin' home."

"Home to what?" said Tayben. "As far as 'the world' knows, we're all dead. But I guess it's in the name of the job . . . I don't see a way back from this."

"You're just not seeing the opportunities," replied Ferron. "After this war is over, you get'ta start *fresh*; you can be whoever you want . . . When we win, the government will give us land and gold and servants like the Crats have now – I am, of course, just talking about the four of *us*," Ferron laughed, "Chent over there's gonna become a hermit and live in this foggy mess."

Chent rolled his eyes and smiled as he continued carving.

"He's not the only one who's grown fond of the forest," said Thephern.

"You like it here?" asked Gallien.

"It's better than civilization. Cerebrian or not, there are people I'd rather not associate with . . . And do you all think that you will be able to hide what you are? Your power? I mean hell, Chent, you could shoot an arrow at a noxberry just by the sound of it falling through the air; and Ferron, you could track an ant in this bloody underbrush. We're almost not human . . . do you really think we could belong in society?"

The group sat silently, listening to the bubbling brook that wrapped around their enormous tree. Insects and small forest scurriers screeched in the dark, but the troops had become accustomed to random calls and growls from hidden places in the forest.

Thephern threw a twig on the small fire in the center of the tree. "We belong here, on the front lines. I've been here long enough to know why I was chosen to be a Phantom – I don't know if any of you do; maybe Chent does. But General Lekshane scouts each of us before we are chosen, and he always has a reason. As for me, I know that the reason for which I was chosen blocks the pathway back to civilization. Each of you may discover something different for yourself; but as for me, I've accepted why I'm here; I've accepted why I'm not going back."

Ferron shuffled, crunching dead leaves on the ground. "But don't you miss Shadowfork? Don't you miss home?"

Thephern shrugged. "Not exactly."

"I do," admitted Gallien.

Tayben looked over to Gallien, and it felt strange, but a feeling of relief came over him that he wasn't the only one who missed it. Tayben sighed. "I miss home too."

"What about it?" said Ferron.

Tayben thought. "I . . . well I guess I don't really know. Just being back in Woodshore . . . maybe I just miss the people there, my parents especially. And the smell of my father's blacksmith shop." Tayben remembered the hot, smoky workshop and the sizzling sound of glowing metal cooled in barrels of water. "After long summer days of working metal," he said, "my father would take me out canoeing on Lake Kiettosh as the sun set." Tayben smiled at the memory of the pink clouds and a pale blue evening sky above wide, placid waters. "Yeah . . . that's what I miss."

"And you?" asked Thephern to Gallien as the fire in the center of them crackled on branches and leaves.

Gallien smiled and leaned his head back on a giant root of the tree. "What's *not* to miss?" He closed his eyes, allowing his mind to wander back to a more peaceful time. "I miss the winter holidays back in Gienn . . . I don't know if any of you have seen it there that time of year, all tucked up next to the mountains. The city streets glow with candlelight from the houses and the moon shines on all the snow and . . . it just looks magical at night."

Ferron rolled his eyes. "Oh, don't get sappy with us."

Gallien laughed. "I'm serious . . . that's what I miss the most. My brothers and I would run and slide down the icy streets in our boots seeing how far we could make it without falling. And I loved those warm dinners with my family on winter nights. I have two older brothers and a younger sister, and we'd read all the classic tales with each other and drink cider by our fireplace."

Ferron shook his head and chuckled. "Yeah, while you got to stay tucked away in your warm and cozy mansion, the rest of us peasants were freezing our asses off in winter."

The group fell silent, and then began to chuckle. Letting themselves loose for once, they grew into full blown laughter. Gallien perhaps got the most fun out of it and took the joke in good sport.

Chent smiled to himself and joined in. "The Aris family should check out the Taurbeir-Krons for their next vacation home."

Thephern burst out with laughter, pushed over the edge. "The man speaks!"

Tayben smiled. "Ferron, I think you've cracked Chent . . . he's going loopy, he's talking now!"

The group gave a round of applause to Ferron and spent the evening joking and reminiscing about life before the army.

As the fire began to die down, steps approached the tree, and Albeire Harkil of the First Platoon called out for them; his voice was gentle and calming, carrying through the forest like light. Easily the most graceful and Nymph-like Phantom, he stepped through roots in the tree into the circle. "Luck," he nodded, "Second Platoon. General Lekshane is ready for the attack. It will be five miles from here to the borders of the camp. Seeing as the camp outnumbers us five hundred to one, we will have no choice but to make this a hit and run."

"What does he want us to do then," asked Thephern, "burn it from the inside?"

"Preferably. Although we must respect our pact with the Nymphs to not harm the forest. We'll sneak into the officers' quarters and destroy all their spies' work, and then steal any leads that we may find."

"And from there we wreak havoc," said Thephern

"*Controlled* havoc. We target the officers first. Slay as many troops as we can. But our existence cannot be known, we only take on as many as we can kill. Lekshane has ordered the Third Platoon to steal Cerebrian uniforms from a nearby battalion, from which they have just returned. We will wear those instead of our cloaks."

Ferron raised an eyebrow. "We might as well go in banging pots and pans with that armor; they'll hear us from a mile away."

Thephern glared at him. "You're capable of being silent."

"Exactly," said Harkil. "And we will not be wearing full armor. Anyway, Lekshane has ordered that unless you are absolutely sure you can take down a group of men and leave no one alive, do not use your full skill. If a man escapes and tells of our powers, our secrecy will be compromised. So if you must defend yourself, and the force around you is overwhelming, act as if you are a regular soldier. Just don't get caught. Do you understand?" The Second Platoon nodded. "Come, we meet in five."

Although he had worn it only a month prior, the armor of a regular soldier now felt awkward. Panels of protection had been removed so as to not cause a clamor when he jumped through trees, but there were still too many. The light from the camp was blinding; even through the fog, Tayben could see roaring bonfires where soldiers kept watch at the gates. Unable to cut down the colossal trees of the forest, the Ferrs were forced to build a battlement under the canopy of the trees. Looking less like a fort and more like a remote forest village, the camp had a collection of barracks and training grounds, but the layout moved with the geography of the forest, including the trees and brooks. A central building, the only one two stories high, sat in a bend of the main river that ran through the camp, and clung to a massive tree sixty feet in diameter. "That's where we'll need to get to first," said Lekshane, scratching once at his reddish-brown beard.

A wall of wooden pikes surrounded the camp. The Phantoms quickly took out the watchmen and guards with both bow and spear. From there, they listened for any footsteps or breathing on the other side of the wall – nothing. The First and Second Platoons jumped over the fifteen-foot wall, landing in the moss on the other side, while the Third Platoon climbed into the trees to enter from the top.

Once the Phantoms successfully infiltrated the central building, it was only a matter of seconds until they were lighting fire to spy documents and leads on the Cerebrian army, and, at the same time, stuffing Ferramish information into their uniforms and boots. While Ferron and Chent were using a burning candle to light them on fire, Tayben looked at the document in his hand, something that he could easily catch on fire if he were in the body of Callenck. *The power given to me by the Nymphs must be similar in some way to what I have in the Evertauri* . . . That last word, *Evertauri*, felt sour in his mind, and although he wanted to hate them, he accessed the feeling in his mind that he used to summon his Taurimous and channeled it into his hand. He jumped back as a stinging pain of an invisible electric current – or something of that nature – cracked through his hand. Almost yelling, he caught himself before making a sound.

Ferron, who saw nothing but Tayben jump back, looked at him with wide eyes and mouthed, *"Are you good, Tayben?"*

Tayben silently mouthed back as he examined his perfectly normal hand with no flame in it, *"Paper cut."* Something seemed wrong, like the Nymphs' power and sorcery made something dangerous when combined. He decided he didn't want to see what happened if he tried it again.

Ferron raised an eyebrow and continued lighting documents on fire then cooling the ashes with quick puffs of air. For ten minutes, flashes of firelight lit the ground surrounding the central building, and then there was darkness. A blur of Phantoms shot out of the building and into a barracks, where the sound of unsheathing daggers, gasps, and coughs echoed out and dripping blood seeped through the floorboards. The green blurs moved into another barracks of sleeping soldiers, and the sound of the bubbling brook and croaking frogs around the building was suddenly replaced by a cacophony of bells chiming and shouting from Ferramish guards.

The sixteen Phantoms quickly severed the throats of the remaining men in the barracks and flew out the windows. As Tayben ran away from the barracks, carrying Ferramish mission reports under his clothes, he saw a mass of soldiers ahead. As if the soldiers ran in molasses, the Nymphs' gift allowed Tayben to calculate everything happening around him, so much that he knew the angle of every sword and spear heaved at him. Knocking swords to the side, he quickly stabbed two soldiers with his spear. As they fell to the ground, he grabbed both swords from their hands, and decapitated two more soldiers on both sides of him. Holding onto a man's shield and ducking from his sword's swipe, he twisted his hands hard, breaking the man's arm, allowing him to take the shield and stab him with the top spike.

Like a bee in his ear, he heard an arrow whiz past him and into the head of a soldier behind him. Chent came to his aid, nocking and loosing an arrow a second. After the group of Ferrs lay dead, he ran to take back each one of his arrows, a sight that Tayben never got used to. While occupied with removing his spear from a man's body, Tayben barely had time to duck when an arrow flew straight for his chest; and to his amazement, Chent sprung out his hand and caught the arrow, loading it onto his bow and taking out the Ferramish archer who tried to kill them. "We need to find the others," he said. He whistled the call of a Slevvnen bird, but with one tiny rhythmic difference. Within seconds, he received the same, off-rhythm call from far off. "This way," he said, and they sprung over the mossy forest floor.

Gallien and Ferron brandished their swords against a platoon of Ferrs. Chent quickly shot the remaining soldiers as he and Tayben approached the two. "Where did everyone else go?" asked Tayben.

Gallien motioned with his body and began running. "I saw Thephern and Albeire bolt into a barracks. The rest, I don't know." Together, Ferron and Chent whistled the bird call and received a response to which the Phantoms ran.

The four Phantoms darted through the dewy brush and screeched to a halt when they heard soldiers — a few hundred strong, including cavalry — moving in the forest. Chent pointed up, and the Phantoms jumped onto a very large and unstable boulder and ascended into a tree to scout out the enemy. They seemed to be forming ranks beneath a group of massive trees which were separated from the rest, and a steep ravine leading to a river created a crescent on the grove's back side.

Gallien peered through the canopy and could see Thephern and Albeire on a large branch. "They're trapped," he said. "There are swordsmen and archers in the middle, and two large sections of cavalry on either side. They could try and run for it — I think Thephern wants to — but Harkil is kneeling. His eyes are closed . . . he's meditating . . . waiting for us to make a move."

"We can't take them all," said Tayben. After a moment of silence, Ferron began to chuckle. The three raised their eyebrows.

"It's bloody stupid," said Ferron, "but it may work."

A crash sounded through the forest. A ten-foot boulder tumbled down the hillside; Ferron and Tayben ran behind it, pushing it and speeding it up. Another crash sounded on the other side – an even larger boulder was pushed by Gallien and Chent. The two rolling mounds of rock and moss crashed and snapped branches and ferns, aimed for the herd of horses. The boulders angled inwards at two side groups of fifty cavalry each. The horses violently turned around to see what the noise was, and when they saw a boulder rolling toward them, they reared and whinnied, bucking their riders off and swinging their heads.

As the boulders rolled nearer, the men began to yell as horses trampled their own troops. The Ferramish army rushed away from the stampede of horses, which converged on them like a giant 'V,' pushing them toward the ravine on the opposite side of the grove. Screaming and neighs sounded through the forest as Gallien, Chent, Ferron, and Tayben pushed the boulders with all their might, making them crash through the forest at remarkable speeds. The first men reached the ravine and turned around, only to find a crowd of five hundred soldiers trying to outrun the stampede. The soldiers cried out to warn everyone of the ravine, but slowly, they and the soldiers were pushed off the edge into the rocky rapids below.

Harkil and Thephern swung down to the forest on vines, running after the boulders, each joining one, helping the Phantoms push them. When they came within a hundred feet of the ravine, they let the boulders go and crushed a line of horses. They each unsheathed their swords, bows, and spears, ready to wipe out the troops that survived. Just as they did, a whistle rang out in the forest. The Ferrs saw a large blur of green streak through the canopy, but Tayben saw Lekshane leading the First and Third Platoons down to the forest below. General Lekshane shouted below, "Take them all!" The ten Phantoms jumped from the trees sixty feet down into the battalion of Ferrs.

Thephern, Gallien, and Tayben jumped over the nearest troops and landed in the throng of soldiers. Thephern, with his two longswords, immediately decapitated a few soldiers. Gallien snapped the neck of the nearest soldier and grabbed his scarlet shield, which he tossed to Tayben. Placing his arm through the straps and holding his heavy spear tightly, Tayben dug his feet into the ground and sprung forward as fast as he could run, knocking down Ferrs and spearing them. From above, Chent picked off Ferramish archers before they could shoot the Phantoms. Ferron grabbed a strong vine and tossed the other end to Albeire, and together they ran at a line of spearmen, hooking them under the neck and throwing them down. "Harkil, the cavalry!" he shouted. A line of five horses with riders were sprinting away from the scene to warn the rest of the camp.

Tayben and Albeire took off after the horses, stepping between the corpses of dozens of Ferrs. Tayben bolted between two of the horses, and as they split around a tree, Tayben thrust his spear up and sideways, catching the tips on the riders' armor and used the tree to stop himself, knocking the troops off. Harkil jumped on a horse, taking its rider out and twisted its reins into the row of horses, colliding with the next. The horses' legs all caught together, and they came down with a thud. Seeming to weigh less than the air around him, Harkil flipped over a soldier and split through his helmet with an iron dagger.

Thephern ran toward them to call them back while Tayben took a rock and swung his arm back to crush the head of the last soldier – a messenger boy no older than fifteen – but before the stroke fell, he stopped. The boy's eyes were wide open, and his face turned pale. Noticing Tayben's hesitation, Thephern took Albeire's knife and threw it into the boy's chest. He then sprung on Tayben and held the knife at his throat. "What are you doing?" he screamed.

"Are you mad?" yelled Tayben.

Thephern pushed him harder. "I saw you hesitate!"

Harkil ordered Thephern to stop.

"I swear if you–"

"Thephern, stop this!" Harkil ripped Thephern off Tayben. "Stay down!" He paused. "Did you hear that?"

"Hear what?" said Thephern as General Lekshane came rushing toward them.

Albeire took off toward the rest of the Phantoms, who were battling off the last troops. Tayben and Thephern ran after him, forgetting what had just occurred, but Lekshane shouted for everyone to follow him.

"Wait, sir!" said Harkil.

"What?" asked Lekshane. "We must go before we are unable to take them. Retter and Brint are wounded, and no troops are coming right now – none that have seen us."

"Exactly," whispered Harkil. "How could all of Camp Stoneheart not hear a stampede of horses? Something is wrong." Just then, as the Phantoms stood in the lush grove, they heard – or perhaps they felt – a force unlike any other. A twinge of fear echoed in their hearts as a pounding sound rushed through the battalion like a front of air, permeating every crevice and hollow both in the earth and their bodies. Steadily growing in volume and intensity, the low, rich, bass note reverberated off of every metal plate, every sword, every helm, and every inch of the platoon. The very earth beneath their leather boots awakened and filled their bones with the overpowering hum, until it grew into a long, harsh roar. Everything went quiet.

Lekshane adjusted the grip on his sword. "What the hell was that–" Another roar filled the air like a crack of thunder, deafening the Phantoms for its duration. "First Platoon, head north, slowly; Second Platoon, head east; Third, head south. I'll check west. Move through the canopy, stay together."

The Second Platoon walked on branches, straining their ears to hear anything. A Ferramish soldier far in the distance could be heard saying, *"stay behind the gate."* Even the frogs and insects stopped their croaking and buzzing. A deep roar echoed around them in the tree, and they drew their weapons.

"I can't see anything," said Gallien. Every Phantom could feel the location of everything around them, even drops of dew, like one could navigate a familiar room in the pitch black; the only flaw was trying to manage all the information coursing into their brains every second. And although they felt a strange presence drawing near, they could not locate its source.

With a gust of air, an enormous, scaled tail swung out of the shadows and knocked the five Phantoms out of the tree. Each of them tumbled like ragdolls to the forest below, immobilized, filled with a force that coursed through their bodies like electricity. The trees cut up their skin as they fell, and they hit the wet soil hard. The roar echoed again and came closer to them.

Tayben was the only one who could move, but only his arm and one leg could function, though they still felt numb. So, starting with Gallien, he dragged each of them into a fallen hollow tree trunk. *Why couldn't we sense it coming? Why couldn't we see it?* With his remaining energy, he gave three loud whistles, *Help.*

Ten feet away from the Phantoms, the wood of the trunk splintered as a set of foot-long claws severed it in half. He gave three long whistles again. The claws and scales crashed through again, and an electric current seemed to flow out of them, but Tayben was unable to tell where the dagger-like claws were until they smashed through the decaying wood.

The pain and immobility worsened, and now only able to move one hand, he grabbed Chent's bow, clumsily loaded an arrow, and, using a knot in the tree to hold the bow, drew it back and shot at the scales of the monstrous thing that smashed the log. The arrow flew through the air and bounced off its black tail without leaving a mark. Tayben fell limp, unable to control his body.

He could hear the yelling of the First and Third Platoons as they sprinted through the forest toward the fallen tree to rescue them. The scales disappeared and roaring could be heard far off in the distance. The last thing Tayben saw before he passed out was Lekshane dragging him out of the tree.

FIRST SNOW
Chapter Twenty One

~Early Evening, October 24th
Seirnkov, Cerebria

Dalah sat on the windowsill with her arms folded on her knees, her breath fogging the glass of her bedroom window. Her loosely braided hair fell over her shoulder; she had not asked Aunika to cut it in months. She ran her fingers through the dark strands, twisting her fingers mindlessly as she peered out into the evening; her freckles dotted her rosy cheeks that were especially red now that it was cold. From up in the window, she watched a little girl chasing a boy in the dim, dusk street lit by the fading light of sunset. Dalah tapped her boots together matching the clip-clop-clip-clop of horse hooves on Winterdove Lane, where there was little more than a foot between each tall and narrow gray house.

The windowsill was her rare escape from the stress of the Evertauri – a life change she had not been ready for; but she, of course, would never tell her siblings that. After all, it was she who followed them out of the house that day and it was her fault for discovering their secret. But wouldn't it all be so much easier, so much simpler and happy if Aunika and Cal had never gone underground?

She had pushed the window open an inch; the cold air helped her think and she liked to listen to feet pattering on the cobblestones. In the distance, she heard the squeaking of the ropes and wheels from the well in the square as a bucket slopped in the icy water, and even the swish of brooms on small front porches and doorways. Lost in thought, she began to hum a tune her mother used to sing her.

As she closed her eyes, a group of Jade Guards marched up the street, entering the occasional house for inspections as usual – the queen was looking both for people worth recruiting into the army and traitors to banish or kill. Dalah had become accustomed to seeing these, now routine, inspections and her head slowly fell to her chest, entranced by the quiet bustle of the street below.

She awoke a few minutes later when she felt a little wet droplet on her hand – a snowflake. Opening her eyes, she saw the wooden window frame begin to turn a frosty white with tiny crystals. She looked up at the sky, which was pinkish gray; a thousand little specks of white floated down. She picked her head up and smiled; *first snow.*

She hopped off the windowsill and took a jacket and scarf off of a wall hook. She flew down the uneven staircase and out the door, ringing a little chime, and once she stepped onto the cobblestone street, she flung her arms out and lifted her chin, looking up at the drifting snowflakes. They landed silently on her freckled face, and she closed her eyes and breathed in the cold air of a waning autumn, not moving for the carriages and wagons that passed her on either side. Many of them stared oddly at her, finding it odd that she stood there in the snow.

An old, bone-skinny driver wearing a tall top hat stopped his horse cart. Dalah put her hands down and looked at his confused but smiling face, from which hung a long white beard and a red and black scarf. "You alright, sweetheart?" he asked.

She nodded. "Sorry sir . . . just taking in the evening. It's the first snow of the season."

The driver gave a jolly laugh. "It is indeed. Makes the city look beautiful. I've always wanted to see what Gienn and Ontraug look like at the holidays – maybe it's something like this."

Dalah nodded and looked around at the lightly snow-coated buildings. A cart driver behind rudely yelled at the man to move forward.

The man with the long white beard rolled his eyes and chuckled. "It seems some people have lost an appreciation for the simpler things." He reached back in his cart, picked out a golden flower, and handed it to Dalah. "Well, happy first snow, miss. Now you better go inside and stay warm." A snowflake landed on her eyelash as he whipped the reins of his horse with a "Yah!"

In minutes, several low clouds rolled in from the south, and the snow and wind picked up in the fading light of day, prompting lanterns to light throughout Seirnkov, like shimmering ornaments in the night. In the still-clear northern sky, huge ribbons of green light danced among the stars.

As Dalah saw her mother rounding the street corner, she lit the fireplace and placed a pot of water inside. Sheilla Bernoil's occasional strands of gray hair blended in as the snowflakes speckled the top of her head. She opened the door, letting a cold draft of night air swirl into the kitchen.

"Hi, Mum," said Dalah. "What's that you're carrying?"

Mrs. Bernoil held a large painting of a bouquet on a candlelit table. "I finally got it. This is the painting I've been telling you about. Your father *forbade* me to get it because of its price, but the artist sold it to me today for half . . . fantastically talented young man."

Dalah helped her take off her coat and hang it. The painting was placed on a nail on the wall, and the faint smell of the fire began to drift pleasantly through the house. Dalah had started throwing together the ingredients for her mother's version of Fjordsman Pie.

Mrs. Bernoil tapped the window, knocking off miniature drifts of snow. "Your brother and sister are late, those rascals. I'm going to start cooking dinner whether they arrive or not."

Dalah lit a candle on the table. "I told you they would come home a while after me; they're probably still helping Uncle Gregt and Aunt Shelln with organizing. But Father is late too."

"He'll be here soon," said Mrs. Bernoil, tying a shabby apron around her waist. "He had an order for shoes on the other side of the city, and this snow is bound to slow him down a bit." Dalah walked toward her and looked out the window at horses and people walking along the whitened cobblestone. Her mother unexpectedly hugged her and kissed the top of Dalah's head. Lost, looking at the night street, she jolted. "Oh damn . . . I forgot to get the potatoes when I was out today."

"I can run to the market and grab some," said Dalah, walking over to put on shoes.

Mrs. Bernoil sighed. "That's if there's still someone there in this weather."

"I can go and check," said Dalah, slipping on her boots. "Do you want them from the market on Waterdale?"

"That would be wonderful; thank you, dear. We won't need them for about a half hour, and hopefully by then your father and siblings should be back." Mrs. Bernoil handed Dalah an argentum as she wrapped her scarf around her neck and put on her coat. As Dalah opened the door, Mrs. Bernoil shivered. "Be careful, there may be ice."

Dalah smiled and shut the door, turning up the street. Mrs. Bernoil checked the pot, and just as she sat down to read, Mr. Bernoil walked in.

Mrs. Bernoil put down her book. "You just missed Dalah."

Hanging up his coat on a hook next to the stairs, Mr. Bernoil immediately went to the window and looked out into the street. His gaze was heavy and worried. "Where is she going?" His face was tense, and his voice sounded uneasy.

She stood up. "Just to get some potatoes for the Fjordsman Pie. What's wrong?"

He kept his gaze locked out the window. "The Jade Guard is going through the neighborhood doing inspections. They're in the house next to us right now."

She put her arm around him. "It's nothing to worry about, Otto; we have nothing to hide. They're just making sure the city is safe." She gave him a half smile to try and ease him. "The death of your friend Rushki was an unfortunate situation because of his meddling, whether it be just or not . . . the Jade Guard is just just carrying out the Queen's orders. We're good citizens; *we* have nothing to be afraid of."

Mr. Bernoil shook his head out of the trance. "I know, I know. They're just doing their job . . ." He looked around the house and smelled dinner and smiled, taking a deep breath in. "Is that pie I smell?"

"Warm pie for a cold evening." She smiled. "Take off your shoes and relax, sweetheart. You look like you've had a long day."

Mr. Bernoil sighed and took off his shoes. "Where are the other kids?" he asked as he walked over to the kitchen to wash his hands in the water bucket.

"They should be here any minute," said Mrs. Bernoil as she walked over to check on the food, "they were staying a bit longer with your brother today."

Mr. Bernoil dried off his hands and shook his head. "Just because I let them go over there doesn't mean they can stay as long as they wish." He continued under his breath, "—all because of a fight with Aunika . . ."

"Otto, you know it was much more than that . . ." Mrs. Bernoil shuffled a few coals around in the fireplace and then put her hand on his. She looked into his gray eyes and spoke softly. "I know it's been hard. We disagreed with her, and *we're allowed* to disagree. But when Aunika left to live with your brother, Cal and Dalah only went because they missed her; they didn't have anything against *you*. I know you may not think so, but things are getting better between you and Aunika. And now that the kids are done with their schooling and Aunika has a job, I think that all this bundled up stress is just gonna fade away."

"You're right, Sheilla," Mr. Bernoil took a soft breath in and gave her a smile, "as usual."

Mrs. Bernoil opened a cabinet to get out five small clay-fired plates for dinner. As she set them down, the front door opened and Aunika and Calleneck walked in – just returning home from the Evertauri after a meeting with Sir Kishk Kaubovfier.

"We're home, sorry we're so late," said Aunika, hanging her coat on the wall.

Calleneck closed the door as a cold draft of air blew in and he sniffed the air, smiling. "Smells wonderful Mum; are you making pie?"

"Dalah started making it while we were waiting on you," said their mother.

"It's *Fjordsman Pie,"* sang Mr. Bernoil like a little kid.

Aunika walked over to her mother and gave her a hug. "Is Dalah upstairs?"

"No, she's getting potatoes from—"

A loud knock on the front door interrupted her. A voice outside called, "Inspections!"

Aunika and Calleneck's faces went pale. *Inspections?*

Mr. Bernoil calmly walked toward the front door. "It's going to be alright everyone." He slowly opened the door, revealing four Jade Guards dressed in similar armor Calleneck used to wear as Tayben.

The tallest of them held up a slip of paper with writing stamped by the government. "City Inspections, sir."

Mr. Bernoil nodded. "Yes, of course, come in."

The four soldiers stepped into the house, closing the door behind them. One of them looked around and smiled. "I smell some good food cookin' in here."

"We'll only be a few minutes," the tall soldier assured them, "and then you can get right back to dinner." The soldier waved to Mrs. Bernoil and the kids in the kitchen. He turned to his men. "You two go upstairs, we'll take this level."

Two soldiers went up the stairs into the bedrooms to search. Mrs. Bernoil put her hands on her children's shoulders. "Just go sit down at the table for a few minutes."

Calleneck and Aunika obeyed, taking their secured bags from the Evertauri with them and hiding them under the table next to the stone fireplace hearth. Calleneck's hands shook as he and Aunika sat waiting at the table. Upstairs, drawers were being opened and closed; books were being taken off shelves, scanned, and put back. On the main level, the two soldiers went through their father's office.

Aunika looked at Calleneck with fearful eyes. The same thought ran through both of their heads – *Is there anything that the soldiers could find?* Their parents stood calmly in the kitchen, looking outside at the beautiful lights of the city in the falling snow.

Calleneck was almost sure Aunika could hear his heart beating outside of his chest. The fireplace just a few feet from him made his nervous sweating increase. The search seemed to last hours, waiting, waiting.

The two soldiers in their father's office emerged and began looking through the kitchen. "What age are you now, lad?" said one as he pulled open a cabinet door with bowls behind.

It took Calleneck a second to realize the soldier was speaking to him. "Um, nineteen, sir. Just three years out of school."

The soldier nodded and opened another cupboard with a loaf of bread inside. "What'cha doing to work?"

Aunika and his parents looked at Calleneck, and he told himself to relax. "Nothing now, sir, just helping out here and there."

The other tall soldier took another scan around the kitchen. "Lad like you should join the army, help protect our country, aye? You can go lots of places you'd never be able to see. Women like a brave army man too." The soldier gave Calleneck a wink and a smile.

Finally, the other two soldiers came downstairs and reconvened in the kitchen. The tall soldier took one last look around and then nodded at Mr. and Mrs. Bernoil. "Thank you for your time." As the soldier was turning toward the door, he stopped. "Oh, let us check those bags."

He was pointing straight at Aunika's lap. Calleneck's breathing stopped, and fear took over. He tried not to let the sheer terror spread over his face. The bag had to be opened with her Taurimous, which their parents and the soldiers would see. Even if she managed to open it, the documents inside were incriminating.

Aunika stuttered. "I— I can't"

The soldier placed a hand on the hilt of his sword. "Excuse me?"

"She doesn't need to open it," said Calleneck, his heart racing.

"You too, young man!" ordered the other. "Put your bag on the table and open it."

The children stood petrified.

"Do as they tell you," said Mrs. Bernoil, wondering why her children were refusing. The four other soldiers stood still with their hands on their swords, but the children didn't move. "Damn it Aunika, listen to them."

Aunika stepped back, looking at Calleneck for help.

The lead soldier stepped forward. "You'll do as I say!" he ordered. The soldier grabbed Aunika's arm and tugged her away from the bag behind her.

Mr. Bernoil rushed in and pulled on the man's shoulder. "Don't touch my daughter!"

The soldier grunted and shoved Mr. Bernoil over. The room went silent when a sickening crunch came from the fall; Mr. Bernoil's head was cracked open on the corner of the fireplace hearth, gushing blood over the stone, turning his white hair scarlet.

Mrs. Bernoil screamed and stumbled back. Calleneck's stomach dropped, and his blood felt frozen in his hands. But quickly, the feeling of ice was overtaken by the burning of fire.

Roaring with anger, Calleneck launched a stream of crimson fire at the soldier, splitting open his armor and slicing through his chest. Screams filled the air as Aunika fired a blast of green sparks into the heart of the soldier beside her. The sound of an unsheathing sword sent Calleneck tackling the next soldier and quickly putting a powerful shock of red light to the soldier's temple.

"Stop!" screamed the last soldier. He had taken hold of their mother and pressed a dagger against her throat. "Stop or she dies!"

The room was silent but for the crackling fire and the soft sobbing of Mrs. Bernoil. Fear filled her eyes — fear of the soldier and the knife and of her own monstrous children. Fire swirled around the children's hands as their father and three of the soldiers lay dead on the floor.

The soldier's face was red, and he gritted his teeth. "Let me go, you freaks!" He pressed the knife harder against their mother's neck, starting to draw drops of blood.

Calleneck stood still, and the fireplace crackled, lighting up the pools of blood gathering around the dead bodies.

Then Aunika sprang forward, sending a blast of green light at the soldier's head. He fell backwards with glazed over eyes, but not before he had sliced the dagger clean through their mother's throat.

Mrs. Bernoil tumbled forward onto the wood. Aunika hurried to cover her mother's throat with her hands, trying in vain to stop the blood that gushed over her fingers. "Help me, Cal!"

Calleneck rushed over to see his mother's fearful eyes lock with his and start to unfocus. "What do you want me to do?!"

"I don't know!" cried Aunika as tears poured down her face. "Please, please, please!" Their mother convulsed below them as her blood gushed over Aunika's hands.

Calleneck turned to his father lying still on the ground. His split head poured open in a sight that made Calleneck want to throw up. This wasn't real. It couldn't be. It was all a nightmare.

Aunika screamed as she cried. "No, no, no, please!" Her mother's eyes closed, and her body went limp. Refusing to stop trying, Aunika sent spells of light into her mother's gash hoping something could clot the blood. But Mrs. Bernoil lay still, surrounded in a pool of scarlet.

"Aunika, stop!" Calleneck found his cheeks covered in tears. He could barely see out of his watery eyes. "They're gone."

Aunika kept her hands on the slit throat. "No, no, they can't be. They're not— they're . . ." She cried out as her falling tears splattered on her blood covered hands. After a few more moments, Aunika collapsed and sobbed into her mother's chest, screaming out in shrill and horrific cries.

Calleneck felt dizzy. Their parent's bodies lay motionless, spilling blood across the floor. *It's not them,* he told himself. *That's not mum and dad . . . no this is all a dream.* Calleneck scanned the room looking at the four dead soldiers. They had killed his parents. Cerebrian soldiers had killed his parents. Xandria had killed his parents . . . but because he and the Evertauri rebelled against her.

He whispered with tears streaming down, "What do we do?"

Suddenly, the front door clicked open and Dalah burst in. "Mum, I got the potat—" She stopped instantly. Her young eyes darted across the carnage of six dead bodies all over the room. She saw her sister crying over her mother. "Wh—What's going on?"

Calleneck looked at her through teary eyes. "Go and get President Nebelle . . . now!"

Dalah dropped the bag of potatoes and rushed out the door.

Not twenty minutes later, the front door opened and Dalah walked in, followed by Borius behind the President.

Dalah quickly shut the door, and Madrick and Borius stared in shock at the scene with his one good eye. Borius whispered, "Great Mother," under his breath.

Dalah, realizing the full scope of what had just happened, began to bawl.

Calleneck sat beside the fireplace next to the body of his father. He looked helplessly at Madrick. "Help us."

Borius knelt down and felt for a soldier's pulse but felt none. "Dead . . . what happened here?"

Aunika's eyes were puffy, and her mouth was dry. "They— they came for inspections. We couldn't open our bags and— I . . . I don't know, it was all so fast and—" She broke down crying.

Calleneck looked at one of the dead soldiers. "They grabbed Aunika and my father tried to step in, but they pushed him down and he hit his head . . . They slit her throat."

In the corner, Dalah ran over and cried in Aunika's arms.

Madrick and Borius pieced together the events that unfolded from the mutilated bodies surrounding them. Madrick's face was grave. "The Jade Guard will be here soon after they realize their men are gone." He turned to Borius. "I knew this was dangerous. What could possibly go wrong letting three young sorcerers live half time unsupervised in the city?" Madrick's face was turning red. "This! This is what could go wrong!"

The room stood in silence. A log fell in the fireplace and a little cloud of embers floated up.

Madrick shook his head. "I trusted you with this, Aunika! You said you had the situation under control!"

Borius put a hand up. "Madrick, they're children! Take it easy . . . their parents are dead."

"And killed by the people we fight against," said Madrick. "We need to get rid of all this evidence before the rest of the Jade Guard comes."

Madrick stepped over the dead bodies to the fireplace. Launching a stream of sparks into it, the fire grew eight feet tall and began to devour the wall of the house. Dalah screamed for him to stop. The flames jumped to the beams of the house and into the cabinets, consuming the room.

Dalah ran past the others and out the door. Calleneck sprinted after her. He turned the corner and saw Dalah far up the street. Leaving the burning house behind him, he ran into the city streets. His bare feet pounded through the snow and the air froze the tears on his face as he continued to cry.

Dalah turned off to another street, and as Calleneck wheeled around, his feet slipped out from under him on cold, wet ice. His body hit the snowy street, scraping his hands and knocking the wind from his lungs. But he ripped himself off the ground, now numb to the cold.

His long legs and adrenaline carried him fast as images of his parents flashed through his head. Around another street bend, Dalah was closer. He followed as she split into an alley reaching for her but causing her to slip and hit hard on the stone.

She sat up, coughing and screaming, "Get away from me!"

Crying, Calleneck grabbed her and embraced her in a tight hug, trying to calm her. Tears streamed down her rosy cheeks as she tucked herself in Calleneck's arms. "It's okay, Freckles, I'm here . . . I'm right here." Calleneck held her long through the evening, crying as the first snow of winter gently covered their heads.

ROYALTY
Chapter Twenty Two

~Midday, November 3rd
Royal Palace, Aunestauna, Ferramoor

To Eston, the paintings on the palace walls now looked dull and grayed, like someone had stolen the color off them. The brown leaves of the trees that covered the entirety of Ferramoor had nearly all fallen, leaving the branches cold and naked. He could no longer count the number of people he had killed or gotten killed between his four bodies. The past ten nights – or really forty – had offered him little sleep, for his dreams were plagued with images of Benja Tiggins, the Bernoils, and the countless Ferramish soldiers he had killed.

The prince lay silently in his bed. The somber light of the overcast afternoon sky filtered through the large, motionless curtains of his lavish bedroom. The room was cold, and for the first time, specks of dust gathered on the floor, for the prince had told his butler Errus not to enter. A chair lay broken on the floor. He grabbed a vase on his nightstand and hurled it into a wall, shattering it. He dropped to his knees and knelt on the wood floor. A drop of blood fell from his hand; a shard of glass still stuck between his knuckles from shattering a mirror.

He wiped the blood on his bed cover and walked to his desk. A drawer held a skipping stone covered in ashes. Eston slammed his fist down and hiccuped after seeing Benja again in his mind as the Scarlet Guard pushed him up the steps of the gallows. *"Eston, listen! There is a paper beneath my mattress; read it and then burn it! Things in this palace are not as they seem. Trust no one, Eston. Trust no one!"* Nearly a month had gone by since the prince rushed to Benja's room to do as he was told before anyone else got there first. On it had been scribbled a single word.

Silverbrook

Sir Janus Whittingale had replaced Benja Tiggins as acting Scarlet Lord in addition to being First Advisor to King Tronum. The vast new responsibilities left Eston without a teacher for the first time in a decade. No one had seen much of the prince at all for the past month, especially the past ten days since the death of the Bernoils. Though he knew logically that they were Calleneck's parents, the loss felt just the same. He *was* Calleneck, and he had lived his whole life, loved his family, and watched his parents die.

Lately, Eston took his meals in private and avoided the councils. He blew on the ashes in the drawer, causing them to fly around the room like thousands of little ravens. *Silverbrook.* That word had consumed his thoughts day in and day out since Benja's death. *What the hell is that supposed to mean, Benja?*

The word on parchment shriveled up and turned black in his memory, engulfed by the destructive flame of a candle similar to the pile of documents his father burned so many years ago. But from his new position – one that he took very seriously – Whittingale was no longer around enough in private to answer Eston's questions about the past, about what Tronum did that long-ago night. He had searched endlessly in the Great Library. *I could ask Senator An'Drui.* From somewhere in his mind, he heard Benja frantically say, "Trust no one!"

Eston walked out on his balcony, dripping splotches of scarlet blood on the concrete, and looking down, he clenched his teeth, knowing that a month prior, he would have cared about a bloodstain on his *pristine, useless balcony.* Eston unbuckled his jewel-encrusted belt and threw it back into his room. The leaves blew across the white courtyards below and passersby crunched them beneath their feet. He imagined the great fire and Tronum standing before it, watching documents burn. The image transfigured into Benja's limp body hanging from a noose. A tear fell onto his ash-covered tunic. *I'm sorry.*

A knock sounded at his bedroom door and Eston bolted from the balcony. He cracked open his door only enough to reveal his face. Qerru-Mai smiled at him. "Hello . . . Umm– Well, no one has really seen you in a couple weeks, and I was wondering if you still wanted to go to the ball tonight to celebrate your father's trip to Ifle-Laarm?"

Eston's heart sank and he hesitated. "Yes, yes sorry. I've just been quite busy."

She tried to look over Eston's shoulder into his destroyed room, her chocolate skin still glowing in the gloomy light. "Do you need a way to decompress? . . . We could shoot arrows in the target courtyard."

Eston hesitated. "Yes, um, . . . yes that sounds good, but maybe some other day. How about I meet you fifteen minutes before the ball starts at the south doors to the library?

Qerru-Mai nodded and smiled, waiting to see if Eston would do the same. "Alright . . . well, I'll see you then." She left and Eston shut the door, turning to his bed which was covered in feathers from a destroyed pillow.

§

Deep in the passageways beneath the palace, Fillian pressed his ear to the door, listening for any sound he could make out. He couldn't unlock it, couldn't get inside. Then he heard it – eleven little clicks. Silence. And then again, eleven little clicks. Something was turning. Eleven clicks, silence. Like wood and metal wheels. A mechanical click, click. Twenty-six times it went through eleven clicks, and then it stopped. A minute later, it resumed. But then he heard louder clicks . . . no, steps. He quickly ran to the other side of the dark hallway and into an unlocked room. Looking back into the hall from the room through the small crack he had left open, he saw Senator An'Drui remove a key from her sleeve and slowly open the door to the clicking room, disappearing into the blackness inside for quite some time. As soon as she reappeared, Prophet Ombern walked into the hallway.

Ombern watched Senator An'Drui as she exited the long underground hallway. She approached him and whispered, "eight, R." She quickly left him alone in the hallway to return to her daughter's room, where Qerru-Mai was getting dressed for the ball. Ombern scratched an 'R' onto a piece of parchment.

He smiled and whispered, "How soon the time comes when Ferramoor shall once again rule." Stroking his long beard, Ombern left the hallway, watched closely through a crack in a door by Fillian.

Fillian waited for a few minutes, thinking to himself, *I need to find a way into that room to see what An'Drui and Ombern are after. Where could I find a key?* Fillian thought for a moment. *The ball . . . Ombern will be gone . . . I'm sure he has a key hidden somewhere in the Great Cathedral.*

Fillian quietly made his way out of the depths of the Royal Palace. But little did the prince know that down the hallway behind a pillar, another man with dark hair had seen the same scene transpire between Senator An'Drui and the Prophet. The man watched Fillian closely and slipped silently into shadow before Fillian noticed.

§

Qerru-Mai fixed her scarlet dress in the mirror. "Mother," she said, and Senator An'Drui walked into her bedroom. "Do you think the prince has been odd lately?"

". . . Which one?"

"Eston of course."

The senator walked out the door saying, "I couldn't tell you yes or no, dear."

"Wait, mother." She stopped. "Where were you this past hour?"

Senator An'Drui hesitated. "Oh . . . Talking with Senator Hillbottom." She swiftly left the room, avoiding further conversation.

Why are you lying? thought Qerru-Mai. She sighed and looked out her window, which overlooked the front gate of the palace. The light of day was beginning to fade, but something down below caught her eye. A cloaked person was leaving the palace on the back of a cart. *Prince Fillian?*

She stood by the library doors as Prince Eston approached. His hand was the first thing to catch her eye – it looked like it has been mained by an animal and a crude attempt at bandaging it made it worse. "What's on your hand?"

The prince looked down. "Oh, that's nothing."

"Eston, it's all cut up and scabbed," said Qerru-Mai.

"I tried to catch a mirror in my room as it fell but it shattered on my hand." Using his other hand, Eston, wearing a white royal robe and scarlet sash, led Qerru-Mai toward the Grand Ballroom in the West Wing. "My father wants to leave soon for Ifle-Laarm with Senator Bardow, so he will likely attend only the first half of the party."

"And he's going to campaign for the war?"

"Well with a few exceptions, Xandria's forces have been getting quieter lately – regrouping. So my father is taking the opportunity to get more troops. Every day, more troops, more troops. One out of every ten Ferramish men are either in Endlebarr or the camps at Abendale and Wallingford."

"And I guess it doesn't help that hundreds of men at of Camp Stoneheart were slaughtered in an attack. I'm sure you've heard about that."

Eston nodded, remembering cutting them down all too clearly from Tayben's eyes. They turned a corner, passing a group of women in floor-length gowns of sparkling pastel.

"How is your brother?" said Qerru-Mai.

"Fillian? I think he's doing alright. I haven't seen him lately."

"Is there any reason he would be traveling outside the palace?" said Qerru-Mai.

Eston halted and looked at her strangely.

". . . I saw him leaving, heading out into the city."

Eston nodded slowly, deep in thought.

"I think it has something to do with my mother," she said.

"And why is that?" He and Qerru-Mai moved into an alcove.

"They've been acting strange around each other, like they're following each other's tails. It's Prophet Ombern too. I'm afraid he's using his power to sway your father into doing something. Benja–"

Eston flinched at the name.

"Benja used to tell me to keep a close eye on them, but for what, I didn't know."

Eston thought back to the night he essentially had killed Benja by stealing his keys. *"The king will not let Prophet Ombern authorize it,"* Senator An'Drui had said, *"and we must follow his orders. Ombern fails to recognize the danger of using those weapons if they were to fall into Xandria's control; but we do need to use them. Tronum is afraid, and I've been here long enough to know he will not concede. We are being pushed back toward our borders, and they grow restless. We have to give them to the army and make it look as though Prophet Ombern did it. This is all for the greater good."* Eston looked into Qerru-Mai's eyes, in which, somewhere deep and far away, there was an unsettling fear. "Has your mother mentioned anything about my father, his past?"

". . . yes. She talked about the night of the fire—"

"—of burning documents beneath the palace. Whittingale told me."

Qerru-Mai nodded. "What do you think they were?"

They stopped in front of the ballroom doors as partygoers entered. "I don't know . . . But your mother and Prophet Ombern do."

Sir Endwin Bardow, Fillian's Mentor, called out to them. "Prince Eston, Ms. An'Drui, are you joining us for dance?"

"Yes, of course," they said in unison, taking each other's hands.

A quartet of string instruments played on a balcony in the Grand Ballroom. An elaborate mural of mythical beasts, coronations, and scenes of battles looked down at the large crowd from the ceiling. Elegant gowns floated over the marble flooring, and ornate tables of Ferramoor's best food sat along the edges. Tronum stood talking to Whittingale, each of them holding wine glasses — all of the wine entering the Grand Ballroom had been checked for poison. As Eston and Qerru-Mai approached them, they caught the last few words of the men's conversation.

"I'll trust you to take care of her while I'm gone," said the king.

"Your palace is stronger than it ever was with Lord Tiggins now that I've made improvements," said Whittingale, as the new Scarlet Lord. "Why, hello."

"Sir, I'm sure you've met Ms. An'Drui," said Eston.

"I have indeed," said Whittingale and Tronum greeted her, smiling with a twitch in his lips. "It's been strange no longer teaching you," said Whittingale "but you've proven to be a fine young man. I must go now, but I wish you two happy festivities." Whittingale left, and Tronum asked for a minute alone with Eston, and Qerru-Mai complied.

"Eston, I will be gone for two additional weeks. Senator Hillbottom convinced me to extend my war efforts north to Bellerush, Oakfoot, Farwater, and wherever else in his district is lacking soldier output. This means that you do exactly what your mother tells you to do." His hand holding the wine glass shook violently, spilling drops of scarlet on him, but he did not notice.

"Yes, sir." Tronum began to leave, but Eston grabbed his elbow. "Wait . . . during my last lesson with Whittingale, he told me about something that happened the night I was born . . . beneath the palace—" Tronum's glance went sour, "next to— next to a fire . . . What did you burn?"

Tronum leaned in and whispered as harshly as a Cerebrian. "You have no right to know about that! This party is no place to have this conversation." Tronum turned his back on Eston and walked away with a noticable limp.

Eradine met the king and he whispered in her ear. The queen called out, "Thank you everyone for coming. The king would like to get a head start on the trip and will be leaving now. I will be accompanying him as he leaves the city." The crowd clapped as the royal couple departed, but Eston stood there without moving.

Qerru-Mai tapped his shoulder as a dance began, and he placed one hand in hers and one on her waist, his mind still off in another world. "What did your father say?"

"What? Oh, nothing." Eston gazed around at the tables of endless food and the sparkling jewelry of the rich diplomats. His stomach began to feel hollow. *Raelynn was looking for a document in the library . . . it was gone.* The drunken laughs of people around him rang like a siren in his ear, and his mind flashed to the cold quietness of the forest of Endlebarr. His stomach dropped again, remembering the young Ferr he hesitated to kill. *He was fighting for me. He was fighting for all these oligarchs.*

"Eston, are you alright?"

". . . I'm fine . . . I just feel a little sick." The floor began to tip sideways and soon people were dancing on the ceiling . . . no, it just looked slightly blue . . . everything started moving away from him.

"You look awful, Eston."

He stepped away. "I just need a little breather." He stumbled dizzily toward a great column and leaned against it. He closed his eyes and in a jarring flash, looked through the eyes of Kyan at the rafters of the Great Cathedral. Standing next to him was Fillian. Only lasting a fraction of a second in Kyan's body, a flash jolted him back into the body of Eston, who had slid down the column.

Qerru-Mai pulled him up off the floor. "Eston, are you okay?"

Dazed, Eston thought, *what the hell just happened? It's not sunrise. I shouldn't be switching bodies right now.*

"Eston?"

He staggered forward without replying. Drunken people around him laughed and hollered, consuming platters of food. A blinding light flashed in his eyes again, and he took a step forward in the tunnels of the Nexus, followed by another flash. Eston lay back on the floor, falling for the brief moment of time when his consciousness transferred to Calleneck. The quartet's song played beautifully through the hall. Another flash of light, and he sat with Gallien in a tree. Another flash, and he lay breathless on the floor of the Grand Ballroom. Picking himself up, he grabbed Qerru-Mai's hand for help standing.

"Eston," she said, "are you alright?"

Eston shook his head. "I– I just feel off." Trying to look around, he felt sick looking at the feasting and the laughing of the party members. *How are they so blind?*

Next to Eston, Senator Mar chuckled to a few other government officials. "I even heard that our teenage soldiers turn loopy in Endlebarr." He laughed and took a sip of wine. He was one of those fifty-year-old men that spend an inordinate amount of time to make themselves look a decade or two younger – styling his greasy hair and dying his fading beard. "For the Great Mother's sake," he snickered, "how hard is it for soldiers to sit on their asses and eat the meals provided for them?" The other men laughed.

Eston's fists clenched. He felt his blood boiling. Finally, he marched up to them and yelled, "STOP!"

Qerru-Mai grabbed his shoulder. "Eston, what are you do–"

"You, sir–" said Eston as he pointed to Senator Mar. "*You are sickening.*"

The other men stepped back in shock with wide eyes as Eston stood in front of the senator.

Eston's hand shook as he pointed at the senator's face. "You have no idea what it's like for those men out there." Eston looked at Qerru-Mai and slowly dropped his finger.

Senator Mar turned red and began to speak. "Says you who's barely stepped foot out–"

"You are a *coward* compared to those boys!" Eston tightened his jaw. "They fight and kill to serve this country and save you!"

Qerru-Mai put a hand on Eston's arm and spoke softly. "Eston . . ."

Eston turned to see dozens of people looking at him. The string quartet's music fizzled out to a silence and the whole ballroom looked at the prince.

Eston turned to the guests with a tear in his eye and spoke. "All of you. You are blind to the suffering. You feast daily and wear gowns as expensive as a poor man's house. You sit and look at paintings and sculptures instead of at your own people. Our soldiers are starving and dying! We have reports of more and more Gypsies fleeing persecution in the Southlands each day and finding no better home on our streets. Our citizens are struggling just to keep their heads above water because you've taken all the damn boats for yourselves!" His voice, and only his voice, echoed in the Grand Ballroom. "You are diplomats, yet you have done nothing! Standing ina palace does not innately make you good!"

Senator Mar swirled his wine glass and shook his head. "What right does a child have to lecture–"

"I AM YOUR PRINCE!" Eston slapped Mar's wineglass out of his hand, staining his clothes with scarlet drops of wine; the crowd stood still after hearing the shattering glass on the marble floor.

Eston's voice fell hushed but raged with anger. "And I will no longer stand for the lack of action being taken in this palace . . . You act like Xandria is just a thought and not a threat. But I will tell you right now that nothing is stopping her and her army from marching right up to our front gates and burning our nation to the ground – nothing except for our brave soldiers who are giving up their lives to defend you."

Eston looked around at the crowd. "You should be ashamed!" he yelled and then fell to a soft voice. "Because I sure as hell am. . . . The party is over; I'm calling a Council meeting in fifteen minutes. And I swear to the Great Mother, if someone doesn't show up, they will be out of Aunestauna by morning." Eston stormed out of the Grand Ballroom, trailed by Qerru-Mai. Shocked by the prince's outburst, the crowd stood silent and then members slowly began to file out.

"Eston, wait!" Qerru-Mai took off her heels and ran behind him. "Eston," she caught her breath. "What you did back there was insane. What were you thinking? Your mother will be back before nightfall."

"I am thinking of Ferramoor; and if taking initiative to get the job done is what I need to do, I'll do it without a care for what my parents think. Thousands of our countrymen are dying – I must do something."

She paused. "Well, you have my support; your integrity and your ideas are bright, and you are right in the sense that this palace is failing in its duties. We'll try to prevent the word from getting to your father so he doesn't try to come back. But your mother will come back soon and–"

"My mother will agree with me that these things have to be done."

Qerru-Mai nodded. "Let's hear your plan then."

The two headed for the Council Chambers in the East Wing. Eston's mind rattled back and forth, still wondering how his mind had switched bodies before sunrise *and* quickly four times. *And why was I, as Kyan, with Fillian in the Great Cathedral? Why was Fillian gone from the palace?*

"The first change starting tonight," Eston announced from Tronum's chair in the Council Chamber, "is that the palace will no longer be taking in unnecessary supplies. That means we will have no more feasts or parties; everyone will receive only what he or she needs to perform his or her job well. The excess food and wine that would normally be shipped here will be given out for free to the farms of struggling people throughout Ferramoor, from Sundale and Diphabee, to Oakfoot and Farwater, to Saerasong and Dawne."

Murmuring echoed throughout the chamber. "This means no more parties, balls, plays, festivals, banquets, or unnecessary events. Every available performer, artist, and otherwise unoccupied person will be put to work helping various shipping caravans that deliver supplies to towns throughout Ferramoor."

Senator Nollard stood up in fury. "And tell us why it's a good idea that we would be fracturing our capital city and giving our resources away to villages that can't fend for themselves. I'll have you remember that Aunestauna is in *my senatorial district.* I think I have a right to worry about my city!"

Prophet Ombern, quite surprisingly, spoke up. "Does it not say in our Holy Book in Chapter 89 Section 5, 'And when the time shall come that your fellow man has need of sword or timber or lamb, I, the Great Mother say – give unto them.'?"

The whole room murmured and waited for Senator Nollard's response.

Eston looked at Qerru-Mai, who smiled back at him with a little nod, *go on.* Eston turned back to the Council and spoke. "And with winter on its way, the rest of Ferramoor does not have adequate supplies for the cold. The stacks of firewood that we don't need for cooking will be given out to the slums of Aunestauna. Senator Elim, I am putting you in charge of these two projects."

The female senator with salt and pepper hair to her waist nodded. "I will order three different shipments of food and wine, one to Longbrush to aid the North, one to Bellerush to distribute to the Spring Rivers, and one to Abendale to cover the Green Rivers and the Burning Hills."

"Thank you, Senator," said Eston. "Third item, this war has gone on long enough. I believe we have the men and the resources to take the fight to Xandria. We can prepare for an offensive assault on the Great Cerebrian Gate and push into Eastern Endlebarr straight for Seirnkov."

Whittingale interrupted Eston. "Eston, I'm sorry but I doubt we have the power to accomplish such a feat. Bringing the fight to Xandria is dangerous, we don't know what could happen. We don't have the resources for it."

"With redistribution and hard work we can," said Eston. "We have more men and more food; we just have to use both more efficiently. Senator Duboiret, I implore you to take what volunteers you can from Seawatch, Dothram, and Landevore – I'm not worried about Paruseans or Northernfolk invading on the North Sea with fishing vessels."

"The little prince is right," said Ombern, voice booming across the chamber. "He's starting to sound a bit more like his grandfather. Some of you barely remember a time before the war. We end it now; we have the means. There are more ways than you–"

"Prophet," said Whittingale, "that's vastly untrue. Look, Eston, you can redistribute supplies all you wish, but you cannot take military command; you simply do not have the authority. Your father and your father alone calls for changes and he's absent. As the acting Scarlet Lord, I only have command over the Scarlet Guard, but there's nothing more with which I can help."

Qerru-Mai looked softly at Eston. "Feeding the poor is a good start. But you won't receive any support if you try to reinforce our military without your father here."

Eston paused and debated it in his head. "Make it a priority then. We fix our broken system, and when we can, we'll push forward in Endlebarr." He scanned the room. Most of the eyes that looked back doubted him; but it didn't matter. "Get started."

§

Prophet Ombern slammed his door to his private wing in the Great Cathedral. He muttered, ". . . Council will damn us all if we don't take the fight to Cerebria. How lost are we that we trust a child with a victory more than our king?" He threw down his coat. He sat down at his desk and opened the *Matrislibereux* to Chapter 89 Section 5 and began to read. After a half hour had passed, Ombern figured it would be best to sleep and save his worries until tomorrow. He blew out the candle and stepped out on his balcony overlooking the moonlit First and Second Districts.

Breathing in the cool air, the old man felt the Great Mother's spirit coursing through him, inspiring him. A voice in his head told him he was right to be doing it; it is not treason if it helps Ferramoor. The king was dying, and Eston would soon take up the mantle. He would support the Prophet; the war would be over, and all this would be saved.

He looked up and spoke to the stars, sighing, "How this world has fallen from its days of glory. Great Mother, bring us back to that time when your law was the king's law and when your voice was the king's voice . . . Save this fallen world."

Stepping back into his room, he pulled out the hidden drawer in his desk just to make sure its contents were still safe. Just then, the bells of the Great Cathedral began to ring, drowning out his scream of pure anger.

BENEATH AUNESTAUNA
Chapter Twenty Three

~Morning, November 3rd
Aunestauna, Ferramoor

"A half argentum?" said Kyan. "You're kidding, right?"

The baker – Mr. Ruben Tumno – raised his hairy hands. "Well 'cause a' t'e war, our prices been goin' up slightly. Is it too much?" The man was about as large sideways as he was tall, but he wore a warm smile and scruffy beard.

Kyan smiled. "It's too little. I have been your customer for ten years now, and you just haven't met me. Here, take twenty."

Mr. Tumno laughed. "Surely you must be a' jokin'."

Kyan was silent and held forward the coins.

"Well, my dear boy, 'tis quite a gift indeed."

"It's the least I can do, Mr. Tumno." Kyan left a bag of argentums on the counter and walked out with two croissants. He ate them as he walked through the beautiful slums of the Third District. The kids at the school were out kicking a ball in the square and when the leather ball rolled by Kyan, he kicked it back into their circle. He laughed and joined them.

§

Vree Shaarine watched Kyan from a high attic window and pressed her hand against it. *Leave the city, you idiot.*

"How cute," said Bay behind her, Riccolo's second. "Little Vree's found herself a boyfriend."

She gave him a dirty look.

"We won't hurt him," he said, stepping right behind her and whispering in her ear. "He's safe not knowing. But it's too bad you can't see him anymore." He moved her hair off her neck. "You have feelings for him?" he slid his hand across her waist.

"Get off me, you rat." She slapped his hand away.

"Now, now," said Riccolo, standing up from a box, "We don't want any tension here, do we?"

A high-pitched laugh broke out from another Nightsnake girl with wild, tangled hair.

"As Bay said, your *boyfriend* will not—"

"He's not my—" snarled Vree.

"—*will not get hurt,* Ms. Shaarine."

Vree's tanned face turned red. "Oh like hell!" She grabbed Riccolo by his trench coat and pushed him against the attic wall and whispered, "Like Grane, and Brethom and all the others that you said the same thing about!"

Riccolo grabbed her throat with his good hand, squeezed, and threw her down. "You don't speak to me that way. I've given you a home." He kicked her in the stomach.

She coughed and struggled on the ground. "You— you took her away. You sold her. You raped her and you maimed her."

He smashed her head on the floor, whispering in her ear with a chuckle. "And you can have her back once you've paid your debts to me. Remember our little deal?" Holding Vree down, Riccolo lowered his knuckle adorned with a steel spike and drew it across her arm, causing a gut-wrenching scream to reverberate in the attic. He clicked his tongue and stood, beginning to pace around the bleeding girl, the dozens of silver bracelets on his arm softly jingling. "You don't trust me. After *all I've done* for you . . . You would have been a frozen corpse on these streets if it wasn't for me. I took you in and gave you a home." He kicked her side. "Respect . . . that's all I ask," he kicked again. "And for some reason," he drove his foot harder into her side, "you are incapable," harder, "of giving it to me!"

Vree coughed and wheezed on the floor. "I h— hate— y—"

"What was that, you little slut?" said Riccolo.

"I— I hate you."

The few Nightsnakes in the room laughed, and Bay smoked from his pipe in a reclined position.

Riccolo bent down, kissed her head, and whispered, "*shhhh,*" He drew cards out of his pocket and shuffled them as he paced. "Let the bitches bite," he sighed. "Bay, tell me again how much money on top of *the reward* we got for Kyan's little adventure."

Bay removed the pipe from his mouth and puffed out a cloud of smoke. "Ten thousand argentums."

Riccolo laughed and threw a cloud of cards at him. "We bet on the right kid!"

§

~Night, November 3rd

Kyan creaked open the door of the Great Cathedral. Last night, no, tonight, when Eston fainted, he saw himself there, and Fillian too. *What was he doing here? . . . It's ten o'clock, five minutes before – or until – the switch will occur. I was in a room with him, I remember seeing it as Eston during the ball.*

The nave of the cathedral was dark and vacant. "Hello?" his voice echoed. Kyan found a staircase leading to another wing of the cathedral. "Hello?" he whispered. He grabbed a single torch that lit the staircase. Opening into a hall, he listened closely and could hear shuffling feet. He approached the room where the sound came from. *Ombern is at the ball right now, no one should be here.* He twisted the doorknob and Fillian jumped out of his socks, diving behind a bed. "Prince Fillian?"

Fillian peeked his head out. "Who are you?"

Kyan had practiced the lie with himself – something to make Fillian trust him. Confidently, Kyan spoke. "I work as an agent for your brother, Prince Eston. The last time he went out into the city in early September, he knew he'd probably be caught and taken back, so he hired me to work for him and operate in the city where he can't. He's been noticing you're up to something, and he wanted me to find out what you're doing and help you."

But Kyan could tell he wasn't convincing Fillian. *I need to tell him something only Eston knows.* Kyan thought for a moment. *That's it!* "Eston also told me that he borrowed your shoes with the little black scuff on the bottom of the sole for the ball tonight. He wanted to match Qerru-Mai."

Fillian's eyebrows showed his nervousness, Kyan's knowledge of the scuff on his dress shoes made him begin to trust the story. Cautiously, Fillian began to stand up. Disregarding the comment about the shoes, he muttered, "–didn't want to take risks himself . . ." he said, looking around the room. "He's been practically locked in his room for a month, of course he doesn't want to get involved in other things." He stared at Kyan. "What kind of agent are you?"

Kyan hesitated. "Well . . . I just update him on things in the city. Sometimes I try to help him crack down on gangs and such. But after the robbery that ended with Benja Tiggins' execution, he wanted me to help uncover whatever mystery Benja was involved with. He gave me what information he knew and asked me to aid you in whatever you're trying to do. If you don't believe me, ask Prince Eston. My name is Kyan."

Prince Fillian cautiously shook Kyan's hand. "I wish Eston would have told me . . . I'll talk to him when I get back to the palace," he said.

Kyan looked at what seemed to be Ombern's bedroom. "What are you doing here?"

Fillian hesitated. "I'm here because I think Prophet Ombern is hiding something. Well, not just him, our father too, and a few others, like Senator—"

"An'Drui," said Kyan in a hushed voice.

". . . how did—"

"Eston told me," said Kyan.

"I think that something happened before my brother and I were born. Something that my father wants to keep secret. But Ombern and An'Drui want to expose it – whatever it is. I've trailed them for the past few weeks, and they keep going down, very far down, to this dark hallway in the palace. There's a door that they have a key to, and it opens into a room where there's this clicking sound. It sounds like wheels, and I think it's an automatic lock; it resets itself."

Kyan paused. Suddenly, a flash of light hit his eyes. His arms slid off a column in a brightly lit ballroom and he fell to the floor. Another flash of light returned his mind into the body of Kyan. He had collapsed to the floor.

"Are you alright? You just fell like a rock," said Fillian.

"Yes, um . . . fainting episode." Kyan switched the subject back. ". . . So, this lock, what do you think it will open?"

"I don't know, something big."

"I think Benja knew. I was walking with Prince Eston once and I saw Benja talking to An'Drui, and he seemed upset, like she wanted to do something he thought was bad. He said that's not what his position was for. And Qerru-Mai said that Senator An'Drui had mentioned the fire before."

"The fire?" asked Fillian

"Prince Eston told me that Whittingale spoke with him about the night he was born," said Kyan. "Whittingale saw King Tronum in a palace chamber late at night in front of a huge pile of burning parchment. Apparently Whittingale said he didn't know what it was, only that it was significant. Prince Eston asked your father what it was and Tronum told him that he has no right to know. I have a strong feeling that An'Drui knows what happened that night; so does Ombern."

"But Whittingale doesn't?" asked Fillian.

"I don't know. But maybe whatever was burned was destroyed because the king didn't want anyone to know what's behind that lock. Maybe behind that lock is the chamber where it happened – beneath the palace."

Fillian stood up and fumbled through more of Ombern's papers. "I've been trying to find anything that hints how to open it. It automatically spins and sounds like it resets after twenty-six sets of clicks, so I think it's letters that open the lock. Ombern and An'Drui have been in that room trying to figure out the letters, but with a Jejjarn lock I'm guessing that it's designed to jam if the wrong code is put in. It clicks eleven times in a set, meaning the lock would take hundreds of years to open if you were guessing. So they must have some way of calculating what the code is that can only get them one letter at a time. But unlike them, we would have no way in."

Kyan's eyes widened. "Wait, what did you just say?"

"We have no way in, we would need a key," said Fillian.

"No, how many times does it click in a set?"

"Eleven."

Kyan counted the letters in his head and thought to himself, *Silverbrook*. He jumped up and started feeling Ombern's desk.

"What are you doing?" said Fillian.

Kyan spoke quickly. "Benja. He knew. The last thing he told Prince Eston was to go in his room and burn a piece of paper that was beneath his pillow." Kyan continued to feel under the desk, seeming to look for something. "It's eleven letters. I don't know what it means but it has to be that code."

"Well, what it is then?" asked Fillian.

Kyan looked around. "It's not safe to say here."

"Okay, but why are you groping the desk?"

Kyan's finger slid across a tiny lever beneath the desk and a drawer popped out. "Ombern wouldn't keep the key on his person." Kyan pulled out a giant rusty key from the drawer. "He would keep the key where he thinks the Great Mother would protect it; in the Great Cathedral."

Fillian smiled. "I can get you into the Royal Palace. I know an entrance."

Somewhat reluctant about stealing the key, Kyan laughed, "So do I."

"You still have it, right?" whispered Fillian, holding a torch. Kyan nodded and slid the key out of his pocket. He could hear the ticking from within the room, and his heart seemed to sink with the rhythm. He turned the lock, and the two slid into the room. On the far wall of the stone room were eleven wheels, each four feet in diameter, embedded in the wall, turning one after another. "Now that's what I call a lock."

"It's massive," said Kyan, stepping close to it.

"Don't touch it! Not yet. See those pegs on the bottom? We have to stop each wheel on its letter once it turns to it, and it will jam if we stop it on the wrong one. Are you sure *Silverbrook* will work?"

Kyan paused. "I trust Benja." He nodded at Fillian and they put their hands on the first wheel's stop, waiting for it to cycle through the alphabet. *Q, R,* "Now!" They pulled it and it stopped on S, while the others kept spinning. "Ten more to go."

Stopping the pegs on each letter, they ended with a K, and the room went silent. Not two seconds later, a great booming sound echoed through the stone, and the wall began to slide open. The two looked at each other, and then down the endless flight of stairs that dove far beneath the palace and the city. An icy cold air blasted up at them and rustled their cloaks as the wall closed behind them. Fillian put his hand on his sword. "You can go first."

For minutes, they walked down the staircase. "Great Mother," whispered Fillian, "how long has this been here? It goes on forever." A giant door appeared ahead, illuminated by his torch. A gigantic engraving lay embedded in the wood, and Kyan traced his hand along it. Fillian grabbed the door handle and pulled.

A thundering crack echoed as the enormous door opened and a gust of cold air blew out Fillian's torch. A very faint light came from inside. Kyan looked to Fillian. "Would you like to go first?"

"I would," said a voice from behind both of them. The dim, dark figure of Senator An'Drui appeared as she walked down the last steps of the staircase.

"You were following us?" said Fillian.

Senator An'Drui smiled. "I've been trying, like you, to get in this chamber for months. *Silverbrook.* I overlooked that simple word." Looking at Kyan, she asked Fillian, "Who is this?"

Fillian responded nervously. "Eston's . . . spy; personal assistant."

Kyan gave a short bow to Senator An'Drui.

"And you trust him?" asked the senator.

Fillian nodded.

She smiled. "I'm sure you are desiring to see what's beyond these doors." The senator silently stepped past Fillian and Kyan and through the doorway.

"What's that light?" asked Kyan. "It's coming from all around." He extinguished his torch. Taking a second for their eyes to adjust, the three saw that they stood in a gigantic domed room nearly a hundred feet high which included both manmade masonry and natural stalactites. A pile of scorched scientific instruments lay in the center, blackened and broken; ash from burned paper coated the floor. The wall around them looked like a liquidy glass, radiating a soft, white glow.

Kyan immediately recognized what the glowing walls of light were — *Taurimous.*

The wall of soft light was divided into five sections by colossal stone columns. The tall panels of Taurimous were unlike anything Kyan had seen . . . except, they reminded him of something. *That light, I've seen it . . . The stone I stole from the vault.*

"What's behind those?" said Fillian as he walked up to touch the cavern's walls of light.

"Don't touch it!" whispered Senator An'Drui.

Fillian jumped back.

"You do not know what those shields lock inside." She walked to the pile of burnt flasks and desks and picked up a bell which sat on top of it. "Get back," she said and then rang the bell with a giant reverberating clang. Immediately, thundering roars shook the air and the stone that held up the cavern. The deafening sound drove them to their knees and through Kyan's mind coursed an image of Endlebarr and a giant scaled tail and claws. The roars increased in intensity, seeming to come from behind the walls of ice-like Taurimous. Senator An'Drui's eyes widened, and her breathing quickened. "This is it," she said.

Fillian stood, shaking. "What in the bloody hell—"

"It's Ferramoor's greatest secret," said An'Drui. She walked in a circle around the underground chamber, looking at the five shimmering walls. "Your father regrets it to this day, but I swear it will win us the war. Just a few years before Prince Eston was born, Tronum anticipated his father's death and also Xandria's plot to take the Empire for herself. Knowing he would need to defend Ferramoor, he found a young sorceress and hired her for protection. But we've now proven that he also convinced her to make creatures — monsters — to defend Ferramoor.

"From what I know, near the time Eston was born, the young sorceress fled the Royal Palace, not wanting to be a part of your father's mad science. *Ms. Silverbrook.* Few people had ever learned her name, and her files were destroyed. How did you know?"

"Benja told Prince Eston," said Kyan with a frog in his throat. "He must have found something with her name and history in his days as the Scarlet Lord."

"I see," said Senator An'Drui. "But recently, I have been trying to find this place. When she fled, she set fire to everything she had created, including this pile of books and scientific instruments here." She touched what remained of an ash-covered book. Another deafening roar came from beyond the walls. "She must have permanently put up these walls of her . . . I guess you could say magic. They're the only thing holding those monsters back."

Fillian pointed at one of the five walls. "Why is that one dimmer than the rest?"

"Prophet Ombern believes one of the five escaped before she left; it fled to Endlebarr and made a nest there. On a mission in the forest, General Carbelle found where it was and reported back to Tronum, who ordered the construction of Camp Stoneheart near it to ensure the Cerebrians would never capture it and use it against us."

Endlebarr and Stoneheart . . . Silverbrook's monster paralyzed my platoon, thought Kyan.

"Did someone release it?" asked Kyan. "How would you get them out from behind these barriers?"

Senator An'Drui thought for a moment. "I suppose you'd have to get a magic user to open it, since it was a sorceress who created it."

Fillian spoke. "Senator, you want to unleash the rest of them to decimate the Cerebrian army."

"To rid the world of your aunt's evil? Yes, I do."

From behind the walls of Silverbrook's Taurimous, a roar like a crack of thunder shook the earth beneath Aunestauna.

THE GREAT CEREBRIAN GATE
Chapter Twenty Four

~Morning, November 4th
Western Endlebarr

Tayben reached forward to touch the glowing white flower, but before his hands could caress its petals, his eyes shot open.

Albeire Harkil, sitting crossed legged in a meditative position, looked up at him. His blonde hair fell down his back and onto the damp black soil of the forest floor. "What did you see?" he said in a melodic, soothing voice.

"I don't know, it was just a lot of dark and light."

"It was *the* dark and light."

". . . I saw a flower," said Tayben. "It was glowing, shimmering."

"I cannot explain what you see when you meditate like this with me," said Harkil, looking far into Tayben's soul, "being connected gives you the ability to see strange visions."

"Connected with what?"

"Everything," said Harkil. "The Nymphs gave us the ability to see everything, to merge our souls with the universe."

"Then why didn't we feel that monster at Stoneheart?" said Tayben, finally knowing what the monster was.

"That's what concerns me. This thing we encountered hid in the shadows between this world and another." Harkil closed his eyes. "And it's what we can't see that motivates us. This monster . . . it terrifies me, yes. It's an evil in the world. But know that it's not the only thing that hides in the shadows."

From behind them, Thephern walked up. "Harkil, you should try spending as much time with your own platoon as you do with mine."

Harkil smiled. "My apologies. We were only meditating."

"And telling stories about *shadow and light*," chuckled Thephern.

Harkil stood up and spoke politely, but close to Thephern's face. "Do not take the Nymphs' gift for granted. I advise you to open your eyes. Have a good one, brother." Harkil walked off through the brush to train with his platoon.

Tayben turned to Thephern Luck, still apprehensive of his platoon commander since he had hesitated to kill a Ferr. But after the encounter with the beast, Thephern's memory of the encounter seemed blank, and his attitude toward him was unchanged. Tayben remembered the claws slashing at his head. After the other platoons arrived, Tayben passed out, his next memory being in the trees once more, answering General Lekshane's questions on what had happened.

"What did it look like?" asked the general.

"I– I don't know, sir. It was black . . . and– and big. I don't know why we couldn't hear it or even sense it . . . it's like it hijacked our minds until it could strike us."

"It paralyzed you?"

Tayben froze, remembering the feeling of helplessness. "Yes, sir. I was the only one not fully immobilized after it hit us – I don't know why . . . after a minute of fighting it, I lost consciousness."

The general put his hands out and squeezed Tayben's shoulders. "What did you feel, Shae?"

Tayben stared blankly into the canopy as he answered. "I felt . . . cold . . . my body felt cold and weak . . . I– I felt like the clarity and light I've had since the Nymphs made me a Phantom . . . it faded. I felt . . . human again."

Of course, he knew now what the beast really was – a sorceress-created monster that escaped from Aunestauna. Tayben shook his head to clear his mind.

When the galloping of hooves echoed far in the distance, Thephern ordered, "Get your spear, Tayben . . . Now!"

The sixteen Phantoms quickly gathered in the trees as the sound of the solitary horse and rider drew near. Many of the leaves in the canopy were beginning to change color, as Endlebarr never truly experienced winter, but only autumn. A familiar whistle rang through the forest. General Lekshane sheathed his sword. "It's Irroy. But what she is doing on this side of the Taurbeir-Krons I do not know." The Phantoms jumped down to the forest floor as Vaya Irroy, Xandria's messenger, came speeding through on her horse. Her lips were cracked and bleeding, and the horse's legs shook as it brought her to a halt. The strawberry blonde dismounted and fell limp on the ground, followed by a thud of her horse collapsing. "What happened Ms. Irroy?" said Lekshane as he ran up to her.

The fastest horse in Cerebria lay collapsed on the ground. "Th– The queen found– I rode for five days straight to get here– Zarranc, my horse, is he dead? – There wasn't–"

"Irroy!" yelled Lekshane. "We can't understand you. What happened?"

"I... I got an order... ran out here as fast as I could," she tried to swallow, but her mouth was bone dry. Gallien quickly handed her his container of water, and she chugged it down, thanking him with her eyes. Breathless, she continued. "The queen's spies . . . they suspect our army is going to be sabotaged." Tayben's stomach dropped, knowing exactly what Vaya spoke of. The Evertauri's plans had begun; his conversation with Mordvitch started it all. Vaya gasped for air. "Our forces are shipping a great deal of . . . explosive weapons . . . through our Great Gate. There are r— rebels that are going to attack the shipment."

Thephern shook his head. "There is no way any civilians could come all this way into Endlebarr just to attack a supply shipment." Tayben shook his head. *They went under Endlebarr.*

Vaya coughed on the ground. "These are no civilians, General — they are sorcerers — 'call themselves the Evertauri . . . and they are going to destroy the Great Cerebrian Gate . . . tonight."

Lekshane stood still.

"Go now!" she said.

"Your horse is dead, miss; you cannot survive in this forest," said Harkil.

"Go!" she screamed, "For the sake of our freedom, go!"

Lekshane scanned the fifteen cloaked figures behind him. "It's thirty miles to the gate. We can make it by nightfall. Sorcerers you say? We'll show them the might of Xandria. Phantoms, follow me East." In a blur of black, Vaya was left in the underbrush of Endlebarr.

The sun had set, but beneath the twilight sky, Tayben could easily see where the snowy peaks of the Taurbeir-Krons dipped down to form a pass between the two halves of Endlebarr. Between the two lowest peaks sat a three-hundred-foot-high wall of black stone, with multiple turrets and an enormous metal gate in its center. "Marvelous, isn't it?" said Gallien next to Tayben. "This has been protecting Cerebria for twenty years." Xandria's Gate had allowed no Ferramish forces to ever pass. For an army with supplies, it was the only way through the treacherous mountains. Lekshane called the Phantoms forward. They climbed up above the gate, leaving the lush forest and stepping into the snow of the mountains. The Phantoms watched from the snowy mountainside just above the wall, on top of which fifty Cerebrian soldiers stood.

Hiding from Cerebrian soldiers behind a snowdrift, Tayben scanned the massive wall, which held rooms of weapons for the hundreds of Cerebrian soldiers it housed — Jade Guards, Cerebria's response to Ferramoor's Scarlet Guard. Chent pointed out into the eastern forest — something was there. From the snow drift, Tayben could see a line of horses and covered wagons coming slowly up the Cerebrian slope to the Great Cerebrian Gate. The seemingly endless brigade of weapons finally stopped emerging from the forest and was pulled up to the gate, ready to be used on the other side to attack Ferramish troops. With a shutter that echoed off the faces of the mountains, the iron lattice wrenched out of the snowy ground and the great doors behind it creaked open. The Jade Guards took another look out into the winter night and began to let their army's supply wagons through.

"Keep your eyes open," said Lekshane. As each of the wagons passed through the Great Gate, they stopped on the opposite, Ferramish, side. Soldiers began stepping off their covered wagons and tying up the reins to their horses. "Why are they stopping?" whispered Lekshane to himself, resting a hand on his thick, reddish-brown beard. The next cart was stopped by a guard and before he could ask the wagon for identification, a flash of yellow light emerged from the hands of a soldier and engulfed the bottom of the gate. Instantly, a hundred cloaked figures appeared from within the wagons on either side of the gate.

"The rebels are driving the carts!" said Lekshane. The Phantoms bolted down the mountain toward the wall, to which the crowd of disguised rebels were running. A rainbow of color rocketed from their bodies toward the side doors of the gate, from which Cerebrian soldiers were emerging. A chorus of bells sounded from the top of the wall as Jade Guards shot arrows from the top. "First and Third Platoons, follow me to the bottom and engage the rebels! Second Platoon, go to the top of the wall."

Tayben's Platoon rushed atop the wall, passing real Cerebrian soldiers in a blur of black and flew through a door to the interior of the wall. As they descended down staircases toward the clamor, Tayben shouted out, "They're going to try and blow the gate! Guard the structural supports." The Phantoms turned around a bend onto a balcony which looked over the eastern forest and the mountains. Snow had begun to fall heavily, and the wind threatened to blow them off the balcony two hundred feet down to the snowy hills below.

A group of cloaked men turned onto the balcony. The Phantoms ducked under a rocketing plane of green light. In that second, Tayben saw the fearful faces of his platoon, not knowing how to fight against sorcery . . . but how much could he tell them? "Don't touch the light!" he yelled as he pounced forward at the group of Evertauri before him. Hurling his spear at them, he stopped in his tracks as an Evertauri produced a shower of embers that vaporized the shaft in mid-flight.

Tayben drew his sword and jumped over the Evertauri, flipping himself in the air to dodge the beams of Taurimous shot at him. From the opposite side, he kicked the knees of a sorcerer and jammed his sword through his head. Chent loosed an arrow at the sorcerers but it was shattered in the air by a ball of sapphire fire. Gallien sprung forward bringing his sword down on a shield of coppery Taurimous. His sword rebounded off the light and cut him on his shoulder. An Evertauri disguised as a Cerebrian soldier threw a knife at Thephern, whom he just saw as a blur of shadow. Thephern caught the knife and swung it back at the Evertauri at five times the speed, piercing straight through the Evertauri's armor. Ferron ripped a door from its hinges and chucked it at the group, sending four men flying off the balcony to their deaths. As the last Evertauri sent a fireball at Chent, Tayben snapped the attacker's neck. The group looked over the balcony to the ground far below, where Evertauri were beginning to remove boxes out of the covered wagons and toward the doors. "We'll each take a central staircase," said Thephern. "That's where we'll find the rebels."

Hearing more and more swords, yelling, and the shimmering sound of Taurimous as he bounded down a stone staircase, Tayben was blown back by a wave of red light. Feeling burns up and down his front, he quickly sprang up with his sword. Seeming to already know Tayben's move, the Evertauri coated his arm in false fire as a shock absorber, and as Tayben heaved his sword down, the Evertauri caught the blade in his flaming hand. The Evertauri squeezed the blade, turning it red hot. Tayben looked in horror at the Evertauri's face in the cloak, and Calleneck stared back at him with animalistic intensity.

With his face shaking, Calleneck screamed, "TRAITOR!" Tayben's sword melted in Calleneck's crimson hand of fire, and Calleneck's fist, covered in a ball of energy, soared into his chest. But as soon as Tayben felt himself knocked off the staircase, his eyes flashed open in the body of Calleneck, who sat up after sleeping on a tunnel floor of the Network beneath Endlebarr.

§

~Hours Before
The Network, Eastern Endlebarr

Calleneck stopped at the end of the cold, damp tunnel. "It's right here." His hand felt along the wall. Hundreds of colorful flames from the Evertauri behind him illuminated the hall with a cold light. Calleneck no longer felt comfortable around any of them. He didn't feel at home with the Evertauri. He had no home anymore. Xandria's troops had killed his parents. But they killed his parents because he challenged Xandria. Nothing seemed right, nothing seemed like the right side to fight for. But this was all he and his two sisters had. At least they might be able to see the fall of the queen who caused this all to start. He was lost, but he knew Xandria had to go.

Calleneck looked at the calculations and maps in his hands.

Sir Borius Shipton stood tall and menacing behind him. "Are you sure?"

"Yes," said Calleneck.

Beside them, Madrick Nebelle placed his hand on the wall, letting a silver liquid-like Taurimous spread. Slowly, the wall disintegrated with large puffs of hot steam; but the heat was replaced by a cold gust of forest air that blew in from the other side, extinguishing briefly all the flames in the tunnel. Calleneck looked forward at the revealed ramp of dirt that led to the twilight surface above. Madrick motioned Calleneck up to confirm they were in the correct location. Slowly, the two walked up the ramp, emerging from a large hole between two colossal tree roots.

Two hundred feet above them, the canopy of Eastern Endlebarr hung dark and still. Just west of them sat the Great Gate in the frigid winter mountains of the Taurbeir-Krons. Madrick nodded to himself and headed back into the tunnel, where Calleneck could hear him address the hundred Evertauri that waited.

"The end of Xandria's rule is at hand," said Madrick. "We are not a large force, but the nation of Ferramoor is. The enemy of our enemy is our ally. If we take down this Gate, and enable the Ferrs to control this pass, we will be that much closer to destroying her."

A murmur swept through the Evertauri.

The President continued. "Target the soldiers in the supply train and only the soldiers," he said. "We will take the explosive weaponry and invade the wall, placing it on the four main structural pillars of the gate. Our engineers will connect the fuses, then we'll light it. The supply train should arrive within a mile in the next hour. We will attack before it reaches the gate. From then on, our navigator, Mr. Bernoil, says we will have to guide the carts through a half mile of forest. Our watchmen will notify us when it is time to engage. That is all; the rest of you have received your assignments. May your minds not falter."

Madrick and the Evertauri emerged from the tunnel to station themselves at the ready in the underbrush.

§

Aunika and Dalah sat together under a fallen tree waiting for orders. A little gold ribbon of fire danced around Dalah's fingers as she leaned close to her sister. Something obviously sat heavy on their minds; the recent events still played in their memories . . . the bodies of their parents lying still on the wood floor, flames engulfing their home. "It's not your fault," said Dalah; Aunika sat still. "All of us are to blame."

"I'm the one who got you into this mess," said Aunika.

Dalah looked her in the eye. "This wouldn't have happened if Xandria didn't start this war."

"Just promise me you will be careful. I can't stand the thought of you getting hurt. Always be analyzing your surroundings; and if you run into trouble, you know how to call for me."

"I'll be fine. We've trained for this. There won't be anything unexpected." Dalah paused. "Aunika, why do we need explosives if we can break stone ourselves?"

"The Great Gate is so enormous that it would require too much energy from us. Even if we did manage to escape the falling wall — much like a crumbling mountain — we wouldn't have enough energy to escape the Cerebrian forces that may come after us."

A long silence followed until Dalah asked, "Do you think President Nebelle is on edge because Raelynn left?"

"He's probably glad she's headed to Ferramoor again; he doesn't want to lose her like he lost Shonnar. I think she left because she was upset with her father — upset about Shonnar's death and Selenora's uprising and . . . Well, I just don't blame her for wanting to get away for a while." A dim silver glow spread throughout the nearby underbrush . . . it was time. The sisters stood and ran to the origin of the light, President Nebelle, around whom the Evertauri gathered.

Calleneck spoke quietly to Borius Shipton, showing him charts and drawings of the gate that spies had collected. ". . . all the way to this side, where the other doors are. If we can split this team into two groups, we'll have a better chance of reaching it in time. The difficulty lies in the actual design; we would have to run the fuse in between floors six and seven."

"But that can be done, correct?" said Borius.

Calleneck was still not used to the way he looked with one eye, the other gouged out by Grennkovff Kai'Le'a in battle. "If we have our engineers work on the explosives in the wagons while we take them from here to the gate, then yes. But that is assuming we take out every guard and there are no Cerebrian reinforcements. If there's little opposition, we'll just have to hurry and blow the thing. But once it ignites, no one in the wall will survive."

"Then we will try our best to evacuate. Thank you, Mr. Bernoil." Borius began to leave.

"Sir Borius, if I may," said Calleneck. "With an infiltration of this scale, won't our secrecy be compromised? Won't Xandria know?"

"It is the extent to which she knows that matters, Mr. Bernoil," said Borius. "After tonight, she will either conclude that it was the work of Ferramish special forces, or a rebel group. Ferramoor will likely take responsibility to intimidate her. But even if she calls the bluff, she will likely not know how we did it. We have also put steps in place to make her think that a rebel group may be located in Gienn, not right underneath her own city. But she will not learn our secrets. At this point, fear of what she does not know or understand is her greatest weakness . . . Thank you for your work, Mr. Bernoil. I must go." Borius left to speak with Madrick as Sir Kishk the Trainer approached Calleneck.

"You've done well," he said as more Evertauri gathered.

Calleneck turned as pale lights circled the Evertauri from a distance. He thought for a moment to point them out to the others around him but stopped himself. *Are those the Nymphs?* His stomach dropped and he felt a sense of dread, like this, the Evertauri, all of it was wrong. He was bringing war and death into their home. As Tayben, he is a sworn protector of the Nymphs and Endlebarr. *We don't belong here,* Calleneck thought. The pale lights flickered in and out of sight, then vanished altogether as quickly as they appeared.

As the Cerebrian supply train approached, Madrick silenced the Evertauri and motioned forward. The noise of wagons moving through the underbrush signaled the Evertauri to move into place. The hundreds of Evertauri stationed themselves behind bushes and trees next to the old forest road which was now overgrown to the point where it resembled only a footpath.

In a matter of minutes, the train of covered wagons reached the Evertauri. Each of the fifty wagons was pulled by two horses flanked on each side by six guards. From behind a bush, Borius conjured thousands of little floating specks of yellow light above the whole train, causing the Cerebrian soldiers to stop their wagons. All of the soldiers looked up at the little stars floating above them, murmuring to themselves. All together, the thousands of lights vanished, signaling every Evertauri to spring forward. Calleneck burst out of a bush and sent a jet of crimson flame into the eyes of the six soldiers nearest him. Crying out in pain, the blind soldiers flailed as Calleneck used his Taurimous to finish them off. In thirty seconds, every Cerebrian soldier in the train and just two Evertauri lay injured on the ground.

Tallius, along with four other boys, joined Calleneck at his wagon. They quickly put on the dark green armor of the Cerebrian soldiers and spurred the frightened horses forward. The Evertauri gently led the explosive wagon train west, ready to infiltrate the Great Gate.

Calleneck recalled the sickening image of his father's head split open and his mother's throat gushing blood. He remembered their faces — faces he knew for so long. Glazed over eyes pierced into his heart with a pain greater than any wound. He would avenge their deaths. *I won't stop until I have . . . until Xandria's kingdom falls.*

Seeming to cross a supernatural boundary between spring and winter, Calleneck's wagon emerged from the forest and instantly slowed on the five inches of fresh snow. A large white hill led up to a giant black wall of stone. Remembering seeing this wagon train, Calleneck strained to see any sign of the Phantoms on the snowy mountain to the south; but it was all a blanket of white and the falling snow hindered his vision. Looking ahead, as he walked in the snow, he sighed when the first wagon went through the gate, even though he had already witnessed everything that was to come in the next few minutes. About halfway through the train, Calleneck's cart was just three behind Borius's, the designated attack cart.

Nearly half of the wagons were already through the Great Gate when the attack cart stopped for inspection like every other and Calleneck held his breath. Giant doors on either side of the archway allowed soldiers to get in and out of the wall. A Cerebrian guard stepped up to ask for Borius's papers and Borius released an enormous explosion of yellow Taurimous, killing every guard at the bottom of the Great Gate. Hundreds of Evertauri jumped from the wagons and ran toward the gate, while others moved the carts of explosives into the wall.

Calleneck sprang forward and ran with Tallius through the snow while the four other boys spurred the horses forward. Bells chimed from the top of the wall and arrows began to pierce the air. Dozens of floors of weaponry and food storage filled the wall; the boys approached one of the four main columns by which it was held up. Taking the cover from their wagon, they began to stack the boxes of explosives around a column that stood in a hundred-foot foyer similar to a cathedral. Each column had branches connecting each floor to help hold the interior of the wall.

Hundreds of Cerebrian soldiers funneled down the main staircases and through the halls as the Evertauri smashed through the main doors with sorcerers and wagons. Tallius looked at Calleneck. "You ready?"

Calleneck put his hand on Tallius's shoulder. "Always."

The two ran toward the staircase sending jets of crimson and sapphire flame at the Cerebrian soldiers who screamed in terror at the sight of magic, glowing fire. More and more Evertauri filled the corridors of the wall.

"Tallius!" shouted Calleneck. "That door has a staircase behind it; take it up to the fifth floor and clear a path to this column! I'll take this one!" Calleneck flung himself through a door and up the staircase. Stopping on the fifth floor, he ran out into a mass of Jade Guards. Disguised as one of them, they had no time to react before he sent a disc of light flying outward, slicing their torsos clean open. An excruciating pain shot through his right shoulder, and he looked to see an arrow jutting out of his skin and armor. Another arrow shot past his ear, and he hurled a weak fireball at the two remaining soldiers. Crawling behind a stone pillar, he tried to pull the arrow out of his shoulder, but it was caught on his armor. Unlatching straps, he pulled off his armor, freeing the arrow, leaving himself in only his Evertauri cloak. *No more blending in.*

Calleneck looked at the giant column and noticed an open staircase on the other side. *Higher is better, we need to secure it from the top,* he thought as he ran along an open balcony toward it, trying not to move his arm. The wind from the blizzard pelted ice against his face as he sent a shower of swirling light toward a group of soldiers, knocking them off the wall and into the blizzard.

Rounding the corner, he bounded up the spiral staircase. A blur of black flashed in front of him, and he instinctively blew it back with a blast of crimson. The black thing turned into a cloaked figure that reached back to grab his sword. A memory of that moment flashed in his head, and knowing Tayben's next move, Calleneck coated his good arm and hand in a protective flame and caught the Phantom's sword as it came down with the force of five men, sending a shock of pain through his hand. Calleneck heated the flame in his hand; he could barely feel the sword's sharp edges. The metal grew orange, then red, and began to bend. Calleneck looked at the horrified face of himself as Tayben, enraged like never before at the disgusting things that Tayben had done in support of Xandria – a Cerebrian soldier the the ones who hiss his parents. The sword began to melt as he shouted the one word, he could think to describe his inner turmoil, "TRAITOR!" Calleneck let go of the sword and struck his fist into Tayben. A blinding light flashed in his eyes and a severe pain hit his stomach. He opened his eyes and looked into the face of Calleneck. Struck back into Tayben's consciousness, the Phantom fell off the staircase, landing hard on a beam of stone below.

CITY OF BLOOD
Chapter Twenty Five

~Night, November 4th
Aunestauna, Ferramoor

Prophet Ombern sat on his balcony of the Great Cathedral overlooking the starlit city of Aunestauna. The Luxuex, as the cathedral was called, sat near the base of the palace hill like a guard tower. Decorated in intricate stained glass and haunting gargoyles, it cast ominous shadows in the moonlight.

In his chair, Ombern stroked his long white beard and peered out west toward the inlet where he thought he saw a little beam of light flicker on the watery horizon. Another light appeared, then vanished. Tapping his foot, he watched a carriage on the street below. He scratched his palm as he watched a flapping flag on the building across the street. Nervousness coursed through his body, and he soon realized he was scratching skin off his hand, bleeding slightly from the wrinkles.

"Prophet?" Ombern jumped at the sound of his name. A relatively young priest stood behind him in long white robes and a scarlet hood. "Prophet, are you alright?"

"Yes, yes, fine," said Ombern as he gazed absentmindedly into the distance. He stopped digging his nail into his palm but continued to tap his foot. Ever since the key had been stolen from his drawer, he'd wondered who had access to the beasts beneath the palace and if they had found them.

The priest looked worried. "Can I get you a glass of wine, Prophet? You seem troubled."

Ombern furrowed his eyebrows. "Yes, that would be good," he said.

"Red or white?" said the priest.

"Red." Ombern glanced back, noticing the priest was new.

The priest exited the balcony and came back a minute later with a glass of wine. "Our best, Prophet." The priest handed the glass to Ombern with a four-fingered hand.

"Ah," said Ombern as he swallowed a large gulp, "the Great Mother's elixir never disappoints." He took another sip, but then coughed some of it up on his clothes.

"Your Honor, are you well?" asked the priest. "Your face is blue."

Ombern's hands shook, and the glass slipped from his grasp and shattered on the stone. The prophet fell off his chair to the floor of the balcony, coughing in a fit and slamming his fist. The priest stood back and smiled, fixing his hair with his mutilated hand. Ombern stopped coughing, and his eyes rolled back.

The priest smiled and unbuttoned his collar, revealing a snakebite on his neck. Riccolo knelt down and whispered to the twitching Prophet, "Stupid, old man." Ombern's eyes closed and he lay still, heart stopped. Riccolo walked silently out of the cathedral, passing a dead, young priest with missing robes. "One prophet down, one queen and a few thousand Ferrs to go."

§

Fillian knocked on Eston's door and entered with a stack of parchment. "Eston," he said, slamming the papers down on his desk, "I'm not fetching any more of these for you. You have to give it a rest. How many trade reports have you read since dinner?"

"Probably forty," answered Eston, beginning to organize the papers.

"Great Mother! Eston, Ferramoor isn't going to collapse in one night. No one is getting any sleep because of us . . . well, mainly you. Father is going to have our heads when he gets back from Ifle-Laarm, just so you know."

"*Both* our heads?" said Eston. "Then who would he have to inherit the crown?"

Fillian sighed. "You can take a break, you know."

"That would make me a hypocrite."

Fillian shook his head. "Seriously, Eston. You've done a fine job. Just take a walk with me or something . . . come on."

Eston reluctantly stood from his chair, grabbed his coat and sword sheath, and followed his brother, noticing the key that hung around his neck on a small chain.

Reaching the large stone bridge near the South Palace Wing, the princes stopped and leaned on the railing. Fillian looked down a hundred feet to a courtyard below. "Bet I can spit farther than you this time."

Eston raised an eyebrow and chuckled. "How old are you? We're grown now, we can't play the games we used to play."

"Oh, come on," said Fillian. "No one's around."

Eston stared at him and slowly smiled. Gathering saliva in his mouth, he spit a white ball that soared out to the courtyard below.

Fillian spat next, and an ocean breeze blew his little glistening ball twice the distance of Eston's.

"I'll give that to you, since it's the first time you've won in five winters," said Eston

Fillian chuckled. "Whatever."

Eston took in a deep breath of the cold ocean air and looked up at the silvery moon. A few snowflakes drifted down from the sky and landed in the princes' curly hair. "It's so peaceful tonight."

"I like it," said Fillian. "There aren't even Scarlet Guards out and about."

Eston laughed. "There probably should be."

Fillian bit his lip. "Say, wouldn't the bells from the Luxeux be ringing just about now? It's midnight."

"Hmm. You're right."

The city of Aunestauna was bustling and brighter than usual, while the palace grounds stood still. The princes watched the dark water of the inlet. Far in the distance, a fleet of Ferramish ships slowly made their way across the waves toward the port. Scarlet banners waved on each of their four masts, and the water slapped on their edges.

Eston pointed. "You see those ships? What are they doing coming in to port this late?" He turned to Fillian. "I thought our naval brigade left three days ago."

His brother shrugged. "At this time of year, rough seas could have turned them back."

Eston squinted and then his eyes widened. "Fillian . . . our ships each have three masts . . ."

Fillian stared at him and again at the four scarlet banners waving on each ship. Fillian whispered in horror, "Cerebrians . . ." The princes sprinted off the bridge and down the senators' hallway toward the Tower of the Guard.

"Fillian," said Eston as they ran, "we need to warn the senators."

"Not until the Scarlet Guard knows—"

Before Fillian finished, Eston had already barged into a senator's room, but stood still in the doorway. "Great Mother!" he exclaimed in horror. His brother knocked him aside to see into the room. A pool of scarlet blood surrounded Senator An'Drui on the floor. Her neck was slit open and multiple stab wounds bled from her chest. Eston whispered, "Check Senator Mar across the hall."

Fillian sped away and returned a minute later. "I checked all the rooms . . . Mar, Nollard, Elim, Resbee, Duboiret . . . They're all dead . . . at least Bardow and Hillbottom are on the road with Father."

Eston stood up and ran out the doorway and down the hall of the South Wing. "We're getting attacked from the inside."

"We need to warn the Scarlet Guard!" called Fillian, running after him.

"Warn them?" said Eston, coming to a halt in the Throne Room lined with great pillars of marble. "Fillian, why do you think we haven't seen a single Scarlet Guard tonight?"

A familiar voice called out in the dark, "Piecing it all together, aren't we?" Rising from the Royal Throne, a tall man holding a bloody dagger slowly approached, flanked on wither side by more than twenty soldiers.

Eston stumbled back. "You?" He could barely breathe. "What have you done?"

Illuminated by a moonbeam, Janus Whittingale stepped toward the princes in his black cloak and raised his hands like a prophet. "You should thank me."

The soldiers behind Whittingale were adorned in gold armor and red cloaks . . . the Scarlet Guard.

Fillian's eyes widened and looked at the men. "You're all traitors . . . You killed them."

"Today a traitor, sure; but tomorrow . . . a patriot," Whittingale explained, speaking like it was just another lecture. "By the end of tonight, the war will be over; countless lives will be spared; and Xandria will regain her rightful throne."

"You coward," whispered Eston, unsheathing his *Queenslayer* sword, engraved with the royal crest and an 'E'. *How could I have missed this all along? Then again, who else would have believed his treason?*

"Coward, you say?" said Whittingale. "No, no . . . Hero . . . Twenty-two years tried my patience, but my loyalty to Queen Xandria never faltered. Bow low and smile often; save Tronum from poison and teach his son; play the part convincingly, and everyone believes you . . . At this moment, forty ships carrying nearly ten thousand Cerebrian troops sail in the bay of this helpless city. Half of the Scarlet Guard has pledged to Xandria; the other half has been killed."

"You follow an illegitimate queen."

"The rightful queen. She always has been. Forced out of her home and her throne by her younger brother. She always was the wiser, the braver, the greater." Whittingale stepped closer to the princes, and Fillian drew his sword. He continued, "We stopped by your rooms, but you were gone . . . The senators are dead, your mother is captive . . . all that's left is you." In an instant, Whittingale lunged forward, ducked under the princes' swings, and drove his dagger into Fillian's side. Fillian screamed and fell to the floor clutching his sliced abdomen. Whittingale dropped the dagger and drew a sword from his waist belt, holding it up to touch Eston's own blade as the Scarlet Guard surrounded them, enclosing them in a circle. Whittingale smiled, an anomaly. "It has been over a month since we last dueled, my student."

Eston looked at his bleeding, cursing brother and drove his *Queenslayer* blade toward Whittingale, who effortlessly swept Eston's royal sword to the side.

"You aren't on the balls of your feet," said Whittingale.

Eston yelled and slashed twice at Whittingale, who dodged both blows. He swiped at his legs, but Whittingale stepped back as the sword barely tore at his pant leg. Eston threw blow after blow at Whittingale, who parried each. Still in his cloak, Whittingale laughed and sliced Eston's thigh. "Eston," he said, "your sword tip is too low." The soldiers encircling them laughed and moved in closer.

Fillian lay groaning on the floor in bloodstained clothes. Limping, Eston charged again, but slipped on Fillian's blood. He rolled to his side just in time to evade Whittingale's downward slash; the sword was stuck in the wood floor, and Eston kicked Whittingale off balance. Whittingale's smile turned to anger. "Enough of this." He punched Eston's side, grabbed the sword, and bashed the handle on Eston's head, knocking him to the ground like a ragdoll.

Eston's vision swirled and he tried to pry himself off the ground. He gasped for air through his blood-filled mouth and coughed.

Laughing, Whittingale clutched Eston by the shirt and pulled him off the floor, putting him in a headlock. He held him and forced his head toward the windows, looking past the circle of soldiers. In the distance, fires began to spring up and light the harbor orange.

"You see those ships?" said Whittingale. "You see your city? We will release a firestorm on you." Eston struggled in Whittingale's grasp, but his head pounded. Whittingale raised his sword to Eston's throat and whispered in his ear. "You have lost."

Suddenly, the sound of galloping hooves and yelling filled the Throne Room. In an instant, a dozen armored horses with riders crashed into the circle of soldiers. Through the clashing of blades and armor, the sound of an arrow whistled through the air followed by a slice into flesh.

Whittingale's grip on Eston went limp and his sword clattered on the ground. Eston spun himself around as Whittingale coughed up blood from the arrow sunk into his back. Blood spurted from his mouth onto Eston's clothes. Whittingale stumbled back, drawing a dagger from his belt. As he made one last lunge at Eston, another arrow planted itself through his chest.

Riding in on her horse and armed with a bow, Qerru-Mai charged through the Throne Room and struck another one of her arrows through a Scarlet Guard. Whittingale crumbled dead onto the floor. The soldiers and horse riders battled around Eston as someone pushed him to the ground. He watched a spear fly over his head and sink into one of Whittingale's men. Within a few more seconds, the yelling and clashing ceased, and Qerru-Mai pulled him up with her chestnut-colored hand.

Holding a bow, Qerru-Mai hugged Eston. "Are you alright?"

Eston looked around at twenty dead Ferramish soldiers. On horseback were more than a dozen palace servants, each with bloody longswords.

Qerru-Mai threw her bow to the floor and knelt beside Fillian. "You're wounded, Fillian," she said.

Fillian looked down at his scarlet side. "I need— need pressure on it." Qerru-Mai cut off a sleeve of Whittingale's cloak and tied it above Fillian's waist.

"How's that?"

Fillian grimaced. "It— It really hurts. But I don't think it's that deep; he got me at an awkward angle."

Eston put a hand on Qerru-Mai's shoulder. "Thank you." He turned to the dozens of palace servants and bowed.

Eston turned back to Qerru-Mai, whose face rested on the verge of tears. She spoke softly, full of helplessness. "Eston, they killed her."

Knowing she referred to her mother, Eston embraced her. He whispered softly, "I'm so sorry."

Stepping back, he saw pure anger take over her expression.

"I'm gonna kill every last one of them," she said with blood boiling. "Every Cerebrian and each of Whittingale's men. I'll do to them what they did to her."

Everyone looked out the windows when they saw a flash of orange light, followed by a *BANG.* Forty Cerebrian ships were now in the harbor, and each of their scarlet banners were being lowered and replaced by jade flags. Multiple blasts of light burst from the ships, followed by cracks like thunder. Explosions of fire erupted from a ship, and a building near it seemed magically torn to shreds. A wall of the palace exploded inward after a set of fire bursts.

"What witchcraft is this?" said one of the servants.

Eston's heart pounded. "It's not magic, it's science. It's the Cerebrians' new weapon." He looked to Qerru-Mai and Fillian. "I need to find where they have our mother and do what I can to stop this."

"I'm coming with you," said Fillian. An explosion sounded from the harbor and a bombardment of iron rocks hit the palace wall. A thundercrack followed a flash of light from the harbor and a wall collapsed down the hallway.

"Are the Cerebrians in the city yet?" Eston asked the group.

A servant stepped forward — Errus, Eston's butler. "My Liege, I was near the gate just five minutes ago, and the Cerebrians have set fire to the streets nearest the waterfront."

"Are you all who are left in the palace? Where are our loyal troops?"

"We're not the only ones," said Errus. "There are about a hundred more servants who all have taken to the streets to fight. Half of the Scarlet Guard has been slaughtered, and the other half is nowhere to be seen. But there are civilians fighting the Cerebrians."

"The rest of the Scarlet Guard is loyal to Xandria now," said Fillian, clutching his wound.

An explosion went off in the Second District, lighting the valley like a flash of lightning. "Qerru-Mai," said Eston, "I want you to lead the rest of these men on horseback to Camp Auness; it's ten miles away, so I want you there in an hour. Alert the soldiers and have them return to the palace immediately. That will give us around four thousand men. With that many reinforcements, the city may stand a chance."

Qerru-Mai looked at him hesitantly.

"Do it for you mother . . ." said Eston, "for our home."

She nodded with a dangerous face of rage. The group bowed and followed Qerru-Mai to the stables.

"Eston," said Fillian, "we need to find out how Whittingale did all this. He must've been in communication with Xandria somehow."

"We can worry about that later; we need to find Mother now. I have a feeling we don't have much time."

Hundreds of screaming civilians flocked into the open palace gates, hoping to find refuge in its walls. Iron rocks soared over the walls and bashed into towers, launched by the Cerebrians' new Gelltzkreiks. Eston shouted to the crowd, "The palace is under fire! Leave now! Leave now!" Only a few people obeyed, returning to the fiery streets.

Fillian grabbed Eston's collar. "The beasts below the palace! We could—"

"Princes!" A woman charged through the crowd of civilians. "The queen, she's at the docks! They're forcing her onto a ship!" Eston hugged the woman and thanked her, and the brothers bolted out the gate and front gardens into the streets. Men and women pushed each other, trying to get away from the shore, screaming to the rhythmic cannon bursts from the Gelltzkreiks. The princes tried to shove their way against the flow of rich First District aristocrats but could barely move a block forward as hands thrashed out and elbows flew into their sides.

Fillian yelled in pain and frustration. "There's no way through!"

Eston looked up at the houses around him and a thought that felt like Kyan's entered his mind. "Yes, there is!" He grabbed the windowpane of a house and pulled himself up. Turning around, he jumped to another window, zig-zagging up the wall.

Fillian put his hand on the window. "You have got to be kidding me." Following Eston, he jumped up to the roof where they could see the massive Cerebrian ships firing Gelltzkreiks from the harbor and unloading soldiers onto the rocky beach.

"That one, there," said Eston, pointing to the largest and most decorated ship which floated beside a main dock in the place of Ferramish trade vessels. "That's it. It's the only one not firing Gelltzkreiks." The two princes ran like thieves across the rooftops of the district, jumping from roof to roof over the swarm of evacuating civilians. Like ants, hundreds of dark green uniforms swarmed the buildings and held torches to indoor curtains, smoking Ferrs out of the safety of their attics and onto their soon-to-be-ash roofs. Dozens of buildings near the shore blazed, and the fire began to slowly creep inland. The street below them echoed with swords. A group of Ferramish men engaged a platoon of armored Cerebrians.

"Eston, the civilians are fighting!" called out Fillian as they ran across the uneven shingles on roofs.

"What choice do they have?" he replied while thinking, *but they could flee . . . why don't they flee or surrender . . . why are they already prepared?* From below, Eston heard a familiar voice seeming to call out orders not to the Cerebrians, but to the Ferrs. "Fight! Defend your city!" When he looked back, the speaker was gone.

The boys reached a house near the docks and jumped off the roof. Fillian grimaced and Eston looked worriedly at him. "Your wound, Fillian?"

"It's fine." Abandoned but for Cerebrians, the streets next to the docks provided a straight pathway to the ship, patched with bellowing fires in the alleyways. A battalion of Cerebrian soldiers marched down a ship's plank and onto the wharf. They had set fire to nearly all Ferramish ships in the harbor, and half the Cerebrian ships had already docked. The princes quickly ducked away and ran toward the towering ship whose silver-plated side read, *The Desolator*.

Eston and Fillian hid behind a pile of wooden shipping containers. "How are we supposed to get Mother off that ship?" asked Fillian.

Eston shook his head and peeked over the containers. Another battalion was leaving its ship, and the Gelltzkreiks continued to fire cannonballs, ripping the palace far above them to shreds. The battalion marched in a line into the city. Eston leaned on a container to get a better vantage point, but it slipped out from under him, causing the whole pile to fall. The line of Cerebrians stopped and turned toward the princes. "Shit . . . Fillian. Run. Now!"

The princes turned away, but the Cerebrian troops began to fire arrows ahead of them to block them. As the green wave swelled toward them, Eston saw no other alternative; he stood firm and shouted, "Halt!" The battalion quickly surrounded the princes with their swords and bows drawn. "We are Princes Eston and Fillian Wenderdehl, sons of King Tronum!" he looked at Fillian.

"We demand an audience with your General," Fillian ordered. The Cerebrian troops silently agreed beneath their helmets.

A soldier stepped forward. "Drop your swords, you little shits." Fillian nodded to Eston and the brothers dropped them to the ground. "We'll take your asses to General Heirmonst." The battalion of troops surrounded the princes and tied their wrists behind their backs, pushing them toward *The Desolator.*

The jade-armored soldiers guided them over the planks of the dock and onto the ramp. The deck of the ship was large and open, filled with Cerebrian troops who began to cheer as they saw the two princes being escorted to the stern of the ship. Turning his head, Eston could see the burning palace on its hilltop. New fires sprang up every second as cannonballs hit its ramparts. Although the air was icy, the entire shoreline of buildings blazed in a bright orange light. *The Desolator* rocked lightly in the harbor as snowflakes fell. The troops walked the princes up a staircase to the elevated stern deck. There, tied to a post, was Queen Eradine with a gag in her mouth.

Fillian looked frantically at Eston. A gruff, muscular man stood near her in a long green cape and silver armor encrusted in gems. A scar ran from his temple to his opposite cheek. He stepped forward. "Sons of the usurper, Tronum Wenderdehl," he said in a cold Cerebrian accent, "Here to join the family get-together? Look at your nation." The princes turned to shore where flames devoured block after block, and waves of green from ships funneled into the city, firing arrows and throwing spears.

"You attack the innocent!" said Fillian.

General Heirmonst slapped a hand across Fillian's face, sending him stumbling back. "You think your citizens are innocent? No one in this world is innocent. Your father and his blind followers stole a throne and continue to take away our right to be free, to enslave us under a false crown! But you started a fire you can't extinguish. Xandria's flame engulfs you now, and it is beautiful." The burning shoreline reflected in his eyes.

Eston struggled against the soldiers holding him. "You call that beauty? That is destruction! That is death!"

"Death is cleansing," said Heirmonst. "They all chose their side; they supported the usurper." He removed a dagger from his belt and held it to Queen Eradine's throat. Eradine looked at him without fear, but with absolute hatred. "Unless you surrender, the attack will continue; Xandria wants nothing but peace and will gladly accept you turning over your nation to her." The soldiers held the princes tightly and Heirmonst pressed the dagger harder. "If you choose not to surrender, your whole nation will burn; your King and Queen will die, and so will you. Cerebria will win with or without blood." He pushed the dagger onto Eradine's skin, beginning to draw blood. "What do you say?"

Eston's heart pounded and he stared at Fillian, who struggled against the soldiers holding him. Eston turned to his mother who gently shook her head. Eston's mouth began to quiver; one sentence of surrender could stop the war and the dagger.

The ship was silent enough to hear the wood creaking as it rocked in the waves. As Gelltzkreiks shot from neighboring ships, Eston looked at the burning city before him. With a tear rolling down his face, he whispered, "Xandria doesn't want peace . . . she will stop at nothing to destroy what she thinks my father stole from her. I can't give up Ferramoor to her." He turned to Eradine but spoke to Heirmonst. He began to cry and could barely force the next words between his lips. "Saving our mother will not save our people."

Fillian watched in horror and Eston's stomach dropped.

Heirmonst nodded. "As you wish." The general drove the dagger inward, and Eradine screamed something before her head went limp. Eston's mind swirled in shock. A bright flash of light seemed to envelop his vision, and he opened his eyes to the ceiling of his ramshackle attic in the Third District.

§

~Morning

Kyan bolted upright and flew out of the door of his attic shack. Immediately turning west, he saw no flames by the shoreline of the city. The morning was cold and cloudless, and his sporadic breath drifted upward from his shirtless figure. The palace looked pristine and unchanged; the people on the street below laughed and chattered; and far away church bells rang gleefully. *The battle hasn't begun. Why should it have? It's this morning.* He looked across at the clock in the square. *November 4th.* He remembered just seconds ago standing on *The Desolator,* watching Heirmonst slit Queen Eradine's throat. *I could stop it. The Cerebrians will come tonight.* Kyan snatched a tunic and jacket, and bounded over his matrix of planks toward the palace.

Robed aristocrats lined the streets near the top of the palace hill, looking distastefully at the panting street urchin that flashed by them, intruding on their otherwise clean domain. Kyan glanced as he sprinted, *they'll be lucky to be alive by next morning.* Kyan rounded the last street and under the tunnel of leafless oak trees of the outer palace gardens, reaching the gate outside of which ten Scarlet Guards stood in scarlet. They each gripped their spears as the ragged boy tore up the last steps. "What business do you have in the palace?"

Out of breath, Kyan pleaded, "I— I have an urgent message for— for the government!"

"We can relay that message," said a soldier firmly.

"No, please, I must speak to them myself!"

"We cannot permit you to pass."

Remembering to whom the Scarlet Guard was really loyal, Kyan clenched his fists. *What am I doing? They're Whittingale's men; they won't help me. If I say anything, they'll lock me up.* Kyan's eyes narrowed, and he spun away from the spears raised at him.

Leaping down the palace steps, he stopped when he reached a square in the First District in the middle of which sat a fountain; he grabbed its edges and plunged his face in, gulping up frigid water. Throwing his long, wet hair back, a group of aristocrats stared at him with disgust. Little ice crystals formed in his hair as the early winter breeze gusted, sweeping leaves along the stone street. Kyan closed his eyes, leaning against the fountain and cursing. *Treacherous cowards.* Kyan eyed two little boys around the fountain with toy swords dueling beside their jabbering mothers, mindless to the raging imaginary battle. There was a whole city of men that could me armed if only they knew of the impending danger. Kyan jumped up, *That's it!*

He rushed down the street, shoving aside a man, and into the Second District. *Left.* Kyan turned hard, knocking over a bread stand. *Right.* The thief jumped over a line of children. *Third to the right.* Kyan skidded to a stop long enough to burst through the door of a smithy.

A dirt-covered, sweaty man yelled from far back in the shop. "Wha'you t'ink you're doin' boy!" He plunged a glowing sword in a barrel of water and removed his ragged gloves. His beard was long enough to be a fire hazard as a blacksmith.

Kyan danced around the anvils and racks of weapons. "Sir!" he panted. "Please listen."

The man raised a calloused finger. "You betta ha' some'in damn good to come bargin' in like this young man. Mourn's chickens get loose again?"

Kyan stumbled forward, reaching a pocket of scorching air from a furnace. "Sir—"

"Aye son, I ain't no sir, I's just Oden Haggahol to you."

He swallowed, "Mr. Haggahol, the Cerebrians are attacking."

The smith raised an eyebrow. "Uh . . . yeah; dey sure as hell is in Endlebarr; dey've been makin' me rich."

"No!" yelled Kyan. He could tell this Oden Haggahol was not the brightest man in the city. "I'm sorry, no, I mean they are attacking Aunestauna."

Mr. Haggahol looked out the glassless window in the brick wall and back to Kyan. "No dey isn't."

"Tonight! Tonight, sorry . . ." Kyan spun up an explanation. "A whole lot of fishermen saw the Cerebrians' naval fleet in the inlet. They're going to attack tonight."

Mr. Haggahol crossed his arms and sat on a stool, seeming to be focused on a bug on the dirt floor. "How many?"

"Probably twenty fishermen saw, but that's not the important—"

"No, how many ships dem Cerebrians got?" asked Mr. Haggagol.

"Forty! But, listen; this city is in danger and because of reasons I can't explain, I think that—"

"Dat's a lot of ships."

"Yes, I know! And we don't have any army here, and the Scarlet Guard isn't able to defend us from them."

"Why not?"

"Arg! It's complicated! But if Aunestauna falls, we lose the war!"

"Wait," said Mr. Haggahol, "if d'ere were twenty fishermen, why is you de only one telling me dis?"

"They are all off in the Third District warning citizens! So I need all the help I can get from you. Do you know any other blacksmiths in town?" asked Kyan.

"Why, I know e'ry smith in dis district and probably a half dozen in the t'ird!"

Kyan stamped his foot in relief. "Alright. I need you to warn every blacksmith, have them distribute their weapons and armor for free to civilians willing to fight. Warn everyone you can that the Cerebrians will attack tonight."

"Give our weapons away for no charge?"

"You yourself said you were already rich!"

"Well," said Mr. Haggahol, "not as rich as I'd *like* to be."

Kyan continued. "You don't have a choice, sir. There is no other way you will survive until tomorrow; do you understand?"

Mr. Haggahol thought hard. "Well, I gotta feed my rabbit first and den I guess I'll help you out. Dis betta damn pay off somehow, kid."

Kyan shook his hand, "Thank you, sir."

"Wait, before you go." Mr. Haggahol walked in a back room where he shouted, "You're a skinny guy, but dis'll fit ya." He came back carrying a belt with a sheath and sword and passed it to Kyan, who took it like it was a glass vase. "Well, if dey really are comin' you need to go, kid!"

"Right, sorry, thank you sir. Tell everyone!" Kyan flew out the door as quickly as he came in but with a large sword sheathed to his side.

~Dusk

Mr. Ruben Tumno, the baker in Kyan's theater square burst through the doors of *The Little Raven,* where Kyan was busy handing out knives to the bartenders and customers at the counter. "Mr. Kyan, sir!" he shouted. "I did like you told me to and went out to the city limits with my family to try an' warn Camp Auness about t'e attack. But t'e Scarlet Guard was dere and t'ey tolds us to 'go back into Aunestauna, t'ey isn't lettin' anybody use t'e roads,' and nobody's horse can go through the miles of corn and cotton fields to get there, 'least not in a day's time."

Kyan swore; they were all fish in a net, but still beneath the surface of the water. Nine out of ten people had ignored him when Kyan had told them the

Cerebrians were on their way, convinced he was crazed or somehow trying to get at their money. But a group of Ferrs who took heed to Kyan's warnings had begun to gather, split, and grow again with more volunteers, filling several neighborhoods of Aunestauna with a ruckus of bells ringing, swords sheathing, and the crack of furniture jettisoned from windows to form barricades. Oden Haggahol had convinced only five other blacksmiths to donate their weapons and armor to citizens to defend against a threat that could not yet be seen, but the supplies circled through the resistance force of Ferrs.

Kyan dumped the rest of the weapons on the counter and exited the tavern with Mr. Tumno. Looking west at the setting sun between the buildings, Kyan nodded in approval at the size of the barricade gathered in the street, where buildings had been emptied and their contents piled on the cobblestone, forming a wall of tables, chairs, frames, and mattresses. A woman shouted at the people in the square that there were no Cerebrians and that they were all safe; no one listened.

Kyan shouted at Mr. Tumno, "Grab that group of people by *Arnday's Apple* and take them around telling people to fill as many barrels as they can from the city wells; the Cerebrians are bound to try and burn the city to the ground."

"Aye, Mr. Kyan, we'll draw water 'till the wells are dry."

Kyan wished him luck and climbed to the roof of *The Little Raven.* Kyan crossed into the Third District and near the shoreline, all the while examining the city below where thousands of people barricaded streets and boarded up houses. To help Kyan's cause, real fishermen and seafarers who saw the four-masted ships of Cerebria in the inlet *had* returned in the last few hours, running to their families and neighbors to prepare them and spread the word. A seagull swooped over Kyan's head as he watched the last glimmer of sunlight vanish over the horizon.

Descending to the streets to help a group of fishermen string their nets between buildings as a trap, he noticed a throng unloading from a vessel. All were in a panic, leading Kyan to assume they had seen and escaped the Cerebrian fleet. "Young man," said a skinny, old fisherman, "will you grab us another net from our boat just on that there dock?" A little boat near the large vessel that had just arrived rocked in the waves and gently tugged on its ropes. This area was commonly known among civilians as the Poor Docks, a joke comparing them to those to the north, which were aristocratic and nicely kept.

Kyan nodded and stepped on the wooden dock where the throng of anxious travelers pushed and shoved to get ashore and see if their families were safe. Kyan weaved his way through, trying to get to the little boat, but he stumbled back as he bumped into a blonde-haired girl exiting the newly-arrived vessel.

"I'm sorry sir," she said in a cold accent.

Kyan stared wide eyed. "Raelynn?"

DETONATION
Chapter Twenty Six

~Night, November 4th
The Great Cerebrian Gate

Tayben fell through the air and landed hard on a beam of the Great Cerebrian Gate after being knocked off the staircase by Calleneck's spell. He looked up at his other self as his future body ran up the stairs and out of sight. Tayben pressed himself up from the support beam and looked down many stories to the flashes of colored light and clamor of swords below. A bead of sweat dripped down his face and the world below him seemed to slow almost to a standstill as he watched the bead fall from his chin down a hundred feet to the clouds of swirling light cast by the Evertauri. *What am I doing?*

Tayben launched himself off the column support to another below, and continued until he reached the bottom floor, which was a battlefield. The Evertauri had pinned the Jade Guards against a wall and were shattering their bones and bursting their hearts with jets of Taurimous. Tayben jumped behind a sorcerer who held a spear and drove his sword through his back. As the sorcerer fell, Tayben tore the spear from his hands and tightened his grip on it, feeling the natural balance of his usual weapon.

At that moment, Harkil and his platoon emerged from the other side of the great atrium around the support column and whistled at Tayben, pointing to the Jade Guards. Tayben nodded, and in what only seemed like a flash of black smoke to the sorcerers, the Phantoms charged toward the front lines and slammed into them. The Evertauri seemed to move through molasses as the Phantoms attacked, unimaginably faster than the humans. Tayben hurled his spear at another line of sorcerers, trying to avoid the jets of Taurimous. The spear skewered the necks of two men, and Tayben weaved through the sorcerers to retrieve it. Only then did the first reactions of fear appear on the faces of the Evertauri. "Get back!" one of them shouted to another.

Harkil's platoon rushed forward with swords and arrows, killing Siti and a group of sorceresses whom Tayben knew well from the Evertauri. The Jade Guards charged forward at the Evertauri and a sheet of teal light coursed through the air, surrounding Harkil as he swung; he began to scream, and Tayben hurled his spear into the attacking Evertauri. The teal light vanished and Harkil lay on the ground as the rest of his platoon and the Cerebrians guards fought in a circle around them. Harkil breathed heavily as Tayben picked him up, and he stared at Tayben with eyes wide open in fear. "Tayben, the monster from Endlebarr – it gives off the same force as they do. It came from came from their sorcery."

Tayben tried to duck, but a jet of gold light blasted him into a far wall, making his joints crack and back sear with pain.

Harkil turned again to face the sorcerers, saying under his breath, ". . . dark magic . . ."

Tayben shot out again delivering blow after blow with sword and spear, hitting the shields of light cast by the Evertauri. Minute after minute he pushed against the Evertauri, with a few other Phantoms who aided him in his defense of the Great Gate. But as they fought, the Evertauri continued to pile up more and more explosives. From the corner of his eye, he watched Tallius and a group of Evertauri ascending the staircase, hanging some sort of rope as they went. *They're connecting the fuse.*

Tayben sprinted up the staircase to the group of Evertauri and rammed into one, sending him falling to the ground below. Tallius shot a sapphire fireball at Tayben, knocking him down and burning his chest. Tayben grabbed another Evertauri and threw him off and hurled his spear through the second to last. Tayben turned to Tallius who stumbled back in fear of the black blur he saw. A memory of talking to Tallius in the Network as Calleneck flashed across his eyes. But Tallius was a rebel, he deserved to die. Yet, Tayben could not bring himself to strike. *Kill another friend,* a voice inside him spoke, *and you die inside as well.* Tayben swallowed a pain in his throat and bounded up the staircase, leaving Tallius alone.

Tayben rounded a corner, trying to find the rest of the Evertauri who were connecting the explosives. His ears picked up voices from another support column of the gate and he quickly followed the sound.

A group of Evertauri stood on a bridge-like beam of the column, which faced the blizzarding mountain air. Although the whistle of the biting cold air rang loudly, Tayben could hear them speaking. "We have three out of four ready. All we need is . . . wait, watch out!" An Evertauri pointed at Tayben at the other end of the bridge; Tayben reluctantly threw his spear at a member of the group; his stomach dropped when an enormous stream of silver light met the spear in the air and vaporized it. Tayben froze. *Madrick.*

Madrick stepped toward him with a cloud of silver swirling around him. Tayben tried to turn back, but a wall of silver appeared behind him, trapping him on the bridge. Tayben froze as Madrick reached forward with a glowing silver hand and grabbed his face with a grip stronger than Riccolo's. The hand felt like it coursed with electricity, and with a snarl, Madrick sent a wave of silver

Taurimous into his body. Tayben felt cold and weak. He felt as if the light given to him by the Nymphs was draining as the pain of Madrick's Taurimous filled his every bone. *I shouldn't be fighting against you,* he thought ina panic. He felt as if Silverbrook's monster was tearing at him again, and he went limp. With a burst of silver, Madrick blasted Tayben's body off the bridge and into the blizzard. His cloak flapped around his limp body as he fell two hundred feet through the falling snow. Tayben watched the gate grow taller and taller. He only felt a brief crack of pain and a burst of light as his body hit a snowdrift.

He opened his eyes in Calleneck's body on the staircase. His fist hurt from punching his other self, and he glanced quickly at Tayben, who pushed himself up from the column support, and ran up the staircase out of sight. His consciousness had just jumped minutes back in time. Calleneck stopped on the staircase. *Did I just die?* He shivered, remembering falling off the gate. He shook his head, the inconsistent flow of time confusing time. Shaking the strange sensation off, he continued to ascend to where he had agreed to meet Madrick and the others, battling his way through the remaining Jade Guards.

Calleneck ran across the bridge that he, as Tayben, would soon approach. Borius and a group of the Evertauri's engineers were already there, working like honeybees on rigging the Great Gate to explode. The blizzard blew hard and slowed Calleneck as Borius greeted him. "Calleneck, are Tallius and your team close behind you?"

"I'm not sure, sir," said Calleneck.

"Well he'd better be here soon. As long as everyone down at ground level has done their job, we will soon be ready to blow this Gate, but we need his fuse for the fourth column."

Another Evertauri interjected, "Otherwise, the chain reaction won't work properly."

A glow of silver from the other side of the bridge alerted them to Madrick's arrival. The man quickly looked around. "How many columns are ready?"

A technician stepped forward. "We have three out of four ready. All we need is . . . wait, watch out!" The group spun to see a blur of black hurl a spear toward them. Before anyone could react, Madrick released a column of silver Taurimous that engulfed the spear. Madrick ran forward and surrounded the black blur with silver light. Calleneck froze as the two figures disappeared in a cloud of swirling silver light. A loud bang sounded when Madrick blasted Tayben out into the blizzard. Calleneck stepped forward, as if trying to save himself, but Tayben's body quickly vanished from view.

Madrick kept a large shield of silver hovering around the bridge as he walked back. Borius asked if he was alright.

"Fine . . . continue with our operation."

§

"Grab the boxes!" Aunika cast a pale green shield around her covered wagon as fireballs of pink and blue soared over her head. Dalah emerged from the wagon with boxes and ran through the crowd of fighting Jade Guards and sorcerers.

"Aunika," Lillia appeared to her side, "is this hallway ready?"

"Two more wagons."

A group of guards spotted them and charged, carrying their pikes low. Aunika knelt to the ground and sent a green lighting bolt cracking through the stone floor until reaching their bodies and crushing their bones. As she turned back to Lillia, a black shadow flew past her.

"Aunika, duck!" Lillia sent a pure white fireball straight over her head. The white met something black, and it flew back with it, swirling.

"What was that?"

"Don't know, but it's coming back." The girls turned around and a shower of green and white embers collided and bounced off a blur of black. More power, and the flakes of Taurimous flew faster. Slowly, the shadow took on a human form in a cloak and no armor, one who carried two swords. In pain, the man jumped back out of the current of sparks and disappeared as quickly as he came.

§

Tallius made sure the black shadow was gone before picking up the fuse to carry to Madrick. Crashes and screams filled the Great Cerebrian Gate, but slowly died down as Tallius ascended the staircase, his foot still aching with pain from Selenora's spell that had stabbed it. The fuse was handed off to technical teams on support beams, who joined it to packs of explosives that Evertauri began to deliver and pack around the supports.

Tallius turned around the last corner and onto the designated bridge where Madrick, Calleneck, and a team of other Evertauri stood. Calleneck ran to him and helped carry the rest of the fuse. Tallius smiled. "Glad to see you alive! Where is Borius?"

"He went back down to the bottom to help continue the fight. The rest of the Evertauri are holding off the Phantom— *shadow soldiers.*"

"Here, grab this; thank you. Are we ready?"

The technical team nodded in sync. Madrick emitted a wave of beating Taurimous that spread to the lowest floor of the gate. "They're evacuating now; once this blows, the whole mountainside could collapse." Calleneck and Tallius finished pulling up the fuse.

An Evertauri held up a box, "We'll connect them in here, it will give us five minutes to get out." Tallius reached forward with the end of the fuse; his hand stopped. The technician stepped forward. "Just pull it further."

Tallius shook his head. "It won't budge." Tallius leaned with it, pulling it taught. "The other teams pulled it as tight as it would go."

"Let me try." Calleneck tugged on the fuse, but it still had six feet to go.

Madrick shook his head. "It'll have to be lit manually." The group stood in silence.

"We can reconnect the first—"

"We don't have time," said Madrick. "The Jade Guards here surely sent messenger birds calling for reinforcements. Cerebrians will be on their way." The snow blew sideways onto the bridge.

The technicians turned red. "President Nebelle, we ran this operation and executed it according to plan — and you expect us to blow ourselves up?"

Madrick clenched his fist. "You took an oath of loyalty to—"

"I'll do it." Calleneck grabbed the fuse from Tallius. "I can light it."

Tallius looked down at the fuse and then back at Madrick. "So will I."

"Tallius," said Calleneck, "we only need one person. I can—"

"I don't care," he said. "We can light it together and then run as fast as we can to the far edge where the mountain is closest and the drop into the snow is the shortest."

"Tallius, your foot; you can't run on it. what about Lillia?"

"What about your sisters?"

Calleneck turned to a technician. "How long from the time we light it until we're cooked?"

"Not more than a minute. The first explosions on the top levels will be minor and will happen within thirty seconds, but then the sequential explosions will be set off causing the whole gate to fall."

Calleneck and Tallius nodded. "For the Evertauri."

"Are they all clear?" asked Tallius.

"They said to give them five minutes," said Calleneck, "and it's been that. We have to do it now."

Tallius paused. "Cal . . . are you scared?"

Calleneck tried to control his heart rate. "Yes." He looked at the fuse in his hand. "But dozens of sorcerers died defending the revolution."

Tallius smiled and looked at the fuse. "In life and death."

Calleneck looked out into the blizzard and then turned back to embrace Tallius. "In life and death . . . we run as fast as we can to the northern edge."

Tallius nodded. "On your count."

Calleneck breathed in. "Three . . . two . . . one." A burst of crimson and sapphire light ignited the fuses, and the boys drove away faster than either had run before. *Faster. Faster.* Calleneck and Tallius sprinted through the halls of the gate, looking for an opening into the air. A loud bang and a burst of yellow light from behind them signaled the start of the explosions. *BANG. BANG.* The roar filled the gate and echoed off the distant mountains.

"Where do we jump?!"

"I don't see!" Calleneck tore off his cloak to run faster through the frozen air. *BANG. BANG.* The explosions got louder, and the floor began to rumble and crack. A stone archway collapsed after they ran through it and the floor fell away to their left. Ahead, a balcony to the outside appeared. "There!" A column crumbled as another explosion sounded. Beads of sweat flew off Calleneck's body. The balcony drew closer, closer. The icy wind blew at them, muffling Calleneck's shout, "Jump!"

The boys lept out into the night blizzard. The sensation of dropping stopped when the final explosion ignited and launched them forward. The Great Cerebrian Gate erupted in blinding flashes of orange and yellow, sending great pillars of stone flying outward. As the searing heat of the fireball approached, Calleneck cast a shield of crimson around himself. The shockwave of the eruption punched him forward as he fell, and his whole field of vision was momentarily concealed in fire.

Calleneck skipped like a stone when he hit the snow, and his shield of Taurimous shattered. Impact. Impact. Rolling down. Cold. A piece of flying stone hit his leg. He rolled through the snow for another ten yards until coming to a stop. The snow now filled his boots and covered his thin underlayer; the fireball around the Great Gate illuminated the mountain pass before turning into a thick cloud of dark smoke. Still, thundering cracks of crumbling debris echoed, but when he looked back, the great wall of black stone no longer concealed the stars. A dozen small fires dotted the snow and rubble where the wall of the Great Cerebrian Gate once stood.

Calleneck breathed in, relieved that it was done. *Tallius.* He shot up and looked around. Nothing but snow, rubble, and fires. "Tallius!" Calleneck pushed himself up out of the snow and sprinted back up through the snowbank. "Tallius!" He looked around in vain. "Tallius!" Calleneck froze when he saw a body on fire, lying still in the snow ahead. The dusty blonde hair began to curl and shrivel, and the smell of burning flesh and the stench of smoke filled the air.

A cold shiver ran through him as shadows began to emerge from the wreckage of the burning rubble. *Phantoms.* He looked at the flaming, motionless body. The shadows. The Body. His heart pounded as he stood there frozen. The Phantoms were regrouping and quickly began streaking across the mountainside toward him.

As Calleneck looked down into the valley, he saw a giant dome of glowing light formed with iridescent, shimmering colors. Beneath it, the Evertauri shielded themselves from the flying debris. Calleneck looked back once more at Tallius as the Phantoms raced toward him. *There's — there's no time.* Calleneck stumbled toward the glowing dome with tears streaming down his face. He cried out as he ran, looking back at the burning body and the shadows approaching him. The Phantoms drew closer, ready to spill his blood. *Faster.* He bolted through the snow toward the dome of swirling Taurimous. Closer. Closer. He could now see that the great iridescent shield of energy was cast by every remaining Evertauri, blocking them from the flying rubble.

The Phantoms were twenty feet behind, ten, five. Calleneck dove forward and passed through the barrier of light like it was mist, and a loud crash sounded behind as a shadow of black rammed into the shield. A few Evertauri rushed forward to aid Calleneck as a dozen Phantoms gathered around the outside of the dome. They darted back and forth, cursing, trying to enter the dome of light but unable to pass the barrier.

"Cal!" Two girls ran toward him and embraced him on either side.

Calleneck buried his face in Dalah's wavy brown hair, feeling what little relief he could and whispering, *"Freckles."*

Beside him, Lillia pushed through the crowd of Evertauri and stopped when she saw Calleneck and only him. "Where is Tallius?"

Calleneck stepped back from her sisters and looked at her through teary eyes.

Lillia's breathing picked up as she started to realize. "Where is he, Cal?"

He shook his head, the image of Tallius's burned body seared into his brain. Calleneck spoke with a pained desperation he didn't know he could. "The explosion, I— I thought I cast a shield around both of us— I tried, I—"

"No!" she screamed out, making a dash for the barrier of light, but Aunika caught her before she could reach it. "No, we need to go back for him— Let me go, Aunika!"

"It's not safe," she said as she helped her back. Phantoms still stood beyond the perimeter of the Evertauri's dome of Taurimous, eyeing the sorcerers inside.

She loves him, thought Calleneck. He didn't want to say the words — didn't want to admit the truth of his best friend's death — but he knew he had to for Lillia's sake. "He's gone."

Lillia fell to the snowy ground sobbing and Calleneck retched from the thought of the corpse smoldering in his mind. Little Dalah knelt beside Lillia and embraced her, soaking up her tears on her cloak.

President Nebelle made his way over just as the shadow shapes of the Phantoms darted off into the night. His cloak was covered in blood and a small cut on his chin had turned his short gray beard scarlet. "Bernoil," he said to Calleneck, "are you alright?"

Calleneck forced himself to straighten up but used his hands pressing against his knees to do it. "Yes, but Tallius . . ." He was still trying to catch his breath, but he felt sick. "Tallius didn't make it."

Madrick nodded with an unphased scowl. Many Evertauri had died that night – Tallius Tooble was just one more name to him. He stepped closer to the barrier of swirling light and looked out onto the snowy mountainside, no doubt searching for signs of Phantoms. "Evertauri," he called out in a gruff voice, spinning around, "we need to get back underground before we have more company. The Gate is destroyed, we've done what we needed. Quickly now!" he ordered, moving back into the crowd of sorcerers to lead them back.

Calleneck's head was spinning, though he couldn't tell how much of it was from the explosion. His stomach heaved again, and he doubled over, vomiting again on the snow. Feeling utterly helpless, he looked up at the ruin that stretched over the mountain valley, where great granite columns lay broken and scattered, fires springing up wherever they could. Where once stood a massive gate of stone sat rubble and an open winter night sky. The wall separating Cerebria from Ferramoor was gone.

He turned to his sisters who helped Lillia to her feet. Tears streamed down her rosy cheeks as she desperately looked toward the mountainside and turned back to Dalah and Aunika. As she walked with them and wept, Calleneck noticed her right hand moving subconsciously to rest on her stomach.

§

Gallien turned to his platoon, whose faces glowed from the iridescent light of the dome that the sorcerers had cast. "It's lost . . . We can't take them. The Gate is destroyed . . . Who's hurt?"

Thephern sheathed his two longswords. "Ferron is burned pretty badly and Shaenler lost a few fingers."

Gallien looked around as more Phantoms gathered outside the barrier of light. "Where is Tayben?"

Albeire Harkil called out as he rushed up to them. "I saw Tayben take a fall off the other side of the wall while it was still standing. Must've fallen a few hundred feet. General Lekshane is already looking for him."

Gallien's stomach dropped, but now was not the time for inaction. "Well help me find him. He could still be alive."

The Phantoms nodded their heads as they walked away from the dome over the remains of the Evertauri they had killed; the Great Gate was rubble. The pass to Cerebria was open, and the long string of Cerebrian victories was over.

Gallien walked quickly through banks of snow with Thephern and his double swords. The mountainside was desolate and silent, and dead Evertauri and Cerebrian soldiers lay scattered all over the pass. "Tayben!" they called. Smoke rose all around them as they stepped over the corpses of sorcerers and Jade Guards in the snow. No sign of life could be seen anywhere.

Thephern nudged Gallien, "Over there!"

The two Phantoms ran over the ruins of wagon carts and the blood-covered drifts to a depression in the snow. Gallien, bleeding from a deep gash on his shoulder, set down his sword and began to dig up snow as Thephern came up the snowbank. "Thephern, help me!"

Once Gallien had brushed aside enough snow to see Tayben's body, he put his hand over his mouth, ready to vomit. Bones from Tayben's legs, arms, and ribcage stuck out of his skin, and his face and chest were crimson with blood. He put a hand to Tayben's neck, and for some time, could not feel a pulse. He breathed easier when he finally felt a weak thump from the veins in Tayben's skin.

"Is he dead?" said Thephern as he came to Gallien's side, recoiling at the sight of his body.

Gallien removed his hand. "Not yet. But I can feel—" He stopped when he saw something strange – impossible. He could see parts of Tayben's body stitching itself back together, forming scars and healing muscles faster than was believable even for a Phantom, like a magic spell was helping to fix the wounds.

Slowly, Tayben opened an eye – the other was bruised and swollen shut. With his head turned to the side, he reached out a shaking hand pointing at the snow.

"Tayben, take it easy" said Gallien, "we're gonna get you back. You're okay."

Two quiet words slipped out of Tayben's bloody mouth in short, weak breaths as he stared at something. *"Flower . . . glow."*

Gallien followed Tayben's gaze and his outstretched hand – nothing was there but barren white snow.

Thephern put a hand on his shoulder. "Let's get him out of here." They began to lift Tayben out of the snow and into their arms. "Careful," said Thephern, "we don't want to do more damage than is already done. He'll recover, we just need to get back into the forest."

Gallien picked up Tayben's body and headed for the trees, walking slowly over the desolate mountainside covered in corpses and burning rubble.

FIRESTORM
Chapter Twenty Seven

~Late Afternoon, November 4th
Aunestana, Ferramoor

Kyan stood on the Aunestauna harbor docks, staring right back at Raelynn – just about the last person he expected to see. As the crowd of evacuees from the incoming ships filtered off the docks, Kyan pulled Raelynn aside.

She looked at him apprehensively. "Who are you?"

Kyan had to think how she would know this body. "I met you in the Great Cathedral."

"Oh, yes. Kyan, right?"

"As I live and breathe," he said, honestly surprised he remembered his name. "I forgot that you were coming back."

"How did you know I was coming back?" she asked.

Kyan's hands turned cold. *Get yourself together; you're only supposed to know that as Calleneck.* "Well, you said you were leaving Aunestauna and that you would be back." Kyan noticed her rubbing charcoal off her fingertips.

Raelynn closed her eyes and pieced together the memories. "Well, it's good to see you again, but you need to know that the Cerebrian navy—"

"The whole city is preparing to defend against an attack," said Kyan. "The Scarlet Guard has been acting strange, and I think they may be a part of this." Kyan knew they were, but acted unsure.

Raelynn picked up her small bag she carried with her. "Well this was an unfortunate day for me to arrive; but I'm here to help."

Kyan turned to the fisherman's boat and the net. "We're stringing traps to stop the Cerebrians."

Raelynn looked out into the calm inlet that was still lit by a fading orange sky. "They'll arrive by midnight tonight . . . What can I do to help?"

~Night

"Kyan! Get up here!" A group of watchmen stood on a spire of a church in the Third District, their silhouettes against the starlight waved him up. Kyan quickly scaled the building and stood next to a group of his volunteers. One of them pointed out into the distance. "See all those Ferramish ships? You can pick'em out in the moonlight; whole fuckin' fleet of 'em. What d'you suppose that's for?"

Kyan looked closely. "It's the Cerebrians."

"But Kyan, the banners are—"

"Scarlet. Don't you think that could give them an advantage? Our ships have three masts; look here in the harbor below us. Those ships out there, they're four-masted. Light the lamps and sound the bells – they're here."

"Aye, sir." The group of boys rushed into the spire. "Give me the torch." A boy thrust the flames into a large stack of firewood next to the bell. "Sound it!" Another boy grabbed the lever of the bell and pulled it, sending a single note reverberating through the nearest neighborhoods. A cathedral in the distance stood quiet and dark, then soon, a light flickered and a fire sprang up and a clear chime rang out from it.

Kyan grabbed the rope pulley of the bell and hit it again and again. Another cathedral in the distance lit up and rang its bells. Soon, the symphony of two dozen beacon churches rang throughout the Second and Third District. Kyan took a break from the bells to look at the palace hill. Nothing there moved, and no lights were lit; it was silent compared to the clamor of the city.

Raelynn stepped onto the roof of the cathedral. "Kyan, we're ready down on the streets."

Kyan looked to the sea. *"We're not ready for anything like this."*

The whistle of Cerebrian cannonballs from the Gelltzkreiks cut through the air over Aunestauna as Kyan held his sword high, alongside Raelynn and forty other volunteers; a fraction of the amount of people who were prepared to fight in the seaside neighborhoods and farther inland. A few thin ropes held a huge stack of barrels together on the sloped street to the docks. A mass of green troops marched around the corner, headed toward the Ferrs. Once they were far enough in to not be able to run back, Kyan yelled, "Cut it!" and three teen boys in the back of the pile severed the lines.

Instantly, forty barrels full of grain and water began to tumble down the steep street. "Forward!" Kyan and the rest ran after the barrels as they rolled down, hitting the sixty troops and all their metal plates with a clash. The Ferrs drove forward and stabbed the soldiers as they lay on the ground. Kyan threw a spear to Raelynn, and they sank their weapons into the Cerebrians. The naval ships in the harbor continued to bash the ramparts of the palace with dozens of cannonballs, and streets beside them now burned bright orange as the soldiers moved in.

Troops farther away had stopped the barrels from rolling and now charged forward. Mr. Tumno, the baker, met one with a powerful blow of a club just before an arrow flew into his neck and another into his heart. Kyan pounced over a barrel and threw a knife into the chest of the archer ahead of them; but Kyan failed to catch the huge body of Mr. Tumno as he collapsed onto the street, bashing his head on the stone.

Kyan knelt next to him, and an unexpected wave of dread passed through his bones. The realization that he could die right there hit him like a draft of winter air. Raelynn shouted from higher on the street, "Archers! Get down!" With no time to think, Kyan dove behind Mr. Tumno's large body as a volley of arrows whistled through the air. Arrows sailed into the flesh of Mr. Tumno's corpse behind him, and in seconds, ten Ferrs who had not ducked lay on the ground screaming with garbled voices as their throats filled with blood. An arrow flew straight at Raelynn but disappeared when she met it with her hand, exploding into a cloud of charcoal.

More explosions from the harbor sent thunder cracks through the city, as the fleet continued to bombard the flaming palace. As more Cerebrian troops funneled into the street, Raelynn ran to a shop on the side and rang a bell over and over. The shutters of all the buildings on the street opened and mothers and daughters threw buckets of boiling water and burning coals on the troops below, some of which were unlucky enough to look up at the coals before they hit their eyes. A steaming rock bounced off Kyan's ankle, stinging him. Kyan froze as he watched the Cerebrians screaming in pain, horrified at the site. He could have passed these men as Calleneck in the streets of Seirnkov or traded with them as Tayben in his little town of Woodshore; he could have had a drink next to one in the *Ivy Serpent.* Kyan grabbed his sword, *No one lives forever.*

Oden Haggahol and a gang of young men rounded the corner, driving past Kyan, and met the soldiers with swords. The huge smith next to him hefted one of the barrels of water and hurled it at the Cerebrians. Raelynn picked up a Cerebrian bow and began firing arrows at whatever troops she could hit, with surprising accuracy for her little experience. Through his other lives, Kyan had learned eleven years of sword fighting from Whittingale and had fought in the Cerebrian army as a Phantom; so unlike the commoners around him, he was no stranger to the art. Kyan raised his sword, "Use whatever you have! This is your home!" The Ferrs roared in a rallying call, and Kyan rolled a stopped barrel down the street. His nimble thief feet dodged the swipe of a sword, and he spun around and sliced a soldier in the neck. "Fight! Defend your city!"

Kyan heard a pounding on the rooftop next to him. Jumping over a chimney, two limping figures darted forward toward the harbor. *That's Eston and Fillian! They're going after Queen Eradine!* His mind flashed back. *The queen, she's at the docks! They're forcing her onto a ship!*

Kyan quickly scaled the shop and ran after the princes, jumping over chimneys and gaps between the slanted rooftops. In the street below, the commoners cried out in joy as they saw the Scarlet Guard approaching them from behind. But they were soon silenced when the Scarlet Guard joined the Cerebrian troops in slaughtering their own people and setting fire to the surrounding buildings.

Once he was close enough to see, Kyan knelt behind a chimney overlooking the harbor. Kyan jolted when he realized Raelynn was behind him. "Holy— why did you follow me?"

"I saw you—"

Kyan put a finger over his lips and whispered, *"Wait."* He pointed to the docks below, where Eston and Fillian stood behind shipping containers. The ships' Gelltzkreiks continued to fire and tear down the palace above them. Every few seconds, another crack rang out.

Raelynn shook her head. "Why are y—"

"Shhhh . . . Listen." From far below, the wind carried Fillian's words up to them, *"How are we supposed to get Mother off that ship?"*

Raelynn looked wide eyed at Kyan. "Queen Eradine?"

Kyan nodded.

"But how—"

"There's no time to explain—"

Raelynn grabbed his wrist and whispered, "How did you know?"

Kyan stared at Raelynn, a girl he knew who did not know him. He thought up the same lie he told Fillian when the two of them found the chamber of beasts below the palace. "I'm an agent for Prince Eston; I'm a spy." He felt it strange to talk about his other lives without being able to tell the truth. "I'll explain later but for now, you have to trust me. The Cerebrians are going to kill the queen; will you help me stop them?"

Raelynn looked at him with confusion, then looked at the burning city behind them and the ship ahead and nodded. To the side, a battalion of Cerebrian troops was unloading from their ship and marching into the city. Down below, Eston leaned on a container to get a better view. Kyan tensed as he watched himself, *No, No, No.* The container slipped, and the whole pile fell over. The battalion of green soldiers stopped, and turned to the princes, who tried to run, but were stopped by a volley of arrows ahead of them.

"We need to do something," said Raelynn as the battalion surrounded them.

Kyan closed his eyes to think. "They'll be escorted to the Cerebrian commander; we need to get on that ship." He grabbed the edge of the building and slid down, Raelynn followed. Kyan saw himself in the distance drop his weapon, along with Fillian, and the troops grabbed them, pushing them toward the ship. Running behind shipping containers, Kyan reached the dock and ducked underneath it, where the edge of a wave grazed his boots on the stony beach. A few snowflakes landed on his jacket.

Raelynn knelt beside him. "There are too many guards; we can't just walk up the ramp to the deck." Her fake Ferramish accent was nearly gone. The platoon escorting the princes approached the dock.

The water of the inlet moved up the stone again, kissing Kyan's boots, on which another snowflake landed. "The water will be cold." Kyan took off his jacket and set it on the stone.

Raelynn whispered as troops began to pass on the planks overhead, "You can't be serious."

Kyan took off his boots and whispered, "This is the royal family, Raelynn. There's a porthole open near the surface of the water to the left of the second mast; we'll enter there." He looked up through the gaps between wood beams and saw himself and his brother pass overhead. Kyan took off his socks and stepped into the water; a searing sting, the heat drained from his feet. He took another step and the stinging intensified until he lost feeling.

Behind him, Raelynn took off her jacket and shoes. Kyan was now waist-deep, and his pants stuck to his skin beneath the freezing water. Raelynn entered behind him as the last soldiers passed. Kyan pushed off the rocky bottom and plunged his body, except for his head, into the inlet. The two swam underneath the dock. The freezing water drained their energy and made it impossible to breathe. Kyan and Raelynn reached the mossy and barnacle-covered edge of the ship. Shivering and teeth chattering, they pulled themselves up into the open shutter.

Their breath froze in the air, which vanished in the moonlight and the light of the occasional fire of a Gelltzkreik. Although his movements were slower, Kyan moved silently through the bottom of the ship and up multiple sets of stairs, followed by Raelynn.

Kyan stopped on one of the middle floors, which was loaded to the brim with a pile of explosives, the same kind the Evertauri was using at this very moment to destroy the Great Gate. *Most likely reserves in case the attack proved harder for the Cerebrians,* he thought. Dozens of Gelltzkreik cannons pointed into the harbor, but the floor was abandoned; most of the troops had been sent into the city and wouldn't risk being vulnerable to friendly fire.

Kyan, shivering horribly from the hypothermic temperature, rushed up the staircase and onto the floor beneath the stern. The room was lit by a small hatchway in the ceiling. Kyan and Raelynn looked through it and saw a group of Cerebrian soldiers, Eston and Fillian, and General Heirmonst standing next to Queen Eradine with a knife. Only a second after arriving at the hatchway, Kyan and Raelynn heard Eston whisper, "Xandria doesn't want peace . . . she will stop at nothing to destroy what she thinks my father stole from her . . . Saving my mother will not save my people."

Kyan's stomach dropped. *No!* He was too late.

The general nodded. "As you wish." Heirmonst drove the dagger forward, and Eradine screamed something in her gag before she fell limp, and blood streamed from her neck.

Kyan stared at Raelynn with his face enraged. "That pile of explosives — blow this ship in two. I'll get the princes off."

"But—"

"Light the fuse and then jump out the stern of the ship." Before Raelynn could say anything, Kyan darted for the ladder to the main deck. He scrambled up, counting as he went. Raelynn lunged down the staircase and into the room of the explosives, taking hold of the fuse.

Kyan emerged on the top of the deck and located the two princes far off in a mass of soldiers; they stood next to a railing in shock from what had just happened. Sprinting, Kyan smashed through the troops, and before they could jab at him with their swords, Kyan dove into the princes and knocked them off the railing. The three fell through the night air off the stern of the ship, trying to position themselves in the air to plunge safely in the water. As they fell, shattering glass sounded next to them as Raelynn jumped out the stern window.

As they fell, Kyan frantically tried to locate the surface of the water and angle his feet toward it. They hit the icy water hard and plunged beneath its dark surface. Bitter cold water surrounded him, and a burst of orange lit the surrounding water. A shockwave of deafening sound pushed the four down further into the water where the pressure tortured his eardrums. Beams of wood began to shoot around him as he located three dark figures beside him. The icy water began to drain his energy as one of his boots slipped off. A huge dark mass blocked the light of the burning ship above them, and Kyan dodged the mast of the ship as it plunged through the water. But the mast hit Eston and Fillian in the head with a thud and knocked them unconscious.

Kyan saw Raelynn's long light hair trail behind her as she dove down to grab Eston's hand while he sank, and Kyan instinctively swam after Fillian, whose body was being dragged down into the black abyss by the mast. He wildly kicked his legs as he touched a finger to Fillian's. The cold stung him and shook his body as more debris shot around him. He dove further and stretched forward, grabbing Fillian's fingers. The pressure of the water around him pounded on his ears so hard he wanted to scream. Fillian's fingers began slipping off Kyan's as the mast sank faster than he could swim; his hand drifted an inch below Kyan's, three inches, six.

A stream of black energy surrounded the mast, shattering it and freeing Fillian. Kyan kicked again and wrapped an arm around him, then he turned back toward the surface and used a free arm and his legs to pull the two of them up. His lungs jerked for air, his vision began to turn black, and he could no longer see the warm light of the exploded ship above. He kept swimming up, but with every second, he slowed. An arm reached out and helped pull Fillian up, and the surface was closer than it appeared. Seconds later, Kyan broke through, gasping for air. He slapped one hand on the surface of the frigid water and held one shoulder of Fillian with the other.

Kyan looked over at Raelynn, who held Fillian's other shoulder and whose wet face reflected the orange light of the burning ship beside them. The two pulled Fillian onto shore, passing the sinking bodies of Cerebrian soldiers and General Heirmonst. Kyan touched the rocks on the seabed with his toes and dragged Fillian up. He saw Eston lying on the stone-covered beach where Raelynn had pulled him up.

Once he climbed onto the shore and set down Fillian, he realized that his second boot had fallen off in the ocean as well. He looked at the two princes, both of whom lay still with their eyes closed. Kyan reached over and put his fingers on Eston's neck, feeling a faint beat. He turned over to Fillian and did the same – nothing. No color could be seen on his face. "Fillian?" Kyan jostled his shoulder. "Raelynn, he's not breathing, help him!"

Raelynn hesitated, then knelt over Fillian and tore apart his tunic, placing her hand on his chest. A pulse of obsidian Taurimous rushed from her palm into his skin. She was trying to restart his heart with shocks of energy, but she was shivering badly, her clothes soaked in freezing seawater. After a few more tries, Fillian's body jerked, and water spurted from his mouth. His eyes opened wide for a brief moment before he blacked out.

Kyan caught Fillian's head before it smacked against the rocky beach, and gently set it down. He turned to Raelynn, speaking through chattering teeth. "We– we need to get d–dry, get th–them dry."

"How– how did you know I could help him?" she said, shaking from the wet cold.

Kyan thought quickly. "You sh–shattered the mast that was dragging him d–down. You're a s–sorceress." He studied Raelynn's nervous look, which was obvious even in the dim light of the fires blazing around the city. "It's okay, just help get them d–dry or they'll die from the cold."

Raelynn nodded and placed her hands over Eston's body first. Little black flames coated her hands as she traced them above his clothes, making them steam. Once she could tell that his clothes were dry, she moved to Fillian, and then to Kyan, careful not to burn him. The warmth felt like the biggest relief in Kyan's life as the water evaporated away into hot steam.

No longer shivering, he ripped open Fillian's tunic further to see the wound. The gash had reopened and was spilling blood over his abdomen. The key strung around his neck was covered in splotches of crimson. Kyan recognized it as Prophet Ombern's key the two of them found in the Great Cathedral. Once Raelynn had dried off her own clothes, she placed a flame to Fillian's wound, clotting the blood. It was crude work and left a gruesome scab, but the flow had stopped and was good enough for now.

Kyan turned to the harbor, where fire burned on planks of wood that floated where *The Desolator* once was. The ships nearby continued firing cannonballs at the Royal Palace, which, far above them, was crumbling and burning. The four had washed up below the cliffs of the Royal Palace, rather than near the shoreline of houses and buildings that blazed in a great orange fire.

As Raelynn checked Eston's pulse again, she spoke. "Kyan— You can't tell anyone you know. Do you understand?"

Kyan heard more fear in her voice than confidence. She had just exposed her gifts with sorcery to him in order to save the princes' lives; of course she would be scared. Sorcerers were supposed to be dangerous, evil . . . extinct. Kyan turned back to her. "I understand." As soon as the words had left his mouth, the clanking of armor and swords sounded from nearby. A few seconds later, a group of twenty or so soldiers emerged around a rock wall on the beach. They rushed toward Kyan and Raelynn wearing red cloaks and gold helms.

The Scarlet Guard, thought Kyan, *traitors.* He had no weapons to defend himself, but he had Raelynn.

The Guard leading the group shouted out to Kyan and Raelynn, spotting the princes on the ground. "Is everyone alright?! We saw the ship explode."

Kyan was taken aback, and Raelynn stood her ground. "Yes, but what are you doing here?" called out Kyan, "The Scarlet Guard—"

"Switched sides," said the commander as he reached Kyan and stopped. "But not us," he said, breathlessly. The soldier had a thick black beard that hung a few inches below his chin. Kyan recognized him as Liann Carbelle, son of a Ferramish General by the same name. "We were attacked by our fellow Scarlet Guards when we refused to turn on Ferramoor," he continued. "But we were able to take a good number of them down. You can trust us." Liann looked at them in confusion, and then at Fillian and Eston laying still on the ground. "Are the princes okay? Who are you?"

"They're okay but they need medical attention," Kyan responded. "I— I work for Eston— Prince Eston. They know us. We pulled them from the ship when it exploded."

Liann seemed like he was about to ask more questions, but Raelynn spoke first in her false Ferramish accent. "There is little time, we need to get them to the infirmary in the palace where someone can take care of them until they wake back up."

Liann motioned a few of his men forward, and they gingerly picked up Eston and Fillian, slumping them over their shoulders. "You said you work for the Prince?" he asked, looking behind him along the shoreline for any Cerebrian troops. The only ones visible from the rocky beach were a long distance off, unloading off rowboats into the city harbor to attack. "Come with us back to the palace; we can see you safely there. I know of a hidden passageway from the shore into the palace."

Kyan and Raelynn thanked him, and hurriedly followed the Scarlet Guards around the cliff face to their north. Horns blasted in the city behind them, and buildings toppled in big billows of embers and flame. At the same time, the Cerebrian fleet was still firing from the inlet, and loud crashes rang out above them as cannonballs slammed into the palace walls. The fires burned so large on the shore that they even began creating their own searing gales.

Kyan looked up to the crumbling ramparts of the palace a few hundred feet above them. "Look up there," he pointed to Liann. "I see five of our trebuchets that they haven't taken out yet. Once you get Eston and Fillian to the South Wing Infirmary, send the rest of your men to man those trebuchets. Knock out the ships that are firing the Gelltzkreiks first."

"The what?" asked Liann.

Kyan remembered he learned the name when Calleneck was with Mordvitch. "Those bloody iron boulder launchers that they've been shooting at the palace."

The soldier nodded. "Aye, we will."

The pebble beach narrowed quickly as they snuck around the giant boulders at the bottom of the palace cliff. The water was soon lapping at Kyan's bare feet, an icy cold that made stepping on the jagged rocks even more uncomfortable. He found himself ascending a slippery rockface, following behind Liann and the soldiers carrying the princes carefully on their backs. Raelynn climbed right behind him, shuffling on a narrow path cut into the nearly vertical rock.

As they snuck around another boulder face, Kyan realized the path was headed into a sea cave that buried itself beneath the palace hill. *We're entering from underneath the palace,* he thought. The sound of the crashing waves changed into violent echoes as they entered the mouth of the cave. Kyan thought the tunnel was nearly wide enough to man a sailboat through, though he couldn't tell how deep the water was that rushed into it. Ahead of him, the soldier carrying Fillian slipped on a wet rock and cursed as he caught himself with Liann's help.

The sea cave went so deep that Kyan could hardly see the firelight glow of the city behind them, only Raelynn's white-blonde hair that stood out in the dark. Ahead, Liann turned and disappeared around a bend, unlatching a door. Kyan and Raelynn followed the soldiers through the ramshackle door just before a swell of seawater splashed up onto the stone.

Liann locked the door behind them, muting the sounds of the waves, and ignited a torch. "Up ahead and to the right, there's a staircase," he said, and the soldiers in front of him made their way through the tunnel. "Prince Eston ordered Qerru-Mai An'Drui to ride to Camp Auness to get reinforcements," he continued, "but she may not be back with the troops for some time. Until then, we need to do what we can to take out the Cerebrians, but our first priority is protecting the princes."

Once Kyan and Raelynn reached the top of the winding spiral staircase, they passed through another series of hidden doorways until emerging in a dark palace hallway, still far beneath the surface. Liann motioned to the left. "We can get the princes to the hospital wing this way. Redward, you take the others and start manning the trebuchets . . . if we have any left. Give the Cerebrians hell." With that, two groups of Scarlet Guards split and rushed off to the defenses and the infirmary, leaving Kyan and Raelynn alone in the hallway.

Raelynn turned to Kyan and spoke quietly in the dim torchlight. "Those trebuchets are not going to stand a chance against the Cerebrian warships. They might sink one out of forty, but probably not before the ships knock them out first."

He was turned away, slowly pacing toward a door a short distance off. Almost to himself, he whispered, "I recognize this place . . ."

Raelynn continued, not hearing him. "Xandria is about to win everything, and we have to stop her somehow. I— I don't have an answer for this battle, but I have information that could help after all of this is over if you tell Prince Eston, since you work for him. Tonight, a rebel Cerebrian group called the Evertauri will attempt to destroy the Great Gate to let the Ferrs through; in the process, they will reveal themselves to the world. I am one of them, but I'm stationed here now. No matter if they fail or succeed, the rebels will demonstrate capabilities that will scare Xandria. You need to convince Prince Eston and the government to take credit for the attack. Say it was Ferramish special forces. This will provide us with secrecy and make your army look stronger. But you know now that I'm a sorceress. The world will suspect sorcery still exists after tonight, so I can fight . . . fight for real. You and I, we can go back out there and defend the Palace. The city is lost. But we could at least try and hold the palace to keep the princes alive."

Kyan was tracing his fingers along the door, lost in thought.

"Kyan? What are you doing?"

He whispered to himself again. "She's a sorceress . . . only she can release them."

"Kyan, talk to me. What's behind that door?"

He broke his gaze and turned to her. "I— I've been down here before. There is something behind this door that could help us . . . I don't know if it will work but— but I don't know what else to do. Our few naval ships are burning and sinking, and it could be hours before Ferramish troops arrive; we have nothing left. You and I alone can't take on the Cerebrian Army . . . so we have to use something that can."

Raelynn studied him, then slowly nodded. "Show me." She walked up and tried to open it, but it wouldn't budge. "It's locked." Kyan held out his hand and opened his fingers, revealing a small, bloody key attached to a chain. Raelynn's eyes opened wide. "You swiped that off of Prince Fillian while he was unconscious?"

Kyan shimmied the key into the lock. "Technically we both stole it from Prophet Ombern." The door unlatched and swung open, and he slipped inside the dark room, where the enormous wooden machine with wheels was turning and clicking.

To light up the room, Raelynn lit a small white flame in her hand— a hue different from her natural obsidian colored Taurimous that provided no light. She looked closely at the spinning, ticking machine, muttering, "What is this?"

Kyan slipped the key and its chain around his neck and stopped each of the wheels one by one to spell out the word *Silverbrook*, and the massive stone wall to their side slid open with an echoing thundercrack. "It's Ferramoor's secret weapon," said Kyan, leading her down the steep staircase to the great domed room. In the middle of the stone cavern that stood multiple stories tall was the same pile of burned papers and scientific instruments that was reduced to rubble. The chamber was surrounded by five panels of light— swirling white Taurimous that seemed to whisper. Behind one of them, Kyan noticed a sound emerging he didn't notice before — crashing waves.

Kyan motioned to Raelynn, who was still looking in awe at the huge cavern around her. "Behind these walls of light are monsters created to defend Ferramoor . . . I need you to release one of them."

She looked at him strangely. "A monster? You— you want me to release it?"

He nodded. "I'm not a sorcerer, I can't. Only you can . . . Aunestauna is burning, and these beasts were created to defend it. Please, you have to trust me."

Raelynn slowly stepped toward the shimmering white Taurimous barrier. Her breathing was deep and heavy, and somewhere in the distance, the echo of cannonfire still echoed through the rock, quickly replaced by more sounds of rushing water and a deep rumble from behind the wall.

Kyan's heart felt like it would pound out of his chest as she pressed her hand to the wall of light, and writhing black flames erupted from her palm, slithering over the barrier like sentient smoke. A sound like shattering glass snapped through the great cavern, and the wall of light burst into a shower of white sparks. Almost instantly, water rushed out from behind it onto Kyan's bare feet like they had released a dam. He and Raelynn stepped back as a gigantic shape materialized from the blackness in front of him. Great red eyes in the shape of thin slits grew wider, and as it emerged from the rushing water, the monster's full terrible form appeared – a colossal serpentine creature with skin of dark seaweed and scales. Ridges of translucent veined webbing lined its snake-like length that disappeared beneath the surface of the water. Its ferocious head was surrounded like a cobra in flapping membranes suspended between spikes.

A hissing sound filled the cavern, and giant flaps of skin along the serpent's chest rattled like vibrating gills. Then the creature opened its jaws and let out an ear-piercing shriek and a torrent of mist that drenched Kyan and Raelynn head to toe as they fell backwards. The deafening sound filled the air like scraping metal, and Kyan had to press his hands to his ears, yelling in pain.

Raelynn stumbled to her feet and ignited a black flame in her hand. "What do we do now?!" she shouted as the serpent coiled and thrashed, sending waves of water rushing onto the floor of the cavern.

Kyan slipped as he stood but regained his footing. "Just wait."

The beast's shriek had turned into a low reptilian rumble, but the three other beasts hidden behind their walls of light had begun to roar as well. Kyan couldn't bring himself to imagine what was behind the other barriers. Towering over them, the serpent slithered and sent another wave of water into the chamber, washing away the bottom of the pile of ashes and debris. But then it lowered its head and its body onto the swamped floor, gently blinking at them and extending a fin of webbing down to their height.

Kyan looked at Raelynn, but her eyes were transfixed in a stare with the serpent. Its eyes swirled with an eerie light that reminded him of the stone he stole. "Raelynn, what is it?"

She spoke without breaking her gaze. "It– it wants us to join it. I can hear it talking to me in my head . . . It's looking at my memories – looking at the ships in the harbor."

"What? Do you mean climb on its back? Wait Raelynn–"

She was already stepping onto the serpent's fin, grabbing hanging masses of seaweed to pull herself up.

Kyan looked at the serpent's snarling jaws that could break a ship mast in two and then up at Raelynn, who sat atop it holding onto its spikes. "You've got to be joking," he muttered. Before he could second guess himself, he found himself climbing up the side of the beast and situating himself rather uncomfortably next to Raelynn. The serpent smelled like salt and decaying fish, and its scales cut into his bare feet.

As soon as Kyan was secure, the beast whipped its body around, making his head spin. The serpent turned toward the darkness of the cave that had held it and the pool of seawater it had lived in. Kyan realized what was about to happen and cursed as he felt his stomach drop, his fragile body plummeting toward the water on the back of the serpent. The creature dove beneath the surface with a scream that dwarfed Kyan's and Raelynn's.

Kyan held his breath, and the cold seawater slapped against his body with such force he thought it impossible he was still holding on. It was pitch black, but the serpent was darting through a sea tunnel, the two of them clutching on for their lives as they were tugged underwater. Just when Kyan thought he could no longer hold his breath, the serpent broke through the water onto the surface. He gasped for air and briefly glimpsed the walls of the sea cave rushing past them before emerging out into the open water of the inlet.

The serpent banked hard to the south, swimming so fast that it churned up a thirty-foot plume of white foam and a massive wake behind it. Kyan looked back and still couldn't tell where the beast's tail ended, but it was at least seventy feet long. Raelynn had held on but could barely keep her eyes open amidst the spray from the water. Up ahead floated the Cerebrian fleet — forty ships unloading rowboats of soldiers and blasting Gelltzkreiks at the palace and into the city. Kyan glanced up at the palace as the serpent sped through the ocean waves — the trebuchets had all been reduced to splinters, and the walls surrounding the main towers were crumbling with each strike. The shoreline of Aunestauana was ablaze, and the soldiers from the Cerebrian ships kept coming.

The serpent was closing the distance between them and the ships with astonishing speed, and Kyan realized the beast was headed for a head-on collision with the nearest vessel. He and Raelynn quickly adjusted their grip, locking arms with each other, preparing for the impact. Waves crashed by them, and the spray of water was blinding as they hurled toward the cannon-firing ship. The soldiers manning vessel turned just in time to see the sea monster bare its fangs and shriek before it slammed into the hull.

The impact was so strong, Kyan felt like his spine had just been crunched. Wood splintered and water rushed by as the beast dove beneath the surface. The ocean smacked against Kyan's head with a jarring blow as they plunged deep. Kyan felt another bone-shaking impact as the serpent slammed up into the hull of another ship underwater, then another, and another. He clutched on as the wild serpent jerked and launched its fightening form out of the water thirty feet into the air. Kyan could hardly tell which way was which as he clung on to the spikes. He heard men screaming as the serpent soared over a vessel, snapping its masts in half with its jaws. In its wake, ships were sinking left and right, and Cerebrian soldiers were jumping into the water as their vessels capsized.

A Gelltzkreik fired from a ship beside them and tore a hole through the serpent's dorsal fin, making it scream a painful metallic roar. Kyan and Raelynn clung on as the beast hurled through the waves toward the ship that fired. It slammed into the bow and brought its head around to bite the mast in half, its spines slicing through the white and green fabric of the sails. The serpent coiled its massive tail around the middle of the ship, constricted, and snapped it in half like a twig, sending wood and debris flying up at Kyan and Raelynn, who blocked it with a shield of black Taurimous.

As the serpent sped toward the center of the fleet, Raelynn hurled balls of obsidian flame at soldiers manning the Gelltzkrieks, sending them flying off the rails of their ships. The serpent slashed at sails and bit holes through the sides of ships as it wreaked havoc on the fleet. Fires were springing up on ships and men were even firing arrows into the serpent's scales. Kyan ducked as a fire arrow whizzed toward him, striking into the beast's armored back. The more the beast got hit, the more it lashed out, diving above and below the surface like dolphins of the Southern Sea to try and shake them off. Soldiers leaving their ships in rowboats screamed as the serpent devoured them in one snap of its jaws, and Raelynn continued to pick off soldiers one by one who were firing at the beast.

A mass of ships ahead had gotten their ships turned around to fire directly at Kyan and Raelynn atop the giant serpent. "Raelynn, ahead!" Kyan yelled. With a flash of light and puff of smoke, the ships fired toward them, hurling balls of iron faster than Kyan could see. Raelynn ignited obsidian flames in her hand and sent a wave of Taurimous forward, shattering the incoming projectiles in a cloud of black smoke. But a few iron boulders passed through, grazing the side of the serpent. Behind them, nearly two dozen ships on the outer edges of the fleet were sinking into the icy waves, but half of the ships still fired from the center, and the serpent had spears and arrows sticking out of its whole length, gushing black blood into the sea.

The serpent dove once more beneath a ship and sprung out in the center of twenty or so ships. These ones at the center of the fleet were larger, and protruding out of their hulls next to the Gelltzkrieks were cones of copper that looked like an animal's tusk. Kyan knew he was freezing cold from the water and the frigid air, but his adrenaline was too high for him to feel anything but his number fingers locked around the spine of the seamonster. He felt the beast constrict in the water, ready to dive into another ship. But before it could launch itself, Kyan felt an unnerving tingling go up his spine.

In an instant, electric shocks of lightning coursed over the water from the copper horns of the Cerebrian ships and wrapped around the serpent. Kyan's vision tumbled, and he felt his muscles twitching and pain coursing through his back. The beast below him let out a hellish scream that made Kyan want to abandon his grip and cover his ears. But he was screaming too, and his field of view was surrounded by bolts of lightning shooting out from the ships into the water, electrocuting the beast and its riders.

Kyan heard the Gelltzkrieks ignite again, and flashes of orange lit the churning water as iron boulders shot through the air toward them. He heard Raelynn yell next to him as she produced a shell of black smoke around them. Deafening blasts rattled his eardrums as the iron boulders slammed into Raelynn's protective shield of energy swirling around them. The beast writhed below them, letting out its terrible scream as the barrage of iron smashed clear through its body.

Raelynn shouted as the serpent thrashed in pain. "Hold on!" But the best threw its neck around, and Kyan's grip on the spikes failed. They slashed through his skin and his body hurled through the air. Just before he hit the water, he saw a glimpse of the serpent exploding in a torrent of water and black blood.

The world went mute, and the water pressed hard against his ears, ringing violently. The world around him was dark, and only the faint sound of explosions made their way into the depths of the sea. A cloud of white bubbles seeped through his clothes and up toward the surface where his feet were pointed. Debris from ships – planks of wood and fabric sails drifted around him, sinking into the black of the sea. Then the darkness lit up with color – a flash of orange light above the surface of the water. Kyan turned his body and swam up to the light. His lungs convulsed as he kicked toward the surface. Closer. Closer.

He broke through the waves and gasped for air, coughing up water. A wave of heat touched his face as he blinked the water from his eyes. The world around him was on fire, explosions were rattling through the air, and he grasped for anything to hold onto. The waves crashed violently around him as he reached for a large plank of floating wood that made a makeshift raft. Once he grabbed hold of it, he saw Raelynn standing on the floating rubble. Still gaining his bearings, he looked around at the storm of fire, a hurricane of flames spinning around them – it was coming from Raelynn.

She stood with her eyes closed and her hands outstretched, screaming from the force of her Taurimous swirling in a vortex around them. Beyond the wall of flames, Kyan could hear ships around them exploding, sending wood flying into the firestorm. The air roared with the ignition of ships and the desparate firing of Gelltzkreiks that shatttered once they hit the swirling mass of obsidian smoke.

Kyan clung on to the wooden debris as the whitecaps swelled and crashed around him in the maelstrom of Raelynn's spell. He looked up at her and jolted in horror; her face was turning black, seeming to be made of ash, and she bled from her mouth as she screamed. The howling wind blew her white-blonde hair across her face as iron boulders shot through the air, shattering in the flames. He had no idea how she was producing such a powerful spell.

Her obsidian Taurimous continued to violently escape from her body and rip apart the fleet around them, churning the water of the inlet. Towering waves swelled and sank with each rotation of the blackness that roared with the fire of the ships. Raelynn's scream pierced through the tornado of shadow and fire as Kyan clutched to the wooden board. His ears throbbed under the pressure waves of the explosions. The never-ending whirlwind of smoke and flame consumed every timber of the ships around them. Raelynn's face seemed to crumble away as she screamed, and all at once, the blackness dissipated, and Raelynn fell unconscious onto the raft of wood, returning to her normal image.

Slowly, the waves around them began to calm, and the rocking subsided. Icy cold water dripped from Kyan's hair as he pulled himself onto the makeshift raft. Shivering and coughing up seawater, he crawled over to Raelynn, who lay unconscious but breathing. He traced a hand along her pale face. Looking around him, he saw a sea of burning debris – fire, timbers, and desolation. A Cerebrian vessel burned brightly in the distance and disappeared below the water. As the wind blew, gusts of hot embers flew through the saltwater air and caught more wreckage on fire – and then the flakes of ash began to fall around him.

Kyan turned around only to see more ships sinking. All their explosives had detonated by Raelynn's spell, sending a large series of waves onto the nearby docks. In the distance, Aunestauna burned in one massive fire that sent a huge column of black into the otherwise clear night sky. Kyan spun around again to examine the inlet, not a single four-masted ship floated, nor any green banner waved. The fleet was destroyed.

Checking Raelynn's pulse again, he brushed her soaked hair out of her face and steadied the raft in the ebbing waves. Reaching out into the water, he grabbed a broken wooden plank and began to paddle through the flaming wreckage of the Cerebrian fleet east toward the shore. Stroke after stroke, he passed burning masts and other floating debris. His head was spinning, and he felt like he was about to faint, but he knew he had to keep going and get to the rocky beach.

About ten yards off, a young boy in green armor trying to stay afloat on a scrap of wood fell off into the frigid water and struggled to grab it again; but he could not keep afloat. Kyan paddled silently by him.

The boy called out for help in a little Cerebrian accent. "Please! Help me! I can't swim much!"

Kyan continued to paddle away, the front of the raft knocking wood aside that drifted away in the waves.

"No! Please!" The boy cried as he tried to stay on the surface of the water fighting against his heavy armor that pulled him down.

Raelynn lay unmoving on the floor of the raft, and Kyan didn't think it could hold another person. Kyan looked at the Cerebrian's puffy red eyes and he struggled to stay afloat.

"Please, sir!"

Kyan looked up at the shore of Aunestauna, which blazed in a column of orange. The Cerebrian army continued to sack the city, colliding with commonfolk trying to defend their home. A tear slid down Kyan's face, and he extended his makeshift oar to the boy. "Grab on . . . reach again, there you go." Kyan grunted as he pulled the boy onto the raft, making it dip down into the ocean a bit further – but it still floated. His head throbbed and his vision was starting to go fuzzy. "Help row," he told the boy, who was shivering and coughing up water. But the boy nodded and shuffled over Raelynn to the other side and grabbed a wooden plank, paddling with Kyan and saying not a word as they passed through the burning wreckage of the Cerebrian fleet.

ASHES
Chapter Twenty Eight

Kyan's eyes were closed, and he felt his chest pressing against cold pebbles. His head throbbed, obscuring his vision, but he could hear the waves moving up and down the rocky beach. It was silent everywhere, save for a very distant screaming. He could tell that it was light out and his clothes were soaked and icy cold. With much effort, he pushed his torso off the rocky shore and opened his eyes to a reddish-gray light. His eyes could only first focus on his hand, on which a couple little gray snowflakes had landed – it was ash. All around him, the beach was ash, and the sky was gray and stank of burning flesh and smoke.

He pulled himself up off the pebbled shore of the inlet and walked along the beach, taking in the desolation. Hundreds of corpses lay sprawled out on the rocky shore, the white foam of waves washing over their limp bodies, spreading scarlet blood over the little rocks and into the ocean. Looking around, he couldn't see the Cerebrian boy who had rowed them to shore, but Raelynn lay not five feet from him on the raft of wood. He looked over the harbor where a dark haze had settled over the water that had become the grave of so many – the beast that helped destroy the fleet, countless soldiers, the queen.

The battle was over. Had Qerru-Mai arrived in time with her reinforcements to take on the Cerebrians? Or had they given up hope when their fleet sank? Either way, Kyan could tell that Aunestauna was nearly destroyed, but the war was not lost. He stepped on a piece of fabric, a torn green banner. He picked up the Cerebrian flag and placed it gently on the raft. Kneeling down, he placed a hand on Raelynn's shoulder and whispered her name. "Raelynn," he said again. She lay still, but breathing softly – weakened from the expense of energy used to destroy the fleet. Carefully, he picked her up into his arms, her head resting against his chest as he carried her inland.

Passing endless piles of rubble and crying townspeople, Kyan carried Raelynn through the city, her blonde hair hung covered in flakes of gray ash. The sky was brightening for the coming sunrise, but it retained its ominous smokey-red glow. After some time, Kyan reached the portion of the city that had not burned down; however, Ferramish and Cerebrian corpses still lay scattered across even these streets. Reaching the theater square, Kyan stopped to look around. *Why was this not burned?* Yes, Kyan helped prepare hundreds of citizens to fight, but still, the number of people who had defended the city was more than Kyan alone could have influenced. *Could Vree have helped save my district?*

Unable to carry Raelynn up to the roof of the theater, he walked through it, and up the staircases to his attic. The shack built into the attic of the theater was mostly untouched, save for a few items blown around by the fire's wind. Kyan set her down on a pile of blankets in the corner and tended to a sword's gash on her ankle.

It was nearly sunrise when she awoke, though Kyan couldn't tell precisely through the orange haze that hung over the city. Raelynn had to open and close her pale blue eyes a few times before adjusting to the dim light of Kyan's shack. Suddenly, they opened wide and she jolted back.

Kyan quickly put a hand on her bandaged ankle. "It's okay . . . it's over."

Raelynn's rapid breathing subsided as she looked at him and studied the shack. "Where are we?" she asked in a weak, Cerebrian voice.

Kyan gave a small smile half out of embarrassment. "Well, um– this is my home. I know it's not much but . . ."

Raelynn tried sitting up slowly, but she grimaced from the pain in her head and her body. "I would think an agent for Prince Eston would have less . . . humble quarters."

Kyan remembered his lie he had told her to account for why he knew so much. "Yes, but the prince likes me to be down here on the streets. I monitor what's going on in the areas that the Scarlet Guard never liked going." The lying made his stomach turn, so he decided to add what truth he could. "This has been my home for a while. I used to be a thief here."

Raelynn looked at the key that miraculously still hung strung around his neck. She pointed to it with a half smile. "*Used* to be a thief?"

He did laugh at that. "I didn't really have time to give it back to Fillian, now did I?"

Raelynn looked around and flinched again at some wound that pained her. "It's too dark in here, let me light a flame and–" Her voice stopped.

Kyan paused for a second, noticing her concerned face. She was looking down at her hands, examining them like something had changed. "What's wrong?"

She made a few motions with her fingers, flicking and twisting, but nothing was happening. "I– I can't make a flame . . ." Raelynn put a hand to her mouth and began shaking, crying.

Kyan put a hand on her arm. "Hey, it's okay. You're tired and you just destroyed a whole fleet of ships. Everything's alright."

She shook her head as tears began to flow from her closed eyes. "I knew the risk when I cast the spell, I just didn't think— I hoped that it would be okay, but now it's gone. It's all gone and—"

"Raelynn, hold on," he tried calming her down. "What happened? What's gone?"

She opened her eyes and looked at him through her tears. "My magic . . ."

Kyan's heart skipped a beat.

"When someone casts a spell that powerful . . ." she said, "there is a chance that they expend all of the magic inside of them. They— they can't use sorcery anymore . . ."

Kyan sat down next to her. He didn't know what to say. She had saved Ferramoor — saved the war. But at what cost to herself? The only thing he could manage to say was, "I'm so sorry."

At that moment, the rising sun peeked through the wooden slits in his shack, and his mind swirled until he was looking up at the vaulted ceiling of the palace infirmary in the body of Eston.

§

A half hour after Eston awoke in the South Wing Hospital, the entirety of Camp Auness arrived in Aunestauna led by Qerru-Mai, pushing back the thousands of Cerebrian soldiers. Eston had been commanding the few loyal Scarlet Guards with the aid of Liann Carbelle until the reinforcements from Camp Auness arrived, and then ordered the officers to move half their platoons, on boats, down the Spring River and west through the city to get behind the Cerebrians, who also had been slowed by the citizens defending their city. The Ferramish troops then formed a double envelopment on the western half of Aunestana, pinning the Cerebrians between the two groups of Ferrs. After hours of fighting, enclosed with no way to push forward through the entire nation of Ferramoor and no way to return home, five thousand Cerebrian soldiers, along with a hundred disloyal Scarlet Guards, surrendered in the streets. The Cerebrians and Scarlet Guard traitors were then marched to Camp Auness to be held captive.

~Daybreak, November 5th

Eston stood in his bedroom just after sunrise. Flakes of ash drifted down from the gray sky where a ceiling previously stood. The palace was destroyed and still smoldering on the seaward side. In the East Wing, the roof and walls of the top floor had crumbled; and from where his bed used to be, Eston could see the entirety of Aunestauna in the open air, as though gazing from a mountaintop. Aunestauna, once a gleaming city, now either blazed or sat in a pile of ash. The shoreline had taken the hardest hit; only the stone buildings still stood. The Great Ferramish Bazaar, normally filled with mounds of produce and other goods meant for thousands of people, was gone. Far in the distance, Eston could see the theater square where his small attic shack remained; the buildings were mostly untouched by the fire; the citizens of the neighborhood who had emptied their wells had stopped the spread of the flames, saving the Third District.

A strong breeze blew his tattered clothing around him and charred papers blew past his boots. His head throbbed from his concussion, which hadn't bothered him during battle due to the adrenaline. The smell of smoke and blood filled the air, and the heavy haze blocked much of the light coming from the orange sky where the sun would soon rise, transferring him into another body. He had come to the conclusion after last night, that the rising sun is not the only thing that could throw him into another body. He had been transferred the night of the royal ball, during the Battle of the Great Gate, and when his mother died. The pain of watching her helplessly slaughtered pounded on his head. Two of his mothers and a father — the queen and the Bernoils — viciously murdered by Xandria's soldiers.

Eston walked over a pile of stone and to his shattered dresser, picked up the small skipping stone, which had fallen on the floor, and placed it in his pocket. Qerru-Mai and Fillian walked up a crumbling staircase and over to Eston. Her eyes were red but held a resilience that inspired courage in the others. Fillian tried to put a hand on her shoulder, but his wound, which was now properly treated, pained him.

Fillian crossed his arms as another cold breeze blew. He turned to Qerru-Mai. "You know you saved Ferramoor by traveling to Camp Auness?"

She looked out into the city of ash and burning timbers. "It doesn't look saved."

"Aunestauna is destroyed, yes," said Eston, "but Ferramoor is not. We will move some of our government operations to Abendale because it's the most naturally fortified city, and evacuees from Aunestauna will travel to Nottenberry, Greenwash, and Willowwood. Meanwhile, here, we'll rebuild and make Aunestauna stronger. I'll bring in the best architects in the nation and we'll create work for everyone who lost their businesses in the fire. Over there, along the waterfront, we'll enclose the docks in an inner harbor, with ramparts on the windward side. We'll send special missions into Gienn to steal the Cerebrian Gelltzkreik Device, and we'll manufacture them here. We'll rebuild streets in the burned areas to make them easier to defend. We'll create channels off the

Spring River to supply the city with better water and transportation. That's just the beginning . . . Fillian, have you received a reply from Father?"

"No, but I'm sure word has reached him. I would guess he'll be here in four or five hours."

"Does he know about Mother?"

Fillian nodded his head, trying to hold back tears. "I told him in the letter."

"We'll need a new Scarlet Guard and we'll need them fast. Those soldiers who remained loyal, they'll lead the new men. There's been enough blood spilled in this city today."

Fillian took a deep breath in. "Most importantly, we need to find out how Whittingale's plan succeeded."

Eston sat on the rubble-covered front steps of the Royal Palace, waiting for King Tronum. Galloping horses not far off signaled the arrival. A cloud of white ash rose behind the pounding of hooves, and the horses were dappled with flakes of gray. The king dismounted his horse. Eston apprehensively walked forward to meet his father. The man's eyes were red and no sign of life registered on his face. Eston flinched when the king reached forward and embraced him. A sound that Eston had never heard before followed . . . the sound of his father crying.

"Father, the city's gone."

"I know," said the king.

"And Mother—"

"I know."

"I tried to save the kingdom—"

"You did exactly what I would have expected and more." King Tronum embraced Eston and looked out into the city. He wiped a tear from his eye; his dear wife was gone. "This city defended itself like I never would've imagined, but somehow you did it. You acted like a king, Eston; a king who puts his people before himself. Eston . . . I'm sure it will take a long time to recover from this, and meanwhile, I want you on the front lines. Although I now know that Whittingale betrayed us, he still doomed Cerebria by preparing you so well. I'm making you the General of our First Regiment. You'll leave for Endlebarr next month."

Eston breathed in deeply. "That would be an honor."

"Where is your brother?"

"Fillian should be here soon; he saw the prisoners off to Camp Auness. His stab wound from Whittingale is still quite bad, but you know him, he's trying to ignore it and tough it out."

The two of them watched the rising smoke from the city. "How did you do it, Eston?"

The prince shook his head. "It wasn't me who saved Ferramoor . . . it was its people."

Tronum began to walk away.

"Father," said Eston, stopping him. "I have to speak with you about things I have found here in the palace; *beneath* the palace . . . Fillian and I know about the beasts. One of them was released to help defend the city, and it took out the Cerebrian fleet." Though that wasn't entirely true, Eston didn't feel like revealing Raelynn to his father, at least not yet. "The beasts could help us win the war and put an end to all of this. Prophet Ombern urged you to use them, but you wouldn't. But they saved us . . . we have to use them."

Tronum stood still for a minute. He scanned the fallen city. His wife was dead, his capital was burned. He turned back to Eston. "Let's give Xandria hell."

~One Day Later

Finally, after searching fervently for any explanation of Whittingale's betrayal, Eston and Fillian found an unfinished letter in a compartment deep within Whittingale's office that was addressed to the vice-supervisor of Xandria's Technological Wing, the day before the attack. Alongside it lay multiple other documents and reports detailing and organizing the rebellion against the throne. Fillian read the letter aloud to Eston.

"Your Honor, In regard to your inquiry as to how this plan to destroy Ferramoor and get the requested object to you unfolded, here is a brief summary – Back when Xandria was Governess of the Cerebrian Territories, but worked under her brother Tronum in the Royal Palace, I served as one of her closest assistants. Over time, my loyalty to her grew more important to me than my loyalty to Tronum. So, when Cerebria succeeded, I became Xandria's core intelligence provider of the inner workings of the Ferramish government – she had promised to fulfill a wish of mine in exchange for the risk I took on my shoulders. While providing Xandria with inside information, I gained King Tronum's trust and served as the principal tutor to Prince Eston. Four months ago, Xandria told me her plan, which she expects to conclude tomorrow night, when King Tronum is gone to Ifle-Laarm. She knew she couldn't win the war through Endlebarr; there's nothing but attrition in that forest. She knew she had to strike Aunestauna directly, but from the sea." Fillian stopped and looked up, "It cuts off there."

Eston grabbed another document and unfolded it. "Let me see if I can find anything here." He took the document and squinted through the handwriting.

"About what?" asked Fillian.

Eston kept reading. "It gives the names of the leaders of the Scarlet Guard who helped him, but we already have them in prison . . . he says again that they had to wait until Benja was—"

"Was what?" asked Fillian.

"Hold on," said Eston as he read ahead. He looked up at Fillian. "Whittingale was the one who put the poison in our glasses many weeks ago."

Fillian thought. "But if he poisoned the wine, why did he stop us from drinking it? Wouldn't he have wanted to take us all out?"

Eston shook his head. "That wouldn't have done it though, he needed to destroy the palace and everyone in it, as well as Aunestauna. He needed the Scarlet Guard on his side."

Fillian's eyes shot wide open. "And the Scarlet Guard was overseen by Benja . . . that's why he framed him."

Eston started putting it all together. "He wanted to throw everyone off his scent by saving Father from the poison that he himself administered. He wanted Father to trust him enough to put him in control of the Scarlet Guard . . . He wasn't trying to kill the royal family because that would be done after the Scarlet Guard was on his side. The whole time he was setting up Benja—" Eston's heart nearly stopped. "Fillian," he said. "Look in that stack for the word Nightsnake."

"Why?" said Fillian, as he began searching through the sheets of parchment.

Eston scrambled for a reason. "Have you ever heard of them?"

Fillian nodded and sifted through the documents. "—gang of thieves. I didn't think they were real."

Eston shook his head. "The final straw against Benja's case was his supposed theft of the palace vault. But what if it wasn't Benja?" Of course, Eston knew it wasn't Benja who stole the stone, it was him. But he was beginning to think that Riccolo didn't just ask him to steal it for the money.

Fillian snatched out a letter. "Here! It's a copy of a contract he gave their leader." He began to read furiously.

"Read it aloud," said Eston.

"It says – 'Our government is gathering quite a collection of files on your group, you will soon be exposed – your numbers, your locations, everything. But if you agree to the following, I could have those files destroyed. You will send one of your thieves to steal the Stone from the palace vault for me.'" Fillian looked up. "Stone is capitalized here." He continued to read. ""'The night of your break in, I will ensure the Scarlet Lord, Benja Tiggins, is set up for the crime.'"

Eston interjected, "Did he ever figure out Silverbrook's beasts were below the palace? Look in the last letter you had. It might explain why she knew how to fight it."

"It doesn't mention the beasts," said Fillian, reading back over the first letter. "But Whittingale says in the contract with the Nightsnakes – 'I've earned Tronum's trust throughout my years as Prince Eston's teacher, and if the plan succeeds, he will appoint me acting Scarlet Lord in Benja's place. From there it will be easy to find the weaknesses in Aunestauna's defenses and exploit them. I have already persuaded a large portion of the Scarlet Guard to join Xandria with a promise of wealth and fame in her new empire, and there will soon be more that join. They will slay the diplomats here in the Royal Palace, while you will take care of those outside the palace walls – Prophet Ombern included. I will give you more details on how we will need your assistance as the time approaches. Long live the rightful Queen.'"

Fillian looked up. "That's where it ends."

"Is it signed?"

Fillian shook his head. "It's just a script-copy." The princes sat in silence, thinking of how everything seemed so obvious now, but not at the time. But there were still missing links. "Eston," asked Fillian, "do you think the stone that was stolen was significant itself?"

"Judge Ratticrad said that it could help Xandria if it ended up in the wrong hands . . ." Eston remembered the last time he saw it, handing it over to Riccolo. "I have a strong feeling that Whittingale didn't just use that to frame Benja . . . I think he wanted the stone as well – knowing him, he would've been accomplishing multiple tasks at once . . . But I have no idea where the stone is." Eston bit his lip, sighing through his nose. "Benja was right . . ."

Fillian lowered the letter. "About what?"

Eston looked out the shattered window at the scorched city. "Things in this palace were not as they seemed . . . and we shouldn't have trusted anyone . . ."

EPILOGUE

~Cerebria

In a dark and cold tunnel beneath the Fortress of Seirnkov, Jade Guards opened a locked door. A group of workers behind them carried a large wooden chest into a barren stone room and set it on a marble table. The door shut behind them with an echoing clap. The dark room was lit by no torches, but a soft white light radiated from the crack in the chest, casting a ghostly glow on their faces.

"Are you sure this is it?" whispered a man.

"Positive. It was shipped straight from Aunestauna and up the River Shirr. Janus Whittingale's seal is on the lock."

"Did the thieves know what it was?"

The other man shook his head.

"Well how can this help us now if the Great Gate is destroyed and our attack on Aunestauna failed?"

"We destroyed Aunestauna."

"Tronum and the sons are still alive, and or army didn't occupy the country."

"Just trust her."

The Jade Guards opened the doors again, and a pale figure walked silently into the room. A long white gown trailed behind her as she stepped toward them like a silent boat on dark, enchanted waters. Reminiscent of the silvery stars in the evening sky, she held her pale, white chin high, moving as gracefully as a cloud drifting over cold, snowy mountaintops. Her long white-blonde hair and silvery blue eyes glistened in the pale glow coming from the chest. A necklace of the rarest blue and white crystals hung from her narrow neck. The white gown seemed to float behind her, and the walls of the chamber seemed to whisper as she stepped forward.

The workers bowed to her. "Your Majesty . . . it has come."

Queen Xandria placed her delicate, white hands on either side of the box as a worker opened it with a key. The lock clicked and Xandria drew open the lid, shining a pale glow of starlight into the room.

Inside the chest, a large, glowing stone lay swirling in light. The stone's edge seemed undefined, and its interior swirled with ribbons of white smoke; the flowing, glass-like orb shimmered as a pool of water in the moonlight. Little stars danced around inside it and melted into the air in wisps of light. Xandria touched her finger to the glowing stone, tracing its shape. Entranced by the soft light, she whispered, "Our victory is sealed."

End of Part One

PART TWO

The Secrets of Silverbrook

PROLOGUE

~Four Years Ago
The Network, Seirnkov, Cerebria

A sliver of torchlight slipped into the dark, stone room as the door creaked open. A young Selenora Everrose snuck into the pitch black of Madrick's office and closed the Goblin-made door behind her. Holding a small crimson flame in her hand, Selenora raised it in the air to examine her surroundings. Strange silver instruments and ornaments, as well as countless books lined the shelves of the president's office.

A whisper shuttered through the air in a long, slow hiss. *"Come here, my child."*

Selenora jolted and frantically looked around the study, but she was alone. That voice . . . it sounded like Raelynn. But it wasn't — it was older and full of power and wisdom.

Again, the voice called out, *"Come here, my child."*

Looking back at the closed door behind her, Selenora slowly approached Madrick's cluttered desk. Sitting down in the wooden chair, she delicately opened each drawer, sifting through the papers and objects inside. She knew it was there somewhere — she had seen it in visions. *Whatever it is . . . it'll show me the memory.*

Continuing to pull out drawers, she found a hidden drawer beneath the desk that unlatched from behind. Pressing a crimson flame up to the lock, she closed her eyes and focused the energy into the mechanism, clicking it open. Selenora slid the wooden box out. Inside it, a small flower glowed with a white-blue light, faint like starlight.

Carefully, she grazed the petals with her finger as energy coursed between her flesh and the flower. The room around her seemed to disappear as light engulfed her, and she felt her body floating weightless in a void of endless light. She felt no need to breathe or move . . . her soul seeped into the world around her. She could feel the room around her slowly melting away like wax under a flame. Memories floated out of her mind and flashed before her eyes in a hazy vision.

The world around her warped into a scene from when she was just a child, deep in a dark cavern of the Nexus. It was the memory again, the one she kept seeing. It had always stopped abruptly here . . . but it kept going this time. She watched as thousands of glowing roses grew behind her eight-year-old self. She saw Madrick rush her out of the cavern and place his hand to her head with a silver flame. She saw Madrick coil the silver light into her mind, taking out a small crimson speck of light that faded black like a cooling ember — the memory.

Selenora had no sense of time or space. As memories and secrets and thoughts coursed through the glowing matter around her, she felt a sense of realization pass over her — Madrick had been stealing her memories. More and more stolen memories weaved into her mind from times when Selenora realized the potential of her powers and Madrick robbed her of her knowledge. She knew not how long she had floated in the void of light or when her mind slowly left the ethereal world and coursed back into her body.

Selenora opened her eyes, and her mind was thrown back into reality. Her heart stopped when she saw Madrick Nebelle standing before her in horror.

Madrick looked at the glowing flower in her hand. "What have you done?" he whispered. His eyes shot up and he looked fearfully at Selenora. "What did you see?"

Selenora froze in the chair, holding the iridescent flower in her hand.

President Nebelle pressed her. "Did you see it? Were you there? . . . Did you connect to the World Beyond?"

Selenora stared blankly at Madrick and ever so slowly nodded her head. "And I saw everything . . . I saw what you've been hiding from me." Selenora stood up from the chair. "You've been hiding memories from me, trying to suppress my power, stealing knowledge from me whenever I grow too strong for you to contain. The cavern of roses. I could've gone there to access more magic than I could've imagined."

Madrick stepped forward cautiously. "Selenora, you don't know the dangers of what you're trying to do. I've seen what happens when someone gets lost inside other worlds — inside magic systems they can't fully understand. They can't come back, the power inside them becomes too great for them to handle."

Selenora shook her head. "It's more power to help cleanse the world of evil. Don't you want that? If you taught all of the Evertauri what you really know about sorcery, we could rule over the world ourselves and establish the peace that has been lost. Imagine a New Evertauri Empire . . ."

President Nebelle reached forward and snatched the glowing flower out of Selenora's hand. "Listen to yourself, Selenora . . ." He placed the flower in the drawer and slammed it shut.

Selenora pointed. "See? You won't tell me what that flower is either! Or why it keeps calling out to me and pulling me toward it. It's a woman's voice that keeps speaking to me . . . And I think you know whose it is."

Madrick's eyes filled with fear, and he raised his hand to Selenora's head with a silver flame, ready to erase this memory. Before Madrick could think the incantation, Selenora reversed the spell with a flash of crimson light, and Madrick fell into a deep sleep, collapsing on the floor of his office.

Selenora knelt over him and coiled her crimson Taurimous through his mind, taking out a silver speck of light. She spoke softly. "You've stolen my memories time and time again. Now the tables are turned. Now, you'll have to live in the dark, not remembering this – not knowing that I've learned the truth about my power . . . This is what is feel like to live in the dark." Selenora closed her eyes, reaching for the spell she had discovered, her mind flooded with all the magical knowledge she had uncovered but Madrick suppressed. Reaching, reaching, her light weaved into Madrick's soul and dimmed there, hiding.

Selenora opened her eyes and smiled at the sleeping face of Madrick. "Now, should you try to tame me again or kill me, I will always be able to come back through you . . . I'll always come back."

THE GLOWING FLOWER
Chapter Twenty Nine

~Afternoon, January 25th
Western Endlebarr

As winter had settled on the world beyond Endlebarr, the great forest itself had fallen into autumn. Preserved by magic either from the Nymphs or some other strange and ancient power, the leaves changed to orange and red, and would simply turn back to green come spring, most of them never falling off the branches. When the Phantoms traveled in the canopy on the system of curving and snaking branches of the immense trees, the world around them blazed with color, painted by millions of yellow and orange leaves. The sunlight traveled farther through the autumn canopy, casting a warm golden glow above and below the Phantoms as they traversed on the colossal branches, making the eerie forest almost beautiful.

A butterfly flapped its wings between the tree trunks beside Tayben, who held out his hand to catch a drop of dew falling from the canopy. Somewhere out in that forest, in another life, he led an army of Ferramish troops toward Cerebria as the Ferramish Prince. Eston's regiment was one of the largest and it moved toward Tayben like a looming storm.

The autumnal forest seemed quieter these days, but not because the bugs and birds had stopped chirping. Tayben strained to hear all the soft sounds he could once so easily discern.

"Tayben?" said a voice behind him. He spun around to see Gallien Aris standing beside a tall fern; he hadn't heard him approaching. "Are you alright?"

Tayben gazed into the forest and tried to make out the shape of the butterfly as it flew away, but his vision seemed to be fogged and his balance wasn't quite as certain as it had been. Nevertheless, he assured Gallien, "Yes, I'm fine."

Gallien tracked the butterfly long after it disappeared from Tayben's vision and heard its fluttering among the sound of falling rain. "You seem out of it . . . ever since the battle at the Great Gate."

Tayben stayed silent and tried to listen for distant sounds but could hear none. He had refused to kill Tallius in battle when he had the chance, but his friend had died anyway. What would have changed if he had just done it himself? But he knew the answer – the pain would be worse, the guilt would plague him like a slow, cursed death.

Gallien picked up an acorn and tossed it in his hand. "You haven't been keeping up with us whenever we travel."

In a trance, Tayben looked out into the forest at a small glowing flower.

Gallien stepped closer to him. "Tayben?" Gallien grabbed Tayben's arm. Tayben jolted and stared in confusion at his friend, like being woken from a nightmare. He glanced back to see the glowing flower that was blooming just in front of him, but it was not there. "Tayben, you're not well."

Tayben looked at his hands and whispered, "I know." Gallien put a hand on Tayben's shoulder. "Your country needs you, Tayben. The Ferrs are pressing through Endlebarr and we're the only thing that's stopping them."

Tayben nodded. "Gallien, are we on the right side of the war?"

Gallien looked around and swallowed. "You think the ancient spirits of the forest would grant us such powers if we were not?" He seemed to be troubled by the question. Changing the subject, Gallien shook his head. ". . . You need to go get some water; then let's get back to the rest of the group."

A calm forest stream snaked through the underbrush near the base of the tree below them. Tayben could feel the thirst in his throat and the ache in his head, and so began to descend the tree, somewhat clumsily grabbing onto knots and ridges of bark to lower himself. After just a few feet, he came to a halt.

Gallien glanced down at Tayben from up on his branch, then in the direction he was looking – empty, golden-red forest. "What are you looking at?"

The single flower appeared again, bursting with rays of light on a branch in front of them, shining with a radiance that lit up the surrounding leaves.

"What is it?" Gallien asked.

"You don't see it?" The flower's translucent petals swirled with the same shimmering white light of the stone he had given over to Riccolo.

Gallien looked scanned the autumnal forest. "See what?"

Tayben shook his head and grabbed another tree knot. It was only in his mind. "Nothing." As he lowered himself, he could hear another Phantom walking through the trees toward Gallien.

"Aris," said First Platoon commander Albeire Harkil to Gallien in his elegant sing-song voice, "how fares your friend?"

Tayben's hand slipped off the bark of the tree, but he latched onto another branch, cursing. He stopped when he was out of sight and listened to the voices.

"I'm not sure," said Gallien. "He's been . . . well I don't even know really."

Tayben looked up at the giant tree above him, and down at the fifty feet left to descend. He couldn't decide if the potential drop bothered him more than his friends talking about him.

"Sit down with me," he heard Harkil say to Gallien. "Close your eyes and listen. Feel. Be one with the forest around you like you were when the Nymphs bestowed your powers."

Tayben stopped to listen. There was a long pause before Harkil spoke again.

"Do you feel it, Aris?"

"Yes." Gallien responded hesitantly.

"That's what we're fighting for, the Nymphs gave us this power, and the amount of loyalty we give them determines how much of that power lives within us. It's fading in some of us."

"It's fading in Tayben, isn't it?" Gallien said, almost reluctantly.

Harkil stayed silent.

"Before," Gallien continued, "when we fought at the hollow and the beast attacked, he wasn't paralyzed like the rest of us . . . that monster had something inside of it . . . a force, a magic, or something of the sort, that fights us . . . It didn't fight Tayben."

"Trust the Nymphs, Aris . . . don't let their power fade in you as well . . ."

Tayben finished his descent to the forest floor and hopped down to the damp and dark soil below, covered in all sorts of mosses and leafed plants. Walking over to the stream, he knelt down at its edge and drank a handful of icy cold water. He could no longer pick out the words above.

Scooping up more water, he splashed his face to clear his head and focus his thoughts. Across the stream, a fat, bumpy toad stared at him with unblinking wide eyes. He hadn't known it was there, but the toad had seen him. It stared back at him with an emotionless gaze, before darting beneath a fallen log. Tayben looked around and took in a deep breath of cold and humid air. The smell of the forest had grown on him so much, the thought of the smokey blacksmith shop back home seemed foreign. It had been so long since he'd come to this godforsaken wood, and he had a feeling he may not ever get to leave.

When Tayben returned to the Phantoms, he found them gathered in the trees on a few branches, with General Lekshane, Thephern Luck, Albeire Harkil, and a few others on the largest in the middle.

"We're right about here," said General Lekshane, pointing at a map of Western Endlebarr unfurled over the mossy bark. "I decoded a message from a bird with the latest intelligence. Our spies say there's a Ferramish force about to leave Camp Stoneheart about ten miles away." He traced a little path through the miles of forest and the rest of the Phantoms listened closely. "They'll be headed northeast, I'm sure, and word has it they've even got their eldest prince commanding them."

"To their own peril," said Thephern. "A child can't command an army."

"He's not much younger than you," said Lekshane, "and he has the best officers in Ferramoor with him."

"Our objective?" asked Harkil.

General Lekshane flipped the map. "To cut their force into two pieces. If we take out this group of Ferrs, it will split their communication chain. Their force is too big for its own good, their supply chain stretches for miles. The further into the forest they go, the more extended it becomes. We strike first at Stoneheart to weaken the camp for attacks by our battalions stationed to the north and south." General Lekshane tapped on the map. "Then strike west of it here, and after drawing more troops away, strike east. If we can get behind their lines, fifty thousand soldiers will be cut off, trapped deep in the forest with no food but that which they carry on their backs."

Tayben's mind jumped around as he listened, images of Ferramish battle maps flashing through his head from his memories as Eston. He could picture the layout of each battalion, he knew all the army's secrets, but he couldn't bring himself to say anything.

"They can still survive for some time with their supplies," said Thephern.

General Lekshane continued, laughing. "You have any idea how much food fifty thousand citybred rookies need each day, Thephern? It's at least another week's march to the pass where the Great Gate once stood, and it's twice that back to Ferramoor. Let's see what this princeling does then."

Tayben's stomach twisted. How could he continue fighting on two sides of the same war? He sat down to listen, eyeing the map from a distance.

"If he knows what's good for him, he'll flee," said Thephern. "But if he marches on, he'll be headed for the ruins of the gate, where the Ferrs now control."

"The most we can hope to get out of the pass is a means to funnel their army and stretch it thin," said Harkil.

"Which is why we bleed the main force," General Lekshane noted, "hit and run, every night. We come in hard, we come in fast, do our work and then we're out before they can make sense of it."

"Won't that raise suspicions?" chimed in Ferron, who sat listening on another branch. "If we hit them again and again but they don't take any Cerebrian lives, they'll figure us out."

General Lekshane smiled. "All the better if they do. Let them know it isn't just men they fight. Let them know the ancient powers of this forest are taking up arms against them. Not only will we break their bodies . . . we'll break their spirits."

"But surely we can't take on this task alone," added Thephern. "They have tens of thousands of men and a whole nation of many more to come after them. Their numbers alone outmatch our manpower."

General Lekshane dismissed them. "We don't have another option. For every step they advance they'll pay for it in blood. By the Great Mother if the princeling doesn't break, his men will. Even if they do still make it into Eastern Endlebarr they'll be half the force they were when they entered Stoneheart; and the queen, with thirty thousand of her best will be waiting to greet them."

Tayben's hands felt cold. He didn't know what to think, what to say.

"And how much time will these attacks buy Cerebria if the Ferrs push through?" asked Thephern.

General Lekshane hesitated. "Maybe a week."

Thephern shook his head. "What does a week matter?"

Harkil glared at Thephern. "Time is all we have at this point . . . The Great Gate was reduced to rubble and our naval forces failed to take Aunestauna."

Tayben had found that Albeire Harkil was often the only one making any sense, and also the only other Phantom who shared a dislike for Thephern.

He continued. "Ferramish cityfolk and farmers are taking up arms in retaliation for *killing their queen.* You can hardly blame them."

Tayben's heart beat hard as he remembered the face of his mother— Eston's mother- before she was killed aboard *The Desolator.*

Harkil breathed in. "What's a week? . . . A week is a chance."

"Harkil is right," said General Lekshane. "We must do everything we can to buy our army time to rebuild and reform to meet the Ferrs. The war will be won or lost in this forest." General Lekshane looked to the canopy. "We can travel by ground until we come within striking distance; then we go to the trees. We'll scout out the Ferrs and decide on a course of action from there . . . I don't want any surprises this time."

After traveling for a few hours, the night fell, and Tayben followed behind Gallien, who ran after nimble Chent on the massive tree branches of the forest. Tayben's legs ached, and his lungs heaved for breath; his muscles burned after running for so long. Slowly, he fell behind the rest of the Phantoms. Trying to keep up, he vainly pounded his legs forward, but his boot slid under a vine on the tree, sending him flying forward, slamming his chest into the wide branch.

The little air he had managed to keep rushed out of his body, and Tayben gasped after falling. Finally managing to catch his breath, Tayben looked behind him at the root jutting up, which he didn't see in the dark . . . the forest was darker every day. *Why didn't I see that?* A feeling of weakness overtook him — a feeling of human vulnerability.

From ahead, running footsteps approached, and Gallien soon appeared from the dark. "Tayben, are you alright?" Gallien, who even after sprinting back, wasn't breathing any different from normally, helped pick Tayben up. "Did you fall?"

"Yes, sorry . . . I– I didn't see a vine."

"You look a little green, Tayben."

Tayben breathed heavily. "I'm just tired . . . I don't know why."

"Well, we need to catch up to the rest, they're going a bit slower for you . . . Is there something you need to tell me?"

Tayben hesitated. "No."

"If there's anything–"

"I'm fine, Gallien!"

Gallien looked out into the fog surrounding them. "Alright, you know yourself . . ." Gallien pointed forward, still concerned. "Let's go."

Tayben nodded and followed, glancing to the side at another bright glowing flower that Gallien apparently could not see.

"Smell that smoke?" whispered Lekshane to the Phantoms who stood in the towering trees. A dim orange light glowed a half mile away from them, and a far-off clanking of armor could be heard. "We're here," said Lekshane. "First Platoon, scan their perimeter and come back here to report. Second, take these branches and scout the area above the Ferramish camp. Come back if you see or hear anything . . . strange."

"You mean the beast?" said Thephern.

General Lekshane nodded and a chill ran through Tayben, who saw flashes of the creature's terrible claws crashing through the hollowed tree. They had not encountered the beast since the last time they attacked Stoneheart, but now Tayben knew what it was – a weapon, and there were three more now waiting for them at Stoneheart.

"I think it will see us before we see it," said Thephern.

"Just be on the lookout . . . Third Platoon, branch out and report any movement; the Ferrs should be settling down for the night. Go." The platoons departed, and Tayben and the Second Platoon followed Thephern toward the lights of the Ferramish camp. A hundred feet below Tayben and the Phantoms, even rows of Ferramish soldiers stood with shields and swords. A commander in a large scarlet cape and helmet addressed his soldiers by torchlight that illuminated the fog and the underbrush. Tayben couldn't pick out what the commander said, but high in the canopy, the others heard and widened their eyes.

Ferron Grenzo turned to Thephern, "Why are they ready to fight? We should've caught them in their sleep."

Thephern shook his head. "I don't know, but there's something strange about this . . . they shouldn't know we're here." From down below, a few scouts looked into the trees, and the Phantoms dodged out of view.

Gallien peeked over the edge of a branch again to see the soldiers. "We have to tell Lekshane that the Ferrs are prepared for an attack; it's too dangerous."

"He's right," whispered Tayben. "We can't take this many of them."

"We did it last time we were here," whispered Ferron.

"Last time," Gallien retorted, "we had them by surprise, and there were far fewer. And keep in mind we were paralyzed by one swing of that monster."

Thephern turned to them. "We haven't sensed it."

"Did we sense it last time?" whispered Tayben, now knowing the full capabilities of the monster and its siblings. "If it wants to attack again, we might not know."

Ferron pointed below. "We don't even know that the thing was Ferramish."

"In this whole forest, the only time we've seen it, it was a thousand yards from a Ferramish camp," whispered Gallien. "That's no coincidence. General Lekshane needs to know we have lost the element of surprise and then decide what to do. Let's go back."

The Phantoms agreed and turned around. Tayben stepped forward and broke a small dead branch, and Gallien caught his arm as the branch snapped and plummeted a hundred feet down. Tayben held his breath as the branch hit the ground not two feet away from the commander, who picked it up and looked straight into the canopy.

"Go!" whispered Thephern as the commander shouted out orders, and the Phantoms sprinted in a blur of black away from the scene.

Reaching the general at the same time as the First Platoon, Thephern and the others told Lekshane what they saw.

"They're in full armor?" asked General Lekshane.

Thephern and the others nodded.

"How do they know they are about to be attacked?" said Lekshane.

"We don't know, sir," said Thephern. "It could just be training."

The general thought in silence for a minute. "We need a win."

"Sir," said Gallien, "how are we supposed to beat a force this size when they're prepared for us? And we don't know if the monster is here."

"We've made it work before; we'll do it again."

"I'm sorry, sir," said Gallien, "but it didn't work the last time we tried."

"Well then why are we here?!" yelled the general with seemingly no regard to the fact that they might be heard. The general sighed and lowered his voice. "We are fighting for something greater than all of us. We're fighting for freedom — freedom from oppression and a corrupt empire . . . There is no other option. We must take risks . . . get Gerreck and the Third Platoon back here and prepare yourselves to attack."

A battalion of Ferramish soldiers numbering around a few thousand stood unmoving in the underbrush with their swords drawn. The fog around them swirled strangely, and they barely had time to turn their heads when sixteen black shadows shot out of the trees.

The clash of swords and steel rang through the forest, and men yelled, trying to duck below the arrows that the shadows fired at them.

Tayben and Gallien stood back-to-back, driving spear and sword into the Ferramish troops as they struggled to group up. Tayben tried to block out the gut-wrenching screams from his mind as he felt his spear slice through flesh and bone – men that had families and memories. Battle horns blared as Tayben ducked from the swing of a longsword. Seconds passed by like minutes as the Phantoms battled off Ferramish soldiers, picking off stragglers, slicing them apart, leaving them dead on the forest floor. But before they had crushed into the center, scarlet shield walls and pikes formed up.

A Ferramish commander yelled out formations and a Phantom named Kallo charged. In the blink of an eye, the shadow darted forward, but was stopped by a thrusting spear skewering his stomach and out his back. The Phantom coughed up a spurt of blood and collapsed. As Kallo hit the black soil, the ground began to shake from the pounding of a charge of cavalry. Turning to meet the Ferrs, Lekshane embedded his sword into the chest of a horse as it drove past. Gallien jumped up and knocked a soldier off a horse as Thephern grabbed another and slit his neck.

As the horses fell dead or ran away, Tayben looked down to see the droves of soldiers lying unmoving on the ground with bloody faces. The sight made him want to wretch. General Lekshane pulled out his sword from a horse and shouted to the Phantoms, "To the trees!"

Tayben followed after the streaking shadows, trying in vain to keep up. His strength was draining from his body by the second. As he grasped the vines and knots of the mossy tree, the commander below ordered another formation. Tayben scurried up the side of the building-sized tree trunk and onto a bridge-like branch far above the forest floor, hidden by a canopy of leaves.

The Phantoms regathered and Thephern spoke up. "We need to get to their watchtowers."

General Lekshane nodded. "Chent, you lead the rest of our archers to the watchtowers. Take out the sentries at the top and climb up to pick off the generals and officers from above."

Chent nodded and motioned three others to follow him, and they jumped off the branch into the canopy, grabbing onto vines as they descended.

Lekshane looked at the remaining cloaked Phantoms. "The rest of us will re-form by the eastern barracks and attack the Ferramish brigade there."

~Ten Minutes Later

Tayben landed on the soft soil of the underbrush next to Thephern and Gallien. The Third Platoon had taken out droves of Ferrs while the Phantom archers were taking the watchtowers in the distance.

Another swarm of Ferramish soldiers rushed toward them with raised spears. The Phantoms drew their weapons, but just before the Ferramish reached them, they stopped at a command from their officer and almost immediately began retreating.

Gallien looked to Tayben for an answer, but Tayben was just as confused. A smile crept over Lekshane's face at the sight of fleeing soldiers, but it vanished when a reptilian roar shook the earth.

Lekshane spun. "Ready yourselves," he said, "it could be anywhere." The forest fell silent, and the Phantoms' heightened senses turned dull. Tayben could tell it was not only him who felt weak – the Phantoms around him all looked ghostly pale with fear, feeling their powers draining out of them. His heart pounded as he waited, standing at the ready. And then, just to his side, Thephern yelled out. Tayben turned to see what had happened, but it looked like Thephern was alone. And then he saw it – a tree root like a living serpent wrapped around Thephern's leg. It tightened and then smashed his body into the ground, snapping his leg.

Tayben then looked forward and saw the whole beast. A monster like a living tree, made of branches and leaves, sprung out from the underbrush, sending roots shooting through the ground and up toward the Phantoms. The beast grew and morphed into a towering giant, its eyes glowing red and teeth like sharpened wooden stakes snapping at the enchanted air. Tayben felt the beast latch onto him as he dug his spear downward into its tendril roots.

With no time to think, Tayben wrenched his foot free and threw his spear into the beast, causing it to roar a strange, rattling noise like the splintering wood of a tree falling. Tayben looked down at Gallien, whose body was covered in roots that were slowly tightening. Tayben jumped forward and slashed the beast's branches off Gallien and pulled him to his feet.

As the two turned back to help the others, who fought off the beast, another shape like molten rock and fire began to form. Gallien looked in horror. "There are more of them . . ."

The molten beast turned toward Tayben and Gallien and sent a fireball toward them, which they barely dodged, singeing the ends of their cloaks. The monster's body glowed with fire, and embers flying off its skin of volcanic rock caught plants on fire around it. The beast's ember wind roar reminded Tayben of the heavy breath of the bellows at his father's blacksmith shop in Woodshore . . . only a hundred times louder.

Tayben stood and drew his sword, ducking to the side to dodge another fireball as it crashed into the ground beside him, setting ferns ablaze. He grabbed Gallien and pulled him through the underbrush over rotting logs and winding brooks to try and escape the beast.

Crossing another stream, Tayben and Gallien stopped in their tracks when a different roar thundered through the forest. The sound rumbled through their bones and then stopped, leaving everything deathly still. Gallien raised his longsword. "We need to get back to—" another roar broke out, and the two whistled for the Phantoms, communicating their location. To Tayben, the forest was silent, but Gallien heard a return call and began to climb a tree. "This way!"

Tayben climbed after him but was far slower. The ache in his shoulders and legs tore at him as he grabbed vine after vine. He could no longer see Gallien's black shadow that had disappeared into the canopy. The energy inside him was fading. Trying not to think of it, he fought up the tree in pursuit of Gallien's trail.

He reached for another vine, but couldn't pull himself up before it snapped, sending his body tumbling through the air, slashing through forty feet of razor-sharp branches. Cut and torn, his body hit the damp forest floor with a crack. Coughing, he pushed himself off the ground and glanced up at a scarlet helmet . . . a Ferramish officer stood before him. The horse beside the Ferr ran away at the sight of Tayben, and the officer held a gleaming sword more elegantly crafted than anything else he'd seen before.

Not waiting for the Ferr to strike first, Tayben lunged forward with his sword, feeling the weakness in his muscles and the pain of his battered body. The Ferr sidestepped and dodged the attack, seeming to know exactly where Tayben would aim. He took another swing at the Ferr; but the Ferr blocked it, expertly trained, and anticipating his movement. Tayben hesitated when the Ferr shouted at him, "Stop!"

Tayben glanced around, and then took another swipe at the Ferr, who blocked his blow perfectly and sent Tayben stumbling down. The Ferr repeated, "Stop!" not fighting back.

Undeterred, Tayben spun and drove his sword forward deep into the foot of the officer who screamed out in pain. Tayben knocked the glimmering sword out of the officer's hands and kicked him back. The Ferr crawled back against a tree root as Tayben stood and raised his sword high with a tear in his eye. *Just kill him, stop hesitating . . . do it already!* But no par of him wanted to bring the blade down. Yet, the fear of the Phantoms overtook him, and he breathed in before the strike.

As Tayben began to swing, the Ferr tore off his scarlet helmet. Tayben stopped his sword a foot from Eston's neck.

The prince looked back at him with terror in his eyes and raised hands.

Tayben dropped the sword and stood in shock, as a roar echoed around them. Tayben looked at his other body in fear, but Eston raised a hand in pain and grimaced. "Wait," said Eston, breathing heavily, "I live this day *after* you do," Eston continued. *"I'm one day in the future for you.* Tayben, please trust me . . . I'm you and you are me . . . *trust yourself.*"

To Tayben's right, a dark shape grew larger in the fog, and his heart began to race. The shape let out a rumbling growl like the crack of an avalanche as it came closer and emerged out of the fog.

Tayben held his breath, gazing at the enormous creature standing in front of him. Glistening like a million icicles, the beast's white spikes and scales jingled and chimed as it stepped forward on four legs to Tayben. Over twenty feet tall with four jagged wings and two scaly tails, the beast expelled freezing gusts of air with every breath; it stood there like a dragon of ice.

Realizing he could not outrun the monster and nearly paralyzed with fear, he chose to stand his ground. The beast lowered its head next to Tayben, where its eyes were the size of his head. From a few yards away, Eston tried to stand, but failed. "Show him the flower," Eston said to the beast.

Tayben shrank back as the creature bent down and its bright blue iris began to swirl like ink in water. But when he looked closely, the eye reflected an image of a glowing flower. Entranced, Tayben inched closer to the monster, gazing in its eye as it seemed to expand and encompass his whole field of vision. As he looked into the eye, all was dark, save for a single glowing flower in the middle. *I know this . . . what is it? I've seen it before.* From somewhere he couldn't see, Tayben heard Eston shout, "You have to go! You have to leave this place . . . leave the Phantoms."

Where do I go? A different voice – a woman's – from another place he couldn't see whispered, *"To me."* The forest around Tayben began to slowly reappear back into his consciousness, and Tayben wiped a tear from his eye as the beast stood back up.

"Where can I go?" asked Tayben, looking back at Eston. "I can't fight for them any longer. I can't go home . . . my family thinks I'm dead . . . I can't go to Ferramoor or Cerebria . . . I was never meant to be a part of this."

The soft voice inside his head whispered, *"I'll lead you."* Looking once more at the icy, dragon-like beast, Tayben hurtled through the forest, running over roots and logs as fast as his broken body could carry him. He was abandoning the Phantoms, Cerebria, the war. Tayben ran through a thicket of trees and sprung over a brook, not knowing exactly where he was going. But a feeling somewhere deep in his mind guided where his feet landed. Only one image remained in his mind – a bright glowing flower leading him toward sanctuary.

THROUGH ANOTHER'S EYES

Chapter Thirty

~Afternoon, January 25th
Western Endlebarr

Despite constant attacks from scattered Cerebrian forces, Eston's regiment of soldiers had finally advanced through enough forest to reach the Ferramish Camp Stoneheart. Although he had seen Endlebarr from Tayben's perspective, Eston could still not believe the endlessness of the wild forest and the sheer scale of every plant that towered over him. He felt like an insect, with ferns rising ten feet above his head. The prince and his officers had successfully blazed a path of scarlet through the forest by consolidating their massive force into one slow-moving but unstoppable fire. One fifth of the entire Ferramish army rested in his command as they trudged through the autumn vegetation, and day after day had been filled with miles of walking, interrupted by occasional skirmishes with Cerebrian platoons. But after weeks of barrages, the regiment finally reached Stoneheart and rested there for a few days of peace.

"Prince Eston," said a commander in the room. General Carbelle, the father of Liann Carbelle of the Scarlet Guard, had white hair and a short matching beard. Though age had shortened his tall stature and wrinkled him, he stood firm, fit, and strong as he was a decade ago. "I'm imploring you to push forward from Camp Stoneheart now," he said, "we can't wait any longer. Every day we tarry gives another day for Xandria to regather her forces."

Ferramish Generals and the Prince stood together in the officer's quarters in a circle with arms folded. The room was large and adorned with scarlet tapestries like the banners of the palace in Aunestauna, with three tables in the middle covered in topographic maps.

"The time to push farther is now," continued Carbelle. "We already have control over what ruins remain of the Great Cerebrian Gate, so we control the north. But in two months, the Southern Pass through the Taurbeir-Krons will be traversable, and the Cerebrians could get through that way. We won't have enough defenses to hold both passes . . . Prince Eston . . . Your Majesty, are you listening?"

Leaning against a pole supporting the room, Eston rubbed his hand on the light, scruffy beard he had begun to grow. Images of the battle with the Phantoms that would come that night flashed in his head as he thought up ways to prepare the camp without revealing he knew about the approaching attack – the attack that would be his last day of fighting for Xandria and the Phantoms as Tayben.

"We can't spread ourselves thin," said Eston to the others in the room. "We need to consolidate our troops in this area while more training camps are emptied and sent here. We took a hard hit a few months ago when the Cerebrians nearly destroyed Aunestauna. Overconfidence is our greatest enemy right now."

"I disagree," said General Tuf from across the circle. "We can't just stay here." The general stood well over six feet tall with greasy black hair. "The reinforcements can take our place here at Stoneheart once we leave."

Eston shook his head. "We do this slowly and we do this right. If we move our forces now before we've gathered more men, Xandria will be able to spread us thin with simple night raids. They could take Stoneheart for themselves if we're not careful. They've been able to defend against us like holding shields up to a volley of pebbles. What we need to do is roll one boulder, one mass of soldiers and cavalry, east. They can't stop that. From now on we move as one army inch by inch . . . we *will* reach Seirnkov."

"But we have the beasts, and I don't think that . . ."

"We have three beasts here and one died saving Aunestauna, but we don't know what the fifth one who nested here is up to. Xandria knew about the beasts; her navy was prepared for the serpent. She could have other traps in store for the rest. We need to stay at Stoneheart until I've figured out how to make the last beast loyal to us so we can use it. Silverbrook never—"

General Tuf pointed his finger at Eston. "You don't know what Silverbrook's intentions were! You were barely born when she fled Aunestauna!"

Eston remained calm. "Even so, I may know things that even you may not and so I—"

"I'm sorry?" said the General.

The rest of the room was silent.

He continued, offended. "What do *you* know that *we* don't?"

"Movements of Cerebrian platoons," Eston responded.

"Of course," scoffed General Tuf as he shook his head. "You know that all the reports go to us as well as you. I get that you're just trying to prove your worth to your father, but by doing so you're endangering my troops!"

Eston leaned forward and whispered, "You mean to say *my* troops. Last I checked, I still am Prince of Ferramoor."

General Tuf whispered through his clenched jaw. "And an arrogant—"

Eston raised his eyebrow, stopping the General mid-sentence. Eston paused and took in the silence of the others around him while locking close eye contact with Tuf. "Well then pray I die in battle . . . You're lucky my father respects you." The room went silent, save for the clicking of horse hooves outside as soldiers tended to the camp. Without addressing the generals again, Eston walked out the door onto the forest floor of Endlebarr.

The forest wasn't as foggy as it usually was, and more sunlight filtered down to the forest floor due to the golden orange canopy of autumn leaves. The training grounds rang with the clash of swords, and horses left and right carried supplies from barracks to barracks.

Eston walked across camp, passing soldiers as he went who would stop and salute him, until finally reaching a large stone structure built into the side of a towering tree that rested as far to the edge of the camp as it could. Distanced from the center of Camp Stoneheart, the conversing and laughing of men was replaced by the songs of birds high up in the canopy and the babbling of a nearby brook. Five Scarlet Guards stood in front of the doorway to a stone building that was shaped like a barnhouse, and they raised their swords up to salute the prince as he approached.

"Good afternoon," Eston greeted.

"Your Majesty," they said in unison.

"How are they?" said Eston.

"Restless as always," said one of the guards. "But they've been acting quite strange now that they're close to their brother – the fifth one."

Eston raised an eyebrow. "Strange?"

The guard nodded. "Their eyes . . ." He seemed unnerved.

Eston folded his arms. "Let me see them." The guards opened the door to the building, which was already overgrown in a tangle of thorned ivy. Inside was a huge, pitch-black room, and the echo of the door around him was slowly replaced by a metallic growl. Suddenly, the floor of the chamber emitted a pale white light from the hundreds of glowing flowers that had grown there since the beasts arrived. Out of the darkness moved three massive shapes. One with shimmering wings glistened like a thousand tiny icicles; one looked like a demon of hell with fire and molten metal glowing from cracks in its rocky limbs; and one appeared to be made of the trees themselves – Silverbrook's war creations.

"Halt!" said Eston, raising his hand. The figures stopped and emitted strange, brass-like rumbles. Each of the beasts had two eyes that glistened with a sparkling light. Looking into their swirling irises, he felt his body transported back into a memory following the Battle of Aunestauna.

Eston reached his hand forward to the wall of glowing Taurimous. The low rumblings of the monsters could be heard inside of the barrier. King Tronum and Prince Fillian stood back in fear, not knowing what would happen.

Eston continued reaching forward with a trembling hand until he touched the wall of light with the tip of his finger. With the contact, an electric shock ran through his body, and in an instant, all of the walls of Taurimous in the room cracked and shattered, sending shards falling forty feet down on Eston, Tronum, and Fillian.

From the light still glowing on the floor, the three of them could see four huge shapes moving out of their chambers. The room filled with rumbling roars that shook the walls of stone. Eston stumbled back and put his hands up, and the terrible beasts before them stopped.

Tronum looked to Eston. "How did you do that?"

Eston shook his head. "I don't know . . . but—"

"What?" said Fillian.

Eston stared deep into the monsters. "I— I can hear their thoughts . . . They're asking what I wish them to do."

Fillian stepped back from the enormous figures. "They must be loyal to the one who sets them free."

Tronum nodded. "Eston, you will take these beasts with you to Endlebarr to Camp Stoneheart. The last beast is nested there . . . They may just give us a chance of driving back the Cerebrians."

Eston jumped as he felt thrown back into reality. *Remarkable,* he thought; the vividness of the memory stunned him. He spoke to the three beasts, who could not answer him. "Why did you show that memory?"

There was silence. "Why?" He got nothing but a low rumble in return. Each of the beasts' eyes seemed to be able to infiltrate his mind and transport him into a memory, but he did not know why. Eston's mind flashed to a summer forest canopy when he first saw the fifth monster as Tayben. Big black claws tearing through a hollowed trunk he hid in was all he remembered, followed by the feeling of near paralysis. *Why was I the only Phantom not completely paralyzed by the beast?*

A knock on the door of the chamber made him jump. A guard from outside asked if he was alright. Eston kept his eyes on the three beasts. "Yes, I'm just taking my time," he said, still wondering how they were going to use these three to get the fifth one whose nest was right outside Camp Stoneheart, the reason for the camp's location. Some years ago, General Carbelle had encountered the beast in the forest and reported the experience back to King Tronum, who knew exactly what it was and authorized the construction of Camp Stoneheart to watch over it.

Trying to come up with a rational plan to prepare the camp for the Phantom attack tonight that only he knew would come, Eston settled an idea that wouldn't prompt further questioning from the generals. Eston raised his hand and commanded the beasts to retreat into the darkness of the chamber as he exited through the door and back out in the dark, autumn forest.

"Your Majesty," said one of the guards outside the door, "how are the beasts?"

Eston sighed. "They're trying to tell me something . . ." Eston looked around at the dark and unnerving forest that felt like it was hiding something in its fog. Eston turned to all the guards. "To whom is your allegiance vowed?"

"You and your family, Your Majesty," they all said in various forms.

Eston looked out into the forest. "The camp is going to be attacked tonight by elite Cerebrian forces. How I know this is classified, not even the generals know. But they won't prepare for a battle unless they have reason to. I'm asking you to report to the generals that you have seen Cerebrian troops in the area getting ready to attack. This will allow me to prepare the camp for battle."

The guards stood silently.

"Do you trust me?" Eston asked.

The guards all spoke up. "Yes, Your Majesty."

Prince Eston nodded. "Say that you saw Cerebrians but that they got away on their horses before we could apprehend them. In twenty minutes' time, sprint to the Generals' Quarters and warn them."

The guards bowed, a little nervous. "Yes, Your Majesty."

"Thank you." Eston walked the long way back to the camp and to the Generals' Quarters, where he waited to see if the guards did as he told them to.

Eston sat in the large room with the generals, discussing supplies. Just when he began to think the guards had failed him, a knock sounded on the door, and four of the guards came bursting in. Eston tried to act surprised and worried but could barely stop himself from smiling. The guards' faces were perfectly scared. All the generals in the room stood up.

"What's the meaning of this?" yelled General Noppton, a bald man with an eyepatch from a battle injury years ago.

The guards all began to talk over each other, breathlessly explaining their lie about Cerebrian troops.

Once they finished, the officers stood still and Eston spoke up. "We must prepare Camp Stoneheart for battle at once."

The generals looked at each other and agreed.

Eston raised his hand to the guards. "You are dismissed." He smiled at them as they left and turned to the generals. "Tell your men to prepare for battle." He turned to a messenger in the corner of the room. "Sound the bells."

~Later that Night

A captain with a bright red war sash ran up to Eston. "Your Majesty! Cavalry on the northern flank is armed and ready!" Night had fallen, and the camp of thousands of soldiers was illuminated by torchlight. The camp rang out with the sheathing of swords and saddle buckles being clipped around horses.

Eston nodded. "Thank you. How many archers do we have on the northern gate?"

"Somewhere around fifty."

Eston dismissed the man and nodded again; but to himself, he thought about how to best prepare the camp. Every soldier thought that a Cerebrian battalion was coming with horses and swords. Nobody but Eston knew that the attack would come from Xandria's Phantoms. *How can we even try to beat the Phantoms?* His mind flashed to his memory of the battle to come that he witnessed through the eyes of Tayben. He remembered fighting himself – seeing Eston rip off his helmet after stabbing him in the foot. Tayben was close by – somewhere in the surrounding forest, yesterday's body was planning an attack on today's. *Can I avoid it?* His mind flashed back to the battle at the Great Gate, when he fought himself as Calleneck and Tayben. *I couldn't stop it from happening then . . . can I now?*

"Prince Eston!" a call from his side diverted his attention. General Carbelle beckoned him, and Eston walked over. "They're ready for you by the east training grounds." Eston thanked Carbelle and walked to meet the battalion that was waiting for him.

Eston stood in his scarlet armor and helmet before hundreds of troops in formation. The cold, wet fog around them threatened to douse the torches that illuminated the camp if it turned into a misty rain. He looked at the men's faces, most around his age. "Ferrs!" Eston projected his voice across the grounds where the troops stood. "Your country needs you to make a stand today . . . a stand against traitors and tyranny." The troops remained silent. He raised his voice louder. "Most of you know what it's like to stand by your brothers and watch them die. Most of you know the pain and, most importantly, the fear of being surrounded by death." Eston paused and looked at the faces of his men again. "But the only thing stopping us from marching through this forest and onto the steps of Xandria's fortress in Seirnkov is that fear . . . When we conquer the fear, we will defeat Xandria! The battle tonight will take us one step closer to an eventual peace."

Far above him, a branch snapped and came falling a hundred feet down to the forest floor not two feet behind him. Immediately, he remembered stepping on that branch as Tayben up in the canopy. Eston picked up the branch and looked to the canopy just in time to see the black blur of the Phantoms before they disappeared into the night.

Eston turned to his men, who were all looking up to see where the branch had fallen from. The prince shouted out, "Defensive formation!"

In unison, the hundreds of soldiers unsheathed their swords and held them to their chests. Eston's heart began to beat uncontrollably. *Clear your mind, damn it!* Eston lifted his own sword. "Third rank, surround the stables! Fifth rank face north! Men in the center of the blocks, I want your eyes on the trees! They'll be attacking from above if they can!" Eston ran to the front of another section of the battalion. "First rank, Pyrot formation!" The troops all responded by creating a semicircle facing outward to bend with the stream that coursed through the grounds.

Eston looked around. "Where's my courier?" A boy not older than sixteen ran up to Eston and saluted. Eston put a hand on the boy's shoulder. "South barracks, I want General Noppton to order forty more archers on the watchtower. Have him cut the ropes that help hold the watchtower steady. The enemy could try and climb them to shoot at us from the towers. Go!" The boy saluted again and sprinted off into the camp.

The forest grew quiet, and soon, the only sound came from the occasional insect chirp and the crackle of the torches. Another young boy brought a black horse over to Eston and handed him the reins. Eston thanked him and mounted the stallion, feeling her strong back muscles twitch in anticipation. The temperature of the air dropped slightly, and horses in the distance began to kick and whinny. "Hold formation!" The fog around them began to swirl and Eston unsheathed his glistening royal sword engraved with an E. "Weapons at the ready!" he shouted. "Soldiers in the middle, keep your eyes up! Eyes up! Eyes up!" The nearest torches all went out. "Eyes up, men!" Sixteen black shadows shot out of the trees from all directions. "Archers, fire!"

A volley of two dozen arrows shot through the air at the Phantoms. The shadows landed on the ground throughout the platoon and a deafening sound of sword clashes and yelling broke out. An arrow whizzed past Eston's ear and he snapped the reins of the horse, rocketing toward another courier. "Distress horn! Now!"

The courier sprinted to the nearest horn, signaling where the fight had begun. Another arrow whistled past Eston and barely missed the young courier. Eston drove his horse into the fray, jumping over the corpses of some of his troops.

A shadow blurred past Eston, who could barely make out the face of the Phantom General Lekshane. He slashed his glittering sword and missed him. The Phantom General sprang up and over him as he ducked right below his sword. Eston yanked sideways on his horse's reins; the horse kicked the Phantom as he landed on the other side of him and tumbled to the ground. A

Ferramish soldier stabbed down at Lekshane, but the General caught his arm and ripped the sword out of the soldier's hand. Jumping up, Lekshane stabbed the soldier and threw the sword like a spear at Eston, who raised his shield. The sword embedded itself in the shield and cut into his arm.

Eston frantically looked around at the battle and tore the sword out of his shield. His battalion was being obliterated. The distress bells rang through the forest camp. Eston scanned what troops he had left and spotted a large cluster of about fifty men to his left. "Form a Parusean, Parusean!" he screamed, and the men fought their way into a tighter formation, with pikes protruding from their shield wall.

Off in the distance, Eston heard the rumble of hooves pounding toward them. "Clear the center!" Eston yelled as a hundred Ferramish cavalry emerged out of the fog, headed full speed toward the Phantoms.

A wave of scarlet robes and their fifty horses passed Eston and rammed into the sixteen Phantoms. Several horses slammed into the ground after being stabbed, and riders were pelted with arrows. One Phantom lay unmoving on the ground with a bloody abdomen, and the rest shot up into the trees after an order from Lekshane. The Ferramish cavalry came to a halt, and General Carbelle shouted orders. "Reform! Flanks one and two join up in the front." Carbelle snapped his horse's reins and came over to Eston. "Damage?"

"Probably half this battalion," said Eston. "We took a hard hit."

"Where are the Cerebrians? And why the hell are they so fast?"

Eston's face flushed red. "I don't know. But they're up in the trees." A bad feeling came over Eston. "Did General Noppton get my message?"

"About what?"

"The watchtowers. Were the support ropes cut? The Cerebrians are going to try and use them to get on top of the towers and fight from there to gain the advantage."

General Carbelle shook his head. "No, the ropes are still up."

Eston's stomach dropped and his heart raced faster. "We need to go there now!"

Carbelle turned to the cavalry and Eston's troops. "Flanks one and four, stand watch! The rest, to the watchtower!" The cavalry and the ground troops sprinted forward after Eston and Carbelle.

As Eston reached the watchtower, his stomach dropped — the Phantoms were rushing to the ropes to the tops of the towers. The Ferramish archers were shooting at them, but the Phantoms had already shot the archer in the tower, so there was no one to cut the ropes. Eston screamed out to the troops, "Burn the ropes! Burn the ropes!"

Just after the Phantoms began to climb the ropes, the Ferramish troops grabbed torches and lit the ropes on fire. Three of the four Phantoms climbing reached the top of the tower before the ropes disintegrated in the middle and snapped, sending the last to the forest floor. Before the Ferrs could apprehend him, the Phantom scurried back into the trees.

At the top of the watchtower, Eston saw little flashes of light where the three Phantoms stood. *Shit.* Eston turned to his troops. "They have flaming arrows! Archers, take them out! Now!" The Ferramish archers fired up at the watchtower, but none of the arrows were hitting their targets. The three Phantoms began shooting streaks of fire into the night and onto all the near buildings in the camp. Eston's heart beat faster and his voice was losing its projection. "Take them out!" The roofs of the buildings began to catch on fire. "I need all troops getting water from the river onto those roofs! They have a limited supply of those arrows!"

Just as Eston finished the order, a fire arrow came directly for him. He ducked, and the arrow sank into his horse's chest. The horse gave a small cry and kicked, then toppled sideways. Another arrow came for him and he ducked behind the body of the horse.

A soldier jumped off his horse and gave it to Eston. "Get out, Your Majesty! They're targeting you!"

Eston thanked him and jumped on the horse as another arrow flew past him. He sprinted away on the horse out of range of the fire arrows. Another distress horn went off in the distance, and Eston drove his horse straight for it.

The screaming and clash of swords made Eston dizzy as General Tuf ran up to him. "We're being overrun! All of my men made a run for it. Carbelle still has more, but we can't last. Where is all the smoke coming from?"

Eston stayed up on his horse. "They're setting the east side on fire."

General Tuf looked at Eston with hopelessness. "You need to unleash them."

Eston paused. "I don't want them revealed yet."

General Tuf urged again, "Release the monsters, Your Majesty! Camp Stoneheart is falling."

Eston nodded and started away, headed for Silverbrook's beasts.

"Open the door!" Eston said as he sprinted up to the large stone building that housed the monsters. The guards opened the door to the building and Eston rode through on his horse. In the dark room, he raised his hand, and three bone-shaking roars rang out. The three beasts stepped forward, each more terrible than the next. "Come . . . Attack the Phantoms." The three beasts seemed to transfigure themselves before shooting past Eston out into the forest where he heard their roars as they met the Phantoms.

Eston snapped the reins on his horse and rode it back through the forest to the camp. The fog was dense, and the horse bounded over the logs and streams. More roars echoed in the dark and shook Eston's helmet. The horse rocketed through the underbrush, pounding its massive legs into the black soil. Without warning, the horse screeched to a halt and whinnied. The air turned cold and Eston heard a branch snap high above him. A black shadow came tumbling down through the trees and landed with a thud on the damp forest floor. The Phantom took off his hood and looked at Eston, who froze in shock – he was staring straight at himself – as Tayben.

Before Eston could say it was him, Tayben lunged forward at Eston, who swiped Tayben's sword to the side. Tayben's fighting was no longer as fast or strong as a Phantom's . . . his power was fading. Eston remembered being in the mind of the body before him and knew exactly how to block the next blow. Eston shouted at Tayben, "Stop!" and Tayben jumped back and looked around. He lunged for Eston again, who blocked his blow. "Stop!" Eston shouted again, trying to get away from Tayben. But stepping on a rock, Eston lost his footing and Tayben drove his sword down into his foot.

Eston screamed as the searing pain took over. Tayben knocked the sword out of Eston's hand and kicked him to the ground, knocking the wind out of Eston, who used every ounce of energy to reach out in his mind to the nearest of Silverbrook's beasts for help. Eston crawled back against a giant tree root, unable to walk and barely able to breathe. Tayben raised his sword. Eston's mind flashed to his memories of this very moment; and as Tayben swung the sword toward Eston's neck, Eston remembered the one thing that saved him and ripped off his helmet.

The sword stopped a foot from his neck as Eston looked at Tayben with raised hands. Tayben dropped his sword and stood frozen when the roar of Silverbrook's beast echoed around them. The pain of Eston's foot took over again, but he could see Tayben's fear of the monster that was coming.

"Wait," gasped Eston with the little breath that he had. Eston stared into his own eyes looking back at him, filled with the strangest feeling. "I live this day *after* you do," he said to himself as Tayben. *"I'm one day in the future for you.* Tayben, please trust me . . . I'm you and you are me . . . *trust yourself.*"

In the distance, a dark shape grew larger in the dark mist. The shape let out a rumbling roar as it came closer and appeared out of the swirling fog.

The gigantic monster stepped with pounding thuds against the forest floor of moss and ferns, and its crystalline scales shimmered in the dim light. Towering over them with asymmetrical glistening wings, the beast inched closer to them, puffing gusts of snowy flurries with each growl.

As it lowered its head next to Tayben, a few feet away, Eston attempted to get up, but couldn't. Remembering what he had seen as Tayben, and knowing it was the only way to get Tayben to see, Eston turned to the beast. "Show him the flower."

Tayben flinched when the monster's sky-blue irises began to swirl like an eddy in a stream, but when he looked closely, the eye reflected an image of a glowing flower. Entranced, Tayben moved closer to the monster, peering into its eye.

Eston watched as the trance took over Tayben, remembering the flower the beast would be showing him at this moment. "You have to go!" Eston shouted at Tayben in his trance. "You have to leave this place . . . leave the Phantoms!"

For a few moments there was silence as the monster communicated with Tayben, telling him to follow the glowing flower.

After a minute, Tayben lurched out of the trance and turned toward him, speaking. "Where can I go? I can't fight for them any longer. I can't go home; my family thinks I'm dead. I can't go to Ferramoor or Cerebria . . . I was never meant to be a part of this."

Eston waited for Tayben to hear the next words in his head, but felt an overwhelming power as he heard them too. *"I'll lead you."*

And with those words, Tayben bounded off into the forest.

§

Gallien stopped when he realized Tayben was no longer with him and immediately ran back. Gallien had heard Eston's scream of pain somewhere in the fog, and he bolted toward it but stopped abruptly when a giant white monster emerged in front of him. The monster looked at him and then vanished into the air. Gallien realized that a young general was lying there wounded next to a tree root, and beside him was Tayben's sword.

Gallien stopped in his tracks, wondering why Tayben's sword was there and not Tayben. Gallien held his sword to the Ferr's neck. "Where did he go?"

Eston's face was white from the blood lost from his stabbed foot.

"Where did he go?!" shouted Gallien.

Eston felt nauseous and weak. Referring to himself in the third person, the prince breathed out, "He— he fled . . . doesn't fight with you any— anymore."

Gallien's stomach churned. "Did he talk to you? What happened?"

Eston's eyes slowly closed as he fainted from blood loss.

Gallien lightly kicked at Eston's side to wake him, but it failed. He yelled out in anger and raised his sword, ready to strike, but momentarily saw a glow of light from a translucent white flower floating in the air over Eston's body. When Gallien blinked, it was gone.

Gallien's body turned cold, and he picked up Tayben's sword and sprinted away through the underbrush shouting for him. Before he had traveled much distance through the forest, dark shadows surrounded him; the rest of the Phantoms heard his cries and came to him.

General Lekshane stepped forward. "Where is Shae?"

Gallien's heart pounded with panic, looking around. "I don't know. He left."

"What do you mean?" shouted Lekshane.

"I should've known," said Gallien.

General Lekshane's face turned red. "He's a traitor?"

"No— no, just that his powers were—"

General Lekshane interrupted and turned to the Phantoms. "Find Tayben!"

The Phantoms nodded and turned to leave when Gallien shouted, "Stop!"

"Excuse me?" said General Lekshane.

"Just . . . just let him run."

"He's a deserter!" screamed Lekshane.

Gallien threw his sword down. "Why should Tayben have to be loyal to people who do nothing but kill for a Queen they haven't even met?! Can't you see?"

The Phantoms were silent. General Lekshane clenched his fist, obviously and deeply offended. "I'll make a deal with you then, Mr. Aris."

Gallien stood still.

General Lekshane grabbed Tayben's sword from Gallien. "I'll let him go. But if we ever see him again . . . *you* will kill him. If you refuse . . . well let's just say I'll pay a visit to your family in Gienn."

Gallien froze. After a long pause, Gallien whispered, "Yes, sir."

§

Two medical soldiers carried Eston's body into the officer's quarters of Camp Stoneheart. The generals who had survived the battle stood up. "Great Mother, is Prince Eston alive?" said General Carbelle.

The medical soldiers set Eston down. "Yes, but he needs to be transported back to Aunestauna at once. We don't have the medicine or medical instruments here to deal with his wound properly."

"It's his foot?" said Carbelle. "That happens to men all the time."

"Yes," said the medic, "but the country doesn't care if one soldier dies from infection . . . This is the prince. For all we know, it could be a poison-tipped blade that stabbed him."

General Carbelle nodded. "Get a carriage for him. He'll be on his way back to Aunestauna tonight."

THE CRANDLES
Chapter Thirty One

~Midday, January 29th
Findinholm, The Crandles

Wedged between the southern Taurbeir-Krons and Cerebria, a land of lakes, rivers, windmills, and pastures served as a home to the peaceful people of The Crandles. Its towns were built on fertile soil and harmonious community, a rarity since the Endellian Empire had fractured. Here, in the low-lying glens, the birds sang and the creeks gurgled without interruption, save for the creak of a waterwheel or gentle slash of an oar. The Crans' sheep, cows, and horses grazed freely without any fences, drinking out of small brooks and placid waters. Every fishing village had its own history, transcribed in lineage quilts or wooden carvings. The emerald grass hills sat quietly beneath the mountains as a refuge and haven from the rest of the world.

Calleneck Bernoil strolled with Sir Borius Shipton and Kishk the Trainer through Findinholm, the capital of The Crandles, headed toward the town hall. Unlike Seirnkov and Aunestauna, the streets of Findinholm were not red or gray cobblestone, but grass with small ruts in them where the wheels of wagons tore up the earth. Every building sat tall and slanted, made from wood with intricate carvings of sheep and fish. The village was not arranged in any pattern; Crans built where they wanted to build, and that was that. From one house, there would be the view of the sunrise over a pasture, while another might lie over a small brook that would run through their bedrooms and living room, joining nature with man's structures.

Calleneck, Borius, and Kishk walked through a village square, which was much more like a park. Although it was winter, green foliage and grass still covered the village. The winters were never cold enough to freeze over the lakes, nor were the summers ever hot enough to make a person sweat. The locals would say — *Fog by morning, sun at midday, rain in the afternoon.*

Calleneck's mind jostled between the present world around him, and thoughts of the much denser city of Seirnkov — of home. But the cold tunnels beneath the city still didn't feel like home. Home was the humble little house on Winterdove Lane – but it was no longer there. His parents had gone with it, killed by the combined strength of Xandria's tyranny and Calleneck's own ignorance. Images from the night they were murdered played again and again in his head. He could see his mother's horror-filled eyes as the soldier held a knife to her throat, her husband lying dead on the floor.

His father's face on the other hand was beginning to fade from memory. The thought filled Calleneck with guilt, but he couldn't help it. It was not so long ago that he sat with him, talking . . . just talking. That's all Calleneck wanted to do now sometimes . . . just sit down with his father and talk, not worry about this war or Xandria or Phantoms or the Evertauri or the Nightsnakes or Tronum or any of it. He wanted to hear his father talk about the prices of potatoes or about the rainy season or about the leather he needed to make more shoes.

His mind turned to his sisters – to Aunika and little Dalah. He didn't know why he still thought of her that way, as *little.* She was growing up certainly, but nothing could erase the feeling of protection he felt for her – she would always be his little sister, his *Freckles.* Aunika had begun her new assignment for President Nebelle working for Sir Mordvitch undercover in Xandria's black fortress. Before she began, she had told Calleneck to watch over Dalah while she was away. She needn't tell him that, Calleneck thought. But this venture south to the Crandles had pulled him away from Dalah and the distance felt wrong, leaving him without much of an appetite. All he wanted was to be back on Winterdove Lane with her, helping her with her sums as his mother cooked Fjordsman Pie and his father hammered away at his shoes in the back shop. *That's all I want . . .*

"Calleneck," said Sir Kishk, pulling him out of his thoughts. "Notice anything interesting?"

He looked around at the people walking by and turned back to Kishk, "None of them are riding their horses."

Kishk smiled at Calleneck's observation. "They see them as equals to humans." Many such peculiar mannerisms could be found only in The Crandles, where nearly the entire population of a few hundred thousand showed off rich red hair. Their pale white faces were often dotted with freckles, much like Dalah's. Borius, being the only dark-skinned person for miles, had received many interesting looks from the Crans; none of malevolence or disdain, more of curiosity and wonder.

The Crandles had been relatively uninhabited in the early ages of history until the Cerebrian Invasion three hundred years ago. When the Church of the Great Mother spread from Parusemare to Ferramoor, a large sect of the population – the "Cerebrals," as they first called themselves – opposed the adoption of a religious government and left Ferramoor to find a new land in the east. Led by the King Dorran Delsar, they conquered the Old Easternfolk and settled the land they named Cerebria. The natives who chose not to fight were granted the fertile lands of the Crandles by King Dorran, and the natives who chose to resist were driven out and banished to the tundra Northlands. Since then, the Crans and Cerebrians maintained an amicable relationship with one another.

The three sorcerers stopped in the road as a flock of roughly thirty sheep crossed in front of them, flanked by a shepherd and two of his brown dogs. A thick wave of putrid sheep-smell engulfed the air as they waddled past, their heavy wool coats covered in flecks of dirt and grass.

"Does Lady Parrine know we are coming?" asked Calleneck as the last of the sheep crossed the road.

"No," said Borius. "And she will most likely not agree with our request, but we must try." Just twenty-five years old, Lady Elsagrid Parrine had already ruled the Crandles for nine years. Committed to the peace-loving lifestyle of the Crans, she had kept her country completely out of the war.

"Will I be able to understand her?" asked Calleneck. "I've only caught a bit of what people are saying around us."

"You will," said Kishk. "Cran is a modification of the Common Tongue, just sometimes hard to understand because of the accent. Cran is a now a hybrid of their old language and the Common Tongue."

The three came to a building only a little bit larger than the others, with a black and white banner on its spire. Kishk and Borius walked up its few wooden steps. Calleneck stood behind for a second. *This is their palace?* The Crans were humble people, disdaining grand shows of opulence and wealth. Calleneck followed Borius and Kishk up the steps. They reached a small porch and a pair of large oak doors hung open with no guards in front. The three passed through and entered a foyer with a statue of a sleeping bear in the center. Two men sat in the corner playing a card game.

"Excuse me," said Borius, "we were wanting to meet with Lady Parrine. We are from Cerebria."

One of the men looked over and smiled. "Fendli, we go'ten ourselven some s'visitors, sains deir wherabin Cerebria. Deir accent sains it too. Wa'tn reason do yea go'ten shoewin' roundabin 'here?"

Borius motioned to Calleneck and Kishk. "We wish to meet with Lady Elsagrid Parrine."

The two men began to laugh.

Kishk looked around. "Is now not a good time? We've come a long way."

The other man played a card. "Why, lad, yea don't go'ten to askains us. Lady Parrine is oiut shoo'in arrow-bow targets in the back'yeard; justa go oiutabin and tal'k to 'er Lady if yea'd like."

The first man put another card down. "Back'yeard's down de 'hall, las door to year right."

Calleneck gave a chuckle of disbelief, *would they let anyone just walk up to their queen without knowing who they are?*

The three of them continued where the men told them to go. Borius cautiously opened the door to the backyard of the building. Sure enough, some ways off, a young, red-haired woman in bare feet drew a bow and arrow and fired it into an upright log with painted rings. The backyard was open to a small grove of forest trees and a 'road' where a group of villagers walked alongside their horses without any reins. Borius continued forward and the other two followed. Calleneck nearly tripped over a passing duck, behind which trailed multiple waddling ducklings. The ducks with green heads and little white stripes dipped themselves into a pond on the other side of Lady Parrine, who still did not appear to notice the Evertauri were there.

Borius coughed to get her attention and gave a bow. "My Lady."

Lady Parrine fired another arrow into the log and looked over and laughed. "I too find the grass interesting . . . Since I am assuming you are from Cerebria, I should speak your language, should I not?"

The three were bowing, but quickly straightened up.

"I was only teasing; you need not bow here; that is an old tradition." Her beautiful Cran accent still bounced off her words.

Kishk stepped forward. "Lady Parrine, we meant no disrespect, quite the opposite," he said, looking at her with his lazy eye and slightly deformed cheek. "I am Sir Kishk Kaubovfier, this is Sir Borius Shipton to my left, and this is Mr. Calleneck Bernoil, our navigator. I am also impressed with your fluency in our language."

"I was taught it at a young age; and you needn't praise me."

"You are, however, their ruler."

Lady Parrine shook her head. "The people of the Crandles do not need me." The little ducks hopped out of the pond and walked around Lady Parrine's bare feet. "Unlike some societies that collapse without order," she said, "everything here goes on as always without government involved. Conflicts resolve themselves, and people help people." Lady Parrine loosed another arrow into the log. "Three years ago, I spent six months canoeing out west near Fennenhogg. Nothing changed. I am simply here for the rare decisions that must be made by a government."

"We may have one of those rare decisions for you today, My Lady," said Borius. "I assume you are aware that three months ago, the Cerebrian military attacked Aunestauna, Ferramoor."

"Please mind what you say about war in our country, Sir Borius."

"Of course, My Lady," he said. "As you know, the Cerebrians stole trade vessels from you and converted them into warships."

Lady Parrine picked up one of the fuzzy ducklings and held it in her arms, where it nestled its head in her flowing red hair. "I am aware . . . May I ask, Sir Borius, why you seem to be referring to the Cerebrians as though you were not one?"

"My Lady . . . we are representatives of a rebel group whose goal is to fix the damage Queen Xandria has done to Cerebria and end its war with Ferramoor."

"By dethroning her?"

"By whatever means possible . . . we too want Cerebrian independence just like the other nations that seceded, but Xandria and her government are tyrannical. It must come to an end, and revolution is the only way."

Lady Parrine set down the duck. "And for some reason you ask my nation to join you in this bloodbath?"

"My Lady," said Borius, "we are a strong presence and are sure that we could bring peace to this conflict, and by telling you this, we request secrecy. We were responsible for the destruction of the Great Cerebrian Gate in the Taurbeir-Krons nearly three months ago."

"You are quite free with your words, Sir Borius."

"Because we are desperate for your aid and trust your character," he replied.

"And you have come to the Crandles in your moment of weakness? You would have me put faith in a failing cause?"

"We are capable of many things," Sir Kishk explained. "Our primary advantage is our way of transportation. Our organization operates underground in a Network of abandoned cities and tunnels beneath Cerebria and sections of Eastern Endlebarr and The Crandles."

"The Goblins' Network," said Lady Parrine. "You wish to take down a person who committed genocide, yes; but you don't find it ironic to house your operation in the catacombs of the race she exterminated?"

"We use the location solely for strategic purposes," said Borius. "We would not ask for men, rather, just some of the vast resources here in The Crandles and a trade ban with Cerebria. We can travel and ship both food and information undetected by Cerebrian troops faster than on the surface. Mr. Calleneck Bernoil here is an expert in the layout of this Network and would lead the operation."

"Sir Borius," said Lady Parrine, "the fact that your country stole our vessels doesn't elicit a violent response from us. We aren't even equipped for it."

"My Lady, we are aware of the Crandles' cultural values; however, we also believe that peace can be found in the very near future between Ferramoor and Cerebria. Is that not something you and your people would wish for?"

"We wish only for peace, but it is not our place to contribute to either nation's demise." Lady Parrine lifted her bow and shot another arrow, missing the exact center by only an inch.

"With all due respect, My Lady, if you do nothing to show that the Crandles is a strong nation, Xandria could trample your country as well. There would be no more peace in your land. Banning Cerebrian trade would show that you have a say in what goes on between the eight kingdoms. The Crandles produce half of all the textiles in Endellia, a third of its cheese and butter, and a fifth of its boats — much of that goes straight to Cerebria. If you cut off trade along the Kettlerush and stopped exporting to Cerebria, they wouldn't have enough clothes for their soldiers for this winter, and their food stores would be depleted."

"If we stop trade with Cerebria, Xandria will invade us overnight," said Lady Parrine, as she bent down to brush the blades of emerald grass with her.

"She hasn't made any indication of violating your sovereignty," Sir Kishk pointed out. A flock of sheep bleated on the distant hillside, herded together into a pack of white by the prancing shepherd dogs that roamed the grass slope.

Lady Parrine looked at Kishk, unphased by his lopsided lazy eye. "Because she knows that invading us would encourage Elishka to go to war with her. Elishka depends on my nation as much as Cerebria does, and if Xandria interferes with that, they will declare war. We trade to keep the peace, and we will continue to. You expect me to rest the fate of the Crandles on a small group of rebels who, apparently, don't have adequate resources for the job you are undertaking? Where are you going to get the manpower if you aren't making alliances with the Ferrs? And food — you have limited donors to your cause, farmers who are probably going bankrupt supporting you, how do you plan to keep up your efforts? . . . I'm sorry you have come so far only to be turned away. Sir Borius, we won't be a part of it. This is not solely a government decision; any of my fellow citizens in this nation would say the same."

Borius began to bow and stopped himself. "We understand."

Lady Parrine smiled as the ducks sauntered through the cattails and plopped into her backyard pond. "I don't think you do . . . we *are* a strong people here. Every morning I wake before the sun does, and I watch the society blossom as the sky turns light. There is no other way of life we would choose. Our Neautrality is the key to our peace. The Crandles are a safe haven from the world and our identity will not be shattered for political interests."

Borius nodded. "We admire your steadfastness and love for your nation. As before, we respect your decision but also implore your discretion and secrecy. Thank you for allowing us to meet with you; we wish you and your people peace and prosperity."

Lady Parrine smiled and shot another arrow into the log. "Before you go, stop by the *Dinpalire's Tavern*; you look weary, and I am sure you have never tried grindsvak – they make some of the best."

The three thanked her and left the way they came.

Following the recommendation of Lady Parrine, they stopped at the small tavern to rest. Although Calleneck felt that they should not be so public about their whereabouts in such a foreign land, Kishk reminded him that the Crans had little concern about what happened in the outside world.

The tavern was homey, with a fire in the corner and candles hanging from the ceiling to illuminate the room on the foggy day. A waitress, with red hair of course, asked for their order; Calleneck requested the 'grindsvak' for the table, although he knew not what it was. When she had left, Kishk traced his fingers along the grain of the wooden table. "Well, we tried the best we could."

"Isn't enough," said Borius scanning the tavern. "We don't have the numbers or the supplies to take down the throne of Cerebria. Now that we have destroyed the Great Gate, Xandria is aware of the threat we pose. Our only advantage at this point is the fact that no one knows where and how we operate, and also there is suspicion that we might be a Ferramish group."

"–which King Tronum claims," said Kishk. Borius picked a splinter off the wood table. "I recently found out that Raelynn Nebelle helped stop the attack on Ferramoor – she aided in destroying the Cerebrian fleet in Aunestauna's harbor. Even so, Xandria's forces have taken a heavy hit and have been struggling to maintain control of the pass where the Great Gate previously stood. We needed support from the Crans if Cerebria is to remain independent after the war. After we've taken down Xandria, the Evertauri needs to hold enough power to convince the aristocrats not to rise in rebellion against us with their own armies. A united Cerebria could ward off Feramish rule."

"Will Tronum stop the war if Xandria and her government falls?" asked Calleneck. "Why wouldn't he just continue conquering?"

Borius tapped a finger on the table and a single yellow spark flew out. "If the rumors are to be believed, the king's health is now fading rapidly. Soon, the eldest prince of Ferramoor will rule. Tell me who you think will follow a green boy-king into yet another fruitless war. We are all tired, and Ferramish forces are stretched too thin to maintain permanent control over Cerebria." He took a moment to look around the tavern, warm and dry from the cold drizzle outside. "Will we return the same way we came?" he asked, turning to Calleneck.

"Yes, sir. Although if we have an hour to spare, I would like to examine a new passageway in the Network about two miles past the turn to Endgroth."

"We don't have time," said Borius.

"Oh . . . Not a problem, that's fine," said Calleneck. The refusal bothered him, as Borius was in no obvious rush to leave, and had not listened like he normally did.

The front door of the tavern flew open and Lillia Hane briskly weaved her way through servers and tables to the three. A smile had not graced her face since the death of Tallius Tooble at the Battle of the Great Gate. A cold knot twisted in Calleneck's stomach every time he thought of his best friend, his corpse burning on the snowy mountainside. But he knew Lillia's pain was much worse . . . she had lost the father to her unborn child, still but a small bump on her abdomen.

"Ms. Hane," said Kishk, "what are you doing here? I thought you were staying back with the group guarding the entrance."

"I was told to tell the three of you to come with me now." Lillia's face was dark and cold. She normally would never speak so abruptly to a superior; the three immediately understood the gravity of the situation.

Kishk stood and dropped two argentums on the table for the food that had not yet come and followed Lillia with Calleneck and Borius out of the tavern. She led them down the grassy streets of Findinholm and into a glade in a deep thicket of trees where a group of ten Evertauri stood.

An Evertauri with a salt and pepper beard down to his stomach stepped forward, a sorcerer from the Council of Mages and one of the first Evertauri – Sir Beshk Prokev.

Sir Beshk looked around at several others. Knowing that this information was classified, he walked up to Borius and whispered so faintly that Calleneck could barely pick out the words.

"President Nebelle wishes for me to inform you that he believes The Rose is back. He wants you to search for any signs of her on the journey back to Seirnkov."

The Rose? Calleneck thought. In his memory he saw the bodies of all the sorcerers who tried to overrun the Evertauri vanishing into clouds of fluttering rose petals. Calleneck's stomach turned. *Is Selenora still alive?* . . .

INTO THE SEWERS
Chapter Thirty Two

~Evening, February 2nd
Aunestauna, Ferramoor

From across the street, Riccolo watched Kyan climb up the theater roof to his shack. The snow was falling, and the sun's evening light was nearly gone, replaced by a biting and howling wind that coursed through the Third District of Aunestuana. Riccolo walked across the snowy square and took hold of the ladder that led to the roof, putting his feet where Kyan's had been.

Once at the top, the wind worsened, and faint orange light from the west cast a silhouette of the shack that sat partly above the roof, and partly below. Riccolo picked up a voice from inside the candle-lit shack, but it was the girl's voice, one that had been there for the last month. *Who does Kyan have in there with him?*

Having listened in on multiple conversations, Riccolo could still not figure out who this girl was except that every few days, she went to the palace, *or what's left of it.* Kyan responded to the girl, and Riccolo walked closer to eavesdrop, careful to put his feet in Kyan's snow footprints. Leaning against the shack, Riccolo closed his eyes.

"Could your mother have something to do with those documents burning?" he heard Kyan say. *"It seems unlikely that there were no records of her. Maybe she—"*

"Maybe she didn't want anyone to find her," said the girl. The voices continued speaking about things that made no sense to Riccolo, until he heard, *"—secret documents about thief gangs in town."* Riccolo's eyebrows furrowed. *"It's a gang called the Nightsnakes."* He clenched his jaw, stretching the white scar on his face. *"From what I've found in just browsing through,"* said the girl, *"Sir Janus Whittingale, Tronum's former First Advisor who actually worked for Xandria, he made some bargain with these people . . . Apparently it was all a setup. Whittingale was going to burn their documents and destroy all of the leads pointing to the Nightsnakes as an incentive for them to steal something he wanted . . . but he died before he could. I think that— What are you doing?"*

Riccolo held his breath as Kyan stood up and looked out a hole in the shack right next to him. After a minute, Kyan sat back down inside. "I thought I heard someone."

After that, the wind picked up, howling over the slanted roofs and chimneys of Aunestauna preventing Riccolo from discerning any more of the conversation in the shack. He snarled to himself. *I grant him his freedom and now he's told this girl! That bitch is on our tail and she'll tell the prince, then Kyan will lead him to us — lead me and the Nightsnakes to the gallows.*

An hour later, Riccolo stood with the Nightsnakes on the snowy roof of the theater. Riccolo turned to Bay, his right-hand man. "You tied up Vree before you left?"

"Yes," whispered Bay, "I think she was going to warn Kyan and the girl that we were coming. You should have sold her with her sister."

Riccolo clenched his teeth. "Don't rush me, I'll do it soon. She's almost made the money she promised me." He looked at Kyan's shack ahead of them. "Get Kyan first," he whispered, "then the girl. But don't knock out Kyan."

"Why?" Riccolo smiled. "I want him to see his home burn to ashes."

Bay obeyed and signaled the rest of the thieves forward. Surrounding it, a few of them silently stepped inside.

§

~Earlier

Kyan brushed light snow off the roof of his shack before entering it to retire for the day. The past week had been unseasonably cold and wet, and little snowdrifts had accumulated in the streets of Aunestauna.

Kicking off his boots, he opened the jammed door and shut it quickly behind him as a gust of snow-blowing wind howled outside. Inside the shack, a candle was lit, and Raelynn Nebelle sat in the corner wrapped in a blanket eating a loaf of bread.

Raelynn glanced at him and covered her mouth. "Sorry for not waiting to eat dinner with you."

He shook the snowflakes from his hair and brushed off his jacket. "It's no problem; I was out later than I said I was going to be. The Tumno's needed me to work an extra hour at the bakery today."

Raelynn coughed and shivered; her nose was red from the cold. As much as they had tried to seal up the shack from winter's chill with panels of wood and blankets, the freezing air still snuck into the small attic space. "Well, now that Prince Eston is away, you have to stay as long as Prince Fillian tells you."

"That's life working as a spy;" he lied, "you would know."

Raelynn smiled and put a piece of paper on the wall where a crack blew in frigid air. For three months, Raelynn had stayed with Kyan in his home. Fighting against an unusually cold winter, the two had spent their days helping rebuild the city, with Raelynn still stopping by the palace occasionally to see if she could find any additional information concerning her mother's disappearance years ago. Kyan had also begun work at the bakery Mr. Tumno used to own. The baker's brother and sister had since come into town to keep it running, and he did what he could to pitch in, rebuilding the place he once stole from.

Raelynn pulled a blanket up to her chin and looked around the shack, which she had helped clean up and organize into a homey space. "Again, I can't thank you enough for letting me stay with you."

Kyan sat down on a wooden chest in the other corner. "Well, with half the city burned down, there aren't too many other places for you to stay."

They sat for a moment before Raelynn perked up. "Did you see they've rebuilt the bridge connecting Wetthern Street to Northmoon?"

"I did," he said. "I assume you crossed it going to the palace earlier?" Raelynn nodded and he picked up the other loaf of bread, one he had baked from scratch yesterday at Tumno's. "So did you find out anything today?"

"About my mother?"

He nodded.

"No," she said, fixing the flap that kept allowing snow to blow inside the shack. "My father said her name was Abitha, but they only file the reports that I've been checking under last names, and there have been no 'Nebelles.' It also doesn't help that a few sections of the library were burned when Cerebria attacked. All of those records are lost."

"Do you think the information about your mother was on one of those documents that King Tronum burned the night I— Prince Eston was born?"

Raelynn straightened up. "What are you suggesting?"

Kyan scratched his head. "Could your mother have something to do with those documents burning? It seems unlikely that there were no records of her. Maybe she—"

"Maybe she didn't want anyone to find her . . ." Raelynn stared at the dancing candle for some time and whispered, "I have to talk to someone . . . someone who knew her."

"King Tronum would know . . ."

Raelynn shook her head. "Sure, and we'd never be able to get close to him. The last time I was in the palace, Prince Eston accused me of trying to poison the Royal family."

He tried to think of anyone else whom she could talk to but couldn't. "I'm sorry it hasn't been productive."

Raelynn sighed. "I just— there's got to be someone who knows something! I have to be missing something obvious. Hell, I've found all kinds of details on everything ranging from secret documents about thief gangs in town to politics of the strawberry trade. If I could just—"

"Wait, what did you say?" he asked, setting down his bread.

"Gangs or strawberries?"

Kyan gave her a raised eyebrow.

She shrugged. "It's a gang of thieves called the Nightsnakes. From what I've found in just browsing through, Sir Janus Whittingale, Tronum's former First Advisor who actually worked for Xandria, he made some bargain with these people."

His heart raced. "What do you know about that?"

"Well, I know it probably wasn't Benja Tiggins who stole from the vault back a month or two ago. Apparently it was all a setup. Whittingale was going to burn their documents and destroy all of the leads pointing to the Nightsnakes as an incentive for them to steal something he wanted and help him assassinate Prophet Ombern, but he died before he could. I think that— What are you doing?"

He had stood straight up and walked toward the door, peeking out of a crack in it to the snowstorm outside.

"What are you—"

"Shhh!" he whispered, staring out into the night.

Raelynn sat still, worried.

After a minute, he sat back down. "I thought I heard someone . . . Anyway, maybe we should bring those papers to the Council. It could give the government an advantage over the Nightsnakes. Or what if we gave them to Prince Fillian?"

"We could . . ."

"And who knows?" he said. "Maybe this could get you access to the files you need to find your mother. I know how much you want to find her."

After a considerable time sitting in silence, Kyan noticed her eyes becoming watery and red. Not wanting to enter a conversation that didn't need to be broached, he kept quiet.

Raelynn sniffed and wiped a small tear off her cheek. Sitting with her knees against her chest, she looked away from him and hugged her shins with her arms. She shook her head in an attempt to compose herself. Looking at the wall of the shack, she spoke to Kyan in a half whisper. "Do you sometimes feel like you can't ever change anything?"

He hesitated and then spoke softly. "I'm not sure what you mean."

Raelynn wiped another tear from her eye. "I mean . . ." she tried to find the words for her thoughts. "Do you ever feel like all your efforts are in vain? That no matter what you do to try and— well, fix things—" She looked at him with glazed eyes.

"—the world throws you another obstacle," said Kyan, finishing her sentence. He looked around his shack and at the small, flickering candle and nodded. "Yes."

Raelynn looked up at the low ceiling, half trying to keep the tears in her eyes from dripping down her cheek. She let out a brief little laugh, but a laugh out of self pity, then softly bit her lower lip. "I—" Raelynn lowered her head. "I hoped that if I could find out what happened to my mother, that everything would be normal again. That somehow I'd have a whole family and I could just —just live in peace for once."

Kyan sat still, knowing that there was more. He wished there was a way to comfort her, but he knew he could do nothing to help. And so, he sat opposite her and quietly let the cold air sank between them.

Raelynn's eyes were red and watery, more tears threatening to come. She clenched her fist. "And—" The words on her tongue seemed bitter and hard to form. "And I was too caught up in my own fantasy to be there for my brother. He was killed by Selenora and her— her demonic followers, while I was busy chasing nothing but a dead hope that my mother would— would just show up somehow." She could barely bring her voice to a whisper through the tears. "And now everything's gone . . . my family and my magic . . ."

Kyan knelt next to Raelynn, putting a hand on her face. The words he needed to say couldn't find their way out of his throat, and instead, his eyes watered up. Raelynn looked at him with tear-filled eyes, glistening in the orange reflection of the candlelight.

Finally, Kyan spoke, trying to smile. "Raelynn . . ." A lump formed in his throat. "I know I'm a solo-act, a rogue . . . And I know how hard it is to feel alone . . . to *be* alone. But you have so much more than you realize."

Raelynn sniffed. "Like what?"

Kyan took a deep breath in and shook his head. He looked at Raelynn. "Like friends."

Raelynn gave a small smile and embraced Kyan. For a few minutes, she cried on Kyan's shoulder, and then she whispered something to herself that Kyan couldn't hear. She leaned back from Kyan and ran her fingers through his long, dark hair before turning around and lying beneath a blanket, placing her head on a small pillow. Within a few minutes, she had fallen asleep.

Kyan breathed out deeply and found his own blanket. Sitting down in the opposite corner, he felt a cold draft seep through a new crack in the wooden wall. He looked at Raelynn's sleeping body and down at his blanket. Putting on another coat, he walked over to her and lightly placed his blanket over her, falling asleep across from her on the cold, bare floor.

In his dream, Kyan raced away from the Phantoms in the forest of Endlebarr. Running over moss and brooks, behind him the Phantoms, shrouded in black shadow, gained on him. Kyan tore around another bush and then yelled as he tripped over a log. The Phantoms surrounded him. Gallien stepped forward, drawing a sword. Someone from behind him grabbed him and forced a hand over his mouth.

Kyan awoke from the dream, unable to breathe. Getting his bearings, he realized that multiple hands secured his arms behind his back while one clamped over his mouth, pulling him up. Kicking and twisting, Kyan struggled to free himself. In the dim light of the shack, he could discern more figures surrounding Raelynn, who writhed in their grasp. Kyan barely saw her draw a knife when a figure bashed her on the head, knocking her unconscious.

There were too many of them for Kyan to overpower. He tried to punch with his arms, but they were pinned back. The figures shoved him forward and out of the door of the shack into the freezing snow and blowing wind.

Pushing himself out of the snow, Kyan found himself on the roof surrounded by Nightsnakes with torches. The Nightsnakes shoved him back down into the snow as a pair of boots stepped forward – the hushed, snake-like voice of Riccolo coiled out in the winter wind. "I gave you your freedom." More Nightsnakes dragged Raelynn's unconscious body out of the shack and into the snow beside him. Riccolo kicked snow over her face. "But you two are conniving little bastards."

Kyan struggled against the thieves who held him. "We've left you alone . . . After I stole the palace stone for you, you said that you would let me be."

"And then you broke your promise to keep quiet about us . . . But I think thanks are in order, Kyan," said Riccolo with a smile, "because until today, we didn't know that Whittingale never followed through on his promise to get rid of the government's intelligence on us. Now we can have those documents destroyed. Apparently, your friend here knows where they are."

Kyan looked up at Riccolo. "What do you want?"

Riccolo seized Kyan by the chin and spoke in a voice like a hiss. "I want to destroy everything you love; and I want this girl to get me those documents."

"You think she'll do what you want?"

Riccolo laughed. "I've found that watching someone's tongue get cut out is a powerful convincer . . . so it's quite perfect that I have two of you . . . isn't it?"

After no response, Riccolo smiled and raised his hand, and a Nightsnake handed him a torch. Kyan's heart raced. "Don't!"

Kyan tried to stand, but the Nightsnakes threw him back in the snow and held him down, making sure he watched as Riccolo tossed the torch inside his shack. Within seconds, the interior lit up in flames and the bit of snow on the top of it steamed away. The crackle grew, and showers of sparks flew out the door and the window. Something wooden fell inside the shack, and the back corner fell in. A timber on the roof fell down into the fire, and the flames rose up out of it to the outside, where they slithered over the entire shack.

Kyan watched helplessly as another wall fell inward. He stopped fighting the Nightsnakes around him and sat frozen in the snow. There, scorched in flames was his home ever since he had left the orphanage. Crumbling, falling in on itself, every last thing he had was burning, sending smoke into the snowy night.

For a long while, the shack burned; and only when nothing was left but a glowing heap of coals did the Nightsnakes put a rag over his face. As soon as he breathed in, a strong smell tingled in his nose and his mind went blank.

Kyan tried to open his eyes; the room around him was completely black. The sounds around him were muted, but he began to hear a faint jingling sound. Lifting his arm, he flinched as something cold and metallic jerked it back. Becoming more aware, Kyan pulled his arms up again, only to be stopped by the chains binding them to a stone pillar. There were footsteps somewhere beyond the pitch-black room; a door creaked open, letting in light. "He's awake, Riccolo," said the figure.

Carrying a torch, The Lord of Thieves stepped past the watchman into the room. Only when Riccolo glanced to his left did Kyan realize that an unconscious Raelynn was tied to a pillar beside him. They were in the basement of the Nightsnakes' manor. Riccolo stepped close to him, staring silently into his eyes. He shook his head and sighed. "You never learn."

Kyan moved in his chains. "You know, truth be told, I'm getting kind of tired of being knocked out and captured as your prisoner."

Riccolo smiled. "It's too easy."

"You're afraid of me. You burn down my home, you knock me out and take me wherever we are now . . . You're afraid."

Riccolo snarled. "When this war is over and you've all died, I'll come back down to the slums from my throne to defile your corpse."

Kyan stood as tall as he could in his chains.

Riccolo breathed heavily, raging with anger. Beads of sweat dripped down his red face as he turned to the Nightsnakes, one of whom held a box. "Bring it over."

The Nightsnake approached and handed the box to Riccolo, who took it carefully, stroking its wooden outside with his four-fingered hand. Kyan's stomach dropped when he realized what it was.

"Our snake has not tasted blood for quite some time . . ." His voice was lost in a trancelike tone, overtaken by the intoxicating, sadistic ritual.

Kyan tried to move away, but the Nightsnakes pinned him up against the stone pillar, holding his head in place.

Riccolo slowly opened a hatch in the box, just the size of a snake. A hissing sound wriggled out, and from the corner of his eye, Kyan could see the green snake coiling up, ready to strike. Its forked tongue flicked and its eyes beamed red. Riccolo released a sinister laugh and spoke to the snake one word, *"Bite."*

Like a bolt of lightning, an excruciating shock of pain ran through Kyan's neck. The snake recoiled and Riccolo grabbed it and closed the box, handing it back to the other Nightsnakes. He then motioned for the Nightsnakes to let go of Kyan and stood in front of him, reaching out his four-fingered hand to stroke Kyan's neck where the snake had just bitten and pulled it back – it was covered in hot blood. Riccolo licked Kyan's blood off his fingers and then smiled. "I told you that you were destined to be one of us."

Overcoming the pain from his neck, he clenched his teeth and groaned. "So that's why you have me in chains?"

Riccolo spun around and turned to the Nightsnakes, "Wake the girl! Alert the other Nightsnakes!" Within a few seconds, one of the Nightsnakes carried in a pail of water and drenched Raelynn. Coughing, she opened her eyes and looked around to figure out where she was. A bit of tension went away when she laid eyes on Kyan. Riccolo stepped in front of her. "Hello deary. You know where we can find the documents that disclose our location?"

"Who are you?"

"Where are my manners?" said Riccolo. "We are the Nightsnakes, and I am the Lord of Thieves. I overheard you tell Kyan here that you've seen the rest of the documents that could send the Scarlet Guard after us – our location, the names of our members, our history. They're somewhere in the Great Library after Whittingale hid them to keep as collateral."

Raelynn kept a calm face. "You heard correctly."

Riccolo tried to match her mood, but his anger showed through. "Here is what we will do – you'll lead us through the palace there, we'll get rid of the documents, and then we'll let you go."

"You're rats," said Raelynn.

"And you care why?"

She bit her lip and then shook her head. "I don't make deals with thieves."

Riccolo laughed and pointed at Kyan. "Except when they sleep with you . . . I'll tell you what; if you lead us there, I'll spare Kyan's life."

After no response from Raelynn, Riccolo clicked his tongue. "Kyan . . ." he said, "Does she know why you're here? . . . Oh dear, you haven't told her who you are . . . and yet, she has sentenced you to death."

From the corner of his eye, Kyan could see a figure approaching slowly. With another glance he knew by the deep olive color of her skin — *Vree.* One step after another, she inched toward them out of blackness. Held behind her back was an ax. Immediately, Kyan knew what was about to happen and readied himself by finding the quickest way out of the room. Before she could be stopped, she swung down with the ax and broke his chains. Riccolo's eyes widened in a flash of fear and anger before he sprang forward. But Kyan met him, slamming into him as Vree brought down the ax on Raelynn's chains.

As a crowd of Nightsnakes rushed into the room, Riccolo pushed himself up from the ground and drove his knife toward Kyan, who jumped to the side. Jabbing again, Kyan grabbed Riccolo's wrist and twisted it up hard. Riccolo's hand slipped, and he dropped the knife.

Next to Kyan, Vree jumped, wrapped her legs around a Nightsnake's neck, and spun, slamming his body onto the floor. Another Nightsnake – Bay – swiped a dagger at Vree. She ducked as it sailed over her head, and quickly knocked it out of his hand. Vree dodged him again as he swung at her with a closed fist, ducking under his arm to sink a knife into his thigh.

As Raelynn fought with her hands, more Nightsnakes funneled through the doorway, Riccolo jumped up and kicked Kyan's chest, hurling him into the wall. Barely able to breathe, he struggled away. The Lord of Thieves picked up his knife and ran for him; but he ducked and tackled Riccolo to the floor.

Before Kyan could grab the knife from his hand, Riccolo spun him around and landed on top of Kyan. Riccolo pushed the knife closer to his neck. He held Riccolo's wrist in his sweaty hand, which threatened to slip at any moment. Out of options, he butted his head into Riccolo's, knocking him back. The blinging pain hurt, but he knew it hurt Riccolo more. During the instant Riccolo was down, he lunged away and headed for the door, seeing Raelynn in the corner of his eye.

He and the girls bolted through the door past more Nightsnakes, knocking anyone down who tried to grab him. From behind, they heard Riccolo scream, "Stop them!" The three ran away from the swarm of Nightsnakes behind them, winding through the hallways of Riccolo's manor, around a corner and up a flight of stairs.

"We need to get out of here!" shouted Kyan from behind as the yells of the Nightsnakes slowly grew distant.

Vree led them to a side room and ran to a painting on the wall. Grabbing the edges, she swung it to the side, revealing a hole in the wall. "Through here!" she whispered. "Riccolo made this in case we ever needed to escape the Scarlet Guard." Raelynn and Kyan followed her through as she put the painting back up from the inside of what seemed like a hallway in between rooms. Planks of wood crossed it every which way, holding it up. The two of them followed Vree through the passageway.

"I don't hear them behind us," said Raelynn.

Vree whispered back to her. "They'll be here soon." Around a bend in the passageway, Vree pried up a plank of wood from the floor, lifting up a hatch to a tunnel below. She lowered herself into the darkness and dropped. A little splash echoed and from below them, Vree whispered, "Come down."

Raelynn lowered herself into the darkness. Again, the sound of a small splash . . . and then Kyan followed them into the hatch, falling a few feet before his feet splashed in a foot of something liquidy. A rotten smell overtook his senses and he nearly vomited when he realized what he was standing in. Kyan reached up and grabbed the edge of the hatch and closed the wooden floorboards above them, jamming the wood so it couldn't be opened.

Vree pointed down the small, stone tunnel in which they stood, even though no one could see her in the darkness. "The sewers lead to the ocean."

The walls were gray and only six or seven feet apart. The rotten smell and cold muck in Kyan's boots only slightly distracted him from what really scared him. "What about Riccolo?"

Raelynn looked back up at the wooden hatch in the stone ceiling. "If they break through it and come for us, they won't have enough room to give us a good fight."

"How well does Riccolo know the sewers?" Kyan asked.

Vree shook her head. "I'm not sure. But there's no way that he spends enough time down here to have it memorized."

He strained to see in the pitch black. "Is there a longer way to the ocean other than a direct path?"

"Wouldn't Riccolo expect us to go for the ocean?" said Raelynn.

Vree breathed heavily. "We have to leave the city."

"We can't," said Kyan.

"Are you saying we should go back into Aunestauna?"

He nodded. "There must be a drain that goes to the Spring River."

"There are a few, yes," said Vree. "But Riccolo will find us in Aunestauna."

"I doubt it," he said. "The city is massive. He burned down my home; he has no way of knowing where we would be."

"Yes," Vree admitted, "but if he got just a hint of our location, he'd be there before we would know. He knows this city like the back of his hand."

"So do I," said Kyan. "He's not the only one that's done this his whole life." Far off, drips echoed off the stone along with the remnants of his voice. Kyan swallowed and continued. "If he comes after us, we'll have the advantage . . . Look, I know how dangerous Riccolo is, but I know what I'm doing."

The three stood in silence, which made it even worse when the hatch above them rang out with a bang. "They're here!"

The three of them sprinted forward through the muck of the sewers. Blindly splashing forward, they ran around a bend in the tunnel. "Where do we go?" said Raelynn.

A crazy idea ran through Kyan's head. It could work . . . "What if we went somewhere he would never expect any runaway to go? Somewhere that already has security . . ."

Raelynn skidded to a halt. "You're not saying–"

Kyan nodded, out of breath. "The last place he'd expect us to go to is the palace."

Vree panted and turned toward Raelynn. "He's right."

"We'd take the Spring River and follow it until it wraps around the First District," said Kyan, "and then go west up to the palace, enter from the docks' side."

Raelynn looked back and hoped that the hatch held shut. "Which way to the river, Vree?"

"North, so that means we'll turn right when we can."

The others nodded and ran forward with her, paying less attention to the overwhelming smell of the sewers. As they rounded another turn, a distant echo of something breaking and splashing rattled through the tunnel. Raelynn flinched, almost feeling it. "They broke through."

"We need to keep going," said Vree. "It should turn soon." They pounded forward through the slime of the sewer, blind in the underground darkness.

Cursing and splashing echoed behind them, and with every second, the Nightsnakes grew nearer. The tunnel bent left and the three of them rounded the corner. Slightly faster than the others, Kyan pushed them onward, while Riccolo's cursing grew ever nearer.

"It should be here!" exclaimed Vree, "where is it?"

"Keep going," said Kyan. Raelynn and Vree ran closely behind. "Vree," said Kyan, "are you sure it splits off?"

"Yes, I– I know it does somewhere."

Feeling along the sides of the wall, they navigated another sewer that ran to the right. The three of them splashed their way to it with Kyan leading the way. The echo of Riccolo and his Nightsnakes chased after them.

Not ten feet into the tunnel, Kyan felt a smack against his head and the clanging of metal. He stumbled back after running into a giant filtering sewer grate that filled the entire tunnel. The clamor rang out, sending a loud rattle echoing through the tunnel system.

"Are you alright?" asked Vree.

"Yeah, I'm fine." Kyan responded in the pitch-black darkness. "Is there a way around this?"

They felt the walls for a way out, but it was a dead end.

"We have to turn back—" said Kyan.

Raelynn shook her head. "Riccolo—"

Vree reached for Raelynn's face and put her hands over her mouth. Listening, they could hear The Lord of Thieves coming closer. As the Nightsnakes bent around a corner, the light from Riccolo's torch illuminated the main tunnel, sending flickering light into their side tunnel.

Kyan and Vree looked to Raelynn, and she nodded back and mouthed the words, *Trust me.* Silently, Raelynn stepped closer to the main tunnel, sliding against the wall up to the corner where the tunnels met.

What is she doing? Kyan thought, as the light from Riccolo's torch grew bright.

As he walked through the muck, Riccolo traced his finger along the wall. "I know you three are near, I can hear you. I can hear your anxious breaths and your racing heartbeats."

As Riccolo emerged, holding his blinding torch, Raelynn jumped out and knocked it out of his hands, sending it into the slush on the floor of the tunnel, where it sizzled and flickered out to total blackness. "Run!" she screamed.

Riccolo yelled out and tried to grab her as she slammed into another Nightsnake. Kyan and Vree came charging through the pitch-black tunnel. A fist clocked Kyan in the ribcage and hands pulled at his jacket. He spun and hit at the Nightsnakes trying to grab him. A knife slashed across his shoulder, cutting into his skin.

Kyan grabbed the arm and wrenched the knife away, pulling the Nightsnake in and stabbing him in the abdomen. The Nightsnake screamed and Kyan shoved him backwards, knocking a few more down.

Riccolo shoved his thieves against the wall and screamed out. "You useless shits – let me through!" Kyan stabbed forward with his knife, trying to hit Riccolo, but he missed. Jabbing forward again, he slammed the knife into the stone wall. Riccolo tried to pull Raelynn down, but she spun around and slammed her fist into his temple.

Riccolo cursed and grabbed his knife, throwing it into the blackness. With a thud, it entered flesh and the sound of a Nightsnake scream rang out before his body splashing into the muck.

Kyan swung with his knife and slashed at Riccolo. Lunging at Kyan, Riccolo tore the knife away from Kyan's hand and jabbed forward, missing in the darkness before Vree kicked him back. Riccolo's splash echoed in the sewer, and he cursed out.

The three of them ran forward with their hands along the wall of the tunnel. The jumbled splashing and cursing of Nightsnakes followed them.

Vree took the others around another bend, and a dim stream of moonlight entered through an overflow pipe into the sewers. From the dim light, Kyan and

Raelynn could see her pointing up to it. Quickly, they each grabbed onto the ledge and pulled themselves up into the pipe and crawled through. Kyan's shoulders could barely fit through, as he pressed up against the stone walls of the pipe. Starlight shone through and ahead of them. Reaching the end of the pipe, Vree jumped out headfirst. Raelynn and Kyan listened to a splash a second after. *The Spring River.* They could hear Riccolo running toward them, not more than twenty feet away.

Raelynn inched toward the exit of the metal pipe and dove out, splashing into the cold water below.

Just as Kyan stuck his head out of the pipe, Riccolo pulled himself up into the tube. But with wider shoulders than Kyan, he cursed out when he couldn't pull himself further toward him. Reaching forward, Riccolo took hold of Kyan's shoe and began to pull him back. Kyan struggled to keep his hand secured on the outside of the pipe. Finally, his shoe slipped off and he fell forward into the night air, slamming into the freezing water below.

As moonlit bubbles floated up around him in the dark river, he could hear muted yelling. The frigid water pressed down on him, digging into his body like stinging icicles. Unable to breathe, Kyan swam up toward the moonlight.

Breaking through the surface of the river, Kyan heard the full strength of Riccolo's scream from the pipe above. Staying above the surface of the water, Kyan looked around for Raelynn and Vree in a panic. A hand grabbed his shoulder. He turned around to see Vree swimming beside him and Raelynn just beyond. Together, they swam through the frigid water and to a boat dock with a staircase leading up out of the canal. Riccolo's cursing still echoed out across the water.

In the moonlight, on the frozen bank of the Spring River, the three of them gathered their breath as their hearts raced. Shivering, their bodies were unimaginably cold from the icy water and gusting air. Without warmth and shelter, they wouldn't make it. Together, they stared up at what remained of the palace, which looked more threatening than ever before in the night, half-burned and covered in soot.

Kyan took a deep breath in. "Are you ready?"

Raelynn looked at the palace. "I'm ready to hear your plan for getting us in."

THREE LETTERS
Chapter Thirty Three

~Morning, February 2nd
Seirnkov, Cerebria

The front gates of Xandria's castle stood before Aunika Bernoil like black, jagged mountains coated in white snow, ready to devour her should her identity be revealed. *I'm the Technological Advancement Vice-Supervisor. Name – Serisa Stinev. Oh, who am I kidding, how am I going to pull this off?*

"Identification ma'am."

Aunika turned to the soldier in silver and green armor. "Yes, sorry sir." She reached into her bag and pulled out a slip of parchment. *Don't be afraid . . . Madrick and Mordvitch picked me for a reason.*

The Jade Guard read it and looked again at her. "Your bag, miss."

She handed it to him to search through.

"Birthyear?" he said, looking at the identification slip.

"780 AHL," she replied, heart racing.

"Business in Her Majesty's fortress?"

She held her shoulders high. "I'm the new Technological Advancement Vice-Supervisor."

The guard looked up at her. "Quite young."

"Her Majesty likes new ideas," she said.

The guard motioned through the gate. "Welcome to the Capitol." Aunika nodded and walked past the check-in, visualizing the map of the castle and where she needed to go.

"You're Serisa Stinev?" said a woman in an expensive black dress to Aunika.

Aunika smiled and shook her hand. "First day."

"Come this way."

Aunika was led down a long, twisting hallway deep within Xandria's fortress and into a cozy room with a crackling fire and a window facing the white mountains outside.

"Make yourself at home. This will be your new office."

Aunika took a deep breath. "This is quite wonderful, thank you ma'am."

The woman in the black dress nodded. "You have a great responsibility now."

Aunika nodded. "And I'm happy to serve."

"Is there anything I can get you, Ms. Stinev?" asked the woman.

"No thank you, I should be fine here."

The woman smiled. "Your meeting with Sir Mordvitch is soon."

Aunika flinched. "I'm sorry?"

"Sir Mordvitch, our Technologies Supervisor hasn't met you yet," she said.

Aunika nodded. "Oh, yes of course. Thank you." She would have to pretend that she hadn't met Mordvitch at all.

The woman nodded and left her alone in her office.

A half hour later, a knock sounded on the door. Aunika finished placing a tea kettle into the fireplace and opened it. "Hello," she said.

A guard stood next to Mordvitch Aufenshiess, the highest ranking Evertauri other than President Nebelle and Sir Borius. Standing slim and tall with tightly curled dark hair, Mordvitch was the mastermind behind infiltrating Xandria's government with the Evertauri.

For the benefit of the guard, Aunika extended her hand to Mordvitch and said, "You must be Sir Mordvitch."

Mordvitch smiled. "Indeed, and you are?"

"Serisa Stinev," Aunika said.

"Come and sit down," she said, gesturing to a tea table next to her office window.

Mordvitch nodded and turned to his guard. "Will you give us a moment, Greshk?"

The guard nodded and stood tall with a sword to his shoulder against the wall as Mordvitch shut the door. He looked around Aunika's office and sat down with her at the tea table, with a view of the snow-covered mountains just beyond.

He turned to Aunika. "It's reassuring seeing you, Aunika. It's been tense working here lately."

"Why?" she asked.

"The Ferrs are winning in Endlebarr," Mordvitch explained, "and the government officials are growing nervous . . . impatient for the Cerebrian Army to turn the tide and push back. They're getting worried that they can't hold them off without the Great Gate. But for business." He pulled out documents from his coat pocket and placed them on the table. "These are the first papers I want you to look over – non-confidential things like our budgets for the technological wing." Madrick pulled out a small, crumpled up piece of parchment. "But this," he said, handing it directly to Aunika, "this is between you and me – information about something I found in the treasury. Hide it."

Aunika shoved the ball of parchment in her shoe. "What is it?"

Mordvitch talked softly. "We all know the rumors of King Tronum's declining health – these rumors are true. It's for this reason the Evertauri has been waiting for the best time to strike Xandria herself, for if we deposed her while Tronum is still at full strength, he would take Cerebria for himself. We've been waiting to kill her until Tronum is on his deathbed."

"I still don't understand," said Aunika, "what is the new information?"

Mordvitch took a deep breath in, glancing apprehensively toward the door of the room. He lowered his voice to a whisper. "Our intelligence suggests that we may have missed our window for assassinating Xandria. I've learned that she had a spy in Ferramoor named Janus Whittingale – the First Advisor to King Tronum and then Lord of their Scarlet Guard. He shipped an object to her, a sorcerer-made creation. It's a stone imbued with magic, stolen from King Tronum's palace vault – it's called the Guardian Stone. We don't know exactly how it works, but we fear that it can protect whoever touches it from harm. And more importantly, the fact that she has sought after the Guardian Stone and now possesses it means that she suspects that she is in the presence of sorcerers – *it means she suspects us.*"

"Protect her from harm? What does that mean?" asked Aunika. "Harm from anything or from magic? Does it prevent her from dying at all?"

"Well, we obviously can't know with certainty, but there's hope that we can still–"

They immediately froze when another knock sounded on the door. Both of them had stood by the time the door opened, revealing a woman in a long, pale blue dress with a small silver crown in her hair.

Mordvitch bowed. "Your Majesty."

Aunika's body turned cold but she curtseyed and repeated Mordvitch's greeting.

Queen Xandria stepped into Aunika's office with two Jade Guards.

Mordvitch straightened back up. "To what do we owe the pleasure of having you here with us today?"

Queen Xandria smiled. "I wanted to meet with you, Sir Mordvitch, but I was informed you were here; so now I get to welcome our new Vice-Supervisor as well. May I join you for tea?"

Aunika managed to summon a smile above her nerves. "Yes– yes, please, by all means, I– I have some warming up over the fire already."

The queen and Mordvitch sat at the table while Aunika retrieved the tea kettle from the fire. Aunika and Mordvitch attempted smiles and relaxed faces, while their insides were frozen in fear. *Why is she here?*

Xandria's white-blonde hair flowed long, and her pale blue eyes shimmered like ice in sunlight. She smiled as Aunika brought the tea over to the table.

Sitting down, Aunika took a deep breath.

Xandria looked at the papers on the table. "I see you've gotten started. You two seem like you'll work well together. Have you met before?"

Sir Mordvitch shook his head. "Not until a few minutes ago."

Xandria smiled and looked out at the mountains. A nervous air filled the room. The queen turned to Aunika. "Well, I apologize for starting you on a day like this."

"A day like this?" asked Aunika.

Xandria sipped her tea. "Oh, you must have not heard yet. We found out recently that we have an imposter in the fortress, a spy aiding the rebel sorcerers who destroyed my beloved Great Gate. But you wouldn't know anything about that, I'm sure."

Mordvitch and Aunika tried to remain calm, not knowing what to do, or what Xandria knew. They shook their heads.

"I am thrilled, however, that we have such loyal heads of this department. Both of you must know how much I value loyalty and honesty. We wouldn't want anything to happen now, would we?"

Mordvitch smiled. "Of course not."

Xandria took another sip of tea. "You know what this tea needs?" She turned back to her guards. "Would one of you happen to be carrying that honey-syrup I love?"

One of the guards pulled out a small vial of golden-brown liquid. Xandria put two drops in her drink.

She turned to Mordvitch. "Would you like to try? I think you'd just *love* the taste."

He swallowed nervously and nodded. "Y— yes I'd love some."

Xandria smiled and put two drops in his tea. "Go ahead, tell me how you like it."

Mordvitch stared at Aunika, trying to summon his courage. He glanced in the direction of Aunika's shoe for a split second, knowing the importance of the piece of rolled up parchment beneath her foot. Xandria smiled, and with a shaking hand, he took the cup of tea and sipped.

Xandria stirred her cup as he set the drink down. "How do you like it?" she asked with a friendly smile.

Mordvitch nodded. "It's quite— quite good—" He coughed a few times. "Quite g—" he put his hand to his mouth and began to choke.

Aunika stared in horror as Mordvitch coughed up a spurt of blood on his hand. Xandria picked up the vial of syrup.

She turned to Aunika. "This is syrup from the BlackHolly tree . . . highly poisonous."

Mordvitch gasped for air as blood dripped down his nose. He convulsed in his chair as Aunika sat petrified.

"This," said the queen, "is how we deal with our traitors. You see," she explained unblinking into Aunika's eyes as Mordvitch writhed in his seat, "Sir Mordvitch here was spying on us for an organization of sorcerers who wish to depose me and take the throne for themselves."

Aunika stared in terror at the blood beginning to cover his face as he gagged.

Xandria reached into a pocket of her dress, pulled out another vial of clear liquid, and handed it to Aunika. "*This mixture* is the one known antidote. I know how horrifying it would be to watch someone you know go through this pain. So, if you know this man and want to save him, just hand him the vial."

Aunika froze, holding the vial. "I—" her mind raced for a solution. But she couldn't escape the thousands of fortress guards. Mordvitch's life lay in her hands. *No, if I save him, we're both dead . . . there's no other way. Xandria has to trust me.*

"I— I don't know him . . ." Aunika lied. She could barely force the words out of her mouth, the only words that would spare her own life. "If he's a traitor . . . he doesn't deserve to be saved."

Mordvitch fell out of his chair and writhed on the floor, spurting up blood. In dying desperation, he conjured a spell of deep violet light and launched it at the queen. But as soon as the light reached her chest, it vanished with a wisp of smoke. The queen hadn't flinched, only kept smiling as the spell died on contact with her skin, leaving her perfectly unharmed from the fire. Xandria sighed and drank her tea, completely unphased by the poison inside. With a final gasp that filled his lungs with blood, Mordvitch twitched and then fell still on the floor.

Xandria frowned and placed a hand on Aunika's. "Oh, my dear sweetling, I'm so sorry you had to watch that. I just had to make sure you weren't with him. You must understand."

Aunika nodded, unable to move in her chair. "Of course."

The queen stood up and placed her hand on Aunika's ghostly pale cheek. Xandria leaned in close to her ear and whispered. *"You chose the right side to fight for . . ."*

Aunika gazed forward blankly at the corpse lying right in front of her.

The queen walked toward the door of Aunika's office then stopped. "Did you talk to him much before I came in?" Xandria asked.

Aunika stared at the lifeless eyes of Mordvitch, glazed over and full of fear. She shook her head and swallowed, forcing words out of her mouth. "No, just— just exchanged pleasantries."

Xandria smiled. "Perfect."

§

~Later that Evening

The air Madrick's office was cold, still, like a frozen crypt of slowly dying hope. He placed down his quill when he heard a knock at his door. "Yes?"

Sir Borius Shipton stepped into the stone room which was illuminated by many small candles with silver flames. Borius came up to Madrick's desk and placed down a letter. "It's from Aunika Bernoil," said Borius in a deep, rich voice, accented both by Cerebria and his native dialect from the Shallow Green Isles.

"What is this?" asked Madrick.

Borius breathed in deeply. "Mordvitch is dead. Xandria found out who he was and poisoned him in front of Aunika."

Madrick felt his stomach lurch and his hands turn cold.

"I know he was your closest friend . . . that he helped you after you lost Abitha. I'm so sorry, Madrick."

Madrick stared blankly at his wall with a hand on his thin, gray beard. ". . . He knew what was worth fighting for . . ."

"But there's something else," said Borius, seeming to dread adding more terrible news to the conversation. "It's what you've been fearing all along."

"Xandria is after the Guardian Stone?" asked Madrick.

Borius took a deep breath. "*She has it,* sir."

Madrick's gaze broke, and he stared at Borius. "How do we know? How is that possible?"

"At the bottom," said Sir Borius, pointing to the letter, "Aunika included a crumpled-up piece of parchment from Mordvitch, the last thing he gave to her. It says that Janus Whittingale had someone steal it for him and he shipped it here to Seirnkov. Mordvitch tried to kill Xandria as he was dying, but the spell he cast had no effect on her – she was protected from the attack. *She drank her own poison, unhurt."*

Madrick froze.

"I recommend you read Ms. Bernoil's letter," said Borius. Madrick picked up the letter and read it through twice, his heart beat faster with every word. Borius shuffled his feet. "I don't understand how this happened. How did Xandria discover what it was or where it was? The only reason we know is because your wife was the one who–"

Madrick looked up at Borius, stopping his sentence there. After a few moments of silence, Madrick put down the letter and crossed his arms. "Janus Whittingale could have figured it out somehow, or . . ."

"Or what?"

Madrick thought for a moment. "Before the Day of the Underground Fire, when the Goblins still lived in these tunnels, my wife sent her findings to them to help prepare themselves for a possible Cerebrian attack — which we now know was the reality. We didn't know if Xandria had sorcerers on her side and we wanted the Goblins to have the power to make their own Guardian Stone to defend against extinction."

Borius leaned forward. "Are you saying that Xandria found out about it from the letters your wife sent to the Goblins once she killed them?"

Madrick nodded. "And those letters might still be there."

Borius folded his arms. "Where did your wife send them?"

"The Goblin capital Rjarnsk; underneath the city of Roshk."

"I can go there and try to find any of the letters. It could help us understand if Xandria still has any weaknesses, if there is a way to still bring her down once King Tronum dies."

Madrick nodded. "I don't want you going alone. Take Calleneck Bernoil with you. He knows half the tunnels in the Network by heart."

Borius tapped his foot. "I'll go talk to him then." He walked toward the door and stopped, looking back at the President. "Have you still not told Raelynn the full truth?"

Madrick sighed. "No."

Borius shook his head. "This may not be my place to get involved, but I think she has a right to know about everything that happened. She has a right to know who her mother really was."

Madrick looked down at his desk and scratched his chin.

"Send a letter to her in Aunestauna," said Borius.

"I'll think on it," said Madrick as Borius exited the room.

Madrick rubbed his beard and opened a desk drawer, revealing a glowing flower. He immediately slammed the drawer shut, hiding it from . . . *no one,* he told himself, *hiding it from no one.*

But he still couldn't shake the feeling that Selenora Everrose was still there somehow. There seemed to be an emptiness in his mind, a void, a lost piece of valuable information he once had. It gnawed at him, constantly reminding him that he was vulnerable, and that she was powerful. He relived the memory over and over again of Selenora vanishing into a cloud of glowing rose petals. He felt as if she was alive, watching his every move, waiting until the right moment to strike. Waiting until he could no longer challenge her.

§

~Morning, February 6th
The Royal Palace, Aunestauna, Ferramoor

Raelynn opened her eyes and immediately shivered from the cold. The window of her lavish palace bedroom had swung open during the night, letting silent snowflakes drift in. She lifted the scarlet bed covers and put her bare feet on the cold, wood floor. She reached over to her bed stand and put on her smallclothes. Closing her eyes again, her mind raced through the last few days and everything that had brought her here.

Four days prior, she had stood with Vree and Kyan below the enormous, half-burned palace gates after narrowly escaping from Riccolo. The palace windows glowed by orange torchlight, but the grounds as a whole still looked newly desolate and abandoned. When Kyan had suggested how they could get into the palace, Vree and Raelynn immediately rejected it. Raelynn relived the exchange in her head.

"What do you intend to tell them?" Raelynn had asked.

Kyan looked at the gate up ahead and the guards that patrolled it. "We have to be as honest as we can if we want them to trust us. We'll tell them that I'm a thief from the Third District who Prince Eston hired, Vree was a Nightsnake, you're a Cerebrian but also a sorceress in the Evertauri, that the Nightsnakes are after us, and that we can help the Ferramish government."

"And how will they know we can help them?" asked Raelynn.

"Because we will."

"And who in the palace will trust us enough to give us a chance?" asked Vree.

Kyan took a deep breath in. "Prince Fillian."

The bedroom that was given to Raelynn overlooked the eastern palace grounds — it was in one of the sections of the palace that had not burned in Cerebria's attack. Raelynn finished dressing and walked over to the window where little snowflakes kept drifting in. Before shutting it, she took a deep breath of the frigid morning air through her nose. Raelynn walked back over to bed. The few things she had brought with her to Aunestauna were gone — burned inside Kyan's shack.

A knock sounded on the door. Raelynn made sure the knife was still on her dresser. "Who is it?"

"It's us," said Kyan from behind the door.

She walked up and unlocked it, revealing the street orphan and the Nightsnake Gypsy.

"Good morning." He and Vree walked in the room each holding some papers. Both of them wore scarves to conceal their snakebites. Vree's skin glowed soft olive-brown, tanned from the southern desert sun; Kyan's long hair was groomed and unmatted for one of the first times in his life.

Kyan sat down on the couch. "You look like you just woke up, Raelynn."

She chuckled. "If I didn't just wake up, I'd be offended."

Vree sat down on the couch with Kyan. "How do our scarves look?" she asked Raelynn.

"Stylish," Raelynn smiled, "no one will think you're a Nightsnake . . . where have you two been this morning?"

Kyan examined the room as he spoke. "We stopped by the palace mailtower this morning to see if they transferred your box from the city up to here."

The Gypsy set down some papers and handed Raelynn a letter. "This is for you from someone named Madrick."

Raelynn took it and froze.

Kyan raised an eyebrow. "Is everything alright?"

She nodded. "Madrick is my father . . ."

"Do you know what's in it?" she asked.

Raelynn shook her head and put the letter in her pocket. A knock sounded on the door and all three of them jumped. "Who is it?"

"Prince Fillian."

Kyan walked to the door, opened it, and bowed.

"Oh, perfect, all three of you are here." The prince walked in the room and leaned over the back of a chair. "Very inconspicuous scarves you two; it'll be safest if you hide those snakebites." He was the only one besides them who knew their story and that they had the marks, for he was also one of the only people in the world that knew about Whittingale, the Nightsnakes, Benja, and the Guardian Stone. "I'd like to thank you for the information you gave me on the Nightsnakes. For now, however, I am the only one who knows the truth of why you're here and who you are. Without telling them why, I had the Scarlet Guard go to the location of the Nightsnake's hideaway – that manor in the Fourth District you told me about. But the place was abandoned."

The three of them looked at each other in disappointment. Kyan shook his head. "Riccolo must have suspected that we would try and turn him in."

Fillian continued, pointing to Kyan and Vree, "I'd like to speak with you two about your experiences with the Nightsnakes to help us catch them. People in this government are starting to get suspicious . . . I want to collect information to prove your innocence. I have half a mind to consult Qerru-Mai An'Drui about this – she's the new Scarlet Lady – but she, along with most others in the palace, has little trust in you."

A new Scarlet Guard had been installed with Qerru-Mai appointed as their commander because of her bravery and leadership in the Battle of Aunestauna.

"So will you two come with me?" asked Fillian.

"Of course." They stood, leaving most of the papers with Raelynn.

Fillian turned back while heading out the door. "My brother is coming back from Endlebarr, just so you know."

Raelynn stood up. "What happened?"

"Injured on the front lines," said Fillian. "Stabbed in the foot and a broken ankle. The letter from the generals said he won't be able to walk for a week or two. My father already has me leaving for Abendale in three days to get some more experience."

Raelynn folded her arms. "Well, the palace could use him back."

Fillian smiled. "Let's just hope my father doesn't send me out to take his place."

Kyan grabbed a paper off the couch. "Raelynn, meet us in the library at noon."

She nodded and sat back down as the others left her room thinking to herself for a while. Wanting more fresh air, she put on a coat and boots and opened the door to her balcony.

The air was cold and fresh with saltwater air, and the sky was mostly gray. Snowflakes still drifted gently down, and Raelynn stood in a half inch of light fluffy snow. The city was white with crystals, and smoke came from the chimneys of hundreds of buildings like her white breath that floated upward. After the attack on Aunestauna three months ago, the rebuilding of the city had gone faster and better than anyone expected, thanks to the hard work of Prince Fillian and Scarlet Lady Qerru-Mai An'Drui.

Raelynn took a deep breath in through her nose, which turned pink like the tips of her ears. She sniffed and took the letter from her father out of her pocket.

To — Aunestauna, Ferramoor, River Mailtower, Box 4057e, R.N.

From — Seirnkov, Cerebria, Orchid Mailtower, Box 1431bn, Madrick

She closed her eyes, breathed out, and opened the envelope.

Raelynn,

I have no doubt that after reading this letter, you will be angry with me, wondering why I did what I did. For months now, and arguably your whole life, you've been searching for your mother. I have not told you all I know concerning her disappearance. Your mother and I met in Aunestauna. I had traveled there from Seirnkov to work for the Empire when she stumbled across me. I had never met another magic user in my life, but I could sense her powers and she could sense mine. She was a palace servant during that time and I worked in the city counting figures for the shipyards, but we became acquainted enough for her to trust me with her secret, and we fell in love.

The night Xandria attempted to kill Tronum, your mother found him on the ground and used her powers to seal his wounds . . . magic beyond compare. So Tronum and I alone knew her gift, and she alone knew mine. Tronum wanted to use her power for his benefit and employed her as his personal servant. Afraid of his sister, Tronum wanted to build up the most powerful defense he could, a defense that Xandria could not anticipate. After seeing your mother's sorcery, Tronum ordered her to begin working on something terrible ~ the creation of subservient monsters meant to destroy Xandria.

Meanwhile, your mother and I had you and your brother. She hated what Tronum was making her do and insisted that I take you and Shonnar far away while you were still babes. Naturally, I refused. But Tronum's thirst for power never diminished, and he asked your mother to create the ultimate protection for him ~ a shield against death. After months, she found a way — the Guardian Stone.

Your mother created a stone that contained part of her own Taurimous. If anyone possessed it, they would be protected by her own Taurimous from harm. After she finished it, she came to me telling me that she placed a curse on the Guardian Stone — a curse that she knew would slowly deteriorate Tronum's health and eventually kill him, while providing us with the time to plan how to take down Xandria. Frightened that Tronum would find out our plan, we agreed together to flee to Cerebria and begin plans to take Xandria down once he died, sparing the world from their endless war.

On the chosen night, as I took you and your brother to board a ship to Cerebria, she gathered all her work, stacks and stacks of documents explaining what she'd done and burned them beneath the palace in her chamber. Your mother agreed to meet us on the ship after that was done. But I never saw her again.

The Evertauri has discovered that Xandria now has the Guardian Stone, that thieves in Aunestauna stole it and gave it to a spy who sent it to her in Seirnkov. While your mother worked for Tronum, she sent letters detailing her progress to alchemist and sorcerer Goblins whom she trusted. We believe the letters are contained in a Goblin library beneath Roshk, which we know was invaded by Xandria during the Day of the Underground Fire. We are sending Borius Shipton and Calleneck Bernoil there to discover if there is any way left to kill Xandria.

Raelynn, up until this point, I refrained from telling you this and I am sorry. It may have been regret or pain or fear over what happened to her, but you need to know now. You need to know that you are part of something complex and fragile. What our family does will tip the world that sits on a knife edge to one side or the other. Please forgive me for the years you've spent in the dark. In this envelope is something that may help to illuminate the way. It was from the last day I saw your mother.

Love,
Your Father

Tears fell down Raelynn's face and onto the letter, smearing the ink. She set the letter down, put her face in her freezing hands, and cried. *All this time . . . all this time I've been searching for my mother. She walked these palace hallways. She created those monsters that fight for the Ferramish in Endlebarr. She – she either left me or . . . or Tronum killed her.* As she sat there trying to process it all, she noticed something emitting a faint light in the envelope. Still sniffling, she reached in and pulled out a small, glowing flower.

THE LAST SAENTAURI
Chapter Thirty Four

~February 6th

"*Tayben, follow me.*" He looked around and could see no one in the midnight fog of Endlebarr. Again, a voice whispered, *"Tayben, follow me."* A faint glow appeared far away in the night mist. He stepped over the mossy forest floor toward it. The fog around him vanished, allowing him to see a glowing white flower in front of him. Kneeling beside it, he tried to touch its radiant petals, but his fingers glided seamlessly through it. Again, the whispering around him said, *"Tayben, follow me."* Pulled as easily as a feather, he drifted upwards in the night air, through the trees, and above the forest canopy far into the sky. From where he floated, he could see a trail of little lights like stars made from the glowing flowers gleaming beneath the canopy of Endlebarr, stretching for miles. His body soared farther into the sky, where he was level with the clouds. From there, he could see the trail of flowers lighting a path over the white peaks of the Taurbeir-Krons and into Eastern Endlebarr. *Where are they taking me?*

Tayben awoke as a clump of snow fell on his face. Brushing it off, he sat up on the freezing floor of a snow cave he had found the day before. About ten feet deep into a massive snow drift, it was the only thing protecting him from the harsh blizzards of the Taurbeir-Krons. It had been almost two weeks since he ran away from the Phantoms; they had not followed him. *Why? They could have; I've lost all my strength the Nymphs gave me. When we crossed these mountains before, it took us less than a day. I've been here for six.*

He looked outside the narrow entrance to his snow cave at the blistering winds of the Taurbeir-Krons. Howling like a demented wolf, it drove volleys of frozen ice shards like arrows past the entrance. The icy air rushed into the snow cave and up through his clothes, which were in no way suited to handle the bitterness of the mountains.

Cupping his hands around his mouth, Tayben blew warm air into them and rubbed them together. Before he had entered the mountains, he stuffed leaves from Endlebarr into his pants and his cloak for insulation and had tied a vine around the hood of his cloak to keep the wind from blowing it off; but it wasn't enough. His hair was frozen at the tips and his feet stung from the cold. His stomach pained him, as he had not eaten in four days; few animals ever ventured into the peaks. As Phantoms, the energy inside them alone enabled them to go days without much food; but in the recent days, his human hunger had returned.

Having gotten only a few hours of sleep, Tayben sat in the back of the cave, dreading going out in the storm. However cold it was, it was warmer inside the cave than in the open. *But if I stay here, I'll die for sure . . .* He breathed into his hands again and tried to picture the path of glowing flowers he kept on seeing in his dreams that lead to the other side of the mountains. *The Taubeir-Krons are forty-five miles across at this point, and I must be about thirty miles through them. That means . . .* He grimaced, trying to concentrate, but the cold and his screaming stomach distracted him. *That means another two or three days if I can keep up the pace. Then I'm back in the forest.* He felt for his knife. He was able to catch a rabbit before entering the mountains, and he longed for anything now – a bird or a rabbit, let alone a loaf of bread or seasoned and roasted potatoes made by his mother.

Another chunk of snow fell from the roof of the cave and onto his leg. A gust of wind howled and the crack of an avalanche somewhere in the distance pierced through the blizzard. *I have to go out there.* Although the storm blocked out the sun, the days were much warmer than the nights – he had to take advantage of any break in the frigid temperatures that he could get. The weight of what he was doing pressed on him – and all because of a glowing flower. *But I've been seeing the flower ever since the night the Phantoms recruited me. I never can remember exactly how I got from my platoon to the Phantoms, but I feel like something from that point in time is missing. Whatever this is, it's my only hope.* He crawled forward on all fours out of the cave.

Standing up, he immediately stumbled to the side from the wind, which changed directions every ten or twenty seconds. The cave was on the side of a mountain, much closer to the bottom of a white valley than the top. The snowy peaks of the Taurbeir-Krons towered around him. The storm was so dense that he couldn't see where the mountains ended, nor where the terrain pitched and turned. But he knew that most of the mountain ridges angled north to south, giving him some sense of direction. Shivering and aching, he marched forward in the snow.

Hours passed, and Tayben's surroundings looked unchanged. The whole world was a cloud of white. Snow crept into his boots and covered his back, blending him in with a storm. The cold drove like needles into his face and his limbs, and no matter how hard he squeezed his hands into balls in his pockets, the cold still seeped in. Closing his eyes, he kept walking forward, bracing himself against the arrows of ice that flew into his skin.

The wind coursed through his clothes and whipped snow upwards, making waves of ice-filled air. The mountains around him cracked and crumbled with avalanches that he could not see, leaving him only to hope that one did not come crashing down on him.

Extreme cold; it was the only thing that he could think about. Never in his life had he thought it possible to experience the excruciating cold that bit at him with every step through the snow. His stomach screamed at him for food. A gust of wind knocked him to his side. Standing back up without taking his hands from his pockets, he shook off some of the snow on his cloak and continued to trudge forward.

Several more hours passed, and the blizzard's fury did not cease. Each step became slower than the last. Climbing up another ridge, Tayben's legs no longer felt any cold; they were no more than sticks strapped to the underside of his torso. Looking up, he surveyed his surroundings — white everywhere, snow everywhere. The light of day was beginning to fade, and the air was getting colder. A few rocks poked out of the snow ahead of him, and he lowered his head again, pushing forward. But he stopped deathly still after hearing a small growl. Slowly looking up again, he realized that one of the rocks had pointed ears and teeth, and its fur, covered in snow, stood up on its ends.

The wolf shifted its hind legs and stared him down as he slowly reached for his knife. His fingers touched the blade, and he pulled it out; the wolf was hungry. It snarled again, taking a step forward in the snow. Its hair stood up on its back. Tayben's cloud of breath puffed away from him rapidly as the wolf took another step forward. For one moment, he forgot the pain of the cold and just stared straight back at the wolf.

The wind picked up, and in a flash, the wolf sprang forward. He drove his knife into the gray blur as a sharp pain entered his neck and chest. He threw the wolf off of him and into the snow, ripping up his skin that the wolf caught in her claws. The wolf thrashed, and Tayben dove down with his knife and sank it into the animal.

He collapsed next to the wolf. Catching his breath, he felt warm blood dripping from his neck and chest. Looking at the ugly animal corpse beside him, he knelt up. He took a minute to gather himself and looked around him at the fading day. *I need to find shelter . . . I have food now.* Fifteen minutes earlier, he had crossed a small ravine in the snow. *I can go back there.* He hugged his now bleeding chest. *I can— I can skin the wolf . . .* he cupped his hands and blew in them. *I can use the skin for more protection. I can use the innards for heat.* He picked up the heavy wolf and heaved it on his shoulders, headed back to the ravine.

Making his way carefully to the bottom of the ravine, he dragged the wolf down with him. The wind didn't reach the fifteen feet down to him, and he curled up at the bottom, examining the dead wolf beside him. He lifted his knife and drew open the flesh. Only slightly recoiling at the familiar sight of blood, he closed his eyes, where he saw in the darkness, the trail of glowing flowers lighting a path over the mountains and into Eastern Endlebarr. *Where are you taking me?*

~Night, February 8th, Two Days Later

Tayben stumbled forward through the snow. Extreme physical exhaustion gnawed at him – he had been getting barely an hour or two of sleep each night. Thankfully, he had gotten a brief break from the cold and hunger after killing the wolf, but it was not enough. Slowly, he trudged forward through the dark and frozen wasteland, unable to see more than twenty feet in the blizzard.

The isolation and cold filled his bones and the snow felt like spikes drilling into his toes and legs. Soon, his legs gave out, and he tumbled forward. Rolling, scraping and cutting his body on jagged rocks, he finally stopped in a large white drift. Lying frozen in the snow, Tayben felt his body's energy and life draining through the blood that circled around him. His mind went blank and accepted his coming death and the inescapable cold around him. His body was broken and spent. The wind had stopped. With a tear sliding down his face, he looked upwards in hopes of seeing the stars one last time.

Thousands of silver specks sparkled in the night sky and began to blur through his tears. Tracing their path for what he knew would be the last time, his mind became once again alert when he noticed the leaves of a tree blocking out their light. Feeling that resurgence of strength that comes with newfound hope, he turned his body enough to look beyond, in the direction he had been walking before he fell.

A dense, misty forest extended in front of him. Next to his hand, on a patch of grass, lay a small, glowing flower. Light streamed out of its petals and into the air. Reaching forward with a shaking hand, he touched a finger to its petals – it was real. It was finally, truly real. Either that or he was so far gone he was hallucinating – a likely scenario in his delirious state.

A shock of pain ran through his finger and through his arm. Slowly, the bloodstained snow turned white again as the blood coursed back into his body. The cuts along his arms and legs sealed together, and the feeling returned to his toes. He lifted his torso, and then his legs. Standing up, he stared at the flower. He turned to the forest. *I remember this place.*

He stepped forward through the seemingly magical boundary between the frigid, blizzarding mountains and mossy, autumn forest. The air instantly grew warmer, and he took another step. The trees closed in behind him in the dark, and far ahead, he picked out another glowing light. Pushing aside bushes and ferns, he made his way toward the light. A glowing flower grew from the forest floor ahead of him. Reaching down to touch it, it shocked him again, and another bruise disappeared on his skin. Looking up, another flower radiated white light in the distance. *I know this place . . . I was healed here before . . . it was the night I left my army platoon . . .*

Out of nowhere, a figure — a woman — appeared behind the next flower and walked slowly toward Tayben, who, in turn, walked forward. He audibly spoke for the first time in days, directing his words toward the figure. "Who are you?"

He approached the figure, who was now illuminated by the glowing flower on the ground, and he could see the woman's face that seemed so familiar. It somehow looked both young and ancient, as if some magic had saved it from the ravages of time. "Who are you?" he repeated.

The woman reached out her hand toward him. In seconds, a small glowing flower grew out of her palm, snapped off and drifted to the ground, where it took root next to its brother. A burst of white light radiated from her hand and swirled up to his head. A wave of memories crashed into his mind — running through the forest after the Phantom shadows, falling from a tree, hurting, bleeding, a woman's voice, and a forest hollow filled with light, glowing plants, magical creatures, and a swirling pool of iridescence.

He jumped back, breathless. "You saved me . . . when I fell from the canopy in the forest as a soldier, you saved me then you let me go . . . Why didn't I know until now?"

The woman looked saddened. "I stole your memory of it."

"Why– why did you–"

"Come with me," said the woman, "then you will see."

He stood in silence and nodded. The woman stepped back into the underbrush, following the same glowing flowers that guided Tayben. "But why did–"

"We will speak when we arrive at my home," said the woman.

He obeyed and said nothing for the hours that he and the woman walked through the fog of Endlebarr, following the glowing flowers all the way.

"Here we are," said the woman. The dark autumn forest of Endlebarr was lit with the light of the heavens; thousands of little white glowing flowers coated the forest floor. In front of them stood a barrier of light, exactly like the walls of light that were used to keep back the monsters in the palace. The woman stepped seamlessly through the Taurimous, creating an opening for him.

As soon as he crossed the barrier, another cascade of memories flooded his head. He gazed around in wonder, remembering the glowing butterflies, the lake of iridescent light that sat in a circle surrounding a towering tree with windows and a door — the woman's home. All around, giant glowing toadstools the size of beds were scattered about, and every step he took sent a faint pulse of white light out of the grass. Behind him, a trail of glowing footsteps faded. Breathless, he tried to say something . . . anything . . . but could only take in the beauty of this forgotten sanctuary in Endlebarr. He turned to the woman, who smiled back at him.

Out of nowhere, a giant creature with wings and a thundering roar pounced out of the forest, causing him to yell in surprise and fall back onto a bed of glowing white flowers. The woman laughed and Tayben stood up to see a magnificent, winged lion standing in front of him. Covered in pure white fur, the lion's mane flowed back to its massive wings. The lion purred a low and frightening sound and walked up to the woman, who wrapped her arms around its thick white mane in a hug. "Sorry for frightening you. Fernox hasn't seen you for quite some time now . . . of course he didn't interact with you much when you were last here."

Tayben walked cautiously toward the winged lion. "Fernox, you said? The name sounds familiar."

"It should." The woman smiled and looked at her house built in the trunk of the great tree that sat on an island in the lake of light. "I doubt you have eaten in some time. How about a meal? We have many things to discuss."

He nodded. "You never told me your name . . . when I was here months ago."

The woman ran her fingers through the lion's fur. "My name is Abitha Silverbrook . . . follow me."

Tayben followed Silverbrook toward the house, or rather, the tree on the island of the lake. He had too many questions rattling around in his mind to sort through them all. *Silverbrook.* That name had followed him for the past months in much of what he'd learned.

All around the house sat a swirling lake of light, which they crossed as they had before, on the back of a Krakleback — a black, turtle-like creature. The lake shimmered with iridescent glowing streams of starry orbs. The heavens sparkled within the waters of the pond and glowed brighter than in the night sky.

After crossing the lake of light, he stepped onto the center island and into the tree and closed the curved door behind them. The interior of the tree was hollowed out, and all the tables and shelves and stairs grew out of the tree itself. The windows were glassless, shaped with the knots in the trunk of the tree.

Silverbrook smiled. "I grew this tree myself," she explained, "and shaped the inside of it like a house so I could live here."

He looked around and marveled at the sight. "I have so many questions to ask you. Ms. Silverbrook . . . you're a sorceress . . . you worked for King Tronum long ago. You created war monsters and—"

"Slow down, my boy," said Silverbrook in a soothing voice. "I will explain everything . . . let me first get the fire started so we can cook the soup."

He waited impatiently for her to begin cooking the meal. He watched her take out two wooden bowls and place them in a fireplace that somehow had no vent. "Is fire in a tree a smart idea?"

A giant white flame sprung out of her hands and covered the bowls, making the soup simmer. She smiled, "I've been cooking for quite a while, sweetheart." She walked over to him. "Sit down, sit down; you've had a long journey I can tell. Do you remember it all now? Being here before?"

"Yes. And I think I now remember the things you had taken from my memory."

Silverbrook sat down at the table with him. "Yes, I'm sorry about that."

"Why did you— I don't understand. Why are you here and—"

"Patience," she said in a whisper, closing her eyes.

Tayben crossed his arms and sat back. "Forgive me, ma'am."

She smiled. "If I do not start from the beginning, you'll have more questions than you came here with."

He nodded and looked at the white fire cooking the soup in the fireplace. He had no idea what talking to her would reveal, but he knew he had few other options. She was, in fact, the only person who knew about his other lives — she had seen them in his memories the last time he was here. Maybe she had answers. He watched the white flames dance around and spoke quietly. "I have nowhere to be anymore."

"Fair enough. But be certain that we will hear your story after mine, about why you are here and not still fighting for the Phantoms of Cerebria."

He agreed and then asked, "The beginning?"

She nodded. "The beginning . . . In the last year you've learned that the world is much more complex than you thought, that powers once lost to time are back and magic is alive. So I ask you to trust in me and what I tell you, even if it defies what you once thought you knew."

"I will," he said.

Silverbrook closed her eyes, seeming to gaze far back into time. "There are powers beyond what you and I can understand, and those powers have long been protected. The forest of Endlebarr is not just any forest, as I'm sure you've come to realize. But there is a reason it is enchanted — it's here to protect something, a power I believe you have now seen firsthand." She looked at him with raised eyebrows, expecting him to respond.

Tayben struggled for a moment to realize what she meant. "The Nymphs," he said.

Silverbrook gave a slow nod. "Beings of infinite power as far as I have come to know. They have been here for thousands of years and are the connection from this world to the World Beyond . . . *They* are the beginning this story must start with."

He didn't yet understand what the Nymphs had to do with her or with him, but he forced his mouth shut and listened.

"But they were not alone," she said. "In this forest, there used to live a people, a civilization far older than the men who built our kingdoms and cities. They were the Saentauri, the first race of Endellia. They served as protectors of the Nymphs and this enchanted forest, guarding their pure light against the darkness from the Old World – Goblins, monsters, men who found their way across the sea and came to conquer."

"Why haven't I heard of these people?" asked Tayben. "These *Saentauri.* A civilization that existed here long before the kingdoms of men?"

Silverbrook gave a hint of a smile. "Tell me, how long ago would you not have believed in the Evertauri . . . or Phantoms? Things remain hidden to us unless we find them or we are told they exist . . . I am telling this to you now."

Tayben shrank. He knew she was right – this last year, he learned that things he once thought to be nothing but common folk stories were true. Silverbrook stood up, quelled the white fire that was cooking the soup and brought it over to Tayben. He thanked her and dug in ravenously, incredibly grateful for his first decent meal in days. "What were they like?" he said between mouthfuls. "The Saentauri?"

She stared off into the distance like she was searching through memories rather than knowledge. "Oh, they were– they were unlike anything else. They grew houses in the trees and giant toadstools. They could run through the canopy like birds diving through air. Great warriors, fast and strong, fighting atop winged lions."

"Were they sorcerers?"

"No, but they controlled magic within themselves and living things. Their magic was not of fire but of growth and life. They were a kind, ancient people with knowledge of pure, light magic. They had unlocked secrets of healing, visions, and even of the soul and its journey from birth to death . . ."

Silverbrook turned back to Tayben and continued. "Eight hundred years ago when Hugor Hedge landed with the first men on the shores of Endellia, a new age began, a war to make Endellia a place of peace – a refuge from the horrors of the Old World. As men sailed from the Lostlands – the continents of old – fleeing disease and famine and *magic,* dark forces attempted to follow. But with the often-unseen help of the Saentauri, the kingdoms of men defeated the darkness of sorcery and settled their new world. What little they knew about the existence of the Saentauri, their protectors, faded into fairytales as the generations passed. Though the kingdoms of men stumbled into the underground world of Goblins and came back to tell the tale, those who traveled into Endlebarr would never return. The Saentauri were never vast in number, but they held Endellia together nonetheless, hidden in the forest, protecting the Nymphs." Silverbrook closed her eyes. "Then the sorcerers returned from across the sea in pursuit of the power the Nymphs held. It was the Great War a half century ago. The Saentauri guarded Endlebarr against them while the kingdoms of men fought them beyond the forest—"

"—led by Gallegore the Great," Tayben finished. "Then he thought the sorcerers were extinct, but they had children with the people of Endellia. That's why there are still sorcerers – the Evertauri." He waited for her slight nod, and then he remembered something she had said. "You said the Saentauri had winged lions . . . Nobody ever knew where King Gallegore came from, but they say he rode on the back of a winged lion with a flaming sword." He felt the words come out of his mouth as a whisper. *". . . Gallegore was a Saentauri.* That's why he seemed to come from nothing – he came from the forest."

Silverbrook looked down, avoiding his eyes. She nodded again, confirming what he thought, but she seemed upset by something he had said. "Then once he won his victory, he stayed in Aunestauna and married a Cerebrian aristocrat named Kliera Dellasoff – she died giving birth to Xandria and Tronum."

He took the last sip of soup from the bowl. "But I don't understand, all these things you've said about the Saentauri being guardians of the forest – of the Nymphs – that's what the Phantoms are."

She smiled at him like he had just said exactly what she wanted him to. "They are, aren't they? Xandria's Phantoms . . ." Silverbrook looked outside into her glowing hollow. Shimmering specks of color danced over the trees, cast by the ripples in the lake of light surrounding her home. "You see, the Saentauri – for reasons you may one day learn – no longer exist. After the Great War, this forest and the Nymphs were left unprotected. When Xandria was Governess of the Cerebrian Territories, she traveled one autumn to Aunestauna on the old forest road – a path Gallegore had cut down to quickly traverse Endellia. In the forest, the Nymphs came to her, and gave the sixteen soldiers traveling with her the powers they had once given to the Saentauri."

He whispered to himself, "The first Phantoms." He looked up from his empty bowl of soup. "How do you know all of this?"

Silverbrook motioned out into the glade of light. "Look around you – the powers you see, my gift of healing and reading memories, this place I've created . . . Tayben," she said, "I am the last Saentauri."

A sense of realization dawned over him but was washed away by a flood of questions. "The flowers. All of this. Your sanctuary . . . How did you create it all?"

"I let my gift flow freely to connect my soul to a greater force."

"What great force?" asked Tayben.

Silverbrook shook her head. "There is no one name for it. But all different peoples and texts on sorcery agree it's there – the Nothing that is Everything, the Great Mother, the Eye of the Universe, the Spirit World, the Cosmic Connector, the Neverending Filament, the Great Tree of Life, the World Beyond. Whatever it is, this— Ether, it's how everything is interconnected, how life and death intertwine, how you exist . . . I mean— how we all exist, really." The house was silent, and beams of shimmering light from the lake outside filtered in through the windows. "My mother raised me on her own in this forest, teaching me all she knew – the ways and the stories of her people. Her name was Aeliara Silverbrook." She said the name as if it was sacred to her. "When she died, I had no one but myself, so I left the forest and traveled to Aunestauna and took up work as a servant in Gallegore's Palace." A little white flame danced around her fingers. She reminded him of someone he knew. "But not long after I arrived there, Xandria poisoned King Gallegore and sent assassins – the first Phantoms – to kill Tronum. They would have succeeded if not for Fernox." She and Tayben looked out the glassless window at the winged lion sitting in flowers on the edge of the pool of light.

He looked back at her. "Fernox was King Gallegore's lion?"

Silverbrook smiled. "Fernox drove the Phantoms away, but they thought that they had been successful in killing Tronum. During their attack, I was walking in a nearby hallway. I heard Fernox roar and I sprinted there to find Tronum covered in blood. I decided it was more important to save him than to continue concealing that I could use magic, so I healed his stab wounds . . . it was the greatest mistake of my life." Silverbrook thought for a moment. "Tronum feared Xandria because she was smarter and more capable; he knew she could destroy him once she had all of Cerebria on her side. But as soon as he knew that I could harness the power of sorcery . . ." She thought for a moment again.

"He wanted to increase his military strength, so he had you create . . ." Tayben's voice trailed off as he pictured her five monsters – a fire giant, a sentient tree, an ice dragon, the water serpent from the Battle of Aunestauna, and the shadowed, smoke-like beast still wandering in Western Endlebarr.

Silverbrook shook her head. "I couldn't say no to him . . . he was the king and he thought I was the one sorceress in existence. So he used me to try and defeat his sister."

"You had all that power and just served King Tronum?"

Silverbrook shook her head. "I tried to find ways to extend my influence outside the palace. All the while I was working for King Tronum, I sent letters to the Goblins in Cerebria. I knew Xandria was about to wipe them out and I wanted to help prepare them by telling them what I figured out how to do – how to create the things I created. But they couldn't do it in time, and then Xandria exterminated them . . ."

Tayben thought for a moment. "How did you escape? Why are you here?"

Silverbrook took a sip of her soup. "Well, you should know that during my time in Aunestauna, I met a man I could sense had the gift of sorcery as well. We kept our secrets hidden from the world, but sorcery wasn't our only one – I had two children with him . . . though we could never marry."

"Who was he?" asked Tayben, though he felt the answer coming.

"Madrick Nebelle," she said. "Our children were Shonnar and Raelynn."

He sat for a moment, trying to take it all in. At first, he was shocked, but then a wave of frustration overtook him. "She's been looking for you her whole life! Why haven't you told her you're her mother? Why haven't you been there?"

Sadness crept over Silverbrook's face. "When I decided I couldn't go on doing work for Tronum, I sealed the monsters up and hid another one of my creations – one that could be very dangerous in the wrong hands. I planned to flee Aunestauna with Madrick and my children to Seirnkov . . ."

Tayben leaned forward. "But you didn't go with him?"

Silverbrook closed her eyes. "Something got in the way . . . something I had to do . . ." Her voice trailed off again, but this time she looked at him with a troubled look.

He couldn't help but feel as if she was upset with him or that she regretted something. He wanted to ask her more but feared pushing too far.

Silverbrook continued. "I took Fernox and flew to Endlebarr on his back. He no longer wanted to be in the palace either and was familiar with Saentauri, so we made a good team. I've been here ever since."

"I have to tell Raelynn that you're her, that you're alive."

She shook her head. "You know it can't come from you; she doesn't know your connection with your other lives. How would the street orphan Kyan know me?"

Tayben sat silently.

Silverbrook looked at the white flame dancing around her fingertips. "She will learn when the time is right."

"So why didn't you ever go to Seirnkov to live with your family?"

Silverbrook stood up out of her chair to warm up her soup again in white fire. "I've told my story and now it's time for yours. The first time I saw you, I learned what had happened to you before from searching your memories; but I can only guess what brought you back here now . . . I could only see blurred visions of you while you were gone."

Tayben thought back to the moment Silverbrook removed his memories. He recalled aloud the events that followed being there at her sanctuary as he remembered them. He told her about wandering through the forest until the Phantoms found him. He told her about Gallien, and the Phantoms taking him to the Nymphs. With a tear in his eye, he remembered the pure light of the Nymphs transforming him into a Phantom. He recalled the strength and speed he had and the battles he had fought side by side with the soldiers of shadow. He explained how every day, he grew more and more separated from the Phantoms until he no longer believed in Xandria's cause.

"As my loyalty to the Nymphs and Cerebria faded," he said, "so did my power. We fought the Ferramish at Camp Stoneheart. I was trying to keep up with Gallien and I fell behind. I ended up fighting myself . . . as Prince Eston. I nearly killed myself before one of your beasts came to my aid. I looked into its eyes and it transported me into a void, where the only thing I could see was your glowing white flowers – the flowers I had remembered the whole time but had not known their origin. I knew I had to go and so I ran, following a glimpse of what your beast showed me. I traveled through Endlebarr and across the Taurbeir-Krons until I reached the treeline and the flowers, which is where you found me."

Silverbrook leaned back in her chair, evaluating his whole story. "You are quite a remarkable person, Tayben."

"Why did you take me in the first time and save my life? And more importantly, why did you let me go back out into Endlebarr to be taken by the Phantoms?"

"Because that's what you wanted then. I knew eventually you would find what was in your heart – what Eston, Kyan, and Calleneck needed to teach you, as I am sure you have taught them. Your bravery has given them the courage to do what they must."

Tayben sat silently for a while, listening to the sound of frogs and birds outside in the night, which was beginning to turn back into day. "Where do I go from here? My family in Woodshore was told I was dead as soon as I joined the Phantoms. I don't have anywhere to go; I don't know what to fight for; I–" He swallowed back his tears.

Silverbrook closed her eyes. "Sleep on it . . . there is a room up the staircase you can use. You haven't truly rested for months."

Tayben nodded, but before he got up, he paused. "Ms. Silverbrook . . . the Saentauri – *your* people – what happened to them?"

She took a long while to respond. There seemed to be a great pain taking over her, filling her head with dark thoughts. "They were destroyed."

"How?" he asked. He could tell she was hurting and was not surprised when he did not receive an answer.

"Go and wash in the stream just outside of the grove. I'll make sure you get across the lake safely. I'll have clean clothes for you as well."

Tayben reluctantly accepted the offer and, after bathing in the stream outside the grove, changed and climbed up the staircase which sat in the center of the hollowed out, but still living, tree. Finding his bed, he took off his shoes and collapsed on top of the covers of a real bed for the first time since he was home in Woodshore.

THE LIBRARY UNDER ROSHK

Chapter Thirty Five

~Sometime, February 9th
The Network, Cerebria

Sir Borius Shipton followed Calleneck around another turn in the cold, stalactite-filled tunnels of the network. The Goblin capital of Rjarnsk lay only a few more miles ahead, directly underneath the Cerebrian city of Roshk. In its library, Borius hoped to find the letters written from Silverbrook to the Goblins detailing her discoveries in magic – specifically if there was any way left to kill Xandria before Tronum dies of his disease. Calleneck and Borius had traveled for two days through the dark tunnels of the Network. Calleneck remained unaware why he needed to lead Borius to the abandoned and destroyed Goblin capital, but he trudged along in the dark with his maps of the subterranean web of Goblin tunnels.

Calleneck stopped and sat down on an outcropping of rock on the side of the tunnel and took out a map. Because the light of bioluminescent worms on the walls wasn't adequate, Borius held a little glowing orb of yellow Taurimous so Calleneck could read it. Calleneck studied his map awhile and traced his finger along it. Borius increased the brightness of the light. "Are we on track?"

"Mostly," said Calleneck. "I accidentally took us down here, but we'll get back on this tunnel right here in about a half mile." Calleneck moved his finger along the map. "And then once we reach here, the tunnel could be filled with water. But right after that, we should be near the ruins of the city."

"Why would it be filled with water?" said Borius, lifting a heavy eyebrow that Calleneck could just make out on his dark chestnut skin. The eye destroyed by Grennkovff's spell had scarred over into a mutilated and disfigured cavity.

"There's an underground river that runs across the path right next to the city, but if the water passageway crumbled on the Day of the Underground Fire, it would have dammed up the river and filled the cavern with water."

Borius nodded. "That makes sense," and adjusted the small pack he wore on his back, which contained a blanket and some vegetables. They had come up to the surface on different occasions to get food from various farmers sworn loyal to the Evertauri. "Do you need to take a break?" asked Borius.

Calleneck stood up and brushed off his back. "I'm fine, let's keep going."

Borius nodded and followed him down the cold and dark passageway, lighting the way with a glowing orb of yellow light.

"So, Calleneck," said Borius as they rounded another bend in the tunnel, looking for conversation, "What brought you here to the Evertauri?"

He thought for a while as they walked along. "Fate?"

Borius shook his head. "No such thing . . . What brought you here, Calleneck?"

He slowed his pace unintentionally as he thought. "My sister . . . Aunika. She was the first one here and now Dalah and I are part of it."

"Why do you contribute so much to something you had but little choice to join?"

"Because I want to do something with my life," said Calleneck.

Borius nodded and thought for a while. "You're impressing your sister."

Calleneck chuckled. "Aunika? No, I– No, it's not that."

"Your older sister is successful, Mr. Bernoil. She is one of the few Evertauri to ever speak with Queen Xandria."

"I guess," Calleneck replied.

"Have you impressed your sister–"

"It's not . . . I–" Calleneck shook his head.

Borius smiled. "My older brother joined the Evertauri before me."

Calleneck continued leading Borius through the tunnels. "I didn't know you had a brother."

Borius Shipton nodded. "Half-brother really . . . Obarius was his name. He was killed three years after he joined, two years after I did . . ." His mind trailed off, navigating the flood of memories. "I joined for him. Of course it's not my motive now, but it was then . . . We had traveled across the world together from the Shallow Green Isles to Seirnkov, but if I ever go back home . . . Well, let's just say it will be hard doing that alone." Borius let a smile sneak onto his face. "I remember when Obarius and I first arrived as immigrants at Port Dellock. They asked us for our surnames, but we didn't understand the Common Tongue well, so Obairus said, 'Just got shipped'in.' The dockworker named us the Shiptons." He turned to Calleneck. "I obviously learned the language after."

After a silence, Calleneck spoke up. "Do you mind me asking how–?"

"How he died?" Borius adjusted the pack on his back. "We were on a mission together – trying to see if Xandria knew about one of Tronum's weapons. We were in her fortress – on our way out we got caught . . . I didn't look back when I heard him yell 'run' . . ." Borius shook his head. "The Jade

Guard killed him. He was strong though, and he knew he had to make a sacrifice."

Borius reached out and put a hand on Calleneck's shoulder, stopping and turning him around. Looking into his eyes, Borius spoke softly. "And should a situation come when you need to make a sacrifice for something greater than you, having already decided to choose to act for the greater good, you will be able to do anything . . . make that decision for yourself, decide what it means for you to be an Evertauri. Decide now, Calleneck, that when it matters most, when your friends and family are dying beside you and you're scared, that you will stand strong and push to the end for everyone who can't."

Calleneck shook his head. "Have I not made sacrifices enough?" He was surprised that he actually said those words, but knew it was how he truly felt.

Borius stood in silence.

Calleneck's breathing quickened. "I've given up everything . . . *my parents were murdered.*"

"By Xandria's soldiers."

"Because we're Evertauri! Because we're rebels! They took the last bit of childhood I had and it's because we joined you and Madrick!" Calleneck waited for a response but got none. "I served in this rebellion at the expense of everything I loved, all the while bearing its scar on my chest!" He pulled off his shirt, revealing the white scar across his upper body.

Borius looked down at the ground. "It's not perfect . . . but we all have to do what's best for the world."

"Can't you see how hard that is?" Calleneck asked.

". . . I know the price, believe me." Sir Borius shook his head. "You don't know how much larger this cause is than any one person . . . but I'll be there for you – and your sisters. *I have been.*"

Calleneck avoided Sir Borius's eye.

Borius peered into the darkness of the tunnel. "Put your shirt on, we must keep going."

It took a while, but the tension between the two began to dissipate, as they left their negative emotions far back in the tunnels behind them. After many bends and slopes, the two of them reached a stalactite-filled cavern that hung sixty or seventy feet high. Without warning, Borius stopped in his tracks.

"Sir Borius," said Calleneck, "is everything alright?"

Borius's eye was fixed on the distant darkness. "I sense something . . . Stay here," he said in a quiet voice. Borius reached up – the yellow orb of light that hung above them vanished, and it took their eyes a second to adjust. Borius began walking alone into the dark cavern.

"What's wrong?" Calleneck called from behind him.

After his eyes adjusted to the darkness, far in the distance of the cavern, Borius saw an impossibly faint red light glowing. He walked alone toward the light for thirty yards in the dark until its shape finally took the form of a dimly glowing rose. He knelt beside it – the flower which grew out of a little patch of grass on the cavern floor. *How can anything grow here? . . . Selenora Everrose . . .* Borius's head jolted upward, and he frantically looked around, but only sensed Calleneck far in the distance. His heart raced as he looked back at the glowing rose and shook his head, whispering to himself, "Selenora is still alive . . . or maybe somewhere in between life and death . . . in *limbo* . . . buying time until she can–"

Calleneck called out in the dark, "Are you alright?"

Borius plucked the flower and put it in his pocket. "Yes," he shouted back, "my mind was just playing tricks on me." Borius headed back to Calleneck and relit the yellow orb of Taurimous above them so that they could see the path they traveled toward the Goblin capital. Borius grew ever more nervous with the glowing rose in his pocket.

As they continued walking in the cold and dark tunnels, Calleneck traced his finger along the damp stone of the caves. "What will we do after this? For a mission, I mean."

Borius stepped over a small stalagmite. "You ask more than I should tell you." He paused. "President Nebelle would like to show off the power of the Evertauri once again."

Calleneck's heartbeat quickened. "Another attack like at the Great Gate?"

Borius nodded. "With permission from her father, Raelynn Nebelle has established a connection to the Ferramish government. She now lives in the palace at Aunestauna. In order to defeat Xandria, we will need the help of the Ferramish."

"Are we allies with them now?"

He nodded. "As long as they leave *us* alone when the time comes. Raelynn has been conversing with Fillian Wenderdehl at the palace at Aunestauna."

Calleneck could tell that he had stopped before revealing too much information. But Calleneck knew the whole story. He'd ridden the back of the serpent with her and watched as she destroyed the Cerebrian fleet at Aunestauna in a firestorm of her Taurimous; he'd housed her in his shack on a rooftop of Aunestauna. It had been so long since he realized his consciousness inhabited four bodies that Calleneck had trouble remembering through which body he experienced events. All four of his memories were now one, and each thought that he had in one body could carry over to any other.

"What's our next move?" asked Calleneck.

"Port Dellock," said Borius. "There are thousands of Ferramish prisoners there. The leaders of the Evertauri think we should free the Ferramish soldiers and destroy the port to cripple Xandria's naval force. We should have done it long ago; we didn't know that Xandria would use that port to launch her naval attack that nearly destroyed Aunestauna . . . Calleneck, what's that up there?"

The two of them looked ahead and saw the tunnel plunge down into an underground lake. The walls of the tunnel were eroded and caved in. Calleneck turned to Borius, "This is what I mentioned earlier about the underground river damming up to create a lake." The tunnel had caved down to the surface of the water; they would have to swim underwater.

"Is there any way around?" asked Borius.

Calleneck brushed aside his overgrown hair. "Six or seven miles back."

Borius shook his head. "Ah, it's not worth it – you've swum before in lakes or rivers I assume?"

"Yes, my father used to take me." Calleneck bent down and felt the glassy, undisturbed water, sending a ripple through it. "It's cold."

A yellow flame burst out of Borius's hand. "We can warm up pretty easily. What do you say, Mr. Bernoil?"

Calleneck nodded. "Let's swim. It should just be about ten yards."

The two of them, with their packs and clothes on, waded into the lake and took a deep breath before completely diving under the surface. The water was cold and dark, but they sent streams of crimson and yellow energy ahead of them to light their way as they swam. Calleneck had underestimated how far they'd have to go, and his diaphragm began to convulse for air before he and Borius broke through the surface of the water on the other side. Swimming back onto the stone of the tunnel, the two used the flames in their hands to dry off their clothes and packs, steaming the water away.

When they finished, they lifted their lights up, but there was no ceiling right above them anymore; instead, it extended three hundred feet into the largest cavern Calleneck had ever seen.

Borius glanced at Calleneck with his one eye. "We're here – the Ruins of Rjarnsk."

Calleneck gazed into the vast cavern at the crumbling ruins of immense buildings of stone, which all once were perfectly crafted by the Goblins who lived there years before. The Goblins had melded their architecture with the cave, carving their buildings out of its walls.

"Remember, this is a graveyard . . . where the Goblins lost their last stand against Xandria." Borius took a deep breath in and walked forward.

"What's that smell?" whispered Calleneck.

Borius looked at him with a saddened face. "Goblin bodies are embedded with many magical properties; they take decades to decompose." He raised his hand and moved the yellow ball of light in his hand forward through the city. The orb of light stopped fifty yards away from them and the light from it spread out across the roof of the cavern, illuminating the whole ancient city in all its rubble and ruin.

The great towers in the underground city of Rjarnsk had fallen and ash coated the ground. A giant mound of something dark loomed in front of them fifty feet tall. The two walked toward it, and Calleneck's heart skipped a beat when he realized what it was, and he put a hand over his mouth and nose. There, in the center of the city, were stacked thousands of Goblin corpses.

Borius led Calleneck forward to the pile, but Calleneck felt sick, not wanting to go any closer. Reluctantly, he stepped forward, following Borius closer to the corpses. The smell seemed to creep on his skin like insects, and the silence of the cavern gave him chills. The closer he got, the more he could see the burned and bloody faces of the Goblins, who all looked more human than Calleneck ever imagined them, just slightly dwarfed. The discovered and flaky skin on their bodies had begun to decompose and peel away from their bones. The awful and sickening sight struck Calleneck and caused him to vomit off to the side.

Borius stopped at the edge of the pile and put a hand on the cloak of a Goblin. With a tear in his eye, he turned to Calleneck, who was still recovering. "Calleneck, this is why we fight Xandria. Anyone who has forgotten the atrocities she committed may one day come down here to see what she really is." Borius stood up. "We need to find what we came here for. Do you know where the library is? Or at least the ruins of it?"

Calleneck breathed heavily and shook his head, still sick from the sight of the thousands of corpses in front of him. "Not many people have been here – we'll need to look around."

Borius nodded and led Calleneck away from the mountain of corpses and into the stone ruins of the city.

After several hours of tedious searching, the two had found nothing but building after building of fallen stone and rubble. Everywhere they went was charred and burned, scorched from the fires of the war. Their boots were covered in ash, and every place they stepped left a footprint.

Borius sat down on a block of stone in exhaustion.

Calleneck plopped on the ground across from him. "If we're looking for things like books or documents, they're all going to be burned to ash by now."

Borius wiped beads of sweat from his balding, dark head. "You may be right. Another bead of sweat dripped from his cheek and fell to the ash below, but it almost seemed to disappear once it hit.

Calleneck tapped his foot. "Xandria probably got here first . . . if it wasn't all destroyed during the Day of the Underground Fire, she would've searched after and found what information she could."

The two remained silent for a moment before Borius spoke. "Unless . . ." he said. "Unless the Goblins *knew* they wouldn't be able to hold Xandria and the Cerebrian army off and they were able to hide their most valuable secrets – to protect them from falling into Xandria's hands."

"What are you suggesting?" said Calleneck.

Borius stood up and scanned the rubble all around him. "We, as sorcerers, can make small illusions like doors and the entrances to the Nexus. But they aren't highly complicated because we don't have many of us working together on the same illusion, and not with such close attention to the minute details that makes it look truly realistic."

"Are you implying that the Goblins could've used sorcery to hide the contents of the library?" asked Calleneck, standing as well.

Borius nodded. "Or the whole library . . . The Goblins were highly intelligent and paid extraordinary attention to detail – they worked together like gears on a clock. With a whole city of them banding together, they could have produced a mass illusion before Xandria's army came to destroy them—"

"—in order to hide their secrets from her," finished Calleneck.

Borius raised his hands up and yellow light swirled into the air, seeming to whisper as it went. It kept traveling all throughout the cavern, coating every fallen and blackened structure in shimmering light. He spoke softly, *"Reveal."*

The light glowed bright and began to descend from the tallest structures. Calleneck could hardly believe his own eyes as huge, beautiful ceilings and intricate archways began appearing hundreds of feet above them where nothing but stone columns had stood before. The ash around their feet began to disappear as it was replaced by glistening marble floors. The sound of Borius's Taurimous shimmered like chimes and small bells as it came down from the vaulted ceiling – the spell was being removed. Where fallen walls and crumbling structures once stood, thousands of balconies and shelves began emerging out of the light all around them, filled to the brim with unscathed scrolls and handwritten books. The truly enormous hall filled with warm light from candle-lit chandeliers.

Borius laughed big and heartily, "Geniuses! Those cunning little alchemists! We were here in the Goblin Library all along!" Borius gazed in wonder at the scene of the spell lifting. "Great Mother, just look at this!"

Calleneck stood awestruck as the yellow light revealed more and more – statues, paintings, tapestries, decorative pillars and shelves upon shelves of writings. It was the greatest, most immense work of architecture he had ever seen. He shook his head in disbelief. "They sure knew what they were doing."

Borius smiled. "Once we win this war, Calleneck, the world will see this. We'll restore it all to its former glory . . . every Goblin city like this." He looked around in amazement at the sight – the most marvelous place in the world he'd seen. He shook his head. "Imagine what other wonders there once were . . . You could fit half of Xandria's fortress in here! They'll have records of the whole world's history from before man even sailed to Endellia."

"How are we going to search through all of this?"

Borius chuckled. "That's a good question."

After hours of searching, they discovered that all the letters delivered to or from outside of the Network – what Borius was searching for – were consolidated in one circular tower of the library with shelves lining the walls.

As they gazed up at the walls of letters, Calleneck asked, "How much did the Goblins know about sorcery?"

"A fair amount, but they were mainly alchemists," said Borius. He thought for a moment. "Look through these and tell me if you figure out a pattern to how they're organized."

Calleneck stepped on a rolling ladder and climbed up to the higher stacks. Sifting through the letters he looked at the addresses and opened a few. "I think they're just organized by date, maybe date and last name."

"Goblins didn't use last names," said Borius.

"Then alphabetical by place the letter was from?"

Borius shuffled his feet. "Look for the section with letters from the year 784 AHL."

Calleneck slid along the shelf with the rolling ladder and looked around, after a few minutes, he pulled out a letter and said, "Here it is! From this letter and to the right are all from 784. Where was it sent from?"

Borius stepped up to the ladder. "I'll look from here, if you don't mind."

"Oh, sure." Calleneck stepped down the ladder and held it as Borius climbed up to it.

Borius scanned the letters and whispered to himself. *"Let's see . . . 784, 784 . . . A, for Aunestuana . . . yes, right here . . . Abar-Kot, Abendale, Arat-Tez, Archtowne, . . . Aunestauna, right here."* Borius pulled a stack of about fifty envelopes filled with letters off the shelf and set them on a step of the ladder. Whispering to himself as he shuffled through them, *"Silverbrook . . . where are you? This isn't Silverbrook, nor is this."* Borius went through the entire stack of envelopes containing letters. *"Nothing,"* whispered Borius, shaking his head. *"We can't search this entire library . . . that would take weeks."*

Borius picked up the stack of letters and began to put them back on the shelf when he saw the outline of a hidden cupboard on the wood behind the letters. Pushing the letters aside and opening it up, a single large envelope rested there, entitled *"Silverbrook"* in Goblin runes. Borius reached forward and pulled it out, opening it carefully. Reading through the latest letters, he found nothing until the very last letter in the envelope which contained only a few sentences –

I will leave the palace at Aunestuana tonight. Queen Eradine has asked a favor of me and I must do it, which means I will not be traveling with Madrick and my children. The Guardian Stone works — it can defend whoever last uses its power from harm. It contains a curse, however, and as Tronum continues to use the Stone, it will slowly kill him. I have done this so that we may plan to take down Xandria together once Tronum is dead — so that neither may triumph over the other and subject the world to their rule. For now, however, I must go. I will burn all of my notes and work as I flee the palace tonight so that no one but you may replicate what I have created. I pray you have all that you need to protect yourselves. Thank you for all you've done.

Abitha Silverbrook

Borius set down the envelope and rested his head on the ladder. *So now that Xandria has stolen the Guardian Stone, the plan is ruined – she can't be killed even once Tronum is dead.* Borius thought hard for a minute. *Unless we steal it back . . .*

From below, Calleneck called out. "Did you find what you were looking for?"

Borius tucked the envelope into his cloak. "I'm afraid not," he lied to Calleneck for fear of him asking what it was. As he stepped back down the ladder to the floor, Borius thought to himself, *We need a thief . . .*

THE TRIAL
Chapter Thirty Six

~Late Afternoon, February 10th
The Royal Palace, Aunestuana, Ferramoor

Kyan sat in the Great Library reading a novel by the famous writer and historian Tomdar Fe with his feet up on a table next to a window. This particular book covered the Zjaari's war with the Guavaanese. In the early seventh century, the Zjaari of the Southlands began capturing Guavaanese vessels in the Shallow Green Isles and enslaving their occupants. Zjaari slavers had already been taking natives from the tropical islands, but the abduction of Guavaanese sent the two nations into a fourteen-year war, only ending when Xingan Yoto seized power and offered a peace treaty to the Zjaari. Enslavement of the islanders and each others' citizens was abolished, and each nation's rights to the Shallow Green Isles were relinquished, leaving it a neutral tropical sea.

Right outside the window, the snow drifted through the frozen air, and the gray afternoon sky was slowly transforming into a menacing overcast — a winter storm was brewing. The candle next to him dripped, and the couch he sat on creaked as he changed his sitting position and adjusted the brown scarf he wore around his neck to conceal his new snakebite.

His mind often wandered off, thinking about his other bodies, where they were, what they were doing. As Calleneck, he was making his way through the Network with Borius back to Seirnkov; as Tayben, he was in Endlebarr with Silverbrook, and as Eston, he was travelling back to Aunestauna after his battlefield wound. He was beginning to feel as if everything he was doing was somehow connected, all a part of one grand purpose.

After another hour of reading, the dusk sky had begun to dim considerably, and ice now coated the edges of the windows. Tired from reading, Kyan looked out the window into the snowy palace grounds and the frosted city beyond, hoping Raelynn and Vree were headed back soon — the girls were going to meet up at the palace baths and then have dinner with Kyan.

Kyan hadn't seen Vree all day, but he had confidence she was fine. *If anything bad happens,* he thought, *we agreed to meet at the docks.*

Two princes were on the road in opposite directions. Prince Fillian had left at first light for his trip to Abendale and was likely nearing the pleasant town of Greenwash. Meanwhile, Eston's caravan of soldiers escorting him back to Aunestauna was scheduled to arrive at the palace tomorrow morning.

What am I doing here in the palace? thought Kyan, looking around the Great Library surrounding him, most of which had been spared from the flames when the Cerebrians attacked Aunestauna. He looked back out past the palace wall into the snow-covered, jagged streets below. *I can't hide up here forever. Riccolo's out there somewhere and he'll find me . . . I'm going to have to leave Aunestauna soon.* His mind wandered back to a conversation with Raelynn the night before.

"You can't stay here," she said, "I can offer you a new life . . . the Evertauri is—"

"But I'm not a sorcerer, I can't help."

"That's not true," she said. "I think there's something you can help us do, but you'll just have to trust me for now."

Kyan came back to reality and shook his head, sipped his hot tea, and continued reading. Not two minutes later, Kyan noticed an unusual amount of noise around him. Kyan set down the book and got up from his couch. Half the people in the Great Library were standing up and leaving through an archway to the hall where a crowd of people was hustling. Sensing that something was wrong, Kyan put the book in his coat pocket and followed the people out of the North Wing.

As soon as he entered the hallway, he was pushed and shoved by dozens of chattering, yelling people who all walked in one direction down the hall. Looking around to try and see what was wrong, he could find nothing. Tapping a man on the shoulder, Kyan asked, "Excuse me, do you know where everyone is going?"

"There's something big going on in the audience chamber," said the man. "Everyone's headed there."

The man moved on with the crowd and Kyan followed, curious to find out what was going on. After a few minutes, he reached the entrance to the central-palace audience chamber – which often served as a courtroom of theater stage – but he couldn't see anything due to the hundreds of people funneling inside. For a second, he thought he heard someone calling his name, but he curiously wandered into the courtroom along with everyone else.

The room had a painted ceiling decorated with scenes from legends of the Great Mother. There was a balcony that wrapped completely around the room for spectators, and the judge's stand sat beneath a section of the balcony in the front of the hall. But looking around, Kyan felt a cold tingling in his hands, as if something was wrong. Again, he thought he heard his name. Looking around, he saw no one. "Kyan!" yelled a familiar voice again in the distance.

He looked far back behind the doorway to the audience chamber and saw Raelynn shoving people to try and get to him – Vree wasn't with her. "Kyan!" she yelled.

He tried to push his way back to her, but the crowds of people pushed him further into the courtroom.

"Kyan!" she yelled again with a horrified face, but he couldn't understand what else she was saying. "I couldn't find– she never showed up– He's here–"

Kyan tried to push his way back through the crowd to get to Raelynn outside of the courtroom. "Where is Vree?!" he yelled in vain. About twenty feet from the doorway, the Scarlet Guards at the door began closing it. "Wait, wait!" Kyan shouted.

As Kyan was just five feet from the heavy oak doors, the Scarlet Guards shut them with a bang, separating him from Raelynn. Kyan ran up to the guards. "Excuse me!" he said breathlessly. "Excuse me, can I please exit back out into the hallway?"

The Scarlet Guards shook their heads. "Sorry, sir, we can't let you back out while the court is in session." The sound of a gavel behind Kyan rang through the hall, shushing the courtroom.

Kyan whispered frantically to them. "Please, my friend is in trouble." He tried to piece Raelynn's words together. *Vree never showed up at the palace baths to meet Raelynn? Something is wrong . . .*

"Sir, it's a matter of security," said the soldier, "same rules have always applied – we can't let anyone in or out while public court is in session."

The gavel sounded again behind Kyan, who felt an overwhelming feeling of dread spread over him. He slowly backed away from the doors and pushed his way through the crowd to get to the balcony that overlooked the floor of the audience chamber. Looking down, Kyan's heart nearly stopped when he saw, standing alone on the courtroom floor in all black, Riccolo.

Stepping back behind people so that Riccolo wouldn't see his face, Kyan felt his heart pounding out of his chest and the blood pulsing through his temples. *He's not on trial,* thought Kyan, *Riccolo is testifying.*

The gavel sounded one more time, and silence spread over the courtroom. The judge – Judge Ratticrad – spoke out with a loud, irritating voice. "Let the session begin." King Tronum sat next to the judge, who spoke again. "This meeting concerns information of an Aunestaunean thief gang by the name of the Nightsnakes." Whispers spread throughout the hall. Judge Ratticrad continued. "Here before us today stands Mr.–"

"Alda," said Riccolo as he handed the judge forged identification papers, wearing a long black coat with a collar pointed up, covering his neck. *Alda,* the surname on Kyan's orphanage record.

"Mr. Alda," repeated Judge Ratticrad. "Will you swear today to testify with candor, may your soul be treated with justice by the Great Mother according to the merits of your testimony today?"

Riccolo nodded and smiled. "Yes, sir."

Kyan's mind ran fast as a horse, thinking of a thousand different reasons why Riccolo was there in the palace, testifying to the judge. *Could he have been caught?* He thought of Raelynn's horrified face. *No, something is wrong . . . Riccolo is plotting something.*

Judge Ratticrad continued. "Mr. Alda has come to the court today with information regarding the Nightsnakes of Aunestauna – Mr. Alda, would you please elaborate on your case to our jury and our gallery spectators?"

"Of course," said Riccolo, with the same chilling voice that haunted Kyan's nightmares. Peeking in between people to see through the balcony down to the courtroom floor, he saw Riccolo standing like a snake ready to strike its prey. Riccolo spoke up and addressed the hall. "The Nightsnakes are an infamous band of thieves that have plagued Aunestauna for years. I'm a private investigator, and two years ago, my men and I began trying to crack down on them and bring them to justice, trying to find out how they operate and who they are . . . but I have had little success until now."

Kyan's heart raced. Hearing Riccolo blatantly lie and talk about his own gang to a judge unsettled Kyan in the worst way possible. *What's up Riccolo's sleeve?* He thought of Raelynn who was outside the courtroom doors.

Down on the courtroom floor, Riccolo continued speaking. "Months ago, former First Advisor Sir Janus Whittingale met with the Nightsnakes' leader. He collaborated with them to help set up a plan that would ensure the death of Benja Tiggins."

The gallery spectators erupted into mumbled chatter, prompting Judge Ratticrad to slam down his gavel. "Silence please!"

Riccolo pressed on. "The plan also ensured that he would take over Benja Tiggins' position as Scarlet Lord, therefore setting up Aunestauna for a Cerebrian naval attack."

From the side of the judge, Sir Endwin Bardow, Fillian's Mentor and the new First Advisor to King Tronum, interjected mockingly. "I think we're going to see a bit of proof that street thieves were involved in the plot to attack Aunestauna."

Riccolo smiled. "I thought you'd never ask." Riccolo drew from his pocket a piece of paper and held it up high. "I present to you the contract from Janus Whittingale to *The Nightsnakes*, retrieved by me after their leader met with the First Advisor the night of September 26th. This details Whittingale's exact intentions. His signature can be seen at the bottom."

The courtroom filled with soft gasps and whispering.

A guard walked down to Riccolo to bring up the paper to the judge, who read it carefully. "And you stole this from the Nightsnakes' Leader?"

Riccolo nodded. "Yes, sir."

"Ironic," said the judge, who examined the signature and then showed it to Sir Endwin Bardow, who shrugged. Judge Ratticrad turned back to the courtroom. "The signature looks authentic."

Again, the courtroom began jabbering; the only ones who previously knew what had happened were the high government officials and the Royal family. Tronum scratched his beard and examined the room below him without expression on his face.

The judge pounded his gavel two times. "Silence please!" The courtroom took a minute to calm.

As Kyan slowly tried to distance himself from the balcony, Riccolo began to walk in a circle, and continued his obviously well-rehearsed lie. "Whittingale asked for the Nightsnakes to steal a valuable stone from the palace vault, as well as to help him assassinate government leaders such as Prophet Ombern the night of the Battle of Aunestauna. In return, he promised them to destroy all the documents in the palace's archives detailing information about the Nightsnakes. Benja Tiggins was set up as the thief that night, and the plan hatched by Whittingale and the Nightsnakes succeeded. I also obtained some of the documents that Whittingale stole from the palace records and was supposed to destroy." Riccolo opened up his coat and pulled out two large envelopes containing many sheets of parchment.

Kyan's eyes widened. *Riccolo wouldn't have trusted Whittingale just to destroy the documents, he would have wanted some of them in his own hands before ever telling me to steal that stone from the palace Vaults. With access to the documents that have a Palace Seal, he could change any information that he wants in those files . . . like the identity of Nightsnakes* —Kyan turned and began slowly pushing his way even farther from the balcony, which hung against the side wall of the room.

Riccolo walked toward Judge Ratticrad's stand and handed him the documents. "I think you'd like to take a look at these."

As the judge read them intently, King Tronum whispered in the judge's ear. Judge Ratticrad nodded and spoke out. "Mr. Alda," he said to Riccolo, "I have been notified by His Majesty that the royal family already knows about the overarching details of Whittingale's sinister plot against Ferramoor."

"But Your Honor," said Riccolo, "this plan took two parties to execute. Your first conspirator is dead, yes . . . but one is still out there. One lowly life form who almost destroyed your nation."

Kyan's stomach dropped and his heart raced as he figured out what was soon to come. *He's sacrificing everything right now. But he wouldn't do this unless he has a plan to divert the attention.* His eyes shot wide open when he realized that underneath his scarf was a fresh snakebite. *If everyone thought I was a Nightsnake, I'd be caught instantly. Riccolo can't catch me himself . . . but with the entire Scarlet Guard on his side, there's no way I can escape . . .*

Riccolo walked back out onto the floor of the courtroom and addressed the room. "I found out where the Nightsnakes were all hiding; but by the time I got to their manor in the Fourth District, they were gone."

Riccolo smiled and projected his voice even louder. "But the Nightsnakes didn't go far . . . You see, the leader of their gang is quite smart and cozied up to the same people who could execute him in hopes that they would never suspect him of being a Nightsnake."

Kyan tried to get through the crowd as far away as he could, but there were too many people.

Riccolo laughed and threw up his hands. "So through an extraordinary course of events and a great deal of luck for my investigation, the *Lord of Thieves* is in our midst today! In this very courtroom!"

The entire hall fell into chaos and Judge Ratticrad slammed his gavel down ten times before the crowd quieted enough to hear him. "Silence!" he yelled. The judge scooted forward in his seat and stared at Riccolo. "Well, Mr. Alda? Who are you accusing?"

Riccolo smiled and looked up to the side balcony where the crowd of spectators stood. "Maybe," chuckled Riccolo, "it's the person who has slowly been trying to press his way through the crowd this whole time so as not to be seen."

The spectators around Kyan who had noticed him pressing toward an exit spun and stared in fear at him. Kyan froze, unable to move, to think, like a fawn staring at a hunter's arrow.

Riccolo threw his arms up to the ceiling and laughed. "Ladies and gentlemen! May I present to you the most wanted criminal in Ferramoor — *Kyan*, the first and greatest Nightsnake! Leader to them all!"

The crowd around screamed and hollered and pushed Kyan over to the balcony for everyone to see. A Scarlet Guard from the front doors came and stood behind him, trapping him against the balcony.

Kyan frantically tried to find words. "But— it's not true, I swear. I'm not a Nightsnake—"

Judge Ratticrad slammed down his gavel close to twenty times before the crowd quieted. Everyone's eyes alternated between Kyan, Riccolo, and the judge. Ratticrad stood up from his chair. "And what grounds do you have, Mr. Alda, for accusing this *Kyan* of something punishable by death."

Riccolo smiled. "Sir, I believe that Whittingale's contract with the Nightsnakes that I handed you has another signature on it. The signature of the person who agreed to help Whittingale, and the person who met with him. Would you care to read it aloud?"

The courtroom was now eerily silent, and the judge spoke. "It— it says Kyan." Ratticrad held up the paper with Kyan's name at the very bottom, next to Whittingale's.

Kyan's stomach dropped. *He's been planning this from day one. He signed my name instead of his when he agreed to help Whittingale. He's going by the name Alda; he's trying to switch identities with me.* Kyan looked around the courtroom in vain for anyone that could help; but the only credible person who knew the truth was Fillian, and he was a city away. The chamber rang out in murmurs as people chattered with their neighbors.

Riccolo turned up his hands. "Perhaps this all would be more believable if we had a witness?" Riccolo turned to the back of the courtroom floor, where two giant doors below the balcony lead to the outside, the only other exit in the courtroom besides the main doors. "Bring her in, boys!" The doors opened, letting in a freezing gust of wind accompanied by snowflakes. Through the doors came two Nightsnakes who dragged between them the limp and bloody body of Vree.

Kyan almost called out her name, but stopped himself, for doing so would surely sentence him to death. *You don't know her; you don't know her.* Riccolo's two Nightsnakes dragged Vree into the chamber and threw her to the floor in front of Riccolo. Her face was bloody, and her limbs were bruised. Her outer coat was gone, so her olive skin was tinted pale from the cold outside. She coughed, and little drops of blood shot from her mouth and onto the white stone floor of the chamber. Riccolo thanked his goons and they left back through the doors, letting another cold gust of air into the chamber.

The spectators on the balcony whispered and glanced between Kyan, Riccolo, and Vree. Stepping uncomfortably slowly toward Vree, who tried to stand up, Riccolo spoke to everyone in the chamber. "We have another special guest with us today that my associates helped track down — another Nightsnake!" The whole chamber mumbled and gasped. Riccolo put his hand on her head as Vree sat there crying. "Her name is Vree Shaarine; she's been staying in this very palace with Kyan, taking advantage of your hospitality right under your noses . . . I think that we all agree we can get some valuable information from her, no?"

The crowd of people surrounding Kyan moved in closer, pushing him up to the balcony and closing him off from any escape.

Judge Ratticrad raised an eyebrow and crossed his arms. "And you know she is a Nightsnake how?"

Riccolo smiled at the judge. "The Nightsnakes have a signature mark . . . one that's easy to hide with a scarf."

Vree's head shot up and she tried to scoot away from Riccolo, but he grabbed her shoulder and ripped off the scarf to reveal a red snakebite. The courtroom gasped, and Riccolo picked up Vree, pinning her head back to show everyone up in the audience the bite. One man from a balcony shouted out, "Well, someone grab him!"

A Scarlet Guard behind Kyan drew his sword, and another grabbed him and pinned him against the balcony. Riccolo laughed and raised his hands to the balconies, speaking to everyone. "Who would like to see this mark on our friend, Mr. Kyan?"

The whole courtroom erupted in yelling. Kyan struggled, but the soldier behind him had his arms pinned back. Another man pushed his way to Kyan and untied his scarf to reveal Kyan's snakebite.

Seeing it, the chamber roared with screams and shouting, and Judge Ratticrad slammed his gavel down again. A sickening dread spread through Kyan, who felt absolutely helpless pushed up against the balcony in front of hundreds of people. The crack of the gavel sounded again and Ratticrad yelled above the crowd. "Silence!"

Riccolo tried to hold Vree up, but she kicked him back. Falling to the ground crying, she sniffed and shivered and tried to clear some blood off her face. She refused to look up at Kyan, who flinched as the guard behind him increased the pressure on his arms by pushing them up behind his back. Some of her hair stuck to her face in the dried blood.

The judge looked up at Kyan. "Let us hear *the girl* speak . . . the snakebites on both of their necks are damning evidence itself, but if Ms. Shaarine here can testify to us today that Mr. Kyan is indeed the leader and founder of the Nightsnakes, I would be so inclined to pardon the worst of her crimes so that her life may be spared." Silence spread over the room. Judge Ratticrad spoke again. "Ms. Shaarine?"

Vree lifted her head and pulled her hair out of the dried blood on her mouth and cheek. Tears streamed down from her swollen eyes.

Kyan closed his eyes, not believing what was happening. He hoped that Raelynn behind the courtroom doors could hear and had a plan.

The judge took a step toward Vree. "Ms. Shaarine," he said, "is Mr. Kyan the leader of the Nightsnakes?" Vree looked up to the balcony where the guard held Kyan. With tears and blood still covering her face, she shook her head.

Ratticrad raised an eyebrow. "Answer verbally, young miss."

Riccolo took a step back and looked straight at Kyan.

Vree shook her head again between coughs and sniffs and mumbled, "No."

The hundreds of spectators turned to each other and whispered. The judge took another step toward her. "Ms. Shaarine, you are under oath, and perjury will send you to the gallows along with your other crimes if you do not tell the truth."

"She's telling the truth!" Kyan shouted from the balcony.

"Silence!" yelled Judge Ratticrad, who stood above Vree and spoke softly. "Tell me who the leader of the Nightsnakes is."

Vree turned around and stared straight at Riccolo, whose eyes widened for a fraction of a section before returning to normal.

The judge laughed. "Mr. Alda? The man who captured you? Why would he risk coming here?"

Kyan yelled down to Vree, "His collar!"

Vree spun around and lunged at Riccolo's neck, but Riccolo grabbed her wrists and threw her down against the stone with a smack.

Deathly silence hung in the room, and then it was pierced by Riccolo's nervous laugh. "They think *I'm the Lord of Thieves?"* Riccolo walked toward Vree who lay on the ground, unable to get up. He looked up to the balconies and raised his voice. "Then surely I would have the mark!" Riccolo then turned his head to Kyan and stared straight into his eyes as he cautiously lowered his collar, seeming to be careful not to touch his own neck.

Kyan's heart sank as Riccolo's neck was revealed, without any trace of a snakebite.

Riccolo raised his hands and addressed the roaring crowd. "It seems as if Kyan's last attempt at saving himself has failed! What a shame – Ms. Shaarine's loyalty to her Lord of Thieves is dooming her. I believe that my case is closed."

The judge nodded. "Silence the girl," he ordered as Vree began to protest, and Scarlet Guards rushed forward, gagging her with a rope. More soldiers surrounded Kyan, and the chambers erupted once more into chaos.

Riccolo knelt next to Vree, helpless and beaten, and whispered in her ear. *"Bites are easy to cover with just a bit of powder."* He gingerly covered up his neck with his collar.

Judge Ratticrad sat back down at his stand. "Thank you, Mr. Alda." Ratticrad looked at Vree once more. "Ms. Shaarine, if you choose to admit that Mr. Kyan here has been your leader of the Nightsnakes, your execution will be pardoned and you will be given ten months of prison sentence. If you do not, you will join Mr. Kyan at the gallows tonight."

Kyan's heart raced as Vree looked up at Kyan with a blood and tear covered face. The whole courtroom looked at her and Kyan. Vree shook her head and let out another sob, crying helplessly on the courtroom floor. She looked up to Kyan with red, tear-filled eyes as she bawled. From her bleeding, gagged mouth, she gave out a horrifying scream, "RUN!"

In one instant, Kyan kicked back the guard holding onto him, and women in the gallery screamed. Raelynn slammed through the doors and into the crowd. A man next to Kyan drew his sword, and, seeing no other way out, he hurled himself over the balcony twenty feet to the stone floor below. He nimbly rolled once he hit the ground to dull the impact, but his legs still stung from the jump and the book in his pocket fell out onto the floor.

Riccolo ran over to grab him, but Kyan dove at his waist, tackling him down. Dozens of guards drove through the mass of screaming people to try and get to Kyan and Vree. Riccolo drew a dagger and stabbed at Kyan, but he lifted the book off the floor and stopped the knife in its pages. Far above, Raelynn pushed and shoved, trying to make her way down the staircase to the courtroom floor.

Yanking the book-lodged knife away, Kyan pushed off of Riccolo. Trying to locate the doors as hundreds of people began to rush after him, Kyan bolted away for the back doors that led outside. Hundreds, including Raelynn, now covered the courtroom floor, trying to grab Kyan as he sprinted away. Vree vainly tried to run from Riccolo, but he grabbed her by the wrist and threw her down, slamming her head into the stone. Vree's body went limp, and Riccolo lunged for his dagger. Ripping it our of the book, he raised it above Vree's unconscious body.

"NO!" screamed Raelynn as she fought her way through the hundreds of frantic people. Before Riccolo brought down the dagger, Raelynn tackled him. As she wrestled Riccolo away from Vree, he stabbed her in the arm. She cried out in pain and rolled backwards across the stone, bleeding from her tricep.

A group of palace servants running out of the courtroom trampled over her body, pounding her limbs into the stone floor and bruising her ribs. Straining to stand, she looked around for Riccolo, scanning the hundreds of moving faces and bodies in dark cloaks, but he had vanished in the chaos. A boot slammed into her head and knocked her dizzy, sending her back to the floor.

She crawled over to Vree and put two bloody fingers to her neck, focusing hard, she felt a faint heartbeat. Raelynn felt her head throb with every pulse of blood. With one arm covered in blood and another badly bruised, she picked Vree up off the floor and looked around in a panic as people shoved and screamed, trying to get out of the room. Pushing through the mass of people, Raelynn carried Vree out of the courtroom in search of the palace hospital wing.

§

Kyan heard Raelynn scream, knowing that something had happened. As Scarlet Guards ran after him, Kyan slammed through the locked doors, breaking them open. Ice cold air swept over him. He quickly registered where he was and ran through the snowy courtyard that sat around the courthouse. The soldiers made it through the doors not three seconds after him. It was dusk and the snow was falling heavily, stinging his face as he sprinted.

Ahead of him, Kyan spotted Ambassador Changereau walking side by side with his light brown horse. In a last-ditch effort, he sprinted up to the stallion, shoved the man off it, and took the reins, climbing on top. "I'm sorry!" he yelled to the ambassador as he kicked the sides of the horse, driving it forward through the falling snow.

A horn blared and bells rang through the frozen air, setting the entire palace on high alert. Kyan snapped the reins of his horse to get it to run faster. The horse hurdled over a half wall into a hallway of the palace. Kyan yelled at his horse, "Yah!" and snapped the reins again; but he immediately pulled them back when he saw a group of twenty Scarlet Guards turn the corner in front of him. Spinning the horse around, he kicked it and spurred it the other way. But behind him, the soldiers from the courthouse had caught up and blocked it off.

Kyan's mind froze and then snapped back, thinking of only one way. "Alright buddy," he said, putting his hand to the neck of the horse, "you're gonna have to jump." Kyan stared down the guards closing in on him and then kicked his horse forward with the experience of a prince. "Yah!"

The horse sprinted toward the guards, who all drew their swords. Kyan kicked the horse faster. "Yah!" Seeing that Kyan was not stopping, the guards put up their shields. Twenty feet, ten feet, five feet. The horse kicked off with its powerful hind legs, clipped the soldiers' shields and hurled itself and Kyan over them. Kyan screamed, "Yes! Go! Go! Go!" and the horse galloped back into the courtyard. Picturing a mental map of the palace in his head, Kyan rode left through the falling snow. "Yah!" The horse shook its reins and took off.

The bells and horns of the palace continued to sound out across the entirety of the grounds, and people had begun to gather. Kyan tore through the crowds on the horse and split off into a hallway that would bring him to the front gate – the only way out of the palace if they hadn't shut them already. The cold air stung his face, and he snapped the reins again after hearing shouting behind him. Left, right, down the ramp. He rode away into the courtyard at the front gate.

The watchtowers' torches were ablaze and the bells on the top of the gate ahead chimed. Hundreds of people were gathered in the courtyard and screamed when they saw Kyan coming on his horse. Fifty Scarlet Guards sprinted out into the courtyard, racing to catch Kyan. The Guards all shouted up to the watchmen on the wall, "Shut the gate! Shut the gate!"

The giant chains of the gate began to crank them shut.

"Come on!" Kyan shouted to his horse. People screamed as he whizzed by.

From up ahead on the watchtower, he heard someone yell out orders. "He's gonna make it! Archers! Fire!" Kyan's heart stopped as he heard multiple arrows hissing through the air toward him. He ducked behind the neck of his horse as the volley shot toward him. An arrow grazed his shoulder, but the horse below him let out a whinny and collapsed at top speed, throwing Kyan off the front.

Getting up, Kyan saw the horse's coat turning red next to an arrow. The crank of the gate yanked his mind back into focus, and Kyan sprinted away from the horse to the closing gate. From above, he heard another command to fire, and another few arrows barely missed him. Kyan's lungs burned as he pounded toward the closing gate. The metal bars had just ten feet left till its teeth hit the ground. A man grabbed Kyan, but he punched his way out of his grasp. Five feet until the gate was closed. Kyan drove his feet as fast as he could through the snow and slid underneath the gate just as it shut.

He tried to stand up, but his jacket was caught in the closed gate. Scarlet Guards from the other side ran toward him with swords and spears. Trying to pry his jacket out of the closed gate, he gave up and tore the jacket off. Pounding through the snow, his bare skin froze in the surrounding air. With his muscles cramping, he ran as fast as he could, but a feeling of dread took over when he heard the galloping of hooves behind him. Glancing back, he saw twenty Scarlet Guards and their horses racing toward him. *I can lose them in the city.*

Kyan ran forward, turning off into a side street between two narrow buildings. Rounding another corner, he shoved his way past a group of street performers into a marketplace. The Guards' whistles behind him sounded, drawing attention to Kyan as he tore through the stands of freezing vegetables. Kyan hurdled over a half wall and into another side street. The Scarlet Guards blew their whistles and shouted behind him, "Catch him!"

Kyan sprinted through the twisted alleyway. His heart pounded and his lungs and legs burned. The whistles grew closer behind him. *I need to lose them.* He was now in home territory – he could race through the streets blindfolded. He knew where he was, and he knew another alleyway was approaching that led to a staircase where he could go up to the roofs. The Scarlet Guard yelled behind him, and he sprinted through the snow. *There it is!* Kyan rejoiced. Overcoming the exhaustion, Kyan rounded the corner as fast as he could, but instantly felt his feet slip out from under him on the slick ice. Kyan hit the ground followed by the smack of his head, and then his vision collapsed.

His eyes took a second to come back into focus and a searing pain coursed through his head. His skin was cold and purple, and his ears rang loudly as he failed to pull himself up from the ice. The alleyway around him spun and he fell back down again from the dizziness. Not able to form thoughts, he heard the muffled sound of hooves and horses through the intense ringing in his ears. His vision closed again, but Kyan could tell the guards had surrounded him, and they were speaking, but he couldn't hear through the ringing.

Kyan felt his body lifted off the ice and his arms pinned behind his back. As his hands were tied together, Kyan could vaguely make out the phrase, "You are under arrest and are sentenced for execution." After that, Kyan's vision completely closed; his legs gave out from under him, and his mind went blank.

THE PAWN
Chapter Thirty Seven

~Night, February 10th
Aunestauna, Ferramoor

A crack of moonlight filtered into the prison cell. Kyan's bare back leaned up against the ice-cold stone wall, and a small snow drift sat beneath the barred window at the top of the room. A dead leaf blew across the gray stone floor and tumbled over his bare foot. His skin was purple from the cold; only a pair of pants covered him. The door was shut and locked with two armed Scarlet Guards on the outside.

A blindfold ran around Kyan's eyes, tied tightly to the back of his head. His arms were bound behind him, and a red rash ran around his wrists from the burn of the rope. Though he was blindfolded, little flashes lit up his eyes with every painful throb of his head. An excruciating pain ran through his foot from the bite – the prison guards had set their hound on him to prevent his escape. The dog had latched onto his heel so hard they had to kick the animal twice to release him. The cold air sat in his lungs, which barely moved. His body lay still but for his shivering chest and shoulders.

For hours, he sat tied against the stone wall, no thoughts coursing through his mind. The prison guards had beaten him with steel-toed boots, hand clubs, and fists. He struggled to think of any way he could get out . . . hoping for help from anyone. But nothing came to him. All that existed was his broken body, the cold prison cell, and the eerie image of the gallows. Tears dripped from his eyes and dampened the blindfold. *What has this all come to . . .*

Kyan shuffled his feet, grimacing from the aching, and tried to move his back; but he was tied tightly to the wall behind him with a rope around his chest. The dread of death overtook him and seemed to fill his blood with ice. The gallows at Benja's execution darted through his mind. The noose being placed around Benja's neck, the fear in his eyes, the door swinging out from under his feet, and the spine-chilling snap of his neck. Kyan hiccuped and let out a sob. *What am I supposed to do now . . .* Kyan breathed in deeply and whispered out with tears, *"I don't want to die . . ."*

A thought entered his mind as he stared blankly into his black blindfold. *If I die, would I only die in this body? Would I keep my memories?* Kyan tried to push through the throbbing pain in his concussed head trying to remember the things he had discussed as Tayben with Silverbrook in her home in Endlebarr. *She said I have one soul, one Taurimous . . .* Kyan shook his head and lowered it to his bare chest.

Riccolo's smirking face in the courtroom ran through his mind. Kyan screamed out into the frozen air of his cell, sobbing and writhing in his bonds, pushing and pulling and twisting – he couldn't escape. The ropes held him like jaws of death that had clamped down and wouldn't let go no matter what he did to escape. Like a bird who's had its wings clipped, Kyan struggled and struggled to get away but got nowhere.

Yelling trying to stand up against the ropes, he slipped back onto the floor and fell limp, crying and gasping for air. Although he couldn't see it, he could feel himself coughing up blood onto his pants and the stone floor. His whole body and mind were drained of energy and hope, and he sat up against the wall crying for some time.

Through his window, he could hear the distant commotion of the crowd that was undoubtedly gathered around the prison's gallows. The prison was located in the Third District so the scum of the streets were kept far from nobility. The volume of the crowd increased, and Kyan's heartbeat quickened, sensing that the time was coming near.

Kyan looked up at a ceiling he could not see and breathed out. *Great Mother . . . I'm sorry . . . for everything I've done, for the people I've hurt . . . for Benja and all the others. I know I don't deserve to live . . .* Kyan hiccuped and began to whisper his prayer. *"But I'm not ready to die . . . I know others have made sacrifices but they're stronger than I am . . . Please don't let me die here. I can't change what I've done, but I know that I can help this world, I swear I can . . ."*

Another minute passed before a knock sounded on the door of the prison cell, and the door creaked open. Kyan's stomach twisted, and he kicked and tried to move away from the door, from the people he knew would take him away and bring him to the gallows. He couldn't see past his blindfold, but he only heard one set of uneven footsteps. Kyan kept silent as the door to the cell closed and the footsteps approached, walking very slowly toward him. Whoever was there spoke to Kyan in a whisper. "If you do exactly what I tell you, you will get out of this cell. Don't speak; the guards may hear."

Kyan's heartbeat quickened. *What is this?* Had the Great Mother really answered his prayer?

The person in the room knelt beside Kyan and began to untie ropes that bound his hands and feet. Once again, the person spoke in a whisper, "Do not take your blindfold off until you are ready to go out of this cell . . . once I get you untied, you will take this cloak and put it on." The person untied the last knot but pressed on his shoulder to keep him down.

Kyan could tell nothing about the person's whisper, but it was vaguely familiar. Was it Ferramish or Cerebrian? He could hardly tell since even his own speech was beginning to sound like a combination of the two. It could have been anyone in front of him. Kyan tried to stand on his bruised and battered foot and whispered, "Who are you? What are you—"

A soft, delicate hand covered Kyan's mouth to keep him quiet. Kyan heard the person rustling a cloak, or some sort of fabric. The gentle hands helped Kyan to stand and held the clothing to guide Kyan's arms through. Now fully clothed, Kyan heard the person sit where Kyan had been tied up.

The person whispered again. "You can walk out of the prison the way you came in. The guards won't stop you. Place the hood of the cloak over your head and keep your head down. Walk slowly and don't look at anyone. Once you turn around, you may take off your blindfold, but do not look back . . . You're free, now go . . ."

Kyan's mind rushed a million miles an hour as he obeyed, and slowly turned toward the cell door, taking off his blindfold, finally able to see the cold stone moonlit walls of the prison cell. Having a strong urge to look back, Kyan once again obeyed and walked toward the door. *Why are they here? Is this some trick? But I have nothing more to lose if it doesn't work . . . Am I really free?*

Kyan reached for the door handle and turned it, walking out into the torch lit hallway of the prison. Two Guards stood at attention beside him and nodded as he walked by, thinking he was the person who had freed him. *Keep your head down.* Though he was blindfolded when first brought into the cell, he had kept track of the turns and steps out of the prison to the gate. Recalling the route in his mind, Kyan slowly limped down the hallways of the prison toward the entrance.

Up ahead was another group of soldiers who stood still as he walked by. Then he quietly exited back into the snowy city streets. In the distance, the crowd of hundreds of people at the prison gallows chanted and roared. The most relief Kyan had ever felt in his life spread over him like a warm blanket in the frozen, snow filled air. And then he stopped and looked around. *Where is Raelynn?*

§

~ Immediately After the Trial
The Royal Palace

Raelynn rushed around the hallway corner carrying Vree's unconscious body in her bloody arms, frantically heading for the palace hospital wing. Vree's eyelids were swollen shut and horrible gashes and bruises covered her body.

Men and women ran through the palace as the chaos from the trial spread. Raelynn's boots clacked against the marble floor as she bolted through the palace halls past groups of anxious officials and Scarlet Guards, some of whom yelled out at her. Raelynn's heart pounded and her vision wobbled as she slowed to a halt in front of large doors blocked by soldiers in gold and scarlet armor.

The Scarlet Guards, upon seeing Vree's limp body, lowered their swords slightly as Raelynn approached.

"This is the infirmary?" asked Raelynn, breathless from running.

The Scarlet Guards nodded and opened the doors slightly, calling into the wing, "We've got a severe one!"

The door opened wider and a young woman with smooth, dark skin walked out and looked at Raelynn holding Vree — a pool of blood was gathering below them from both their injuries. The young woman quickly ran up to them and looked at Vree's face, introducing herself. "Qerru-Mai An'Drui, Scarlet Lady. Did this happen just now in the courtroom?"

Raelynn nodded as Qerru-Mai took Vree into her arms.

"I wasn't there," said Qerru-Mai, "—getting the infirmary ready for Prince Eston's arrival. I found out about this all just a minute ago." She saw Raelynn's blood covered arm. "You're in bad shape too. We'll get you in."

Raelynn stumbled in dizziness. "Thank you."

Qerru-Mai stopped — Raelynn's cold accent left the air around them frozen. Qerru-Mai narrowed her brow, failing to hide her internal conflict. "You— you're the Cerebrian girl staying in the palace? This is the Nightsnake?" She held Vree carefully.

Raelynn brushed aside her eastern blonde hair with a bloody hand. "Yes."

Holding Vree, Qerru-Mai looked through the open door into the hospital wing. "I— I can get her in, she's badly hurt." Qerru-Mai turned back to Raelynn with a face of pain. "—just . . . give me a moment."

Raelynn waited as Qerru-Mai disappeared with Vree into the hospital wing, unsure whether she would see her alive again. The Scarlet Guards stood in silence, clearly uncomfortable and trying not to look at the disheveled, wounded Cerebrian girl.

After a moment or two, Qerru-Mai emerged holding a roll of cloth and a pail of water. She walked past the Scarlet Guards and up to Raelynn, unrolling the white cotton. "Arm," she prompted Raelynn to lift her injury. Qerru-Mai lifted the tin, pouring water mixed with some clear solution over Raelynn's arm, splashing scarlet over the floor.

Raelynn grimaced from the sting. "Why are you helping me?"

Qerru-Mai set down the pail and began wrapping Raelynn's arm. "You're hurt . . ." She pressed down on the cloth and carefully spun the roll around the wound. "Fillian cleared your stay with me, and I trust his heart and good intentions . . . but you are Cerebrian, and there are many things going on in this Palace tonight that are out of my control – it's my job to keep it safe."

As Qerru-Mai finished rolling the cloth, Raelynn ripped the end and secured it. "You're telling me to leave?"

"No one is sure what's happening or who is telling the truth, so I must take precautions. You must understand . . ." Qerru-Mai's eyes showed sincerity.

Raelynn nodded. "Yes, of course."

"I'll make sure your friend is tended to," said Qerru-Mai, picking up the pail and dropping the cloth in it, "and once everything is sorted out, once the chaos stops, we can revisit this."

Raelynn took one last look through the open door to a distant bed where Vree lay. "Thank you . . . I have to find my friend."

Qerru-Mai's expression went somber. "I'm sending more of my Scarlet Guard after Kyan, it's my job . . . you may get wrapped up in this. But go." Raelynn began to turn, but Qerru-Mai spoke up once more. "You'd risk your life for him?"

Raelynn stopped and looked back. She knew she had to try and save him. "He'd do the same for me." Walking past the golden-armored guards, Raelynn headed for the city in search of Kyan.

§

~Morning, February 10th
The Ferramish Countryside

Eston woke up in a sweat. Soft light filtered through the canvas of the carriage he rode in. A hundred memories flashed through his head as he tried to figure out which body he was in. What happened? Eston lifted his body up and flinched in pain from his bruises, but mostly from his stabbed foot. He looked around the carriage. The flap of the door let in wisps of freezing cold air that made him shiver even beneath his blankets.

The generals had put him in a carriage as soon as the battle at Stoneheart was over – two weeks ago. Despite his adamant refusals, the carriage horse-master and the soldiers accompanying him had pressed forward to Aunestauna to return him to safety. Their company traveled almost non-stop through Endlebarr and the forested hills of Ferramoor, headed for the palace where he could get treated for his stab wound. So much had happened to his other bodies since that battle. As Tayben, he had crossed the mountains and now rested in Silverbrook's forest sanctuary; as Calleneck, he had journeyed to the Goblin capital with Borius; and as Kyan– Eston's heart pounded again, remembering escaping from the Nightsnakes, going to the palace, but then the courtroom and his failed escape. Hyperventilating, Eston called out for his servant.

"Yes, Your Majesty. Is it your foot?" The little boy said.

Eston shook his head and tried to breath slowly. "What day is it?"

"I believe it's the 10th, Your Majesty."

Eston tried to remember. *It's the same day . . .* Eston searched his memories. *Riccolo will come to the palace today . . . then the trial will be held . . . then I'll try to escape but get captured . . .* Eston tried to remember if it was in a dream or reality that someone came to his prison cell and let him go.

"Your Majesty?" said Eston's servant.

Eston whipped his head and looked at the boy with wide eyes.

The boy, who sat on the other side of the carriage, slid away from Eston. "You're breathing very heavily, that's all — I was worried. You should lie back down."

Eston shook his head. "I'm fine."

"Are you sure it's not your foot that's hurting again because—"

"It's okay," Eston reassured him.

The carriage went over a pothole on the dirt road that spanned from Wallingford to Aunestauna. The cold air filtered in along with several snowflakes that landed in Eston's uncombed hair. The little servant boy looked at him in fear. Eston bit his lip from the pain in his foot and then his mind jumped back to the events he knew would occur today. *I need to stop all this. I don't know where Raelynn or Vree will be after the trial. I need to catch Riccolo.*

Eston turned to his servant. "How long until we get to Aunestauna?

"We're supposed to get there by next morning, one full day."

Eston shook his head. "No, no, I need to get there today."

"Your Majesty, I don't think—"

Eston slammed his fist down. "I have to get there today! I have to be in the Palace tonight!"

The carriage was silent, and Eston breathed heavily, feeling bad for raising his voice, but there was no way for the anyone to understand why he needed to be there for something that hadn't happened yet. Cold air filled his lungs; it had been nothing but wet and bumpy for the long journey home. Lying there bloody, infected, and sick to the stomach, Eston fought with himself. The whole way, he had argued for them to take him back to the front lines; but now, all he just needed to get back to Aunestauna as soon as he could, to stop the trial, catch Riccolo, and save Kyan.

The boy looked out a shutter of the carriage wall. "The snow isn't helping us go faster. And plus, I don't think—"

He pulled at his hair and clenched his teeth. "I don't care, I need to get to the palace!"

"Your Majesty, our horses are tired and—"

"Whip them or spur them or get new ones. There are plenty of farmers out here, just take theirs and—" Eston stopped, hearing the cruelty in his voice. The boy looked at him in concern, and Eston shook his head. "Just go and tell them that we mustn't take breaks and we have to be back to the palace this afternoon. Do whatever it takes – lighten the carriage, attach the soldiers' horses. Go!"

The boy bowed and jumped out of the carriage into the snow to go talk to the driver and the soldiers. Eston closed his eyes and bit his lip . . . the throbbing in his foot came back and the jostling carriage made his upset stomach rumble. He leaned over, picked up a bucket, and vomited into it. Breathing heavily, he lay back down, feeling powerless.

He shut his eyes and let images run through his head – the hundreds of corpses that were left behind after battles, the blood dripping from their noses and mouths, their glazed over, unfocused eyes. Eston clenched his fist as another sickening feeling spread through his body.

His mind wandered more – to the image of the monsters in Endlebarr he left behind. *I'm one of the only ones who knows about them . . . The generals can't control them . . . they're useless to Ferramoor without me . . . not even weapons . . .* The little boy came back into the carriage.

"Your Majesty," said the servant boy, "we did what you said and lightened the load and attached the soldiers' horses to help pull the carriage faster. We were going to stop for the night, but we'll keep traveling. Even so, the carriage driver says that we can't possibly make it back to Aunestauna until nightfall."

"Thank you." Eston closed his eyes and hoped. Would it be enough?

The boy left the carriage, leaving the prince by himself. He put his face in his hands, which were cracked, dry, and callused. His mind played back the memories of what was to come later today to Kyan, Vree, and Raelynn. Riccolo's smug grin stabbed into his brain. *That slimey bastard! That fucking madman!*

He felt sick, knowing what was going to happen, unable to stop it. There wasn't going to be enough time to get back before the trial. He knew he couldn't stop Riccolo from capturing Vree or the trial accusing Kyan as the leader of the Nightsnakes; he knew he couldn't tell himself to not go into the courtroom, tell himself that it was a trap, tell himself to run sooner, tell himself not to turn the corner in the alley where he slipped on the ice, tell him to get out while he still can. *I should've left Aunestauna when Vree told me to.*

Eston cried silently into his hands and felt the tears turn cold on his face from the blizzarding air that blew into the carriage as it traveled along the road to Aunestauna.

By the time Eston and his soldiers reached Aunestauna, night had fallen, and dread filled him to his core; he knew the trial was already over, Riccolo was gone, and he – as Kyan – was locked up in the prison. Eston's carriage wound through the dark streets up to the palace, passing buildings that had suffered no damage, and others that were still piles of ash mixed in with the snow. It was pulled by horses through the streets and up to the palace steps, but Eston couldn't think of anything but the cell in which he sat as Kyan at that very moment and the person who came to save him.

The carriage pulled through the giant gates of the palace, and for a moment, Eston could smell the saltwater breeze of the inlet. A crowd of Palace servants gathered around the caravan as a crew of doctors entered the carriage and assisted him in walking on one foot. The doctors reassured him he would be alright once they gave him the proper medicine. Eston couldn't pay attention, his thought occupied by the prison and the gallows.

The doctors and servants guided him to the hospital wing where a large fireplace crackled near his designated bed to keep him warm. The nurses brought over various medicines to drink, and the doctors resewed the stitches in his foot, pouring stinging medicine over the wound. After they had tended to the largest of Eston's wounds, he asked to leave.

A doctor shook his head. "I'm afraid I can't let you go yet, Your Majesty. You were stabbed in the foot and bruised badly on your side and shoulder."

A nurse placed a warm damp cloth on his forehead. "But the good news is, your wounds don't show signs of bad infection. If you keep taking this medicine, you should be out of here in not much more than a week."

Eston shook his head. "I need to go and—"

"Your Majesty," said another doctor, "you need to rest and heal."

The doors to the infirmary flung open and King Tronum entered with Scarlet Guards behind him. He walked over to Eston's bed and smiled. "Thank the Great Mother, you're alive," he said.

Eston looked around the hospital wing. "I need to talk with Fillian."

Tronum looked at the fireplace, his gray eyes reflecting the dancing orange light. "He left this morning to Abendale."

"I know; I need him back here."

"I sent him to head government operations there for the next few months."

Fillian needed to be here to vouch for Kyan. Eston slammed his fist down. "Father, he's my brother, you shouldn't have sent him off the day I came back!"

Tronum shook his head. "He'll see you in a few—"

"I have to talk to him!" shouted Eston. "The man on trial is innocent!"

"Mind your tone, boy!" Tronum bellowed.

The whole hall went silent, and doctors stared at him. *Who else can help?* thought Eston. *Fillian is the only one who knows the truth about Kyan, Raelynn, and Vree—*

Eston stopped as he saw Vree's bloody body lying on a hospital bed across the hall. She was clearly unconscious, and doctors anxiously tended to her injuries. *Where is Raelynn?* he thought. *No one here in the palace will believe me. Why should they have any reason to think I know the truth about the Nightsnakes? . . . I need to get to the prison before the execution.*

Eston looked up at King Tronum. "Qerru-Mai, she's the Scarlet Lady now, correct?"

The king nodded.

"Send for her. I can try and speak with her since Fillian isn't here."

Tronum looked at his Scarlet Guards. "You, come with me. And you, send for Lady An'Drui. Eston, I'll come back to check on you in a few hours." The soldiers bowed and left with their king from the hospital wing.

Eston impatiently waited for Qerru-Mai to arrive. All the while, scenes of the courtroom passed through his head. He looked over to the doctors tending to Vree. *I'm sorry this happened . . . but it'll be alright, I'll fix everything. Once I make sure I escape from prison, I'll write to Fillian, asking him to vouch for Kyan and confirm that Riccolo is the head of the Nightsnakes and not me.*

Qerru-Mai burst through the doors of the hospital wing and ran up to Eston. "You're safe!"

". . . Were you here earlier?" asked Eston.

Qerru-Mai nodded. "Yes, there were many people hurt after the chaos in the courtroom today, I'm sure you heard about—"

Eston pointed to Vree. "Did you see who brought her in? Was it a blonde, Cerebrian girl?"

Qerru-Mai looked over at Vree concerned. "Yes, I told her the Nightsnake girl could be treated here, but she had to leave."

"Why?" asked Eston.

Qerru-Mai looked shocked that it was even a question. "Eston . . . She's a Cerebrian . . . as the Scarlet Lady I can't risk something happening."

"Something *did* happen but it's not *them.* It's someone named Riccolo. That girl over there," he pointed to Vree, "she's innocent . . . so is the person they accused today."

"How do you know?" said Qerru-Mai.

Eston looked at Qerru-Mai in her dark eyes. "You just have to trust me . . ."

Qerru-Mai looked around the hospital wing nervously. "What are you asking of me?"

"I need you to mobilize the Scarlet Guard to get to the prison and free the accused Nightsnake."

Qerru-Mai shook her head. "I can't do that without proof he's innocent. That's an abuse of my power and authority."

Eston shook his head. "Then get me out of the palace; I know that someone is going to help him get out, and I think I know who it is. But in case I don't find her, send the Scarlet Guard to help search for the Cerebrian girl and protect her. Let me leave . . ."

"You really have a thing for using the commander of the Scarlet Guard to sneak you out, don't you?" said Qerru-Mai sarcastically, but with a worried face.

Eston closed his eyes. "You have to trust me; multiple innocent lives are at stake . . . my friends."

The hospital wing was silent, save for the soft crackling of the fire and the howling of the snowstorm outside. Qerru-Mai shook her head and bit her lip. "Okay."

Eston whipped the reins of Qerru-Mai's horse forward and passed through the gates of the palace, where many people were being questioned by the Scarlet Guard about the "Nightsnake leader" – Kyan. Eston lowered his head in his cloak as he rode her horse into the snow-covered city.

Navigating the streets, he headed toward the prison in the Third District. He knew nothing of Raelynn's location, only that if something were to go wrong, he had told her – as Kyan – to meet at the inlet docks; but only one thought drove Eston forward – getting to the prison and making sure Kyan and Raelynn get out safely. At least that was who he assumed came to save him.

Eston snapped the reins again. The cold air and snow pelted his face as he shot through the streets headed for the prison, which loomed in front of him illuminated by torchlight. The snow fell hard all around him in the night as he approached the front gates to the prison. Slowing the horse down, Eston stopped it behind a corner of a nearby building that allowed him to hide but still watch the front gates. Off in the distance, around another side of the prison in a courtyard open to the streets, a crowd of hundreds of people with torches yelled and chanted around the gallows. Eston's stomach dropped, seeing the noose loom tall and black in the torchlight. He felt sick, hearing the people of the city shouting with their torches, demanding they bring out the Nightsnake.

Adjusting his seat on Qerru-Mai's horse, Eston looked around in the freezing night air for Raelynn. People were still funneling toward the gallows, but no one was approaching the front gates. *Where is she? . . .* Eston kept searching, breathing into his hands to warm them up. Eston replayed his memory as Kyan, trying to remember what happened; but no one approached the front gates.

Nearly fifteen minutes had passed, and Eston's heart pounded – Raelynn was nowhere in sight – no one had come to the front gates – no one had come to take Kyan's place. The crowd at the gallows had tripled in size as news spread of the Lord of Thieves' capture, and their roar pierced through the blizzard. Judge Ratticrad had taken a seat on the stand opposite the gallows.

Every time a cloaked figure passed by the gates and the guards to the prison, Eston held his breath, but none entered. In the distance, the crowd began to quiet for the first time. Eston's stomach dropped and his hands turned even colder when he realized it was because the judge was speaking. *It's almost time.*

Eston frantically looked around. *Did I just miss something? . . .* The judge said something and the crowd yelled, making Eston breathe faster. *Come on, come on,* he thought, looking at the gates to the prison, but no one was speaking with the guards, entering, or exiting. *Come on! Time is running out!* Eston looked back to the gallows where the judge continued to speak and the crowd murmured. Torches lined the edge of the gallows, symbolizing the fires of hell in which the criminals would pay for their misdoings.

The crowd roared again, and Eston's heart pounded. *Come on! Why is no one coming to help?* He looked around again for Raelynn's shimmering blonde-white hair and saw nothing. The crowd around the gallows grew louder and Eston tapped his fingers together in nervousness. *No one is coming – why is no one coming? Time is running out! They're bringing out the prisoner soon! I swear someone came; I remember it, someone came to my cell and freed me – took my place . . .*

It was at that moment that Eston realized the plan – he realized there was a way to fix all of this. *That's it! That's the solution. It was never Raelynn. I was the one who set myself free the first time around, I just didn't know it was me!*

Suddenly he felt hope again. He ran his mind through it all. *Of course! I'm the Prince – the only person who the Scarlet Guard would ever let into the prison. I won't be able to stop the execution if they think it's a criminal, but if I free myself and escape, then I'll stay behind in this body and stop the execution. When they see who I am they'll stop the trial, let me go, and look for Kyan – but he'll be far enough away to be safe.*

Eston looked at the gallows and the torches around it, the roaring crowd, and the judge. *I can do this . . . I already did.* Eston limped up to the gates, slowly; his foot still throbbed. Eston approached the guards, who raised their swords. Eston removed his hood, and the Scarlet Guards on prison duty stepped back. "Your Majesty . . . what are you doing here?"

Eston slowly exhaled. "Let me see the prisoner."

The guards looked at each other. "They're almost ready for the execution, Your Majesty, I don't think–"

Eston raised his hand and spoke softly. "Do as I say."

The soldier bowed and opened the gate and led Eston through the torchlit hallways of the prison to the door behind which Kyan was held. Eston turned to him and raised his hand again. "Return to your post."

The prison guard nodded and left Eston with the other soldiers blocking the cell door. Eston spoke quietly, "Let me see the prisoner, and hand me the head cover . . . I want to put it on him myself." The guards bowed and handed him a cloth bag and opened the door.

Eston stepped into the dark cell and the door closed behind him. He saw himself sitting tied against the stone wall, blindfolded. His shirt was gone, and his body was bruised and bloody. Eston looked at himself, but his other body could not see him through the blindfold. It was the strangest feeling, seeing himself, knowing what thoughts were coursing through Kyan's head. Eston slowly stepped toward Kyan — toward himself.

Eston whispered the first words that came to his mind. "If you do exactly what I tell you, you will get out of this cell. Don't speak; the guards may hear." Eston knelt beside Kyan and grabbed the ropes that bound his hands and feet and began to untie them. Once again, he spoke in a whisper, "Do not take your blindfold off until you are ready to go out of this cell . . . once I get you untied, you will take this cloak and put it on." Eston untied the last knot and removed Kyan's ties but pressed on his shoulder to keep himself down.

Kyan whispered, "Who are you? What are you—"

Eston put his hand over Kyan's mouth to shut him up. He then removed his cloak and shirt and allowed Kyan to stand so he could hold it and guide Kyan's arms through. Then Eston sat down where Kyan had been tied up.

Eston whispered again. "You can walk out of the prison the way you came in. The guards won't stop you. Place the hood of the cloak over your head and keep your head down. Walk slowly and don't look at anyone. Once you turn around, you may take off your blindfold, but do not look back . . ." A tear slid down Eston's covered face. "You're free, now go . . ." Eston's heart pounded as he heard himself leave the room and walk down the hallway — set free. He breathed a sigh of relief — it had worked.

But Eston's stomach lurched when he heard several armor-clanking footsteps coming down the hallway a minute later. *Shit, they're too early — there's not enough time for Kyan to get out far enough.* Eston's heart began to race. *I need to give myself more time to escape.* Eston quickly scanned the jail cell and grabbed the rope and the execution headbag. *They have to think I'm Kyan for just a bit longer.* He quickly put on the headbag, which hung to his shoulders, and in twenty or so seconds, he tried to tie knots around his own ankles and wrists behind his back.

Just as he pulled a crude knot tight, the door swung open. Anxiety spread through him as multiple soldiers walked into the cell. They grabbed him and untied him from the wall, pulling him up to his feet. A guard spoke. "Get up, you filthy scum . . . the gallows are ready for you." Eston walked along slowly with the guards and a bag over his head, blinding him. His body was bruised and cut enough from battle for him to pass as Kyan.

Eston shook his head as they pushed him forward. *This isn't enough time.* The noise of the crowd outside drew near. *But I have to reveal myself . . .*

Hoping that he had given Kyan enough time to escape, he pushed back against the guards and shouted, "Stop!"

His stomach dropped when they kept pushing him forward. "Stop! I'm the Prince! I'm Eston Wenderdehl!"

The Scarlet Guards laughed. "And I'm your daddy King Tronum. Prince Eston just left a minute ago. Nice try little shit." They pushed him forward and around a turn toward the noise of the crowd around the gallows.

Eston's heart beat out of his chest. "No! Stop! Take my headbag off! I'm the Prin–"

Suddenly, a piece of cloth tightened hard around his mouth, pressing the headbag into his teeth – they were gagging him. Eston tried to yell, but all that came out was a pitiful muffled cry. He began to writhe – pushing and kicking at them. Shouting in vain to let him go. He thrashed and tried to hit, but the prison guards just tightened their grip on him.

Eston screamed out of his gagged mouth. Then a shock of pain rang through his skull as he felt the hilt of a sword bash into it. Another hard hit to the head made his mind swirl as the guards dealt blows to his knees and shoulders – he was completely limp.

Dragging Eston through the prison hallway, they opened the latched doors to the outside. The roar of the unseen crowd pounded against his ears. People spat at him, waved their torches, and chanted curses against him – the *Lord of Thieves.* The Scarlet Guards pushed Eston forward to what he knew were the gallows. Eston tried to struggle, but the pain overtook him, and the guards' grip on his body was too strong to overcome.

Images of Benja flashed through his head. Eston pictured his face at the gallows as the door opened beneath him. The crowd chanted more, and Eston was pushed up the stairs of the gallows. He tried to yell, but his voice was hoarse and weak. He was breathing too fast to get anything out. The cold night air and snow mixed with the smell of smoke from all the torches. Eston's head pulsed and his breathing quickened; his body lay limp in the hands of the guards.

Suddenly the world seemed to close in around him as the dread filled his blood. His senses were muted, and neither the snow nor the air seemed cold. The crowd's roar began to sound muffled as a feeling of sickness spread through his body, threatening to make him vomit. His blood felt chilled, and a darkness spread through his soul. Eston barely breathed, but his heart pounded so that he felt every pulse go throughout his entire frozen body. Eston tried to think clearly, but nothing else went through his head.

Judge Ratticrad pounded his gavel and the crowd quieted. Above the howling wind, the judge spoke out. "Citizens of Ferramoor! We have gathered tonight to witness the execution of the head conspirator and leader of the infamous thief gang – The Nightsnakes. *The Lord of Thieves* has tarnished the sanctity of this glorious city in the eyes of our Great Mother, defiling Her law and harming Her children, murdering and robbing hundreds. He killed our Prophet, kidnapped our Queen, and conspired to overthrow our government and destroy our kingdom. He has therefore given up his right to live."

The crowd below Eston roared and cursed and spit toward the gallows.

Ratticrad continued, "The head cover shall be kept on the criminal for the remaining minute of his life; the Great Mother wishes not to see the faces of her disloyal and vain children. By the power of the Great Mother and the Crown of Ferramoor, I now commence this execution."

The crowd roared once more as the guards pushed Eston forward onto the trap door and placed the noose around his neck. Expanding his last bit of strength he had, Eston kicked a soldier and yelled from his gagged mouth. Another shock of pain in the back of his head from the hilt of a sword made his vision spin. Eston's heart pounded so that every inch of his body felt the pulses. Images of Benja shot through his mind again, and his breathing quickened. In his blurry mind, he could manage one thought. *This is it . . .*

Judge Ratticrad slammed the gavel down once more and quieted the crowd. The snowstorm around the gallows howled and the torches of the hundreds of spectators crackled, but Eston could hear his heartbeat above it all. A precious thing that never meant so much — a heartbeat. The judge spoke out, "Let it begin!"

Tears streamed down Eston's face like never before. Faces flashed through his head – Aunika, Dalah, and Fillian. *I'm sorry,* he thought. He didn't want to leave his little brother alone in this cruel, cruel world . . . He remembered Fillian running up behind him to mess up his hair and spitting off a bridge with him. But he also remembered Fillian's face as he watched Aunestauna burn, and he remembered Fillian's tears for their mother. Eston pictured his smiling, selfless brother. He cried helplessly beneath the dark headbag. *It's your turn, Fillian . . . I love you, brother.*

Sobbing, Eston shut his eyes and shouted gagged words that no one could hear. The door beneath his feet opened, and Eston felt a brief sensation of falling before a crack of pain . . . and then darkness.

IRIDESCENCE
Chapter Thirty Eight

The only thing he could see was light . . . pure, iridescent light swirling softly around him. His whole body floated in glowing streams of energy. Vibrant colors danced across his skin, and streams of light twirled around his legs. As far as he could tell, he wasn't breathing, but he didn't feel the need to. Like a galaxy was being created around him, thousands of little specks of light sprung into existence as his body slowly drifted into more light. His mind was blank, as rivers of light seamlessly drifted into and out of his body, lighting up his skin and veins. It was silent, save for a small sound inside his head that could only be described as a shimmering. His body felt weightless as it drifted in the light. He couldn't tell how long he floated there before he heard the muffled sound of someone calling out his name — a name so long forgotten he hardly recognized it. *Tayben!*

~Morning, February 11th
Silverbrook's Hollow, Southeastern Endlebarr

Suddenly, Tayben was pulled up onto the grass and mossy shore of the pond of light in Silverbrook's hollow in Endlebarr. Silverbrook quickly turned Tayben over as he coughed up water that vanished into the air. The pond of light rippled and sent tiny stars dancing underneath the golden canopy of the hollow. Tayben's heart raced, as if he had just awoken from a nightmare.

"Tayben!" said Silverbrook in a panic. "I couldn't find you this morning! Are you alright? Tayben, look at me, what happened?"

Tayben coughed up more water and his chest convulsed. He shook his head and kept trying to calm his breathing.

Silverbrook quickly put her hand to his head and let a stream of white Taurimous course into him. She closed her eyes, trying to read his thoughts and memories. Her eyes shot open, and she grabbed Tayben forcefully. "You died as Eston— that body — the Prince of Ferramoor – you died . . ."

Tayben coughed again and she rushed a stream of light into his chest to try and slow down his racing heart.

"Tayben just breathe, you'll be alright. You're safe; you're with me; you're okay . . . you're alive."

Tayben's eyes darted around at the enormous trees of the hollow with frightened eyes.

Silverbrook put a hand on his face. "Look at me, Tayben. It's okay . . . you're alive in this body, I promise you . . . Tayben, breathe and try to calm your mind . . . you're safe."

Tayben's breathing slowed, and Silverbrook sent another stream of light into his head to try and calm him. His eyes stopped darting around and began to focus more.

Silverbrook felt his thoughts and memories and began to cry with him. "It's alright, Tayben . . . You're safe." She sat there with Tayben for some time, staring into the lake of light as he tried to comprehend everything in tears. "How did you fall in?"

Tayben tried to get up, but his limbs were weak. "I— I was sleeping in this body— I think— and I— now I'm here. I d-don't remember how I—"

Silverbrook nodded and stared at the light. "The Ether does work in mysterious ways . . . I wouldn't be surprised if it moved your body to the lake at the moment of Eston's death to protect your soul, allowing Eston's memories to transfer to you while he was in *limbo* before he was lost into the void . . . Did you see anything after death?"

Tayben finally sat up and breathed heavily with his arms crossed over his knees. "I— I didn't see anything, feel anything." His cloak was drenched in water, and little beads of light dripped from his bottom lip and his nose. He whispered to himself, "I'm alive . . ." He stared at the lake of shimmering light. "I'm dead b— but I'm alive as well." He turned to Silverbrook. "Is my other body gone? Eston— am I—"

"Dead," whispered Silverbrook. "Yes . . ." She put a hand on his shoulder. "I'm so sorry, Tayben . . . I don't know what to say."

Tayben stared blankly at the pool of stars in front of them which surrounded the center island of the hollow with Silverbrook's treehouse. He watched the specks of light dance around in the water. "What's going to happen?"

"That's a question with many answers," said Silverbrook.

"Fillian will take my place as heir?"

She nodded.

"I'll be living every day only three times . . ."

Silverbrook stared with Tayben at the lake of glowing water.

"I—" Tayben couldn't think of what to say. "I don't know whether to be grateful or saddened."

Silverbrook brushed a tear from her eye for a reason Tayben couldn't figure out. "It's bittersweet. You have to leave that life behind, but you get another chance to live . . ." Silverbrook's mind trailed off somewhere distant, whether past, future, or present, it didn't matter. "You are something extraordinary, Tayben . . ."

Tayben sniffed up tears and tried thinking of something else. "I'm assuming it's sunrise?" he asked, "because I switched bodies?"

Silverbrook nodded. "Sunrise, yes . . . I felt a disturbance in the air and rushed out of the house to see you motionless in the lake of Taurimous." She looked at Tayben, who was still drenched and shaking. "I think you need something to calm you down. Your mind is racing a million miles an hour right now. You've also lived after death – something no one has ever done . . . Let's start with a change of clothes, shall we? You're drenched. I'll make you something to fill your stomach. I'm here for anything you need, alright?"

Tayben nodded and slowly followed her into the colossal tree that served as her house and walked up to his room to put on new clothes. Tayben stood by the dresser and slowly opened the drawers, his mind still haunted by the sounds of the crowd at the gallows. He couldn't feel the presence of Eston's part of his mind. The vacancy felt so big, so empty and lonely. A vast void had been hollowed out in his soul. *If I can't feel that . . . does that mean there's nothing after death?* Tayben's heart rate picked up, but he pulled out a pair of clothes to distract his mind.

From downstairs, Tayben heard Silverbrook call. "Tayben, are you alright?"

Tayben stared blankly out the glassless window into the golden autumn forest before replying, "Yes, I'll be right there."

"Noxberry juice or renberry juice?" she called up to him, with a little hint of anxiousness in her voice.

Tayben opened the door and walked down the crooked spiraling stairs. "Renberry, please." Each step was angled and curved, growing from the tree itself, and soft light filtered through the openings into the center of the tree. He stepped into the twisted and gnarled wooden kitchen, where Silverbrook was mixing something in a cup with a small oak rod. Tayben looked around the small kitchen within the tree. The tiniest breeze blew through the openings for windows.

Silverbrook handed him a wooden cup. "I picked the berries when I was out in the forest yesterday."

"Thank you." Tayben took the juice, and both the fragrance and the sugary sweetness running down his throat helped calm him down.

"Do you want to talk?" asked Silverbrook.

Tayben looked out the window into the glade which sparkled with the light of glowing butterflies. "I don't know what to say right now, or even what to think . . . I'm just . . ."

"In shock," said Silverbrook.

Tayben nodded and said to himself more than to her, "I guess you could say that." Tayben looked at Silverbrook and could tell she had been crying. "I just need to sit down and think for a while."

She nodded. "Yes . . . yes, do that." She looked outside and sniffed. "I'm going to go tend to Fernox and then I'll check in on you." She left the kitchen to see her winged lion and disappeared out the front door, leaving Tayben alone to his thoughts running wild.

For a few minutes, Tayben's head ran through the memory of his death. Feeling scared and alone, he got up and opened the front door, following where Silverbrook had gone. On the island in the lake of light, Tayben walked around the giant tree that was Silverbrook's house, and saw her standing there with her enormous, winged lion. Fernox's white body shimmered ahead of her, and she seemed to be in a trance. Tayben noticed something strange happening with the lion's eyes as he approached.

"What is that?" he asked. "Your beasts do it too — their eyes. They suck you into another reality, but your body truly does still stay here."

"One of my favorite experiments — if you can call it that. It's the way I can communicate with my beasts . . . and Fernox as well."

"How does it work?" he asked, stepping close to Fernox and putting his hand on his soft fur. The lion let out a deep but gentle purr.

She paused. "You've asked me about the Ether, the World Beyond, the universal force of many names . . ."

He nodded, feeling nervous.

Silverbrook put her hand on Fernox's massive, snow-white forehead. "It's what connects life, time, space, light, magic, everything all together. It's what makes a flower grow and what makes love strong. When you wield a Taurimous in the body of Calleneck — when I wield mine — you are manifesting your connection from your spirit to this world, in a physical form."

Tayben stood there thinking, finding everything very abstract.

She looked into the lion's eyes. "Fernox's mind connects souls with space and time — that's what our memories are. He taps into that Ether to show us memories — his, ours, other people's." Silverbrook looked out onto her gleaming lake of iridescent light and her glade of glowing flowers and butterflies. "Everything exists through the Ether. It's what I've studied my whole life, how I was able to discover new forms of magic and new uses for it. All I was doing was tapping into the preexisting connections between everything. And I know that there is still so much more to learn and to do . . ."

The air hung silent and still for quite some time before Tayben was able to find words. "How do you know that's how the Ether works?"

Silverbrook motioned around her. "Look at what I've created . . . You're proof of it."

Tayben raised an eyebrow. "What do you mean?"

She looked out into her glade of glowing water and plants. "What do I mean? I mean you, yourself, don't live time linearly. Once you live a day and go back to live it again in another body, you practically know the future. That power comes from the Ether. Your soul is connected to time in a strange way, and it exists across space to inhabit four – now three – bodies. You used the magic of the Ether, given by the Nymphs, inside your body as a Phantom and outside your body as an Evertauri. In moments of stress or intense emotion, your soul can sporadically jump through time on its own. Tayben, you are proof of how the Ether can exist fully within the human form. How your soul can perfectly connect with the world . . . It was my greatest—" Silverbrook stopped herself.

Tayben looked up at her with a fast-beating heart. "It was your greatest what?"

Silverbrook looked away from Tayben and back to Fernox. "I was going to say that it was my greatest wish to be able to connect to the Ether the way you do . . ." Her voice trailed off as she petted Fernox.

Tayben got the sense that she was hiding something but decided not to push further.

Silverbrook turned to Tayben, "That's why I protected you."

Tayben studied her gaze. "Protected me?"

Silverbrook took a leaf out of Fernox's mane as he ruffled his wings. "You can't have thought you were all alone these past months as a Phantom. Why do you think you kept seeing my flowers?"

Tayben looked into Fernox's eyes and felt himself transported back into a memory of his first battle of Camp Stoneheart where Silverbrook's beast first attacked the Phantoms and paralyzed them. Tayben heard the slashing of the claws of her beast as he dragged Gallien into the hollowed tree trunk.

In a second, Tayben was thrown back into reality, and he turned again to Silverbrook. "That's why I was the only Phantom not paralyzed . . . your protection dulled the effects of your beast so I could escape. But why did that beast still attack me?"

"I lost control of it shortly after I left Aunestauna. But the others, I kept an influence over. Why do you think my beasts became loyal to *you*? Why do you think the walls of Taurimous dissolved around them as soon as *you* touched them? To let *you* control them."

The thought sank into Tayben. "You entrusted me with your beasts so that they could protect me. I healed so quickly after my fall off the Great Gate because of your spells. Everything you've done was to protect me . . . Why?"

"It wasn't perfect. But overall, yes, I did what I could from afar."

"But why did you do it? You're the one who sent me back into the forest after coming here the first time."

Silverbrook ran her hands over Fernox's strong wings. "I wanted you to have a chance to decide for yourself what you wanted — what you thought was right. If I had kept you here instead — if you were never forced to make that decision on your own, risking your very life — you could not have truly trusted the outcome; it wouldn't have been genuine."

Tayben walked around the winged lion. "You wanted all of my bodies and minds to influence the others, to figure out the true path, to decide which side of the war I want to fight on."

Silverbrook smiled. "There are not just two sides to this fight, Tayben, but thousands. Everyone's motives and beliefs are different."

"Is that why the Nymphs still gave the Phantoms their power?"

Silverbrook stopped petting Fernox and turned to Tayben. "Why do you say that?"

Tayben chose his words carefully. "If someone's motives are noble, then the Nymphs would see them as pure, no matter what side they're fighting for, as long as they protect Endlebarr and the Nymphs. Would they not?"

Silverbrook smiled. "You're exactly right, Tayben." Silverbrook paused and looked at the grass and moss beneath her toes. "That's the lesson it took me many years to learn. The enemy we're fighting . . . they aren't necessarily evil. They're not any less human than the rest of us. Xandria has done bad things, yes, but she's done everything for her people to build a strong and safe land for thousands."

"Then why is everyone fighting?" asked Tayben. As soon as he said it, the words settled heavily in his mind.

Silverbrook shook her head. "Because people hate each other . . . and people love each other. We fight those we fear to protect those we love."

Tayben thought for a while and looked out into Silverbrook's forest sanctuary, watching a glowing violet butterfly briefly land on a flower then take off again. "But if Xandria is not entirely evil, why does she need to fall?"

Silverbrook spoke again. "I see into the future. Not full events but feelings and pictures and people . . . Tayben, you know King Tronum is ill; he will soon die. I see two paths in the clouded future following his death. On one path, Xandria dies with her brother, leaving their rivalry to the ashes of history. But on the other path where Xandria lives and remains in power, I feel death and pain on a scale I've never felt before as she conquers all of Endellia. If the new world, however, is handed off to Fillian as king over Ferramoor, there could be peace . . ."

Tayben her words sink in for a moment. Half to himself and half to Silverbrook, he asked, "Why was I chosen to be a Phantom?"

Silverbrook sighed. "That's one question to which I have no answer."

For a while they stood with Fernox and said nothing, listening to the lion's low purrs. Tayben thought about his situation, how he couldn't return to his home in Woodshore, nor could he stay here his whole life. Tayben tried to keep his breath steady. "What do I do now?"

Silverbrook thought for a moment. "This lake of light around my home is a place I created to let the Ether exist fully without restraining it. I thought you had died in this body when I found you in it this morning. How could anyone survive being surrounded by the Ether in its purest form? But the Ether seems to exist within you more than anyone in the world, even me. I can't step in that lake for long without losing consciousness, but you can."

Tayben gazed into the swirling lake of light as she continued.

"The connection to the Ether that exists here; how I could watch you as a Phantom from here in my hollow. With years of practice, I could access little pieces of space and time. Trying to watch most people is like trying to remember a face in a dream – very vague and blurry. But I could always see you more clearly – your soul is part of the Ether. The connection that dwells here is how I can see that the Ferramish and Cerebrian soldiers are headed for each other to one spot in this forest where there will soon be a bloodbath like no other."

Tayben's heart beat quickly. "What do you want me to do?"

"See what you can glimpse by going back into the lake of Taurimous. I don't know what you'll find, but I think it will help."

Tayben looked again at the iridescent glow of the lake. "Before, I need to ask you one more question."

Silverbrook nodded.

Tayben spoke slowly. "If space, life, and time are all one and the same," he said, choosing his words carefully, "if time doesn't exist in a line but rather all at once, if I can experience time differently than everyone else, does that mean if I see something happen in one life, I can change it in another?"

Silverbrook stood silently. But rather than giving Tayben a reassuring answer, she simply whispered. "I don't know . . . I would think that's not the case."

Tayben felt a feeling of nervousness overtake him. "So if I see something in there; if I see what the future could be and how to get there, do I not have a choice?"

"You have a choice to create the future you want," said Silverbrook, "but you have to weigh the costs. There may be much pain on the path to peace."

Tayben felt helpless, but slowly stepped toward the pool of light until he stood at its edge. Before he stepped in, he turned back. "You need to connect to your beasts, talk to them; you need to tell them what to do and to stay with the Ferramish Army. Fillian will take my place commanding forces in Endlebarr. You need to get them to follow Fillian when he arrives."

Silverbrook nodded. "I will . . . I promise."

Tayben turned back to the lake of Taurimous. Beams of light swam like minnows through its endless depths. Taking a deep breath, Tayben took his first step in, letting the light swirl over his foot and around his ankle. He took another step, then another, letting his body drift slowly into the lake. He could no longer feel his legs, but he kept moving slowly into the pool of Taurimous.

He did not know when he was fully submerged, how long he had been there, or where in the pool of light he was. Time and space seemed to melt around him — his body could be miles tall or that half his mind was in the future and half was in the past. He felt weightless as the little shimmering specks of light circled around him. He no longer felt the need to breathe, and his heart even stopped beating, letting his consciousness exist outside his body and in the light surrounding him. Like in a dream, where time seems to pass in strange ways, Tayben felt his mind drifting. It wasn't with sight that he saw the thousands of soldiers crossing through the forest hundreds of miles away, and it wasn't with sound that he heard the cries of grief-stricken Fillian and Tronum, but he felt all of it. Without consciously thinking, the knowledge of what was to come sank into his body, and the emotions of all the people close to him shimmered like little stars, dancing around him. Like a dream, flashes of events coursed through the endless world around him — crashes of swords, the flapping sail of a ship, the tightening of the noose, the roar of a lion, a blinding flash of white lighting up a valley, the death of his mother the queen, the sting of snow, the cut of a blade, a glowing rose petal, raindrops pelting his skin, falling rock, blood covering his fingers, three different hands wielding Eston's gleaming sword, the crimson red light of Calleneck's Taurimous, the beating of Fernox's wings, falling ash, the trumpeting of horns, tears falling onto his body, endless blood and death. For a time unknown to Tayben, he drifted in a state of dreamlike existence.

Without knowing whether only seconds had passed or whether it was years later, Tayben became aware of the grass beneath his toes. He looked up, disoriented, and saw Silverbrook standing there.

She walked forward and put her hand on Tayben's face. "What did you see? You were in there for over a week. I was afraid you were gone. Tayben . . . what did you see? What happened to your other bodies while you were in there?"

Tayben looked at Fernox, standing tall with his wings and mane glistening white. A flood of memories from what he had done in his other lives in the past days entered his mind, colliding with his visions of the future. He looked back to Silverbrook. "I know what I have to do."

PASSAGE TO THE HEAVENS
Chapter Thirty Nine

~Late Night, February 10th
Aunestauna, Ferramoor

Raelynn pushed further into the roaring crowd, trying to get closer to the gallows. Her insides turned cold at the sight of Kyan being brought out from the prison through the crowd of spectators holding blazing torches. A dark bag was covering his head and Scarlet Guards walked him up the steps of the gallows. She could see him trying to fight his way out of their arms, but he seemed weak, like he had suffered severe beatings. He also seemed to be injured in the foot, limping like he hadn't before. The deafening crowd chanted and spat at him, and Raelynn struggled to get closer to the gallows. She shouted out his name, but she knew he couldn't hear her in the crowd.

The judge cracked his gavel and spoke out the sentence. The Scarlet Guards placed the noose around the prisoner's neck and Raelynn wished he could see her through the bag on his head.

Raelynn's body froze as the door opened and his neck snapped. She screamed out in horror, her face flushed red. She slammed her way through the crowd, which began to quiet, hearing her cry. She reached the base of the gallows next to the guards and fell to her knees. A Scarlet Guard ceremoniously ripped the head cover off the hung corpse to reveal the thief but instead gasped in shock. A woman near the gallows shouted, *"The Prince! It's the Prince! The Prince is dead!"*

The crowd erupted in screams and the Scarlet Guards quickly cut the noose and took it off Eston's neck, pressing his chest and blowing into his mouth to try to revive him. Many other Scarlet Guards formed a barrier around the gallows to prevent people from trying to see the prince's body. The judge waved his hand, but there was no hope of quieting the crowd. The Scarlet Guards tried to force people to exit the scene, but the mob fought back and broke their line. Shouts of conspiracy and fear filled the air. "They killed him! The Scarlet Guard killed him!"

A man snatched a shield from a Scarlet Guard, knocking him down and slamming the point into his head, spewing a fountain of red onto the rioters.

Another group forced a Scarlet Guard to the ground, kicking him and spitting on him. Up near the gallows, the Scarlet Guard were too busy defending the Eston's corpse to prevent the mob from getting to Judge Ratticrad, who fell into the sea of rioters with a horrifying scream. "Murderer!" The crowd screamed as they stabbed and mutilated his body, tossing a fat, severed arm into the air.

The brawl did nothing but intensify as Raelynn pushed her way against the flow of people and away from the gallows. Running down the street, she saw a platoon of Scarlet Guards rushing her way toward the commotion. She ducked into an alley in case they were looking for her. *What is going on? Why was the prince at the gallows? Was it Riccolo? Was it Cerebria? If the prince is dead,* she thought, *then where is Kyan?*

§

~Hours Later

Prince Fillian's mind drifted in dream as he slept in his canvas tent in the countryside. En route to Abendale, his royal caravan had stopped just south of Greenwash on the southern fork of the Green River, whose banks had begun to ice over in the storm. He had been ordered to oversee government operations in Abendale while the capital was rebuilt to its full strength. *"To get practice as the diplomat you'll need to be,"* in his father's words.

He turned over beneath his wool blanket, shivering from the cold, heavy air. Half awake, he could hear the rustling trees around the tent and the breeze that blew snow through the campsite. His tent was erected beneath a willow tree, and the gusts of wind made the switch branches whip and snap. He turned over again, struggling to find a comfortable spot where rocks or roots didn't stick up into his back. Feeling his dreamy thoughts wandering, he was pulled back out of sleep by the sound of snow crunching under boots outside his tent.

The sound stopped just outside the tent, where a Guard was posted. Fillian could only make out a few whispers.

. . . in Aunestauna. No one knows where the Nightsnakes are or how they were able to . . . chaos in the city streets and the palace . . .

. . . bring Prince Fillian back?

He fully awoke when the guards pulled aside the tent flap and walked over to him. He stirred and sat up from the ground, wiping his eyes and yawning. "What's going on?" he could barely make out the guards in the torchlight.

One of the guards spoke. "Your Majesty, something has happened to your brother. We have been ordered to return you to the palace."

Fillian's heart raced. "What happened? Is he alright?"

"We don't know the details, but we know you may be in danger. Please come with us."

Fillian put on a coat. "Where?"

"Back to Aunestauna. Quickly now!"

Fillian nodded and followed them out of his tent, preparing to depart back to the palace.

The sky to the east was beginning to brighten into day by the time Fillian and the guards reached the capital and the gates to the palace. Bells were ringing and Fillian could hear shouting in the distance. Navigating their way into the palace, Fillian ran with two Scarlet Guards on either side of him, following them down the hallways of the palace. "Will someone please tell me what's going on now?"

The Scarlet Guards ignored Fillian and shouted at people blocking the hallway as they ran through, trying to get Fillian to the Safe Room. Fillian's breathing was fast, and his stomach felt queasy. *What's going on?*

Finally, the guards reached a doorway in front of which a dozen Scarlet Guards stood. The soldiers opened the thick metal doors and led Fillian inside where he found Tronum sitting on a chair with his own guards on either side. The doors shut behind Fillian with a bang. "Father, what's going on? What happened to Eston?"

King Tronum's eyes were red and his body looked weak. He remained silent.

"Father! What's going on?! Why are we here and where is Eston?!"

Tronum looked at Fillian with tears in his eyes. "Your brother died at the gallows last night."

Fillian looked at the guards to try and see if his father was hallucinating. "W— What?"

Tronum spoke again. "They thought— they thought they were executing the Lord of Thieves — the trial from yesterday evening. They— they hung him and took off the headbag and somehow it was your brother. We still don't know how . . . Some trickery from those Nightsnakes, those vermin!" Tronum slammed his fist down in rage. "I should have scattered them like insects and killed them all!"

Fillian's world stood still. His mind seemed blank, trying to find some way to wake up from this nightmare; but looking at his father's tears, he realized the reality of what had happened. His father began to cry into his hands and the doors to the room opened again. Surrounded by his own Scarlet Guards came Prophet Ombern's successor, Prophet Mirriotus.

The ebony-skinned man with a long white beard walked up to Fillian and put a hand on his shoulder. One of the soldiers in the room was Liann Carbelle from the Battle of Aunestauna. He stepped forward and spoke. "Prince Fillian, you are now heir to the throne of Ferramoor. You will take over your brother's duties immediately. Prophet Mirriotus is here to make the change official."

Fillian's mind was still blank, trying to understand what was happening.

Prophet Mirriotus stepped forward. "I know you are in shock right now, Prince Fillian; but you must clear your mind and listen."

Fillian's eyes still stared off into the air, but somehow his head slowly nodded.

Prophet Mirriotus opened a scroll and read with a deep, commanding voice, accented subtly from the Shallow Green Isles. "Will you, Fillian Wenderdehl, son of Tronum Wenderdehl and Eradine Lameira, assume the position of Heir to the Throne of Ferramoor, take responsibility for the wellbeing of your people, swear to the Great Mother to act justly and courageously, and assume the title of King of Ferramoor should your father die?"

Fillian looked at his father and allowed the first tear to roll down his face. "I–" he swallowed a lump in his throat and breathed in deeply. "I, Fillian Wenderdehl, do swear this."

Prophet Mirriotus bowed. "May the Great Mother bless you."

Tronum embraced Fillian and looked at him with his pale gray eyes. Tronum's hands shook from his disease, but he placed a firm hand on Fillian nonetheless. "Ferramoor looks to you. You'll be leading it soon." Tronum reached back and lifted a shimmering longsword off the table with a Royal Crest engraved in the hilt, along with a letter 'E.' "This was your brother's . . ." said Tronum. "I want you to keep it as a reminder."

"I can't . . . I was never supposed to be your heir; I'm not ready."

The king looked him in the eye and spoke with a weary but unwavering voice. "You have to be."

Fillian looked down at the sword and slowly took it into his hands, letting a tear fall onto the shimmering silver blade. Covering the bottom of the engraved 'E' with his thumb, an 'F' for Fillian emerged. Fillian had always been there behind Eston; this was always a possibility, no matter how remote it seemed.

Anger took over the king once more. "Liann," he said to the soldier, "find the men responsible for the death of my son and bring them justice! Anyone withholding knowledge of their names, their location, or any rumors they've heard will stand trial and hang like my son!"

Prophet Mirriotus stepped forward. "We should exercise caution dispensing the Great Mother's ultimate justice until we know more about–"

"I don't care about *Her* justice; THIS IS *MY* JUSTICE! *MY* SON!" His face shook with rage as he looked back at Liann, speaking in a furious and unstable whisper. "Find them. Find them if you have to tear down the city. Question everyone, look through every brothel and sewer and pit where these creatures hide . . . Avenge my son."

§

~Dawn

Raelynn sat against a wooden post on the dock as the sun rose – arms and knees tucked to her chest, waiting for any sign of Kyan. A dense cloud of rising steam formed over the ocean and filled the freezing morning air. Mist seeped up from the cracks between the planks of wood, clouding the air with a heavy fog that muffled the distant sounds of the city shoreline. Raelynn closed her eyes, listening to the icy water a few feet below ebbing and sloshing. The docks creaked with every passing swell, and the waves softly lapped against the rocky shore. Boats with soft bells lightly tapped against the wooden docks, pulling on their ropes.

The rhythmic sounds of the water and docks were interrupted by a distant voice calling out. Raelynn opened her eyes and looked east through the swirling fog lit by the obscured risen sun. Walking toward her was a dark figure, who called out again. "Raelynn?"

Slowly, the figure's face came into view and tears of relief streamed down her face as Kyan ran up and embraced her. She dwelt for a second in the warmth of Kyan's arms, putting her head to his shoulder and crying. "What happened? I– I don't know what's going on. I–"

"It's okay," said Kyan, holding the back of her head. Waiting until Raelynn calmed down, he explained what had happened and told her the truth – that Eston made the choice himself to take Kyan's place, that Eston thought he would be able to save himself at the last minute but couldn't.

After the story, Raelynn looked over to Kyan as they sat on the dock in the morning fog. "We have to tell Vree you're okay," she said. "I brought her to the palace infirmary, but there's no way to get back inside now that they're searching for you." The frigid water below them churned and bubbled, filling the silence.

Kyan looked up through the misty shoreline air at the silhouette of the palace atop its cliff. "She's being looked after by Qerru-Mai and the palace doctors; she'll recover. If Fillian is back in the palace, we can get a letter to him and Vree explaining what happened."

After a while, they made their way back into the city, staying low and discreet. Nailed to the walls of shops and inns were warrants for Kyan's arrest, along with rewards for any information on the Nightsnakes. As they hurried through the streets, they passed mobs of rioters burning down the Bazaar. A bald man stood atop a barricade of fruit crates shouting out conspiracies. "It's the Cerebrians who done it! If the Prince ain't safe, none of us are! They're here in the city!" Another man shouted back. "It was the little brother! He killed Eston to take the throne himself!" More voices, more rumors. "It was the wrath of the Great Mother striking down another cursed Wenderdehl! Soon they'll all be gone!"

Scarlet Guards marched through the smoke-filled streets, trying to contain the grounds. A man caught stealing bread was clubbed by the hilt of a sword and pinned to the ground as he screamed in pain. A group of women scurried into a tavern as more Scarlet Guards marched by.

Kyan and Raelynn ducked into an alleyway and onto the next street, where a group of young men were throwing rocks at a shield wall of Scarlet Guards, cursing and screaming at them. "Motherfucking traitors! Prince killers!" One man rushed at the Scarlet Guards, but they cut him down and reformed. "Traitors!" yelled the mob. "We're coming for you! You can't stop us all!"

Street after street was filled with absolute chaos as rumors and fear spread throughout the city. Finally able to find sanctuary at *The Little Raven*, they penned a letter to Vree explaining what had happened. They told her that she was in good hands with Qerru-Mai, and to not fear telling the truth to anyone. Kyan finished the letter with the words, *"I'll come back for you."* They addressed it to Prince Fillian and sent it off with a messenger bird at a mailtower.

~Night, February 11th

Together, they walked through the moonlit streets and up to a rooftop in the Second District to watch the Passage to the Heavens – a nationwide homage following a royal funeral. The emptiness in Kyan hurt him physically. There seemed to be a vast void in Kyan's mind that needed the presence of his other body. As he and Raelynn watched the people gather in the dark streets below, he reflected on his memories of being a prince with a sadness in his heart. Each citizen dressed in white and scarlet if they could afford it, gray and brown is they couldn't. From young to old, each member of the procession held small candles.

The night was cold, but the sky was clear and starry. Nearly every light in the city had been blown out for the ceremony. At the sound of the bells from the Great Cathedral of the Luxeux, tens of thousands of Aunestaunans lit their candles. The streets of Aunestauna lit up in a glowing yellow light, like veins filled with gold – all radiating from the palace.

Sitting on the rooftop in the chilled night air, Kyan and Raelynn gazed at the constellation of candles appearing throughout the city of Aunestauna. Raelynn turned to Kyan. Her blonde hair and pale skin still seemed smooth and healthy even though she hadn't slept much in the past weeks. She pointed to the candlelit streets. "Why do they do that?"

"It's supposed to symbolize a sun," said Kyan. "So from the heavens, the dead royalty would see the streets of light as rays of sunshine all coming from the palace. It's just a way to send them off properly." The same ceremony had been held for Queen Eradine, but they had been too weary from the Battle of Aunestauna to participate.

Raelynn nodded and rested her arms on her knees, and they sat watching the candles for a while until Raelynn looked up at the moon. "Riccolo is still out there. He found you in the palace; he'll find you here . . . We have to leave."

He stared out into the night. "I know." The two watched a snowflake fall that seemed to come from nowhere in the clear night sky. "Where do we go?"

Raelynn thought for a while. "Cerebria."

Kyan turned to her. "Cerebria?"

Raelynn nodded. "My work here in Aunestauna is done . . . we could use you in Seirnkov."

Kyan remained silent, wanting her to go on.

"Not all Evertauri are sorcerers." Raelynn explained. "There are farmers and smiths and all sorts of people who've joined our cause . . . you could too."

Kyan thought for a while. "How would we get there?"

"The same way I've been coming back and forth – we'd board a boat to the Crandles and then take another from there to Port Dellock in Cerebria. After that, we just go underground to Seirnkov." Raelynn put a hand on Kyan. "The war is close to over and you could help us end all of this."

Kyan put his hand on hers. "When is the soonest we can leave?"

"Tomorrow morning, there's a ship headed for Catteboga. I'll write a letter to let my father and Borius know when we'll be arriving."

Kyan nodded. "Then I'm an Evertauri."

~February 16th
The Southern Sea

Their ship had sailed through rain for three days, but the wind was pushing them quickly toward the southern tip of the Endellian continent and then off to the Crandles. Raelynn sat across from Kyan in the small ship cabin they had rented out. The space barely large enough to stand up straight or stretch one's arms, but then again, Kyan's old shack had been the same way. Both were trying to read small, hand-copied books, but were distracted by the storm and the uncertainty awaiting them in Cerebria.

They had used all but their last argentums to pay for tickets on their ship, saving a few for the cheaper journey to Cerebria. Kyan looked out the window at the storm and the endless waves. For some reason, his mind had only been switching back and forth between his bodies of Kyan and Calleneck. *I must still be floating in that light as Tayben. . . I'm probably still switching bodies, but I don't notice when I'm in Tayben's because I'm in a different state of consciousness.* The time he was spending as Tayben in the pool of Taurimous in Silverbrook's hollow searching for answers was clearly much longer than it felt like.

Raelynn set down the Tomdar Fe history book she was borrowing from the ship's cook. For a while, she stared out at the rolling waves of the ocean. "When we get to Port Dellock, we'll meet up with the Evertauri and attack the port. They've wanted to attack it for a while now, but they want to meet us there to ensure we get to Seirnkov safely."

"Why do they want to attack Port Dellock?" asked Kyan.

"It's the main place Cerebria trades its foreign supplies, and it's where their navy is based."

"But you destroyed the Cerebrian navy in Aunestauna," said Kyan.

"And you don't think they're rebuilding it?" she said. "There's also a prison camp on a peninsula right next to Port Dellock where we think a few thousand Ferramish soldiers are being kept. If we free them, we can destroy the Cerebrian port and take the city ourselves – significantly blockading Cerebria from trading with the rest of the world. Then those Ferramish soldiers could help make a second front coming from the south up to Seirnkov."

"Or," Kyan suggested, "they could occupy the southern cities like Roshk and Endgroth. That way, they prevent militias from keeping control of Cerebria."

Raelynn nodded. "I assume we'll dock in the city, meet with the rest of the Evertauri, then make our way to the prison camp to free the Ferrs."

Kyan turned to her. "So what would you like me to do?"

Raelynn thought for a moment. "I know someone named Calleneck you'd work well with – he's our cartographer and could plan something for you."

Kyan smiled and looked out the window at the raging sea.

Raelynn chuckled. "Now that I think of it, you remind me a bit of him."

Kyan tried to hide his grin. "You don't say?"

Raelynn tilted her head. "What's that face for?"

Kyan shrugged, thinking for a moment. "It's just– well I don't know– but I feel like there's an end coming."

"And that doesn't scare you?" she asked.

"It does," said Kyan, "but . . ." He struggled to find the words. "It's resolution. Even if things go south when we get to Port Dellock and Xandria wins, it's resolution. We can't do much after that point to stop her reign."

"I'd never stop fighting," said Raelynn, solemnly.

The words made Kyan almost feel bad for what he had said.

Raelynn seemed to be lost in thought, but then spoke to Kyan as the ship rolled over another wave. "It still hasn't fully sunk in that my brother died for all of this last year . . ."

Kyan looked at her, expecting her to say more.

"Death became more real to me then," she said, staring blankly at the wall of their ship cabin. The blue in her eyes seemed to grow pale and icy, frozen over in the hellscape of war and loss, where what once was vibrant now was dead.

"Are you scared of dying?" asked Kyan.

Raelynn thought for a moment. "Yes." She turned her gaze to Kyan and looked him deep in the eyes. "I'm terrified."

Kyan's mind flashed back, remembering the feeling of the noose slipping around Eston's neck. *What happens if I die again? Am I actually losing that part of me? What if I die in this body and all my others? Is that the moment that I truly die?* A dark cold hole swallowed up his chest and chilled his veins with the notion of death – the thought of not seeing, hearing, feeling the world around him, the idea of not having thoughts and not speaking to others, the thought of being so unimaginably alone but not aware of it, the thought of never getting to breathe in cool air or run over grass or watch the clouds roll by or the rain fall.

"Kyan?" Raelynn's voice returned him to his senses.

He turned to her. "Sorry– just thinking . . ." He breathed deeply. "This world is just a lot more complicated than I ever thought it was."

Raelynn gazed out toward the rolling waves of the Southern Sea, watching gulls gliding on updrafts. "I miss the days when I saw the world in a kinder light." She turned away from the porthole and stared at the wall of their ship cabin. "My brother always used to say that things will never be like they are right now, no matter how much you try to keep it that way."

Kyan sat down next to her, noticing how deep her eyes looked. *You just have to remember the important moments,* he thought, as he remembered the golden sunset light filling the Great Cathedral the day he spoke with Raelynn for the first time. His mind drifted through the past that was forever gone as their ship sailed east through the rocking ocean waves.

PORT DELLOCK
Chapter Forty

~Late Afternoon, February 21st
Port Dellock, Cerebria

Dalah saw Lillia at the end of the pier and walked over to her. After receiving a letter from Raelynn, around sixty Evertauri had spent days traveling south through the Network to Port Dellock and planned to meet up with her to release the thousands of Ferramish soldiers reportedly kept in the prison camp there. The Evertauri waited in hiding throughout the city, preparing for their attack until Raelynn and Kyan arrived and night fell. Since Aunika was working as a spy in Xandria's fortress and unable to be around, Dalah had found a new sisterhood with Lillia over the last few weeks.

At the end of the pier, Lillia had taken off her shoes and was gently swirling her feet in the calm seawater, looking out at the lush, green peaks rising steep out of the water into the low hanging clouds.

Dalah gazed out into the fjord, her freckled cheeks rosy red in the brisk winter air. The great, white-sailed ships drifted between the mountains soaring up into the low-lying clouds. Dalah now viewed Lillia as a second older sister like Aunika. She looked back down at Lillia, able to tell that she was upset. It had been just two months since she had lost Tallius at the Battle of the Great Gate. Not wanting to address it, Dalah simply asked, "Are your feet cold?"

Lillia half smiled and nearly whispered. "Yeah, a bit." Lillia swirled her bare feet in the ice-cold water a bit more and laughed. "Actually yes, it's freezing." She lifted her feet out and shook them a bit before putting on her warm socks and boots.

Dalah chuckled and sat next to her. "How are you, Lillia?"

Lillia spoke through chattering teeth. "Cold."

Dalah smiled back. "I meant— well—"

"I know," said Lillia, her smile fading.

Dalah looked down at Lillia's stomach, which was starting to grow more. She turned away, watching her own dangling feet above the black seawater. They sat in silence for quite some time, listening to the birds gliding in the overcast sky and the occasional splash of fish popping up to the surface. A large ash gray bird landed next to them and waddled around for a second, twisting its head looking for food, then flew off.

Lillia broke the silence. "I hate it . . ."

Dalah looked up at her, confused. "Hate what?"

"All of this . . . the Evertauri." Lillia began to turn red, tears forming in her eyes. "If I could just go back in time and restart this, I would've never been a part of this— this rebellion."

"Lillia, don't say that."

"It's true, Dalah." Lillia looked out into the foggy fjord with watery eyes. "I had no idea what it was going to be like . . . the things I've seen, Dalah, and the people I've hurt and the people I've lost . . . I just . . ."

Dalah looked down at the rippling water on the dock. She had lost just as much. There were days where nearly all she could think about was the image of Aunika crying over their mum, her hands covered in the blood from the gash. If it wasn't that, it was the sight of her father's head split open on the corner of the fireplace hearth. She still hadn't truly accepted that it had all ben real — that her parents were gone, and that it was their own children's fault for joining such a cause that would get them killed. The memories had often been too much to bear, and she had spent sleepless nights crying — but softly enough not to wake Lillia. Dalah's life was gone, the little narrow house on Winterdove Lane burned to ash forever. It was all gone because of the Evertauri — because of her.

Knowing the images would still come back, Dalah pushed those momentary thoughts away to help her friend — just to be strong now. "I know how you feel . . . but there's no backing out now."

Lillia threw her hands up. "Am I just supposed to do this for the rest of my life?"

Dalah shook her head. "Of course not. Soon, they'll take down Xandria and then we'll be free."

Lillia turned to Dalah with a helpless expression. "We're sorcerers. Do you really think President Nebelle would let us lead normal lives again? We're all just pawns in Madrick's grand scheme; he doesn't care about us."

Dalah remained silent, knowing that part of Lillia's anger was trying to rid the sadness from her heart, the void left after losing Tallius. She knew what Lillia was thinking about but didn't want to press it until Lillia spoke.

"Do you think—" Lillia stopped for a moment, trying to get rid of the lump in her throat. "Do you think it should have been me that—"

"Died?" finished Dalah. "No . . . and I also don't think it should have been Tallius . . . It should have been no one." Dalah thought back to the explosion of the Great Gate in the Taurbeir-Krons. She could tell that Lillia was holding back tears.

Lillia had stopped shivering, but her nose, cheeks, and ears were a deep pink from the cold. She sniffed up the tears she knew were coming. She shook her head and looked out across the water, lost in memory of that night. "I should have been with him. It could have been me instead; it could have been Calleneck—" She stopped, wishing she could take back her words. "Oh, Dalah, I'm so sorry I didn't mean to say that—"

Dalah put her hand on Lillia's back. "It's okay, I know what you meant." Dalah paused for a while. "I know you miss him . . . we all do. Tallius was . . ."

"Perfect," said Lillia.

Dalah nodded, looked down again at Lillia's rounding stomach, and closed her eyes with sadness. *I'm so sorry, Lillia,* she thought. *And I know Cal is too.* Dalah looked behind her to the shore, where Calleneck was speaking to another Evertauri. Her love for her brother made her heart ache, remembering that it could have as easily been Calleneck who had died at the Great Gate instead of Tallius. She watched Calleneck as he pointed into the fjord at an incoming ship with a black and white flag – a ship from the Crandles. Dalah turned to Lillia and pointed at it. "Look there, I think Raelynn's on that ship."

Lillia wiped her tears and looked up at it, happy for a change in subject. "Yes, I think you're right." The ship seemed to cut through the misty fog that hung in the fjord. "And she's bringing that Ferr with her," said Lillia. "What's his name?"

Dalah shrugged. "I forget."

§

Kyan stood near the bow of the ship, watching the waves crash by as they sailed through the fjord. Port Dellock sat nestled in the valley ahead of them, with towering green peaks rising into the low-hanging clouds on either side. The cold water below slapped against the wooden planks of the ship, and Kyan leaned up against the railing to feel the misty wind stinging his face.

A few others, including Raelynn, walked around on the deck. She came up to Kyan and stood next to him. "Aren't you cold? I'm going to go down to our cabin. It'll be another forty minutes at least before we dock."

Kyan nodded. "I think I just want to stay up here. I like the mountains."

"Probably quite a sight for an Aunestaunan," said Raelynn. She noted Kyan's slight smile and then continued, "I'll be below until we dock." She turned and headed down to the cabin while Kyan watched the waterfalls cascading off the overgrown cliffs.

They docked at the port a while later, and Raelynn and Kyan walked together down the ramp onto the wooden pier. Kyan turned to Raelynn as they walked onto the shoreline street. "Where are we meeting the group of Evertauri?"

"It's a garden off of Greenpeak Street — by entrance to the Network."

Oh, I know right where that is. Kyan studied the city with rolling and bending streets, its hundreds of ivy-covered buildings nestled quietly between the clouded peaks of the fjord. "Do you know how to get there?"

Raelynn pointed ahead, where Lillia and Dalah were walking toward them from another boardwalk. "They'll take us."

As she and Lillia approached, Dalah waved at Raelynn, who smiled back. Though Kyan got to see Dalah as Calleneck, he felt as though he were looking at a long-lost sister. He wished badly that he could pick her up and hug her and kiss her on the head, calling her *Freckles* like he always did, but he resisted the urge.

"Raelynn, we missed you," said Lillia.

Dalah gave Raelynn a giant hug. "We're so glad you're back with us . . . Everyone has been talking about you and what you did in Aunestauna — giving up your Taurimous to destroy the Cerebrian fleet. If you hadn't made that sacrifice, Xandria would've won the war . . . You're a heroine in the Evertauri."

"I had no choice," said Raelynn.

Dalah shook her head. "You did . . . and you chose to save us."

Raelynn smiled, but with sorrow deep in her eyes. "I did what had to be done . . . Anyway, this is Kyan."

The two others introduced themselves to him, which almost made Kyan laugh, as they had no idea they were essentially shaking hands with Calleneck.

"Will you lead us to the meeting spot?" asked Raelynn.

Lillia nodded. "Of course, it's just up this hill." She led the three of them and walked up the gray-stoned, puddle-filled street. "Don't you have bigger bags," she asked, lifting an eyebrow, "traveling all this way?" Both were carrying only small wool sacks.

"We ran into trouble back in Aunestauna," said Raelynn, "and neither of us had much to bring back."

Kyan recalled the image of his burning shack, feeling truly homeless.

Lillia pointed ahead at a gate covered in vines. Behind it grew a lush, dense forest of evergreens, crooked maples coated in moss, and purple flower beds. Kyan followed them through the gate and into the garden. After a few bends in the path, they came into a clearing where Borius stood with several other Evertauri.

Borius Shipton greeted Raelynn in his low, rich voice, "It's good to have you back . . . I can't thank you enough for the sacrifice you made in Aunestauna. You saved the rebellion."

"That means a lot, Sir Borius." Raelynn responded. "This is Kyan."

Kyan gave a little bow to Borius and shook his hand, again finding it humorous that Borius did not know him. "It's a pleasure, Sir."

"You're brave for coming here, Kyan," said Borius, his one eye seemed to understand Kyan and look into his heart, like Kyan was the exact person he needed to join his cause.

"How can I help, Sir?" asked Kyan, subconsciously trying to make himself look taller than he really was.

Borius chuckled. "I appreciate your enthusiasm, but we will not need help with our operations in this city tonight. Your skills will be used another day. You will stay beneath this garden in the Network entrance with our guards until the Evertauri starts to make its way up to Seirnkov tomorrow morning – hopefully after we have freed the Ferrs and taken control over this port."

Raelynn crossed her arms. "So he's not joining us in the attack tonight?"

Borius shook his head. "We need him for important things back in Seirnkov and can't risk him getting hurt in the mission tonight." Borius turned to Kyan. "Fair enough?"

Kyan nodded. "Yes, sir."

"I'm trusting you with a great deal, young man," said Borius, "I also trust Raelynn's judgment. You're entering a dangerous conflict at dangerous times."

"Yes, sir," he repeated.

"The entrance is right here," said Borius, touching his hand to a moss-covered boulder. A soft yellow flame bled out of Borius's hand and onto the boulder, which began to shimmer and ebb like water. He spoke through the rock. "He's coming down." Borius turned back. "Just step on this boulder and you'll fall right in. It will be alright, trust me."

Kyan knew exactly how these entrances worked. He placed a foot on what looked like the boulder, but was really as thin as air, and fell a few feet down through the Taurimous entrance, landing on his feet on the floor of the Network. He examined his dark surroundings – a guard, a vaulted ceiling, a few stone benches carved into the wall, and a dozen candles.

"Hello," said Kyan to the guard.

The guard nodded. "Hello . . . we know this isn't the nicest place to stay with us your first night, but you're safe here."

Well I've certainly stayed in worse places. Kyan tried to think about what they might want him to do when they got to Seirnkov. He wished that he could be a part of the action tonight. *But I guess I should be thankful to be safe for now.* Kyan ate a small portion of bread for dinner and talked a while with the guard about his journey to Cerebria until it was time to fall asleep.

Drifting to sleep as Kyan, he awoke in the eyes of Calleneck the morning of the same day – backwards in time for him. The Evertauri arrived in the city a few hours after midday and waited in various places around town for Raelynn to arrive, and for nightfall to attack the Dellock Prison, release the Ferramish soldiers, and take control of the harbor.

§

~Night

The sky was dark, and the prison camp sat alone on its peninsula in a cloud of heavy fog that filled the fjord. Fifty Evertauri had loaded onto the small boats that would carry them around the back side of the prison camp so that they could invade it through the boathouse, the only other entrance to the camp besides the front gate, which sat on the isthmus of the peninsula. Calleneck sat rowing a boat with Dalah, old Sir Beshk Prokev from the Council of Mages, and a few others. The water around them was black and cold, and the fog hid them from the eyes of the sentries at the prison camp. The Evertauri had silently rowed past the main port and were now circling their way around the camp. It loomed dark and foreboding in the distance as they maneuvered their boats around the peninsula.

Calleneck looked over at the older Evertauri, who sat with a pure blue dagger in his hands. Sir Beshk was one of the first Evertauri to join Madrick nearly twenty years prior; he had long gray hair to his chest and a white beard that hung to his stomach.

"Where did you get that?" Calleneck said, pointing to the dagger.

Sir Beshk looked up at him, and the dagger turned into a thick blue fire and then vanished.

Calleneck's eyes opened wide. "I've never seen anyone use their Taurimous to create weapons. How did you—"

Sir Beshk smiled. "'Learned it a long time ago. It's the same way we make fake doors and entrances to the Network with Taurimous." His light blue Taurimous swirled like smoke and took the shape of a longsword that looked as if it were made of pure blue topaz.

Dalah stared in amazement. "It's beautiful."

Another Evertauri spoke up. "We're almost there. Be silent; get ready."

The vessels slowly approached the boathouse on the water's edge, which connected to the prison camp's interior. Dellock Prison was made by a series of small stone buildings and streets surrounded by a wall with a boathouse entrance. The boathouse grew nearer, but the fog hung so heavy that they could barely see it. The cold seawater lapped up against the wood of their rowboat, which was the first in line. Raelynn, Lillia, Kishk, and a few other Evertauri that Calleneck was close with rowed in the boat directly behind them.

Slowly, the figure of the boathouse sentry became discernable. They could tell he was trying to see through the fog. Suddenly, he sprinted inside the boathouse. Old Sir Beshk turned back to Calleneck and the others with a worried look. He pointed forward and whispered, "Keep going."

The Evertauri all slowly rowed into the boathouse. They looked around at the inside – it was completely deserted. Once inside, Borius, from the boat behind them, carefully stepped onto the floor of the building. Dalah began to whisper, "Where did that sentry—" Borius quickly put a finger to his lips. *Shhh.* Borius motioned the others out of their boats, and they all carefully and silently tied their boats and stepped onto the floor of the boathouse. A large door sat at the end of the boathouse, connecting it to the prison camp. Borius motioned forward and thought to himself. *"I don't like this . . ."*

The Evertauri stood behind Borius as he slowly opened the door. They stepped through the doorway and into a deserted courtyard. Calleneck's stomach began to feel uneasy. Something was wrong. Ahead of them, they saw a giant mound of something in the fog. As they stepped closer, they realized what it was – the corpses of Ferramish soldiers. Borius stopped abruptly and turned around horror-struck to face the Evertauri.

With a face of grim determination, Borius commanded, "At the ready!" Shrill and high, the horns of the prison camp began to sound. Hundreds of Cerebrian troops funneled out of buildings and barracks. Calleneck grabbed Dalah and turned around for the doors to the boathouse, but the doors slammed shut and locked from the inside. A burst of light filled the courtyard as Borius sent a wave of yellow Taurimous at an oncoming group of soldiers, the sound shimmering like thousands of miniature windchimes. Up ahead, Lillia made a shield of her white Taurimous around herself and Raelynn.

The soldiers collided with the Evertauri and drove forward with their swords. The sorcerer next to Calleneck screamed out in pain as his hand was cut off. Green and violet fire flew over their heads and into the Cerebrian soldiers bringing their swords down on Evertauri. Calleneck looked over and saw bearded old Sir Beshk fighting off Cerebrian soldiers with his blue sword of Taurimous. He ducked as Borius sent what looked like a lightning bolt of yellow at an archer, who got thrown back into a wall but still managed to shoot an arrow. Borius vaporized the arrow as it flew into a shield of his yellow Taurimous. Scores of additional Cerebrian troops still poured into the courtyard.

Calleneck saw a giant plume of blue Taurimous from Sir Beshk crush the heads of ten soldiers. He looked over to see Raelynn fighting off soldiers left and right with a longsword, striking one down every few seconds. The prison grounds were filled with nothing but soldiers and vibrant, colored flames from the Evertauri.

Calleneck looked around for golden light. *Dalah.* He saw a stream of gold embers fly at a soldier. A sickening convulsion filled his chest and made his bones feel like a skeleton of ice slowly freezing his body. *This is a warzone; this is no place for her.* He felt the full weight of her young age, her innocence, his *Freckles* that couldn't be harmed. Yet, he had led her to this place of danger and death. He yelled her name and sprinted for her, sending a shockwave of crimson Taurimous forward to knock Cerebrian troops off their feet. "Dalah!" She heard his voice and ran toward him, but stopped at the sound of a faint, low-pitched battle horn.

Calleneck recalled that sound from Tayben's memories in Endlebarr — *the Ferrs.* Calleneck called to his sister. "There are still Ferrs somewhere! We need to find them! But stay next to me! You don't leave my sight, okay?"

Dalah nodded, her face far braver that it should have been amidst the carnage.

Sir Beshk knocked aside a group of soldiers with a wave of blue light and raced over to the siblings after hearing Calleneck's conjecture. "Aye!" he shouted. "Let's try and find—" He was interrupted by another faint note from the Ferramish horn.

Dalah pointed toward a barracks in the distance. "There!"

Together, the three of them forced their way through the chaos, taking down Cerebrians as they went. As they approached the barracks, they could hear the horn again. A group of Cerebrian archers shot down at them from the top of the barracks, but Sir Beshk disintegrated their arrows with a series of blue fireballs. The horn from inside sounded again, and Calleneck collapsed the stone wall with a crimson pulse of light.

As the stone came crashing down and the dust settled, a deafening sound of cheering broke out as Ferramish men pushed to get out into the night. Standing in front was a simple soldier holding a gold and scarlet Ferramish horn.

The man bolted over to Beshk, shouting in joy, "We heard people fighting and we figured it might be our own men . . . what do you need from us?"

Sir Beshk nodded. "Help us take Port Dellock, then the city is yours and we'll send a messenger bird to Aunestauna. They'll send enough soldiers in the next few weeks to help secure the Fjordlands. Take your men to the armory and grab weapons. Once you've gotten into the city, burn their ships."

A Ferramish messenger boy shouted over at them. "There are four more barracks, hundreds of captured soldiers in each!"

Calleneck called back. "We'll get them out!"

"Thank you," said the soldier as the rest of the Ferramish soldiers rushed toward the armory. "We thought we'd end up like . . . them." He pointed to the mound of dead soldiers in the distance. "They were taking us out to slaughter one by one every few hours to keep us compliant . . . The ones who resisted their orders got executed . . . it would be my honor to fight."

As fireballs lit up the night sky, Calleneck, Dalah, and Sir Beshk wound their way through the streets to the other barracks to free more Ferramish soldiers.

~An Hour Later

Calleneck ducked behind an overturned wagon as a volley of arrows shot through a street of Port Dellock. Looking over his shoulder, Calleneck sent a wave of crimson hurling toward the Cerebrian archers. The Evertauri and the Ferrs had taken hold of Dellock Prison but met hundreds of Cerebrian soldiers in the city. Running into an alleyway with Dalah, Calleneck crossed over to the next street.

A great green fireball flew by at a frightening speed, blowing the Bernoils' hair back as it passed with a wave of heat. Calleneck and Dalah peeked around the corner and each sent jets of light at the Cerebrian troops.

The tall, blonde Evertauri who had sent the green fireball swung his Taurimous like a rope to slice the shields of the soldiers. He turned to Calleneck and Dalah. "Cal! Sir Beshk said to retreat to the entrance! We're being overrun and the Ferrs are—" He ducked as an arrow flew past. "The Ferrs are pushing in from the east."

Calleneck launched a shower of crimson sparks like a swarm of insects at the Cerebrian swordsmen charging down the narrow street. "Garner, you go and get Dalah to safety!" Calleneck disintegrated an arrow with a shield of crimson light. "I'll hold them off!"

The blonde Evertauri, Garner, nodded and signaled to Dalah. Together, they sent waves of green and gold flames at more troops and ducked away through a side alley. Out of the corner of his eye, Calleneck saw a flash of lilac light as Sir Kishk the Trainer rounded the corner downhill.

Kishk called up to Calleneck. "Aye! Follow me!"

Without hesitation, Calleneck bolted down the street to Kishk. "Do you know the way to Greenpeak Street?" said Calleneck breathless.

Kishk exploded the side of a building in purple fire, sending a cloud of debris between them and the Cerebrian swordsmen. "You're the cartographer! I know it's somewhere up this street." Sir Kishk pointed to the right.

The two of them wound through the streets fighting Cerebrians until finding Greenpeak Street – the entrance back into the Network. A whole group of Evertauri were funneling into the garden off of the street, escaping from the city as the Ferrs secured it from the outside.

Sir Beshk with his waist-long white beard was guarding the gate and rushing the Evertauri through. "Go! Go! Get back!" he yelled.

Kishk and Calleneck ran toward the gate to the garden. A raspy Cerebrian war horn sounded as dozens of soldiers rounded the street corner and spotted the Evertauri.

"Fall back now!" Sir Beshk bellowed at the Evertauri as he launched a bright blue disk of Taurimous up at the Cerebrians.

But before Calleneck reached Sir Beshk and the gate to the garden, he stopped at the sound of his name. He looked back down the street; two blocks away Dalah came sprinting toward him with tears rolling down her cheeks. As Sir Kishk bolted inside the garden, Calleneck spun around and ran back to Dalah.

Behind him, Sir Beshk yelled, "Calleneck Bernoil! Get back here now! Don't leave!"

Calleneck raced down the puddle-filled street to Dalah, who ran up to him. "What are you doing? I told you to go with Garner!" He grabbed her and pulled her back up the street with him.

Tears fell down her face as she ran with him back toward the gate. "I'm sorry, I came back to find you because everyone was evacuating, and you hadn't come yet!"

At the top of the street, Cerebrian cavalry charged down at Sir Beshk.

"Damn it, Dalah!" Calleneck cursed. "You need to take care of yourself, don't worry about me."

Forty more troops rushed between the Bernoils and Sir Beshk. Arrows began to fly down at them, and Calleneck shielded himself and Dalah with a ribbon of light.

Sir Beshk shouted down at the Bernoils. "Hurry!"

A Cerebrian commander shouted an order, and lines of soldiers charged down toward them. The Bernoils slammed into them with their Taurimous, but there were too many. Sir Beshk wielded his bright blue energy, trying in vain to fend off every troop. Calleneck and Dalah shattered multiple men's swords, but they were slowly losing ground, being pushed farther and farther from Sir Beshk. The Cerebrian troops were shouting, "They're using the Goblin tunnels! They're going underground!"

Calleneck shouted over the clamor to Sir Beshk. "We can't make it, just go! Seal off the entrances to the Network! They know!"

Sir Beshk blew two soldiers six feet in the air. "How will you get back—" he stopped himself before he revealed the location of the Nexus and sliced through the abdomen of a Cerebrian with his glowing longsword of blue Taurimous.

Calleneck yelled back. "Just go! Seal it off! We'll find a way back!"

Sir Beshk looked at Calleneck with sorrowful eyes, begrudgingly turned away, and vanished through the gate into the garden. Dozens of soldiers charged after him, but a shuttering sound indicated that Sir Beshk had sealed off the Network entrance.

Calleneck grabbed Dalah and sprinted away from the troops, turning into an alleyway. Both of them stopped when they saw it was blocked off. Behind them, another war horn blared.

Dalah turned to Calleneck. "What do we do Cal?"

Calleneck looked up at the walls of the alleyway that had plenty of outcroppings. A thought came to him almost from the mind of Kyan. "To the roofs," he said. "We'll escape the city that way."

Dalah nodded, and they scaled the building unseen onto its roof as the Cerebrian troops raced through the streets below.

Calleneck pointed northeast through the cold night into the mountain valley beyond. "Once we're out of the city, we can make our way back to Seirnkov on the surface."

Dalah looked at Calleneck with watery eyes. "This is my fault, I'm so sorry, I was stupid and—"

Calleneck hugged his sister tightly in his arms. She was alive and safe — nothing else in this whole world mattered, not the war, not the Evartauri, but his little Dalah. He promised himself he would never let her come so close to harm again. "It's okay, Freckles, we're gonna be alright." He leaned back and wiped the tears off her cheek. "Just follow me, okay?"

Dalah took a deep breath to calm her racing heart. "Okay."

A MEMORY OF REVELATION
Chapter Forty One

~Morning, February 22nd
Silverbrook's Hollow, Southeastern Endlebarr

Tayben, having returned to consciousness after weeks of floating timeless in the lake of Taurimous, stood awake on the grassy shoreline. He slowly looked around at the forest glade and back to Silverbrook. Tayben's clothes still glittered with beads of light from the pool of light surrounding Abitha Silverbrook's house.

Silverbrook put a hand on his cheek. "Are you alright?"

Tayben nodded, and a tear dripped down his face. "I know what I have to do . . ." Tayben looked over to Fernox across the lake, glistening white and majestic with his wings spread. Tayben breathed out, trying not to let tears run. "I need to go back."

"Where?" said Silverbrook.

Tayben closed his eyes. "To battle – I need to finish what I started."

Silverbrook realized what Tayben meant, and her hand dropped from his face. She paused for a while before speaking. "You're going back to fight with the Ferrs?"

Tayben slowly nodded. "In the lake of Taurimous . . . I– I saw my brother– Fillian. I know where the Ferramish army is. They're about to collide with the Cerebrians. Thousands of men on thousands of men. Your monsters with the Ferramish under Fillian's control, the Phantoms with the Cerebrians."

Silverbrook looked at Tayben with a deep sadness in her eyes. "You know that if you go you may not come back . . . Tayben, it's going to be a bloodbath."

Tayben nodded. "I've seen enough blood for a lifetime already . . . but that doesn't mean my fight is over. I can't stay here forever, and I can't just leave my friends and family to die. It's not something I can abandon now. I've died once already."

Silverbrook stood silently. "You're seeking out death."

Tayben shook his head. "I'm seeking out a world where people are no longer afraid. You said it before — soon, Tronum will die. If Xandria still sits on the throne, the whole world will collapse into war. Defeating her and crowning Fillian *is* our last hope. I understand now that this world never revolved around me . . . but I may be the only one who can make the sacrifice for peace. The way this all ends . . . it's more pain and death than I ever could have imagined. I've seen it, just glimpses — like you said — and I know what has to happen to succeed; but if I tell anyone how it goes, it won't happen."

A tear dripped out of Silverbrook's eyes. "I know, Tayben . . ." There was something wrong in her voice.

"What's wrong?" asked Tayben.

Silverbrook looked away and wiped a tear from her face. She turned back to Tayben, looking deep into his eyes. Softly, she began to speak. "Tayben . . . the reason I found you in the forest when you first met me, the reason I've been protecting you, it's because I know you . . . I've known you since the moment you were born."

Tayben stood still. "How?"

Silverbrook extended her hand to Tayben's head, and a smoke-like stream of light flashed. "Let me show you," she said.

Tayben took her hand and felt like he was ripped off the ground and thrown tumbling through the air. Tayben's vision swirled and, trying to orient himself, he looked around, finding himself in a dark hallway in the palace of Aunestauna. It was as if he was actually there in the memory.

Silverbrook stood there beside him in the vision and spoke. "I told you the truth before, that I had created the beasts for Tronum, and that I planned to escape Aunestauna with Madrick and my two children . . . but I did not tell you the whole truth — the story of who you are."

From one end of the dark, dreamlike hallway Tayben saw two figures. The first was a young-looking Madrick Nebelle, before his face grew dark and cold, ravaged by loss and the passage of time. The second was Abitha Silverbrook, who held a baby in her arms, followed by a toddler boy who clung onto Madrick's hand.

The two stopped and Silverbrook handed the infant Raelynn to Madrick, speaking in a whisper. "Take them to Cerebria. I'll meet you in Seirnkov, there's something I have to do for Queen Eradine."

A young Madrick looked at his small children and then back to Silverbrook. "You said you would come with us on the ship."

"Madrick, I can't . . . Queen Eradine needs me. The future of the kingdoms is in danger if I don't help her."

"*I* need you . . ." said Madrick.

Silverbrook lowered her head. "I promise I'll find you. Take Raelynn and Shonnar, head to the docks."

The toddler — young Shonnar Nebelle — looked up at Silverbrook and spoke in a high little voice. "Mommy, where are we going?"

Silverbrook knelt to Shonnar's height. "You're going on a ship to a faraway place where you'll be safe." Silverbrook kissed his head and stood up, looking into Madrick's eyes. "Everything will be okay." She kissed him, kissed Raelynn who was cradled against his chest, and headed back down the dark hallway.

Tayben and Silverbrook followed behind the memory of herself, down the hallways of the palace that he had known as Eston until they came to Queen Eradine's bedroom. They stood behind the young Silverbrook as she knocked on the door quietly. The door opened and a palace nurse stood there. Silverbrook tried to look inside the room. "Is she here?"

The nurse nodded. "Come quickly, the child's health has worsened."

Like ghosts in the memory, Tayben and Silverbrook followed the younger Abitha through the door and into Eradine's room. The queen lay on her bed holding a newborn. She looked young, but tired and weary. Tayben held his breath, seeing her alive once more, giving him the strangest bittersweet mixture of joy and grief.

The memory of Silverbrook approached the queen's bedside. "Your Majesty," she said.

Eradine picked up her head. "Abitha?"

She nodded. "I'm here."

Eradine, breathless, looked at the memory of Silverbrook. "My child is dying, Abitha."

The memory of Silverbrook looked at the newborn in the queen's arm. She placed her hand on its head.

The real Silverbrook turned to Tayben. "I could feel the life leaving you."

Tayben's stomach dropped. "That's me?" Silverbrook extended her hand to Tayben's head and the world around him spun until he stood back in the forest grove in Endlebarr. Slowly, the sounds of chirping forest insects reappeared.

Silverbrook spoke with a tear in her eye. "If a soul is halfway between life and death, in *limbo* between the world and the abyss, a certain spell from a powerful sorcerer could bring someone back into life — back into mortality before they drift away. As you died, I tried to use my sorcery to catch your soul before it slipped away . . . but as I tried to pull it back into the world, I felt it fracture."

Tayben looked at Silverbrook with a locked gaze. "Into how many pieces?"

Silverbrook stared straight back into his soul. "I think you already know the answer to that."

Tayben paused. "Four . . ." He stood still, trying not to believe her.

She continued. "But after seeing what happened when both Tronum and Xandria thought they had a birthright to the throne, your mother knew that only one of you could stay. So I flew away on Fernox carrying you and the babies that would be called Kyan, Tayben, and Calleneck. I gave Kyan to Madrick's friends, the Aldas, in Aunestauna. They were a kind and loving Gypsy family, I never imagined they would give you up to an orphanage. I flew to Woodshore in Cerebria and found a young couple I could tell were honest and good people – the Shaes. That was where you grew up in this body. I flew to Seirnkov to wait for Madrick and my children. I gave your body of Calleneck to the Bernoils. I could sense that Calleneck's body was the one that possessed magic blood, and I could sense that same magic in the Bernoil's first young daughter. I wanted to surround you with people like you, in a family with magic blood. Mrs. Bernoil thought she couldn't have another child, so she eagerly took you in when I offered you to her. I kept your minds separate until I thought it was time to ease them back together . . . when I thought you could help end this war."

Tayben stood in shock, trying to find a reason to rebuke what he'd just heard.

Silverbrook continued to speak. "But my Taurimous' strength was growing out of my control with my creations for Tronum and then with the spell I cast to save you. I was afraid for my family until I knew how to control my powers. With Fernox, I fled to Endlebarr where I could hurt no one – where my power could be fully unleashed; and I created this." She motioned to the hollow around them, a grove of light and life. "But after years of abandoning my family . . . I just couldn't bring myself to come back, not when I still don't know how dangerous my powers are and how they might hurt people . . . This is my home. It's the one place I know is safe for me to be because this is where I grew up. I'm Saentauri . . . I'm meant to be here."

Tayben sat down on the grass to think. For minutes, he sat there unraveling the story in his head. *This whole time . . . it all comes back to the night of my birth; it all comes back to Silverbrook. I was once one person, but through her magic, my soul split into four? How can that be possible? How can I believe her? . . . I have to.* He thought back to his other lives and had a realization. *The Olindeux . . . the silver necklace. The Aldas must have given one to me to keep me in Aunestauna, where my family really was. It kept me close to the palace, to my mother and father. The three carved lines were for my three other bodies I was leaving behind.* Other realizations poured into his head from all his lives, and everything began to make more sense.

Tayben looked up. "I owe you my life."

Silverbrook shook her head. "I cursed you."

"You saved me." Tayben stood up. "You brought me out of *limbo* before I died and gave me a chance to live. I wouldn't change anything that happened.

Through the connection I have with my other bodies, I've learned the truth, and what side I'm really on. Right now, I have to go . . . I have to fight."

Fernox flapped his wings and flew over to Tayben and Silverbrook. He nuzzled his giant head into Tayben's side, seeming to read Tayben's thoughts and confirm them.

"If Fernox wishes to accompany me, I would be grateful to you to let him fly me to the Ferramish army, where I'll join their ranks."

Silverbrook nodded, looking at the great white lion rustling its wings. "He is dependable and unimaginably loyal. He wishes to take you there."

"Thank you," said Tayben.

Silverbrook put a hand on Fernox's soft mane, speaking to Tayben. "You'll be fighting against the army for which you once fought."

Tayben nodded. "I know."

Silverbrook shook her head. "The Phantoms will hunt you down and try to kill you. You don't have their strength anymore."

"I know," said Tayben.

"I can restore some of that power you once had, with my magic. It won't rival the Nymphs', but it may help you stay alive." Silverbrook extended her hand and touched his head. A stream of white light coursed gently into his head and illuminated his body for a moment.

Tayben opened his eyes, and saw Silverbrook, who looked weary.

"Thank you . . . I'll need every advantage I can get." Tayben jumped up onto Fernox's muscled back, leaving room for Fernox's wings to move.

"I connected with them," she said, "with my beasts. They listen to Fillian and obey him now, with a little help from me of course."

"So he's protected?" he asked.

"Yes . . . they'll watch over him." Silverbrook reached up over the lion and put a hand on Tayben's knee. "Before you leave, there is one more thing . . ." She could barely bring herself to say the words. "You aren't the only person I've been trying to reach through the Ether. This whole time, all these years, there has been someone else . . . Years ago, I began seeing visions of a little girl capable of creating life — flowers — like I have done. She was always with Madrick, being watched over and cared for and taught. So I thought it was Raelynn . . . I pulled her closer and closer to me and my power through the Ether, through giving her visions and knowledge, through the glowing flowers. But over time, I realized it wasn't Raelynn; it was someone with an unquenchable thirst for power. I don't know who it was, but in all my years she is the one person I have sensed whose Taurimous has a raw natural power that matches, maybe even surpasses my own. But she has not yet realized and released her full potential. If she does, I fear she may present an even greater danger to the world than Xandria and Tronum."

Tayben knew instantly who it was. "Her name is Selenora Everrose."

Silverbrook nodded. "She has grown even more powerful in death than I am. I just wanted to tell you now, in case—"

Tayben finished the sentence. "—you don't see me again . . ." He thought back to the vision Silverbrook showed him, and everything came crashing down on him once again. "If all my bodies really came from one soul, descended from King Tronum and Queen Eradine, then how can I use magic? Why am I a sorcerer as Calleneck? Who passed down the gift to me?" He looked at Silverbrook's worried face. "And— and if you came from the Saentauri, the people of the forest who couldn't use sorcery, how are you a sorceress too?"

Silverbrook's face seemed ghostly pale, like the blood was drained from her skin. After a moment, she spoke softly. "A story for another time."

Tayben wanted answers but knew he would not get any further. Fernox shuffled his great paws below him. "Your story isn't over yet, you know," he said to Silverbrook, "you still have more to give the world." A tear ran down Silverbrook's cheek as Tayben put his hand to Fernox's mane and whispered. "North . . . I'll guide you."

Fernox gave a growl and kicked his legs, running over the ground faster than a horse. Tayben felt the power of the lion beneath him as Fernox leaped up into the air over the lake of Taurimous. Seeing the ground get smaller beneath him, Tayben felt the rush of cold air against his skin as Fernox flapped his wings.

The two of them broke through the canopy of the forest, emerging over an endless sea of red autumn trees. Tayben looked down, where hundreds of feet below, the light of Silverbrook's pool of Taurimous shone through the trees. Golden leaves stretched hundreds of miles in the distance. Below him, Fernox roared, making Tayben's insides shake. The cool air blew back Tayben's hair, and he felt like part of the clouds above him. The sun continued to rise in the east and cast a golden light over the land as Tayben and Fernox flew north to the Ferramish army.

§

Prince Fillian stood at the entrance of the generals' tent on a blanket of moss. Supervising the soldiers filled him with a sense of vigor. Men adorned with scarlet belts and reddened armor crossed left and right, each trying to hasten the preparation. Over the last weeks, the Ferrs had taken a hammering from Cerebrian assaults. Though Silverbrook's beasts seemed to be listening to Fillian and following his orders, he didn't know how to fight back against the Cerebrian night raids. It seemed as if shadows came through their camps and slaughtered soldiers without a trace, and night after night, he lost more men to these ghost-like soldiers. But despite being pushed back and having their supply chains ravaged, the Ferrs were almost ready to engage in their largest assault of Cerebrian forces since the war began – Fillian estimated that his forces ranged from fifty to sixty thousand men. Tronum had ordered a ninety percent deployment of troops from the camps at Abendale and Wallingford; they had arrived at the Great Gate three days before and had just reached the bulk of the Ferramish army.

Most troops however, remained unaware of Silverbrook's monsters because the army moved them at night. Fillian had tried to figure out a way to tame the shadow beast of Camp Stoneheart before the forces left, but it had proven elusive and dangerous. Every day he failed was another day lost in the march toward Seirnkov, one more day of food that was starting to run scarce.

But three beasts were better than none, so Fillian pressed on with monsters of fire, ice, and tree. The prince hoped that it would be unnecessary to use the beasts he did have in the assault, but he would not hesitate if the battle turned against them. He didn't know why they had begun answering to him, but he was learning not to try to unravel the mysteries of a magic he did not understand. Cerebrian forces had raced to an elevated forest hill and hoped to beat the Ferrs before their reinforcements came from the Fjordlands, which were now under their control following last night's Port Dellock prison-break. The battle would be fought in the underbrush of Endlebarr in no more than a day's time.

A call from a nearby officer interrupted Fillian's thoughts, "Archers, look above!" Twenty longbows pointed skyward as a dark shadow flew over the trees. Because a layer of fog hung in the canopy, Fillian could just barely make out a pair of wings. Another second later, the figure of a winged lion emerged.

Fillian instantly thought of his father's stories about Gallegore's winged lion. "Hold!" he called. "But stand at the ready!" *Were all those stories true? And if so, how is the lion here now?*

Descending from the mist, the white lion landed with a thud on the moss next to Fillian. Advisors emerged from the tent to see why soldiers were gathering. Atop the winged lion, a young man around his age wore a black robe and a white blouse underneath. As he dismounted the lion, Fillian drew his sword and raised it to the stranger's throat with a look of apprehension in his eyes.

The boy nodded. "My Liege."

Fillian held Eston's old *Queenslayer* steady and looked at a line of pikemen. "Contain the lion," he ordered, nodding toward it. The soldiers surrounded the beast with spears as it shuffled its massive paws in the black soil.

Fillian turned back to the boy and stepped forward. "Who are you?"

"My name is Tayben Shae – I bring no harm. I'm loyal to you."

"Says your Cerebrian accent," said the prince with a scowl.

"I didn't say I wasn't Cerebrian, My Liege; I said I am loyal to you."

"How am I supposed to believe that?"

"I can tell you how to defeat the Cerebrians." Tayben pointed behind him at Fernox sitting on a bed of moss. "I also flew here on your grandfather's lion."

Fillian's eyes widened. *It is true.*

Tayben gently raised his hands in submission. "Would you prefer to discuss this privately?"

When Fillian noticed the crowd surrounding them stirring, he dismissed them and focused again on Tayben and then on Fernox. "Come," he said and led Tayben into his tent after guards searched him for weapons.

As they walked toward it, Fillian looked at Tayben and his stomach dropped a bit. He stopped Tayben. "You—" Fillian paused, staring into Tayben's eyes, "You remind me of someone I know—" Fillian's face went blank as he paused again. *". . . knew."*

§

Gallien stood on a giant tree branch beside General Lekshane, hearing the rhythmic marching of the Cerebrian army in the underbrush below. "Are you sure?" he asked. "How can you be sure?"

General Lekshane nodded to himself and scratched his reddish-brown beard. "I can feel it . . . Tayben Shae is close."

"Did he join the Ferrs?" asked Gallien, already guessing the answer.

Blue veins bulged from Lekshane's neck. "I should've never listened to you – should've never let him go."

Gallien stood in silence.

Lekshane looked down at the other Phantoms and back to Gallien. "Our lives are in danger as long as Tayben Shae lives, Mr. Aris. He has no doubt explained to Prince Fillian how the Ferrs' monsters affect us."

"Then the damage is done," said Gallien. But as the words left his mouth, he knew he had made a mistake. Lekshane's hand shot out and grabbed Gallien by the throat, holding him still.

Lekshane looked into Gallien's eyes like a hawk. "The damage is done? Yes, by *you* who refused to track him down."

Gallien's face turned purple as he tried to breathe.

"So, you have a choice – *you* kill him, or we all take out your family back home in their mountain mansion. The Ferrs and our army are at each others' doorstep as we speak . . . by the time the night has fallen, either you or Tayben will be dead. Understand?"

He frantically nodded, and the general released his grip on his throat. Gallien fell to his knees and gasped on the branch. A battle horn blared . . . the Ferrs.

§

Tayben stood beside Prince Fillian as their army's horn sounded, followed by a higher pitched Cerebrian horn not far in the distance. Fernox stood with his wings out behind Prince Fillian, who seemed as if he had darkened, hardened himself to the world around. He looked older than Tayben remembered, even though he saw him through Eston's eyes only weeks ago. A small shadow of a beard even stretched across his jaw, and his eyes looked sorrowful but fierce with adrenaline. Thousands of Ferramish footmen, archers, cavalry, and pikemen stood in ranks beneath the red and brown forest canopy, unable to see far into the ever-present fog of the forest. Tayben had told Prince Fillian everything about the last month – Silverbrook, Fernox, the beasts, the Phantoms, the Saentauri, everything except for the fact that he was indeed Fillian's blood brother.

Prince Fillian took a deep breath. "Tayben," he said. "Can I trust you?"

Tayben nodded. "Like you'd trust a brother." His heart felt heavy for Fillian. He couldn't tell him that his brother was still here in a way – still alive inside this body. *I'm Eston, Fillian. I'm still here.*

Prince Fillian nodded and looked far behind them, where three of Silverbrook's giant beasts stood – a glistening winged dragon of ice, a giant with enormous limbs and body of roots, vines, and leaves, and a monster of fire and stone seeming to spawn straight from hell itself. "These soldiers, *Phantoms,* they're disabled by Silverbrook's monsters?"

"Correct," Tayben confirmed. "I believe the monsters could kill them too. But Phantoms are nearly impossible to locate or fight."

Prince Fillian looked concerned. "Then how are we supposed to set our beasts on them?"

"They'll try to kill me . . . I'll be the first one they come for." Tayben took a deep breath as another Ferramish horn sounded, and a Cerebrian horn responded, getting close. "Once they find me, that's when you'll set them loose. Silverbrook said her beasts would be drawn to the Phantoms and fight them. They can sense the magic the Phantoms hold."

The prince nodded and thanked Tayben, noticing his awfully pale face. "Are you alright?"

"I've been in many battles," he said. But his face remained nervous, and his breaths were deep. "You?" he asked Fillian, to be polite.

Fillian shook his head. "None like this . . ."

The Ferramish horn sounded once more, but there was no response. The whole of the Ferramish army went silent, listening. The forest was quiet, save for the whinnying of horses. Tayben's heart raced when a flock of black birds in the distance took off, screeching.

Prince Fillian spoke. "They're here . . . this is it." He turned to his generals and nodded. The generals gave signals to their platoons, who silently raised their swords and bows.

From the canopy above, a soft pattering grew louder as frozen rain began to drizzle down, clinking against the armor of the soldiers. In the fog, a deep rumbling noise grew. Tayben's heart pounded . . . *cavalry.*

The thundering of Cerebrian horses shook the forest floor. Prince Fillian climbed up onto his horse and yelled out, "Pikemen! Form in front! Archers at the ready! Soldiers, this is your day! This is Ferramoor's day!"

The rumbling grew closer, and the horses with Cerebrian riders appeared out of the fog — two hundred across. Tayben turned to Fernox, whose white fur glistened in the drizzling rain. Tayben put his hand on Fernox's head, "Don't come after me until I call for you."

Prince Fillian called out, "Defense position! Shields up! Archers ready your bows! Hold!" The Cerebrian cavalry charged forward. "Hold!" The archers stood with arrows nocked. "Fire!" Three hundred arrows were loosed over the pikemen and into the cavalry ahead, knocking dozens of horses to the ground. The Cerebrian cavalry covered the remaining ground and slammed into the front line of pikemen, and the Ferrs sprang forward into the Cerebrians, shooting, slashing, stabbing. From the fog ahead, hundreds of Cerebrian archers shot at the Ferrs.

Tayben grabbed his shield and held it over his head. An arrow punched itself an into the shield just an inch above his hand. He ran forward into the bloody spray of soldiers and horses. An arrow whizzed past his ear through the frozen rain as he blocked a sword swipe from a young Cerebrian. Tayben tripped the attacker and stabbed him on the ground. A gut-wrenching punch of guilt coursed through his body, these were his countrymen, his people. But he knew he had to keep fighting, this war had to end.

Yelling in anger at himself, the war, and the world for pitting him against his own men, he threw his spear into a Cerebrian on a horse and knocked him off. Jumping onto the horse and grabbing the reins, he kicked the horse forward, stomping on a row of infantry. Tayben raised his shield to block another volley of arrows. He snapped the reins and rode the horse through the endless mass of Cerebrian and Ferramish soldiers, bashing in the helmet of a Cerebrian he passed. A pikeman stabbed Tayben's horse, and he flew forward into a tree as the stallion collapsed beneath him, knocking the wind out of his lungs.

Completely soaked from the ice-cold rain, Tayben struggled to get up, and rolled away before a screaming soldier missed him by inches. Tayben reached for his spear and his stomach dropped — it was ten feet away. The Cerebrian lunged again at Tayben, who grabbed the Cerebrian's spear and stopped it inches from his chest. With his renewed strength from Silverbrook, he snapped the spear in half and drove the splintered piece into the soldier. Running to grab a sword in the mud, he ducked below another arrow. As he grabbed the sword and looked up into the freezing rain, he saw a flash of shadow in the trees above him. *Phantoms.*

Tayben looked back in the direction of Prince Fillian. "Fernox!" he called out. A few seconds after, the winged lion emerged, flying beneath the canopy of trees and landing beside him with powerful flap of feathered wings. Tayben climbed on Fernox's back. "The Phantoms are here, send a message to Silverbrook's beasts. Fly me up to the trees."

Fernox roared and sprung up, carrying Tayben up and over the battle to a massive branch a hundred feet up. Fernox landed and Tayben hopped off. "Is a beast on its way?"

Fernox pulled Tayben's soul into his eyes and mind, where Tayben felt the presence of an answer, *yes.*

Tayben jolted back into the real world. "Are the Phantoms near—"

Before Tayben needed an answer, he felt the uncomfortable chilling presence that he did in the forest so many months ago as part of the Cerebrian army. Tayben turned around to see fifteen Phantoms throughout the canopy with swords raised and bows drawn. General Lekshane stepped forward. "Mr. Shae," he called to him, raising his arms. "I'm glad we meet again."

Tayben stood silently with his hand on his sword. Fernox grumbled, and Tayben felt the presence of another creature in the canopy. He looked behind him to see Silverbrook's ice dragon waiting on a huge branch in the canopy, ready to pounce on the shadows. The Phantoms' faces flushed white, feeling their senses dulled by the power of the beast.

Lekshane stepped forward on the branch the size of a bridge and hesitated when he saw Fernox. "That's the wretched animal that stopped me from delivering the final blow to King Tronum . . . I could've stopped this war from happening altogether right then. But I see you have also brought a creature of hell to fight alongside you," said General Lekshane.

Tayben turned to Fernox. "Go, protect yourself." Fernox nodded his massive head, and sprung off the tree branch, and glided out of sight into the soft, drizzling rain.

Tayben turned to the general, who continued to walk toward him. "All of you to fight us?" Tayben said as Silverbrook's beasts stood behind him.

Lekshane shook his head. "One on one will suffice."

Tayben raised his sword toward Leshkane. "Then what are you waiting for?"

Lekshane laughed. "You misunderstand." He turned toward his Phantoms and signaled one forward. The Phantom removed his hood.

Tayben's stomach twisted. "Gallien?"

"Tayben," responded Gallien, the color draining from his face.

Lekshane smiled and walked back, allowing Gallien to walk up to Tayben.

Gallien shook his head. "Tayben – they'll kill my family, my brothers and sister . . . I have to."

Tayben whispered, "I know."

Gallien raised his sword to meet Tayben's. Neither of them moved, standing in silence and refusing to strike first. Tayben's mind flashed back to fighting alongside Gallien, defending him, protecting his friend. *I can't do this.*

Lekshane screamed out, "NOW!"

Gallien lunged forward and Tayben knocked his sword away. The sound of metal clashing rang out, and three monstrous growls thundered behind Tayben. In a flash, the ice dragon sprang at the other Phantoms. Tayben lashed at Gallien's side, who ducked below the blade and stabbed at Tayben's feet. Tayben lunged aside across the branch as the beast flew past him tearing its claws at another Phantom. Gallien jumped up and brought his sword down on Tayben, who dodged to the side. Gallien's sword embedded itself into the branch, and Tayben kicked him back, grabbing his sword. Tayben held up the two swords, and Gallien dove at his legs, knocking him down. Tayben could tell that Gallien had lost some of the Nymphs' power, he wasn't as fast and strong as before.

The monster roared above them as it tore at the Phantoms, chasing them away through the canopy. Gallien flipped and wrenched his sword out of Tayben's hands and bashed it into Tayben's side. He yelled out and rolled behind Gallien, stood to his feet, and slashed at him, but Gallien knocked aside the blow and kicked Tayben in the chest.

Tayben stumbled back and slipped off the wet bark, falling twenty feet down to another branch below. Landing with a thud, Tayben used all his strength to stand as Gallien jumped down. Their clothes and armor were soaked from the freezing rain.

Gallien lunged at Tayben, who swiped his sword to the side. Tayben bashed the hilt of his sword into Gallien's head, knocking him over. Gallien cried out in pain and grabbed Tayben's cloak, pulling him to the branch beside him, and elbowed his ribs. Gallien sprang over Tayben and swung down his sword, but Tayben diverted the blow and jumped up, meeting Gallien's blade again. Tayben slashed again and again, pushing Gallien back. But Gallien locked his sword with Tayben's and held it there.

Tayben leaned into the locked swords, his face inches from Gallien's. He looked into Gallien's eyes and pushed his sword into his, but neither could push harder. A tear slid down Tayben's grimacing face. Gallien's feet began to slip on the wet branch. Tayben leaned further, and Gallien's feet slipped more.

Gallien looked Tayben in the eye and said the words that Tayben knew were coming. "I should've followed you when you left the Phantoms . . ."

In a last hope movement, Gallien twisted his blade, knocking Tayben's aside, swung around and jabbed the blade through Tayben's abdomen.

Shock spread through Tayben, as he looked down to see Gallien's sword stabbed through his body. Blood began to soak through his cloak and armor. Gallien stood in horror, pale-faced at the sight of his best friend gushing blood.

Tayben fell to the branch and lay there coughing up spurts of blood. Gallien fell to his knees beside Tayben and began to cry. "I'm sorry."

Tayben lost all feeling and convulsed, coughing up more blood. Gallien put his hand on Tayben's face and screamed out curses.

Fear spread through Tayben as he grabbed onto Gallien's arm. Tayben tried to speak through the blood that bubbled in his throat, but he just coughed up more blood onto Gallien's hand and began to shake horribly. A pool of blood formed around him, and rain fell onto his pale face.

Gallien shook his head. "You had the courage to do what I couldn't . . . I should have followed you . . ."

As his vision began to close and his body began to shut down, Tayben summoned the remaining strength left in his body to push out just a few fractured words through his blood-filled mouth – the words he knew he had to say. "Be loyal to your heart . . . nothing else matters."

Slowly, Tayben's mind went blank as he stared up into the forest canopy. He convulsed again and struggled to breathe. His body was shutting down. The red and gold leaves overhead became blurry and bright as freezing rain drizzled down on his body. The sound of birds and drops of water pattering on leaves calmed him as he felt his soul slipping out of his body. Light filled his vision and covered Gallien's face and the leaves overhead until every single one disappeared. Distant swords clashed out, and then there was silence.

THE LAST DAYS OF WAR

Chapter Forty Two

~Afternoon, February 24th
Central Cerebria

Calleneck and Dalah walked side by side on a dirt pathway through the tall pine forests of central Cerebria. Headed north to the capital, they were a little way southeast of Weirkoff Nocht by Calleneck's mental map. After the battle at Port Dellock, Sir Beshk and Sir Borius had completely sealed the entrances to the Network throughout Cerebria – except for Seirnkov – afraid that the soldiers who saw the Evertauri escape had notified the government. If Xandria had a sorcerer – or sorceress – the Network could be breached. So the Bernoils had made their way up through Cerebria without the benefit of the Goblin tunnels, stopping by an Evertauri-loyal farmer in Tangle Took for packs and supplies.

A gaping hole filled Calleneck's soul after the death of Tayben. That body, that life was now gone forever. The hopelessness and emptiness darkened his thoughts. But despite the loss, he still kept Tayben's memories of the pool of Taurimous – he still knew what he had to do. He didn't know if what he saw would become reality, but it was the only chance to win – the only chance to end the war.

Walking through the forests gave Calleneck's mind a chance to wander. He thought lately about his childhood home, about his parents and old school-friends. He had half a mind to find Gilsha Gold and warn her about the impending danger of the coming conflict – he hadn't seen her since his parents died, and guilt for abandoning her and her sickly mother made his stomach uneasy. *Hopefully one day I can go back to her and explain,* he thought, *maybe then we could start a life together . . . once this madness ends.* Another thought plagued his mind as always – the lingering guilt for the death of Tallius. If he had taken just a second longer to make sure his shield was protecting Tallius in addition to himself, he could still be here, and Lillia's unborn child would not have to grow up fatherless.

He thought back to his conversations with Silverbrook, and he felt as if he had more questions than answers. *If I am really Tronum and Eradine's son, how do I possess sorcery? If Silverbrook was descended from the Saentauri, how does she possess sorcery too? And why didn't she tell me how her people were destroyed?* The questions bounced around in his head, but he couldn't find any solutions, any way to explain it all. Names coursed through his mind, though some of them, he did not know why. *Gallegore Wenderdehl, Tronum Wenderdehl, Xandria Wenderdehl, Kliera Dellasoff, Abitha Silverbrook, Aeliara Silverbrook, Raelynn Nebelle . . .*

Dalah stepped over a puddle of mud, but her boots were already wet with snow and speckled with dirt. Calleneck looked around the evergreen forest as they walked, trying to match the streams he saw with the streams on his map. The trees here were uniquely green, wet from daily precipitation, their branches sagging and hanging moss overgrowing on half-fallen trunks.

Dalah adjusted the leather straps over her shoulders. "Do you think the Evertauri have sent anyone to look for us?" she asked Calleneck. "Aunika is probably worried sick."

"I think it's more likely that we're on our own," said Calleneck. The two of them walked up a slope on the forest trail. Patches of snow lined the sides, but some of the plants were still green. "We should be coming up to a junction between this trail and the main road," said Calleneck.

"Which do you want to take?" asked Dalah.

"I'm not sure yet . . ." Calleneck's stomach grumbled, but he knew he had to ration the food. "Will you be fine waiting for dusk till we finish off the bread?" he asked Dalah.

She nodded. "I'll be alright."

At the same moment, Calleneck and Dalah stopped in their tracks. Just twenty yards ahead was the main road. On it sat a series of carts and carriages – a Cerebrian war supply train. Dozens of Jade Guards in dark green and silver armor loaded huge boxes from one train to another.

The Bernoils ducked behind a fallen tree trunk, sitting in a depression of wet soil and fallen pine needles, and listened intently to the guards. "These crates are all going to Seirnkov," said one.

"Nothin' else is getting in the capital," said another. "Whole city is blocked off to civilians trying to get in. They're only lettin' people out."

Calleneck looked at Dalah, who had the same idea. This could be their only way into the city. Calleneck quickly whispered a plan to Dalah, and then they quietly made their way toward the main road. Before jumping out into the open dirt road, they hid beneath the cover of the hemlock bushes that lined it. Needing a distraction, Calleneck raised his hand and shot a little burst of sparks across the road behind the soldiers, breaking a large branch off a tree.

The guards all turned to the other side. One ordered, "Go check out what that was."

While the guards' attention was focused on the sound, Calleneck and Dalah ran up next to the crate being loaded and used their Taurimous to create an illusion around them of a large wooden box. Surrounding themselves with fake planks of wood, they sat silently, listening to the muffled sound of the soldiers around them.

Before long, a soldier tapped on their box, shouting to another. "We've got one more right here!"

Several troops walked over and heaved the crate carrying the Bernoils up onto a wagon. On the inside, Calleneck and Dalah held their breath, hoping for their success. After another minute, they felt the wagon lurch forward carrying them in their box toward Seirnkov.

§

~The Royal Palace

King Tronum sat silently at a great oak desk in his dark study. A fireplace lit the room, illuminating the hundreds of books and scrolls along the walls, and the overcast, snowy sky filtered in a soft gray light through the window. The faint crackling and popping of the burning wood in the fireplace was the only sound.

Tronum's eyes were focused down at his shaking hands, where he held a silver and gold ring, unsuccessfully trying to roll it across the tops of his fingertips like he used to. A knock on the door caused his heart to jump, and the ring dropped onto his lap.

The king slid the perfectly crafted ring back onto his left hand. "Come in." he called out. Slowly, a Guard opened the door and Qerru-Mai An'drui stepped through. Her eyes looked heavy and tired, but her chestnut skin glowed warmly in the firelight. "Your Majesty," she said and gave a slight bow.

King Tronum nodded in return. "Have you any news of the campaign in Endlebarr?"

She stepped forward, taking out a letter from her coat pocket. "I received this from your son." She walked up to Tronum's desk and extended the letter.

"Just set it down," said Tronum, whose hands still slightly shook.

Qerru-Mai placed the letter on the walnut wood and continued. "Fillian says that four of our regiments — tens of thousands of troops — engaged with a Cerebrian force of roughly the same size. We won and drove them back, but we also suffered heavy casualties."

"How many?" asked Tronum.

"Between twelve and fifteen thousand."

Tronum's stomach lurched, and a wave of cold rushed through his blood. He shook his head without words. *So much death . . . thousands of our young men's corpses on the far side of the mountains.* It had been the largest death toll since the Battle of the Burning Hills. Tronum scratched his chin. "The beasts?"

"They're in good condition," said Qerru-Mai. "They engaged with Xandria's special forces unit and caused its retreat."

King Tronum stared over at the crackling fireplace. The sound of popping wood filled the otherwise silent room.

After waiting through the pause, Qerru-Mai spoke. "The rest of the information is in that letter from Fillian if you wish to read it."

Tronum didn't respond but instead continued to watch the dancing flames in the fireplace.

Watching the reflection of the fire in Tronum's eyes, Qerru-Mai added, somewhat quietly, "I, um— I also wanted to let you know that I'm leading an investigation into your son's death . . . I'm working with a former Nightsnake named Vree Shaarine to uncover the truth. The chain of events is a bit complicated at first glance, but the man ultimately responsible for Eston's death goes by the name Riccolo. He was the man at the trial falsely accusing the young man named Kyan. We believe Riccolo knows we're searching for him, and we've found evidence suggesting that he has fled with his loot and his thieves to the Southlands . . . I plan to board a ship in two days to Zaabu."

King Tronum swallowed with a sore and dry throat. "I want you to stay here."

Qerru-Mai stuttered. "Oh— I'm sorry, why, Your Majesty? Don't you want to find Riccolo?"

"In time," said Tronum, "I hope you're able to apprehend him, as well as the thugs who helped him . . . but you are now the Scarlet Lady, your obligations lie here."

"Someone else can take my position. Liann Carbelle led the loyalists in the Scarlet Guard during the Battle of Aunestauna. He would make an ideal Scarlet Lord; he helped save the city."

"So did you," said King Tronum. "If I'm not mistaken, you were the one to put an arrow through Janus Whittingale's heart before he could kill my sons, and you were the one to ride through the night to Camp Auness to lead reinforcements into battle and reclaim the city." Tronum coughed a few times into his arm. "To be candid with you Qerru-Mai, the only reason you are not currently my First Advisor instead of this oaf Endwin Bardow, is because people in this government aren't comfortable with me heeding advice from someone as young as you."

"I thank you for the compliment, Your Majesty, but that does not diminish the qualifications of Liann. You're still lacking a new Ambassador to the Southlands. I can resign as Scarlet Lady and—"

"You are not resigning, Qerru-Mai, and that is a final order from your king."

Qerru-Mai looked down at her feet in silence.

Tronum leaned back and sighed. "I need you here; I need someone competent to run this palace when I am gone."

Qerru-Mai shook her head. "I'm sorry, but I don't understand. When you're gone, where?"

Tronum looked at her with a solemn, ill gaze and held forward his shaky hands, severely taken over by the spreading disease. "Soon, before Fillian returns . . . when my health runs out. My time grows ever closer."

Qerru-Mai slowly nodded and took a deep breath in. "I understand."

Tronum looked Qerru-Mai in the eyes and then turned back to the fire. "I never did express my condolences for the loss of your mother . . . She, like your father, was an ally and a dear friend to me."

"I hope only to serve as well as she did."

Tronum nodded. He could hear the deep hurting in her voice. "You will; and you will do so much more – for Ferramoor and for the world . . . You're dismissed, Lady An'Drui."

Qerru-Mai gave a small bow and left the King's Study.

Tronum sat silently for some time before walking over to the fireplace and dousing the flames with a tin of water. Grabbing a long, heavy coat, Tronum walked out of his study, leaving Fillian's letter on his desk, and headed across the half-destroyed palace grounds with two guards behind him.

The palace grounds were desolate, cold and burned. A few new senators, ambassadors, and Scarlet Guards walked the halls and courtyards, but the palace was otherwise silent. Windows were still shattered, and walls were still crumbled. A void had enveloped the palace over the past months, and the world seemed filled with strangers.

Tronum stopped near the edge of the palace, where the stone breezeway overlooked a sloped hillside on the north end of the grounds. He signaled to his Scarlet Guards. "Wait here, I'd like to go alone."

The Scarlet Guards bowed and stood at attention as King Tronum stepped off the walkway and into one of the thin patches of snow that covered the hill's dead grass. Small snowflakes drifted silently down in the late afternoon sky, and from this view, Tronum could see the blackened walls of the palace, large columns that were being rebuilt with new stone, and fallen turrets that had not yet been repaired.

Tronum continued his small steps down the hill, passing large marble statues and headstones. Finally, he stopped beside four headstones and reverently brushed the snow off them. He stepped back and took a deep breath. "Father," he said to the largest. "Mother," he said to the next; "My Love" to the third; and to the last, "My son." He took a few steps and knelt between the last two. Feeling the snow's cold seep into his skin, he closed his eyes and took another deep breath. Slowly, tears filled his eyes as he reopened them to see the names that were inscribed in stone – King Gallegore Wenderdehl, Queen Kliera Dellasoff, Queen Eradine Lameira, and Prince Eston Wenderdehl.

"We're in the last days of war," he said to his departed loved ones. Hoping that somehow, they were listening, he continued. "Our forces are closing in on Xandria, Father," he said. "She has caused this world great pain, and I need your strength to still love my sister despite what she's done . . . what we both have done."

He looked at the whitest gravestone. "Eradine . . . not a day goes by where I don't miss your presence, your courage."

He closed his eyes. "Eston . . . I'm so sorry. I wronged you in many ways and didn't value what I had – a brilliant, worthy son."

Tronum clenched his teeth to try and suppress tears. "My days grow short. I can feel the sickness that I've long ignored overtaking me. I feel the wings of death approaching swiftly, not waiting for me to finish what I started . . . But Fillian will avenge all of you. He's not ready yet, but I know he will be." King Tronum stood up, renewed. "I'll see all of you very soon."

§

~Two Days Before
Eastern Endlebarr

Fillian unclasped his metal helmet and took a deep breath. The foggy air of Endlebarr stank with the smell of blood and war. He looked around at the complete devastation. The forest floor was covered in bodies as far as the eye could see – thousands of Ferramish and Cerebrian soldiers lying dead, sprawled on top of each other, blood soaking into the black soil beneath.

In the distance, Ferramish generals rounded up the survivors into new battalions. Fillian shivered from the cold of his rain-soaked clothes and armor. The sound of gently rushing air, pushed by giant feathered wings descended from the canopy. Fernox glided down and landed softly next to Fillian, but he looked angry and growled low.

Fillian cautiously stepped forward. "Where is Tayben?"

Fernox growled again and lowered his head.

"He's dead, isn't he?"

The lion backed away slowly as Fillian raised a hand toward the winged lion.

"I'm not going to hurt you," said the prince. "Do you know who I am? Do you remember my father, Tronum?"

Fernox gave a snarl and dug his claws into the soil.

Fillian nodded. "My grandfather then? Gallegore? You were his . . . then you left Ferramoor . . . come, I won't hurt you." *He can surely hurt me though,* Fillian thought.

Fernox stood still for a moment, then ruffled his wings and stepped forward.

Fillian extended his hand, and with a racing heart, placed it on Fernox's nose. "Stay with me. Fight alongside a Wenderdehl again." As he ran his fingers through the lion's thick white mane, he felt the ground rumble, and a tree-giant emerged from the soil, followed by a beast of ice and another of fire approaching out of the fog. Fillian spoke out. "You drove away the Cerebrian Phantoms?" Suddenly, he felt as if he were being sucked into the mind of the beasts, where he felt a reassuring confirmation.

Fillian nodded and looked around at the carnage from the battle, and the bodies that lay scattered across the underbrush that would soon be swallowed up by the vegetation. "It won't be the last we see of them."

§

Gallien knelt on the forest floor with Tayben's body in his hands. After carrying his corpse away from the battle, Gallien gently set him down at the base of an enormous tree. He removed his own sword from his belt and situated Tayben's cold, stiff hands around the hilt, giving Tayben one last piece of his heart to hold on to. Tayben's last word echoed in his head – *"Be loyal to your heart . . . nothing else matters."*

Choosing not to block out the past, Gallien let the memories flow. He remembered the first time meeting his tentmate, feeling scared of the army, scared of the forest, and seeing Tayben's bravery through it all. He remembered being taken by the Phantoms, then learning that his best friend would too join the ranks. He felt the hollow hole in his heart after Tayben had left, and the chill of seeing Tayben's pale, dead face in front of him.

Gallien flinched when he felt a hand on his shoulder. Turning around, he saw Chent and Ferron standing behind him with solemn faces. Gallien shook his head. "I can't do this."

Ferron knelt beside him, glancing at Tayben's body, and then back to Gallien. "None of us thought we could. But you have to push through."

Chent spoke, unlike his usual silence. "General Lekshane doesn't understand the hardship . . . but we do. Soon this will all be over, and the world will be at peace."

Gallien wiped tears from his eyes. "I'm fading, brothers. My powers are—"

The three sat in silence for a moment, all looking over Tayben's body. Ferron attempted a smile and patted Gallien on the back. "The rest of the Phantoms are still a distance away . . . Let's send Tayben off right, shall we?"

The three stood up beside Tayben's cold body. Gallien bowed his head but picked it up when he heard the sound of humming from Ferron. On his other side, Chent began to hum as well. Gallien hadn't heard the music in years, yet the melody of the old tune wound its way out of his memory. Softly, Ferron let the old soldier song flow –

O'er forest, hills, and dales I've gone,
Defending what I love,
I will not tremble anymore,
I'm off to worlds above.

No longer pained with mortal life,
Or hid from winter's grasp,
No longer grieved with earthly strife,
My new home everlasts.

Wiping tears from his face, Gallien looked once more at his dear friend before turning back to the forest. "You're right," he said, looking east toward Seirnkov. "Soon, this will all be over."

THE BLACK FORTRESS
Chapter Forty Three

~Morning, February 25th
The Network, Seirnkov, Cerebria

Kyan awoke to a knock at his door. He opened his eyes and stared at the cold stone ceiling above him. Most of the Evertauri had been able to escape from Port Dellock after the Cerebrians discovered their entrance. Barely getting away but suffering only a handful of casualties, they had made their way north to the Nexus with Kyan. Someone knocked at the door again. Kyan put his feet on the cold gray floor and walked over to the Goblin-made door and opened it.

"Hello Kyan," said Raelynn, standing there in a black robe looking drained and stressed.

"Good morning," Kyan greeted.

"How was your first night in the Nexus?"

"Couldn't sleep very well, it's cold down here in these tunnels." Kyan reached to the side to put on shoes.

"It's colder up on the surface, your Ferramish winters are much milder than Cerebria's."

Kyan nodded. "What'd you come here for?"

Raelynn attempted a smile. ". . . The meeting with my father."

"Oh shit," Kyan smacked his forehead, "I'm sorry, it's hard to keep track of time down here. You still won't tell me what it's about?"

"Follow me," Raelynn said with a smile.

When they arrived at the office dedicated to the Council of Mages, Madrick, Borius, and Aunika sat around a long table along with a few others Kyan recognized from his memories as Calleneck. *You don't know these people,* Kyan reminded himself. *You don't know much about the Evertauri.*

The people in the room stood up, and Madrick walked over to Kyan, extending a hand. "Welcome."

"President Nebelle," said Kyan, trying to act as though he'd never met him as Calleneck, "it's a great honor."

"Please sit," said Madrick.

Kyan took a seat at the table, noting the additional presence of Sir Kishk, Sir Beshk, and a few more Evertauri.

After introductions, Madrick spoke. "Kyan, we've heard about your experience spying and thieving . . . we want to put those skills to use for us." The room was silent, the only movement was from the little silver ornaments and instruments that spun and glittered. "There is a stone that Xandria possesses; it was created by a sorceress named Silverbrook."

Kyan's insides turned cold with the realization.

Madrick continued. "Based on evidence that Aunika Bernoil has discovered while working undercover at Xandria's fortress, and based on evidence her brother Calleneck and Sir Borius Shipton found in the Goblin capital of Rjarnsk, we believe that this so-called Guardian Stone can protect who weilds it from most or all physical harm."

Kyan's mind raced. *Of course! Silverbrook created the stone, Tronum had it, Xandria wanted it, Whittingale recruited the Nightsnakes to steal it, Riccolo got me to steal it, I gave it to Riccolo who gave it to Whittingale who shipped it to Seirnkov before he was killed! That was the other half of Whittigale's plot.*

Madrick continued. "We need you to steal the Stone and bring it to us."

Kyan's heart pounded. *Steal it? . . . I'm the reason it's in Xandria's hands in the first place . . .* But he remembered the vision he saw in Silverbrook's Lake of Taurimous — the Guardian Stone was one of them . . . *I have to do this.*

Madrick spoke again. "It's the only way we may be able to win. The Guardian Stone currently protects Xandria from any attack. If we have any hope of killing her, we have to take it from her."

Kyan froze for a minute. "Do *you* intend to use it?"

Madrick looked at Borius and then back to Kyan. ". . . We will do with it what we see fit for the situation. Our spies tell us that, although they suffered many casualties, the Ferramish forces defeated thousands of Cerebrians in Endlebarr. Prince Fillian and the Ferramish army have taken Tallwood Watch to resupply and have pressed their way through the countryside. We think they will arrive in Seirnkov within a day or two. The entire remaining Cerebrian army has been regrouping in Seirnkov the past two days — numbers in the tens of thousands. The training camps at Vashner and Roshk have been emptied and all sent here. Xandria is ready for battle while Tronum lies on his deathbed."

Borius, who had not yet spoken, added, "Tomorrow night may be the last battle of this war. If the Ferramish army and its allies can overcome Xandria's forces and kill her, Cerebria will surrender. If they cannot, we will be trapped in the city with the Ferramish army and will die. Two thirds of all Ferramish troops will soon arrive in this city. If they all die, there will be few left to defend Ferramoor. Xandria would take Ferramoor and then begin her conquest over the entire Endellian continent – The Northlands, Elishka, The Crandles, The Southlands, Parusemare–"

Madrick rubbed his thin beard. "We will have lost."

The room sat in silence.

"But you can help us," Madrick continued. "The battle will happen soon no matter what we do. Thousands of Ferrs will flood the city and battle against thousands of Cerebrians. While the Cerebrians are well trained and well rested, the Ferrs have traveled hundreds of miles and are weary. I doubt they will succeed without our help."

Kyan knew his decision but still struggled to respond. *It's my fault Xandria has the Stone . . . I have to do this.* He sat up straighter. "I'll get you the Guardian Stone."

Borius smiled in relief. "Aunika Bernoil will give you the information you'll need on the whereabouts of the Guardian Stone, all the people you will need to get past, and the best passageways for you to reach it and then hopefully escape."

Kyan looked over at Aunika, who reached down and pulled out five different scrolls. "These are maps of Xandria's fortress," she said, unfolding them. "It will be difficult getting in and even harder getting out. There are guards stationed at each entrance to every wing. Eight different watchtowers line the grounds, with guards constantly scanning the streets below and the courtyards within the fortress . . . not to mention the fact that for three blocks around it, aristocratic mansions with their own guards line the streets."

Kyan studies one of the maps depicting the south side of the fortress. "Who will be with me?"

Sir Kishk spoke. "You'll have a team of a few others waiting at various points in the fortress–"

"Including me," said Aunika.

Borius turned to Kyan. "They'll be there to help you and take over in case anything goes wrong."

Aunika pointed to locations on the maps. "You'll have Evertauri here on the south side, here on the east, and I will be here by the bell tower. We hope to be ready to begin tonight an hour after sunset."

"Where do we enter?" asked Kyan.

"Through the main gate," said Aunika.

"How will we go unseen?"

A silver flame danced around Madrick's fingers as he spoke. "Aunika will enter normally; she works there. You and the other four Evertauri will enter inside a cart of potatoes we will ship to the fortress. One of our Evertauri, Lillia Hane, is placing an order for that cart of potatoes to be transported tonight. Lillia will guide you through the gate where you'll be carted into food storage."

Aunika pointed to the map. "Which is here." She then explained to Kyan the route to the technological wing and the room where the Guardian Stone was kept.

Madrick clasped his hands together. "Kyan, if anything should happen, give the Stone to one of the Evertauri." Madrick then pulled out of his pocket what looked like a tiny black bean and handed it to Kyan.

"What is this?" said Kyan, taking it. From the silence in the room that followed, Kyan could tell exactly what it was. Kyan whispered to himself, "It's for if I'm captured." His heart pounded, and he put it in his pocket and shut it with a button.

Madrick looked around the table. "Be ready by sunset. Good luck to you all."

~Dusk

The golden rays of sun had just begun to dip toward the horizon when Kyan, Lillia, and four other Evertauri arrived in a small cobblestone alleyway on the surface. A light snow had begun to drift down from the sky, and the very last light of day was disappearing to the west. The Evertauri set down their giant bags of potatoes they had hauled up from the Nexus.

Lillia turned to them. "Do you have everything you'll need?"

Kyan and the others nodded.

Lillia scanned the alleyway. "Alright, you all just get in the cart, and then I'll cover you up." The others nodded and climbed into the cart, using the wheel to step up.

Just as Kyan stepped onto the wheel, he heard footsteps running toward them. Alarmed, he turned to see Raelynn running up to him and asked her if everything was okay.

A little out of breath, Raelynn nodded. "Yes— yes, everything is fine . . ."

She looked at the others getting into the cart. "I just— I wanted to wish you luck."

Kyan felt as if she was holding something back. He nodded, noticing the way her hair glowed in the light of the sunset — the same as when he had first seen her in Aunestauna. "Thank you." He gestured toward Lillia, who was occupied speaking to the other Evertauri. Kyan looked back to Raelynn. "Lillia's going to take care of us."

Raelynn nodded, but her face hung sad and heavy. "Kyan . . . Xandria's forces are dangerous; the Ferrs are coming and the city is going to burn and—"

"It's going to be fine. We have it all planned out." He gave her a small smile, but it faded. They both knew how dangerous the mission would be, and that he might not come back alive. "I have to do this."

Another tear dripped down her cheek, shimmering in the golden light streaming through the alleyway. "Just—" Raelynn took a deep breath. "Just promise me you'll be careful." Then faster than Kyan could respond, Raelynn flung her arms around him into a tight embrace.

"I promise," he said to her.

A few tears dripped from her eyes onto Kyan's shoulder, then she softly pulled away, turned, and exited the alleyway. Kyan felt her presence leave like a candle blowing out into smoke. He turned toward Lillia and the others, took a deep breath in, and climbed up into the cart.

§

A minute or two later, Lillia dumped the last bag of potatoes onto the cart. "Are you all okay?"

From within the cart stacked with potatoes, five voices all responded, "Yes."

"Can you breathe alright?" she asked.

From beneath the potatoes, Kyan grinned, "Better than ever."

Lillia looked around the alleyway and took a deep breath, which puffed into the cold air like a chimney as she climbed onto the cart pulled by two horses. She reached inside her pocket to feel for the little black bean-looking object. Her fingers grazed it, and she closed her eyes. Her heart pounded and she shook her head. *Just do what you need to do, then it'll all be over.* She grabbed the reins and snapped them, driving the horses into the streets of Seirnkov.

Xandria's black fortress loomed up ahead. Its towers pointed up like the teeth of a monster, and its heavy gates stood like an iron mountain. Lillia guided the cart forward, trying to breathe normally. Winding through the streets of panicking Cerebrians, Lillia and the multiple Evertauri hidden beneath the potatoes reached the gate of Xandria's fortress.

"Papers?" said a Jade Guard. Twenty other armed soldiers stood there, blocking the gate. Lillia hopped down from her place on the cart of potatoes and pulled out papers from her coat. "Delivery for the main kitchen. Ms. Rostner is the name."

The guard read the papers and looked up at Lillia. "We aren't letting anything through at this point. The Ferramish army is headed toward the city we speak. Seirnkov is on full defense protocol."

"It's just a quick delivery," said Lillia.

"Not allowed . . . who are you? I haven't seen you before."

Lillia's stomach lurched. "I— like I said, Ms. Rostner is my name . . . I'm the assistant imports manager."

"I've never heard of that. Why are you making a delivery yourself and not your staff?"

Lillia's heart pounded. *Think quickly!* "My staff is part of our city's military reserves . . . called to action to help defend the city."

The guard furrowed his eyebrows. "I think I'm going to have to—"

A voice from behind Lillia approaching the gate spoke up. "Let them in."

Lillia turned around to see Aunika walking up to them and the cart of potatoes. Lillia sighed a breath of relief.

Aunika went up to the guards and signaled to Lillia. "I helped interview her. We need the food stores in case of an extended siege with the Ferrs."

The guards made a slight bow. "Our apologies Ms. Stinev . . . but please move quickly, the whole city is secured; the Ferrs are approaching."

Aunika nodded and the guards opened the gate to let the cart through. Lillia jumped back on and snapped the horses' reins. Aunika followed the cart through, and the giant gates shut behind them.

§

Lillia stepped off the cart and shut the doors of the food storage – a vaulted room filled with grain and vegetables. After scanning the room, Lillia whispered, "We're clear." The potatoes on the cart came tumbling down as four Evertauri and Kyan pushed their way through.

One of the Evertauri, Garner, stretched. "Feels good to be out of that."

Kyan jumped down from the cart. "No changes?"

Lillia shook her head. "Just as we've planned. Aunika should be at her post near the bell tower. Everyone else, to your posts to guard." Lillia gave Kyan a hug, surprising him a bit. "Good luck."

Kyan gently hugged her back, noting her rounded stomach. "Thank you."

"You have your dagger?" asked Lillia.

Kyan reached down to his belt and pulled out a longknife.

"Are you sure you know the way?"

Kyan nodded. "I'm sure, as long as those maps were correct."

"Be invisible," said Lillia, half joking, half serious.

Kyan breathed out heavily and made his way to a side door in the vaulted room. He thought back to his days in Aunestauna. *This is part of me . . . it's no different than any other time I stole on the streets . . . step lightly, be quick, be unseen. I stole this stone once; I can do it again.* Kyan turned the door handle and entered the maze of passageways inside Xandria's fortress.

Kyan stopped in his tracks when he heard voices. He quickly moved behind a door frame and watched as two figures rushed by the next hallway. He waited to move until they were long gone then scanned the dark stone hallway for anyone else. He turned the next corner and hurried down the narrow, winding passageway. Kyan rounded a bend and stopped when he saw a soldier guarding a door. Before the guard could yell out, Kyan drew out his dagger and lunged forward. The soldier fell to the ground, and Kyan stepped over him through the door he had been guarding. He shut it behind him and beheld a long staircase. *It should be up there.*

He climbed up the staircase and slowly opened the tall door at the top. He stuck his head out and into another dark hallway. *It's close.* At the end of the corridor, two guards stood in front of a doorway to Xandria's Vault. *The Guardian Stone is in there,* thought Kyan. *How do I get past them?* He reached for his dagger. *I can only take out one at a time.*

Kyan stepped back into the stairwell. The door to the main hallway sat beneath an arch above him. Kyan climbed up onto the archway, sitting like a bird perched on a branch. He pulled out his dagger beside him, set it down, and took off a shoe. Holding it in his hand, he took a deep breath in and then dropped it, sending the pattering sound echoing through the stairwell.

The guards in the hallway heard it and ran toward the noise. "Who's there?" Kyan held his breath. He could hear the guards looking around in the hallway behind him. Then, beneath him, the door to the stairwell opened and the two guards walked in. "Who's there?" they repeated. He gripped his dagger tightly. One of the guards spoke to the other. "Look here." He was looking at Kyan's shoe. *Here we go.*

The guard bent down to pick up the shoe, and Kyan jumped down from the archway onto the soldier's neck, snapping it. Before the other one could stab him, Kyan pierced his dagger into the soldier's collarbone. The soldier gasped and his eyes went blank. Kyan caught him as he fell so as not to make noise. He gently set the dead guard down and took the keys off his armor.

Kyan put his shoe back on and stepped back out into the hallway, scanning to make sure no other guards had heard, then quietly crept to the door of Xandria's Vault. He stuck the key into the lock and slowly twisted it.

Stepping silently into the vault, he moved past shelves filled with medicines, weapons, machines, and treasures. His eyes strained for the glow of light that he remembered from Aunestauna where he had stolen the Guardian Stone from the palace Vault. Rounding another corner, he saw it – a small box with soft, white light streaming out of it. Walking up to it, he slowly unlatched the lid.

Inside the box, a large stone radiated a pure white light. He couldn't exactly tell where the stone's edge met the air, and its interior seemed to swirl with drops of starlight from the heavens. It looked identical to when he had stolen it for Riccolo in Aunestauna.

Kyan picked it up; light danced around inside of it and seemed to melt into his hands. A strange sensation passed through his arm and the Guardian Stone felt cold to the touch. He could tell it held an immense power, though he knew not how to access it. Kyan shook his head out of the trance that had sucked him in, and he looked around the massive, vaulted hall. He placed the Stone into a big pocket on the inside of his jacket. *Now to get out . . .*

The only light that entered the hall came from a large fireplace in the back. Since there was only one, he assumed it was the same one Aunika had mentioned when explaining how to get out. He quickly made his way to the fireplace and located the pail of water next to it that the guards would use to put it out. Kyan threw the water onto the fire, plunging the room into darkness. The water sizzled and hot steam came up. As soon as Kyan took a step into the fireplace, the sound of yelling and banging echoed on the locked door to Xandria's Vault – it was Aunestauna all over again. *They know I'm here.*

The banging on the door continued, and Kyan quickly stepped over the wet, charred logs of the fireplace and put his hands and feet on either side of the chimney – a trick he had learned in his years thieving in Aunestauna. His heart pounded uncontrollably as he heard more and more soldiers gather at the entrance to Xandria's Vault. Kyan used all his strength to slowly climb up the inside walls of the chimney.

About five feet from the top, Kyan heard the door to the room below him break open and dozens of soldiers spill in. They yelled and ran between the aisles, trying to find Kyan, who continued to climb up the inside of the chimney. Kyan's body turned cold when he realized that there was a metal grate covering the top of the chimney. Just one more foot to go. He could see the stars in the night sky above, along with the shimmering glow of the auroras glowing in the north. The grate's holes were big enough to slip his fingers through. He could hear the soldiers below who kept searching the aisles, looking for Kyan. Kyan could feel his hands getting sweaty and slippery as he held himself thirty feet up in the chimney. His left hand slipped, and as he fell, he grabbed onto the metal grate with his right hand, sending a loud metallic rattle echoing through the chimney and Xandria's Vault.

A guard stepped into the chimney and yelled, "He's up here!" The guard tried to heave his sword up toward Kyan like a spear, but it didn't reach high enough and bounced off the sides, falling back down.

Kyan secured his feet back on either side of the chimney, grabbed hold of the grate, and shook it hard. Finally, something came loose, and the grate crashed off the top of the chimney. Kyan grabbed the rim of the stone chimney and pulled himself up onto the roof just as an arrow shot up past him.

Kyan looked around, getting his bearings. He stood atop a tower of Xandria's fortress, and he could see the whole moonlit city of Seirnkov. A gust of wind nearly blew him off the precarious roof. *I don't have much time until the guards sound the warning bells. I can do this . . . I've been doing this my whole life.*

Kyan sprinted off to the left, running along the ridged edge of the roof. He bounded forward, ignoring the hundred-foot drops to either side. He jumped onto another tower, nearly slipping on the shingles. The chimes from the bell tower rang out all over the fortress, sending a warning that the Evertauri were there. Soldiers began streaming into courtyards below, and fires along the outer wall were lit to help locate the intruders. Kyan spotted the rooftop doorway he was supposed to enter and ran through it, bounding down the staircase. *Just a bit more, and I'll meet with Aunika at the base of the bell tower.* Kyan raced through the halls as fast as his feet could carry him. He rounded a corner and jumped clear down another flight of stairs. Kyan sprinted into the next hallway and plowed into someone, who fell from the impact. He quickly drew his dagger and stood up but stopped when he saw that it was Aunika.

"Kyan, they know—"

"—know we're here," finished Kyan, pulling her to her feet.

"I was going to meet you where we had agreed, but the bells went off and so I went as quickly as I could. Do you have it?"

Kyan nodded.

From down the hallway came the echo of guards approaching. "We need to go now!" said Aunika.

"No. *I* need to go," said Kyan. He pulled the faintly glowing stone out of his pocket and handed it to her.

She immediately sensed the power it held.

Kyan continued. "They know you as one of Xandria's advisors. They've seen me, and they know I stole it. I'll be a diversion. Take it and slowly make your way out. We'll meet back at the Nexus."

"But I—"

"Take it, Aunika!" he whispered.

Aunika nodded and put it in her jacket. "Good luck."

Kyan hugged her, letting his emotions from Calleneck boil over in love for his often-unlovable sister. She had no way of knowing how good it was to hold her just this one time as her brother, and she probably had no clue why this boy was hugging her. The embrace only lasted a moment, and he sprinted off down the hallway as Aunika ducked into a side room to wait for the guards to pass.

"Over here!" shouted the guards.

Kyan tore away down a side hallway and through a door, trying to find his way out. Kyan's heart pounded as he ran forward through an empty ballroom lined with huge thirty-foot-tall windows. The guards burst through another door at the end of the hall and more funneled in from behind him.

Kyan looked for another way out as they closed in but could see none. The warning bells chimed all around. He vaguely remembered where he was and did the last thing he could think could get him out. He took a deep breath and sprinted forward at one of the towering windows, driving into it with all his force. The whole thing shattered as he flew out of it twenty feet down to a grass courtyard. Although the fall had knocked the wind out of him, Kyan stood up to try and run. But he stopped when he felt a dark, cold presence fill the air around him. His skin felt like ice and the hairs on his arms stood up. Shadows shot around him. *Phantoms.*

Kyan stood tall and closed his eyes until he could feel the Phantoms had stopped around him. He opened his eyes and tried to breathe slowly, staring at the ten or so Phantoms surrounding him – Thephern and a few others were gone. He recognized all of them, knew them by name, knew where they were from and what they could do. He refused to speak first.

General Lekshane stepped forward. "It's over, you're out of options."

Kyan breathed in, feeling for the small black pill in his pocket. "I know," he responded.

"You can't overpower us . . . you know what we want; just hand it over."

Kyan stood silently.

"Hand it over – the Stone," said General Lekshane.

"I don't have it," said Kyan.

"Hand it over!"

"I don't have it!"

"He's telling the truth," said a different, calm voice. Queen Xandria walked toward them in the night. Her blue eyes reflected the moonlight, and her white and silver dress seemed to glow like ice. "I can sense it." Xandria stepped close to Kyan. "So you handed it off to one of the others, did you? Why aren't you trying to fight? Who are you?"

His fingers held the small black pill in his pocket. Kyan's heart beat faster than ever before. "I'm not a sorcerer;" Kyan reached inside his pocket and pulled out the black pill. "I'm just a thief from Aunestauna."

Kyan bit down on the black seed and let the poison inside run down his troat. He expected pain, but there was nothing . . . Nothing was happening.

Xandria smiled. "Poison won't work so shortly after you've touched the Guardian Stone. It's a fortunate thing you're protected for the time being; you're no use to us dead . . . besides, we captured another one of you."

From the other side of the courtyard, Thephern Luck dragged Lillia by the hair and threw her to the ground. She sent a stream of white light at the Phantoms around her, who dodged it. The Phantoms quickly tied her hands behind her to prevent her from casting effective spells. Lillia struggled against them and Lekshane kicked her mouth with his spiked boots, knocking her over.

Xandria raised her hand. "That's enough, Lekshane. Take the thief to the dungeons and leave her with me."

General Lekshane complied and grabbed Kyan.

Kyan tried to turn back. "Lillia!" he shouted. "Don't give them what they want! Don't tell them anything!"

General Lekshane knocked Kyan on the head with the hilt of his sword to silence him as he dragged him away. Xandria walked up to Lillia and knelt beside her. Tears streamed down Lillia's hopeless, bloody face. She closed her eyes, letting out a sob as the blood dripped down, and subconsciously touched her hand to her stomach.

Xandria noticed and put her hand on Lillia's cheek. "Oh, my sweet, sweet darling, look what they did to you. The Evertauri does not want what's best for you; they only want to rule this nation for themselves. The Evertauri stole your life from you, stole your innocence and made you do awful things. Don't you want to make them pay? Don't you want to right their wrongs?" Xandria put her hand on Lillia's shoulder. "Let me see your eyes, little one." The queen picked up Lillia's chin. Looking deep into her, she nodded. "And they killed someone you loved . . ." Xandria looked at Lillia's stomach *". . . the father."*

Lillia cried, covering her bleeding face and avoiding the queen's eyes.

"I'll tell you what," said Xandria. "If you want to make the world better, if you want to make it a better place for *your* little one to grow up in, show us where the Evertauri are hiding and how to get inside. If you help me, your child will live. You can see him grow up . . . see him smile, hear him laugh . . ." Xandria put her hand again on Lillia's face. "But I'm afraid if you choose not to do what I say . . . your child will have to die."

Lillia sobbed and looked down at her stomach.

Xandria wrapped Lillia in her arms. *"Shh, there, there.* Don't cry; it will all be okay. I know you'll make the right decision. You are a good person . . . Will you help me, dear? For your child?"

She looked up at Xandria and the Phantoms with a quivering lip. Lillia's chin sank her head back to her chest and whispered, "Okay . . ."

XANDRIA'S WEAPON
Chapter Forty Four

~Evening, February 25th

As soon Lekshane hit Kyan, a flash of light brought him into Calleneck's mind, which sprang into action. He rolled over within the fake crate he had created with Dalah to sneak onto the supply train. The wagon cart jolted to a halt – it had carried him and Dalah the rest of the way back to Seirnkov over the past night and day. Thinking of the event to come – the stealing of the Guardian Stone – Calleneck tried to control his breathing. He looked over at his little sister. Though she was grown, she still seemed so young in his eyes, her childhood freckles dotting her cheeks like they always had. She was sleeping peacefully, somehow still able to do so despite the recent months' nightmarish experiences. He leangently leaned over her and made a tiny crack in the Taurimous wooden crate to try and tell the time of day.

The very last light of day was fading to the west and stars had already emerged in the dark sky. Snowflakes began to drift down and cover roofs with a thin layer of white. *The sun has set for some time, so the Evertauri who are helping Kyan steal the Guardian Stone have already left the Network, and Fillian and the Ferramish army must be closing in.* It made his head spin that his memories were of the future to come. He looked out the crack in the fake crate and saw a building sitting in a grove of evergreens that he recognized and a few battalions of Cerebrian soldiers marching south.

Our supply train must be just a few miles in front of enemy lines. We must only be five or ten minutes outside of Seirnkov. The cart jolted again and continued to move. Once we get into the city, we'll be a few streets over from the Ivy Serpent Inn where we might be able to enter back into the Nexus . . .

Calleneck watched through the crack in his fake crate as they slowly entered the city. His stomach pained him as he longed for food. But the far worse aching in his body was the fear of what was yet to come tonight. He thought of stealing the Guardian Stone and handing it off to Aunika, only to be cornered by the Phantoms. *Did Aunika make it back safely with the Stone?* He wanted to visit Gilsha while back in Seirnkov to help get her and her mother to safety, but he needed to first warn the Evertauri that he and Lillia would be taken captive.

Ten minutes later, the cart pulled into the city. Calleneck recognized the buildings that surrounded them. *We need to get out now.* He thought quickly and decided on a plan. Peering out the crack, he located a small shop up ahead.

Calleneck tapped Dalah to wake her up.

Her eyes shot open. "Where are we, Cal?" she whispered.

He looked again outside the crate. "We're in Seirnkov on Middleton Street. I'll cause a distraction. Get ready to run for it."

Dalah nodded and sat up.

Calleneck looked at his little sister. "We can do this, Freckles." He put his hand in hers; it was soft and gentle. "Look at me . . . I love you."

She breathed in deeply, trying to calm her nerves. "I love you too."

Inside the crate of Taurimous, crimson fire began circling around Calleneck's hands. *Focus . . .* Calleneck controlled his breathing and pictured what he wanted his Taurimous to do. He thought back to the night he became an Evertauri against his will – the night he cracked and destroyed a street corner. He was going to do it again. *Three, two . . . one.*

Calleneck channeled his Taurimous through the ground and into the shop beside them. With a brief blast, an explosion of fire shot out glass and bricks into the street and over the cart. The people in the streets screamed and pushed each other to get away. Most of the soldiers lay wounded from the explosion. He evaporated the fake crate around him and Dalah then pulled her off the wagon. A few of the nearby guards noticed and immediately surrounded them, drawing their swords; but Calleneck knocked them over with an explosion of crimson light. The mob of people in the square screamed and pushed each other over in the streets of shattered glass and flaming debris. Calleneck grabbed Dalah's hand and rushed her into a side alleyway.

Dalah looked around as she ran with Calleneck, figuring out where she was and what his plan was. The *Ivy Serpent Inn is close!* The two of them ran out into the next street, where people flocked through, trying to see what had happened. People were screaming, "The Ferrs are here!"

Calleneck and Dalah ran into another alleyway between two tall houses and into the next street. Fearing more soldiers were behind them, Calleneck and Dalah sprinted up the street, Xandria's black fortress looming ahead in the evening sky. Around another street corner, the Bernoils spotted the *Ivy Serpent* Inn up ahead. They ran through the crowds of people trying to board up their windows and get water from the wells that had now been completely emptied. Sprinting up to the steps of the *Ivy Serpent,* they saw that a mob of looters filled the tavern floor, stealing wine to prepare for the attack and water shortage.

They walked through the door and pushed through the crowd of fighting citizens, ducking beneath punches. The two pressed their way into the back of the inn and into a side room filled with mirrors, locking the door behind them.

Quickly, Calleneck put his hand to the mirror and covered it in crimson flames; nothing happened – it was sealed off. He pounded on the mirror and yelled. "It's the Bernoils! We're alone and safe. Let us in!"

After a few seconds, the mirror began to ripple like water and they stepped through it and into the Network. A guard stood before them with dark blue fire circling his fingertips.

"It's us," said Calleneck.

The guard breathed out in relief. "We thought you two were dead."

"We snuck into a supply wagon and rode it up from Port Dellock."

The guard nodded. "Quickly, go down into the Nexus!"

"Where is Aunika?"

"She hasn't been through my gate, but possibly one of the other entrances."

Dalah ran after Calleneck through the hallways and down a massive staircase into the cold and dark Nexus. The two of them sped into the main atrium of the underground buildings where a crowd of Evertauri had gathered. They all turned toward the Bernoils. "Cal, Dalah! We thought—"

"—that you were dead," they all said in a jumble. "Are you alright? What happened?"

"Where's Aunika?" asked Calleneck.

Hearing them, Raelynn ran out of a hallway up to them. "Aunika and the other Evertauri from the mission are with my father and Borius. A few of them went to Xandria's fortress but not all returned – Kyan and Lillia didn't come back."

Calleneck nodded. "I need to speak with your father."

Raelynn sensed the worry in Calleneck's voice and nodded. "Follow me."

§

General Lekshane and the Phantoms walked beside Lillia down the streets of Seirnkov. Behind them marched a battalion of the Jade Guard easily several hundred strong. Their armor rattled with the rhythm of their steps down the cobblestone streets as commoners rushed to safety inside their houses.

Lillia's face still bled, and the defeat inside her felt like a knife to the heart. She stopped in front of the *Ivy Serpent Inn* where a mob of people fought over getting the last bits of resources in the tavern, but quickly stopped at the sight of the Cerebrian army. "It's in here," she said weakly.

General Lekshane motioned forward. "Show us."

Lillia slowly walked into the *Ivy Serpent,* followed by the Phantoms and a small stream of the hundreds of Cerebrian troops. Everyone in the inn immediately felt the chilling presence of the shadowed warriors; silence fell over the room and the looters stared in fear at the Phantoms.

General Lekshane looked around and shouted, "Out!" and the tavern quickly emptied.

The Phantoms and a throng of troops followed Lillia to the back of the building into a sideroom full of mirrors. Lillia looked down at her stomach, her unborn child, and she began to shake. The thought of Raelynn, the Bernoils, and all the others in the Evertauri filled her head. Lillia cried, slowly raising her hand up to one of the mirrors. Almost inaudibly, she whispered, "I'm sorry."

White flames circled around Lillia's hand and covered the mirror, making it ripple like molten silver. She looked back at the General Lekshane who motioned her forward. With her head down, she silently stepped through the mirror like a ghost. In the dark tunnel, Evertauri guards stood in front of her.

"Lillia!" said a guard. "You're back, we didn't think you survived—" The guard paused. ". . . What's wrong?"

Lillia looked up with tears streaming down her face. "She would have killed him . . . *I'm so sorry.*"

Fifteen shadows crept through the mirror behind her. The guards launched fireballs at them, but not before the Phantoms streaked past and sliced swords through their backs and out of their chests. General Lekshane stood behind one and raised the sword up, making the guard groan out a dying scream and cough up a spat of blood, before shoving him aside and pulling out the sword.

Kicking over the dead body, Lekshane put his hand on Lillia's shoulder. "You've done well . . . now open the other entrances for the rest of our troops and then leave the city, or what's left of your Evertauri will hunt you down for giving your loyalty to the queen."

Lillia nodded and left the dark tunnel, sobbing as she went.

§

Calleneck, Dalah, and Raelynn stood outside Madrick's office. Raelynn pounded on the door and Sir Borius opened it. "Ms. Nebelle—"

He was interrupted when Aunika shot through the doorway to hug her younger siblings. Aunika's heart raced and she buried her head in Dalah's shoulder. "I thought you were both dead."

"We're okay," said Calleneck.

President Nebelle stood and demanded answers, "Why are you here?"

Calleneck looked over and saw the glowing Guardian Stone sitting on Madrick's desk, guarded by a shield of silver light around it. "Who came back from the mission to Xandria's fortress?"

President Nebelle looked at Borius. "Everyone except Kyan and Lillia."

Borius nodded. "But they're surely dead by now."

Calleneck shook his head. "I don't think so." Everyone looked at him as he continued. "Ever since we revealed the Evertauri at the Great Gate, Xandria has wanted to infiltrate us. But the reason she hasn't is because she doesn't know where we are or how to get to us. However, if she's captured Lillia—"

Borius nodded in understanding and finished the thought. "—then why would she kill her only way into the Network?"

Calleneck nodded. "Xandria's most dangerous weapon—"

"—is one of us," finished Madrick. ". . . Lillia Hane."

The silence that followed was broken by screams and explosions off in the distance. They all realized at the same moment what had happened. Borius turned toward the gut-wrenching sound. "They're here."

Madrick quickly grabbed the Guardian Stone as they heard the Evertauri fighting the Phantoms and Cerebrian troops in the distant hallways. Borius and a few other Evertauri darted out of the room toward the commotion to fight.

Calleneck pointed at the Guardian Stone and stared at Madrick. "We need to get that out of here! The Evertauri are compromised. Xandria is going to get the Stone if it stays here. We need to get it to Prince Fillian – It'll be safe with him . . . *it must go to him.*"

Madrick took the glowing stone and looked into its depths, and for a moment, it seemed like he was going to keep it himself. But Raelynn put a hand on his arm, breaking his trace, and he handed it gently to her. He spoke with words clear and precise and looked her in the eyes. "You run. You get the Stone out of here to Fillian Wenderdehl."

The fighting sounded closer, and they could see the colored lights of Taurimous down the hall. Raelynn took a deep breath in and then nodded. She placed the Stone in her coat pocket and then dashed out the door away from all the commotion. The shadow of a Phantom streaked by in pursuit of Raelynn; Madrick launched a massive jet of silver light at him, knocking him into the wall. Calleneck ducked as Albeire Harkil lunged at Madrick, but the President sent a silver fireball into the Phantom, sending him flying down a tunnel.

Another Phantom ran toward the Bernoils, and Aunika shocked a green bolt of electricity through the ground, rippling through the rock and knocking pieces down from the wall onto the Phantom. Aunika pointed down another hallway. "Run!"

Calleneck and Dalah rushed down another hallway and into the atrium of the Nexus where shadows and glowing Taurimous flew through the air. Hundreds of Cerebrian soldiers were flooding into the Network in a wave of rattling armor and unsheathing swords. Everywhere there were Evertauri fighting Phantoms and Cerebrian troops, and bloody corpses on the ground, both Evertauri and Cerebrians.

Calleneck locked eyes with a Phantom, Thephern Luck, twenty feet from him. "Dalah duck!" he yelled as he sent a fireball toward Thephern, who flipped over it and landed in front of them holding twin longswords. Dalah created a glowing golden shield of Taurimous and held it up. Calleneck focused his crimson fire into his own swords and swung at Thephern, who met the blades with his. Calleneck attacked again, the muscle memory from Tayben expertly guiding his movements. Thephern parried the blow and swiped with his second sword. Beneath her shield, Dalah sent a wave of glowing embers at Thephern's feet and knocked him off balance.

With only a moment to strike, Calleneck severed Thephern's hands and stabbed a glowing, crimson blade through his abdomen. "That one's for Tallius." He grunted and lodged the second Taurimous blade into Thephern, watching the Phantom's face of silent shock. "And that one's for Tayben." Thephern coughed up a spurt of blood and crumbled dead to the floor as Calleneck evaporated his swords into red smoke.

A wall of shields marched forward onto the floor of the Nexus; the Jade Guard trampled over the corpses of the sorcerers and then locked their shields together, planting their feet as a volley of arrows flew over their heads into the Evertauri. Calleneck's Taurimous soared into the air as a wave of light, splintering multiple arrows as they whizzed overhead.

To Calleneck's side, the old, bearded Evertauri – Sir Beshk Prokev – hurled a blue beam of light like a whip at the wall of Cerebrian soldiers and slashed their shields, sending them flying into the air. Immediately, the Cerebrian Guards raised their swords and pikes and drove forward, slamming into the Evertauri.

Countless colors of light sprung up as sorcerers produced shields and weapons to counter the hundreds of troops that still streamed into the Nexus in a never-ending torrent. The forces collided as the guards charged forward, driving their pikes into the disorganized mess of Evertauri. Cerebrian archers shot down from the high balconies lining the Nexus. Shadows of black streaked through the battle at impossible speeds, slicing through the Evertauri.

Calleneck looked around in a panic. Pools of blood seeped over the floor as Cerebrian troops and Evertauri crushed each other. Sickening sounds of dying screams and spattering blood filled the air.

"Cal!" screamed Dalah.

Before he could understand why she yelled, he felt a sharp pain in his shoulder, and he saw a dark shadow on his side for a moment before Dalah blasted the Phantom away with a jet of golden sparks. Calleneck yelled in pain and looked at the gash in his shoulder that began to bleed.

He heard another "Cal!," but from Aunika, who ran up to him, seeing his bleeding shoulder.

"I'm okay," said Calleneck through clenched teeth.

Aunika launched a green ball of fire into the Phantom Ferron Grenzo, driving him away. Her face was bloody on one side, and she had a gash from an arrow on her fingers.

Calleneck groaned, trying to overcome the pain. "Did Raelynn make it out?"

"Yes," answered Aunika as they all ducked under a jet of Madrick's silver Taurimous. "She's on her way behind enemy lines to give the Stone to Prince Fillian." The Cerebrian soldiers and Phantoms were closing in and forcing the Evertauri into a tighter area. The Nexus was dark, lit only by a few torches and the flashes of colored light from the Evertauri who were still alive.

Suddenly, a giant wave of reassuring and powerful silver light flashed through the chamber — Madrick. A powerful yellow fireball from Borius joined a column of silver embers from Madrick and exploded over a group of soldiers, crushing their bodies into the stone floor.

Purple, blue, and green balls of fire shot over their heads, burning up the arrows fired from archers above them. Beside them, Sir Kishk and Sir Beshk fought side by side with lilac and sky-blue flames, blasting away the Phantoms and soldiers. Kishk's stream of purple embers rippled through the ground as Beshk's blue flames swirled in a storm above their heads.

But it wasn't enough, they were being completely overrun as more and more soldiers swarmed the Nexus, raining arrows down on them like sheets of hail. Phantoms skewered Evertauri on spears, raising their writhing, screaming bodies in the air and hurling them back into the ground, smashing their heads open. Cerebrian troops found the Evertauri crippled by broken bones and pulled them up by the hair to slit their throats open.

Calleneck focused his flames into a glowing crimson sword and brought it down on a passing Phantom, who lunged back at Calleneck. Aunika kicked the Phantom away from Dalah, but he jumped back on Aunika and drew his dagger. Calleneck swung his glowing sword at the Phantom, who had to roll off Aunika to dodge the blade. Aunika sent a coil of light at the Phantom's sword to try and knock it out while Calleneck took another swing, which was blocked. From the corner of his eye, he saw another Phantom knock an arrow. "Watch out!" He tackled Aunika to the ground as the arrow whizzed over their heads, but his body went cold when he heard a thud and a small gasp.

They looked up in horror at Dalah. The arrow stuck straight out of her chest, and blood began to stream down. Little Dalah stared at them in shock as her legs gave out. Aunika jumped forward and caught her as she fell to the ground.

A giant wave of yellow light blasted the Phantoms and soldiers away from the Bernoils, and Borius ran up to them. Calleneck knelt over Dalah as Aunika placed her on the ground. Dalah coughed blood onto her cloak and looked at Calleneck with wide eyes of fear.

Tears streamed down Aunika's face as she gently spoke to her. "Dalah, listen. Listen. You're okay." Aunika put her hand on her shoulder as her body shook with pain. "Stay with me, alright? Stay with me . . . Shh, you're gonna be okay."

As fireballs and arrows soared over their heads, Borius stood over them, protecting them with a great yellow shield. Aunika began to sob.

Calleneck placed a hand on Dalah's face as her eyes began to lose focus. Her body convulsed as scarlet blood bubbled out of her mouth and onto his hand. Calleneck's vision blurred with tears as he began to cry. "It's okay, Freckles, I'm here . . . I'm right here."

Her face was filled with fear as the light in her eyes died, and the golden flame dancing around her fingertips vanished in a wisp of smoke. Aunika bawled and hugged Dalah's bloody, limp body. Dalah lay there unmoving, her face slowly draining of its warm rosy color.

An explosion knocked Calleneck over before he could cry more. Borius picked him up with a burned and blistered hand. "You two need to get out of here!"

President Nebelle ran over to them as balls of purple fire flew through the air around them. "Borius!" yelled Madrick through the explosions. "We're being overrun! It's over!" he said, out of breath. Madrick stopped when he noticed the arrow sticking out of Dalah's corpse. "Borius, take those two and get out, now. I have to collapse the Nexus. It's too late, but Xandria's best men are all here now – I can take them out, and the troops too." Madrick unleashed an explosive silver fireball to drive back Phantoms and knock down a line of troops. "They've killed almost all of us, but I think I can hold them off until you and the others get out. The Ferramish army won't be able to get to Xandria until the Phantoms are dead."

Borius looked around at the Phantoms and Cerebrian troops fighting against the Evertauri, most of whom lay dead on the ground. He turned to Madrick, "There has to be another way–"

Madrick stared Borius in the eye and swallowed hard. "Take them and run . . . Finish what we started. Go!"

Aunika sobbed and pleaded. "No! We can't leave her!"

"You have to go! Now!" said Madrick as a violet fireball exploded near them. He reached forward to Calleneck's shoulder. "Forgive me . . ." Madrick's face showed sorrow and hopelessness like Calleneck had never seen.

Calleneck looked at Madrick with watery eyes and nodded.

Borius didn't hesitate. "Come!" he ordered the Bernoils.

Ducking under a jet of silver light from Madrick, the Bernoils had no choice but to run after Borius, who sent yellow fireballs at five soldiers ahead of them.

Calleneck turned back to see his little sister one last time as Aunika yanked his arm forward.

They sobbed for their sister as they left her body behind. Both crying, Calleneck and Aunika each made shields of Taurimous to block themselves from the explosions. Borius sent wave after wave of yellow light ahead of them to pave a way for the Bernoils to escape. Running past the corpses of their friends, they turned into a hallway. Aunika wiped the tears from her face as they turned another corner, trying to get as far away from the Nexus as possible.

Pushing as fast as they could, they rounded another corner as a burst of silver light filled the Network tunnel, followed by a deafening explosion – Madrick's spell.

Borius yelled, "Run!" as the walls of the tunnels began to shake and crack. The noise continued as rock began to fall from the roof. And with a thundercrack from the Great Mother herself, the Nexus caved in, buildings and caverns crumbled under the weight, sending up a massive gust of air and debris.

Fragments of stone flew past them, hitting their backs as they dove to the floor. The raging wind screaming past them blew out the torches of the tunnel, plunging their world into blackness. The earth shook and around them as the great Goblin halls and underground towers came crashing in. A landslide of rocks filled the tunnels. For what seemed like minutes, the Nexus, the great Goblin city, crumbled and roared until the last few pebbles tumbled down next to their feet. Then silence.

A small yellow light sprang up, lighting the rubble-filled tunnel. Borius groaned as he stood up, with bleeding legs cut by rock shards. Calleneck slowly picked himself up, knocking off the smaller rocks that covered his legs and back. He was coated in gray dust, debris, and blood. He looked around for Aunika, but saw no one, until a green light moved rocks out of the pile of rubble and Aunika gasped for air.

Calleneck rushed forward to help her out of the rubble. "Are you alright?"

She nodded with tears in her eyes. Coughing up dust, the two looked to Borius. "What do we do?"

Borius looked around with his one eye, trying to breathe. The Nexus had collapsed, but the surrounding tunnels were still holding up for the time being. All the other Evertauri – with the possible exception of Raelynn – were most likely gone, buried under stone and dirt. Calleneck and Aunika began to let it sink in. Their sister was gone. Madrick was gone. Everything was gone.

Borius coughed from the dusty air. "We need to get out of the city. No doubt Xandria will be sending her troops down here to look for survivors."

"Where will we go?"

Borius shook his head. "I don't know . . . our best hope would be the mountains above Seirnkov. From there we'd be safe, but we could still look down on the city." Borius looked down the tunnel. "Calleneck, lead the way; you know these tunnels the best."

Calleneck stood in shock, but he had to force himself to think and process. He mentally planned a route that could take them to the mountain forests as long as the tunnels weren't severely damaged in that direction. "We'll go right, southeast toward the mountains."

Borius and Aunika followed Calleneck around the twists and turns of the tunnels, stepping over burned and bloody corpses as they went. Soon after, they reached another mountain of rubble on the edge of a cavern, and Calleneck stopped dead in his tracks. There in the rubble of fallen rock, trying in vain to get out from underneath a fallen stone building, was Gallien.

Gallien's face was covered in blood and sweat, trying to pry the giant stone boulder off of himself. His arms seemed completely weakened, with no power left to lift the rocks off. Gallien cursed and hit the rock and as he tried to wrench himself free but couldn't.

Calleneck stepped closer, as Gallien clenched his teeth and yelled in pain, blood from his gashes and burns dripping into his mouth.

From behind Calleneck, Borius stepped in front with a swirling ball of yellow fire, his one-eyed face filled with rage. Aiming at Gallien, Borius froze when Calleneck yelled, "Stop!"

Borius looked back at Calleneck and Aunika. "He's our enemy . . ."

Calleneck shook his head. "Leave him."

Borius's fireball in his hands grew larger. "They killed our men!"

"—and we killed theirs!" yelled Calleneck. ". . . let him be." Calleneck couldn't bring himself to help Gallien, knowing that Dalah lay dead underneath rubble, but he couldn't watch his best friend die, even if Gallien never knew Calleneck. ". . . He can't harm us."

Borius cursed and threw his fireball down at the ground in anger. "Then let's go! Leave him here to die for all I care!" He turned and followed Calleneck and Aunika away from Gallien, taking the light with them, plunging him to darkness . . . alone.

They knew that Raelynn was somewhere out there with the Guardian Stone, and they only hoped she would survive the night and make it safely to the Ferramish Army.

Borius stepped over a glowing rose petal as Calleneck led them into the mountains above Seirnkov, leaving behind hundreds of bodies of friends and family buried in the Nexus beneath the city.

THE SILENCE BEFORE THE STORM

Chapter Forty Five

~Hours Before Sunrise, February 26th
Blackpine, Cerebria

After narrowly making her way through Seirnkov with the Guardian Stone in her pocket, Raelynn had stolen a horse and sprinted to the Ferramish troops, who were attacking the small town of Blackpine three miles from the mouth of the valley of Seirnkov. The Ferramish troops pressed into the town, battling against a regiment of Cerebrian soldiers there, hoping to take it by morning to use as a base for their attack on Seirnkov.

Raelynn ducked behind a burning carriage as another volley of both Cerebrian and Ferramish arrows soared over her head. She looked back at her black horse lying dead with two arrows through its side. She checked to make sure the glowing stone was still in her jacket pocket. All around her, the Ferramish and Cerebrian troops were fighting, slashing swords and jabbing spears. Another volley of arrows whistled through the snowy air as Raelynn ducked. The Ferramish war horns sounded. *I'm close.* She figured that Prince Fillian would be near the horns, a heavily guarded part of the army. She darted into a side alley between two narrow shops and listened to the horns blare once more. *They've got to be just a few blocks away.*

Raelynn jumped out into the snow-covered street, running past the burning cart. She heard a Ferramish officer yell, "Get down!" and she ducked as a shop on the side of the street exploded. Glass flew at her and cut the skin on her right side. A plume of smoke from the explosion went up into the snowy sky as ten Ferramish cavalry charged up the street into Cerebrian pikemen. Citizens screamed from within their houses, unable to escape through the streets out of the city.

Raelynn dashed ahead and down another sidestreet, jumping over a dead Ferr. Turning the corner into more fighting, Raelynn knocked aside a Cerebrian swordsman with the hilt of her dagger. Up ahead, she could see a wall of scarlet Ferramish shields forming a blockade.

Raelynn sprinted toward the blockade with her hands up. Someone shouted, "Fire!" and suddenly, a volley of twenty arrows whizzed toward Raelynn from the Ferrs. Instinctively, she ducked behind a handcart as the arrows lodged into the wood. Realizing the Ferrs thought she was with the enemy, Raelynn shouted, "Fillian!"

The wall of shields and spears marched toward her as another volley of arrows came flying forward and smacked into the wooden cart. Raelynn screamed again, "Fillian! It's Raelynn!"

Just before the Ferramish archers loosed another set of arrows, Fillian shouted, "Hold fire! Hold fire! Let her through!"

The wall of red shields parted down the middle, forming an aisle. Raelynn quickly ran through it to the other side, surrounded by Ferramish troops. An explosion went off a block away, sending a fireball into the sky.

Prince Fillian, in full body armor minus a helmet, ran up to her. "Raelynn! I thought— well I don't know what I thought . . . After Riccolo and the court trial and Eston and . . . you and Kyan were just gone."

Raelynn frantically nodded. "We came back here, but I can tell you about that later. Right now," Raelynn reached inside her pocket and touched the glowing stone, "there is something urgent, but it has to be private."

Fillian nodded. "Come quickly to my tent."

Raelynn followed him through flanks of troops and wagons to the royal tent, and the two of them slipped inside.

"What's going on?" asked Fillian.

Raelynn pulled out the glowing stone from her pocket.

Fillian looked at the Guardian Stone with a mixture of curiosity and fear, staring into its starry light. "What is that?"

"It's the Guardian Stone; it will protect you," said Raelynn. "Xandria had it but Kyan stole it back. However, the Phantoms have overrun the Evertauri and were battling them under Seirnkov when I fled with the Stone. My father wanted me to bring it to you. He said that you and your army could protect it."

Fillian nodded. "We surely can do that."

Raelynn breathed out deeply and handed him the Guardian Stone. For a moment, Fillian marveled at it until white-haired General Carbelle burst into the tent. "My Liege, we're taking down Cerebrian troops, but we're losing a lot of our own. I don't know if we'll have enough men left to take Seirnkov."

Fillian felt sick to his stomach. "We could try and take our archers to the—"

Suddenly, a massive crack like thunder rumbled through the valley, followed by the booms of an avalanche coming from the direction of Seirnkov.

Fillian looked at Raelynn with a panicked face. "What hell was that?"

Raelynn's worried mind raced. *The Evertauri . . .* Without thinking, she rushed out of the tent.

Fillian yelled at her to come back, but he lost her in the swarm of Ferramish soldiers. She was undoubtedly trying to get back in front of Ferramish lines and up the valley to Seirnkov. Fillian shook his head and whispered to himself, *"She's not gonna make it back to the Evertauri alive."*

Fillian walked toward the center of his forces and opened the flap of his officer's tent. Pulling out the glowing, starlit stone, he felt the power surging through it like a wave that builds higher and higher until it breaks on the shoreline. In the corner of Fillian's tent, a white lion with powerful feathered wings stood up and walked over to the prince.

"Hello, Fernox," said Fillian.

Fernox the lion seemed transfixed by the Guardian Stone and apprehensively approached it, grumbling low in his chest.

"What's wrong?" said Fillian.

The lion's eyes grew as he stepped closer, tilting his head at the sight of the Stone. The reflection of starlight bounced off Fernox's infinitely deep eyes. Suddenly, Fernox lunged forward at Fillian with claws and a growl. Tackled onto the ground and held down by Fernox's paws, Fillian dropped the glowing stone on the ground.

Before he could grab it again, Fernox snatched it in his paws and leaped backwards, keeping Fillian at bay with a flap of his wings.

Fillian lunged forward. "Fernox! What are you doing?!"

Fernox jumped out of the tent and Fillian followed him, only to see the dim white outline of Fernox as the lion took off into the predawn sky with the glowing stone.

§

~The Black Fortress

Kyan's eyes shot open as a bucket of ice-cold water poured onto his face. Gasping for air, he looked around at the dark chamber around him. He felt the tight pressure of chains on his wrists, ankles, and chest. An armored Jade Guard stood in front of him, holding the empty water bucket.

Kyan shook his freezing wet hair to get it out of his face as the guard turned his head to the side. "The boy's awake . . . get the branding iron." A few guards outside the metal bars of the chamber marched down the hallway.

The thought of trying to escape flickered into Kyan's mind, but vanished as quickly as it came. The memories of the night before coursed like fire through his head – stealing back the stone, handing it off to Aunika, the attack on the Nexus, the Phantoms, the swarms of Cerebrian soldiers, Dalah, Madrick, the hundreds of Evertauri buried beneath Seirnkov. *Who's left to fight?* A cloud of dread suffocated him as he strained his mind, telling his body to give out, wanting it to end.

The guards reentered with a glowing red iron bar. Ripping Kyan's sleeves, the guards lowered the molten metal slowly. The soldier looked Kyan in the eye. "Tell us where the Guardian Stone is."

Kyan shook his head as the heat radiated from the red-hot iron. "I don't know."

The soldier nodded and pressed the branding iron into Kyan's forearm. Unimaginable, searing pain tore through Kyan – it was just like Evertauri's brand on Calleneck's chest. He couldn't hold back his screams. The guard lifted the metal and asked again. "Where is the Stone?"

Kyan shook his head hopelessly. "I don't know."

Kyan's cry from the pain echoed through the chamber as the smell of burning flesh wafted up. Again, and again the agony of the pain hit him as his vision started to blur; and with a flash of light, his mind ripped him out of consciousness, and he felt frigid mountain air on his face.

§

~Afternoon

The cold of the cloudy winter day sunk deep into Calleneck's bones. Huddled by a fire, he looked around at the snow-covered forest, where the evergreens leaned from the weight of the snow beneath an ominous gray sky. Around the fire sat Aunika and Borius, as well as the only other survivors who had found on their way out of the collapsed Network – Sir Kishk the Trainer, and white-bearded Sir Beshk of the Council of Mages. The five survivors had made their way into the mountains above Seirnkov and gone into hiding after the attack.

In the middle of the city, a crater of rubble four blocks wide marked where the Nexus beneath had collapsed. Buildings there had crumbled to ruin on top of the fallen earth. Powdery snow and dust from the Nexus covered the roofs of Seirnkov, and chimneys all over the city sent little smoke columns into the sky. Bells rang out across the valley, warning citizens to prepare for the coming attack. Somewhere down there, Calleneck hoped, Gilsha Gold was getting her mother to safety.

Looking southwest, he could see the Ferramish army approaching. In nearly every neighborhood, fathers were boarding up their houses as mothers collected their playing children, bringing buckets of water from the wells into their homes.

In the mountain forest overlooking Seirnkov, Calleneck's breath swirled into the cold afternoon air like a puff of smoke. His body ached and protested with exhaustion. Looking over at Aunika, he could see her eyes were red and swollen from crying. They had lost everything. From the hundreds of sorcerers who could have fought against Xandria at the last hour, only five they knew remained.

Raelynn was still nowhere to be found. The little fire crackled and engulfed a log, melting the patches of snow off as it flickered from crimson and yellow to green, lilac, and blue.

Borius broke the long silence. "From what we can see in that clearing there below, the Cerebrian troops seem to have made multiple rings of barricades within the city. Xandria has set up trebuchets to catapult fireballs at the Ferrs if they breach the city. We destroyed most of Cerebria's explosives at the Great Gate, but I'm sure Xandria kept some in Seirnkov. On the other hand, the Ferramish have three beasts with them that I'm sure will inflict heavy damage."

Sir Kishk shook his head, his lazy eye glancing off in another direction. "Xandria has at least as many troops in the city as the Ferramish have, if not a thousand more . . . you just can't take a city with fewer men than the defender."

"Are you saying the Ferramish are going to lose?" said Calleneck.

Sir Beshk shook his head and responded in a heavy, rough voice. "Xandria will walk over my cold dead body before I concede defeat."

Sir Kishk turned the fire lilac with an outburst. "The Ferrs cannot win. There's no way for us to win! We're outnumbered, we're on the run . . . I mean look at us . . ."

Aunika's head hung down.

Borius shook his head. "Madrick wouldn't have collapsed the Nexus unless he thought we had a chance . . . we may not have many Evertauri left, but now the Phantoms are gone as well."

Sir Kishk stood up. "But what if Madrick was right about Selenora . . . wh—what if she's still alive and she's with Xandria . . ."

Borius took a deep breath in. "There's no way to know . . . All I know is that we started something that we have to finish. The Ferrs march on Seirnkov tonight. This is the silence before the storm. You may decide for yourselves whether or not it's hopeless to fight; but as for me, I'm joining Prince Fillian and the Ferrs tonight. It's our duty to avenge everyone who has fallen."

The group sat in silence until they heard footsteps in the snow, walking through the forest up to their fire. Quickly standing at the ready for a fight, Borius and old Sir Beshk formed yellow and blue flames in their hands. The figure walking toward them was alone, blonde hair trailing down past her shoulders. Calleneck's eyes strained. "It's Raelynn . . ."

Raelynn reached the clearing of trees and stopped, staring at the group around the fire. Calleneck walked over to her. She looked like she had been on the run since the attack on the Nexus, but there was no stone with her. Her face was weary, her body at the point of exhaustion. At the sight of Calleneck, she began to sob with relief. She rushed forward through the snow and wrapped her arms over him, crying on his shoulder.

Trying to speak through her tears, her body shook. "I— I thought that everyone was gone— I gave the Guardian Stone to Fillian and rushed back to the Nexus but— it was all rubble, and I thought everyone was gone. I looked and looked until I found tracks in the snow leading up into the mountains."

Aunika stepped forward and embraced Raelynn, beginning to cry with her. Raelynn raised her chin and wiped tears off her face. "Where's Dalah? Kyan?" She looked around at Borius and the others. "My— my father?"

Borius stepped forward. "He was the one who collapsed the Nexus . . . he held off the Phantoms and the Jade Guard long enough to let us escape. By that point, almost everyone else had been killed. We're the only ones left . . . Raelynn, I'm so sorry."

Raelynn stood there in shock, trying to hold herself together. Anger coursed through her veins that bulged on her temple. She shook her head with teeth clenched. "We're going to kill her . . . Xandria . . . we're going to kill her."

Borius nodded. "At nightfall, when the Ferrs march up to Seirnkov, we'll join their front lines."

Calleneck looked over to Aunika. "We'll stay by each other's side." He turned to Raelynn. "Your father made his sacrifice so that we could finish shat he started."

Raelynn looked through the trees down at the snowy, glistening city below, where platoons of troops marched through the streets. "Then let's finish it."

~Nightfall

The sky had turned black by the time Prince Fillian and the rest of the Ferramish forces reached the edge of Seirnkov.

"We're almost there," said Borius to the surviving Evertauri as they descended through the snowy forest.

Calleneck stepped through another snow drift and between two tall evergreens. Above their heads, the green auroras of the night sky cast an eerie glow over the white valley. The mountain city of Seirnkov glowed with lights of battalion torches. Its city bells clanged and chimed, warning people to stay inside, as flanks of Cerebrian infantry marched through the streets.

Up ahead stood the Ferramish army, with flickering torches and waving scarlet banners. Dressed in battered armor, thousands of soldiers stood at attention in the potato fields and evergreens outside of Seirnkov. Platoons of Cerebrian cavalry, archers, pikemen, and infantry readied their formations. Near the front, Prince Fillian and his generals gave orders in front of three of Silverbrook's beasts that each released reptilian roars.

The group of six Evertauri broke through the trees and into the fields where the thousands of troops stood, approaching the side flank of the army.

Immediately, a sentry spotted them and called out an order. Fifty soldiers turned toward them. Following Borius's example, all of them raised their hands above their heads. Borius produced a glowing yellow flame in his hand to show who they were. A few seconds later, a General Carbelle called out, "Let them through to the prince!"

Platoons of soldiers lowered their weapons, sheathing them in one synchronized movement, and parted down the middle. Calleneck, Raelynn, and the others then lowered their hands and ran down the aisle of soldiers to the front of the army, where Prince Fillian sat atop a sturdy black stallion, with three of Silverbrook's hellish beasts behind him. The prince dismounted his horse as they approached. The troops reformed their positions and the six Evertauri stood before Fillian and the beasts. Fillian removed his helmet and stared at the six sorcerers in front of him, seeing them distraught, covered in snow and dirt. "What happened?"

Raelynn, the only one who had met Fillian before, spoke. "Xandria captured one of our own and forced her to let the Cerebrian army into our Network. It was a surprise attack, and we lost almost everyone. My father collapsed the tunnels to kill the remaining Phantoms."

Fillian stared in disbelief. "You're the only ones left?"

Raelynn nodded.

Fillian looked at Calleneck and the others in anger. "You were supposed to fight with us, help us take the city!"

"We are," said Borius, low and rich.

Fillian shook his head. "I meant all of you. Hundreds of sorcerers, that's what we were counting on going into this battle."

"We were too!" said Borius. "But we've only got one shot at this and we're here to help. We were the ones who sent hundreds of Ferramish troops free in Port Dellock who are now helping you occupy southern Cerebria. We were the ones who destroyed the Great Gate to let your army pass through the Taurbeir-Krons. We are the only reason you're here today. And if I may ask, where have these beasts been? It seems with them you should've taken the city by now with these monsters on your side."

"I'm not sending out our beasts without first knowing what defenses Xandria has set up against them. One beast was already killed in the Battle of Aunestauna by the Cerebrian navy. They electrocuted the serpent and were only defeated because of Raelynn's sacrifice." Fillian looked at her, then toward the city he had to take. He breathed in the wintry night air to clear his mind. "Thank you for coming to our aid."

"Where is the Guardian Stone?" asked Raelynn. "Is it protecting you?"

Fillian's insides turned, knowing the Stone was gone, taken by Fernox. He nodded and lied, reassuring her, "Yes— It's safe."

Raelynn breathed a sigh of relief and stepped forward, marveling at the three beasts before her with Calleneck at her side. One with four colossal wings shimmered white like it was made from millions of icicles; another grew straight out of the ground like vines and branches twisting together to form an enormous creature; and the last looked like an erupting volcano, its eyes and body made from molten rock and embers of fire. The beasts all turned to her, looking deep into her soul through their transformative eyes. Raelynn received the powerful impression that they knew her somehow.

Fillian interrupted her with a hand on the shoulder. She turned around to behold a glistening longsword in Fillian's hands.

Calleneck instantly recognized the sword.

Prince Fillian extended the hilt to Raelynn. "You may want this."

She took it in her hands. "Thank you—" She stopped when she saw the intricate Royal Crest on the handle, with the letter 'E' inscribed. She looked up at Fillian. "This was Eston's, wasn't it?"

"You saved our lives in Aunestauna," he said. "He'd have wanted you to have it."

Calleneck's heart tugged at him, wishing he could tell them who he was — that he was Eston and Tayben and Kyan too. They were all her inside of him.

Raelynn nodded and hugged Fillian as the sound of Cerebrian troops marching toward them through the city grew near.

Calleneck's body turned cold, fearing the inevitable fight — the closeness of death. He ignited a crimson flame in his hand, at the ready for any arrows from enemy archers.

With bells chiming in the distance, Prince Fillian turned to his generals Carbelle, Tuf, and Noppton. "We're ready."

The generals nodded and turned to the thousands of Ferramish troops behind them. "Sound the battle horns!" A single thundering note blasted from giant horns and echoed through the valley. Another, higher pitched note sounded from the city — the Cerebrian horn.

Fillian climbed onto his black stallion and looked up at Xandria's looming fortress at the center of the city. With thousands of troops behind him, he breathed in deeply and yelled loudly enough for the wind to carry his voice to his men. "We are not here to sack the city; we are here to kill Xandria and take hold of the fortress. On your honor as soldiers and men of Ferramoor, harm no one who cannot harm you. This city is fortified, and we have thousands of brave men standing between us and the Queen. This is it. This is the night that will end the war in either death or victory." Fillian raised his sword. "But we will have victory!"

The thousands of troops behind him bellowed and marched forward toward the city. The ground shook with every step the army took, and the beasts roared toward the night sky, sending a rattling thunderclap through Seirnkov.

Ahead, the Cerebrian troops marched through the city toward them, swords raised. But all at once, they stopped, frozen in the streets.

Calleneck looked to Raelynn and Aunika in fear. *What are they doing?*

Fillian repeated his thoughts. "Why aren't the Cerebrians marching?" He stopped and froze. "Halt!" he commanded the army; and in a few seconds, the Ferramish came to a stop.

Calleneck looked forward at the empty thousand feet between their armies and his body turned cold. Floating in the night air were dozens of glowing rose petals, suspended in the ice-cold breeze. Slowly, they began to spin around each other. More and more petals appeared out of thin air, swirling in a vortex around each other until they stopped, and silently drifted to the ground, revealing Selenora Everrose.

THE ARMY OF THE DEAD
Chapter Forty Six

Selenora silently stepped toward the Ferramish army as the snowy winds blew sideways. Behind her, rose petals flooded the streets of Seirnkov like a fog, revealing her hundreds of masked sorcerers, who began to march forward. All dressed in the same eerie, crimson cloaks, sparks shot out from their boots as they clinked down the cobblestone. Cerebrian soldiers ran aside into shops and smithies as the horrifying army of the dead walked through the streets, resurrected from the rose petals they vanished into months ago. Their skin seemed to be made of ash, and large flakes of gray flesh peeled off in the cold breeze, drifting in clouds behind them. The hundreds of dead sorcerers chanted in low, hypnotic voices, and colored fire flashed from their fingertips as they marched.

On the other side of the snowy field in front of Seirnkov stood the Ferrs and the Evertauri.

Borius looked back at Prince Fillian and Raelynn. "Get behind us, now."

Fillian snapped the reins on his horse and turned it back as Raelynn stepped behind the other Evertauri.

Calleneck's blood felt frozen inside him like ice. *She's back. They were right* . . . Selenora's face too seemed to be made of ash. Deep, black cracks lined her translucent skin and her mouth was but a black hole beneath her skeletal nose with gnarled, blackened teeth. All her form showed death and decay, except her eyes, which shimmered black, gold, and crimson. *She's halfway between life and death . . .*

Borius ignited a yellow flame in his hand, ready to fight. He turned to Calleneck. "She did it . . . she and her followers have been existing in *limbo* this whole time."

Raelynn trembled. "She just waited until my father was dead to come back. She knew that he was the only one who could challenge her again."

Selenora raised her hands of bone and ash, and her voice echoed across the army, amplified by her magic. "You have come to kill a queen with whom you are displeased . . . Kneel before me — your true queen — and no blood other than Xandria's will be spilled."

Behind Calleneck, Silverbrook's beasts rumbled. In the distance, dozens of Cerebrian soldiers began to kneel.

Fillian looked back at his army. "Stand your ground! Weapons at the ready!"

Selenora smiled with her flaking, gray face. "Then you have made your choice . . ."

Borius looked at the other Evertauri – Calleneck, Aunika, Kishk, and Beshk. "Now."

At once, five fireballs shot through the air toward Selenora. But instead of colliding with her, they passed seamlessly through her body as if she were a ghost. Calleneck's stomach dropped as he sent another stream of fire at her, and it sailed right through her into the mass of masked sorcerers behind her, where they disintegrated it in a shower of little flashing lights.

Prince Fillian raised his sword. "Archers! Fire!" A volley of arrows sliced through the air toward Selenora and her followers. As they whistled toward her, a cloud of crimson embers surrounded them, and they slowed to a halt in mid-air, levitating above the ground. Selenora raised her hand of ash and turned each of the arrows backwards. With a flash of light, the arrows whistled back through the air toward the Ferrs. The sound of arrows piercing through armor followed, along with the screams of pain from fifty soldiers, who writhed and fell to the ground, dying slowly.

Selenora smiled with blackened teeth and sent a crimson shockwave through the ground, knocking down a battalion of cavalry and infantry. Fillian shouted for the men to hold their ground.

Calleneck turned to Fillian. "The beasts!" They had taken down Phantoms. They could buy them time.

Fillian turned back to the massive monsters. "Forward!"

The horned beast made of smoking embers shot forward twenty feet over Calleneck, sending a wave of searing heat down to the ground, melting all the snow. Landing in front of Selenora, it roared, sending a firestorm of embers and sparks into her sorcerers. Truly like a monster from hell, the beast of molten rock slashed at Selenora and dodged a blast of her fire. But a flash of crimson light shot out from within the beast, and it exploded into the air in a shower of sparks and rock that came falling from the sky like volcanic ejecta. Fire circled around Selenora as she stepped forward, followed by a hundred masked sorcerers.

Calleneck looked to Aunika for comfort, but she shook in fear. He turned to Borius, who yelled in full fury, and charged forward. Sir Beshk followed, sprinting ahead of the troops toward Selenora, his long white beard trailing behind him. Aunika too began to rush forward, sending green fireballs toward the masked sorcerers. Summoning what courage he had left, Calleneck ran forward into the snowy night toward Selenora. Soon, the safety of the Ferramish troops was behind him as he sent a volley of embers toward her ghostly body.

An explosion threw him back as Selenora deflected all the spells from the Evertauri. Borius threw a spinning disc of yellow light toward Selenora, who severed it in half like a splitting river and spun it back around at Borius, knocking him to the side. A purple fireball soared over Calleneck's head as Kishk tried to distract Selenora.

Sending blast after blast to no avail, Calleneck's body began to freeze up after every crimson light passed through their ghostlike bodies without any effect. *We can't kill them . . . we can't kill them.* The snowfall began to intensify, and behind him, Calleneck heard Fillian call out. Following the order, the ground began to rumble like an earthquake, and Calleneck fell to the dirt as a moving tree root sliced through the ground below, digging its way through at unimaginable speeds. Fifty feet in front of him, a house-sized giant made of roots blasted out of the ground, sending a cloud of soil and rock flying into the air.

The beast's roots rippled and reformed, trying to stab and surround Selenora, who sliced through the roots with discs of light. The beast's roots quickly grew back, trying to lock Selenora into a cage of branches and crush her into the ground. But with a thundercrack of sound and a flash of crimson fire, a shockwave of light rippled through the system of roots and turned the beast to black ash. The charred skeleton of the beast stood for a moment, then crumbled and drifted away in the wind.

Fillian turned back to the remaining beast – a dragon of ice. "Stay, we can't lose you." He shouted to the army as he saw fire from Selenora. "Shields up!"

Crimson Taurimous coiled around Selenora's ghostlike form, as she sent fireballs toward the Ferramish troops. Calleneck and Aunika sent shields of light into the air to block the attack. Selenora shot a cloud of embers like a flock of burning ravens screeching toward the Ferrs, flying around Calleneck's and Aunika's defenses. The fire birds sailed like arrows into a platoon of soldiers, who screamed in pain from the fire as they thrashed on the ground.

Sir Borius and Sir Beshk sent blasts of yellow and blue light into the mass of undead sorcerers, hoping that they would inflict any damage. But they kept marching forward, fire scorching the earth wherever their ghostlike bodies stepped.

Sir Kishk yelled and rushed toward them with violet flames circling him. Barrelling himself into the disfigured, masked sorcerers, he knocked several down as they tried to push on. Green and orange fireballs soared past him as the undead fought back. Overrun by magic, Kishk formed a cloud of purple light, enveloping the nearby battlefield to obscur the vision of Selenora's followers.

Calleneck's world turned into that same violet fog, and he strained to see the other Evertauri around him. A glowing, green fireball whizzed by his ear and he turned to where it had come from. A crimson-cloaked sorcerer formed another ball of fire with skeletal hands and hurled it at Calleneck, who ducked beneath it. Calleneck blasted the mask off the sorcerer, revealing the rotting, ashen face of Grennkovff Kai'Le'a.

Calleneck focused his crimson Taurimous into a glowing longsword of fire and stabbed it up into the undead sorcerer. The blade crashed through bone and blackened flesh, but Grennkovff looked down at Calleneck with a deformed smile from hell and effortlessly pulled out the sword from his abdomen and stabbed back. Calleneck barely jumped back enough to avoid the swing, and as he ran away, a spell lifted the violet fog from the battlefield.

As the cloud lifted, Sir Kishk found himself surrounded by undead sorcerers. "Borius!" Kishk called out for aid, but the others were held off by Selenora far closer to the Ferrs – he was stuck behind enemy lines. A torrent of spells flew at him, and he tried to hold off the storm of fire until someone came to help. But the fire circled around his limbs and slammed him to his knees. He screamed in pain as his body bent backwards until his spine snapped in half and he fell lifeless on the ground.

Standing before Selenora, Sir Beshk moved in front of Borius and Aunika with a giant blue shield, trying to block the others from her. To his side, Beshk saw Calleneck running toward them. "Get behind me!" yelled Beshk, but Selenora turned her gold and black eyes away from Sir Beshk and toward Calleneck. Beshk ran toward Selenora to block her and as she raised her hand, he sent out a disc of blue light; but with a flick of Selenora's bone fingers, it came spinning back at him and sliced straight through his body.

Aunika covered her mouth at the horrific sight and stumbled as Calleneck and Borius formed crimson and yellow shields of their own. Desperate, Fillian ordered another volley of arrows that Selenora's followers disintegrated in the air. She moved closer to the Ferramish army, sending blast after blast, knocking Calleneck, Aunika, and Borius back. Calleneck stood up from the cold, snowy ground only to be hit by another fireball that singed his arm.

Weak and broken, Calleneck pulled himself back up again, grimacing in pain. Selenora locked eyes with Calleneck, and at that moment, Calleneck knew it was over. A beam of crimson light soared toward him, blinding him until it was replaced by a flash of green, and then went dark. Calleneck looked beside him, and the glazed-over eyes of Aunika stared lifelessly back at him.

The battlefield was muffled in his ears as a blast went off between Borius and Selenora. Calleneck stared at Aunika, whose face still held the fear and pain of death. The light had died . . . light that had been there his whole life. Another explosion of yellow and crimson Taurimous shook the air as Calleneck reached forward and placed a hand on Aunika's face and closed her eyes forever. The whole world seemed to move in slow motion.

Calleneck looked up with tears in his eyes at the muffled sound of his name. Borius and Selenora's Taurimous were colliding together in a blinding ball of yellow and crimson fire. Borius grimaced, trying to hold her off. He looked at Calleneck and called his name again, throwing Calleneck back into reality.

"Calleneck!" called Borius, who strained to hold his footing as Selenora forced her full Taurimous on him. "Calleneck!" said Borius again, shaking from the force of the spell. "Remember what I told you Calleneck!" He yelled from the pain, fighting to hold her off.

Calleneck finished Borius's words in his mind . . . *push to the end for everyone who can't.* Borius yelled out, and in an explosion of yellow light, Borius fell to the ground, mutilated and covered in blood. Calleneck looked back to the Ferrs; he was the only thing between them and Selenora. Directly in front of the army, Fillian and Raelynn stood with their swords drawn and a glistening beast behind them. Their eyes were hopeless, filled with fear of the death that was approaching. Standing on the burning battlefield, Selenora focused a stream of fire toward Calleneck.

Summoning all the strength left in his mortal body, Calleneck spun around and blasted against it with an iridescent shield of light. Through it, he could see Selenora stepping closer, pressing the fire harder. Calleneck strengthened his shield and widened it as the masked sorcerers began to send fireballs toward Raelynn and the prince. His feet began to slip on the blackened earth. Screaming in pain, he pushed back harder as the army of the dead marched forward.

Feeling his Taurimous begin to fail, he turned back to Fillian and Raelynn with a tear in his eye. "Run! Damn it, run!" he screamed. The force of the blasts overtook him, and the shield began to crack. Memories coursed through his head of the people who had given their lives to save him — from his mother to Aunika, they had made their sacrifice. Calleneck looked to Fillian and Raelynn who remained unmoved. Another tear fell down his face. "I'm sorry . . ."

Like breaking glass, the shield shattered, and crimson fire enveloped his body. Immense pain took over his body until he felt the cold snow on his chest and the world around him went silent and still.

§

Raelynn and Fillian stared at Calleneck's bloody corpse in the snow. Fillian looked around at his army in vain. Selenora and her army of the dead pushed forward, sending fireballs into their ranks. Horses and men flew twenty feet in the air before landing with sickening sounds on pikes. Men writhed and screamed on the ground to rid themselves of the flames that scorched their skin, trying to unclasp their molten hot armor from their bodies with blistered fingers.

A crimson fireball soared toward Fillian, who pulled the reins of his horse, rearing it up on its hind legs. The fireball hit the stallion and knocked Fillian to the ground. He gasped for air and stayed still on the ground; he felt hope drain from his body like blood from a wound, hollowing him out. But a hand reached down and pulled him up on his feet.

Raelynn looked him in the eyes. "I'm going to die standing on two feet . . . and so are you."

Fillian swallowed and nodded, unsheathing his sword. The ground in front of them exploded upward in a shower of rock like a cresting wave. Raelynn's heart beat quickly as the end neared.

Selenora raised her hands, and a torrent of crimson fire the breadth of the battlefield came soaring toward them like an inescapable cloud of death. Raelynn held tightly to the sword, ready for the wave to hit, ready to die. The whistling air pounded against their eardrums as it blasted toward them, shaking the ground.

I'm ready, thought Raelynn, and she closed her eyes.

And at that moment, the thundering wave of fire vanished in a flash of white light, replaced by a soft gust of cold, whispering air. From the dark sky behind them, the booming roar of a lion thundered through the valley.

Raelynn barely looked up before a blinding flash of white fire struck down from the night sky. A bombardment of building-sized, pure white fireballs slammed into Selenora and her followers, sending boulders of earth flying out across the battlefield. A deafening ripple of white light split through the ground like a shockwave, sending the ghostly masked sorcerers in front of them to their knees. In a flash like lightning, the mighty winged lion Fernox landed on the ground in front of them with a torrent of air from the flap of his massive wings. On his back, glowing in white fire, sat Silverbrook.

THE END OF WINTER
Chapter Forty Seven

Silverbrook stepped off Fernox and onto the scorched earth of the battlefield. With white flames circling her hands, she inched toward Selenora, whose ghostly arms pulled herself off the burning ground. Selenora stared back at Silverbrook with a flash of fear in her dead eyes.

Raelynn's heart nearly stopped as she gazed forward at Silverbrook. Somehow a magic flowed into her mind that confirmed the feeling of family, filling the void of the loss of her father; and Raelynn knew that, for the first time she could remember, she was looking directly at her mother.

Fernox roared behind Silverbrook as she produced a towering shield of light between Selenora's sorcerers and the Ferramish army, stretching hundreds of feet tall. Silverbrook turned back as the undead sorcerers began to fire at the barrier. "Raelynn!" she said, looking back at her grown daughter. "Raelynn, there's no time . . . take Fernox and Fillian – go get Kyan in the fortress, then kill Xandria."

Raelynn locked eyes with her mother, eyes just like her own. She found herself unable to speak, unable to express what she was thinking – her mother seemed to know everything.

An endless firestorm of Taurimous smashed into Silverbrook's barrier of light from the opposite side, threatening to shatter it. Silverbrook strained to hold it up. "Raelynn! Go, now! Take him with you." She pointed to the giant, four-winged beast behind them that glistened like ice – the last one left.

Fernox roared and pounced toward Raelynn and the prince. The giant shimmering beast sent out a rumble and crouched down. Fillian climbed atop Fernox and addressed his generals, "Take the army in two flanks around this battlefield and invade the city from the sides!"

Raelynn slowly stepped forward and grabbed onto the icicle-like scales of the beast, climbing atop its back. The beast flapped its enormous wings, sending out a gust of air across the battlefield. With two different roars, the ice dragon and Fernox leapt off the ground, headed around the city toward the fortress.

Freezing wind rushed over Raelynn as she desperately clung to the shining white scales of the beast, climbing into the night. Fifty feet below her, Fillian held onto Fernox as the winged lion followed her skyward. Raelynn looked over the side of the beast to the battlefield below and saw the giant barrier of light separating the Ferramish army and Selenora's followers shatter. After a few seconds, torrents of white and crimson Taurimous collided between her mother and Selenora.

The Ferramish army split down the middle and charged around the sides of the battlefield, cavalry leading the way around the immediate battle to attack the city. The Cerebrian troops in the street sounded off shrill battle horns that pierced through the snowy night. As the Cerebrians re-formed to protect the sides of the city, Silverbrook faced the army of the dead.

Fernox flew up beside the ice dragon as they streamlined to Xandria's fortress — and Kyan. Fillian shouted over to Raelynn and pointed toward it, "Watch out ahead, we have incoming!"

Raelynn looked forward and her stomach churned. The Cerebrian soldiers of the fortress had ignited their oil-soaked boulders for their trebuchets. Twenty catapults swung and rocketed giant fireballs toward them, streaming trails of smoke behind them as they flew through the night.

Raelynn latched on to the beast's shimmering scales as it flipped sideways, barely missing a fireball. Fernox and Fillian ducked under another that soared over them. Another volley of flaming, oil-soaked projectiles flew through the night toward them. Raelynn and her ice dragon spun in the air as the heat singed her back. "Watch out!" she yelled as a fireball smashed into a stone mailtower that came crashing down. As the debris fell through the air, Fernox banked sideways around the falling turret.

Fillian heard the whistle of an arrow streak past him as another clipped Fernox's wing. The lion let out a cry and dove to the side, out of the line of fire. A flaming ball came roaring toward them as Fernox flew behind another building that came crashing down from the impact. Below them, buildings burst into flame after being bombarded by fireballs from the trebuchet launches. War horns continued to sound off through the city as another volley of arrows from Cerebrian troops flew through the air up toward Raelynn. Ahead, the fortress ballistas shot giant iron arrows toward them.

The ice dragon soared up into the air as arrows flew past. In the distance, the Ferramish soldiers collided with the Cerebrians in the streets on both sides of Seirnkov. Cavalry charged in droves into Cerebrian pikemen as their archers fired over the rooftops into their ranks. Screaming and clashing of metal broke out on the rim of the city as blinding explosions of white and crimson fire from Silverbrook and Selenora thundered at the mouth of the valley.

The fortress battle horns blared, and another volley of flaming boulders roared through the snowy air toward Raelynn and Fillian. Fernox and the ice dragon climbed high above the streets of the city as the shower of fire soared toward them. Fernox and Fillian twisted and dodged the fireballs as the volley screamed past them with smoke streaming behind them. Suddenly, a bone-shaking roar split through the air as a flaming boulder smashed into the side of Raelynn's beast.

The fire exploded over Raelynn and the beast as it impacted them. Raelynn's body flew backwards and her grip on the scales slipped. Trying in vain to hold on, she slid off as the beast began to fall from the sky. The wind and snow rushed past as Raelynn's body tumbled through the air. Fillian and Fernox dove down vertically, plummeting through the sky toward Raelynn and the beast.

One of the beast's four wings caught on the wind and whipped it around, smacking Raelynn. Fernox flew around the falling beast toward Raelynn, and Fillian extended a hand, unable to reach her. The buildings below fast approached with only a few hundred feet left. As the ice dragon's tail whipped around, Raelynn latched onto its scales, pulling herself onto its back as it opened its wings to slow the fall before it crashed into a school roof, crushing it inwards.

Raelynn reoriented herself as Cerebrian soldiers on the streets below shot arrows up at her. In a few flaps of its injured wings, the beast bounded off the crumbling school and onto the next building, where the roof and rafters collapsed under its weight. *We can no longer fly,* thought Raelynn, *but we can still get to the fortress.*

A platoon of Cerebrian troops entered a city square below and began to fire arrows at Raelynn and the beast. Another arrow clipped one of its wings, and the beast roared, jumping down to the streets with a giant collision. With another bellow, the beast opened its mouth and launched a snowstorm of ice at the troops, knocking them dead onto the cobblestone.

As more soldiers funneled through the streets, Raelynn placed her hand on the neck of her mother's ice dragon, "To the fortress."

The shimmering beast below her let out an earth-shaking roar and pounced forward, shattering glass windows with its wings as it thundered up through the streets. Just a hundred feet above flew Fernox and Fillian, staying with Raelynn the whole way. The sounds of battle horns echoed again through the snowy night air as the Ferramish collided forces with the Cerebrians in the streets of the city. In the distance, white and crimson explosions from Silverbrook and Selenora lit up the sky like lightning flashes.

Crashing back onto the streets, the ice dragon let out another roar and slashed a charge of cavalry with its razor-sharp tail. Ahead, a giant barricade blocked the street with archers behind it. Raelynn clung tightly to the icicle-like scales of the beast as energy coursed through it and blasted out of its mouth as a hurricane of ice, exploding the barricade and the soldiers behind.

Flapping its wings, the beast pounced forward with Raelynn on its back, following the outline of Fernox and Fillian toward the center of the city. Raelynn held on for her life as the beast leapt up onto a collapsing roof and jumped from building to building, crushing its way up toward the looming black fortress.

§

Silverbrook watched as her daughter flew off into the night on the back of her ice beast. The iridescent shield of Taurimous was beginning to crack against Selenora's crimson flames. With another blow from Selenora, Silverbrook's barrier of light shattered and fell to the blackened battlefield. Selenora's ghostly figure ignited a crimson flame in her hand and stepped closer to Silverbrook. "You think you stand a chance against us?" she said.

Silverbrook armed herself in a circling white light. She lifted her hands at the ready and looked the disfigured, darkened Selenora in the eye. "Madrick sent you halfway into the abyss . . . I can finish the rest."

With the force of a hurricane, jets of crimson and white light smashed into each other, releasing a thundercrack that echoed over the valley. Silverbrook's constant stream of white fire toward Selenora allowed Raelynn and Fillian to gain a safe distance over the city. As she held Selenora's powerful spells away, the Ferramish troops escaped around and marched into the streets of Seirnkov.

Thrown back by a crimson explosion, Silverbrook picked herself up and looked up into the sky ahead, seeing her giant ice dragon dodge a fireball from the fortress. Another jet of crimson from Selenora sent her to the charred ground. Selenora raised both of her hands in crimson fire as her army of undead, masked sorcerers rushed toward Silverbrook. With green and violet sparks shooting from their feet as they ran, the masked followers sent a shower of spells at Silverbrook.

She cast a dome of light over her head as the spells hit. Extreme pain coursed through her body as she tried to stand. Her arms were soaked in blood, and beads of red dripped from her nose. But slowly, she stood, lifting her aching body off the scorched earth.

She stepped forward through the frigid night air toward the half-form of Selenora, who stood there like a ghost, deformed, fallen from her mortal state. Raising her voice toward the sorceress across the burned battlefield, Silverbrook spoke. "You won't win through sheer force."

Selenora smiled and raised her hands. "Of course not." Like a nightmare come to life, the earth around them seemed to be bending upward and overhead, pulled by crimson fire. The falling snowflakes froze still in mid air as Silverbrook felt gravity shifting sideways. Her feet slipped out from under her, and she felt herself falling through the air.

Silverbrook quickly sent out a burst of light to hold herself in place as the world warped around her, where the aurora-shimmering sky was now simultaneously below her and above her like a different dimension. Rocks and burning earth morphed and twisted around her like in a dream as Selenora tried to disorient her. In a mystifying illusion, Selenora's followers multiplied by the hundreds into a sea of crimson cloaks and terror-inspiring masks surrounding Silverbrook in all directions, above and below her.

Through the warped air around her, Silverbrook spotted Selenora sending a volley of crimson embers in her direction, and Silverbrook vanished them in a wisp of white light. *I can't kill her followers, but I need to fight Selenora one on one.* With blood-soaked hands, Silverbrook cast a spell with an enormous burst of light into the air that only Selenora could block with her Taurimous, and instantly, the warped earth around them returned to the same scorched battlefield.

Selenora stared in shock around her — floating in the wind, frozen in time by Silverbrook's spell and unable to move, were her hundreds of disciples. Suspended in the night air, their bodies were stuck in one instant in time. Silverbrook wiped a drop of blood from her nose. "Now it's just you and me."

§

Kyan's eyes shot open as a thundercrack rumbled in the distance. He looked around his chamber in a panic after feeling the pain of death from Calleneck and tried to control his sporadic breathing. His heart beat like he was sprinting as he gasped for air. The memories flashed through his head of the crimson fire overtaking his body as Calleneck — seeing Borius and Aunika lying lifeless on the battlefield. The frightened faces of Raelynn and Fillian scarred his mind. *They're all dead . . . Selenora must have won by now.*

In the distance, a low rumble shook the walls, and dust came showering down from the ceiling. Jade Guards rushed through the fortress hallways toward the commotion. Another thundercrack rocked the walls; a few stones from the ceiling came falling to the floor.

Kyan began to shake in his bonds. *This is it . . . Selenora has come to kill everyone. She's broken into the fortress.* Kyan's mind raced as the explosions and yelling grew louder. *This is my last body . . . this is the end.*

Kyan clenched his teeth and closed his eyes as a deafening crash collapsed the wall of his prison cell. Kyan balled his fists and prepared for death. But he froze when he heard a familiar roar — the roar of Fernox.

Kyan opened his eyes and saw an ice dragon shaking bricks and stone off its back as Raelynn and Fillian ran toward him. Fernox spread his wings behind them and pounced on a Jade Guard, pinning him to the ground.

Kyan stared in shock. "How did you— I thought you were both dead."

Raelynn unsheathed a dagger and sawed through Kyan's bonds. "We thought you might be too."

Fillian helped pull off Kyan's ropes. "Fernox brought Silverbrook to Seirnkov."

"Selenora and her followers are back, but she's holding them off."

At a loss for words, Kyan stood up and hugged them. Fernox purred and stepped toward them.

Raelynn put away her dagger and unsheathed her sword — Eston's sword. "We need to get to Xandria while we can. The Ferrs are fighting with the Cerebrians in the streets; my mother and Ferramoor are buying us time."

Barely having time to digest Raelynn's words, Kyan nodded. "Let's go."

Fillian put a hand on Fernox and climbed on his back, raising a sword and shield. Raelynn grabbed Kyan's hand and led him onto the back of the ice dragon, which bellowed, rattling Kyan's bones. Feeling a surge of energy beneath him, Kyan grasped onto the pale white scales of the beast as it blasted through the wall with a storm of ice from its breath. Pouncing forward, the ice dragon slashed through a group of Guards with its claws as Fernox roared and sank his teeth through their armor.

Fillian swiped away blows from atop the winged lion and sank his sword into the chest of a Jade Guard. Fillian turned to Raelynn and Kyan. "Where will Xandria be?"

Kyan looked around, getting his bearings in the fortress. "The Throne Room . . . it's the most heavily defended." He held onto the beast's scales as it flapped its wings and bounded up a flight of stairs, crashing into a grand dining hall, where arrows whistled through the air at them. In seconds, the platoon of archers was buried in a snowdrift and speared by flying shards of ice. "Up ahead and to the right! That bridge across the courtyard is the entrance to the Throne Room!"

The ice dragon smashed through the walls and Fernox flew behind. Kyan turned around when Fillian cursed in pain. A crossbow had crushed his shield, and his arm looked broken. He ducked as another volley of arrows whizzed through the air. Fillian cursed again as he sheathed his sword and held on tight with one arm to Fernox.

Raelynn and Kyan grabbed onto the ice dragon's scales as it sent another storm of ice down a hallway at a new platoon of soldiers. With a growl, it smashed through another wall and glided into the night air. Soaring to the next tower over, Raelynn, Kyan, and Fillian could see the city on fire around them as the Ferrs and Cerebrians battled in the streets.

Landing on the bridge to the Throne Room, the beast knocked over a line of Guards as Fernox tore them apart with his claws. Raelynn and Kyan slid off the back of the beast and drew their swords, and Fillian did the same. Dozens of Cerebrian troops funneled onto the bridge as a last line of defense to protect Xandria. The doors to the Throne Room sat there, not thirty yards away.

The beast swung its massive tail, knocking a cluster of soldiers off the bridge, screaming as they fell. It coiled back and released a jet of ice that impaled more infantry with spikes of ice.

Kyan charged forward into the army of Jade Guards. Parrying swings, he sank his sword into two different Guards as Raelynn did the same. Kyan ducked as a sword swung over his head, and he rammed into the soldier, knocking him over the edge of the bridge.

Fillian regripped his sword and with one arm, jabbed forward, swiping away spears and swords before Fernox jumped on the soldiers. Raelynn jumped behind the ice dragon as it released another blast, and then ran forward into the swarm of soldiers. But as more troops funneled onto the bridge, the three found themselves fighting on both sides, wedged between throngs of Cerebrian troops. Fernox roared in pain as an arrow embedded itself into his leg.

Kyan turned around to help Fillian take on the soldiers attacking them from the back. Trying in vain to push them back, Kyan slowly retreated to the side of Fernox and the beast. Out of the corner of his eye, he saw the flash of a sword just before a blast of ice knocked Kyan's attacker off the bridge.

Yelling, Fillian drove his sword into another Cerebrian. "I can't hold them off, Kyan!"

The ice dragon leapt forward, crushing two soldiers beneath its claws. Craning its neck back, the beast aimed a storm of icy breath at the great doors to the Throne Room. But before the first cold winds could pass its jaws, an explosion lit up the bridge as a vat of boiling tar spewed out from above the doors. Fire and heat filled the air, and Kyan ducked behind a Cerebrian soldier as burning potions and boiling tar flew by, searing soldiers' flesh. But the ice dragon had taken the full force of the explosion, and the burning, black liquid coated its scales in a blanket of flames.

The ice dragon let out a bone-shaking screech as it writhed in pain, melting away in a huge cloud of steam. Men screamed too, and a few were pushed off the bridge before the beast disintegrated completely.

More soldiers arrived on the scene, jumping over the flames to get to the three of them and Fernox. Kyan's body turned cold as he looked toward Fillian, and time slowed to a halt as the army closed in — there was no way to fight this many without the ice dragon.

Kyan knew what he must do to protect Fillian. Just before a soldier swung at him, Kyan dropped his sword and shouted, "We yield!"

Raelynn looked at Kyan with rage. "No! We can't—"

"They'll kill Fillian!" yelled Kyan. The Cerebrian soldiers around them had stopped.

Prince Fillian clenched his teeth as he dropped his sword to the bridge. Raelynn dropped the weapon she held as well — Prince Eston's royal sword. Fernox growled and lashed out at one more soldier, but then backed away in submission. The metal clashed against the stone and the three of them raised their hands above their heads in surrender.

§

Silverbrook put a hand to her mouth as she felt her beast die, and it took all of her strength to not fall to her knees. She looked out in the night toward Xandria's fortress, straining to see anything. *They're not going to make it if I don't buy them time . . .*

Selenora stood in front of her, hands raised, streaming dark energy at Silverbrook, who diverted the river of fire onto the battlefield behind her.

She looked helplessly at Selenora, trying in vain to take her down. She looked at her own shaking, cut-up hands as blood and sweat dripped down her face. Every fiber in her body screamed at her to give up. Silverbrook sent spell after spell toward the undead figure in front of her, but they sailed right through her ghostly body. *I can't get the upper hand . . .* she thought, as her feet slid back in the dirt. Her blood began to turn cold as the torrent of fire pushed her further and further back, overpowering her. *I can't kill her . . .*

Selenora sent spikes of earth shooting up at Silverbrook, which she barely dodged — one sliced a gash up her calf. With a sound that seemed to shatter the air, the undead sorceress began to tear apart Silverbrook's white Taurimous as it coiled out of her, sending her to her knees.

Silverbrook looked in horror at the half human face staring at her, killing her. Flakes of dying white light fluttered up into the sky and dimmed like cooling embers. The agony grew too much for her to take; she screamed out in pain. Images coursed through her mind of Kyan, Tayben, Calleneck, and Eston.

Silverbrook's world stopped as the thought overtook her. *The four of them exist because I tried to pull them into mortality when they were halfway to death; I pulled them out of limbo.* Silverbrook stared back into Selenora's half-formed, golden eyes. *The only way to kill you . . . is to bring you back to life . . .*

Silverbrook channeled through her mind, reaching for every place that still had magic left to give, reaching for the memory of catching a soul on its way to death. Summoning every piece of light she could find, she raised her hands and cast a spell over the battlefield — the spell she had failed that night nearly twenty years ago. A wave of light soared through the air, taking hold of every masked sorcerer and Selenora herself. The light dimmed and Selenora stood there with a fully formed body.

Selenora froze and looked at her hands, feeling the soft skin. She slowly reached up and touched her truly beautiful face with a delicate, shaking finger. Her hand ran through her silky hair once again. Her followers, entering back into consciousness, felt their mortal flesh again, many removing their masks to see with their old blue or green eyes — the sorcerers before Silverbrook were once again human.

Turning toward a breathless Silverbrook, Selenora slowly let the word roll out of her mouth. "How?"

Having taken it from inside her cloak, Silverbrook held a glowing, white stone — the stone that had been given back to her, its creator, by her noble winged lion. Silverbrook slowly held it up above her head and spoke, answering Selenora. "I did it right this time."

The Guardian Stone in her hand began to glow with the intensity of the sun, lighting up the entire valley with a blinding white brilliance. Both whispering and booming like thunder, the Stone radiated a cloud of pure, white light that charged over the scorched earth like a thousand cavalry, trampling forward into the army of the living. The air whispered and sang out as the light filled the city and softly vanished as gently as it arrived.

As the darkness of the night returned, the Stone in Silverbrook's hand was no more, destroyed and transformed into light. Before her lay a field of death. Droves of sorcerers lay unmoving, scattered on the ground as the winter wind gently rustled their crimson cloaks. Selenora lay among them, her journey to death finally complete.

Silverbrook stumbled forward and fell to the scorched earth below. The Stone was gone, as was the piece of Silverbrook's soul that went with it. Her body was spent, and the last bit of magic left in her body was beginning to fade. Silverbrook tried to stand, even using her powers to assist her, but they were exhausted. The curse inside the Stone had magnified as she used it to survive against Selenora, and now the disease ran through her blood as much as it had through Tronum. Her head turned sideways as he lay on the smoldering battlefield, hearing distant chaos in the city. She felt life fading as the city bells rang out and explosions rattled the air, all slowly beginning to get quieter and quieter to her. *Please,* she thought, trying to connect to the World Beyond, *let me see my daughter one last time.*

§

Kyan, Raelynn, and Fillian stood frozen in the frigid night air as a throng of Jade Guards surrounded them on the bridge. War horns sounded in the city below as the armies slaughtered each other in the streets of Seirnkov.

"We yield!" Kyan repeated with raised hands. As Cerebrian soldiers took hold of them, Fernox rumbled out a harsh growl.

Their commander stepped forward. "Surround that beast," he ordered. The pikemen quickly circled Fernox and lowered the points of their spears just inches from his fur. The commander looked at Kyan, Raelynn, and Fillian with a scowl. "Kill them."

The soldiers kicked their knees and forced the three of them to the ground. Fillian struggled against the soldiers and broke free for an instant. "I am Fillian Wenderdehl, son of Tronum, and Prince of Ferramoor. If you men have any honor, bring us to see your Queen."

Kyan frantically looked up at the soldiers. "You have no right to kill a prince . . . he's your Queen's nephew . . . bring us in."

An eerily familiar voice spoke up from the doors of the Throne Room. "Do as he says."

The green-clad Cerebrian soldiers hesitated, and then grabbed the three of them, lifting them to their feet. With iron grips, the soldiers pushed Kyan, Raelynn, and Fillian forward, stepping over the royal sword of Prince Eston lying ownerless on the stone.

Kyan looked to see who had given the command to take them to Xandria, but he couldn't see through the crowd of guards. The pikemen stood firm on the bridge, surrounding Fernox with a dozen iron-pointed spears. Before them, great iron doors opened with a loud creak, and the soldiers shoved them through. Kyan heard Fernox growl once more, but the slam of the doors closed off the lion from him.

The Cerebrian Throne Room was lined with enormous stone pillars and walls of windows that looked out into the destruction of Seirnkov below – a city on fire. At the end of the hall, on a green and silver throne sat Queen Xandria.

The soldiers marched them forward toward the white queen before them. She raised her chin and lifted her hand, halting the soldiers, who threw the three down to their knees before the throne of Xandria. She sat just ten feet in front of them, raised slightly by the stone step beneath her throne.

The queen smiled and spoke in her timeless, dreamlike voice. "And who do we have here, separated from their army?" She scanned them and looked at Fillian. "You look like my brother . . . Fillian, is it?" She smiled at the sight of Tronum's son at her feet and then turned to Raelynn. "The young sorceress? Though . . . not a sorceress anymore as I heard from your old friend Lillia." She turned her piercing gaze to Kyan. "And you are the Guardian Stone's thief?" She smiled again. "Would it amuse you to know that, though you stole the Stone from me, yes, I have already used its power to protect me? You and your men simply cannot kill me . . . you cannot win."

Kyan clenched his teeth together, not wanting to believe her.

"How fate has blessed me by bringing all three of you here," said the Queen. "Once you are dead, Ferramoor won't last the night." She looked at Fillian, tones of rage and fear in her voice. "As soon as they hear they have no king or prince to fight for, they will shatter like glass and concede victory to me and my people."

Fillian stared back with confusion and apprehension.

Xandria raised her eyes. "Has the news not yet reached your ears?" she said. "Why, Fillian, your father is dead."

Kyan's stomach lurched. Was it true? Had he seen this in his vision in the forest? He couldn't be sure, but if it was, Xandria had won everything.

Raelynn broke the silence. "You killed him, didn't you? Poisoned like your father."

Xandria smiled. "Oh no, young one, this Wenderdehl left this world without any help from me."

"So you admit to killing King Gallegore?" said Kyan.

"Of course I do," said Xandria, "and I hope any of you would have done the same if you'd learned what he'd done."

Fillian's face turned purple. "We would have never harmed our family."

"Oh really?" said the queen. "Then I would love to know what your plan was with me, nephew." The soldiers behind them sniggered and Xandria sat up taller, looking out to the city below as it burned. Battle horns continued to blare, eerily echoing through the valley. "We can wish death on even those closest to us if we know their monster inside . . ."

The three of them remained silent.

Xandria leaned forward on her silver and green throne, studying them. "You don't know, do you?"

"Know what?" said Fillian.

"What my father really was," she replied. Her eyes stared even deeper into their faces, looking at each one of them in turn. "Who *you are . . .*"

The hairs on Kyan's back stood up. She seemed to know everything about him, and more. Chills ran down his spine as he spoke. "Maybe not, but we know you. You murder anyone who stands in your way, and you won't stop until you've conquered all of Endellia. You and your brother have ravaged this world on your quest for domination over the other. There will be no peace until you have gone to the grave with him."

Queen Xandria's face turned pink with anger. "I built this empire to end the evil my father brought into the world, to end the reign of darkness and to protect the sacred powers of this land . . . to protect my people. Killing the three of you is the final stroke in bringing peace to the world. With you gone, the bloodline ends, and I can finish what I was meant to do."

The three of us? thought Kyan as he looked around the Throne Room at the throng of armed soldiers and back at their three, helpless figures. Suddenly, the windows to the city shone with a blinding light that quickly died.

The queen turned to the windows. "What was that?"

Kyan's spirits lifted momentarily as he earnestly hoped it meant Silverbrook had been successful. "That was probably your precious Guardian Stone." Xandria turned back to the three of them, a hint of dread running over her face. She was scared now.

"Aris!" she yelled, calling to a soldier standing next to a stone column.

Kyan's blood turned cold as Gallien Aris slowly stepped forward through the ranks of soldiers – it *was* the voice he had heard earlier. He had gotten out of the collapsed Network. Gallien's boots clicked and echoed on the stone floor, unlike his silent steps fighting in Endlebarr. He was cut up and bruised but adorned in silver armor and a jade cloak.

Xandria placed her hands on the armrests of her throne as Gallien stood between her and the three prisoners. "Aris," she said, "my last Phantom . . . kill them."

Explosions echoed outside and lit up Gallien's face with light from fire. Gallien nodded, and a tear fell down his face. Kyan shook his head . . . *please, Gallien . . . please see . . .*

As Gallien drew his sword, Kyan's heart stopped. Engraved on the hilt was the royal crest of Ferramoor and an 'E' for Eston Wenderdehl.

Xandria smiled as Gallien stepped toward Fillian, Kyan, and Raelynn. "You chose the wrong side to fight for," she said, "and now you pay the price."

Gallien took a deep breath in, hands shaking as he held Eston's sword. He spoke quietly, almost to himself. "The bravest person I knew once told me . . ." Gallien swallowed as his face turned pale. "He told me to be loyal to my heart."

Kyan's eyes widened as he finished the words. *Nothing else matters . . .*

And as a look of horror spread over Queen Xandria's face, Gallien spun around and stabbed the blade through her heart. The queen gasped and coughed a spurt of blood as her gown turned scarlet red. Fear filled her eyes as they slowly went blank. The room fell still, as Gallien clenched his teeth and dug Eston's sword further into Xandria's chest. He stared at her with a face of rage. ". . . You *earn* loyalty."

Suddenly, an arrow whizzed past Gallien as a few archers fired. Shouts of "Traitor!" and "Murderer!" echoed out from the crowd. Most of the Cerebrian troops stood stunned, not knowing what to do, but a few raised their swords and charged forward. Gallien drew the sword out from Xandria's chest and jumped in front of the soldiers, standing between them and Fillian, Kyan, and Raelynn.

At that same moment, Fernox smashed through a window into the hall, roaring fiercely, shaking the very air of the room. Fernox pounced in front of the Cerebrians and bared his bloody teeth. With another roar from Fernox, the air seemed to shimmer with a strange kind of magic as little wisps of light collected around the sword Gallien held. Within a second, Prince Eston's *Queenslayer* sword was ablaze with writhing white flames, and Gallien stood tall, looking like the legends of Gallegore come to life. The Cerebrians stopped in their tracks from fright – beholding the winged lion and the flaming sword.

Gallien handed the sword to Fillian, who addressed the Throne Room. "Enough! There will be no more blood spilled." One by one, the clattering of swords against the stone floor rang out as soldiers dropped their weapons.

Beside Kyan, Gallien stood tall and strong. "Sound the horns of surrender," he ordered. Within the minute, the horns of the fortress rang out in unison, blaring their surrender across the valley of Seirnkov. Distant cheers from the Ferramish army broke out in the city streets below as they raised their swords to the sky.

Raelynn rushed up to Kyan and threw her arms around him, feeling the same weight lifted that he did. "It's over," she said.

Kyan held her close. "I think so." There would surely be much more to do – local rebellions to calm, Cerebrian generals to surrender, and a whole nation to rebuild. It would take some time to cool the boiling war; but Xandria was dead, entering and leaving this world together with her brother.

Raelynn stepped back and glanced at Fernox, then back to Kyan. "I need to find my mother."

Kyan asked no question and nodded to Fernox. Raelynn quickly climbed onto his back, and Fernox jumped out the smashed window and into the morning sky.

Kyan watched for a few minutes as she flew away. The Cerebrian soldiers had taken Xandria's body off the throne and carried her away as Ferramish troops occupied the fortress. Kyan walked up to Gallien, who stood beside the bloody throne in shock. "Aris, was it?" said Kyan, holding himself back.

Gallien nodded with a grim look on his face.

Kyan couldn't tell if Gallien was relieved, horrified, or some other mix of emotions impossible to explain in a few words. Kyan breathed in deeply trying to keep in his tears. "I– I'd like to thank you for what you did . . . for all of us."

Gallien shook his head, "It didn't come soon enough." He turned to leave but stopped for a moment. "You should know . . . I'm going to fight to keep Cerebria free from you." He looked toward the silver and green throne. "Just because she's gone doesn't mean your king gets to rule over our people. We'll have a freedom of our own, no longer subject to the whims of Wenderdehls." When Kyan didn't respond, Gallien walked off to breathe the morning air of a nation he had changed forever.

But Kyan was proud. From the day he had emerged from the lake of Taurimous as Tayben, he had done all he could to give them a chance to win, no matter how hard the choices were. But everything he had seen in the visions had come down to a decision that was out of his control, Gallien's choice of freedom from tyranny.

Kyan slowly stepped toward the window, where he looked out on the city as people doused fires and hugged in the streets. His heart sank as he remembered who lay dead down there — all of the thousands of men, the Evertauri, the Phantoms, Madrick, Borius, Aunika, Dalah. He turned around to Fillian, who was staring at Xandria slumped over in her throne. "We need to give them all proper burials," said Kyan. "Ferrs and Cerebrians alike, Evertauri and Phantoms . . . no one should have needed to die."

Fillian stepped forward and hugged Kyan with his good arm, patting him on the back. He nodded, trying to hold back tears himself. "Yes— we'll make sure that happens."

"Fillian . . . your father . . ."

The prince took a deep breath in, trying to hold back a whole storm of emotions. He didn't have the words to speak how he felt, but Kyan knew what must be going through his head. Everything would change now.

Kyan turned out toward the city as horns rang out and a black banner rose above the fortress signaling defeat. Tired of trying to hold it in, Kyan broke down and fell to his knees. It was over . . . the war was over. Kyan sobbed as the emotions rushed out of him. Relief, pain, sorrow, joy all flowed over him like a flood of new air to breathe. From the visions he saw in the lake of Taurimous, the one way he knew they had a chance to win, the sacrifices he knew he had to make but could tell no one, the people he had to lose . . . it was all worth it. He thought back to his old shack in Aunestauna and shook as he cried, thinking of the long journey he had survived — one that so many others hadn't.

THE LAST SUNRISE
Chapter Forty Eight

~Before Dawn, February 27th

The wind blew gently across Raelynn's skin as she flew on Fernox's back above the city of Seirnkov. Together, she and the lion glided softly through the air, heading toward the field at the front of the city, now scorched and blackened from fire. The sky was beginning to show the first light of day, turning into a soft yellow glow from the east. Raelynn looked below as the lion's strong wings flapped and rustled in the breeze. In the streets, men and women were dousing fires, and the Ferramish army was rounding up Cerebrian weapons and helping repair the damage.

Ahead, the battlefield where Raelynn had left the presence of her mother to take the fortress and find Kyan lay barren and smokey, with patches of both snow and fire dotting the landscape. As Fernox descended to the earth, Raelynn picked out hundreds of corpses lying motionless in crimson cloaks. The lion's paws gently thudded on the ground as he landed, and Raelynn slipped off his back. The air was filled with a ghostly haze turned orange by the soon rising sun. Raelynn scanned the scene around her – dead sorcerers everywhere. Some still had their masks on, while others revealed faces she knew from long ago.

Raelynn knelt by the bodies of her friends, Calleneck and Aunika, and by her mentor Borius Shipton. She looked around for any sign of life but found none. Still in shock, she hardly noticed the faint coughing in the distance. Immediately, she rushed toward it, with Fernox walking in big strides behind her. Raelynn ran fast when she saw who it was. Kneeling down beside Silverbrook, she could see that she was still breathing, though her body was bleeding and scarred. Raelynn gently touched her hand to Silverbrook's face.

Silverbrook's eyes opened, and upon seeing Raelynn, shed tears that dripped down her temple. "My Raelynn . . ."

Raelynn burst out into tears and smiled, "I'm here, Mum. I'm here."

Silverbrook placed a shaking, weak hand in Raelynn's palm and closed her eyes, sighing a breath of relief. Seeming to barely be able to get the words out, Silverbrook looked her daughter in the eyes and spoke through dry, parched lips. "My– my little girl . . . look how you've grown."

Raelynn nodded and let out a laugh as tears streamed down from her face onto Silverbook's neck.

Her mother looked sorrowfully into her eyes, as a drop of blood trickled out her nose. "I wish I never left you . . . but I can rest knowing I did what I could to protect you in the final hours . . ."

Raelynn sniffed and looked at her mother's wounds. "We need to get you help."

Silverbrook, with the tiniest of movement, shook her head from side to side. "No, darling . . . I'm going to see your father and your brother."

Raelynn shook her head. "You can't." She let out a sob. "You can't leave me again."

Tears streamed down her mother's face as she put a hand on Raelynn's chest. "I'll always— be right here."

Fernox, having been observing from the side, gently walked up and lay down with his head right next to Silverbook's body, giving a low, sad grumble.

Silverbrook coughed and clenched Raelynn's hand. "T— take me back to my hollow . . . Fernox will know th— the way. There I can rest and see you again. But first, you— you must go to Fillian and Kyan. Fernox will show you my memories and— and you will understand everything. Will you go to them?"

Raelynn tried to control her sobs to be brave for her mother. "I will."

Silverbrook smiled. "You are strong." Silverbrook coughed once again as another tear dripped down her face. "My little flower . . . My Raelynn."

Raelynn could feel something in between her hand and her mother's. Growing with the last ounce of life left in her mother, was a small glowing flower. Silverbrook gazed peacefully at her daughter, and then gently closed her eyes.

Raelynn smiled and let out another sob, taking the white flower and standing up. Through teary eyes, Raelynn looked at Fernox, who let out another forlorn grumble. She then wrapped her hands around the lion's white mane and cried for a moment in his long, thick fur.

As the sky began to brighten above the white mountains, Raelynn climbed onto Fernox's back, and Fernox scooped up Silverbook's body gently, taking a fair amount of dirt with it. Raelynn leaned down again on his back and hugged the lion's powerful shoulders and soft mane. She looked up and peered out into the chilled morning sky that seemed just an hour until sunrise. Putting a hand on Fernox's shoulder, she spoke gently to him. "You heard — to Fillian and Kyan." With a gust of wind, Fernox opened his powerful wings and bounded into the sky.

By the time Raelynn arrived at the black fortress sitting atop its hill at the center of Seirnkov, droves of Ferramish soldiers had made their way into its halls. She had flown over burning buildings being doused with water and cheering throngs of scarlet cloaks as they raised banners into the sky. Small fights between soldiers pushing each other in the streets or trying something more stupid were broken up quickly. The only civilians that had yet left their homes were those who needed to escape from fires. It would take time to rebuild, and the animosities between Ferrs and Cerebrians would not be so easily repaired.

Even from the height of the fortress, she could hear the bells and horns still echoing out over the mountain valley. Though the castle infirmary was almost overrun with soldiers and nurses, Raelynn found a bed on which to lay her mother. A few soldiers had graciously agreed to watch over her body as Raelynn took Fernox to find Fillian and Kyan.

After asking directions from a handful of guards – all of whom were quick to help her with a lion staring down at them – she found her way to the top of a tower near the Throne Room. Stationed outside two intricately carved doors were four Ferramish officers, each with scarlet feathers adorning their golden helms.

"I wish to see the prince," Raelynn said, not hiding her Cerebrian accent. Fernox let out a growl.

These men were braver in the presence of Fernox, but still shuffled. A general with a white beard and hair coughed. "I, um– I can't let anyone in to–"

The doors opened behind him, and Fillian stood there, only halfway still dressed in armor and mail. "I thought I had heard Fernox," he said with a smile. "Carbelle, let her through, she's with me. And the lion too."

"Yes, My Liege," said General Carbelle.

Even with both doors ajar and his wings tucked in, Fernox barely fit through. Raelynn followed him in as Fillian shut the doors behind her. The room seemed to be a study or royal lounge of some sort, with shelves of books and embroidered green couches. Large glass windows let in the soft yellow glow of the coming sunrise in the east.

Kyan stood up from a jade armchair. "Raelynn– your mother, what happened? Is she–"

She took a moment to speak. "She's gone . . . her body is in the infirmary being guarded for the time being." Raelynn surprised herself with how she spoke. Her sadness seemed inexplicably resolved. Though maybe it was just the importance of the moment – she still had something to do.

Fillian put a hand on Raelynn's shoulder. "I'm sorry to hear . . . she was quite brave from what I've gathered . . . brave like you."

Raelynn looked at Kyan. "She said I needed to speak with you. With both of you. Do you either of you know what for?"

Kyan took a deep breath in. "I think I do."

§

At first, when Kyan told them, they didn't believe him. He didn't expect them to have believed something as strange and inexplicable as his connection to his other bodies, but he knew they deserved to know. He told them everything that happened in the last months and all he had learned from Silverbrook – from her, to the Nymphs, to the Saentauri, to Gallegore. After Fernox showed Fillian and Raelynn the same memory Silverbrook had showed him in the forest – the night of Kyan's birth in the palace of Aunestauna – the room had gone quiet. They sat across from each other in silence, Raelynn and Fillian trying to wrap their heads around what they saw, and Kyan waiting for their response.

Fillian was the first to speak. "So you have every memory Eston had?"

Kyan nodded and tried to figure out the words. "I– I still feel like I *am* him, and the others too. It's not like he was someone else, I was him and he was me – those four bodies *were* all me, all one person."

Fillian's face sat somewhere between tears and confusion, but he stayed composed. Tracing his finger along the woven designs of the fabric couch he sat on. "So I guess that makes you my brother . . ."

Kyan didn't know what to say, or how Fillian felt, until the prince chuckled.

"And I thought those damned beasts were the strangest thing I'd ever see."

Kyan allowed himself to smile but stopped when he saw Raelynn looking down at her hands. She sat on another soft armchair in between Fillian and Kyan. "Raelynn?" he said, unsure why.

She looked up at him, moving a strand of white-blonde hair out of her face. "You could have told me where my mother was . . . that my brother was dead."

Kyan didn't know how to respond. Part of the reason her mother never came back to her was because of him.

"But I understand why you didn't," she said. "I wouldn't have believed you if Fernox didn't show me the memory – my own mother there at your mother's bedside." She looked out the window at the white mountains beyond and the slowly brightening sky. "It's just a lot to take in . . . I just don't know why my mother needed us three to talk together. This explains a lot but–"

She stopped when Fernox nudged her leg with his wet nose.

Fillian stroked the stubble on his chin. "What was Xandria saying when she spoke to us? She mentioned that we didn't really know who Gallegore was. She said we didn't know who we were – the three of us. She said the bloodline ended with killing us." He turned to Kyan. "You said when Xandria was younger, she traveled through Endlebarr and was approached by the Nymphs. They gave the Phantoms the powers they had given the Saentauri." He turned to Raelynn next. "And your mother told Kyan that Gallegore was a Saentauri who was chosen to lead the Great War against the sorcerers and unite Endellia . . . So what if the Nymphs showed Xandria something in Endlebarr? Something that made her go back to Aunestauna wanting to kill her father."

Kyan's hands felt tingly, and he leaned forward in his chair. "Fernox was Gallegore's lion. I don't think the night of my birth was all he needed to show us . . . There's something else."

Fernox purred, and his eyes began to glow and swirl like the beast's eyes had done. Suddenly, the world felt like it was spinning. Up was down and down was up and suddenly the three of them were standing in a dark forest. The soil was black beneath Kyan's bare feet, and the trees around him stood hundreds of feet tall, shrouded in fog – *Endlebarr*. But something seemed different – the forest seemed less dangerous and more enchanted, brighter and livelier than he remembered it. *Almost as if I'm looking at it as it was in another time.*

Not ten yards off, a group of cloaked figures approached Kyan, Fillian, and Raelynn, but could not see them. The three of them were like ghosts in a memory, just watching the cloaked figures. They wore masks over their faces so similar to the ones Selenora and her followers once wore. Fire circled around their fingertips as they trudged through the underbrush – blue, green, gold, violet flames. They were sorcerers. It wasn't until the figures passed through Kyan like he was made of mist that he realized there was a child walking with them in a cloak of his own.

Before Kyan could make anything of it, the sorcerers stopped in their tracks. They had noticed something Kyan hadn't – darting down from the trees like shadows were warriors carrying wooden bows and spears that glowed with shimmering light. Kyan could hardly catch a glimpse of them before they attacked with such speed and ferocity, Kyan almost thought to run before remembering it was only a memory he was seeing. Fireballs and sparks flew through the air toward the woodland warriors, who shot past the spells to deliver quick strokes of death to the sorcerers. Shields of light glowed brightly as the warriors from the forest elegantly glided through their ranks, slashing them down as swiftly as a river current. Kyan realized who they were – Saentauri. He was looking at a memory decades in the past, though he knew not how far back – sometime during the Great War.

The battle was over as quickly as it had begun. Fillian and Raelynn watched silently with Kyan as a group of Saentauri warriors circled around the bodies of the sorcerers. They seemed to wear no iron or steel. Their armor was made of woven plants Kyan thought must have been grown into fortified plates to cover them. The swords hanging on their belts were made of some wood as sharp as a blade, endowed with spells and magic from the Nymphs. They had incredibly long and skinny arms and legs, but they seemed undoubtedly strong, nonetheless. Their faces were long and their chins prominent and sharp – in fact, every feature about them seemed remarkably defined. As they approached, Kyan noticed that the child sorcerer was still alive, nervously backing away from the Saentauri into a bush.

One of the warriors reached down and pulled the little boy out. The child couldn't have been older than five or six, and his fearful eyes looked out on the dead sorcerers he had traveled with. The Saentauri spoke to his comrades in words Kyan could not understand, then he turned to the child and spoke in the Common Tongue. "Are there more of you?" The child said nothing. "How many did you come here with? Why did you enter this forest?" The little boy stayed silent. "He does not understand even the Common Tongue," the Saentauri said, "he's a Lostlander like the rest of them. They've come to try and take the power of the Nymphs. What do we do with this one?"

Another warrior stepped forward, even taller than the first one. "The boy is a child. Look at the fear in his eyes . . . We can erase his memory; we can take him in as one of our own."

"Raise a sorcerer from the Lostlands? They've come to destroy us."

The taller Saentauri pointed at the little boy. "This one hasn't." He knelt down to the trembling child and put a hand on his forehead. Soon, the crying stopped, and the child fell asleep into the Saentauri's arms.

As he picked up the boy, the first Saentauri asked, "Did you find a name for him? In his memories?"

"Yes . . . his name is Gallegore."

Kyan's stomach turned upside down. He looked sideways at Fillian and Raelynn and could tell they were feeling the same way. *Gallegore was a sorcerer? The Saentauri raised him as one of their own? A foreigner and an enemy?*

Before Kyan could talk to Fillian and Raelynn, they were tumbling through the air again, light swirling around them as Fernox took them to more memories. One after another, they saw Gallegore grow from a child to a man, chosen by the Saentauri to lead their war against the sorcerers and the false kings. Memory after memory, Fernox hurled them through space and time, showing battles, Gallegore atop Fernox wielding his great flaming sword of Vaeleron. They saw him with a Saentauri woman with skin that shimmered like silver. He called her by her name – Aeliara . . . Aeliara Silverbrook. They were kissing, lying with each other atop a giant bed of forest mushroom. Kyan, Fillian, and Raelynn were tumbling into more memories. A coronation. A wedding. Kyan saw a woman he recognized only through paintings as his grandmother Kliera Dellasoff. They were falling through the air again and soldiers were marching through a Goblin tunnel, then a forest was burning, then a grave was being dug. Too many images and all too fast to take in; too much to understand.

Then the sickening feeling of falling stopped, and the three of them stood in a quiet study – but it wasn't in the true world yet. This was Tronum's study in Aunestauna, but the books and the room were all different. And instead of his father sitting in the great chair, another man sat with a crown of silver atop his head, matching his silvery gray hair. Kyan could see in the man's face that he was Gallegore grown, weathered by the years. Opposite him stood Xandria, younger, but with the same silvery blonde hair from her late mother, Kliera.

Tears streamed down her face as she looked at her father. In a soft voice, nearly a whisper, she spoke to him. "I know what you did." She seemed barely able to look him in the eyes. "The Nymphs of the forest showed me everything."

King Gallegore sat back in his chair with a stern, unyielding gaze. "And what would that be?"

Xandria shook her head, clearly not wanting to speak, but forcing herself to. "That you were one of them, a Warrior of the Forest. That they chose you to end the Great War and to unite us. They showed me the woman and the child you fathered with her before you realized you weren't one of them – you were a sorcerer from the start and that's why they picked you to lead the war. You were the strongest of them all – you possessed sorcery and the gift of the Nymphs."

Gallegore stared at his daughter with rage. "The Saentauri used me as a pawn. Raising me, pretending that I was one of them, making me annihilate my own kin, my people."

Xandria couldn't look at her father anymore, but the tears kept coming. "And you killed them for it. All of them. The Nymphs showed me what happened. You left the forest and took your crown here in Aunestauna. You married our mother, but before we were even born, you went back into Endlebarr to take back your child. *Your bastard child.* And when the Saentauri wouldn't turn her over or the woman you bedded–"

"Her name was Aeliara."

"–you killed them all! The Saentauri are all but extinct because of you. And in exchange, you agreed to let those vile Goblins live in peace if they built you a tunnel under the forest for you to bring your army of men. You destroyed them all while they protected your bastard daughter from you . . . and you never found her, did you? By the time you had finished off the Saentauri, Tronum and I were already born, and mother had died because of it . . . and you weren't there. You weren't there for your first true daughter – your heir."

Gallegore's face was purple, and his teeth and fists were clenched. "You are no daughter of mine."

Xandria shook her head. "I wish now that I was not. But I am the eldest truborn child and I must rule after you. It's my right."

"Silence!" shouted Gallegore. "You are dead to me . . ." He looked out the window of his study. "You will no longer govern the Cerebrian Territories, and Tronum will inherit the Empire."

The world swirled and turned around Kyan once more, sending him tumbling and falling until he found himself resting in the jade armchair across from Raelynn and Fillian. It took a moment for his eyes to adjust, but the fortress room around him came back into focus, and the light in the east over the white mountain Seirns brought his senses back into the true world. It seemed as if no time had actually passed while they were peering through the eyes of the lion. Kyan looked at Fernox, whose glowing eyes dimmed until they were the normal deep irises of an animal.

His world felt like it had been spun upside down, in more ways than one. But everything made sense. It explained why he had the gift of sorcery as Calleneck, why Silverbrook had been so powerful — she had the blood of the Saentauri and the sorcerers. It explained why Silverbrook went to Aunestauna after her mother died — to be with her father Gallegore and her half-siblings Tronum and Xandria, the only family she had left. It explained why the Saentauri were destroyed, and why Gallegore disowned Xandria. Why had everything been so complicated? Years ago he had nothing more to worry about than getting a loaf of bread.

Kyan turned his mind to the present world, looking at Fillian and Raelynn who both sat silently, undoubtedly trying to take in all that had just happened. It was a few minutes before any of them spoke, and it was Fillian who broke the silence. "She knew this whole time. Xandria saw what had happened and must have seen some of what was to come. She knew the forest needed protection, knew who Gallegore was and what he did."

Kyan stared blankly at the ornate couch on which Fillian sat. "She still killed her own family. She still destroyed the Goblins in retribution for the help they gave Gallegore. She was still too dangerous, too set in ridding the world of everything her father was. This war had to end with her death." Kyan looked at Fillian. "With both her death and our fathers'. There wasn't another way for peace . . . but we can forge our own pathway to peace now."

Fillian shook his head. "But the bloodline . . . Gallegore first fathered a child with a Saentauri, Aeliara Silverbrook. The child was Abitha Silverbrook. And if that's true, that makes the heir to the throne—"

Kyan and Fillian turned to Raelynn, who was sitting silently, looking at Fernox. "—me," she said simply. The word seemed to hang in the air for a moment before she spoke again. "But I can't take the throne."

"Says who?" asked Fillian.

"Says reason," she responded, "not to mention half the laws in Endellia. If what Fernox showed us is true, my mother was Gallegore's bastard child, which makes my claim to the throne a bastard's claim, even though she was his first child." She shook her head. "And how would anyone believe the story? We can't show every person in Endellia what Fernox showed us. My mother knew who she was, but she decided to let everything run its course. If she thought taking the throne was a good idea, she would have done it herself. I'm a bastard's bastard. It's not for a Silverbrook to hold."

"Then you," said Fillian, turning to Kyan.

Kyan stumbled on his words. "I— I can't — for the same reason. Who would believe that I am really Prince Eston, that I have a right to the throne over you?"

"It doesn't matter what they believe," said Fillian, "we can choose who takes the crown."

"It *does* matter what they believe," Kyan responded. "It's a ruler's subjects who grant him power through the very belief that power resides in him."

Raelynn leaned forward and breathed in. "Kyan's right, Fillian. Who in Ferramoor or Cerebria would follow someone they don't know; someone they don't think has any royal blood? Would we rather risk more war? More chaos and death? Or would we rather move forward with what everyone else already sees as the natural next step. To the world, you are the one heir to Gallegore, to your father. We three are the only ones in the world who know the truth, and the secret is safe between us."

"You would have me live a lie?" said Fillian.

"We would have you be good," said Kyan, a tear threatening to pool in his eye. "We would have you rule with love and justice and kindness, learning from the mistakes of all those before us. A king who does not want power is exactly the king most deserving of it."

Fillian's eyes began to water.

He just lost his father and won a war in one night, thought Kyan, *no wonder his emotions are running high.* It took all of Kyan to stay composed as well. "Fillian," he looked him in the eye and forced himself to speak over the lump in his throat, "I would be proud to call you my king."

"As would many," said Raelynn. "And the world will be a better place for it."

Fillian thought for a moment, then stood. "So what's next?"

Raelynn looked out the window at the white mountains beyond and the brightening sky. "I'll take my mother back to Endlebarr to lay her to rest . . . It's her home."

Fillian nodded. "Take Fernox with you, he'll see you there safely. He is as much your blood as mine, and I have a soldier or two who will keep watch over me." He gave her a smile. "*That's an order,* Ms. Nebelle."

Raelynn allowed herself to smile back. "Yes, *Your Majesty.* It will be an honor to fly with Fernox again." The winged lion stepped closer to her and nuzzled his nose against her side as she put a hand on his soft white fur.

"And you?" Fillian asked Kyan, putting a hand on his shoulder. "Maybe you can help me find a way to sow peace between two nations that hate each other?"

"If you'll have me," said Kyan.

Fillian smiled. "There will always be a place by my side for family . . . for my brother."

EPILOGUE

The morning air was cool to the skin as Kyan and Fillian stood on the bridge overlooking the fortress grounds and the city below. In the east, the sky had brightened to a soft orange and yellow glow where the sun would soon rise above the snowy white mountains. The sight took Kyan's memory back to a sunrise long ago over the forest of Endlebarr, where he had absolutely no idea what life lay ahead of him.

A few birds glided by, floating on the wind above the city. Many of the fires had been extinguished, and the boarded-up windows of shops and houses were opening. But far above the streets, the morning was quiet and peaceful. In the western sky, he could see Raelynn atop Fernox, flying gently into the clouds until disappearing from sight.

As Kyan and Fillian stood, leaning on the balcony of the bridge, they smiled at the sight of the sunrise. Fillian turned to Kyan. "What do we do now?"

Kyan stared out as the sky over the mountains brightened. "Well, all of this is yours if you want it."

The prince shook his head. "No . . . at least not permanently." Fillian thought for a moment and chuckled, gazing out over the edge of the bridge.

Kyan smiled. "What?"

The prince shook his head and grinned. ". . . In Eston's memories, do you remember the bridge in the palace in Aunestauna where we used to see how far we could spit?" Fillian laughed and bit his lip to prevent his watery eyes from showing.

Kyan felt his throat choke up. "You'll have to remind me who was better."

Fillian chuckled as his eyes began to fully tear up. "Oh, it was always him. . . but of course I'd never admit it." He smiled big, an understanding passing between them.

Kyan felt his own tears forming and breathed in deeply to try and hide it.

The prince shook his head, and Kyan could see the sunrise reflecting in his eyes. "This is going to be hard . . . without Father."

Kyan nodded, holding his emotions back. "I know," he said, turning to Fillian, "But you will always have family beside you. I'll be here."

Fillian wiped a tear from his cheek and nodded, looking out into the white mountains beyond. "And for that, I am grateful."

And ever so slowly, the golden sun peaked up above the mountaintops. Kyan breathed in the crisp air as it rose, shedding rays of warm, spring light over the valley. His lips formed into something of a smile as he felt a sense of long-lost peace settle over the world. His mind wasn't traveling into another body; he was himself, all four lives in one – watching the sun continue to rise for the first time.

The End

APPENDIX

Characters

The Royal Family

–KING TRONUM WENDERDEHL of Ferramoor, second Wenderdehl to sit the throne

–his eldest son, PRINCE ESTON WENDERDEHL, Prince of Ferramoor, heir to the throne

–his youngest son, PRINCE FILLIAN WENDERDEHL, Prince of Ferramoor

–his twin sister, QUEEN XANDRIA WENDERDEHL of Cerebria, former Governess of the Cerebrian territories and current queen of the Kingdom of Cerebria

–his late father, [KING GALLEGORE WENDERDEHL], also called Gallegore the Great, King of the former Endellian Empire, Saentauri, led the Great War against the Sorcerers

–King Gallegore's wife, [QUEEN KLIERA DELLASOFF] of Cerebria, mother of Tronum and Xandria Wenderdehl

–King Gallegore's winged lion, FERNOX

–his wife, QUEEN ERADINE LAMEIRA of the Kingdom of Parusemare, Queen of Ferramoor

–Eradine's late mother, [LADY ANETTE LAMEIRA], former Queen of Parusemare, former Governess of the Parusean Coast

–Eradine's late father, [LORD PHILAR TOUSSOIS of Luquette]

–Eradine's elder brother, KING PHILAR LAMEIRA II, current ruler of Parusemare; and Philar's wife QUEEN CHARLETTA FONTIGNE

The Ferramish Government

—in the Council

—SIR JANUS WHITTINGALE, cunning First Advisor of King Tronum and Prince Eston's mentor

—LORD BENJA TIGGINS, the Scarlet Lord, palace overseer and commander of the Scarlet Guard

—QERRU-MAI AN'DRUI, quick and intelligent Council Scrivener

—her mother, SENATOR QARA AN'DRUI

—her late father, [LORD JARRO AN'DRUI], former governor of Southern Ferramoor, killed in the Battle of the Burning Hills

—PROPHET OMBERN, stern leader of the faith in Ferramoor 'the Church of the Great Mother', lives at the Cathedral of the Luxeux

—his successor, PROPHET MIRRIOTUS

—JUDGE RATTICRAD, petulant Palace Judge responsible for hearing cases and administering the King's justice

—other senators: SENATORS BARDOW, DUBOIRET, ELIM, HILLBOTTOM, MAR, NOLLARD, and RESBEE

—others in government: Eston's Butler ERRUS; Fillian's Mentor SIR ENDWIN BARDOW, brother of Senator Erdwey Bardow; Parusean Ambassador to Ferramoor CHEVEIR FONTIGNE; Ferramish Ambassador to Parusemare THOMET CHANGEREAU, and more

—in the army

—GENERAL LIANN CARBELLE

—his son, LIANN CARBELLE II of the Scarlet Guard

—GENERAL TUF

—GENERAL NOPPTON

The Streets of Aunestauna

—KYAN of the Third District, street thief, orphaned since early childhood, also known as Kyan Alda

—Nightsnakes

—RICCOLO, sadistic leader of the Nightsnakes, also called the Lord of Thieves

—his second in command, BAY, Nightsnake

—"VREE" VRIISHA SHAARINE, thief of the Nightsnakes, runaway Gypsy from the Southlands

—her twin sister, VENESSTA SHAARINE, maimed by Riccolo and sold to the Zjaari slave trade

—others

—ZOGO BLACKBLOOD of the slums, the pawn shop trader, the giant

—RUBEN TUMNO, the baker

—ODEN HAGGAHOL, the smith

The Forest of Endlebarr

—TAYBEN SHAE of Woodshore, Phantom, Cerebrian soldier, blacksmith apprentice for his father

—in the Phantoms

—GALLIEN ARIS, Tayben's best friend in the army, Phantom in the Second Platoon, from the aristocratic Aris family of Gienn

—GENERAL LEKSHANE, leader of the Phantoms, the last remaining original Phantom

—THEPHERN LUCK of Shadowfork, leader of the Second Platoon

—FERRON GRENZO of Vashner, charismatic Phantom of the Second Platoon

—CHENT VANTTE of Tangle Took, quiet and deadly Phantom of the Second Platoon

—ALBEIRE HARKIL of Tallwood Watch, pensive leader of the First Platoon

—other Phantoms – SI-CHEN VANTTE, KALLO, and RETTER of the First Platoon; GERRECK, BRINT, and SHAENLER of the Third Platoon

—in the military

—BIRG NORR of The Iced Bank, Tayben's and Gallien's tentmate in the Cerebrian Army

—CAPTAIN FENLELL of Endgroth, captain of Tayben's army platoon

—VAYA IRROY, courier for the Phantoms

—other soldiers: HASHT of Whitetree; GENERAL KORKOV of the army; GENERAL HEIRMONST, leader of the Cerebrian Navy

The Evertauri

—CALLENECK BERNOIL of Seirnkov, sorcerer and cartographer for the Evertauri, joined after discovering his gift through a dangerous outburst of magic

—his elder sister, AUNIKA BERNOIL, the first Bernoil child to discover and join the Evertauri, also assumes the alias Serisa Stinev

—his younger sister, DALAH BERNOIL, last Bernoil to join the Evertauri, also called Freckles by Calleneck

—members of the Council of Mages

—PRESIDENT MADRICK NEBELLE, founder and leader of the Evertauri

—his son, [SHONNAR NEBELLE], murdered presumably by Klytus Kraine

—his daughter, RAELYNN NEBELLE, also assumes the alias Endra

—SELENORA EVERROSE, the most gifted sorceress, trained and raised by Madrick Nebelle as his own

—SIR BORIUS SHIPTON, second in command of the Evertauri

—his half-brother, [SIR OBARIUS SHIPTON], killed by the Jade Guard

—SIR MORDVITCH AUFENSCHIESS, aristocratic spy leaking information from Xandria's Fortress to the Evertauri, third in command of the Evertauri, cofounder of the Evertauri with Madrick Nebelle

—his butler, KOSOV

—SIR KISHK KAUBOVFIER, also called Kishk the Trainer, responsible for overseeing the training of newcomers to the Evertauri

—SIR BESHK PROKEV, old and experienced sorcerer on the Council of Mages

—SIR GRENNKOVFF KAI'LE'A, disciple of Selenora Everrose

—other Evertauri

—LILLIA HANE of Fellsink, newest Evertauri, girlfriend of Tallius Tooble

—TALLIUS TOOBLE of Seirnkov, Calleneck's best friend, boyfriend of Lillia Hane

—[KLYTUS KRAINE], presumed murderer of Shonnar Nebelle

—others: GARNER; SITI; VORROV; EDDRI and more

The Surface of Cerebria

—MRS. BERNOIL of Seirnkov, mother of Aunika, Calleneck, and Dalah Bernoil, formally Sheilla Vontammin Bernoil

—MR. BERNOIL of Seirnkov, father of Aunika, Calleneck, and Dalah Bernoil, formally Otto Bernoil

—his elder brother, GREGT BERNOIL, called Uncle Gregt, relocated to Bordertown

—his sister-in-law, SHELLN BERNOIL, called Aunt Shelln, married to Gregt

—his best friend, [RUSHKI], killed by the Jade Guard

—GILSHA GOLD of Seirnkov, childhood school friend of Calleneck

—her three brothers – GARNER; GIMB; GLINE

—others: THE INNKEEP of the *Misty Wharf Inn*; THE INNKEEP of the *Ivy Serpent Inn*

Other Figures in Endellia

—LADY ELSAGRID PARRINE, young, elected leader of the Crandles.

—ABDU FAAZERNAN, sultan of the Southlands

—SIJONG YOTO, king of Guavaan

—[KING XINGAN YOTO], ancient King of Guavaan that seized power to end the slave war between the Guavaanese and the Zjaari

—[KING DORRAN DELSAR], the first King of Cerebria, who conquered the central east and split the natives between the Crandles and the Northlands

—[HUGOR HEDGE], the first human explorer to land on the main continent of Endellia, starting the age of exploration and 'year 0' of the modern calendar

—[TOMDAR FE], famous writer and historian

Setting

The Eight Nations

–FERRAMOOR, a central-western nation ruled by King Tronum Wenderdehl, with plentiful fields, river valleys, northern deciduous forests, and a southern warm-temperate climate

–AUNESTAUNA, capital of Ferramoor, an oceanside port city divided into class districts, home of the Royal Palace

–CEREBRIA, a central-eastern nation ruled by Queen Xandria Wenderdehl, with vast evergreen forests, snow capped mountains, misty fjords, and a humid continental climate

–SEIRNKOV, capital of Cerebria, a mountain valley city centered around the queen's black fortress

–ELISHKA, the easternmost nation in Endellia ruled by city-state aristocracies, with snowy northern forests, southern woodlands, and a large inland sea

–GUAVAAN, a mountainous jungle island and the southernmost nation of Endellia, ruled by King Sijong Yoto

–PARUSEMARE, the religious, westernmost nation of Endellia, ruled by King Philar Lameira II, with open plains, moors, cliffs, and seafaring cities

–THE CRANDLES, a small, peaceful nation southwest of Cerebria, full of lakes and pastures, and ruled by Lady Elsagrid Parrine

–THE NORTHLANDS, the northernmost nation in the brutal tundra of Endellia, divided into seven clans

–THE SOUTHLANDS, a desert nation in the southwest of Endellia, with a divided population of Zjaari and nomadic Gypsies, ruled by Sultan Abdu Faazernan

Other Locations

–ENDLEBARR, a dense, enchanted forest spanning between Cerebria and Ferramoor. The forest remains in a cool summer state for most of the year, shifting into a golden autumn during wintertime. Home of the Nymphs

–CAMP STONEHEART, a Ferramish camp in western Endlebarr settled near the nest of one of the five beasts

–THE TAURBEIR-KRONS, a tall, treacherous mountain range stretching north to south through the forest of Endlebarr. These mountains have a SOUTHERN PASS accessible only by summer and a central passage blocked by the GREAT CEREBRIAN GATE

–THE NETWORK, an abandoned system of underground Goblin tunnels and cities spanning the length of Cerebria; home of the Evertauri

–THE NEXUS, center location of the underground Network; Headquarters of the Evertauri; abandoned city

–RJARNSK, abandoned Goblin capital city beneath Roshk

–THE SHALLOW GREEN ISLES, an archipelago of tropical islands in the Southern Sea

The Endellian Saga
has just begun . . .

Made in the USA
Monee, IL
05 March 2022

92331356R00301